# Room

## in the

# Inn

# Room in the Inn

Rhea Jean Fish

Scripture quotations are taken from the King James, the New King James, and the New Living Translation versions of the Bible.

ISBN-13: 978-1493690787
ISBN-10: 1493690787

Edited by Laura Pollard

Artwork by Deac Mong

Book design by Sarah Misko

Additional Editing & Layout by Mandy Davidson

Printed in United States of America

> *"Love never gives up, never loses faith, is always hopeful, and endures through every circumstance."*
>
> *1 Corinthians 13:7*

*Room in the Inn* is dedicated to the glory of my Lord and Savior Jesus Christ, who, as I prayed to Him every day before writing, helped me write this book. It is also dedicated to the wonderful family God has blessed me with: Red, Ardelle, Jay, David, Andy, Jennifer, Andrew, Logan, Caleb, Lindsey and Kory.

Special Thanks to Kandy, Mary Ann, and Lanny.

# Room In The Inn

# CONTENTS

# Foreword

How perfect that this part of the book is called 'forward,' for we as Christians are to walk 'forward' with Christ and leave the worldly part of our lives behind.

I have been writing this book (on and off) for around thirteen years. I actually finished it seven years ago but at that time it was worldly and bland at best—kind of like my Christian walk. My friend Emma wrote a book entitled *God Is My Salt.* What a great and thought-provoking title! Matthew 5:13 says, **"You are the salt of the earth; but if the salt loses its flavor, how shall it be seasoned? It is then good for nothing but to be thrown out and trampled underfoot by man."** 'Good for nothing'—yep, that pretty much sums up me and the book back then. It was only when I read *The Purpose Driven Life* and rededicated my heart to Christ that my life (and the book) started to *open up.* As I started reading my Bible and praying before I wrote, I slowly began to walk the walk as the book began to talk the talk. It was a miracle; I was getting *salty!* No longer was I like a bland French fry lying under the great heat lamp of the world for I had salt, and not only that, my book was getting *salty!*

All of God's children got to be salt, so if I'm in*sulting* you or you're tired of getting burned by the world, come to the Father and let your life become a pleasing sacrifice to Him. He's the only one who can sprinkle you with life-fulfilling salt. It would honor me if you read this prayer and meant it from your heart: *Lord Jesus Christ, I believe You rose from the dead and sit at the right hand of God the Father. Please forgive me for all my sins. Come and live in my heart forever, and I will make You the Lord of my life. Through Christ my Lord, Amen.* All glory to God! Now get a Bible and start reading in John (in the New Testament), just a couple of chapters every day. Remember *slow and steady wins the race.* Mark this day on your calendar because one year from now, you will be amazed by how salty *you* are!

TYG!

*Blessings,*

*R. J. F.*

# Room In The Inn

In loving memory of my Daddy,

## Red

# 1
# Leaving

As I stand at the kitchen sink arranging daisies in a vase for Bobchia's* birthday, my Christian, Croatian/Polish/Italian grandmother, the song she sang to me as a child comes to mind:

**"You are the precious daisy in my garden, your heart is so full of love; like the sunshine that surrounds me, God has sent you from above."**

Through the plaid curtains, I watch snow fall lazily on the red barn, remembering my childhood in this Inn. The memories of my Bobchia are as clear as the days I lived them. Mother, Father and I had lived with her and Grampie David until I was four. In those four short years, I learned a wealth of knowledge from Bobchia, like how to crack eggs when we made chocolate chip cookies and how to feed the barn animals, but the most important thing I learned from her was how to pray. It seemed insignificant at the time but it was the one thing that sustained me in the darkest moments of my life.

From the moment I got out of bed in the morning until we said our prayers at night, I was Bobchia's shadow. After we completed our chores in the red barn, I'd sit at the wooden kitchen table watercoloring while she made pies for supper. She'd fix my hair in an upsweep and dress me in clothes like the little blond Sunbeam bread girl wore in the Sunbeam calendar that hung in Bobchia's pantry. One year a Little Miss Sunbeam lookalike contest was held in Erie. Even though the judges told Bobchia that there was a striking resemblance, I had to be at least five years old to enter. "Sweetie Pie, you're a shoo-in for next year," Bobchia said, but unfortunately that never happened.

The day we left the Inn was a bright summer day in 1955. Mother and I were in the field beside the red barn. I was picking daisies for Bobchia as Mother looked nervously toward the Inn.

*Pronounced "Baht-chee" or "Botchie."*

2

I could hear faint arguing, but I was oblivious to anything other than the thought that the more daisies I picked, the more of a fuss Bobchia would make over them and me. I tugged on a handful. It came loose faster than I expected, and I fell backward onto the ground. Mother quickly came over and brushed me off. "Be careful, Jennifer. You'll get your pinafore all dirty." I took the green ribbon from my hair and tried to tie a bow around the daisies with one hand as I held them tightly with the other. Mother was straining to hear the argument between Bobchia and Father as I ran past her onto the porch, through the squeaky screen door of the mudroom, down the hallway, and into the kitchen. Mother came in fast pursuit, but I had a head start, running straight into Bobchia's arms. She scooped me up, hugging me hard. I held the daisies in front of our faces.

"They are sooo beautiful," she whispered, smiling through her tears.

"Why are you crying Bobchia?"

"Oh, Bobchia has something in her eye," she sniffled.

"Let me see." Our noses met. "Just big tears."

Father looked at me sadly. "Honey, Mommy, you and I are going away for a while."

"Is Bobchia coming too?"

"No, honey girl," Father said.

"I want to stay with Bobchia!"

"Now Sweetie Pie, you go with your Father."

"I want to stay with you!"

"I know, Sweetie," she said as she wiped the tears from my cheeks, trying to compose herself. I hugged her with all my might and buried my face in her neck. Father tried to pull me away.

"Bobchia! Bobchia!" I cried.

"Paul, please don't do this!"

"I have to mother. I'm sorry." Tears flooded Bobchia's cheeks as she pulled my arms from around her neck. I grasped her necklace breaking the chain. Father held me tight and hurried toward the door. I pounded his back with my fists, daisies falling to the wooden floor.

"I want my Bobchia! I want my Bobchia!" I screamed as we went out the door, Mother was just steps ahead. Bobchia picked up the daisies and followed, holding the daisies to her cheek.

"I love you awful Sweetie Pie!" she yelled.

"I love you awful back!" I screamed, hitting Father with all my might while he carried me down the steps and over the little bridge leading to the cobblestone driveway. I threw the remaining daisies back toward Bobchia, but they fell into the brook. Once in the car, Father set me on Mother's lap, but I pushed her arms away and turned to the back window to see my Bobchia waving frantically at the car. "I want Bobchia! Bobchia!" I cried hysterically, pounding on the seat. I held up her dangling, gold cross necklace as Father drove fast down the lane and across the covered bridge.

I didn't know it then, but it would be twelve long years before I would see my Bobchia again.

We moved to Florida, but I might as well have been a million miles away from my grandmother in Titusville, Pennsylvania. Even though I would talk with her on the phone and hear smiles in her voice, they were never as good as real hugs and kisses. For years I begged to spend my summers up north, but somehow at the last moment the plans would always fall through. Eventually I quit begging, but I *never* quit praying to be with my Bobchia.

I was around seven years old when I got my map. Father had picked me up from school for a dentist appointment. Afterward, I opened up the glove compartment to look for some gum.

"What are you looking for?" Father asked.

"Nothing."

"You're looking pretty hard for nothing."

"My mouth tastes funny."

"Your Mother doesn't want you chewing gum, if that's what you're looking for."

Bored, I got out my geography book and unfolded a map of the United States that my teacher had discarded.

"Where did you get that?"

"Out of Mr. Rainey's wastebasket."

"Oh, you want to make sure we are on the right road?" He chuckled. "If you're wondering what state we're in, we're in Florida." I scrunched my face at him.

4

"I know what state we're in, right here!" I exclaimed triumphantly. And then, "Why can't I have gum?"

"Why did you have to go to the dentist? Because you keep pulling your fillings out with gum, that's why."

"You just asked me a question and then answered it. Can't I have gum for the rest of my life?"

"When you're sixty, you can have gum."

"Sixty? I won't have teeth by then! I want gum now!"

"No gum. But maybe some vanilla ice cream—how about that?"

"How about chocolate?" I said.

"How about vanilla?" He smiled.

"Ok…chee." I scrunched my face at him behind my map.

He made a U-turn to go back to the ice cream stand that we had just passed. While we stood in line, I held the map out trying to find Pennsylvania. A gust of wind blew it out of my hands.

"Stay in line and order!" Father demanded.

He chased the map around the parked cars coming back out of breath, just as the girl handed me two large chocolate cones.

"I told you vanilla!" He sighed.

"It's her fault!" I said, pointing at the girl behind the counter. "She asked me what I *wanted* and you told me never to lie to anybody!"

Father laughed as he paid. I handed him his cone, and we found a picnic table and sat down. He stretched the map out on the table using his elbows to hold his side secure while I held the other side down lest the wind reclaim it.

"I can't find Titusville." I moaned.

"You need to find Pennsylvania first. Do you know where it is?"

I leaned over the map. "Nope!"

"It's right up here."

"Oh, it's just little. Where's Titusville?"

"Well, I don't think Titusville will be on this map, but it's right under Erie, up in the upper left corner of Pennsylvania. Erie is right there. See the E?"

Father slid closer, and I leaned my body over the map.

"How far is it to Bobchia's?"

"Oh, honey."

"I want to visit her! Please, Father, pretty, pretty please! For Bobchia's birthday, please! I miss her awful!"

5

"I know you do, honey girl, but interns don't get vacations."

"Will you mark it for me, the road from here to Bobchia's, just in case you get a vacation?" Knowing I would be satisfied with a straight line, he took a pen out of his shirt pocket, marking the way up through the states, his cone dripping on the destination.

"Oops, chocolate marks the spot, honey girl."

He wiped it off with his napkin, smearing Pennsylvania. I looked at the distance that separated me from my grandmother and put my head down, whispering, "She's too far away from me."

When we got home, I tacked the map to my bulletin board and ran my finger along the inked line every day as I prayed for Father to get a vacation so I could see my Bobchia's face once again. It was my secret wish for twelve years, whenever I blew out all the candles on my birthday cakes.

The years passed slowly. Father finished his internship and worked in a clinic where he enjoyed helping the less fortunate. My first brother Logan, who had a habit of spelling everything out, was born when I was eight years old. Then, two years later, Andrew, the redhead, came along. Around that time Father 'got a more secure job' (as Mother put it) on staff at Ocean View Hospital, where the wealthy go when they *think* they are sick. When we moved into the big house by the ocean, Mother hired our wonderful nanny, Greta. Soon she was like part of the family, entertaining us when Mother held parties for her elite friends.

We were not permitted to have pets in the house on the white carpet, so we spent hours out on the beach feeding the seagulls or chasing small fish in the shallow water of the bay. We were, as Mother put it, 'on top of the pile.'

On my thirteenth birthday, my parents surprised me by painting my room pink and installing a TV, a stereo and a pink telephone—but the best gift was setting on my dresser in a plain white box from Pollards' Jewelry Store: Bobchia's mended cross necklace. I never wore it for fear of losing the only thing I had of hers, but I gently held the cross in my hand every night when I prayed for us to be together again.

I was almost fifteen when the unexpected happened. Father grew very ill. He held onto his position at the hospital as long as possible, but his treatments made him so weak that he could only work a few days a week, then half days, then none at all. As the months passed, Greta stayed on helping Mother, working for just room and board. Unfortunately, when her own mother fell and broke her hip, Greta was forced to move in with her. Greta brought sunshine whenever she visited. She knew how to chase the dark clouds away with peanut butter cookies and countless games of hide and seek. She was always trying to persuade Mother to pamper herself with a facial or go to the hairdresser's or, at the very least, to take a drive—Father would, of course, be well taken care of until she returned. Mother refused, knowing that Father's time on earth was short; she did not want to miss one precious moment with him.

When Greta moved out, I was forced to become the babysitter of my fighting brothers while Mother attended to Father's every need. Whenever I'd correct the boys, they'd whine to Mother until she gave in. Andrew's goal in life was to play ball, but Logan, being older, made fun of him for it, so Andrew was constantly begging Father to play "just a little catch" outside.

"Andrew, sit here a minute and tell me about your morning." Father said.

Andrew sat on the bed, tossing his baseball into his glove, over and over. "Mommy sent us with Greta to get new shoes, look! They make me slide better and turn circles for a double play. She got me this new baseball too! Want to watch me slide, and play catch with me?"

"Maybe tomorrow, Red, when I'm feeling better, I'll play with you, okay?"

"Daddy, promise?"

"I promise, when I feel better, we will play catch from sun up to sun down."

"Tomorrow will be the *best day of my whole life!*"

"Will you sign my new baseball? I'll keep it special, just for when *we* play."

"There are some pens on the desk."

"Oh good, a red one…here." Father concentrated, trying to steady the pen as he autographed the ball.

"You write slow but real nice."

"Thanks. I don't know why I'm so tired today, honey boy, I think I'll lie down for a little while. Why don't you go play with Logan outside? He'll play catch with you."

"He laughs at me."

"Tell him I said to play catch with you, okay?"

"Okay, but I want to play ball with *you* not him!" Andrew walked slowly to the doorway and looked back. Father had closed his eyes, so Andrew went outside to find Logan.

Andrew flagged Logan down. "Stop your bike and play ball with me!" Soon they were in an argument on the rules of baseball. They came back in to the house to get Father's deciding opinion, but I quickly ran ahead of them, shutting Father's bedroom door and waving a wooden spoon.

"Shhh! Father is sleeping!" They would have to go through me to get to him!

"Where did you get that wooden spoon? I hid them all!" Logan said.

"Under the couch. And I found two more in your bathroom. So there!"

"You're snoopy!" Andrew pointed.

"I'm telling m-o-t-e-r!" Logan said.

"What did you just spell?" Andrew asked.

"Mother!" Logan retorted.

"Mother said that we have to be quiet! Father is trying to rest," I said blocking them from the door.

"No he's not! I just talked to him!" Andrew held up his baseball glove, showing me Father's signature on the ball inside. "See! He's going to play baseball with me all day tomorrow—he promised! Get out of the way!"

Andrew kicked me in the knee. "Ouch! BRAT!"

"Come on Logan! Hurry!"

They pushed the French doors open, banging them into the wall, and ran to Father. "The safe place, meet you in the safe place!" Andrew yelled as they dove under Father's covers, shaking the bed. Father flinched in pain, straining to laugh. (Father did not for the world want the boys to know how ill he was.)

I stood beside the bed, holding the spoon high, waiting for one of them to stick a head out so I could 'bop it' with the spoon. "I'm going to let both of you have it!"

Father laughed at me. "Jennifer, if only you could see yourself!"

"I hate them! They're nothing but little brats!"

"They're just children trying to have fun!"

The boys stuck their heads out.

"We're just trying to have f-u-n!" Logan crooned.

"Yeah!" Andrew agreed.

They made faces at me and disgusting sounds with their hands in their armpits.

"Excuse me! I have gas!" Logan said.

"Me too!" They laughed, ducking back under the covers. Father laughed, coughing. I hit the first thing that moved under the quilt.

"OW!" Father said, "That was my knee!"

I hugged his neck. "I'm so sorry! I wouldn't hurt you for anything in the world!"

"It doesn't even hurt now." He said, kissing my cheek.

"Honest?"

"Honest."

Father hugged me with arms that were as frail as a willow's branches—the same arms that used to be as strong as an oak when I had hung on them as a child.

"I love you awful," he whispered.

A tear ran down my cheek. "I love you awful back."

The boys laughed, making more sounds in their armpits. Father choked trying to laugh.

"What on earth is all this?" Mother asked as she came in with Father's dinner tray and set it on the bedside table. "Your Father needs his rest! Jennifer, get up!" She grabbed the end of the quilt, throwing it to the floor. "Get out of there!" The boys scrambled to their feet.

"Clair, they're just being boys. I love it—really!"

Mother quickly covered him again and gave me a dirty look as he started to choke. "Honestly! I was only gone fifteen minutes."

Father started to gasp. We stood beside the bed, scared and silent. Mother took a deep breath. Her face that had once been confident and serene was drawn with dark circles under her eyes, making her look older than her years. Her once perfectly coiffeured hair was now shoved on top of her head in a knot for the task at hand. The last months had taken their toll.

Father quit coughing. Mother gently wiped his lips. As calmly as possible, she turned to me and said, "Jennifer, dinner is on the table." No one moved. She closed her eyes. "Jennifer, please take the boys to the kitchen." I looked concerned. "Please take the boys!" She said sternly.

I shook my head, and without taking my eyes from Father, tried to turn the boys toward the door. The baseball fell from Andrew's glove and rolled under the bed and into the hallway as he stared at Father.

"Is my Daddy going to be okay?" Andrew's eyebrows scrunched together.

Mother said, "Let the boys eat in the living room tonight and watch cartoons."

The boys ran to the living room. I walked slowly after them, glancing back to see Mother kiss Father's forehead and put a pillow behind his head.

"Clair, please recite the twenty-third Psalm again."

"Of course, dear.

> 'The Lord is my Shepherd; I shall not want.
> He maketh me to lie down in green pastures: he
>   leadeth me beside the still waters.
> He restoreth my soul: he leadeth me in the paths of
>   righteousness for His name's sake.
> Yea, though I walk through the valley of the shadow
>   of death, I will fear no evil: for thou art with me;
>   thy rod and thy staff they comfort me.
> Thou preparest a table before me in the presence of
>   mine enemies: thou anointest my head with oil; my
>   cup runneth over.
> Surely goodness and mercy shall follow me all the
>   days of my life: and I will dwell in the house of the
>   Lord forever.'"

Father coughed again, and she wiped his lips. Then she got up and shut the door.

I had no idea that on that very night he made Mother promise to take us to the Inn to live with Bobchia. Father knew in his heart, that no matter what had happened between them, that she would help Mother raise us. That was the last time I saw Father alive for he died in his sleep that night.

Mother waited until just hours before the funeral to call Bobchia. She wouldn't have time to come to Florida for the funeral. I heard Mother hang up on Bobchia and told her that 'I hated her for doing that!' We had a terrible fight.

Our lives were falling apart! I thought I would never be able to live a single day without seeing my Father's face. Night after night I'd lie in bed, flooding my mind with memories of him, willing him to be in my dreams so we could be together once again.

Every week like clockwork, Mother received a letter from Bobchia. I'd dig them out of the garbage. They all asked the same question: 'When are you coming?' I could tell Bobchia was careful not to write anything that would offend Mother, because with Father gone, we were all the family she had left. The letters must have included money because the P. S. at the bottom always read, 'I know this isn't much, but I thought it might come in handy this week.' Bobchia also begged for pictures of her grandchildren and wrote, 'Tell Sweetie Pie I love her awful.' Mother never told me, nor did she respond. Every time I put another letter under my mattress, I'd get down on my knees and pray to move back to the Inn. As sure as I knew there was a God in heaven, somehow, some day, I would be with Bobchia again!

Mother waited well over a year after Father's passing—until the last possible moment—to move. Father's illness had drained most of our funds, and the cost of living in our big, beautiful house was more than we could afford. At this point, Mother was depressed, and the boys were uncontrollable. The house went into foreclosure. All Mother's society friends had long since deserted her, and we had sold everything we possibly could to keep afloat. Time had run out.

Mother confided in us one stormy night at the dining room table of her horrible news. We thought it odd that she would let us eat there when it typically was restricted for Christmas and birthdays. The table and the buffet were the only things she had left of her parents. (Mother often told us of the day the furniture had arrived from England for her parents' twenty-fifth wedding anniversary. She was appointed to take our grandmother Joanne shopping, as Grandfather Bode had the set delivered as a surprise.) Mother had guarded the table all these years—for this final meal of French fries and hot dogs. Smiling, she ran her hand across the shiny surface, sliding coasters under the boys' glasses to protect the table that would be sold the next day.

Mother hung her head, dreading the words she had to say. "I talked with your grandma Rhea this afternoon. We'll be moving to Pennsylvania next week." I couldn't believe my ears! I stared at her. I felt as though my heart would leap out of my chest. But then I saw a tear trickle down her cheek.

In the midst of such overwhelming loss, I struggled to contain my joy. So many things—too many things—had happened since I had picked Bobchia the bouquet of daisies beside the red barn. I tried to contain my enthusiasm, but I couldn't ignore the fact that my prayers were being answered! No, they weren't being answered the way I *thought* they would be, but they were being answered just the same! At last I would see my grandmother! Mother sighed. "I can't believe we're leaving our beautiful home."

The boys whined about leaving their friends. I had mixed feelings about leaving my girlfriends and my boyfriend, Tyler. Mother called it 'puppy love' and asked me to trust her, saying, "You'll find other friends." She also promised before that I would be able to spend my summers up north, and that had never happened, so it was hard for me to believe her. Besides, nobody could ever replace my best friend, Tiff.

Tiff was so wonderful having a surprise pajama party for me the weekend before I left, inviting Theresa, Megan, Shelly, Ericka, Amy and Peggy, my closest friends. It was a bittersweet time as we looked through scrapbooks and mementoes, promising to write to each other every week and to attend the same college. After hugs and tears, I knew I would never find a friend like Tiff in Pennsylvania! With two days left in Florida, I hardly slept, instead spending my time trying to comfort Mother as she walked through the empty rooms sobbing. I had my teary moments, but the thought of seeing my grandmother again kept me busy packing boxes. The boys enjoyed playing catch and running through the vacant rooms, their laughter echoing throughout.

The day before we left, Mother traded in her baby blue Cadillac for some cash and an old, beat-up station wagon. She cried, but I laughed as I saw her pull in the driveway.

"Don't worry; we'll leave before sunup, so hopefully no one will recognize us!"

"It doesn't matter to me how I get there, just so I *get there!*"

Mother gave me 'the look' and climbed the steps into the house. I hurried after her, grabbed a box from the hallway, and carried it to the station wagon.

Mother came outside, "Tiff just called. I told her you'd call back when you finished packing. There are still a lot of boxes in there and I don't have the money to rent a tagalong trailer, so anything that doesn't fit will have to go into the Salvation Army boxes."

"But..." I started.

"No exceptions! We need every cent we have for gasoline."

I ran upstairs and dragged my two remaining boxes down the steps, securing their space for the trip. I thought *if we run out of room, the boys will have to sacrifice their junk!* After all, I had had my junk the longest. I carefully packed Mother's china, placing the boxes on the boy's sleeping bags, and went to return Tiff's call.

I walked into the family room where Mother was putting items into the Salvation Army boxes. She screamed when she realized that she was about to give away her wedding shoes. "Oh, no! Oh, no!" She sobbed, frantically digging into a box, pushing it over and rummaging through it. She hugged her shoes to her heart and ran to her bedroom, weeping, and slammed the door.

I ran after her "Mother? Mother!"

"I'll be fine," a shaky voice said through the door. "Please finish packing."

I went back to the family room to find the boys rooting through the boxes, taking things out that Mother had just put in.

"She was gonna give away my fire t-e-r-c!" Logan cried.

"Your what?" Andrew asked.

"My truck! Here's my roller skate, it's only missing *one* wheel! And look—my G. I. Joe without a head! It's still good!"

"Hey, how come none of your junk is in here, Jen?" Andrew asked.

"Because, *I* know how to pack!"

"Will you put this stuff in the car so Mother doesn't see it? Pleaseee?" They begged.

13

I sighed. "I guess."

The boys piled their prized possessions on the porch replacing them with old stuffed animals and newspaper. Climbing into the back of the station wagon, I became very skillful at squeezing things into the tiniest of spaces. The old car looked like a giant tick, ready to explode! There was just enough room for the last suitcase to be packed in the morning.

I went to the kitchen to get a Coke and call Tiff when I heard the boys playing catch in the great room.

"Mother told you to do that outside! You're going to break a window!"

"Shut up! You know I can throw straight!" Andrew said proudly.

"So what if we do, we're moving anyway!" Logan said.

"How many more baseballs do you guys have? I just shoved some under the back seat."

"Just this one," Andrew replied, "My special one. I'm going to look at it on the trip."

The doorbell rang its familiar chimes, but this time they sent a haunting echo through the empty rooms. Mother came out of her bedroom wiping her swollen eyes and slowly walked to the door.

It was the banker, Mr. Trimmer. "Mrs. Matko, I've brought my niece to see the house."

"Not 'the house,' Mr. Trimmer, our *home.*"

"Not any longer," he said with certainty and a smile, pushing past her. "I'm sure you know Mrs. Snodgrass."

"Hello Clair." Mother reached out to hug her.

"Rosemary, I'm so glad you came to see us before we left!"

"Yes, well, I really came to see the house." Mrs. Snodgrass walked swiftly past Mother, checking the condition of the room.

Mother squinted. "See the house? You've been here a hundred times!"

"Well it's been a while," she fidgeted. "I wanted to see if everything was intact." She sneezed.

"GBY Aunt Rosemary!" Andrew said.

"What?"

"GBY—God bless you!"

Mr. Trimmer looked down his nose at Andrew. "I didn't know you two were related."

Rosemary quickly said, "We're not. Clair and I used to be good friends, and well, the children used to call me *aunt.*"

Mr. Trimmer dismissed her reply and asked, "Well, do you think Tiffany will like this house?"

I looked at Aunt Rosemary. "Tiff, like this house? She's always liked this house, why?"

"I may be buying it for her."

"Huh? Tiff live here...by herself?"

"Sweet Jennifer, she's not going to live here by herself." She said, shaking her head with disgust. "She told me she was going to tell you the other night at the party."

"Tell me what?"

"Well, now that she isn't going to college next year—"

"Not going to college? That's all she has talked about for months!"

"Well, you know Tiffany Marie. Now that she's engaged—"

"Engaged?!"

"Oh, dear. I would have thought she would have told you *that* too." Rosemary gathered her composure. "She's engaged to Mr. Tyler Young." She said it like it left a bad taste in her mouth.

I felt like someone had stuck a knife in my back. "Ty and Tiff?" I said under my breath.

Rosemary looked at Mother. "It's rather cute, wouldn't you say?"

Mother looked back in disbelief. "Cute? She's barely a woman!"

"I know, Clair, but whatever Tiffany Marie wants, well, you know, she gets."

"And she wants my home?"

"Well, she has always loved this quaint house and commented on it often; and now that it's such a steal..." She paused and took a step backward when she saw Mother's eyes well with tears. I struggled to hold Andrew back from kicking dear Aunt Rosemary in the shin. "Wouldn't you be happy knowing that someone you *know* is living here?"

We stood there trying to make sense of all the things Aunt Rosemary was saying.

"Tiffany has always loved those crystal door knobs and the beautiful crystal chandelier." She said as she walked to the archway of the dining room and peered in. She gasped when she saw the electrical wires hanging from the ceiling. "My land, someone stole it!"

Mother walked toward her. "I only *wish* someone had stolen all the lovely things Paul and I so painstakingly picked out together! No, Rosemary, it was not stolen nor were the paintings. They were sold."

"Sold?"

"Yes, sold to buy medicine for Paul and to put food on the table!"

"Oh dear! I had no idea!"

"Well, you might have if you had been a true friend instead of a *vulture!*"

"V-o-l-t-u-r," Logan spelled it out.

"What did you just spell?" Andrew asked

"Vulture."

"Well, I never!" Rosemary placed a hand at her chest in disbelief.

"A well is a hole in the ground!" Andrew huffed back, pointing his ball glove at her.

Rosemary looked down at him. "So it is."

Mr. Trimmer walked over to Rosemary. "At least the crystal door knobs are still intact."

"Thank goodness!" she said as she walked to the winding stairway and looked up. "I hope the Tiffany stained glass window…"

"It's gone too." Mother sadly said.

Rosemary looked annoyed at the wood that replaced it, then to Mother. "Is there anything of *value* left in this house?"

"Memories!" Mother said, squaring her shoulders. "And you can't foreclose on those, Mr. Trimmer!" She took a deep breath walking to us. "I used to love this house and everything in it. It was a very difficult lesson to learn but now I know that memories are the most important things in this house, and we are taking every one of them with us tomorrow morning!" She walked toward the banker. "We do have one last night here, do we not, Mr. Trimmer?"

"Well, of course…"

"Then I would appreciate if you would **leave us alone**! We will be out in the morning and then you can bring over all the vultures in your family, to pick the bones of whatever is left of our wonderful home!" Mother swung open the door.

"I'm sorry you feel that way, Mrs. Matko." He walked out onto the front porch and wiped his forehead with his handkerchief.

I was proud of Mother as I stood there thinking of Tiff and all the good times we had shared in this house. People always asked if we were sisters. We would reply 'yes' and then laugh. After all, she was the closest thing I had to a sister, spending her weekends here before Father's illness. Her father, Doctor Snodgrass, the head surgeon of Ocean View Hospital, had caused quite a scandal when he left town with a nurse who was half the age of *dear* Aunt Rosemary. I had helped Tiff through that heartache, and now she was engaged to *my* Tyler and going to live in *my* house? I couldn't believe she didn't even have the decency to tell me! What kind of a friend was that?

This had to be a dream—or, a nightmare! I needed to wake up and see Father in his chair smoking his pipe, reading his medical journals and Mother on the lanai, planning a party with Aunt Rosemary as Greta prepared dinner and watched the boys from the kitchen window. I would be in my beautiful pink room on the telephone with Ty. *I have to wake up!* I thought. *I have to wake up!*

Out of the corner of my eye, I saw Rosemary start up the stairs. I let go of Andrew. He ran and kicked her in the shin. "Ouch!" she cried.

I blocked Aunt Rosemary's next step. Logan ran to assist us. "Mother has had enough, Mrs. Snodgrass! Now leave!" I demanded.

"Yeah leave ya old Aunt Vulture!" Andrew yelled.

She stuck her nose up and walked gracefully down the steps, trying to avoid Andrew, but he stepped forward and kicked her again. "OW! You little brat!"

"Watch who you're calling a brat!" I said, taking a step down to her level.

Mother hurried over. "Get out of my home, Rosemary! Get out! **Get out now!**"

I grabbed Andrew's hand, just as he drew back to throw the baseball at her head. Mother ushered her out and slammed the door behind her. She turned, crying, and embraced us.

"Why is Aunt Rosemary doing this to us?" Logan asked.

"I don't know, honey." Mother wiped away a tear. "I never in a million years thought this would ever happen to us. This is so hard, but thank God I still have you, the *loves* of my life!" She looked into our sad faces. "Come on. Let's forget about her. We'll never see *her* again. I know—how about an ice cream cone?"

"Yeah, I want an f-u-d-s-y-k-l!" Logan cried.

"What did you just spell?" Andrew asked.

"A fudgsicle!"

"Me too!" chimed Andrew.

Mother looked over at me. "How about you Jen?"

"No thanks, I have something I have to do."

Sobbing, I went to the back of the station wagon and pulled out boxes until I found the one marked 'personal.' I took out all the journals and photo albums labeled 'Ty & Me' and threw them into the brick fireplace on the patio. Then I poured charcoal fluid on them, lit it, and watched them burn.

Mother came out and put her arm around me. With tears streaming down my face, I took off the bracelet Ty had given me for my birthday and tossed it into the flames. She hugged me and said, "I don't know why young love is so painful. You didn't deserve this Jen, as loyal as you were. I know this hurts now, but in time you'll forget."

"I may forgive them but I'll never forget!"

"Know what we need?" Mother asked. "A 'Walk and Talk' night like we used to do in the family room, remember? That'll be a good way to get all these hurtful feelings out, and now that we don't have any furniture to move, it will be a lot easier to walk in a circle. How about it? Come on, Jen. It's our last night here. Do you think we could go in with the boys and have a 'Walk and Talk' about all the good times we had in this house, as a memorial to your Father? Do you think we could do that?"

I shook my head yes. "But do we all have to sleep in the same room? The boys snore."

"If we're going to do it right we do, and that includes all of us sleeping in the circle."

"I can't remember where the flashlights are, but we can dim the lights over the fireplace."

Slowly, we walked arm-in-arm up the porch steps. As we opened the door, we heard the boys playing tag. Mother quickly turned to me and tapped me on my shoulder. "You're it!" She ran through the kitchen door, and I followed. The boys quickly joined in. It was wonderful hearing Mother's laughter fill the house again!

The best way to describe our 'Walk and Talk' was 'therapy.' We took turns sharing and laughing about the wonderful memories of Father, this house, and the little house we had by the clinic. Andrew was the first to leave the circle jumping on the pile of blankets, then Logan. Mother called a time out and left to get warm washcloths for our teary faces. We laughed as Logan wadded his up, gently touching only his eyelids. Andrew held his by the corners, barely touching it to his face as he moved his head back and forth.

"I packed my blankie and teddy bear!" Andrew pouted.

"Me t-o! I want them and my sleeping bag."

"You'll both be fine for one night. You can hardly keep your eyes open as it is."

"No Fair!"

"No Fair!" They wrestled while Mother and I took turns, telling memories from opposite sides of the room, neither of us breaking stride. Soon the boys were asleep, snoring quietly.

"I can't go much further, Jen." Mother admitted. "You're the champ!"

"Father always used to be."

"You are now, honey."

We hugged goodnight. I could have walked all night I was so excited! I lay down but tossed and turned, dozing before the alarm went off.

The boys were still snoring when Mother left to gas up the wagon and drop off the Salvation Army boxes. She wanted to get started as early as possible because we only had enough money for one night in a motel.

As I lay there half-awake, I repeated last night's visit with Rosemary in my mind. Then I got up, got a screwdriver, and took off all the crystal doorknobs. *This will shake up Aunt Rosemary the next time she visits!* I thought as I hid them under the kitchen sink.

By the time I had taken a shower, gotten dressed and put my hair in a ponytail, I was starving! I hurried downstairs and looked hopelessly into the empty refrigerator.

Mother came in the door with coffee and a box of doughnuts.

"Mother…doughnuts?" I questioned.

"I'm in a hurry! One doughnut isn't going to make you *fat,* I promise! Boys you can have doughnuts after you get out of the tub, it's getting late!" She hollered up the stairs.

I ate half a doughnut and took a couple swigs of the Coke I had opened the night before. I carried it, my purse and my cherished map to the car while Mother walked through the rooms, summoning the courage to leave. The boys ran down the stairs, slapping each other with their wet towels.

"Well, I guess this is it." Mother announced. "We'd better get going."

The boys grabbed a couple doughnuts each and then hurried to the bread box and ran out the door with the bread bag.

"Where do you think you're going? Come back here!" Mother yelled after them.

They ran to the bay to feed their seagull friends for the last time and then ran back to the house and used the downstairs bathroom. They nearly knocked me off the porch laughing, when they came racing out to the car.

Mother came out of the house wiping her eyes, just as I was walking in. "I have to go to the bathroom."

"First the boys, now you! We'll never get started!"

"Sorry!" I hurried to the bathroom, covering my nose as I opened the door. "Ouu!" Apparently the boys had left a *surprise* for dear Aunt Rosemary! I smiled at my discovery—a better place to hide the crystal doorknobs!

# 2
# Where I Belong

Mother kept her eyes on the rearview mirror as she pulled out of the driveway and turned onto Franklin Avenue. Our beautiful home would soon be just a memory. Leaving the shore we traveled inland, stopping at Kandy's Karnations.

Andrew yelled; "Mother! Logan's got his smelly breath in *my* face, spelling stuff on *my* side of the car!"

"No s-i-r!" Logan defended.

"We haven't even gone five miles yet and already you're fighting! Logan, keep your breath on your own side of the car! I am not going to put up with fighting the whole way to Pennsylvania! Do you understand?" Mother got out, slammed her door, and hurried up the steps to the flower shop.

"Hey Jen, listen!" They started making disgusting sounds in the back seat, so I grabbed my coke and followed her.

Mother was looking at the beautiful, red roses.

"Hello, Mrs. Matko."

"Hello, Kandy."

"It's been a while since you've been in. Do you want me to check in the back for lilies or hydrangea?"

"Not today, thank you. I'll take four of those red roses."

Kandy started to get them for her, but I interrupted. "Hello, do you have any daisies?"

Mother gave me 'the look.'

"What color?" Kandy asked.

"Just white."

"I believe I do, next to the palms over there." She turned to Mother. "I have some beautiful mums that just came in for autumn, in case you are interested."

From several bouquets, I picked the biggest, prettiest daisies. Mother waited impatiently as Kandy smiled.

"That will be two dollars and sixty eight cents, Mrs. Matko." She said wrapping the roses in paper and handing them to Mother. I handed her the bouquet.

"You have a keen eye for daisies young lady."

22

I thanked her. As she started wrapping the daisies in paper, I chugged my Coke. "Would you please fill my Coke bottle with water, and put them in it? Sorry, I guess I picked too many."

"I have a jar in the back room." She headed for the back.

Mother sighed. "We'll never get there at this rate!"

Kandy came back with a jar half full of water and put the daisies in it.

"They're for my Bobchia," I explained as I arranged them. Kandy looked puzzled. "For my grandmother."

"Oh, well then let's make it real pretty!" She winked as she poured the water from the jar into a plastic vase. Mother paced. Kandy placed the daisies in the vase and garnished them with a few pieces of fern. Mother sighed. Kandy added a little yellow bow.

"Her favorite color is green."

"Jennifer!" Mother scolded.

"No problem, green it is! There, how does that look?"

"Groovy! Thank you very much!"

"You're very welcome."

The radio playing in the background announced that Denver had gotten a foot of snow overnight. "Thank goodness we won't see snow around here, Mrs. Matko!"

"Thank goodness." Mother said shaking her head, as we headed for the door.

"Oh my, I hadn't even thought about snow in Pennsylvania, ech!"

"Not Pennsylvania, Mrs. Matko, Colorado!"

As soon as we walked out the shop's door, we could hear the boys fighting in the car.

"He punched me!"

"He k-e-c-k-d me!"

"Stop fighting right now!" Mother handed the roses to me as she got in.

The boys calmed down when they saw the flowers. "What are those for?" Andrew asked.

"We are going to the cemetery before we leave." Mother asserted.

The car got very quiet. It had been a while since we had gone to Father's grave. It was just too painful to go.

We drove through town, passing several orange groves before reaching the stone columns that marked the cemetery's entrance. I got a lump in my throat as we passed the rows of headstones, wondering if there could possibly be anyone there that was loved as much as my Father.

We came to his row. The car stopped. I wanted to run. No one moved.

"Come on." Mother got out, holding the door open for the boys.

We slowly walked to Father's grave. Mother handed a rose to each of us. Then she touched Father's name on the headstone and bowed her head. We bowed our heads, sobbing.

"Thank you Lord for Paul," Mother prayed. "He was a wonderful husband and Father, and even though he suffered, he never wavered from his faith. We know he is with you in heaven and that we will see him again. We miss him, Lord. In Christ's name, Amen."

"Amen," we echoed.

We laid our roses on the grave and hugged her.

"We will love you forever, my darling." Mother whispered.

Andrew sobbed running to the car.

"Andrew! It's okay, honey!" Mother called.

He ran back sliding, as if on home plate, beside Father's grave. "I slide real good now!" Andrew tried to smile. He got up and placed a baseball in front of the headstone. Mother put her arm around him. "Why did my daddy have to die? I wasn't done with him yet!"

"I wish I knew, honey. I wish I knew." She gently kissed his cheek.

"Jesus, please hug my daddy for me. I miss him awful." Andrew bowed his head and then said, "Look, a toy from Father!" Half-hidden in the ivy beside the headstone was a little, faded, wooden horse, lying sideways.

"Honey, I don't think—" Mother started.

"It *is!* A toy from Father!" He ran to Logan and then to me, showing it to us.

"Father couldn't get you a toy, honey, he's in heaven. I'm sure a child dropped it…"

"Oh. But can I pretend?"

She put her arm around him and we walked back to the car. I watched as she held the door open for the boys, wiping the tears from her face. How devastating these last years had been for her, for me, for all of us!

We got into the car.

The trip to the cemetery calmed the boys for a while, but I knew it wouldn't last. They fought over the wooden horse.

"Come on boys, *share!* Please share!" Mother chided from the front seat.

"I'm t-o bored!" Logan said.

"I'm more boring than you!" Andrew proclaimed.

The boys grew restless, so I had them count all the red cars, then blue, then green. We then played a license plate game but soon they were bored again! They talked of how much fun they would have in the snow as soon as they got to the Inn.

"Ouu, snow!" Mother shivered despite the heat. "There won't be snow there for at least a couple of months, I hope!"

"No snow?" Andrew said sadly.

"How are we going to make a snowman, if there ain't no s-n-o?" Logan asked.

The boys had never seen snow, except on television, so it was all they talked about—snowmen, snow forts, snowshoes, skis and skates, Mounties and horses. I couldn't remember snow, but I did remember that when it was cold Father used to carry me everywhere shielding me from the freezing wind.

Mother broke me out of my thoughts with, "Look, only twenty-seven cents a gallon! I'm pulling into this gas station and filling up! That's six cents less from the last station!" The gasoline wars were a pleasant surprise to her.

Unfortunately, a pattern soon emerged that whenever we stopped, the boys would hit the ground running, climbing trees, playing catch, running in and out of the station, and then just when they were within Mother's reach, they'd hurry into the men's room laughing! After she had replenished the cooler and cleaned out the clanging, empty pop bottles from under the seat, she'd go back into the station only to fight with them at the register, making them put the souvenirs they had gathered back on the shelves and their quarters back into their plastic horseshoe wallets.

As I leaned over the hood of the car putting X's through city names, that we had passed, the boys ran around the car with Mother in hot pursuit.

"Jennifer, help me get the boys!" She called exasperated.

"Pull out of the station. They'll run after the car." I said matter-of-factly.

"Jennifer!" She scolded.

"Fine!" I folded my map and noticed the teenage station attendant smiling at me. I smiled sweetly at him, pointed at my brothers and shrugged. He grabbed the brats by their arms and dragged them to the car.

"Hey s-r-a-g-h-e-r let me go! You're hurting my arm!"

"What did you just spell?" Andrew asked.

"Stranger!"

Andrew twisted and kicked the teen in the shin.

"Ouch!"

They dove into the car and locked the doors. Mother rushed to the teenager. "How *dare* you touch my children! I could have you arrested! Get away from my car, this minute!" Mother quickly got into the car and was appalled when I called the attendant over to my window to thank him. When he asked me for a date, she peeled out onto the highway.

The boys gulped down one Coke after another and soon begged Mother to find another gas station so they could relieve themselves.

She shook her head. "You just went!"

"Bad, I have to go real bad!" Andrew held his pants.

"On a scale of one to ten, how bad do you have to go?" Mother demanded.

*"Three hundred!"* Andrew whined.

Mother pulled over to the berm and slammed on the brakes. "Go behind those trees over there!"

They pushed open the back doors and held them open with their feet, while Niagara Falls gushed from both sides of the car.

"Ouu! Boys are so *gross!*" I ducked down in the seat as Mother covered her face, flinching when the truck drivers blasted their horns at the boys. The boys slammed their doors shut, laughing.

"Well, I hope you're proud of the spectacle you made of yourselves! It's a wonder we didn't get arrested!" Mother chastised.

Logan paid her little attention. "Those trucks were sure k-o-l!"

"I think those truck drivers liked us! I might drive one after I become a Mountie. I like those horns!" Andrew said.

"I'm bored!" Logan said.

"Me too!" Andrew slumped in his seat. "How much longer to Grandma Rhea's?"

Mother looked at me, and I laughed. She sighed. "We won't get there until tomorrow."

"*Tomorrow?* You mean when I wake up, we'll be there?" Andrew asked.

"Well, it is a very long way, so don't ask me again until tomorrow, okay? Find something to do like color or draw. Jen, can't you think of something for the boys to do?"

My nose was buried in the map. "I tried, but they got bored with all the things I suggested."

Mother sighed while starting the car.

Andrew suddenly yelled, "Logan! Did you stick your tongue on my hair?"

"N-o!"

"He stuck his tongue on my hair! *Feel it!*" Andrew leaned toward Mother.

"I did n-o-t!" Logan turned his head franticly wiping the hair from his tongue.

Andrew tossed a baseball hitting Logan on the side of the head.

"Ouch! Mother! He threw a baseball at me!" Logan whined.

"Did you throw a baseball at Logan?" Mother asked.

"I can't know!" Andrew shook his head.

"What do you mean you don't know if you threw a baseball at Logan? So help me Andrew…" She turned the car off.

Andrew talked fast. "Okay, I *tossed* it. I *tossed* a baseball at his head for licking my hair! I did not *throw* it."

"It felt like he *threw* it!" Logan rubbed his head.

"Give me that baseball right now!" Mother extended her arm into the backseat.

"Can I put it under my seat, with the rest of them? Please? It's my special one, and I have to look at it once in a while."

"Put it under your seat and leave it there. And Logan, keep your tongue in your mouth and off of his head! I mean it!"

I laughed behind my map. Logan rubbed his head. "Isn't my head at least bleeding? It hurts like it's bleeding!"

Mother got out of the car. The boys hurried out the opposite side. She opened the back of the car, reached into a clothesbasket, and pulled out a belt. The boys ran to the front of the car. I got out, laughing. *Retribution at last!* The boys ran behind me.

"Help us, Jen!" Andrew cried.

I quickly turned, grabbed their arms, and pushed them toward Mother so she could let them *have it.* They kicked me. "Ouch! Stop it! Ouch!" No amount of pain would make me let them go.

"Leave g-o of me! I hate you." Logan thrashed from side to side.

"Let go, pig face!" Andrew kicked me again. The boys looked at each other and then grunted and farted!

"Ahhhhhh!" I ran to Mother. "Gag a maggot! They farted on me! Ouu, I think they pooped their pants!" I franticly waived clean air into my nostrils. "You guys stink like pigs!"

"You are a p-i-g!" Logan pushed up his nose at me.

Mother opened the back door and crawled on her knees onto the back seat. Ever so carefully, she tucked the belt in a hole in the top of the seat and draped it down. "Whoever owned this car before me must have had boys! There, now get in and keep your bodies on your own side of the car."

I was disappointed. "That's *it?* That's all they get?"

"You didn't think I was going to *hit* them with it, did you?"

"I was hoping!" I gave the boys a look.

"Pig face!" Andrew retorted.

"Yeah, p-i-g face!"

"Quit the name calling!" Mother said and pushed the boys back into the car.

The belt gave the boys a whole new thing to fight about. They taunted each other and blew their breath over the belt.

"Stay on your own side, Logan!" Andrew hissed.

"Say it! Don't spray i-t on my side!" Logan said.

Mother threatened to stop the car a hundred times to spank them, but she never did.


We passed a billboard with a picture of animals on it. "If you don't quiet down, I won't take you to Deer Park after supper."

"Deer Park? Okay, we'll be good!" Andrew sat up straight.

"Can we get souvenirs there? How f-a-r is it?" Logan asked.

Andrew pulled on Mother's seat. "What kind of animals do they have? I hope they have *deer!*"

We passed a dead animal on the road. "There's one that escaped from the p-a-r-c!"

"P-a-r-k," I corrected.

From then on the boys played 'guess the road kill' game, taking turns describing in great detail, the dead animals that were splattered all over the highway. Andrew made Logan say the gross stuff instead of just spelling it, which prompted me to put in my earphones and turn the volume of my transistor radio *way* up.

That night after supper, the boys petted all eighty-five animals at Deer Park, and refused to get in the car until Mother let them buy a souvenir.

"Chee, please just let them get a stupid plastic deer. It's almost nine o'clock!" I begged.

Mother rubbed her temples. "Okay, okay, go get a deer!"

The boys took forever, examining the shelves of fawns and antlered bucks proudly carrying their bagged deer to the back seat.

Logan danced a doe across Mother's headrest. "I'm naming mine Bambi!"

"Mine is Buck!"

They soon fell asleep with their souvenirs tucked under their tee shirts to keep them warm, while Mother drove from motel to motel, looking for the cleanest accommodations for the least amount of money. Finally, she struck an agreement with a motel owner, and we carried the boys to their rollaway beds.

"The room is small, and they snore!" I pointed at the boys, exasperated.

"Quit complaining, Jen! You can put up with their snoring for one more night." Mother pulled the covers over them. "Besides the room is not *that* small. Stick in your earphones!"

The next morning Mother and I got up early to take showers.

"You were right." Mother said, "both of them snored…loudly! I hardly slept a wink."

I shrugged. "Told you." I eagerly put on my makeup and my emerald green blouse that Mother had gotten me for my birthday and set my hair in rollers.

Andrew yelled from the bathtub. "I'm hungry!"

"Me t-o!"

"I saw a sign for a diner just down the road. So the sooner you two get out of the tub, the sooner you'll eat." Mother explained.

I plugged in my table top hair dryer, but Mother pulled the cord from the wall. "I'm not waiting around for two hours, while you sit under that thing and do your hair!"

I reached for the cord. "Mother, I want to look *pretty for Bobchia!*"

"We'll have the windows down. Your hair will dry!"

"Please!"

Mother gave me 'the look.'

"Chee, fine!" (I knew there was no use in arguing—she hadn't had her coffee yet.)

Adding to Mother's good mood was the surprise of the boy's thievery, not realized until we had driven to the diner, when the 'supermen' proudly emerged from the backseat with stolen towels reading **Mildred's Midnight Motel**, tied around their necks along with washcloths stuck in their sleeves for muscles!

Mother tugged the towels from their necks. "I don't care if you two Supermen are starving. We have to take these things back to the motel! Get in the car!"

The boys kicked at the back of her seat until she parked the car at the scene of the crime. She looked over the backseat. "Well?"

They handed the stolen washcloths to her from around the cooler lid they were using as a shield.

"I'm the one that should be *hiding!*" Mother ran sheepishly to the room returning the ill-gotten gain, then she jumped back into the car and stepped on the gas. The car spewed black smoke, and with the smell of burnt rubber filling our nostrils, we made our get-away back to the diner.

Mother and the boys got out, but I stayed in the car, not wanting to be seen in rollers and scotch-taped bangs.

"Jen, are you staying here with those *bug tunnels* in your hair?" Andrew pointed. I nodded. "Mom won't let me take in my ball glove. Will you watch my special ball back there while I'm gone?"

I promised.

While they ate, I eagerly wrote in my journal. Then I stretched my map out on the dashboard and added several more X's. "In sixteen hours, I'll see my Bobchia!" I said to myself.

I heard Mother sigh, and I looked up. She handed me an orange juice and a bag with toast. "Just a little butter, no jelly."

"Perfect. Thank you." I smiled at her.

"You're welcome. Keep an eye out for the boys, will you?" She asked. "They're in the men's room. I'm going to go to that little store over there and get sandwiches for lunch."

As I ate my toast and studied the map, the boys came running out of the diner laughing to my car door.

"How much further?" Logan asked.

I held up the map. "Well, we're here," I pointed, "but we need to get way up there."

"That's not so f-a-r. Look Andrew." Logan stepped to the side.

I opened my door, he came beside me.

"Where's Sylvania?" He asked.

"We're here and need to go up there." I repeated.

Andrew smiled. "That's not so far!"

Mother heard him as she returned and opened the cooler to fill it with the sandwiches. She burst their bubble by saying, "We won't get there until after dark tonight."

"*After dark?* We just got up!" Andrew's shoulders dropped.

Logan put his arm around him. "Don't worry. We should see a slew of dead stuff on the r-o-d by then!"

"What did you just spell?"

"Road."

An hour down the road, the boys were whining for the sandwiches in the cooler.

"Why can't I get out the sandwiches? I'm gonna die back here, if I don't eat!" Andrew pretended to pass out.

"Me t-o!" Logan leaned over on top of him.

"Get off!"

Mother rolled her eyes. "You just ate a big breakfast. Besides, I don't want you getting food all over the back seat. Get out your comic books. I'm not stopping until noon!"

"Do ya got gum then?" Andrew asked.

Mother shook her head. "You know better than to ask that question!"

"But my mouth is hungry now!" He complained.

Just then we passed a chain gang digging a ditch. The boys watched them through the back window until they were out of sight.

"Wow. Are those men b-a-d?" Logan questioned.

I spoke up. "Yes they are bad because they were mean to their sisters, so they're getting what they deserve!"

Mother laughed.

It was almost noon when I read the sign announcing that a roadside rest was just a couple of miles down the road.

Andrew tried again for lunch. "Can we have a sandwich *now?* My stomach sounds funny!"

"A couple of minutes and we'll be there!" We pulled into the rest stop. Big yellow arches glistened in the sunlight.

"I don't want a bologna sandwich now. I want a hamburger with American cheese!" Andrew said definitively.

Logan looked at the sign and said. "Me too! Wow! Over two m-i-l-l-i-o-n sold. I wonder what I just spelled?"

"I can't know," Andrew answered.

They went in to eat, and I got my curler caddy and hair spray out of the back of the car and went to the ladies' room. I took great pains to get my long hair into a perfect flip for Bobchia. When I emerged, Mother was sitting at a picnic table drinking coffee as the boys played tag around her.

"How do I look?" I asked, turning slowly.

"Beautiful, as always." Mother said, taking another sip.

I stopped turning. "I mean *really.*"

"Really. There's a hamburger and fries in the bag."

I gave her a look. "Don't look at me like that! It wouldn't hurt you to gain a pound or two. I wish I could be as disciplined as you are about your weight. All right, all right. Give me the fries."

"Did you get me—"

"Ketchup is in the bottom of the bag."

"Thanks." I gobbled my burger and was ready to go before she finished drinking her coffee. "I'm going to the car," I said.

"I'll be there in a minute."

"Mother, hurry!" She took another little sip. "Mother!"

"Okay, okay, it's inevitable. Boys, in the car!" They ran around the car. "*In* the car, now!"

"I want a milkshake." Andrew said.

"Me too!" Logan agreed.

"Get in the car, and I'll get it."

As they climbed into the back seat, Logan whispered, "watch this" to Andrew. "Hey Jen," he said. "I thought you combed your hair, but you got s-p-y-t-e-r-s in it!" He messed up my perfect flip! I screamed trying to climb over the seat to hit him. He kicked open his door, and I chased him around the car.

"You little maggot! I'll get you!" I yelled.

"Run, Logan!" Andrew called from the car. "Run! Look out! She's hiding on my side!"

People stared as Mother ran out the door, shaking the shakes. "Stop, Jennifer! Now! I mean it!"

I stopped. Logan jumped into the car and locked it.

"Look what he did to my hair! He *ruined* it!"

She made a face. "Well, go fix it!"

"That's it? Go fix it? And he still gets his shake?"

"Please, Jen. I have enough to think about!"

I tried the door. "I can't get my stuff!"

"Logan, open the door this minute!"

He didn't move. "She'll p-o-n-d me!"

"She will not pound you!"

"Yes, I will!"

"Make her stand over there, and *you* get her stuff." Logan bargained.

Mother relented. "Jennifer, go stand by that picnic table over there."

"But—"

"Just do it! Now unlock this door!" He opened the door for her and she handed them their milkshakes and then got my hair spray and teasing comb. I went back to the ladies' room, but this time my perfect flip wasn't as *perfect*. I came out and threw my stuff in the back of the station wagon.

"Hey pig face! I thought you were going to f-i-x your hair," Logan taunted.

"Logan! That is enough! If you say one more nasty word to Jen, I'll put Andrew up here and Jen back there with you!"

"Oh boy! I'd like just five minutes back *t-h-e-r-e* with you!" I shook my fist at him.

He pushed himself into the seat. "Sorry, Jen!"

I narrowed my eyes. "Sorry doesn't cut it, maggot!"

"Enough is enough! *Get in!* I'm not moving this car until everyone is quiet!"

We fell silent. It started raining, and Mother made the boys roll up their windows as we pulled back onto the highway. The humidity made my flip *flop*. The boys got hot, and opened the cooler and stuck their stinky feet in it. Then they took the bologna out of the sandwiches, folded it and stuck it into their mouths. Andrew took his out of his mouth and unfolded it and then held it up to me, laughing. I shook in disgust. Then he folded it as small as he possibly could, bit little holes in it and opened it to reveal a snowflake design. Then he set it on his coloring book to design a new piece. I shook again.

"W-o-w!" Logan tried the same thing and they voted on the prettiest ones and then ate them. I gagged at their germ-swapping, but at least they were quiet. I would have had to be starving to death to go near that cooler!

We drove for endless miles. The further north we went, the crisper the air. The clouds soon parted and the sun came out, shining on the brilliant red, yellow and orange leaves. Every year God painted these trees but this year, they were just for *us* to enjoy! The closer we got to Pennsylvania, the more frequent were our roadside stops. It wasn't easy getting the boys back into the car as they gathered the colored leaves as treasure. I decided not to pound Logan within an inch of his life. (Only because I didn't want to get perspiration stains on my birthday blouse.) "The next time you get out of that car, maggot, will definitely be your last!"

I crossed off cities on my map as we passed them and as the number of x's grew, so did my excitement. I read aloud the road signs and announced the miles left to the Inn.

Mother drove with one hand on the wheel and another around a coffee cup, staring at the open road. She started to talk nervously. "I can just *imagine* what Rhea will say about my not telling her that Paul was so ill."

(To be honest, it was hard for me to forgive my Mother for that one too—especially when she caught me calling Bobchia and grounded me for doing so!)

Over the years, I had been Mother's sounding board. Every time I would say something *nice* about Bobchia, she would say something *negative,* contemptuously referring to her as 'Saint Rhea.' (Whatever that meant.) I had learned to hide my love for Bobchia deep in my heart, but the closer we got to the Inn, the more I thought it was going to explode! I loved my Mother, but the only side of my Bobchia I had ever seen was loving eyes, kisses, hugs and the best chocolate chip cookies in the entire world! I was the apple of her eye for four short years, and I was looking forward to being that again!

We pulled into a gas station. "Good grief! Gas is up to thirty-five cents here! You save at one station to spend it at another!" Mother announced. "Potty break time!" She grabbed her head when she saw the top of the cooler off and the mushy pieces of bread floating. "I need an aspirin."

Andrew and Mother went inside. Logan had passed up the last two potty breaks, and when they came back to the car, I was reaching to smack him.

"Help! Help!" Logan cried. He couldn't even *spell,* he was so scared!

"Jennifer, sit back down! Logan, your face is beet red and your eyes are going to float out of your head if you don't go to the men's room!" Mother chastised.

"I'm going to try to p-e in this pop bottle."

"Young man, you get out of this car right *this instant!*" Mother's face reddened.

"Jen's going to rip my hair out!"

"No, she's not!" Mother retorted.

"I am!" I said defiantly.

"Well then, Jennifer, if he goes on the seat, you can clean it!"

"Me? He's the one who messed up *my* hair, remember?"

"You are the one keeping him from the men's room! I will not drive out of this parking lot until he goes to the men's room, understand?"

"Okay, I won't rip your hair out...*now.*" I said with a smirk. I laughed as he held himself and ran to the men's room. I took my purse and my curler caddy to the ladies room, to touch up my makeup and put curlers around the edges of my flip. When I came back to the car, Logan stuck his tongue out at me.

My desire to punch Logan was soon replaced with anticipation to see Bobchia. I studied the map and recalculated the mileage.

We drove another two hours and parked at a little diner. I took my curlers out and went into the ladies' room to comb my hair *again.* I took the little white box out of my purse and put on Bobchia's beautiful cross necklace. The last time it had been worn, *she* had worn it. I couldn't wait to show her how well I had taken care of it and longed to fasten it around her neck.

I came out of the ladies' room, and was pleased, noticing guys noticing me as I walked through the restaurant. Then I slid into the booth next to Mother and across from Logan.

"How do I look?" I asked Mother.

"She's going to k-i-k me!" Logan interrupted.

"Shut up!"

"Okay, you two. We are in a public place, so settle down. Jen, don't you dare kick him! I ordered you a salad with dressing on the side."

"Thanks."

Logan sat with his legs on the seat, just in case my foot happened to slip over to one of his boney kneecaps. After supper, the boys played tag behind the diner and searched for bugs in the field.

"Look Andrew. These kind of b-u-g-s in Florida are bigger then these."

"Maybe these are the babies!" Andrew said excitedly.

I went to the car and waited impatiently, going back and forth from checking the map to admiring the cross necklace. I delighted in the trail of black X's that sometimes crossed over the straight mark Father had drawn on the map. I only needed a few more X's, then I heard father say; "X marks the spot, honey girl!" By my estimation, we had about four hundred miles to go. *What is with these stupid boys anyway?* I thought. *If they only knew they were going to the best place in the whole world, they'd be in the backseat!*

I watched Mother impatiently as she tried to persuade the boys to get back into the car. She chased them until she ran out of breath and then yelled at them as she dumped out the cooler. Finally bribing them with beef jerky, she got them into the back seat. Mother shoved the cooler under Andrew's feet.

"Where's the Coke-Cola?" He immediately asked.

"You've had enough for one day." She got in.

They kicked the back of her car seat in protest as she ran her fingers through her bangs and tried to start the car. It stalled. "Oh, no! Please start! *Please!*" Mother begged.

I prayed silently. (*We were so close and yet so far away!*) With a cloud of black smoke, we coasted down a ramp and out onto the highway. *Please start, please!* Thankfully, it did. We sputtered down the road.

It didn't take long for the boys to again amuse themselves with road kill. For me another city, another black X.

We could have made better time if Mother would have quit stopping for coffee. Every time she stopped, we'd waste precious time retrieving the brats from whatever trouble they worked themselves into. Our last potty break at a McDonald's was around eleven o'clock. Mother complained about the weather and searched in the back of the car for light jackets. We put them on and went inside. I got a Coke and then hurried back outside and paced. Bright lights shown on a row of pine trees against a fence that stretched into the darkness. The pines were so much bigger and fuller than the ones in Florida. I got excited thinking of Christmas in the Inn and knowing my Bobchia would have a big Christmas tree like those if I asked her to. *Why is it taking them so long?*

I got into the car, turned on the interior light and stretched the map out on the dashboard. *Not much further now!* (We had been on the chocolate stain for the last hour.) Mother and the boys finally came out. Logan walked safely behind Mother until he saw me in the car.

"Only a hundred and eight miles left to go!" I announced.

Mother got into the car. "Jennifer, I have had it with that *map!*"

"I was only telling the boys—"

"I know! Now put it away or I'll throw it out!"

"You'd actually throw out my map?" I stared in disbelief.

"Put it away!" She answered.

"Chee…" I reluctantly folded it, leaving the stained side out so I could glance at it whenever we passed under streetlights.

Andrew started to whine for his Teddy bear.

"Why didn't you tell me to get your bear when I was looking for the jackets?" Mother asked.

"I didn't want it *then!*"

"I want mine t-o." Logan kicked my seat.

Mother turned to me. "Jen, what box did you put the boys' bears in?"

I scoffed. "What box did *I* put the bears in? I started to pack their stuff and then they threw that big fit and broke their alarm clock, remember? Then you told me to let *them* pack their own stuff, remember? Andrew marked his boxes with a red crayon and Logan with an orange one, if that helps."

Mother got out of the car. I reached into the back seat to hit Logan, but he yelled for Mother.

Her muffled voice came through the window. "Jennifer!"

"Okay! All right!" I quit. Then I looked Logan squarely in the eye. "But if you ever, ever, *ever* lay another one of your crummy little fingers on my hair again, I swear I will throw your bear in the toilet and I will flush, understand?"

"Y-e-s!"

Mother pulled some boxes out of the car and rooted around in them until she found Yogi and Boo-Boo. She handed them to the boys through the window and then pinned the side of her hair back up.

"Where's my blankie?" Andrew asked.

"Yeah," Logan reached out.

"I didn't see them in your toy boxes.

"They weren't in the toy boxes," Andrew explained. "They were in the box with the towels and fudgsicles, to keep them cold."

"What? Why on earth didn't you put the fudgsicles in the cooler?" Mother sighed.

"The box wouldn't fit!"

I laughed.

"Those blankets will be ruined by now! I'll never be able to get the stains out! You're just going to have to wait until I can get you new blankets."

"I don't want a new one! I don't care if it's stained!" Logan whimpered.

"Me either. I want the old one that I play Superman with!"

"Yeah, the one I s-l-e-p with!"

"What did you just spell?"

"Sleep."

Mother replaced the boxes and got back in the car. They kicked the back of her seat. "STOP." She gave them 'the look.'

"Will my blanket be stained forever and ever?" Andrew questioned.

"Come to think of it, your grandmother can get the grass stain out of grass, so don't worry about it. '*Mrs. Clean*' will clean them!"

I smiled at Mother's positive reference to Bobchia.

Mother peeled out of the station, leaving a long trail of black smoke behind us. The boys kicked at her seat for a while, but fifteen minutes down the road they were fast asleep, using their bears for pillows. Other than Mother mumbling to herself, all was quiet.

I looked at the speedometer we were barely going fifty. "Chee! Please let me get to Bobchia's before *my* hair turns gray!"

"What?" She shook herself out of her drowsy lull.

"Nothing. Never mind." I looked at the daisies when we went under a street light, straightening the green bow. Although I had knocked them over when I'd tried to get to Logan, they still looked pretty good. I held the vase tightly and closed my eyes, envisioning Bobchia's smiling face upon receiving them, trying to remember her real—not her telephone—voice. It came to me from across the years. *"Let's give those little hands a scrub, with soap and water, now rub, rub, rub!"*

I looked down at the map, any time now. **Welcome to Titusville**, a sign read. I looked at Mother. No reaction. As much as she was exhausted, I was excited. My hands started to shake. I slid my jacket off, straightened my blouse, and touched the edges of my flip. My heart pounded fast. It was 1 a.m. on the dot.

I sat on the edge of my seat straining to recognize anything in the dim streetlights, but nothing looked familiar. We went down a side street that forked and then went through a covered bridge that had **Plum Alley Lane** written across the top of it. As we rounded a bend, we could see emergency lights up ahead. We passed a big brick house and then a long white fence with big bushes on one side.

"The fence!" I said excitedly.

A fire truck was hosing down what was left of a funeral home. I read the sign. "**Parker's Funeral Home**." The noise of the trucks and the bright lights woke the boys.

Logan rallied first. "Wow something burnt to the ground! It stinks! PU!"

"What did you just spell?" Andrew asked.

"PU." Logan held his nose.

The firefighters motioned for us to go around the trucks. The lane came to a dead end as we pulled onto a cobblestone parking area, full of cars.

"We're here." Mother said quietly. She sat motionless and stared ahead.

I didn't think the boys even heard her; they were gawking out the back window, too fascinated with the firefighters.

"We're here?!" I clutched the vase of daisies and leaned over the dashboard, squinting out the windshield. "The little bridge!" Nothing could have held me down at that moment! I bolted out of the car, ran over the little bridge and then stopped short. Even in the dim light, the Inn was more beautiful than I had remembered. It looked like a big dollhouse with blooming window boxes adorning the bottom of the long windows.

In front of the towering pines, a familiar yard light illuminated the carved Inn sign of a horse looking out a barn window at a bird on a snowy pine. At last I could read the sign! "**1849 Red Barn Inn**. *I'm back!*"

Tears flooded my eyes as I looked past the pines to the dimly lit kitchen porch with its lattice stretching from the steps to the Inn's stone foundation, my favorite hide-and-go-seek hiding place from Bobchia. From there my eyes slowly followed the charm of the Inn to the front door then further to the glowing cove of the windows in the great room, biding me to come inside. "Nothing has changed!" I said stepping backward, smiling to heaven, and to the faint emerald green light shining from the cross-topped cupola, reflecting the moonlight.

"I'm finally *home!*"

Turning, I could barely make out the red barn's silhouette. "It's still there!" The moon's glow lit the field separating it from the Inn, where I had picked daisies twelve years earlier. I ran up the front porch steps and looked through the leaded glass window of the vestibule, aglow with the Tiffany Lamp squinting to see through the lace curtain and the archway into the great room, but I couldn't see anyone. I ran down the steps following the sidewalk to the kitchen porch and up to the door of the mudroom.

It was through this very door that I had run down the long hallway, past the kitchen and into the great room, jumping into Bobchia's hug—only to be pulled out of her arms! I blinked back tears as I thought of how I had pounded Father's back with all my might. Strange, I had thought this moment would be the *happiest* moment of my life, yet I felt sad. I looked down at the storage bench where I had played many an afternoon with my doll and white pebbles. I eagerly opened it only to find it now full of gardening tools.

Mother struggled with the boys trying to pull them up the porch steps, but they were determined to watch the firefighters wrap their hoses. "Can't we watch? Pleeease?"

"Only if you stay in the back seat and keep the windows rolled up." Mother ceded. "Keep an eye on them, Jen, while I go talk to Rhea."

"*Are you kidding?* I'm going to see Bobchia!"

"Jennifer!"

I opened the screen door. Its squeak was music to my ears! I turned the copper doorknob to the heavy wood door of the mudroom and went inside. The wooden church pew still hugged the mudroom wall and had several pairs of shoes tucked under it. I smiled at the needlepoint sign framed in painted daisies hanging over it, proclaiming, "**The dirt stops here!**" I quickly sat on the bench and rubbed the wooden seat as I slipped my sandals off and closed my eyes, remembering Father patiently lacing up my white, high-top shoes. The faint odor of the dinner that had been prepared hours earlier still lingered. Was I *really* back or just dreaming that I was, as I had done a hundred times before? I stood, and slipped into my sandals. I seemed to move in slow motion as I opened the lead glass door to the hallway. It was as if I were floating on air walking down the yellow hallway once again. My hand touched the rungs on the stair railing like I'd done all those years ago—only now I didn't have to stand on my tiptoes. I closed my eyes and made a promise to myself that I would never, *ever* leave Bobchia again!

I heard Bobchia's voice coming faintly from the kitchen. I rushed toward it until I heard a man's voice say, "Thanks for letting me put Mrs. Archer in the brown parlor. I'll have the viewing tonight at seven and the funeral tomorrow. Cecil said he'd ride with me and check the intersections so I won't have to turn my head. Hopefully the hearse will be out of the shop by then."

"Lead foot!" I heard Bobchia exclaim.

"I can't imagine what started that fire. I feel terrible that I couldn't get Mr. Bimber out, but the good thing is that he wanted to be *cremated!*"

"Harold, you should be arrested!" Bobchia said.

Then I heard a laugh, a laugh that made me feel like I had never left this Inn. I followed it to the archway with the writing above it that I could now read: "**Oh taste and see that the Lord is good.**" I peeked into the green kitchen and saw Bobchia and a man in a foam neck brace holding hands across a wooden table in the corner. I took a deep breath but could only manage a whisper. "Bobchia...Bobchia."

She looked over. "Sweetie Pie!" she squealed, standing and throwing her arms up.

My reaction was to do what I had done a million times before; I ran into her embrace! "Bobchia, I missed you so much!"

"Me too, Sweetie Pie! I love you *awful!*"

"I love you *awful* back!"

All the kisses I had missed for the past twelve years were now on my face and hands! Something seemed odd while looking down at her...That was it—I was looking *down* at her!

"Let me get a good look at you," she said, stepping back and pulling her glasses up to her eyes from the chain that hung around her neck. "You are so beautiful, awful thin, but my, oh my, just look at that a gorgeous head of hair! Just beautiful! Beautiful and *tall!* What have you been eating, beanstalk vitamins?" She beamed with joy. Now I finally could replace the sad face that haunted my memory for the past twelve years. She was smaller than I had remembered but still had that unmistakable twinkle in her teary eyes, but now with little wrinkles at the edges.

"You look so like Paul," she smiled.

I shook my head. (I was proud to resemble the most handsome man in the world!) "I know, and you're…*blond?*"

Well, they say blonds are supposed to have more fun, and I must confess that I've gone to too many Doris Day movies! "*Que sera sera!*" She laughed and snorted. (How could I have forgotten that she snorted?)

"Bobchia look, I took good care of your necklace. See? Father had it fixed." I started to take it off.

"Aw, how dear of him." She held her hand up. "No, no, you keep it, Sweetie." She wiped away tears. "Your grampie David gave that to me on our first Christmas together after we were married. He'd want you to have it and—"

"Oh my, how did you get those scars on your hand?!" I interjected.

"Battle scars from fighting with the oven door! I finally replaced it with these ovens. But enough about me! I can't believe you are finally here with me in my very own kitchen *again!* Oh, how I've prayed, prayed and *prayed* for this moment!"

"*Me too!*" She hugged me again.

"I watched out the window for you all day. This evening before the seven o'clock news I went up to the dome and lit the green lantern and prayed again for traveling mercies for my family, and when I looked down the lane for you, I spotted the fire in the back of the funeral home and then the thing blew up! Let me tell you, it's been pretty hectic around here! I figured you were in a motel somewhere and wouldn't get in until tomorrow—mercy, that's just what you did! It *is* tomorrow!" She threw her arms around me again, but this time I felt something squirming in her cobbler apron. I backed up and looked down. "It's only Minnie, the runt of the litter. It was touch-and-go for a while, but she's gaining speed." Reaching into her apron pocket, she pulled out a tiny puppy. "She's just a mutt."

I eagerly traded the daisies for the puppy. She held them to her cheek, kissing them, just as she had that last awful day; then she went to her china cupboard and got out her best porcelain vase, filled it with water and carefully arranged each daisy just the way she used to.

"Bobchia, can I always stay with you, forever and ever—the *rest* of my whole life, I mean?"

"You can do anything you want, Sweetie Pie!"

Just then Mother came into the room. "Some things *never* change!"

"Clair!" Bobchia looked hurt. "I choose to ignore that remark. I'm too happy to see Jennifer to have *you* spoil it!"

Mother bit her lip. I gave her 'the look.'

"Of course, you're right. I apologize." Mother took a deep breath. "I appreciate your taking us in."

"**Taking you in?** I take in puppies and strangers. *You're family; this is your home!* It is *wonderful* having my family here again, and if I die tonight, I die a happy woman!" She hugged me again, looking to the ceiling and whispering, "TYG!"

"Thank you, God," I translated. See, Bobchia, *I remembered!*

She smiled, and Minnie growled as she shoved her back in her apron. "Miss Minnie, quit acting like a *dog.*"

The man at the table stood up. "Have mercy! Where are my manners? Jennifer, Clair, this is my gentlemen friend, Harold Parker. Harold, this is my daughter-in-law, Clair, and my precious granddaughter Jennifer!"

Harold turned to me. "Jennifer, it's a pleasure. I have known Rhea for six years and I can't tell you how many great stories she has told me of you and Paul!"

"It's nice to meet you too."

Mother looked at him and cocked her head, "I suppose she told you a few stories about *me* as well."

"No, none that I recall,"

Bobchia recovered. "Harold is the owner of the funeral home that burnt down."

"What happened? Hurt your neck?" Mother asked.

"I had a little fender bender yesterday. As for the funeral home, I wish I knew what happened. There were enough chemicals in the basement for World War III. It just blew up, I guess. I'll know more after the firemen go through the rubble. Luckily I got Mrs. Archer out in time!"

"Who?" Mother asked.

Harold continued, "I put her in the parlor. I hope it's not too much of an inconvenience."

Bobchia tried to get his attention to be quiet, but before she found a way to change the subject, he said, "The viewing had to be pushed to tonight because of the fire, but it will only last a few hours. I'll be back around six tonight. Is that okay with you, Rhea?"

Bobchia shook her head defeated. Mother was in shock. "Do you mean to tell me that we have to stay here *with a dead body?*" She grabbed her head and sat down.

"Well she won't *hurt* you!" Harold grinned. "It's only until she's buried, and I'll bury her first thing tomorrow morning—I promise!"

Bobchia kissed him on the cheek. "I'll hold you to that. Do you think you can drive home all right with that brace on your neck? You could sleep on the couch."

"I took the back way over here, hardly any traffic. I'll roll the windows down and listen for cars at the intersections. It'll be okay. It was nice meeting you two." He winked at Bobchia and left.

Bobchia turned to face Mother. "Well, where are my grandsons, is what I want to know?"

"In the car, watching the firemen."

They stood staring at each other. Bobchia broke the awkward silence. "Oh, mercy, I bet you are all starving after that long trip. We ate dinner later than usual, thinking you'd be here. I waited and waited and then I thought you probably stayed at a motel. TYG that Harold was in here having coffee with me when the funeral home blew up or I'd be having a funeral for *him* and I don't know where I'd have it!"

I laughed. Mother didn't. "Why don't you get the boys and I'll get out some meatloaf and scalloped potatoes and whatever else I can find around here."

"Yum, my favorite!" I exclaimed.

"I know!"

Mother stomped out.

Bobchia went to the photo-covered refrigerator and stuck her head in. "Mercy, I'm having a hot flash. Feels good in here!"

A long, rectangular oil painting hung above one of the tables, a picture of a radiant sun shining brightly through a rainbow as sheep grazed on a mountainside. The scripture at the bottom read, **"But let those who love Him be like the sun when it comes out in full strength"** Judges 5:31. The signature in the corner was signed Mary Galmish.

Minnie's little head popped out of the apron when Bobchia put the potatoes and meatloaf in the oven along with a roaster. "It won't take long for this food to heat in these new ovens." She lit the stove and dropped the match into the mouth of a bronze pelican sitting on the back of the stove with '**1939 World's Fair**' etched on its webbed feet.

"Don't forget the ketchup!"

Bobchia giggled. "How could I? It was the only way your Father could get you to eat meat. Never fear, I have stocked the pantry with five big bottles. I hope you don't still suck off the ketchup and keep the meat in the side of your mouth for a midnight snack."

"Did I do that?"

"Yes, you did. You always looked like a chipmunk with a toothache!"

We laughed while I washed my hands and looked beside the green plaid curtains at a picture of me and Bobchia hugging two ponies in the barn.

Bobchia looked from me to the picture. "Do you remember Sally and Flash?"

"Vaguely, do you still have them?"

"Of course, after you left, nobody else could ride them, so I gave them to Wesley Woods. It's a camp for disabled children. I visited them a few times. They were sure enjoying all the attention they were getting from the kids."

"Can we go see them sometime?"

"Well, I don't know if they're still there, but sure."

Next to our picture was a plaque. I read, **"But as for me and my house, we will serve the Lord."**

"Joshua said that," Bobchia said, following my gaze.

"Joshua who?"

"The Old Testament Joshua, the man of God who conquered a mountain at eighty-five—my hero!"

"Oh."

On the other side of the window was another plaque. "**In the darkness, the believer shines the brightest.** Who said that?" I asked.

"You're looking at her!" Bobchia smiled. "It's *true,* ya know!"

"I like it." I sat at a table. She slid a tin of cookies down to me.

"I made them for you this morning—well, yesterday morning I mean."

"Thanks Bobchia! I hope they are—" I ripped the lid off. "*They are!*" I shoved a big, fat chocolate chip cookie into my mouth. "Yum!"

"Twice the chips, Sweetie, just the way you like them!"

I smiled with cookie teeth. "I knew you would remember!"

She carried more food to the table and touched my face. "I remember every single thing about you, Sweetie, *every single thing.*" She hugged my shoulder and hummed then fussed gathering food from every corner of the kitchen. "Oh and here's the banana bread Mrs. Dunham made today, delicious! I suppose, she'll be fighting you for the bananas, now that you're back." She giggled.

Mother finally dragged the boys through the archway to meet their grandmother. Bobchia bent over with open arms. "Give your old Bobchia some *sugar!*" They quickly hid behind Mother. I could tell she was pleased they responded that way. Bobchia eagerly walked over to them, pulled up her glasses and studied their faces while they ducked from side to side behind Mother. "Well, the apple sure doesn't fall far from the tree, now does it? Let me see, your strawberry redhead looks so much like Paul's when he was little, and you have his coloring and those dark eyelashes I wish I had, so you must be Andrew."

He shook his head yes. "Strawberry?"

She looked at Logan. "I can see the Florida sun has bleached the hair around your face and that you have Paul's eyes too. You must be Logan."

"Y-e-s."

Bobchia's eyebrows went up as she smiled tearfully, kissing the tops of their heads. They frantically wiped the kisses off with their hands. With one hand on her hip and the other pointing at them, (making her finger go back and forth like a windshield wiper) she said; "I'm your grandmother and grandmother's kisses *never* wipe off!"

"They're there forever?" Andrew cocked his head to the side.

"*Forever and forever!* And you can call me Bobchia."

Mother nudged them. "H-e-l-o Grandmother Rhea, Bobchia."

Her eyebrows went up again as she intently looked into Logan's face. "H-e-l-o, yourself!"

All Andrew could say was, "That birthday cake sure looks yummy!"

"That's because it is, and you must have some this very moment. We had a surprise birthday party for Mrs. Pratt today who just turned eighty-five. Anyway, when we all yelled 'SURPRISE,' she fainted dead away to the floor! I thought she had *a coronary!* The hospital is keeping her for observation."

Mother rolled her eyes.

Bobchia cut five big pieces of cake. "We'll have a picnic, like my Bobchia and I used to have—dessert first, then the feast. Sweetie, you can pour the milk."

"S-w-e-a-t-e?" Logan asked.

Bobchia chuckled.

Andrew asked "What did you just spell?"

"Sweetie."

"Do you remember where the glasses are, Sweetie?"

"Yes," I said, going to the cupboard, no longer needing the stepstool under the butchers' block to reach them. On the outside of the cupboard door was a weekly food schedule, held up by two pieces of green duct tape. Friday was circled with a big green star on it: *Sweetie's meatloaf and scalloped potato homecoming day!*

I got out the mismatched glasses and filled them with milk.

"Bobchia will put some meat on those bones of yours!"

The boys jumped into wooden chairs and shoveled cake into their mouths as fast as they could.

"Mer-cy!" Bobchia fanned herself with a napkin. "You're welcome and TYG for this food, Amen!"

Mother gave her 'the look.'

"Clair, have a seat. Jen, you must be starving!" She patted the chair next to her for me to sit in.

Andrew finished his cake first, licking his lips. "Do you got any cheese?"

"I believe I have some sharp cheese in the fridge."

"I'm not allowed to eat anything with a p-o-n-t on it." Logan said.

"What did you just spell?"

"Point. Don't ya have American cheese?"

Bobchia quickly went to the refrigerator, desperately wanting to please. "I don't see any, but look—did you boys notice the side of the refrigerator with the pictures you colored and sent to me?"

"I don't remember coloring you anything," Andrew said.

"Well, it was when your…well, it has been awhile." Bobchia wiped her brow. "I'll put cheese on my list right now for Cliff and Gladys to get at the Golden Dawn tomorrow. They will be tickled to see you. They are your relations, second cousins on my mother's, your great-grandmother Regeena's, side. They buy the staples for the Inn."

They blankly stared at her. "Hello, are you in there?" Bobchia teased.

"I just want American cheese!" Andrew frowned.

"There are lots of other good things here to eat, in the oven." Bobchia grabbed the hot pads.

Mother whispered, "She cooks; therefore she is." I gave her 'the look.'

"Clair, how do you like my Garland commercial gas ranges and the Kelvinator refrigerators? They make my life a lot easier, I can tell you that!"

"Nice."

"I made some golumpki—you know, pigs-in-a-blanket—for you, Clair." She pulled the roaster out, proudly setting it in front of Mother. (A peace offering no doubt.) Steam bellowed to the ceiling when she took off the lid. "I remembered how much you liked them."

"You did? I haven't had them in years!"

"Twelve to be exact, but who's counting? Dig in!" Bobchia stood smiling in front of Mother, hands on her hips, waiting.

Andrew and Logan ran over to the roaster.

Andrew squinted his eyes. "Where's the *pig?*"

"I don't see any p-i-g in there!"

"Well mercy, there is not a *live* pig in there! It's what us Croatian and Polish people of which I am proud to be part of, call pork wrapped in cabbage."

Mother stared at her plate. "Rhea, I…I appreciate you making these, and they smell delicious, they really do, but I'm afraid I've turned vegetarian."

"*Turned vegetarian?*" Bobchia forced a smile. (Vegetarian is a *curse word* to all great cooks!) "A *full-blown vegetarian?*"

Mother winced. "Once in a great while, I may eat some chicken or turkey, but I don't eat any *red* meat."

Bobchia poured herself a shot of coffee and downed it, pulled out her sleeve hankie and wiped her forehead. "Another hot flash. My doctor told me to cut down on the caffeine, it makes me chatty." She took another shot of coffee. "So let me get this straight, you don't eat anything with a *cute* face—just *ugly* birds."

I laughed.

"Once, in a great while."

"Once in a great while, an *ugly* bird." Bobchia whispered as she squinted at Mother, thinking. She took another shot of coffee and solved the problem. "Clair, you can take the blankets *off* the pigs and just eat the blankets!"

Mother shook her head no and cut a piece of banana bread.

"You're going to starve around here! This is a *meat* and potato crowd I'm cooking for!"

"I'll be fine. You cook other things."

"Yes I do but every meal has *meat!*" Bobchia took a deep breath and shut her eyes, shaking her head again. "I know, I know, I'll cook extra veggies for you. How's that?"

"Sounds good, thank you." Mother took a bite of banana bread.

"Clair, next time cut a thicker slice; I can read the newspaper through that one."

The boys giggled as Minnie watched the food being passed.

"Come on now, eat as much as the law will allow! Bobchia's food will put hair on your chest!"

"It will?" Andrew tugged his shirt to check.

"Yes, look what it's done for Minnie!"

Bobchia giggled watching us pile ketchup on everything. "Mercy, can you even *taste* the meatloaf?"

Mother looked over at my brimming plate. "I'm glad you didn't eat those French fries. *They* are soooo fattening!"

Bobchia giggled watching the boys scoop ketchup into their mouths from the sides of their plates. "I better add a case of ketchup to my list."

"Get t-o!"

"Good idea! It's better to be safe than sorry."

Bobchia's voice captivated me as she talked with Mother, side-stepping any mention of Father.

Suddenly Bobchia jumped up from the table. "I have to get a picture of my family!" She opened a little drawer and got her camera out. Black duct tape held the battery in on the side of it.

'Pop!' A huge flash went off, capturing us stuffing ourselves.

"Your first day back!" Bobchia beamed. "I love my pictures!"

"I see spots." Andrew complained.

Logan waved his hands in front of his face. "Me t-o!"

"I'll have to get a new camera, now that I have my family to take pictures of! I think this is the same one I used when you were little, Sweetie. Smile!"

'Pop!' She sat back down.

Mother looked daggers at her as Bobchia slowly rubbed my back with her fingertips, just like she used to do. It was as though I had *never* left her side. (The unconditional love that oozed from every pore of her body could actually be felt!) Needless to say, Chocolate chip cookies, meatloaf, scalloped potatoes and golumpki made for the greatest welcome home dinner a girl could have! I think if she would have given me a worm sandwich, I would have eaten it. Mother cut a thicker piece of banana bread.

"Now that's what I call a slice of bread, Clair!"

I sighed with contentment. "I've never eaten so much in my life!"

"You had better left some room for..." Bobchia rushed into the pantry and proudly carried out two big pies. "Apple pie! Your favorite, Sweetie!" She cut one pie into four big pieces.

Andrew shook his head. "I don't like apple pie."

"M-e either." Logan turned up his nose.

"I dare you to taste it. It will melt in your mouth." She winked at me. "Go ahead, boys. I double dog dare you. No, I *triple* dog dare you!"

They both took a bite and their faces lit up. "Yum!" They said in unison.

"See there? Bobchia knows!"

Andrew asked with his mouth full, "Can I have some more for breakfast?" Logan nodded in agreement.

Bobchia snorted. "I think it could be arranged. That one will be on the counter waiting for you to wake up, and I'll make more tomorrow."

Mother rolled her eyes back and sucked in her cheeks.

'Pop,' went the camera!

"Rhea!"

"Clair, don't be sad. There will be plenty for you too!"

Mother stabbed her slice repeatedly.

The boys jumped up from the table to look into the pickle crock.

"This would be a great place for frogs to live!" Andrew said as he looked it over.

"Have one of Cliff's pickles. The fork is on the inside of the lid."

Andrew lifted the lid and turned around with big eyes "Wow! They are as big as cukes!" They each took a pickle, licking the juice that ran down their arms as they walked across the kitchen.

"I think I like it here even if everything is *old"* Logan said.

"Glad to hear it!" Bobchia exclaimed.

They found Minnie's ball under the butcher's block and threw it to each other a few times before Bobchia caught it.

Andrew cocked his head. "You catch good, for a *old lady!"*

"Thank you, I think." Bobchia smiled. "But when you're inside the Inn, *roll* the ball, okay?"

"I can throw the ball real good, Bobchia!" Andrew boasted.

"Yeah, he can. He just can't h-i-t a ball!" Logan chimed in.

"Can too! Liar, liar, pants on fire!"

"Can, not!"

"Can too!"

Bobchia looked to Mother to stop the arguing, but when she didn't, she downed another shot of coffee and put Minnie on the floor to avert the boys' attention.

Andrew patted Minnie's head. "I'm glad you got a dog! We couldn't have a dog in Florida because they poop on the floor!"

"We don't say poop here, we say *bowel movement,"* Bobchia corrected.

I felt a little tinge of jealously watching Bobchia watch the boys laughing, as Minnie eagerly ran after the ball, from one boy to the other.

"May I have another cookie?" I spoke louder: "May I have…" Bobchia handed me the tin without taking her eyes off the boys and patted my back, reassuring me.

"Minnie's stuck to my wallet!" Logan said, standing up with the pup hanging from his back pocket, growling.

We laughed while Bobchia stuck her finger in the dog's mouth to work her teeth clear. "I hope she didn't put a hole in your trousers!"

"Trousers?"

"Your pants! She chews on everything, especially bedroom slippers. And look here." She turned to show us the back of her right shoe. It had a piece of black duct tape across the back. "These shoes aren't even a month old, and now I can't even wear them to town! That's why she's in my apron. She acts like a *dog!*" She kissed the pup and stuck her back in her apron and then washed her hands.

Eventually the boys tired of the simple ball game. "I'm bored!" Andrew whined.

"M-e too!"

Bobchia forced a smile. "Mercy, you've just arrived. How could you possibly be *bored?*"

"Don't ya got any *boy* stuff to do?"

"Well, inside that window seat there are some Superman coloring books and crayons."

"Superman?"

"We **Love** Superman!"

They ran and got them, shuffling through the pages as Mother and Bobchia made more careful small talk.

I quickly volunteered to tell Bobchia of my childhood but when I reached sixth grade, Andrew yawned and one by one, yawns went around the kitchen. The hall clock chimed startling the boys.

"You'll eventually get used to that clock," Bobchia smiled. "It's called a grandfather clock and is over a hundred years old."

They curiously walked around the corner to look at it, then ran back in. "WOW! That is the hugest clock I've ever seen in my whole life!"

"Me T-o-o! Mother, want to see it?"

"I've seen it more times than I can count, thank you."

They walked to the counter where they discovered several magnifying glasses stacked in a little wooden mushroom box; and laughed looking at each other's distorted faces. Then they noticed a handful of marbles in a green dish and rolled them across the counter.

"I used to play with those when I was your age," Bobchia told them.

"Wow! They must be a hundred years old too!" Andrew said.

Mother giggled.

Bobchia smiled. "Well, almost."

52

The boys yawned again as I was telling of the summer that I had learned to scuba dive.

Bobchia yawned, smiled sweetly and held up her hand. "Mercy, where are my manners? You all must be totally exhausted."

Mother shook her head.

I was wide-awake, wanting to stay up all night and talk of my childhood and hear of Father's.

It was like Bobchia read my mind. "Sweetie, I'd love to stay up all night and listen to your stories *but* I'll hardly get any sleep as it is. Breakfast time comes fast around here. We'll talk then; I promise."

"I don't know if I'll be able to sleep." I said

"Once you hit those down quilts, you'll be sawing logs!"

The boys looked puzzled.

Mother broke in, changing the subject. "I noticed that you've added a few rooms."

"Your room is all ready, so let's get this show on the road."

They looked puzzled again.

"Only *one* room, in this big Inn? Oh please tell me our room is *not* next to the corpse!" Mother said nervously.

"No, Luella is down the hall and you're upstairs in number four. I guess, over the years this old Inn has turned more into a boarding house, than an Inn. People travel through and fall in love with this part of the country and my cooking then they never leave."

Mother smiled, "But, when a room eventually becomes vacant… "

"I really don't foresee any vacancies, unless of course someone moves out in a *pine box!*"

That comment revived Mother and she gave Bobchia 'the look!'

"I originally had three rooms set aside for you but a lady showed up in a cab on my doorstep. I almost called The Brady House downtown to see if they could take her but thought better of it after she told me she was recently widowed. We are to look out for widows and orphans, ya know."

"That's what I think we are, ain't we?" Andrew asked.

"You children are most certainly not *orphans!*" Mother said giving Bobchia another look.

"Where was I, oh yes, anyway to make a long story short, the widow had just sold her houseboat, sooner than she anticipated and needed a place to stay, so I gave her room two, the little room I had made up for the boys, next to mine. Her name is Ginger Star and she's 'in mourning' after her fourth husband that she met on a three hour cruise, passed away when they were stranded on some island somewhere, anyway she told me she only had six more weeks left to mourn, whatever that means. She's shy! She told me she worked with Red Skelton, when he had his radio show back in the forty's. Isn't that kippy? She's such a plain woman and always dresses in black, easy to spot in a crowd." Half asleep, Mother was lost in the story as Bobchia continued with another shot of coffee. "I had room sixteen for you Clair but I had to give it to the family that lived in the back of the funeral home because they had nowhere to go after the fire. I couldn't turn her away, not with the babies! They barely made it out alive and lost everything!"

"Oh my!"

"Your old room, number eight, is rented to Paul's widowed aunts, Ardelle, a retired cosmetologist and Wanda. I don't know if you ever met them or not."

Mother's eyes were shut. I kicked her under the table, she jerked. "No, well… maybe."

"The things you left behind are in boxes in the attic. So, I switched the twin beds from the boy's room for Ginger. Then I put some mattresses in the walk-in closet for the boys.

"We have to sleep in a closet?" Andrew questioned.

"On the s-h-o-u-s?" Logan scrunched his nose.

"No, you don't have to sleep on the *shous!* That closet, next to mine, is the biggest in the Inn. You'll be like sardines in a can but you'll just *sleep* there then be down here with me!" We were all confused, trying to follow her hands and where the beds where but it didn't matter to me, as long as I was under the same roof with Bobchia, I was where I belonged!

Mother's eyes were shut. I kicked her again. She said slowly; "Oh, we'll be fine in one room."

We walked from the kitchen into the hall. Two sets of stairs curved around a landing that connected to the main stairway leading upstairs. On the side opposite from the kitchen was the archway to the great room. Under the landing's railing stood a long mahogany table. Which was covered with rows of our baby, holiday and school pictures in beautiful frames on starched crocheted, daisy covered doilies.

Mother looked at them curiously then at Bobchia.

"Paul sent them." Bobchia said coyly.

"Oh..." Mother said tightlipped.

"Who's that with you?" Andrew said.

"That is Andrew David, my husband, your grampie David."

"Hey he has the same name as me!"

"That's right, you were named after him."

"Does he live here too?"

"No, honey, he died."

"Is there any dead people with my name?" Logan asked

"No honey."

"Why not?"

Bobchia looked at Mother for help. Mother quickly said, "Okay, enough questions, upstairs."

Harold had brought our suitcases in the entryway so we grabbed what we could carry and made our way up the winding staircase. (I knew it would take forever to get to the top, for Bobchia and I always stopped at the halfway point to eat a cookie. It would sustain us for the long journey upward.) I counted aloud to the eighth step and paused in front of the little arched door on the left that led to the dome on top of the Inn. I looked at Bobchia. She counted the remaining eight to the top of the stairs.

"Here we are. Good old number four. It's one of the biggest up here." Bobchia turned on the bright, overhead light. The room was white, trimmed in green lacey curtains. Red and green plaid throw pillows leaned against feather pillows in embroidered flowered pillowcases.

"It's beautiful!" I cried.

"It's a girl's room! Lace, ick!" Andrew snorted in disgust.

"Sorry, remember I thought this was to be *Jennifer's* room. Your room that I gave to Ginger was the same color as your eyes, honey boy, blue."

"Can't ya k-i-k Ginger out?" Logan wondered aloud.

"Mercy, no! She may be an *'angel unawares'!*"

"Living *here?*" Mother said under her breath.

The boys looked to the ceiling. "I thought angels just lived in heaven."

"Yeah!"

On the farthest wall were the twin beds sitting between two long windows. They had tall mahogany headboards and were separated by a heart-shaped nightstand. On the wall with three windows were tall wooden chest of drawers nestled in between.

Knick-knacks were displayed on starched daisy dollies covering the surfaces of the dressers and tables throughout. Overlooking the front of the Inn was a large window. With emerald green cushions piled on the window seat. Short caned rockers were positioned for viewing the lane and the covered bridge beyond. On the other side of the room a vanity, with a concave mirror sat next to the closet, along with a secretary and a caned, high-back chair. At the foot of the beds were cedar chests, piled high with down quilts. I picked up a feather pillow and examined its pillowcase.

"This is beautiful!"

"I got into my cedar chest and did up those sheets and pillow cases that your great grandmother Kay, Grampie David's mother, embroidered." Bobchia explained. "She would be thrilled to know her great-grandchildren were sleeping on them! Look at the tree on that quilt. The leaves are made from pieces of clothing that were actually worn by the members of her family, your family. See the names of your ancestors and their birthdays?"

I spread the quilt. "Groovy! I claim this bed!"

"Hey Andrew, look! There's holes in the floor!" Logan said.

Andrew ran over.

"They are heat grates. Be careful. They will hurt your feet." Bobchia explained.

Bobchia walked to the closet and turned on the light, plus a nightlight.

"You boys will sleep in here for now."

The closet was painted brown. "Yeah, the d-i-r-t color!" Logan cheered.

"What did you just spell?"

"Dirt."

"We like dirt! Do you got a lot of dirt in Sylvania?" Andrew asked.

"Our share and I'm sure you'll find it!"

Two thick mattresses were on the floor in the big walk-in closet, with wood shelving all around. Blankets and quilts in a variety of patterns were heaped on the mattresses separated by a little round blue rug. "It's been a hot autumn, but the nights get pretty cool, as you can feel. This big, old place gets a little drafty, so I turned the furnace on to take the chill off. You'll want to hop into bed as soon as possible, so you don't catch a chill." She smiled as she watched the boys jump on the mattresses. Mother told them to quit.

"Bobchia told us to hop into bed and that's what we're doing hop, hop, hop!" Andrew giggled.

"H-o-p, h-o-p, h-o-p!"

Someone in the next room pounded hard on the wall! The boys stopped, frightened. Bobchia put her arms around them. "That's just Mr. Pill, in room three. Ignore the old coot! He used to work for the railroad, and all he cares about is these stupid train sets he has, so if you dream of trains it's probably because he's running them over there. Just slam on the wall!" She slammed on it. Mother's eyes got big. "I've been trying to get rid of him for years. So far nobody has claimed him! On the other side of you in number five is a barber who's as timid as a little mouse. He got here last Saturday. I couldn't turn him away either."

She kissed the boys on the tops of their heads. They tried to wipe them off. She windshield-wipered her finger at them, smiling. "Remember…" She sighed and took the camera out of her apron pocket. Minnie growled. "Sorry, Minnie. Boy, I've sure missed a lot." she said.

'Pop,' went another flash. The boys grabbed their eyes and fell backward onto the mattresses.

"Please leave me out of *future* pictures, Rhea." Mother squinted.

"Gladly, oh, sorry Clair." She held her hand up to Mother and made a motion as if erasing a blackboard, saying, "Erase, erase, erase. I mean, whatever you want, Clair. I aim to please!" Bobchia grinned and looked at Mother. "I am so thrilled that you are here!" She waited for a response.

Mother gave her a weak smile.

"Where does Minnie sleep?" Logan asked.

"With me—"

"In the rainbow room," I interrupted.

"That's right. Across the hall, on the wooded side of the Inn is my room. Anyway, if I forgot anything, just ask me in the morning, and I'll fill you in."

I walked over, kissed her cheek, and whispered, "I love you awful."

"I love you awful back." She started to walk out and turned. "Oh, before I forget, now there are four big bathrooms up here, Clair. The one across the hall is just for you and the kids, but you'll have to share the washer and dryer with the others on this floor. To respect your privacy, I told the tenants to use the washer and dryer only on Tuesday and Saturday mornings. So make yourselves at home, because that *is* what it is!" She smiled at the boys. "They'll be out like a light in five minutes. Sleep tight and don't let the bedbugs bite!" She started down the steps. "But if they do, hit them with your shoe… then they'll turn into pooh!" She snorted. My eyes followed her until she was out of sight.

Mother quickly switched on the desk light and turned off the overhead. "Why do I feel like I just landed on another planet?" She looked at the desk. "Could she have possibly found a *bigger* Bible to put in here? I bet Billy Graham doesn't even have a Bible *that* big! It must be some kind of a hint."

"Bobchia wouldn't do that. I bet all the rooms have Bibles in them." I reasoned.

"Believe me when I say that your grandmother has a reason for everything she does."

I yawned and stretched. "I will wake up in the Inn, an answer to prayer!"

"You prayed for *this?!*" Mother's mouth gaped.

"Only every night for the past twelve years!"

"Well, thanks a lot!" She gave me 'the look' and walked to the closet.

The boys had pulled the sheets off the mattresses to look for 'cool bedbugs.' Mother had a hard time convincing them that Bobchia had been kidding when she'd talked about bedbugs, because Bobchia kept things 'so clean you could eat off the floors!'

Andrew looked confused. "Why would we do that? She has a slew of plates!"

Mother took the boys to the bathroom and then came back in rubbing her arms. "I hate being cold!" She wrapped herself in a blanket and sat on the edge of her bed and stared into space. "I hope the boys can sleep with all that sugar Rhea pushed at them." She got up and looked through the boys' suitcases. "I bet everyone that lives here has *rotten teeth!* Where on earth did I put their toothbrushes? We'll have to find a good dentist. Remind me tomorrow to get appointments for check-ups. It's been awhile."

"Mother," I said.

"What?"

"You're *chatty.*"

She blew her bangs out of her face just as Andrew came running into the room pulling Logan's pajama bottoms off of his head screaming, "Logan's being mean!" Mr. Pill pounded the wall.

We froze. Andrew ran to hug Mother. "This place is *scary,* Mommy!"

"*Tell me about it!*" Mother escorted Andrew and the toothbrushes to the bathroom.

When I looked for a nightgown in my suitcase, I found the picture of Ty and me at an amusement park that had sat on my dresser in Florida. He had lied to me when he said he loved me and would come to see me over Christmas break. How did he and Tiff get together? How did that happen under my nose? I must have been a big joke to them! I wiped tears as I dropped the frame into the wastebasket.

Mother came back in the room and stood over a heat grate, rubbing her arms. The boys came in running past us and dove into their mattresses in the closet. "Did you brush all the sugar off of your teeth?" Mother called.

"We spit it out in the sink!" Logan said.

"It's still in there if you don't believe him and want to take a look at it!" Andrew confirmed.

Mother went to tuck them in and listen to their prayers as I hurried into the bathroom and got ready for bed. She came in with her nightgown. "Mother, do me a favor?"

"What?"

"Be nice to Bobchia! She's trying harder than you are. You know it hasn't been *easy* for her, without her family for twelve years and…"

"Okay, okay, I'll *try* harder." Mother rolled her eyes. "I'm freezing in this old barn of a place! I'll have to buy flannel nightgowns *again!*" She rolled her eyes noticing the Ten Commandments in a black frame directly across from the toilet. Then she got really perturbed at the daisy needlepoint rules for using the washer and dryer. "Get this! '**Anyone washing clothes on Sunday will be asked to leave the Inn.**' Do you believe *that?* She always has to be in control, that one does!"

"I thought it was one of the Commandments not to work on Sunday. Yeah, there it is number *four!*" I giggled and ran across the hall, pulled my journal out of my purse and jumped into bed. I couldn't wait to write that Bobchia said I could *stay here for the rest of my whole life!*

Mother came in and checked on the boys. "They must have been totally exhausted." She turned out the light and got into bed.

"Sorry, you'll have to finish that later. I've just got to get some sleep. Good night, Jen."

"Good night; don't let the bed bugs bite."

"Very funny."

"If they do—"

"Jennifer!"

I lay in bed watching the shadows of the pine trees on the wall. They seemed as restless as I was. I closed my eyes and saw Bobchia's happy face. I put my head under the quilt and came up gasping. I was too excited to sleep. I listened to Mother breathing slowly, noticing the green glow of the heat grate in the ceiling across the room. I got up, put on my robe and investigated it, then tiptoed down to the eighth step. I went through the narrow door and up the steep steps leading to the dome. There alongside the green glass lantern was a Bible sitting on a little table, dwarfed by a high-backed, caned chair matching the one at the desk in our room. I looked down the lane. A trickle of smoke ascended skyward from the basement of the funeral home. I turned to the other window facing the enormous pines, imagining them covered with snow. I sat in the chair as Bobchia did earlier, looking to the covered bridge. I touched her Bible. *Maybe she's still up!* I thought with excitement.

I crept down the stairs, stopping when I heard her talking. "I can't remember when I have ever been so excited! They are really and truly here! *TYG"* I crept further. "Jennifer is so beautiful, just the way I knew she would be, and those boys! Mercy, will they ever be a handful—especially that redhead! I will definitely be calling on *you* to keep them *corralled!* Clair sure threw me a curve ball with that vegetarian thing, loving every minute of it. And to think I just ordered a side of beef from Wayne! Oh well, I guess I'm thankful she isn't any *worse!* Erase, I mean I am *thankful,* really and truly I am!"

I stretched my neck over the rungs from the forth step, straining to see who she was talking to. "You know, I really didn't give up believing that I would see my Sweetie Pie again although I came pretty close! The desires of my heart, you *always* give me the desires of my heart! TYG for giving me that extra measure of faith I needed to see me through! You are so faithful to me! Point out anything in me that offends you and lead me along the path of everlasting life."

I went down another step. Her head was bowed. One hand rested in the dishpan as the other was stretched to the ceiling. "Help me to forgive Clair and to be patient, loving, kind and merciful to her as *You* are to me. It won't be easy but what You did for me *wasn't easy* either! Help me to never take these precious days you have given me with my family for granted ever again, and help me not to be prideful of my cooking. TYG for always answering my prayers! What a gracious and merciful God you are! *I love you awful and will praise your name forever!* Through Christ, my Lord, Amen."

I wiped away tears as I ran up the stairs and tiptoed into my room. I snuggled under Great-Grandma's family tree quilt, wishing I knew the stories of my relatives' lives to pen in my journal. "TYG *I love you awful too,* and I will praise your name forever and forever. Thank you for bringing me back to the place *where I belong!* Through Christ, my Lord, Amen."

# 3
# Tenants

I awoke the next morning under great grandmothers quilt. *"It wasn't a dream!"* I said and hurried and covered my mouth as Mother rolled over. I took a deep breath. The smell of bacon and cinnamon rolls was rising through the heat grates. I sat up. The room was even more beautiful with natural light streaming in from the tall windows. I jumped out of bed and put on my robe, walked to the window and watched the rain fall in puddles on the lane. I grabbed some clothes and went into the bathroom, dressing while looking out at the smoldering remains of the funeral home. I noticed a flag painted on the side of the red barn. "Huh."

I pulled my hair back into a ponytail, splashed water on my face, and headed for the cinnamon rolls. I counted down eight steps, then eight more. How I loved this old Inn! The smell of bacon was like a magnet, pulling me through the archway of the kitchen. I was shocked at the crowd of people. The ladies' hair looked like a field of cotton candy in a variety of colors ranging from dark gray to light blue, from pink to various shades of orange, and every whipstitch a bald head shined forth, reflecting the bright overhead lights.

A stocky man walked up to me. "Hello, I'm Spike, Rhea's cousin. I bet you don't remember me, do you? You look just like Paul. This is my wife, Carolyn. Where are the boys?"

"Sleeping."

Two couples came through the archway, and Spike introduced me to "Mr. and Mrs. Cecil Dunham and Mr. and Mrs. Frank Galmish."

"Oh!" I exclaimed, "You're the lady who painted that pretty picture."

"I'm glad you like it." She said.

A woman wearing a red sweater, pink blouse, yellow skirt, and red sandals with little white socks walked over to me and gave me a hug. "Remember me? I'm Gladys, and that's my better half, Cliff—that tall drink of water over there. Oh, Cliff!" Sitting, Cliff was the same size as everyone else, but when he stood and waved, he was as tall as the dish cupboard behind him! I waved back. "Remember him now? You were always climbing on him and hanging from his arms like he was a tree! Ah, those were the good old days! Remember when Rhea had you looking like little Miss Sunbeam and you came to our house and made Christmas cookies?"

I creased my forehead. "Sorry, I don't."

"We'll never forget it! You were so cute, covered in frosting from head to toe! Rhea was always taking pictures of you. I'm sure she has one around here some place."

A woman tapped my shoulder. "I remember when your folks brought you to church all dressed up."

Another woman, as neat as a pin, with gray hair that defied gravity as it was combed upward and tucked together at the top of her head, walked over. "I'm your great Aunt Ardelle, on your grandfather's side. My, oh my, *you are* the spitting image of your Father, young lady."

"Thank you!" She kissed me on the cheek and pulled me by the arm over to a lady who had straight, chopped hair that was eating toast.

"And this is my aunt, your great, great Aunt Wanda. She's just six years older than me. We grew up together."

"Just call me Wanda," the lady said.

Bobchia came out of the pantry, carrying a bottle of Geritol in one hand and a bottle of prune juice in the other. "Sweetie Pie!"

I giggled, looking at the prune juice.

"Ya know; it makes ya *go!*" She laughed. "Dora hand this stuff out will you?" She wiped her hands on the front of Minnie's face and her apron as she walked over and kissed me on the cheek. "How did you sleep?"

"Like a log."

The people laughed.

"Everyone, this is my precious granddaughter, Jennifer! Jen, these are some of the nicest people that you will ever want to meet! There are some more flitting around here somewhere; I'll introduce you later. Sit here, Sweetie." She removed a dirty plate and then grabbed the dishtowel that was draped over her shoulder and 'cracked' it onto the table, scattering crumbs to the floor. Then she grabbed a fresh plate off of a large stack and piled on bacon, scrambled eggs, home fries and pancakes and set it in front of me.

"Thank you."

She pointed. "There's Cliff's homemade syrup, off of our very own trees!" She saw me eyeing the pan of cinnamon rolls sitting in the middle of the table. "Ah ah, eat your eggs first!"

"Bobchia!"

"I'm sorry. I know you're not a baby anymore! *Where have the years gone?*" She said under her breath. "Don't forget grace." I said it silently and fast, stabbing the eggs.

'Pop!' went the camera! Spots surrounded my eggs.

"Her first breakfast back!" Bobchia captioned.

(As time went on, spots in midair became a regular part of our lives.)

I glanced up from my plate at a man across from me, eating eggs with a Q-tip sticking out of his ear. (My brothers would nickname him Antenna Man.) He smiled at me, and I saw that he had a front tooth missing. *Too much sugar,* I thought and gobbled my food. A man sitting beside him stared at my ponytail. I found out later that he was the barber who was staying in room five. He cut the tenants' hair for free, competing with the cosmetologist, Aunt Ardelle, who charged a small pittance for her time.

"You have beautiful long hair." He said, smiling. "Any time you need a little trim, just let me know."

I smiled at him, looking curiously at his toupee. It looked like a crazy rainbow of colored hair piled atop his head. (My brothers would nickname him Mr. Hair.) The man sitting beside him—with no hair on his head but plenty in his ears—would become known as Mr. Plants. Then I noticed a lanky, quiet woman, sitting by herself next to a window, wearing a high-necked, black, flowing gown. She had flat, tight hair pulled into a bun with a tiny black bow atop. I thought she must be the lady with only six weeks left to mourn; *wow,* she must be the lady who knew Red Skelton! Everyone looked old and odd, but I figured if Bobchia liked them, then I would too!

A knock came at the side kitchen door. Bobchia stopped flipping pancakes, looked to the ceiling and clapped her hands. "This may be my *'angel unawares'!*" she said peeking through the curtain at a man in a wheelchair.

Bobchia flung the door open. "I smelled your cooking way down the lane, Ma'am. Do you have any extra for a vet who's down on his luck?"

"Clear down the lane? You've got a good smeller, feller!" Bobchia snorted. "You're more than welcome to some food, if you're willing to pile up some wood in the back when you're done." The man nodded that he would.

"Well, get in here then! Veterans get the best seat in the house!"

"That's what I've heard, ma'am."

The man looked down. "I'm kind of wet to come in. Maybe you could just hand it out to me?"

"You'll catch your death in that wet shirt! There's the bathroom with soap and clean towels, and I'll hunt you up a shirt." The man started to protest, but Bobchia wouldn't have it. She pushed him through the door and into the bathroom.

"Thanks so much!" A few minutes later she knocked on the bathroom door.

"Somebody left this shirt here, but it's laundered and looks to be about your size. Waste not, want not."

A hand reached out to grab it. "Thank ya ma'am."

"Quit calling me ma'am."

"Okay…ma'am."

Mother and the boys came into the kitchen. The barber stood up and held his stomach in while brushing off a seat with his handkerchief. The bathroom door opened and Bobchia pushed the stranger in the wheelchair over to the table. Mother stood there taking in all the strange looking people, pulling the boys back to her.

"Hey! I'm h-u-g-r-e!" Logan whined.

"What did you just spell?"

"Hungry."

"Me too!" Andrew said.

Bobchia picked up a dirty plate from in front of the stranger and 'cracked' her towel, sending crumbs scattering to the floor. "Good morning, Clair. Boys, how did you sleep?"

"On the m-a-t-u-s, Bobchia!" Logan beamed.

"Ha! On a mattress. You're quick, Logan."

She heaped a plate and set it in front of the stranger, along with a glass of prune juice. "Thank you, ma'am."

"You are welcome." The boys looked at the stranger's motionless legs and his wheelchair, watching as he silently gave thanks to God.

"Sweetie, clear a place for Clair and the boys." When I got up, the boys squeezed into my chair, grabbing cinnamon rolls and shoving them in their mouths. "Mercy! Were you two brought up in a *barn?*"

Mother's face turned red as she gave Bobchia 'the look.' The words hung heavy in the air. Bobchia winced. "Oh, I'm sorry! Erase, erase, erase." Bobchia waved her hand, erasing the words, and took a shot of coffee.

I confidently walked to the sink, took a towel that hung over the dish drainer and draped it over my shoulder. Then I went back to the table, picked up some dirty plates, and 'cracked' the towel on the table. The egg crumbs pelted Mr. Hair's hair. He didn't even flinch! The boys laughed so hard they slid off their chair! Bobchia spit coffee back into her cup.

Completely unaware, Mr. Hair eyed mother's head and said, "If you ever need a little trim, I'm available."

Mother looked at the egg bits on top of his head and then at me. I put my head down, quickly setting plates and silverware on the table.

"Make yourselves at home!" Bobchia said as she set plates full of eggs, toast, bacon, pancakes and home fries in front of them along with their apple pie. "Don't forget grace."

"Is Grace one of these *old ladies?*" Andrew questioned. Bobchia laughed.

Logan took the plate of bacon and counted out each piece, placing them on his and Andrew's plates. "One for you. O-n-e for me. Two for you. T-o for me. Three for you. T-r-e for me and four for me."

"Hey!" Andrew cried.

"I have m-o-r-e!" Bobchia rolled her eyes.

You could have heard a pin drop, as all ears were on them.

As the boys ate, the others at the table made comments about how cute they were and how much they looked like Father. Mother was as cold as ice to the people who recognized her, and when she looked at Antenna Man, she moved her and the boys' plates to the other end of the table. There the boys looked curiously at a man who introduced himself as Ken. He was wearing a rare pair of eyeglasses. The brown pair had the left lens and the black pair the right, but when fastened with duct tape at the bridge of his nose, they made the perfect pair.

"Hello, what swell young lads you have, lady." Ken nodded at mother.

"Thank you. Now boys, please quit staring!"

"But they are staring at us!"

Mother turned back to her plate but then slowly lifted her eyes toward Mr. Hair who had slid down four chairs until he was right next to her. "If you ever need a little trim, I'm your man!" He held his fingers like scissors, snapping them in front of her face. "Snip, snip, snip!"

"It's like I *never left.*" She said in unbelief. Bobchia heard her, rushed over to her and hugged her shoulder.

"I'm so glad you feel that way! For a while there, I didn't think we would get along any better than we used to, but I can see you have *matured!*"

Mother rolled her eyes as Bobchia held her camera at arm's length to capture the tender moment.

'Pop!' went the flash and spots floated across the food in front of them.

"Rhea!"

"Sorry, Clair!" She erased the air but couldn't erase the film.

When the stranger finished eating, he thanked Bobchia for the delicious breakfast.

"Do you have a place to stay?" Bobchia asked.

"Yes ma'am."

"Do you go to church?"

"Oh, yes ma'am, at the mission."

"Great people down there. That Carl and Mae can sure make a body feel at home. Do you have family around here?"

"The wife divorced me after the war, and the kids don't come around."

"Well, you're always welcome here. My husband was a veteran; he lost his leg at Normandy."

"Sorry ma'am. War changes everything."

"Everything except our *faith in God.*"

"Yes, ma'am. It's done raining, so thanks again."

"Hold on for a minute!" Bobchia hurried out of the room and returned with a trench coat. "This looks about your size, don't you think? Let me help you put it on."

"Thank you, ma'am. *Thank you!*"

"That should keep the next rain off," she said, helping him out the door.

He wheeled down the ramp, as she watched him through the curtain, whispering. "Inasmuch as ye have done it unto one of the least of these my brethren, ye have done it unto me."

69

The sun poured in the tall windows, reflecting the items in the corner cupboard. One was my favorite. The Howdy Doody cookie jar that I remembered being on top of the refrigerator.

I launched back into the story of my childhood where I had left off the night before. Mother looked on edge. The boys paid no attention, instead craning their necks to see a man whittling into a shoebox at the end of the other table.

Logan piped up. "Can we go watch that guy down there?"

Mother shook her head. "He has a knife; maybe he wants to be alone."

Bobchia chimed in. "Who, Henry? Na, he's a halfway decent guy, he'll enjoy them." The boys clamored over to the other table.

Two sisters came in; waving to Bobchia as they fixed their plates at the stove. Venal and Izora were their names. Venal wore hearing aids and was as fat as Izora was skinny, wearing thick glasses. Their straight, gray hair had bushy ends and was pushed behind their long-lobed ears that dangled with heavy gaudy earrings.

Bobchia whispered, "You won't believe this, but they're *twins!*" We looked at them wide-eyed. "They taught school in the forties and fifties. Venal taught physical education, and Izora taught home economics. They married twin brothers, isn't that funny? Anyway, when their husbands were gone the same year—"

"Oh, how *awful!*" Mother said with her hand on her chest.

"They didn't *die,* Clair, they were just *gone.* They up and left and we've never seen hide nor hair of them since!"

Mother said something under her breath, leaned back and closed her eyes. Mr. Hair quickly slid his chair closer to Mother. Mother sat up, leaning as far from him as possible. Bobchia gave him 'the look' and continued. "They receive a little pension and help me with chores for half of their room and board. I'm the one getting the better half of that bargain!"

When the women finished eating, Bobchia introduced us. The women took to the boys right away. Venal got into Andrew's face, pinched his cheeks and told him he was "just soooo cute."

"Well your breath is soooo *atrocious!*" Andrew retorted.

"Andrew!" Mother scolded.

"Well, it is! Come here and *smell it* if you don't believe me!"

Luckily Venal's hearing aid was squealing, so she didn't hear a word! Logan saw Izora's *fuzzy upper lip* and dodged her as she tried to kiss him. Defeated, the ladies turned to their household tasks.

Izora swept the floor while Venal gathered dishes, deliberately bumping Izora with her hip, sending the frail woman into a chair. "Sorry, sister dear. My hip got away from me *again!*" When Izora shook her boney fist at her, the boys giggled. Then their attention went back to halfway decent Henry.

A man came in and sat at the table. "Where's my breakfast?"

Bobchia shook her head. "Homer, you were the first one at the table this morning. You *already* ate!"

"Did not!"

"Look at the napkin around your neck."

He looked down at the egg stained napkin. "Oh, yeah. Was it good?"

"Same as always."

"Did I have coffee?"

"I think so, but you can have another." But by the time Bobchia had filled a cup and turned around to hand it to him, he had left. "Homer drives me nuts! He's the husband of Mrs. Pratt, the lady that fainted at her birthday party yesterday. She usually keeps an eye on him, but now that she's in the hospital I guess I've been elected."

Halfway decent Henry told the boys that he had grandchildren about their age and asked them if they liked sports.

"I love baseball." Andrew said.

"Me too. Wow! Andrew, look! What he's carving looks just like a b-e-r-d!" Logan said.

"What did you spell?" Andrew asked.

"Bird," Logan answered, then asked; "How do you get that bird out of the wood with that knife?"

"Well, I just whittle away everything that doesn't look like a bird." Henry chuckled.

"Will you show me how to do that?" Andrew asked.

"It takes a pretty sharp knife…"

"*No!*" Mother said empathically.

A few minutes later, Henry handed the bird to Logan.

"Thanks!"

"Will you make me one? I want a bigger one than Logan's!" Andrew said.

"Get me a flat piece of wood over there, from beside the potbelly stove."

Andrew handed him a piece of wood. "Show me where the bird is in that wood."

He chuckled again. "Well, let me see. I think I see a *butterfly* in this piece."

"Wow! A butterfly? Where? Show me!" He pointed. "I don't see it! Is it red?"

"It isn't red, but when I cut it out, you can paint it red, okay?" Andrew nodded.

The boys grew impatient watching Henry whittle.

"When is it going to be a butterfly?" Andrew asked. "How much *longer?*"

He smiled. "Just like it takes God a while to make a real butterfly, it will take me a while to make a wooden one. I think by tomorrow it will be a butterfly."

"You mean when I wake up tomorrow, it will be done?"

"Yes, when you come down for breakfast, it will be beside your plate. Where will you be sitting?"

"Right here, next to you." Andrew tapped the chair.

"Mercy, it's nigh on to ten!" Bobchia exclaimed, glancing at the clock. "I'm behind on my work!" She gathered some plates taking them to Venal who was washing the dishes. Izora was quickly drying them, impatiently waiting for the next plate.

"Look at this plate, Venal! It still has egg on it!"

"It's a poor dish dryer that can't wipe away the food that the dish washer *missed!*"

Bobchia giggled then turned and said. "Clair, bring your coffee cup. Come on kids! I can't wait to show you!"

Mother lagged as we followed her down the hall. Bobchia pointed us to the great room and got beside mother staring down into Mr. Hair's beady eyes.

"Don't you have to give someone a 'little trim'?" Bobchia asked.

"I was just looking at..."

"I *know* what you were looking at!" he put his nose in the air and left.

"Bobchia, that guy wanted to cut my hairs!" Andrew said.

"Mine t-o!"

"Mercy, boys, what did you say to him?"

"Drop dead!"

"What did he say?"

"*Pull my finger!*"

The great room was just that—great! It had high ceilings and red-and-green paisley wallpaper. The cove of tall, leaded glass windows that protruded from the side of the house, were framed in red satin drapes that cascaded to the floor, pooling at the foot of a baby-grand piano on a green and gold Persian rug.

The boys ran over to the piano and pounded on the keys. "Please take it easy, boys! I just had that tuned!" Bobchia turned to Mother. "Do you still play, Clair?"

"I haven't in years. I guess I just lost interest."

"What about you, Sweetie?"

"I quit taking lessons after…well, I quit."

"Well, feel free to tickle the ivories whenever you want. Your grampie David was the one who filled this old Inn with music, remember? Of course all he knew, by ear, were polkas." The boys pounded their ears on the keys. "Mercy, stop that! You'll go deaf! Let's keep the piano off limits, shall we?" Bobchia hurried over and pulled bed sheets off the furniture. "*Finally*, I can get rid of these!" The couches were emerald green, and the overstuffed loveseats were bright red. There was a variety of matching plain and striped winged chairs.

"W-o-w!" Logan said.

"I like the red part!" Andrew smiled.

"This is beautiful Bobchia." I said beaming.

"Thank you. I knew you'd like the colors. Do you like it, Clair?"

"Well, it's better than that ugly mustard color."

In the middle of the back wall was a stone fireplace, and on either side of it were mahogany window seats decked with red cushions and green-striped pillows. Lacy valances hung from the top of the leaded glass windows. The furniture's trim, the mantel and the antique bookcases were mahogany. Some of the furniture was arranged around a strange-looking television set.

"Your TV looks funny!" Andrew said giggling.

"We always watch cartoons on Saturday." Logan said.

"Well, let's see if they'll come in." Bobchia said.

"Do you get Carol Burnet in Sylvania?" Andrew asked.

"I do!"

"I like it here!"

Mother looked at the TV set, shook her head and thumbed through a magazine.

"Just because it *looks* funny, doesn't mean it's no good, that's my motto!" Bobchia walked over turning on the set. We looked wide-eyed at the coat hanger that stretched from one rabbit ear to the other, covered in a variety of different sized aluminum foil balls. Some dangled from strips of red duct tape—some from green that swayed when she fine-tuned (pounded) on the TV set. A little dot finally appeared and then the screen looked like a snowstorm. *"Hold the phone, Gert!"* She ran out the front door and inched her way behind the pine tree beside the window. The boys ran to the window seats, stretching upward looking at the antenna, watching her struggle to turn it. She yelled at them through the window. "Don't look at me, look at the TV and tell me when you see a picture!"

"It's the stupid news man!" She hurried back in, turned the channel twice…yea Bugs Bunny!

"See what I mean? It might be old *but* it still works!"

As the boys lay in front of the set, Bobchia took pillows from the window seats and gently tucked them under their heads. Her eyes welled with tears as she saw Father's face in theirs. She kissed her hands then patted their heads.

'Pop,' went the camera.

"Clair, you may be interested in the brochures on top of that puzzle on the coffee table. I picked them up for you the other day."

"Thank you, Rhea. That was thoughtful of you."

"It *was?*" Bobchia said in surprise, looking at me and winking. "Sweetie, you enjoy what's left of your morning. I have a few things to do and then I'll look you up. I'll be back"

Mother leafed through the nursing pamphlets. "I've got to go back to nursing school and get my degree so we can get our own place."

"But this *is* our place," I countered.

"This is *Rhea's* place!" she said sharply. "Until then we'll need a good dentist and definitely a downtown barber!"

I looked out the window and saw the stranger in the wheelchair struggling to pile the firewood. I was puzzled and frankly upset that Bobchia, who gave so freely, was actually making this poor man work for his breakfast! I went into the kitchen where the sisters were helping her make pies. Bobchia was wiping Minnie off in the sink. "Second time in a week she jumped into the pie dough!" Bobchia saw me heading for the door and asked where I was going.

"To help that man pile wood!"

"Oh no, you're not!"

I gave Bobchia a puzzled glance.

"The war took the use of his legs, not his dignity." She paused. "If he didn't have it, he would have left with a full belly, and we'd never see him again. This way he feels useful, and if he gets down on his luck again, he can come back and work for a meal. *Understand?*" She whispered, "It's like Mutt and Jeff over there making pies. It gives them the satisfaction of helping me. They enjoy it; and believe me, we will sure enjoy eating those pies!"

"I'd rather be in here with you than with the boys. They've done some pretty nasty things to me. I'd rather be in here, please." I followed her outside, where she put Minnie on the lawn. We heard the car door slam.

"Hi, Grandma!" Andrew yelled, waving his ball and glove.

"Hi, Andrew!" She hollered back.

"Watch this, Grandma!" He threw the ball high into the air and caught it over and over.

"You're a *crackerjack* the way you throw and catch that ball, a real *crackerjack!*" Bobchia beamed.

He looked puzzled but knew she had complimented him. "Thanks?" He walked to the door.

"Don't throw that ball in the Inn, okay?" She called after him.

"I won't."

"He won't, will he?" Bobchia asked me.

"No, he just likes to push it into his glove."

"I'm a little concerned about Logan. Tell me—why does he spell so much?"

"Ever since he watched me in the spelling bee last year, he's been doing it. I guess we're just used to it."

"I hope *I* get used to it." She smiled looking down at Minnie. "I can't tell when she goes, her legs are so short. I usually have to *feel* the grass, to make sure."

"Uck!" I made a face.

She giggled. "It makes the pie dough taste better!"

"Bobchia!"

She laughed. "See those pine trees over there, the three in front of the huge ones? That tall one is the one your grampie planted the day you were born. Those other two are the ones I planted when the boys were born. Old people say the years come around fast but not these last twelve." Minnie walked up to the sidewalk, where she 'did her business.'

"Why she prefers the sidewalk to grass, I'll never know. At least I can see what she did and by the looks of things, she could use some *prune juice!*" I laughed. "Mercy, Minnie, now I'll have to wipe your tooty wouty!" She picked up the pup and held her away from her as I followed her into the kitchen's bathroom where she wiped the pup's tooty wouty.

"Well, Sweetie, I hate to tell you this, but living here is a group effort. The only way to keep cost down is if I don't have to hire help. Minnie, I don't know why you can't go in the grass, like all my other dogs did! I have no idea what you're going to do when it snows! Hold her while I wash my hands. Where was I? Oh, yes…some of the tenants like to help out, it gives them something to do and I shave off some of their rent. Lots of hands, make the work light, you know."

Needless to say, I was not thrilled.

"Remember when you helped me feed all the animals?" She asked.

"We had fun."

"We did. I held on to those memories of you, and every day when I did those things myself, I thought of how much fun we had together."

"Every day?"

"Every single day!" She took Minnie, kissed her and put her in her apron. We hugged. I turned to leave. "Where do you think you're going?"

"To check on Mother and the boys."

"Leave Clair to tend to the boys. I need you to do me a favor."

*Oh brother,* I thought, *scrub the floors, clean the toilets, ick!* I tried one last plea. "Mother expects me to watch the boys."

Bobchia took two containers out of the refrigerator and ran warm water over them and then wrapped them in a towel. "Come with me."

Bobchia led me down the hall and pulled apart pocket doors to reveal a bright orange room. "A hundred or so years ago, this room was the Inn's tavern, but your grampie converted it into this game room. Your grandfather sure had a flair for color, didn't he? I couldn't bear to change it and don't you dare mention this room to the boys. Spike and Harold had the pool table refurbished and they are fussy about it. How Paul loved playing pool with your grampie! He'd stand on a milk crate when he played, make a shot and then shove the crate underneath the table to the other side to make another shot. He also loved playing on that old shuffleboard table over there with your grampie. You did too, remember?"

I smiled as the memories came back to me. "I remember getting my fingers pinched."

"You sure did! I can still hear you screaming, blaming your grampie."

Bobchia pointed to the closet. "I keep the rollaway beds in there, in case someone needs a place to rest their weary head."

We walked further down the hall. "I added this wing a couple of years, after you left because there was no room in the Inn." Bobchia struck herself funny. '*No room at the inn*'—where have you heard that before?" She snorted.

We kept walking. "Gents *older then dirt*, stay in these smaller rooms. They don't need much space. They're widowers who get pensions from Cyclops, the steel mill. They have a good life here with their buddies, and every spring they help with the cleaning and the painting. They're a great bunch of guys." She pointed to each door and gave a name: "Mr. Hollinsworth, Mr. Carlin, Mr. Zerbe who used to play semi-pro football with your grampie, and Henry." She paused before continuing. "Oh, and there's Mr. Baker. He has twin grandsons named Jamie and Justin, who you'll probably meet at school. Then there's Archie, Gus the Q-tip man, and Mr. Zdarko. They all share those bathrooms and those two parlors." She waved at two of them as they were hunched over a checker board. "When Mr. Yoder, the barber, came, I had to put him in number five upstairs with us widows because we were all full down here. He had been staying at the Brady House downtown, but they kicked him out. For some reason, I always seem to get their *rejects!* I just pray he fits in with the rest of the strays around here, but it's too early to tell. I feel sorry for him, so I won't show him the road just yet, but he better watch his manners around your mother. This isn't a *flophouse!*"

We passed a bright red laundry room where we waved to Gladys and Cliff Pachnick folding clothes. We walked on. "Cliff is my window washer; only needs a stepladder! He's a gem alright. Let's see, this is Gladys and Cliff's room—number nine. They share that bath with Homer and Mrs. Pratt in number ten. You met Frank and Mary Galmish; this is their room, number eleven.

They share their bath with Mr. and Mrs. Dunham in room twelve. Spike and Carolyn are in number thirteen, and they share a bath with Tom and Ann in number fourteen." Bobchia got a glimmer in her eye. "Those baths used to have water closets that hung over the creek. Your grampie David told me that when he was a boy, he proudly caught the same two headed fish more than once. When he gave it to his mother, it somehow ended up back in Plum Creek, if you get *my drift.*"

She smiled as she opened the door to number fifteen, the brown parlor. "This is where Harold put Mrs. Archer last night. It's not the prettiest room for a viewing, but everything else is full up. After David passed, I gathered all his deer heads that he had scattered all over the Inn and put them in here. I thought they went well with the brown plaid wallpaper. What do you think?" Minnie peeked out of the apron and growled at the deer. "Quit acting like a dog, Miss Minnie!" The deer's eyes *followed* me as I paced behind Bobchia. Some had orange hunting hats on, some camouflage. One was mounted on a mirror with its four stuffed feet at the corners!

Bobchia motioned for me to come closer, but I refused to go into the *death room.* "Harold did a good job on Luella. She looks pretty *natural* for somebody dead." She bent over the casket and loudly said, "Luella, I hope we won't be disturbing you. Blink twice if you can hear me." Horrified, I walked backward until I ran into the opposite wall.

"Oh, erase, erase. Sweetie, I'm just *teasing* you! Luella's gone on to her reward, but I must say that turquoise chiffon jumpsuit does look better on her then it ever did me! She was taller than me but with that flowered blanket over her legs—nobody will ever know she's wearing *high water pants!* Now that I get a good look at her, she looks a little like Marilyn Monroe, with my $10.95 GIGI blond wig and red lipstick. She always was a plain Jane, but she's going out like a *movie star!*"

I could see the top of the expensive wig from the hallway. "Lucky for you Luella, Harold had some coffins stored in his garage!" She looked at me and smiled as she came into the hallway, handing me the containers. "Those deer never had anything to look at until Luella. She was a sweet lady, had eleven children and outlived three of them. Mercy, I'm chatty. I've got to cut down on the coffee!"

She went back into the room to the closet and dragged out a fan with a loose leg. "It's going to be another scorcher!" Then she reached into her pocket and pulled out a handful of rolls of duct tape in a variety of colors. With a quick glance around the room, she put the brown roll in the corner of her mouth and (like a pro) ripped off just the right amount to sturdy the fan. "It's going to be a hot one today, Luella." She turned the fan on and pointed it toward the drapes.

She paused beside the dead woman and then went to the little table in front of the window that had a lamp made out of a log with a stuffed raccoon on it. "Hi, Rocky!" She said as she rummaged through the drawer. "You don't remember seeing a pair of tweezers in here, do ya, Rocky? I know there has to be a pair in here somewhere because David used to tie flies in here. Ouch!" She pulled a hook from her finger, looking to the ceiling. "David, you caught me *again!* Oh, here they are." She walked to the casket. "Now hold still, Luella, those black hairs around your lip have bugged me for years!"

"Bobchi-chaaaa!"

She giggled. I nervously teetered from one foot to another watching the top of her hand move up and down over the dead woman's face. "*Ouuu!*" I looked up the hall for any sign of Mother.

"There. Now she doesn't look so much like Groucho. Luella made the best elderberry pies I ever ate." Bobchia smacked her lips as she entered the hallway. "Most of all she was a great wife and mother. When she and Matthew didn't have children, they adopted two sons, brothers. Then all of a sudden they had two of their own plus seven girls! They put all four sons through college, but they never came around much. Back in the day, mostly boys went to college while girls were trained for housework."

*Oh brother,* I thought, *here comes my lesson for the day.*

"Janet, Connie, Barb, and Brenda were the good daughters, but the others lost interest once she divided all her stocks and valuables. But I'm sure they'll show up tonight. That's something I never could understand."

"What?"

"Why people come around to visit the *dead* when they won't visit the *living.* Whenever I went to her house, she talked of her children as if they had just paid her a visit, repeating the same stories over and over with her Tommy cat on her lap. Great company, cats. Tommy was nearly starved when she found him one winter. Which reminds me, I wonder who is feeding Tommy *now?* Well, anyway, I need you to help me with the family that was burned out. They're down here."

I was hoping to have a long visit with Bobchia (if I could ever get a word in edgewise), but I would never refuse her anything. We walked to the next door, which didn't have a number on it. "This is my tiny emergency room, if all the other ones are full. I guess I could always move the Barber down here.

It used to be the washer room. I can still see your great grandmother, Kay, using her wringer washer in here. What a hard job *that* was! David wanted to buy his mother a modern, automatic washing machine, but she would have no part of it. She was 'old world' and as stubborn as a mule! She'd say, 'This washer is modern enough for me!' Compared to beating clothes on rocks in Croatia, and getting bloody fingers, I guess it was pretty modern!

I'll never forget the time she had that window open and a snake crawled up the ivy and into the room. Kay spotted it hanging over one of those rafters, got David's rifle and shot it—putting a hole clean through the roof! That's when we started to notice she was one bubble *shy* of a bubble bath. David hid his guns after that."

The room was just big enough for a twin bed and a small dresser. "Not a good room for anyone who is claustrophobic. However, it doesn't seem to bother Mr. McStall who stays here every whipstitch, whenever his wife kicks him out of the house. She always cools down after a couple weeks and begs him to come back home. He teaches music and theater at Pitt campus. He stutters when he talks, so he *sings* instead. What a hoot!"

"When he sings, he doesn't stutter?"

"I don't get it either."

We walked past a broom closet to room sixteen. "This is the last room on this wing, not counting the cold room next door with the stone wall, the outside wall of the Inn."

"Cold in this heat?"

"I kid you not, come here, I'll show you." She fiddled with the latch. "Sometimes I run in here when I'm having a hot flash. It cools me down, right now."

"No wonder, it's really cold in here."

"Strange, huh, but that's how they built them in the old country. Look at that craftsmanship. Go ahead, touch the stone."

"It's so cold."

"It's because of the stream. It's really, really cold in the winter. It's amazing how your ancestors carved those stones. It's a work of art, that's what it is, a work of art!" On one wall, from the ceiling to the floor was thick shelving. "And look at those shelves. I bet you couldn't buy one of those long, mahogany boards for less than a fifty cent piece today!"

The walls were dark purple, and except for two little framed parchments trimmed with needlepoint daisies that hung on a wall, it was empty. I rubbed my arms, walking to read the parchments while Bobchia recited them from memory. "Jesus said in Matthew 5:16, **'Let your light so shine before men, that they may see your good works, and glorify your Father which is in heaven.'** He also said in Matthew 25: 40, **'Verily I say unto you, Inasmuch as ye have done it unto one of the least of these my brethren, ye have done it unto me.'** I framed those; they were written in your great grandmother's hand. It's a reminder to me to not take the praise for good deeds but to tell people to give glory to God instead."

I studied the beautiful penmanship.

"She was self-taught, think of that. You come from a long line of God-fearing people who had very high standards and a strong work ethic. It's up to you and the boys to carry on the tradition that they started. Be proud!"

I mustered up a smile; she smiled back. It was too much for me to grasp! All I had wanted to do for the last twelve years was come back and live a contented life with Bobchia—that was all! How could I ever measure up to my ancestors who quoted the Bible, taught themselves how to read and write and worked until their fingers bled? It was overwhelming to me, and it was *quite evident* that Bobchia didn't know my brothers!

I opened the window and stuck my head out, taking a couple of deep breaths, checking the vines for snakes. I was distracted, looking at the thickness of the stone wall that was just as thick outside as it was inside. The sun shining on the stone made them sparkle. In my thirty's, as I thought of this conversation, I would understand what she meant but today, all my sixteen year old brain could grasp were things as deep as the shallow creek that flowed beside the Inn. "Bobchia, look two ducks!" They lazily rode the babbling water past the Inn, headed for the covered bridge.

"Probably Daisy and Donald. That reminds me, we're having gooseberry pie for supper." She stuck her head out. "Yeah, that's them. They fly up the lane, and jump in up there, for a ride down. Cute, huh?"

"I love this Inn, Bobchia, *It's where I belong.*"

"I know."

Across the hall from the cold room was a door with red-checkered curtains. It looked out onto a little whitewashed porch with a bright red porch swing and red wooden chairs.

"That's a cute porch," I said.

Bobchia looked out the window, irritated. "Somebody in this Inn *smokes!* Look, cigarette butts! If I catch who it is, there will be a room open for the barber! Our bodies are a *temple,* ya know. Besides, if a person can throw away thirty-five cents on a pack of cigarettes, then they had better be generous when the collection plate is passed come Sunday morning! That's it—Fort Pitt!"

We walked back to room sixteen. She looked up the hall before unlocking it and was careful to lock it after we went in. "These old latches..." The room was bright pink and was trimmed in white. As she opened the blinds, sun poured onto a brass bed that was embellished with flowered pillows resting on a pink spread flowing down to a pastel braided rug. A basket filled with flowery washcloths and various flowered soaps was on a cedar chest at the foot of the bed. In front of the tall windows was a pink cushioned white wicker chair and matching desk, with a glass top completed with a brass lamp. Corresponding wicker dressers and tables were throughout. It was a pretty room that reminded me of my bedroom in Florida.

Bobchia walked over to a dresser beside the bathroom. The bottom drawer was halfway pulled out. "I need you to put this ointment on her feet and face where she got burned." I leaned around the bed and saw a cat lying on some towels.

"Ahhh."

"She got burned rescuing her kittens from under the porch of the funeral home. Harold said she cried when the porch caved in because she still had kittens under there. Good mama." Bobchia checked her feet. "No infection yet." A commotion broke out in the bathroom. When I opened the door, kittens came scampering into the room, sliding on the hardwood floor and climbing up the curtains. We hurried and grabbed them before they could snag them.

"Ouch! Their claws are sharp!" I said smiling into a kitten's face

"They are the problem!" Minnie stuck her head out of the apron, growling. "Now Miss Minnie." Bobchia windshield-wiped her finger over the dog's head in front of her face.

Bobchia handed me a container of food. "Here, you feed the little ones, and I'll take care of mom." She carefully carried the cat over to the bed, laid her on a towel and applied the salve then fed her.

I finished feeding the kittens and came over to pet the cat. "Aw, what's her name?"

"Poor thing doesn't have one. Harold just called her 'Cat' when he fed her. She tried to stand, favoring one foot, then another. You name her, okay?"

"I'll have to really think about it. She deserves a special name, being a *hero.*"

A kitten climbed up the side of the bed, but Bobchia grabbed it and put it back on the floor. "These kittens won't leave her alone. They're too big to nurse. I'll run an ad in the paper next week.

"They are so cute. I don't think *I* could give any of them away!"

"That's why I have a barn full and that's why they are all *fixed.* Besides, these deserve their own special person to love. We'll have to keep them in the bathroom until then. Help me shred this newspaper for her litter box. It won't aggravate her paws like litter but it will have to be changed at least three times a day. The kitten's box is in the bathroom and should be scooped daily. I know your Mother doesn't like cats, so don't say anything to anyone about them being in here! Your great aunts Ardelle and Wanda hate them too. Mercy, I don't know how anybody could *hate* a cat! Well, one reason is because when Ardelle's mother died, she willed them Lucky, her little, green parakeet. The poor thing hasn't chirped since the old lady passed. Anyway, last year Cutie Boy, one of the strays from the barn, climbed up the tree outside their window, jumped through their screen, and tried to kill the poor bird. I thought Ardelle and Wanda were going to have coronaries! I had to put bars on their windows so they wouldn't move out. It sure spoiled the looks of the Inn on that side, but oh well. Your grampie David and I had a *pact* that we would take care of our relatives if they ever needed a place to stay, so they're here for the *long haul.* Every Easter I go to Erie with them for the Matkovich reunion. Next year you can go with us. We have to take that stupid bird with us, stopping now and then to change its papers. Or I suppose we could drive with the windows *down!*" She giggled. "You'll be surprised what a fuss the relatives make over that bird. I have pictures on the side of the refrigerator of your relatives at the reunion last year. Remind me to show them to you."

The cat meowed. "Ahh that's alright, girl." Bobchia said to her. Then she turned to me. "I'll give you a key. You'll have to feed the mom three times a day and check her head and feet for infection and also feed the kittens and clean the litter boxes. We'll have to keep these cats our little secret for now."

"You mean this is it? All I have to do is *babysit cats?*"

"Well I guess you could clean some toilets if you get bored."

"I don't think I'll get bored..." I smiled.

"I didn't think you would." She carefully picked up that cat and put her in the litter box.

"The boys like cats."

"She needs TLC. They can play with the strays in the barn for now. Let's keep this to ourselves until she's healed, okay?"

"No problem."

The cat carefully got out of the box, and Bobchia put her back on the bed, while the kittens tried to climb up the bedspread to get to her.

"I'll have to get her fixed, when she's up to it." The cat leaned down, licking the kittens faces as they jumped at her. "My, they sure are a rowdy bunch!"

"Meow."

"I've got to find homes for these kittens!" We pulled the kittens off of the bedspread then she laid the cat back in the drawer.

We laughed at Minnie's little growl as the kittens scampered across the braided rug and slid on the hardwood floor. Bobchia put her down to play but the kittens turned on her, chasing her until she yipped, trying to climb Bobchia's leg. "Not so brave now, huh, Miss Minnie?" Giggling, she scooped her up, putting her back into her apron. "You better put the kittens in the bathroom."

"Okay."

Minnie got brave, stuck her head out and barked. "Shh! You'll wake the dead... down the hall."

"Bobchia!"

We went back to the kitchen and washed our hands. Bobchia slid the tin of cookies down to me.

"Thanks."

"How do pork chops for dinner sound?"

"Sounds great!"

She opened the refrigerator and sighed. "If I've told Gladys once, I've told her a hundred times, I don't have room for linen blouses in my fridge!" She pulled out six rolled-up blouses and put them on the counter beside the pork chops to thaw. "She'll have to spray starch, like the rest of us!"

Just then the boys burst into the kitchen, dripping wet. Mother yelled from behind them, "Take off those shoes and go directly to the bathroom and get in that tub!"

"Why do we have to get in the tub? We're already w-e-t!" Logan moaned.

When Mother came in, she shook her head. "I don't know what on earth possessed them! I turned my back for a second to get their blankets out of the car when Logan jumped off the little bridge. Andrew, of course, had to do the same dumb thing!"

Bobchia whispered to me, "Well, that *answers* that age old question!" I snickered.

Mother turned back to the boys. "Don't you look at me like that! Get into the tub! You can stay inside for the rest of the day!" Bobchia handed Mother a towel to wipe up the steps.

I got back into the tin and looked out the window. "I don't remember there being a flag painted on the red barn before."

"That's because it wasn't there when you were here before. I have a truck driver friend named Caleb, who wanted to go to Vietnam and fight for our country, but for whatever reason, he couldn't go. God gave him the gift of painting, so one day a couple of years back he got the idea to make the red barn patriotic. I like how he put 'One Nation' across the top of the flag and 'Under God' across the bottom, don't you? His Uncle Ed is a World War II Vet and owns the Valley View Turkey Farm, anyway, one day, when he was delivering turkeys here and saw Caleb painting the red barn; he talked him into painting his barns too. We'll take a ride out there so you can see how beautiful they are. He's even a little famous. Whenever he traveled the interstate in Virginia, he'd pass a huge dairy farm on a hillside. He got permission to paint flags on those barns and someone from *Look Magazine* took pictures of them and did a story on Caleb. I have a copy of it upstairs. I'll show it to you. After that, he got several offers from farmers all over the United States to paint flags on their barns. That's his dream—to paint flags on barns in memory of Veterans but unfortunately painting barns doesn't pay the bills. It's a down right pity he can't make a living out of painting, especially when he's so good at it."

Mother came downstairs and poured herself a cup of coffee. "We were just talking about my artist friend Caleb. He's the one who painted the flag on our red barn and on his Uncle Ed's barn at the Valley View Turkey Farm. I thought you might enjoy taking a ride out there, now that it quit raining. Not only do they have turkeys; they have sheep, cows, all kinds of animals. I think the boys would enjoy it. "

Mother nodded. "Sounds good. The boys are getting dressed and then they were going to count the money in their piggy banks."

Just then the boys ran downstairs with towels tied around their necks, carrying their banks.

Andrew ran up to Bobchia. "Do you have any change that you ain't usin' for nothin' right now?"

"Andrew! I told you not to ask your grandmother for money!" Mother blushed.

Bobchia shook her head. "It's okay. I have a couple of dollars in my purse. Let me get it."

Logan stopped her. "We don't want d-a-l-e-r-s."

"What did you just spell?"

"Dollars."

Andrew explained, "We want change because it fills the bank up faster. Mom says when it's full we can get a toy and put the rest in the bank."

"Well then," Bobchia said, "I have a couple of quarters."

"Don't ya got any *pennies?*" Andrew's shoulders dropped.

Mother chimed in, "One quarter a piece will be plenty. Thank you, Rhea. Now I don't want you boys asking your grandmother for any more money, is that understood?"

The boys hung their heads and nodded. (They never *asked* again, but whenever they left their banks in front of Bobchia's bedroom door at night, they were heavier by morning.)

To the Turkey Farm we went. The paintings on the barns were beautiful.

"Man, look at that ship with a flag on it!"

"I like that round flag on that plane!"

A row of tanks with flags hanging from their gun barrels were painted on the backs of the low, red-white-and-blue turkey pens.

"Boy, I wish I could paint like that!" I said. Bobchia stuck her head out of the car window and gobbled at the turkeys, and the turkeys gobbled back. She smiled watching the boys in the rear view mirror 'talking turkey.' We counted the sheep in the fields and visited the pigs and laughed watching Farmer Ed demonstrate cow milking, spraying the kittens with milk wheneven they got close.

The boys did not want to leave, and kicked the back of Bobchia's car seat as the tour continued in Titusville.

"Ya know something boys? 'Seat kickers' are not allowed apple pie!" They stopped kicking. Up and down the town she drove. She showed us the stores and pointed out Penn Theatre, Benson Memorial Library, Pitt University and Colestock High School, where I would go, across the street from the newer built Colonel Drake Elementary School, where the boys would attend.

"It's a shame they don't read the Bible before school starts anymore," she said. "Mercy! I feel bad for the children who don't go to church. How are they ever to hear the Word of God? Mark my words—when you take God out of anything, *chaos follows!* I suppose that *next* they'll take Jesus out of the school's Christmas program!"

"Bobchia, they would never do that!" Andrew said.

"Yeah, we *always* got to celebrate Jesus' birthday. It's f-u-n!"

Mother barely lifted her eyes from her fingernail filing as Bobchia proudly enlightened us on Father's scholastic and athletic achievements.

"That school is o-l-d!"

Bobchia stopped the car.

"Are we going in this old place?" Logan scrunched up his nose.

"Not today, I was thinking we could go to Islay's for an ice cream sundae." She pointed down the block. The boys squealed and jumped out of the car.

We ate our sundaes in the park gazebo across the street. "When I was a kid, I'd make what I called ice cream 'gerish' and then drink it." Bobchia stirred and stirred, and the boys followed suit.

"Yum, *gerish.*" They drank their sundaes, getting ice cream on their noses.

"This is a nice town, Bobchia," I said.

"It's the best," she smiled.

"How would you know?" Mother asked. "You've never lived *anywhere else.*"

"I don't need to go anywhere else, Clair, *I love it here.*"

"But how do you know for sure? You're *sheltered.* You've never seen the world."

"Clair, I know for *sure.* Your treasure is where your heart is, and mine is *here.* I've never come into town and not had someone wave at me. Why would I ever move?" Someone yelled hello at Bobchia from across the street and waved. "See there?" She drank her sundae getting ice cream on her nose. She giggled.

We heard thunder in the distance and soon it started to sprinkle.

"It sure rains here a lot." Logan said.

"That's what makes the trees so pretty, honey boy."

"Can we have a huge Christmas tree with popcorn garland? I saw it in a movie." I blurted.

"I think that can be arranged." Bobchia smiled sweetly.

The rain snapped Bobchia into action. "Mercy, we better get this show on the road. Dinner's at six. How does pork chops sound?"

"I want mine with American cheese on top!"

"Me T-w-o!"

"What, no ketchup?"

"Ketchup on top!" We hurried to the car. She giggled messing Andrew's hair as he climbed into the back seat.

Lightening flashed as we drove up the lane to the Inn. Just as we got out of the car, the rains came. We ran onto the porch and watched the water wash the land.

"I want to go to the barn and see the animals!" Andrew said.

"You'll get soaked." Bobchia shook her head. "Besides, the animals get spooked when it thunders and they are hunkered down by now."

"Please," Logan begged.

"Tomorrow will be better, besides I've got to get supper on the table." Bobchia said definitively. She cringed watching them stomp across the porch.

After dinner while I was feeding Joan of Arc, (an appropriate name for a burnt hero cat); I glanced out the window and saw Spike under an umbrella, kicking over the woodpile that the stranger had piled up. I stood there thinking about what Bobchia said, about people's dignity, not realizing that I must not have latched the door. The kittens had managed their way down the hall, to Mrs. Archer's room where her family had gathered to pay their last respects! I panicked, creeping down the hall just in time to see a kitten make his way between someone's feet and onto the fringe of the drapes, blowing from the breeze of the fan.

"Mother looks like a *floozy* with that red lipstick on!"

"I hardly recognized her!"

"Her mustache is *gone!*"

"How did her hair get so *thick?*"

"Look how thick it got!"

"She must have gotten that ugly pantsuit from the Salvation Army!"

A kitten played with beads dangling from a lady's hand, while she prayed at the casket. Another had made her way through a fern and onto her wig, pulling it to one side as it fell into the coffin. A woman screamed! I ran in not thinking of the looming deer heads, franticly trying to gather the kittens. A woman yelled; "I have never seen anything so disrespectful in my entire life!"

A man got into my face. "Who let these beasts in here?"

Everyone was screaming at me. Bobchia and Harold rushed in. "If this gets out—I'll be *ruined!*" He said nervously.

All the mourners yelled, threatening them. I could see the panic in Bobchia's eyes as she straightened Mrs. Archer's wig, then grabbed a kitten from the casket. She gave me a disappointed look as she turned to face the mob. She looked down at Mrs. Archer. "I'm sorry, Luella."

"*You should be sorry!*" A son said. "Desecrating mother's body! First a fire..." He looked at Harold, then the deer heads, then at Bobchia's apron with Minnie's head poked out, growling at him. "And now this make-shift *zoo* funeral home!"

I could almost see the wheels turning in Bobchia's head as she turned to speak into the casket. "I'm sorry that everyone is so upset, Luella. I know how much you loved animals." Bobchia turned back to the mourners. "This is what Luella would have wanted, to be *surround by kittens.*" She looked to Harold for help, but he was speechless, dead in the water. He was afraid to even blink! A kitten climbed up his pant leg, across his chest and onto his shoulder. Another kitten fell from a fern.

"Meow." She walked over and picked it up.

A huge man cornered Bobchia by the casket. She looked at him and just as he put his chubby finger in her face she rallied and continued, "If Luella told me once, she told me a million times that she wished people would take in strays and give them a good home, like she did. She called cats her *only* friends." She sniffled, continuing, "How appropriate that these kittens could have run into any room in this big Inn yet chose this one to be a part of *this* solemn occasion."

"What do you mean *only* friends?" her son asked.

Her daughter asked, "Were these all mother's cats? I thought she just had a sickly old tomcat."

Bobchia looked sternly at Luella's children.

"When was the last time any of you visited Luella? It doesn't matter if these cats were hers or not. She would gladly have taken all these kittens in and loved every one of them. It's a tragedy that so many people dump defenseless animals! *God sees all!* Of course, I don't know what will happen to these sweet little ones."

A granddaughter said, "I'd take one, but I don't know how to take care of a cat."

Bobchia took the one off of Harold's shoulder. "It's not at all hard. Just food, litter and the most important thing—" She handed the teen a kitten.

"What's that?"

"*Love.*"

A son sobbed in the chair next to the casket. "I wish I would have visited you more often, Mother. Now it's too late." Bobchia made her way over to him, pulling a stubborn black and white kitten off the drapes on her way.

"It's going to be all right," she said as she patted his shoulder. "And I'm sure your mother would have wanted you to have little...*Oreo.*" The son looked up at her and smiled and in one smooth move, she handed him the kitten, patted his shoulder sympathetically, grabbed Harold's shirtsleeve and pulled him into the hallway. I was on her heels.

We hurried to Joan of Arc's room. She latched the door. Harold grabbed Bobchia by the shoulders and kissed her. "You are the most amazing woman!"

"Mercy, Harold! Jennifer's here!"
She grinned. "You have to *strike* while the iron is hot!"

A little orange kitten scampered out from under the bed.

"Oh no! Not another one!" Bobchia scooped it up. "Mercy, I guess I'll just have to keep you, you little *pumpkin,*" she said, as she kissed its little head.

"Hey, that's a good name for it!" I said.

"It is isn't it? I'll give him to the boys to teach them responsibility."

Harold peeked out the door. "I think were in the clear. At least I don't hear any ruckus. I'll check."

As soon as he walked out the door, I turned to Bobchia. "I'm so sorry that the kittens got out! They just sneaked out, honest!"

Bobchia pulled out her hankie from her sleeve and wiped her forehead. "That was quite a scare. It was like being in a lion's den, but I do so like a *challenge!* No harm done! So have you named the cat yet?"

"Joan of Arc."

"How appropriate!" She giggled.

Harold returned. "They're all gone."

"Kittens too?"

"*Kittens too!*"

"That's music to my ears! Now remember Harold, when you bury dear Luella tomorrow, only put *half* the flowers on her grave and take the other half to Pine Grove Care Home, like last time."

"Okay." She kissed him on the cheek.

"Wonderful! *TYG* for blessing me with homes for the kittens, and please bless all of Luella's relatives." Bobchia looked at the ceiling. Her eyes caught the clock on the wall. "Mercy, I'm missing Lawrence Welk! Tonight he was having a tribute to Glenn Miller and I'm missing it! Oh, and don't forget the hymn sing in the great room at 8:15 sharp! We always start with *Amazing Grace*, my favorite. For your information, Sweetie, it was written by a reformed slave trader named John Newton." She looked to the ceiling. "*No sin is too horrid for my Lord and Savior to forgive. TYG*" She started down the hall.

"How does she *know* all these things?" I asked Harold.

"Beats me," he said.

"Oh, Bobchia," I called after her. "I'm not a very *good* singer!"

"None of us are, but when we make a *joyful noise,* it's music to *His* ears!"

# 4

## Sunday

Early the next morning I heard a knock, knock, knock on my door, accompanied by Bobchia's cheery voice declaring, *"This is the day that the Lord has made! We will rejoice and be glad in it!"*

It was Sunday, and everyone that lived under Bobchia's roof went to church except for Mr. Pill, who blamed God for everything that ever had gone wrong, or *will ever* go wrong, in his entire life! Bobchia took great pleasure in knocking on his door the loudest until he grunted at her to leave him alone.

After the Cutie Boy incident, Aunt Ardelle and Wanda had an understanding with Bobchia, alternating their church going so Lucky would never be left alone again. Today it was Wanda's turn to *bird sit* and to man the Garland commercial gas ranges that were cooking our dinner, until Bobchia returned.

At the breakfast table, Andrew divvied out bacon to Logan and himself as Mother confessed to Bobchia that we hadn't been to church since Father's passing.

"For almost *two years*, Clair?" Bobchia looked at the boys. *"Well, that sure explains a lot!"*

"What was *that?"* Mother pursed her lips.

"Oh, sorry Clair. Erase, erase, erase! So let me get this straight. You *blame* God for taking Paul? That's *nonsense!* If you are going to blame someone, Clair, blame the *devil!* Yes, from time to time we all deal with rough sailing, but God is our compass and will guide us to our destination! He is *love."*

"But—" Mother started.

"No buts about it. People in other countries *die* because of their faith in Jesus and here we sit in America where *all roads lead to church!* Everyone should talk to *the Man Upstairs!* Mercy, think of the *children!* They need to know right from wrong, and they'll enjoy meeting new friends in Sunday school."

Andrew piped up. "I want to go!"

"Me t-w-o!" Logan mumbled through his bacon.

I smiled remembering the fun I had had in church and how close the family had been back then. "I really do *miss* going to church, Mother."

Bobchia looked triumphant. "See! Now, don't dilly-dally. Hurry and finish eating!"

Mother didn't look convinced. "I had planned on going back to church *someday,* really. I just don't know if *today* is the right day for us."

"Well, if a farmer waited for *perfect weather,* the corn wouldn't be knee high by the fourth of July! That's it, Fort Pitt! Now, I have to change my clothes and help Ginger find her specs. She couldn't find them last week either. I know I have another chain for glasses somewhere…anyway, I'll meet you all by the front door at 9:45."

Mother mumbled something about Bobchia being *'Mrs. Perfect'* as she and the boys climbed the stairs.

I took another cinnamon roll. "Stuff that roll in your mouth and help me put these dishes in the sink. I hate to leave a mess for Wanda." Bobchia said.

Curiously I asked; "Do you ever have people stay here who *won't* go to church? What about the guy that banged on the wall? Does he *go* to church?"

"While it pains me to say it, I give folks like that *three Sundays* (like three strikes), and then they are O-U-T. I realize *I* can't *save* anyone because that's God's job, but I can *persuade* people to go to church while they're under *my* roof. I know my limitations, which is why I made a *vow to God* a few years ago to show the person the road after the *third* Sunday. Mr. Pill is my only exception to the rule. Some people, Sweetie, ruin their lives by their own foolishness and then get angry at the Lord for *letting them do it.* Mr. Pill is getting ready for a *breakthrough;* I can feel it! At any rate, I have too many prayers invested in that old coot to throw him out."

I was mulling over what she had said. "What does it mean that you 'made a *vow* to God'?"

"I think of it as my highest promise to God, to make sure *I* keep my word to Him. The way I look at it, if the Apostle Peter, who *ate* with Christ and *saw* with his own two eyes all the *miraculous things* He did, and he *still* denied Him, who am I to think I couldn't be *swayed* by someone? At the drop of a hat things could turn the other way, and I *refuse* to let the devil get a foothold in this Inn!"

"Well what if they don't go to church and they *refuse* to leave?"

"That's happened before. And that's why I have my formidable team of Spike, Cliff and Cecil. They have helped me out more than once, or I should say that they have helped *others out to the front lawn."*

I had a sudden awful thought. "What if Mother would have *refused* to go to church today and next week and the week after that? Would you have kicked *us out*, Bobchia? Would you have put *me* out on the front lawn?"

"TYG that didn't happen!"

"But what if it *did* happen?"

"Oh Sweetie, I drew that line in the sand years ago when I made God *first* in my life. If Clair would have refused to take you kids and go to church, I…I would be upstairs right now *praying and fasting* until I got a clear word from the Lord. He *knows* you are the most important person in the world to me and that I'd sooner burn down this Inn than not have you in it! *He is first in my life.* He has to be! God should be the most important person in your life too. *Is He?*"

I hesitated. "Yes, but—"

"No buts. He either *is* or He *isn't!* Now let's not make a mountain out of a mole hill! That's it, Fort Pitt! Now get dressed; I'm ready to worship!"

We were waiting by the front door promptly at 9:45. "Bobchia you look so pretty." I said.

"Plain, simple and in good taste, is what my mother always said besides seersucker is the *only* way to go in this heat!"

"You look skinny without Minnie." Andrew complemented.

"Where is she?" Logan asked.

"She is still in the apron but in her bed upstairs."

"Can we take her?" Logan pleaded.

"Mercy, to *church?*"

"God loves animals!" Andrew shook his head.

"Yeah, why can't she g-o?" Logan asked.

She looked at them, "He does *love* animals but honey boys… the apron doesn't *go* with the dress! My, you boys look quite handsome when you're all scrubbed up!"

Mother smiled saying "Cleanness is next to Godliness!"

"That's really *not true* Clair but at least we won't have to ride with the windows *down!*"

Mother rolled her eyes as the misfit tenants strolled past us to get into the vehicles. The women wore skirts and blouses with various 'themed' sweaters of humming birds, puppies, kittens, birdhouses and flowers. Except for Gladys, who said it was too hot for a sweater so instead had a fox fur hugging her neck. The boys begged to ride in the van, to pet the 'dead furry thing.' "It's impolite to stare and **no** you cannot pet it! You will ride in the car!" Mother insisted.

The old gents strutted by. Bobchia whispered; *"Moth-balls on parade"* Then she sneezed.

"GBY, Bobchia."

"Thank you Andrew."

Mr. Hair stood smiling up at Mother, until Bobchia guided him out the door. Ginger was at the end of the pack in a black flowing dress and a big, black hat cocked on her head. The netting concealed her face. Her spectacles swaying on a long, imitation mother of pearl chain, completed her ensemble.

"Sweetie, you are as pretty as a picture!" Holding the camera at arm's length, Bobchia took pictures of me and her, then the boys and her, then me and the boys, while mother stood in the hallway, irritated. We saw spots the whole way to the quaint, stone church that had a sign in front reading: '**Evil will win, if Christians do nothing!**'

Bobchia parked the car and said; "I was glad when they said to me let us go into the house of the Lord! This is a *blest* day to have my family in church with me *again!* You will love it here as much as I do!"

Along with Andrew's ball glove, Bobchia convinced Ginger that her mourning hat should be left on the seat as well; otherwise the view of Pastor Jay would be obstructed. The fox went in.

We walked into a gathering of welcoming Christian people and as we proceeded past the sanctuary to the Sunday school classrooms, the boys tried to read the long, brightly woven banners hanging down the high walls of the church, with Mother's help.

"**Jesus is the way, the truth and the life.**"

"**Come to me, all ye that labor and are heavy laden, and I will give you rest.**"

"**For God so loved the world, that He gave his only begotten Son, that whosoever believeth in Him, should not perish but have eternal life.**"

Pastor's wife, Lois, was the boy's Sunday school teacher and a gifted pianist, playing the piano during church. The words of Pastor Jay's sermon; "God gave his only Son to die for us" resonated in our hearts.

When the service had ended, we stood in line waiting to meet the pastor and his family, as they stood on the church steps. Mother quietly tried to explain to the boys that "the older ladies do not have *tattoos* on their legs!"

"That one looks like 'Starry' our starfish!" Logan pointed.

"I know!" Andrew hunkered down in front of a lady.

Mother pulled the boys to her "Shh. Those are not tattoos, those are *varicose veins.*"

"What's that?" Logan asked.

"Shhhh, I'll tell you later. *Be quiet!*"

At last we were the next in line to shake the Pastor's hand. Bobchia glared at the boys then turned to introduce us to Pastor Jay and his wife, along with their six year old twin daughters, Samantha and Amanda and their toddler Cora Rose. They looked quaint standing on the steps straight backed, the tallest to the smallest, with the Pastor sporting a polka-dot tie matching Lois and the girls' pink and white polka-dot shirt waist dresses. (For years, Pastor Jay had prayed for our family to be reunited, and this was the *moment* that Bobchia had waited for.)

"Our prayers have been answered, Pastor Jay." Bobchia said beaming.

The Pastor's family extended their hands to shake Mother's, then mine, as Bobchia proudly introduced us but when the boys stuck out their hands, Logan whispered to Andrew; "On the count of three, ready?"

"One... two... three!" Andrew blurted out *"Pull my finger!"*

"Andrew!"

*"Mercy!"*

*"Logan* made me say it! *He* made me say it! Well he *did!*" Andrew kicked Logan!

*"Ouch!"*

Bobchia put her hand on her heart. "Oh my and right on the *church steps!*"

Mother, mortified said through clenched teeth, "Tell Pastor Jay *you are sorry,* right this very minute! Go on! Tell him right now or *so help me young man...*"

"You are sorry right this very minute but *he's the one that made me say it! Honest, he did!*"

I was so embarrassed! I hurried down the steps and saw some teens standing beside the church sign. A couple of girls motioned to me to come over. I slowly walked to them. They were all so friendly—especially Beverly Jean and Dawnette. They invited me to go with them to Teen Action at church on Wednesday nights. (Little did I know at that time that those friendships would span over the next sixty years.) Dawnette had written her phone number on my church bulletin and made me promise to sign up for the second lunch period at school so I could sit with her and Beverly Jean. I was relieved to know I'd see a few friendly faces on my first day of school, but I was *cautious* to make new friends since I had been hurt in the past. I quickly said goodbye seeing Mother push the boys to the car. "I have never been so *humiliated* in my life!" Scolded Mother.

"That's what you said *last* time!" Andrew pouted.

Bobchia was red as a beet taking out a hankie from her purse then tossed her purse into the back seat.

She wiped her forehead and turned to me with a smile. "I'm glad to see you met Dawnette. Her parents are the most wonderful Christians! Ramona and Garwood come over every Wednesday for Bible study and sometimes to play cards." She paused and patted her face again with a hanky. "Anyway, everyone in the car! Roast of beef, here we come!"

Once we were in, Bobchia asked if we'd enjoyed the service.

"We did," I answered quickly.

"Boy that Lois sure can make that piano *sing!* Speaking of singing, I noticed you didn't sing this morning, Logan."

Logan stuck his lower lip out. "I was singing, but I had my voice turned o-f."

"Ah. Well, have it turned o-n next Sunday, or the TV will be turned o-f! There's no church service tonight because Pastor Jay's mother is in the hospital with a broken leg. What a shame!"

Andrew picked up Bobchia's New Testament, which had fallen out of her purse along with her camera. "Hey, why is your Bible so *little?*"

"It's not the *whole* Bible, honey it doesn't have the *Old* Testament in it. It's just the *New* Testament."

Andrew thumbed through the pages, "I think this is the *Old* Testament, Bobchia."

"You do?"

"Yeah… because all the pages are *bent!*"

We laughed, then sang ***Jesus Loves Me*** on the way back to the Inn. Bobchia was right; going to church was *just what we needed.* I noticed that even Mother had a tear in her eye as we rode down the lane.

As soon as Bobchia parked the car, the boys ran to the little bridge and began throwing stones into the water.

"Don't you *dare* jump off that bridge!" Mother hollered. We caught up to them.

Bobchia glanced up at the sky. "TYG for chasing the clouds away."

"Hey Bobchia, why did you wave at the preacher when we were singing in church this morning?" Andrew asked, cocking his head.

"Oh, honey boy, I wasn't *waving.* The song touched my heart, and I was holding my hand up *agreeing* with the words. '*I'll cherish the old rugged cross and exchange it someday for a crown.*' Understand?"

"Nope."

"Well, let me ask you a question. What is it on TV that makes *you cheer and throw your hands up into the air?*"

"*A homerun!*" Andrew said without hesitation.

"Whenever a song touches my heart and I wave my hand back and forth, it's like *cheering* for the words of the song like you do for a homerun, understand?"

Andrew was silent as he thought it over. We continued our walk to the Inn. Bobchia spoke up, "Oh, before I forget, do you see those three trees over there?" We nodded and she continued, "One is named Jennifer, one Logan and one Andrew. They were planted on the days you were born. Walk over there so I can get a picture of you in front of them." I walked over and the boys slumped after me. "Now smile! You are not smiling. Good! Hold it right there. I hope that didn't put too much strain on your smilers!"

Mother was at the front steps, reading aloud the daisy motif plaques on either side of the door. "**My Country and my Inn, love them or leave them!**" She leaned to read the other. "**Welcome to the Red Barn Inn, where smoking and drinking is a sin. You're welcome to stay, then be on your way; come**

**back again when you kin!"** Mother mumbled something about *Looney Tunes* as she slowly walked inside.

The kitchen smelled of the roasts and baked beans that Bobchia had put in the ovens before leaving for church. Aunt Ardelle rushed to the dining room's bookcase to check on Lucky as Spike went right to work, pouring the drippings from the roasts into saucepans and adding some potato water from the boiling potatoes so Bobchia could make gravy. We hurried to change our clothes.

Just as we were returning to the kitchen a car sped down the lane and came to a squealing halt in front of the little bridge. Bobchia shook her head. "It's only *hot rod* Harold in the hearse!"

The boys ran to the window to look at the funny car. "Wow! I never seen a car like that!"

Harold hurried into the kitchen. "The bad news is that I *missed* church, but the good news is that *I planted Mrs. Archer!*"

Mother gave Harold 'the look' and he quickly put his head down and mumbled, *"Bless her little heart."*

"Can we ride in your long car?" Andrew asked Harold.

*"No!"* Mother said emphatically.

Bobchia looked at Harold. "Mercy, how could you drive the hearse with that neck brace?"

Harold smiled. "Slowly."

"You? *Slowly?"*

"Through the intersections, I mean!"

Bobchia ordered "Get some of Wayne's corn out of the freezer, the water is boiling, Harold."

He poured the corn into the boiling water telling us we were "in for a treat."

Cliff mashed the potatoes and Bobchia poured the bubbling gravy into gravy Boats as Harold told us that his son, Wayne and his wife Jody and their kids live on his old homestead and that they keep the Inn supplied with fresh vegetables and beef. He told us about the fun he had picking corn with his grandchildren.

Bobchia rang the old school bell in the hallway. "Dinner in a *few!"* Aunt Ardelle, Wanda, Mother and Bobchia lifted the dinner while the tenants gathered. Bobchia said grace with her hands palms up, and the boys mimicked her. "Dear God, You are so merciful to us. TYG for this beautiful Lord's Day and for *blessing* me to go to church with my family once again! Thank You for answering *all* my prayers! I love You awful! Bless this food to the nourishment of our bodies and keep us in the palm of Your hand. In Christ our Lord, Amen." She smiled at the boys. "You're learning fast."

Mr. Hair came in and slid into the chair beside Mother. Bobchia gave him 'the look.'

"Bobchia! Guess what you forgot?" Logan said

"The ketchup is on the table."

"But the American cheese ain't!"

"Isn't." Mother said as she volunteered to get it, hurrying away from Mr. Hair. When she returned she sat at the other end of the table.

Bobchia smiled as we enjoyed our ketchup-covered meal. Everything was so delicious!

She proudly listened to the boys repeat their Sunday school lesson of Noah on the ark and got a kick out of watching them line their green beans and corn two by two around the edges of their plates.

She answered the boys' questions of "How did the snails climb up the ramp of the ark without getting stepped on by the elephants?" and "Why would Noah build a ark when it ain't even rained one drop in the whole world yet?"

Frank, a retired pastor, had a trick question of his own, to the boys "In Genesis, the first book of the Bible, how do you suppose God knew to tell Noah, over 4,000 years ago, to build an ark six times its width so it would *float* and not sink?"

Andrew was ready. "I can't know what *that* means, but my Sunday school teacher said that God knows *everything*—even how I act when my Mother ain't in class with me."

Frank beamed. "You are right! *God knows absolutely everything!*"

The boys ate their corn but pushed their beans around the edges of their plates.

Bobchia scowled. "You're making me dizzy. If you want to go for a walk with me, you better eat those green beans before dark!"

Andrew shrugged his shoulders. "I can't know if I can eat them."

"I *don't know* if I can eat them!" Mother corrected.

"Me either!" said Andrew.

Bobchia laughed. Aunt Ardelle and Gladys got the zwiebach pies out of the refrigerator, but we were all 'stuffed to the eyeballs,' as Bobchia put it, so we decided to eat the pie after we'd 'walked off' some of our dinner.

"Come on Sweetie, *you and I* will take a walk and look at the cute animals in the barn."

That caught the boys' attention. "Okay, okay, we'll eat the stupid beans!" With plugged noses they downed the beans making gagging noises.

I laughed at them as I took my plate to the sink. Venal hurried and washed my plate and handed it to Izora to dry; the ladies were in a hurry to get into their favorite rockers on the porch, to watch the horseshoe tournament.

Finally we made our way to the porch where people were cheering for Cecil, the horseshoe champion, who was playing against Spike. The boys ran the length of the porch, dodging the rockers, then down the steps to the side yard, looking up the flagpole at the American flag blowing gracefully in the breeze along with the Croatian, Polish and Italian flags blowing beneath it.

Logan followed Andrew's gaze. "Wow, it's our American flag and somebody else's in Bobchia's own y-r-d! Remember what Father said?" Logan asked.

Andrew shook his head. "'Spect the flag. That's what Father said."

Logan nodded and put his hand over his heart while Andrew mumbled after him, "I pledge allegiance to the flag of the United States of America, and to the republic for which it stands, one nation *under God* indivisible, with liberty and justice for all....*Play ball!* Want to?"

Bobchia sniffed. Her right hand was over her heart but her left hand held her camera, snapping a picture of them. Mother smiled with pride until she saw Mr. Hair waving at her, then she ran down the steps, pulling the boys from getting their baseball gear from under the car seat to join her sprinting down the lane.

"Hey!" Andrew protested.

"We're going to play ball!" Logan said

"You're it!" She cleverly said as she tapped Logan. Logan tapped Andrew and ran after her.

Mr. Hair followed until he got winded then leaned against a tree to straighten his toupee.

Bobchia and I watched from the porch. "I never knew your Mother was so *athletic*, Sweetie!"

"Me either."

Bobchia and I walked along the white fence with tall bushes, passing Mr. Hair. "Those are the rhododendron your grampie David planted from seedlings, the summer after we were married. They remind me so much of him. How that man loved working outdoors, now look they are taller than Cliff!"

Mother walked backwards, to keep an eye on Mr. Hair. Some tenants rode past us on bicycles saying 'hello.'

"Those bushes are not much to look at now but you just wait. They get beautiful pink and purple blooms in the spring. People drive down the lane, just to look at them! You'll love it here in the spring, Sweetie!"

"I'll love it here in the *spring, summer, fall, and winter!*"

Mother turned, giving me 'the look', noticing Mr. Hair was gaining ground and ran past the boys who were playing tag in the pumpkin patch, on the other side of Bobchia's fence.

We waved passing the boys and while walking passed a brick house, Bobchia said "Hello" to a young boy and a girl on the porch drinking soda pop. They smirked at her. "That's Lucy and Ricky. He's ten and she's seven now, I guess."

"*Lucy and Ricky*, are you kidding?"

"It was Sue's favorite TV show. They have an older brother, Lanny, around twelve. The best of the litter, Luke, got married a while back. I pray hard for Lanny, he's as ornery as his father, Butch." She smiled back at the porch. "They sure look sweet sitting there, don't they?"

"Yeah, I guess."

"A couple of times I caught them calling Dollee Doll to the fence only to throw stones at her but that only made me pray **harder** for them to go to Sunday school!"

"Who is Dollee Doll?"

"Spike's horse."

"Spike has a *horse*? Is she *tame*? Do you think he will let me *ride her?*"

"Yes, yes and yes! Can I finish the rest of my story?"

"Yes cheee."

We passed the house and stopped.

"Anyway, Benjamin and Judith lived here and had one child, Butch. They were good decent people. They never missed a church service, and they did charity work to beat the band. Then Butch married a nice gal named Sue and moved away. When Benjamin passed, Butch, Sue and the kids moved in with Judith. Judith brought them to church with her, and they were the nicest people. Then, about a year after Judith passed, Sue got ill and had to go into Pine Grove. When she died, Butch grew very bitter. The kids used to come visit me on Fridays when I baked cookies, but Butch called it charity and made them stay home. He's as stubborn as the day is long. I used to drop off meals every now and then, but he kept returning them, so I finally quit. But I put them on the prayer list at church. It's so sad. Sometimes bad things happen to good people. But they were raised to believe in God, and His word says that they will come back to Him."

The boys screamed! We ran back to the pumpkin patch where Lanny was chasing them and shaking his fist.

"*Get out!* Get out now or I'll call the police!" he yelled.

"Andrew, Logan, come here right now!" Bobchia yelled.

"We were only *looking* at the stupid pumpkins, Bobchia!" Andrew protested.

"H-o-n-i-s!" Logan spelled.

"Hey, shrimps! Are you sissies, hiding behind an *old lady?*" Lanny taunted.

Bobchia wheeled to face Lanny. "Watch your mouth! I'm not too old to give *you* what for! You need to go to church and learn some *respect!*"

The boys made faces at Lanny behind Bobchia's back and then looked sad when she turned around. She nudged them toward the Inn. "He used to be a nice boy, coming to the Inn to play with the strays, but once that child grew *armpit hair,* I thought the school would close down!"

"Bobchia, that is so funny!" I laughed.

"And the truth! A bully is only a *coward* in disguise—remember that!"

Mother came running, dodging Mr. Hair's open arms. "What was all that screaming about?"

"That big kid chased us out of the pumpkin patch!" Andrew whined.

"He did? But it's on your grandmother's property!" Mother looked questioningly toward Bobchia.

"*It used to be.* I leased it to Butch for a dollar when he wanted to raise some beef cattle. That's was when Lucy and Ricky were just little."

Mom guffawed. "*Lucy and Ricky?* You're kidding!"

"It was Sue's favorite show…"

Andrew jumped up and down. "I got a dollar! Can I buy some land from you?"

"Someday you'll have land, honey boy."

"Me t-w-o? 'Cause I want *that land* with the p-u-n-k-i-d-s on it!"

"What did you just spell?" Andrew asked.

"Pumpkins!"

Bobchia laughed as a gust of wind caused the leaves to dance around us. "You'll have land too, Logan. Now, come on! There's a piece of pie with my name on it!"

Mr. Hair finally caught up to us and asked Mother, "May I please have the pleasure of your company and escort you to the Inn?"

"Um, excuse me!" Mother said and took off running as fast as she could with the boys on her heels. We laughed as Mr. Hair ran after her, his toupee flying up in the front.

Bobchia took my hand walking me to a corner of the Inn. "Do you remember *that?*"

I looked at the words **Christ Our Cornerstone** carved deep into the stone.

"Your grampie David sure was proud of that. His grandfather Edjew carved it! That oil painting hanging in the hall across from your room is of him and his wife Mineya with their daughter Rita."

"Sorry, Bobchia." I smiled at her. "I don't remember seeing that stone before. Besides, I couldn't *read* then."

"Have mercy, I guess not at four years old! I just want to catch you up on your heritage, in case the Lord calls me *home*. There are so many things that you haven't been privy to."

"Bobchia, I'm planning on being here for a while and—"

"You're right, absolutely right! No point in telling you everything I know about the family all in *one* day! Slow and steady. I'll spread it out and trust that the Lord will keep me around long enough to fill you in on the good history of the family and pray that nobody tells you about the *outlaws.*

"Outlaws? Really?"

"If you remember nothing else, remember that family is everything. Some of the people who live here never get a single visitor. Do unto others, as you would have them do unto you – *the Golden Rule*. Remember to come visit me when I get old, Sweetie."

I shook my head. "I won't visit you!"

Bobchia stopped. "What? Why?"

*"Because we'll be living here together."*

*"I know."* She patted my hand. "Well, my mouth is watering for a big piece of one of those zwiebach pies that Ardelle has been bragging about!"

(I had no idea what 'zwiebach' was, but I figured if Bobchia thought it was delicious, I would too! Sunday was shaping up to be my favorite day of the week!)

As we came around the corner of the Inn, an ambulance was coming down the lane. The boys waited for it on the little bridge, cheering while it parked. The attendants wheeled the gurney with Mrs. Pratt on it over the little bridge and up onto the kitchen porch where we stood.

"Mrs. Pratt, I didn't mean to scare you *to death* on your birthday!" Bobchia apologized.

"Where should we take her?"

"Through the mud room and to the left, past the laundry room, and it's the second room on the right," We followed the attendants as they squeezed passed Homer in the hallway.

"Homer, your wife is back!" Bobchia grabbed his hand and U turned him.

We entered the turquoise room as sunlight streamed through the tall windows framed with tapestry draperies. A settee and twin beds were at opposite ends of the room, embellished with tapestry pillows depicting fox hunts. Above the massive headboards was mahogany shelving, filled with sculptures of hunting dogs and horses.

"Look at all the dogs and horses!" Andrew exclaimed.

"Let's count them!" I'll count the d-o-g-s." Logan pointed.

I walked around the room looking at the chocolate marble stands and dressers with various cast-iron hound and horse coin banks covering them. The marble dressers had stair step shelves framing the sides of the mirrors, with rows of miniature iron dogs.

"Mother, look at these cute little dogs."

"Jen, look at these." Mother stood in the middle of the room looking upward to the gold framed oil paintings depicting fox hunts and the English countryside, stretching to the tall ceiling.

"Wow, Bobchia who painted these?"

"Homer did." Mother and I looked at each other in disbelief then looked at the paintings.

"Mrs. Pratt is from England, where she used to raise fox hounds. Homer met her there, when he was in the service."

"These paintings are exquisite." Mother said in awe.

"Her bed is over there." Bobchia told the attendants. They lifted her off the gurney and carefully onto the bed, handing her some papers and an envelope of pills.

They looked skyward to the oil paintings of the hounds. "Hey Bill, that looks like Sis and Little Miss."

"And, how! Boy, someone can sure paint! Ma'am, Doctor Williams wants you to use a wheelchair until you're steady on your feet. Do you have one?" She looked at Bobchia.

"There is one in the attic."

"If you need anything, call the doctor. His number is on the papers."

"Thank you for bringing me home," Mrs. Pratt said with an English accent.

"You're welcome." The boys walked over to her, waiting to hear her talk again.

As the attendants started to wheel the empty gurney out, Homer tried to get on it. Bobchia took his hand, leading him over to his wife. "Don't you want to welcome your wife home?"

He leaned over her with his lips puckered. Mrs. Pratt looked up at him with her lips puckered, but he just stood there. "Well, are you going to *kiss* me, or are you looking for a place to *lie down?*"

He bent down to kiss her, but rolled over her instead and faced the wall. He just lay there until all of a sudden, the bed slid from the wall and he fell on the floor!

*"Mercy, Homer!"* The boys howled with laughter! Bobchia and Mother quickly pushed the bed out helping him to his feet.

"Your bed is over *there!"* Bobchia pointed. He walked over and lay down, got up, then left the room. We shoved Ms. Pratt's bed back to the wall while Mother tried to quiet the boys.

"That was so funny!" Andrew slapped his knee.

"Yeah! First he was there, then he's n-o-t!" Logan hit his forehead.

Bobchia windshield-wipered her finger at them slowly bringing it to her mouth to hush them. Mother pushed the boys out of the room. Their laughter followed them down the hallway. Bobchia shook her head then looked at me, standing with both hands over my mouth.

"Sweetie!" I quickly turned to the paintings. Bobchia went to the foot of Mrs. Pratt's bed.

"Can I get you anything, Mrs. Pratt?"

"No, thank you."

Bobchia gathered Homer's dirty cups from the stands, scattered throughout the room.

"I was wondering where all my cups were. Grab some, Sweetie."

Mrs. Pratt piped up, "Well, maybe a piece of my birthday cake, would taste good, that is, *if* you saved me a piece!"

"*Of course I saved you a piece!* I'll go get it." She started to leave.

"And maybe a little spot of tea."

Bobchia turned at the doorway. "Tea it is!"

"With a teaspoon of honey."

"Naturally."

"And a wedge of orange."

"Right away!" she said going down the hallway. I followed her to the kitchen.

"The Pratts never had children. She's told me on more than one occasion that she and Homer have willed their belongings to me, to be sold and the money used to help keep the old Inn going. As long as I am doing the Lord's will, *He* will keep this place going."

After delivering the birthday cake and tea, Bobchia cut the zwiebach pie and dished us each a piece.

Andrew stared at his slice. "Bobchia?"

"Yes, Andrew?" "I saw a horse with a funny back on TV a long time ago, and—"

"That's *swayback. This* is a *zwiebach.*"

Aunt Ardelle gave Andrew a dirty look. "I assure you there isn't any horsemeat in *my* pie, young man! Why, I never!"

Andrew looked unconvinced. "Can I have a cookie instead?"

"Me too!" Logan shook his head.

Bobchia slid the tin down to them. "Speaking of horses, grab a cookie, and I'll introduce you to my four-legged tenants in the barn."

I, for one, couldn't wait to meet Dollee Doll and gulped my pie. I tried to hurry Mother, but she wanted to savor hers. That is until Mr. Hair slid into the chair next to her. Then she downed her last few bites in a flash and became an *instant animal lover!*

As we walked toward the red barn, my mind raced back to the last time I had been in this field picking daisies. I reached for Bobchia's hand and squeezed it.

"I know, Sweetie," she whispered. *"Let it go and let God."*

She patted my hand looking at a tear roll down my face. "Now, tell me how do you like that flag on the side of the red barn?" I shook my head. We walked up to the painted flag, proudly depicting the stars and stripes.

I noticed Caleb's signature. Caleb Mar+in. "A 'cross', instead of a 't'. Groovy!"

The boys ran to the two dog coops under the lean-to beside the barn. The name '**Poochie**' was stenciled on one and '**Nikki**' on the other. They startled a gray muzzled collie out of her sleep when they slid on their knees in front of her and petted her.

"This is Spike's old dog, Nikki. Poor old thing has seen better days."

Logan leaned back to look at the stenciling. "She's in the wrong house."

Bobchia explained, "She's *waiting* for Poochie, has been for years." Bobchia and I hunkered down petting her as Minnie peeked out of the apron, growling. "Nikki's a good old girl." She wagged her tail.

"Where is Poochie?" I asked.

"*Doggie heaven.* Remind me later, and I'll tell you the story. Oops! Here comes Tootie." A calico kitten ran sideways and jumped on Nikki's tail. "Cute, huh?"

Mother looked beyond the coops at several old bicycles that were leaning against the barn wall. "I sure could have used one of those bicycles, earlier."

"Use them whenever you want."

"We had to give our bikes to people in the a-r-m-e." Logan said seriously.

"The *Salvation* Army," I whispered. Bobchia snorted.

"I got a couple of boys' bikes at the *army* myself last week."

Andrew pushed his bottom lip out. "I want a *new* one!"

"Maybe for your birthdays next summer. So get that 'birdie poop' off your lip, Andrew! In the meantime you can paint these. I'll have Spike pick us up some pink paint." She winked at me.

"I want red paint!"

"I want o-r-n-g!"

"Not pink?" The boys shook their heads hard. Bobchia pretended to mull it over and then declared, "Red and orange it is!"

We walked into the timbered barn. "I remember Popeye, the bull."

"He's long gone, Sweetie, natural causes. We had such a hard time getting him out of his stall. Remember how gentle he was letting the kittens swing on his tail? People don't believe me when I'd tell them that he ate right out of my hand. I cried for a solid week after that big guy died!"

Logan looked up at the words carved deep into a rafter. "What does that say? A right…A right…"

Bobchia recited it. "**A righteous man regards the life of his animal but the wicked are always cruel.** Proverbs 12:10."

"What does *that mean?*"

"That means that animals have feelings too, and it's our responsibility to make sure they have food, water and shelter."

"*And love?*"

"That goes without saying, honey boy."

A kitten pounced on bale twine. She picked it up and held it to her cheek.

"This is tiger."

"Sweetie, do you remember that every time we'd get a stray, you'd name it Daisy? We had a cow, chickens, two dogs and a car full of cats you named Daisy. That made feeding time easy. We just yelled '*Daisy*' and everything came running!"

The boys started to run down to see Dollee, but Bobchia put her arm out. "Patience, kids! We don't want to slight these other animals; they need attention too! They came here under duress."

Logan looked at her wide-eyed. "*Under a dress?*"

Bobchia shook her head laughing. "Mercy, Logan! Not a dress, *duress*—meaning they'd been mistreated. But believe you me, they are *spoiled* now!"

"Like me!" Andrew said.

"And Me!"

Bobchia shook her head saying "Unfortunately, so we have to love them awful, *every day!*"

Mother took a few steps back as Bobchia proudly pointed out her menagerie. "Let's see. Girls first. I have just one cat named Daisy; she's over there stretching. Snowball is playing with her tail, and Cutie Girl is the shy one on the windowsill trying to catch a miller. Kitty and Lacey must be playing in the field. I don't see them. The boy kittens are Vic and Cedric on the bales, Larry and Moe on that rafter, and Curley on the saddle over there." We heard a meow and looked up. "There you are *outlaw!* The culprit over our heads is Cutie Boy. He likes to sneak up on me. You get down here this minute! Come on, I'll catch ya, bad boy." He jumped into her arms. She hugged him to her cheek then put him over her shoulder like a baby hugging him as she walked from stall to stall. "Here are the goats, Fred and Ethel. In that cage hanging in the corner, hopefully high enough so Cutie Boy can't get to him, is Jet, a robin with a bum wing. Cecil almost ran over him a couple days back. He was flapping around on the covered bridge. Cecil gave him a splint, and he comes in every day with a fresh can of worms."

"Can we feed him worms too?" Logan asked.

"I'm sure, but you'll have to work that out with Cecil. Did you meet him?"

"I don't remember."

"He was the man Spike was playing horseshoes with this afternoon. I'll point him out to you at supper." Cutie Boy jumped down from Bobchia's shoulder and sat below Jet's cage with his tail twitching. "This pig is Twiggy and in the stall next to her is Little Porker. They were blue ribbon winners at the county fair. I was offered a good price for them, but I can't bear to have them b-u-t-c-h-e-r-e-d."

"What did you just spell?" Andrew asked.

"Ask Logan."

"*Buttered!*" He said confidently. We laughed.

"Let's see, in that cage is Ike the rabbit, and in that cage is Meme; they're separated now for obvious reasons. And in this corner, in a stall all his own, in a cage without a door, weighing anywhere between thirty-two and thirty-five pounds or more, is one-eyed Rocky the second!" We looked at the sleeping raccoon resting on a pillow. A 'DO **NOT** DISTRUB' sign on a little chain hung down where the door once was. "He leaves nights but insists on coming back in the mornings."

"Don't touch him!" Mother said, "He might have rabies!"

"He's harmless. He runs into trees instead of climbing them. The hens don't like him, but we have a mean banty rooster that won't let him near the henhouse! Last but not least is Dollee Doll."

"She's beautiful!" I said as I pet the black and white pinto. The boys and I fought over Dollee's affections using cubes of sugar Bobchia pulled out of the pockets of her old barn coat, hanging on a nail beside the stall. Dollee shook her graceful head and flicked her long black tail, hitting Mother on the side of her head.

"Oh, my!"

"It's okay, Clair, she won't hurt you," Bobchia said.

"I thought I heard a bat flapping." Mother looked at the rafters.

"That's just Jet the robin in the cage."

"A bird?! I *hate* birds!"

Mother hunkered down on the other side of Dollee.

"I assure you that nothing in this barn will hurt you, Clair."

Cutie Boy jumped down from the rafter in front of Mother *hissing* at her. "I've seen enough animals to last me a *lifetime!*" Mother headed for the back barn door but then staggered to one side and sat down hard on a hay bale. "What's *that* over...over..."

Bobchia giggled, walking to her. "Nobody would buy that *coffin* for some reason! Harold has had it for years; it's a discontinued model. I guess 'Guaranteed for Death Time' never quite caught on as a catchy phrase! Anyway, Harold got tired of listening to me complain about the rats out here and decided to kill two birds with one stone so one year for my birthday—voilà, there it was with a big green ribbon tied around it! *Thoughtful, huh?*"

Bobchia walked over to the casket and lifted the lid. Mother gasped. "With the oats and grain in here, I am *rat-less,* thanks to Harold!"

"Ah, r-a-t-s!" Logan said.

"Can we *crawl* in there?" Andrew asked.

"*No!*" Mother yelled.

"I'm actually glad you asked that question. I'll have Harold take the lock off."

"Why would a casket have a *lock* on it?" I asked.

Bobchia shrugged. "To keep people from crawling *out,* I guess." The boys looked scared. Mother gave Bobchia 'the look.' "Sorry! Erase, erase, erase."

"Don't you *DARE* crawl in there! *And I mean it!*" Mother rubbed her forehead and headed for the back door, mumbling, "We haven't even been here forty-eight hours and already—oh no, *chickens!*" We watched her run toward the Inn with her hands over her head, screaming.

"Not much of an *animal person,* is she?" Bobchia snorted.

We took turns riding Dollee as Bobchia lead her up and down the field over and over. The boys stuck their tongues out at Lanny as he shook his fist from his front porch. Bobchia rolled her eyes. "Pay that boy no mind!"

Logan had other concerns. "Will Dollee b-a-c-k me off?"

"She's as gentle as a kitten, this one is."

"Bobchia, does she eat like a horse?" Andrew questioned.

Bobchia laughed and then looked down at her watch. "Mercy, it's almost 6:30. This day has *flown!* I'm getting tired, guys. This old gray mare ain't what she used to be." She laughed again and led Dollee back into the barn. "We'd better get in the kitchen for a bowl of Cliff's potato soup. Then it's into the tub to be ready for school tomorrow."

"School *tomorrow?* Yuck! I thought we were on *vacation!*" Andrew protested.

"Yeah, why do we have to go to s-k-o-l?" Logan asked.

"To learn to *spell* would be reason enough! And who told you that you were on vacation?"

"Coming here is sorta like vacation, I think."

"It's f-u-n being here, Bobchia!"

"Good! I hope you *always* feel that way." She helped the boys get down and then slid Dollee's saddle off.

Andrew's eyes brightened. "Can't we stay here tomorrow and learn from you? Mother says you know *everything!*"

Bobchia giggled. "Well, as much as I enjoy having you around, you don't want to spend all your time with old people, do you? Some of the best years of your life are in school." Bobchia rubbed the top of Logan's head.

"Some of my best years are when I'm on v-a-k-a-o-n!"

"What did you just spell?" Andrew asked.

"Vacation!"

We gave Dollee more sugar and hugs and went out the back door of the barn.

In the back field, looking through the fence, the boys discovered an old claw-footed bathtub that had water running into it through a pipe from a spring. Andrew looked around him. "What's a bathtub doing way out here?"

"For the cows and Dollee Doll to drink from."

"Where're the cows?" Logan asked.

"Probably in the upper fields. They like the shade trees up there."

"What're their names?" Andrew asked.

"I just call them Bossy."

"All of 'em?"

Bobchia nodded. "Yup, all five. You and Logan can name them, okay?"

"Can we pet them?" Logan asked.

"Probably, they're pretty tame."

"Let's go Andrew! We'll chase them down here and squeeze milk in the cat's face like Ed did!" He unlocked that gate and ran to the tub.

"They are not *those* kinds of cows!"

"Are you *teasing* us again?"

"They are beef cows, not milking cows. Besides, you have to get your dinner and get in the tub."

"How about in this tub?" They splashed each other.

Bobchia pulled them away from the tub and told them to get moving. They stomped the whole way through the field.

Logan whispered to Andrew, "We'll milk them anyway!"

"Yeah!"

I closed the gate.

"I just had a bath before church. I'm not sweaty now." Logan said.

"Me neither! *Mine dried.*"

I laughed. "You guys might not be sweaty, but you both smell like a horse!"

"Well, you're a pig, Jen!"

"And *smell* like one t-o!"

"There will be no more name calling as long as you are living under my roof, *understand?* **Bonanza** will be on later, so if you want to watch it, get in the kitchen, eat and then hop in the tub! Nobody wants to smell a *horse* when they're watching a western!" I laughed.

After supper, while Bobchia was 'fine-tuning' the TV, the boys ran downstairs in their pajamas with their blankets tied around their necks.

'Pop,' went the camera.

The boys grabbed pillows from the window seats and got as close to the TV as Mother would let them. Every seat in the great room was filled for **Bonanza**, a show with cowboys for *women of all ages:* Ben for the blue hairs, Adam for Mother, the boys loved laughing at Hoss, and Little Joe in his dark green jacket was the dreamiest for me! At every commercial the old timers visited the bathrooms and the boys hid behind the couches, making disgusting noises as they sat back down.

I pleaded with Bobchia to let me stay home from school the next day so we could visit without interruptions from the boys.

"We can visit after the boys hit the sheets. Besides, that would just be postponing the inevitable. If you stay home, the boys will want to, and I don't think this Inn can put up with them running around another *whole day!* Mercy, and to think they've *just arrived!* I better double up on my vitamins and *warn* the beef cows!" She looked over at the boys in their brown and red **Lone Ranger** pajamas, holding an eye open with one hand while eating a cookie with the other. She took a shot of coffee. "TYG *I think."*

After **Bonanza** the boys hemmed and hawed, as Bobchia put it, then hugged her goodnight and begged her to let Minnie sleep with them.

She shook her head. "Not on a school night. Maybe next weekend, okay?" They stomped up all sixteen steps. Bobchia rubbed her forehead and hollered after them, "Don't forget to say *your prayers!"* She walked toward the kitchen. "Come on Sweetie, I need more coffee...and *a bottle of aspirin!"* She slid the cookie tin to me.

"Thanks."

Do they always have an attitude at bedtime?" I shook my head with a mouth full. "I thought they'd be *sweet little boys,* like your father was."

I choked! She patted my back and poured me a glass of milk. I caught my breath. She rubbed her forehead with her eyes closed. "*Mer-cy me!*"

I smiled. "What was that story you were going to tell about Poochie?"

"Oh, yes, dear Poochie. You would have *loved* that dog, Sweetie. She was like Nikki—not much to look at, but there was never better natured dogs that lived, than Nikki and Poochie. Stole my heart right away! Spike found the two of them abandoned alongside the road when they were pups. God will deal with whoever dumped them out, but anyway, they were the last two out of eight that were still alive; the others had starved to death or got hit by cars. When Spike brought them here, they were horribly emaciated. We bottle fed them and it was touch-and-go for a while. Finally they grew strong enough to eat food. Even though their growth was stunted, they were inseparable, running together in the woods and splashing in the creek. I can still see them tumbling in the field behind the red barn. It was comical, whenever Spike called one, they'd *both* show up!

"When they were a couple of years old, the strangest thing happened—they went missing. First we thought they were holed up somewhere because of the rain. Then we thought that because they were so friendly, somebody had probably found them and took them home. Spike looked for them for four days straight, never saying out loud that they might even be…dead. Upon inquiring about the dogs in town, he found out that several other dogs from the area were missing, so he set out to solve the mystery. He and Cecil searched from morning until night in that awful rain to find them. On the forth night they were sitting here in the kitchen—drinking coffee and drying out, studying a map that Cecil had drawn of some oil lease roads that he had driven on when he worked for Quaker State. They were devising a plan for the next morning, when we heard a faint scratching at the back door. Spike threw the door open, and Nikki was standing there, soaked to the bone and ravenous. He grabbed a flashlight and ran out onto the porch, looking for Poochie. She wasn't there. He looked in the field and down the lane, nothing. We watched Nikki gobble her food fearing the worst for Poochie.

"Spike got the blanket off of his bed and put it in front of the potbelly. Nikki lay there until she got some strength back then she stood at the door whining. Spike tried to coax her back to the blanket, but she paced, whined and *howled*—making the hair on the back of my neck stand up! Spike and Cecil pulled on their rain gear and followed her past the covered bridge, until too weak to walk, they carried her, periodically putting her down, following her as she guided them along the bank of the stream. About a mile up from the bridge, *on my very own property* mind you, they found Poochie with her leg in a trap and her head bashed in. We figured Nikki had fought off the trapper and stayed with Poochie as long as she could. *I hate traps! They should be outlawed!* I've seen animals that have chewed their legs off just to get out of those *miserable things!* Anyway, where was I?"

"They found Poochie."

"Oh yeah, they found Poochie, but she was barely alive. They carried the dogs back here. She lay right there in a low box beside the potbelly for weeks. She was a heart-wrenching sight, I'll tell you that! The vet didn't give us any hope and suggested that we *'put her down.'* Spike wouldn't have it. He told the vet to do his best and that we'd count on God for the rest. That vet knew he didn't have any medicine to make her well, as he bandaged her head and put a splint on her leg. But he didn't count on the best medicine— *Nikki!* She never left Poochie's side. She climbed into the box with her to keep her warm, and she licked her face."

"*Puppy love!*" I said wiping a tear.

"*Exactly!* I have been around animals all my life but that was the strongest animal devotion I had ever seen! Nikki hardly ate anything herself in sympathy for Poochie, I guess. I prayed and prayed for her. Spike doted on her, trying everything to get Poochie to eat, but her teeth were broken from gnawing at the trap so the most he could do was get her to drink a little milk.

"One day as I was fixing vegetable soup, I got the idea to mix some broth with cold milk and put it in a turkey baster. I'll never forget the first time Spike squeezed it into the side of her mouth and saw that pink tongue of hers lap it up! I kid you not the big guy looked up at me with tears in his eyes! We both cried that night over Poochie eating soup! Every week, for the next couple of months, there was a big pot of vegetable soup cooking on the back burner *just for her.* It was a great day when she stood up on her own. Well, slow and steady does win the race, and as the days went by, she grew stronger. Her leg healed pretty good, although she walked with a limp and her ear never fit her head as good as it used to, but other than that, she was as good as gold! Spike and Cecil posted all my property and found a couple more traps downstream. One had a dead coon in it. They took turns patrolling the stream but never saw anyone. Anyway, Poochie gained strength, as Nikki walked slowly beside her. Soon the inseparable dogs were again running and playing in the fields and things got pretty much back to normal. Spike would call one and both would come running. He kept pretty close tabs on them after that, making sure they stayed in the backfields where he could keep an eye on them and away from the stream beyond the covered bridge. He bought an old, red pickup to haul the dogs whenever he went past the covered bridge to his fishing hole and for trips around town. He never caught any fish with those two dogs in the creek, but he was happy they were together again.

"A year or so after that, Spike broke his fishing reel, so he and the dogs drove to town to get one at Hoppy's sporting goods store. Hoppy had a Lab, Shady, that went to work with him and kept him company, so Spike often took the dogs in the store for a visit. That day when he parked the truck and let the dogs out, they immediately ran over to a truck and circled it, growling, the hair on their backs stood up! Spike called them back, but they were intent on getting *inside* that truck, jumping and scratching at the doors. A man came out of Hoppy's yelling. The dogs ferociously ran to him and he barely made it back inside the store! Hoppy held Shady back while the man yelled and pounded on the door at the dogs, as they viciously attacked it, biting at the handle and jumping at the window. Spike got a rope and forced the straining dogs back into his truck. The man opened the door yelling at Spike. Shady ran out and Hoppy grabbed her by the collar. Spike went to apologize to the truck's owner.

'I'm sorry, mister! I don't know what got into my dogs! They have *never* acted this way before!' At the sight of the man, the dogs went berserk inside the truck clawing and biting at the windows. The man walked over laughing and pounded the windows.

'*Shut up, you mangy mutts! Good for nothing dogs!*' Then the man walked over to his truck. 'Look what they did to my truck! I'll sue you for this!'

'I'll make it right...' Spike started. The guy pushed Spike.

'Hold it right there! I said I'd make it right with you!' He threw a punch, and Spike ducked. The guy didn't stand a chance; Spike had boxed in the Navy. One punch and the guy was on the ground! Spike looked over his shoulder into the bed of the man's truck. It was full of traps! Among the traps was an old rusty steering wheel with several dog collars fastened through it. Spike pulled it out and threw it on the man's chest. 'Now I get it—you tried to *kill* them!'

'What?'

'*Dog killer!* I should let them out of the truck to give you what you *deserve!*' Spike looked at the men standing around. 'Poochie was in a trap. This man here tried to *kill her,* but Nikki wouldn't let him finish her off.' Spike looked back at the man. 'I'd like to let her finish *you* off right now.' Spike walked over to open his truck door.

The man got up, begging. 'Please mister, *please.*'

'It's going to take more than that for me to not let these dogs out!'

'I'll never set another trap as long as I live. *I swear!*'

'If you're telling me the truth, you won't need any of those.' He pointed to the back of the man's truck and grabbed a trap. 'How would you like one of these *stuck to your leg?*' He threw the blood-stained trap at the man.

'You can't *prove* nothin'! I found those traps and that wheel along the road. You can't *prove* nothin'!'

'You're right, I can't prove anything, but my dogs can. Every one of these men knows me and my dogs. They know that nothing ever riles them. I bet if I let them out of my truck right now, they wouldn't bite anyone here but *you!* Want to find out?' The men made a tight circle around the man. Spike walked toward him. 'All these men have dogs, and some of them are missing.'

One of the men picked up the steering wheel and looked intently at a red collar. 'Jake, what's the matter?'

'Trooper! *He killed Trooper!* Why I otta...' He went over and grabbed the guy's arm and twisted it behind his back.

'Leave me alone!'

'You're coming with me!' The man hit Jake. Jake hit him twice, and he went down. 'Come on! Get up and hit me again you creep! Stay there. You belong in the dirt! Just for the record, I named my dog Trooper, because *I am one.* Hoppy, call the station and have them send a car over here. Tell them we have a truck to impound.'

'It will be my *pleasure!*' Shady barked.

The man looked at Jake with contempt. 'You're going to arrest me?'

'*Cruelty to animals!* You're gonna sleep on the county's dime tonight! You killed the best friend I ever had, my Trooper!' He wiped his eyes.

"Jake brought charges against him and so did a couple of other men in town that recognized their dogs' collars, but he got away with paying just a small fine. Can you imagine? Just a *fine,* for all the misery he caused those poor dogs! But things that are done in *secret* will someday be brought into the *light.* We *all* have to give an account someday, not just on how we treat animals but how we treat each other!

"Mercy, look at the strange ones under this roof that God sent my way! Believe you me, some days I could throw in the towel, but then I remember He died for *everyone* and made us all different and with a *purpose!* I know some of the stories of the people that God has blessed me with here in the Inn. People act the way they do because of their circumstances. Everything that breathes has a *story,* some better and some worse, so remember—*only God can change a bad story into glory!* That's my motto. My Mother always said, 'Never judge a storybook by the cover; you never know what is really inside!' Well, there you have it, the story of Poochie and Nikki and a little *sermon* to boot! Sorry I'm so chatty. I'm two coffees over my limit." I giggled. "Mercy, look at the time. I know you don't need beauty sleep, but I need *every drop I can get.* Plus I still have to do my devotions. I didn't get to them this morning."

"I want to stay here with you tomorrow, please? *Pretty please?*"

"Now Sweetie, we already went over this. I know you were hurt in Florida, but believe me when I tell you that Dawnette is a sweetheart. Remember, you didn't learn to scuba dive without getting your big toe *wet!*" She kissed me on the cheek. "Get to bed, sleep tight and don't let the bed bugs bite. I'll see you at breakfast; I love you awful."

"I love you awful back." I said with 'birdie poop' on my lip.

She smiled saying "Quit looking at me like you did when you were little. It'll be okay; honest…*I'll cook extra bacon!*"

That night would be one of many spent under Great-Grandmother's quilt with a flashlight and an ink pen, barely able to keep up with my brain as I filled page after page of my journal quoting her sayings and the day's events. I wrote, "People are the way they are because of their story, and only God can change a story to glory!" I then wrote the story of Poochie along with some profound questions: 'How can people be so cruel to animals? What was Nikki's favorite treat? Will Spike teach me to ride Dollee? What duress had the tenants and the animals in the red barn gone through before Bobchia got a hold of them?' I hurried and crossed that last question out because just knowing about Poochie and Nikki was sad enough. (I didn't know if I could bear knowing why some *people* are the way they are!) I had lots of questions, but one thing I knew: as sure as I was lying underneath my great-grandmother's quilt, the animals in the red barn were more loved here than anywhere else in the entire world because... I knew *I was!*

# 5
# Settling Inn

The alarm went off at five-thirty the next morning. I rubbed my eyes and looked around. "Yea, I'm still here!"

Mother rolled over and said, "*Ouuu, I'm still here!* What on earth is the matter with you? Have you totally *lost* your mind? It's only 5:30!" She rolled over. "I hope you don't think you're going to get up *every* morning at 5:30, young lady! I'll never be able to get back to sleep now!"

"*Sorry!*" I hurried to the bathroom with my makeup and curler caddy. I'd been in there primping for an hour when the boys knocked on the door.

Andrew mumbled. "What are ya doing in there, Jen? I have to go really *bad.*"

"Me too! Really b-a-d!"

"Use one of the other bathrooms!"

I heard Logan whine. "I can't walk that far or I'll p-e myself!"

When I unlocked the door, they pushed past me and had the lid up before I was even in the hall! "Ugh. Boys are so *gross!*"

When I went back into the bedroom mother was making my bed. "Thanks."

"I was trying to wake-up a little before facing your...before I go downstairs. You know, I'm not a morning person, so I hope you're not planning on getting up every morning at 5:30 young lady!"

"Sorry! Chee...How does my hair look?"

"You know it looks perfect, as usual." Mother took the boy's clothes to the bathroom.

I took several blouses to the mirror and held them up to my face to see which one showed off my tan the best. I put the peach one on and hung the rest up. Then I pulled on my yellow and peach madras skirt. As I was checking out every angle in the mirror, Mother stuck her head in the doorway, yawning. "How do I look?" I asked.

"The same way you did the *last time* you wore it."

"Mother!"

"Beautiful. Are you ready? We should get there a little early so I can get you kids registered."

"I'm ready."

She yawned again. "I need some coffee."

Bobchia cornered Mother when she stepped into the kitchen looking frazzled and rubbing her forehead. "Clair, the teeth in the false tooth cups were *switched* in the downstairs bathrooms last night!"

"What?"

"I think the boys—"

"They fell asleep as soon as their heads hit the pillows!"

"But—"

"I checked on them *twice!*"

"Well, I *never* had a problem with people putting their teeth in someone else's cup *before* the boys moved in!" The boys howled at the sight of people running to the sink, rinsing and trading dentures. It was enough to *gag a maggot!*

Ken hurried over to the laughing boys and looked at them through his duct taped glasses. Then he took out the wobbly dentures and chased the boys around the kitchen, clacking the teeth at them. "You little brats, where are *my* teeth?" The boys dove under the table and grabbed at Mother's legs. They scrambled out and clung to her back as Ken ran over clacking the teeth over Mother's shoulder.

"*Leave my sons alone!*" The boys buried their faces into Mother's blouse as the tenants gathered around them, holding out teeth. "Leave them alone! They don't *know* where your teeth are!"

Bobchia's face was beet red as she rushed in front of Mother and fended off the *toothless, ticked tenants!* Sadly, one by one, they left the kitchen... *with someone else's teeth.* To keep the peace Bobchia gave into Mother's outrageous rant that "Homer must have switched the teeth!"

"Homer? Homer?"

"Yes, Homer! Why not Homer?"

"Mercy, Clair, you can't see the forest for the trees!" Mother's eyes bulged. "Erase, erase, erase." Bobchia erased the air, downed three gulps of coffee and then set plates of hot food in front of us as platefuls of cold food sat at the vacant tables.

In just two short days the boys had gone from being called 'little darlings' to *(the more appropriate)* 'little brats!' In Bobchia's own kitchen, the boys taunted her, smirking and giggling. Mother pushed her plate away and drank her coffee with her eyes shut. You could have cut the tension with a knife. Bobchia didn't dare say another word for fear that we would be uprooted. I read Bobchia lips as she counted to ten and prayed for patience. As her face grew more calm, Mother's turned more red. Bobchia took deep breaths then smiled lovingly at the boys.

As soon as we were done eating, Mother ordered us to hurry and brush our teeth and get to the car. "I don't want to go to stupid school!"

"Me e-h-u-r!"

They stomped up the steps. Mr. Pill pounded the floor. Bobchia shook her head and hollered up the stairs; "Don't forget your lunch buckets here on the hall table! How long have I lived here and it's never dawned on me to carpet those stairs." I hugged her and went to brush my teeth. She smiled as I tip toed up the stairs.

"TYG, for school! By the way, you look very beautiful this beautiful day!" She walked into the dining room. "Mrs. Dunham will just have to make banana bread next week!" She said ripping off two of the four bananas from the fruit bowel on the dining room table. She giggled and shut her eyes, taking deep breaths. The boys passed me on the way down, jumping down the last two steps landing in front of her. She forced a smile. "Here take these bananas, in case you don't like what I put in your buckets, ok?" She teased them by holding the bananas out to them, then behind her back, wanting a hug.

"Two things to remember at school today: Do unto others as you would have them do unto you that goes for **here** too, by the way and I love *you* awful! And *you* awful!" She said kissing the tops of their heads. "Be good, and you be good too!"

"We will!"

"We w-i-l!"

They tried to wipe the tops of their heads off with the bananas, as mother hurried down the steps and pushed them out the door.

"Mercy!" I kissed her on the cheek. "Thank you. I sure needed that!"

"Any little gem of *wisdom* for me?" I smiled.

"Let me think...something for a teenager. Um...bad company corrupts good character. How's that? Oh, by the way, I called the school this morning. Lunch tickets are now up to a dollar thirty-five a week. Mercy! Here's a dollar fifty."

"Thanks, Bobchia."

Mother came in. "Give that *back* to your grandmother! I have money for my child's lunch!"

"Sorry, Bobchia. I love you awful." I handed her the money.

"Me too." She smiled weakly.

I gave Mother 'the look' as she grabbed the lunch buckets off of the hall table, hurrying me out the door.

"I have got to get back into nurse's school and *get us out of here!*" Mother said hurrying down the sidewalk.

We looked curiously at the boys with their noses plugged hanging out the car windows. *The car reeked!*

"Oh my word!" Mother said as we got into the car.

*"Gag a maggot!"*

"I'm gonna p-u-k!"

"What did you just spell?"

"Puke!"

"I'm gonna throw-up *worser than you ever thought!*"

We rode to school with the windows down. I sat on the edge of my seat, praying the hardest that I ever had in my entire life! Chee, after all, I had just gotten here and didn't want to leave Bobchia over something as stupid as… *false teeth!* The boys didn't help Mother's mood, sword fighting with their bananas the whole way to school.

"Stop that!" Mother demanded.

"Mine is kind of mushy. Want to trade?" Logan asked.

"Okay."

"It's the same!"

"Stop that or you'll smell like bananas!"

Mother came back to the Inn and after searching under the back seat, pulled out the smelly bread bag with the *dead hermit crabs.* At 10:15 the morning went further downhill when she received a phone call from the boy's principal, Mr. Fish. It was either by fate or coincidence that *each* of the boy's teachers had sat on a mushy banana, making their dresses gooey! Mr. Fish requested a visit. Mother went to the school defending the boys, demanding to speak personally to their teachers! "I'm sorry, Mrs. Matko, you cannot speak to Mrs. Chamberlain or Mrs. Hummer because they had to go home to change their dresses. I assure you they would not *plot* against your children or *lie* about the situation, Mrs. Matko!

Logan and Andrew will *not* be permitted to have recess for the rest of the week and I think that it is only appropriate, that you should *reimburse* their teachers for the cleaning of the dresses."

Mother stormed back to the Inn in a rage, telling Bobchia of Mr. Fish's injustice. Without thinking, Bobchia had blurted, "Even a *child* is known by his deeds; whether what he does is pure and right."

"What?"

"Face it Clair, if it *looks like* a skunk and *smells like* a skunk, chances are, *it's a skunk!*"

Mother's eyes bulged! Bobchia grabbed her mouth, erasing as fast as she could, but the words hung thick in the air and before she finished erasing, Mother stomped up the stairs to her room, slamming the door!

Later that same week, Mother was *summoned again* to Mr. Fish's office—this time because the boys had been running in the cafeteria. They'd stood at one wall with heads down and arms flailing and then, as if a giant magnet was pulling them, they'd run screaming to the opposite end of the cafeteria, bouncing their heads off of the wall! The students thought it was funny; Mr. Fish did not. That little incident caused their recess privileges to get pushed back another whole week and Mother to rush back to the Inn, slamming the kitchen door!

"Mercy Clair, what is it?" Bobchia asked.

"I'd like to know what kind of mother with a last name of *Fish* would name her son *Gil?*" Then she told of Mr. Gil Fish's allegation of how the boys bounced their heads off of the cafeteria wall! Bobchia started to blurt out the skunk scenario again, but when Mother gave her 'the look', she rushed (erasing all the way) to the pantry where she stuffed a dishtowel in her mouth muffling her laughter!

Meanwhile, when Mother dropped me off at school, I was relieved that Dawnette and Beverly Jean met me at the brown-and-gold doors of the high school. At lunchtime they introduced me to Mary Ann, Betty Ann, Donna, Nancy, Darlene and Karen.

It didn't take much of the girls' persuading in the following days to get me to join the debate team, the girls' ensemble and the acting club. After writing a test paragraph on Titusville (with information from Bobchia's tour), I was picked to be a reporter for *The Rocket Recorder,* the school's newspaper.

New teens in school are always popular, and I was asked out on a couple dates, but I was hesitant to say yes after the whole Ty and Tiff fiasco. I was content to hang out with my new gang of friends at Teen Action or at Grady's Soda Shop.

Everything was secondary compared to being with Bobchia in the Inn. I followed her around like Minnie, listening to her quips and watching how she interacted with the tenants. In less than a month, I had filled *three* journals as Bobchia had filled the front of the refrigerators with photos of us kids.

In the cool of the evenings, Spike was kind enough to teach me how to saddle and ride Dollee. When I asked him about Dollee Doll's story so I could record it in my journal, I was relieved to hear she didn't have a sad history like the other animals in the red barn. Dollee had belonged to Spike's friend Barney who had worked for Universal Cyclops, the steel mill in town, and who had been transferred to New York City. There, he bought a townhouse and couldn't take Dollee, so when Spike told Bobchia the situation; she eagerly offered Dollee a stall in the red barn. Dollee had a gentle spirit, and whenever I wanted to get away from my brothers, I'd ride her along the deer paths on the hillside behind the Inn.

My grandparents' bedroom looked out onto the hillside and on their balcony is where Grampie and I used to sit at dusk to watch the deer lick the salt licks he had put out and drink from the creek. Bobchia called the hill *Red Barn Mountain,* her very own mountain where we used to have picnics with Daisy, my doll and Daisy the white tipped beagle pup of Grampie's that she carried in her apron. I remember us throwing rocks in the pond up there but I called it Bed Rarn Yake. (I got my R's and B's mixed up and had trouble with my L's until first grade.) She'd giggle. 'Now, what's the name of the lake again? I didn't hear you the first time.'

When I grew more confident running Dollee through the fields, Spike taught me how to race her around the barrels behind the red barn and timed me with his stopwatch. My jealous brothers would watch from the fence and beg to have a turn, running to tell Mother whenever I *refused*. She'd storm out to the field, and I'd reluctantly get off Dollee and carefully help them up. As she watched, I'd lead them around the barrels in a *nice slow walk,* but as soon as she left, *I'd run as fast as I could,* weaving Dollee in and out of the barrels with the brats *holding on for dear life!*

Mother felt obligated to try to help out in the Inn, but cooking and housework were never her strong suits. Plus with Bobchia's everyday rituals, the Inn ran like a *Swiss watch.* Life in the Inn regrettably…was *not* for my Mother. Mother told me in confidence that she had applied for a loan to start nursing school because she'd rather pay interest than borrow money from Bobchia. "Not a word to your grandmother, understand? She'll insist on giving me the money, and I already *owe her,* promise?"

"Okay." I said chewing on a cookie.

"Are your fingers crossed? Jennifer! Now promise me again with both hands where I can see them."

I promised, reluctantly. The fall classes had started weeks earlier, but Mother was determined to catch up. She said that until she could get us a place of our own, she'd be at the library, reading medical books, in anticipation of the loan being approved, and that I was in charge of keeping track of the boys' *sugar intake.*

After school each day, Bobchia would watch us come up the lane from the corner kitchen window as she cut veggies for a salad or stirred a bowl of something yummy for dinner. The boy's routine consisted of running from the covered bridge past Sterling's to Bobchia's property line with Lanny hot on their heels. Bobchia would cheer them on and swing the door open as they bounded up the steps out of breath. "It's a good thing you guys are *wiry!* He was biting at your heels!" They nervously looked at the back of their shoes. She laughed welcoming us home with a big hug then she'd pour us glasses of ice-cold milk while we washed our hands. If Mother was there, she'd give us *one* chocolate chip cookie each. If Mother wasn't, she'd slide us the tin to fight over. After that, she'd shove the boys out the door to get *the stink blown off them* before dinner, shouting at their backs, "Remember the rules!"

Now Bobchia had rules for everything but the rule for fishing under the covered bridge included 'adult supervision.' The boys, eager to catch some Sylvania fish, ran into the red barn, coming out with Spike's fishing poles and Jet's can of worms. They looked high and low for Spike but his truck was gone so they ran to the Inn to get a *chaperon*. With the 'false teeth episode' still *afresh* in everyone's mind, no one volunteered to go with them so unbeknownst to anyone…they *coxed* Antenna Man under the bridge! That night at the supper table, when his chair was empty and the men were doing thorough search number four of the Inn, she slowly came down stairs *snapping* one of Grampie's belts…just to help *jog* the boys' memories. They quickly confessed. "We forgot to bring him *b-a-c.*"

"Back from *where?*"

"The covered b-r-a-g-e."

"What did you just spell?"

"Bridge."

"Mercy! MERCY!, *MERCY!*" Bobchia franticly called the fire department and thankfully before midnight, they found him wandering in the woods unscathed.

"We thought all *old people* knew how to fish under bridges!" Logan explained.

"He liked throwing rocks!" Andrew smiled.

It was humorous listening to Bobchia explain to the boys; why Antenna Man could never go with them again because even at seventy-nine years old, he was really not an *adult!* They were *confused and confined* to the premises after that. *'A bitter pill,'* She said, 'for all to swallow.'

The boys were in constant motion, in and out of the Inn. They never walked but always ran, bumping into tenants and causing several to threaten to leave. The thought that Mother could pack us up at any given moment, kept Bobchia in a *slow boil* and kept her from disciplining the brats. There was, however, one thing she was emphatic about—the hand-blown hurricane lamps in the dining room (her inheritance from her mother, my great grandmother, Regeena). One day, as Bobchia and I were sharing the cookie tin, the boys came running through the Inn. "No *running* in the Inn!" Bobchia yelled. They ignored her and ran into the dining room where they played tag around the tables. She quickly went in. "Come here you two, I would like to share a little word with you."

Andrew went into protective mode. "I'll tell Mom if you yell at us."

"Or h-i-t us!" Logan added.

"I'm not going to yell at you." She bent down, speaking softly and secretively. "But you two will have to face *the consequences* if you don't quit running in the dining room."

"What's a conquents?" Andrew looked at her suspiciously.

"The definition of the word *consequence* is an old Croatian word meaning *the exact second a wooden spoon meets with your little duppas,* that's what consequences are. Do you know what a wooden spoon is?" They nodded. "Do you know what your duppas are?" They nodded again. "Good, because if I ever catch you playing tag in here again, near my Mother's two hand-blown hurricane lamps, it's *consequences* for both of you. So *much consequence* in fact that you won't be able to sit down for an *entire week! Understand?"*

"Yes."

"Y-e-s."

"Good, let's get a cookie." They followed her into the kitchen, quietly. (They knew she was serious because she didn't erase after the definition.) While smiling down into their little horrified faces, she shoved cookies into their mouths and pushed them back outside to get more *stink* off their tiny bodies. She watched them out the window and laughed when they ran straight through one of the leaf piles Spike had just raked to burn. He shook his fist at them! "What a caution those two! At least they're not saying that dirty word 'poop,' anymore. I've got them saying 'bowl movement!'"

I rolled my eyes. "*Gag!* I'd rather they say *poop!* Besides, I've never heard them say bowel movement."

"That's because they can't pronounce it." She shook her head. "They say 'owl moose' instead."

"*Owl moose?!* That's hilarious. There's one for my journal!"

After that the boys *walked* in the Inn for the most part, but they were still 'a caution' outside, swinging on the barn ropes, scattering the laying hens, and frightening Dollee Doll out of her stall. They found great sport in racing garter snakes in the claw-footed tub and in chasing me around with them. (Bobchia's laughter only encouraged them.)

When the rabbit population in the barn exploded, everyone had their theory. The boys finally confessed they'd thought Ike looked lonely in his big cage all by himself, so they had been putting Meme in his cage for *overnighters* and then back in her cage when they brought Dollee an apple before school; thus they were talking to the Man Upstairs on a regular basis. (Especially when Mother wasn't around.) Sometimes, to our amazement, they would actually go talk to the Man Upstairs *without* being told to! That baffled Bobchia as she quickly checked her Mother's lamps, summoning me on a *scouting expedition* throughout the Inn, only to discover a broken window or a gouge in the woodwork. When she confronted the boys, they denied knowing anything about the matter. They'd run and hide behind Mother and smirk at Bobchia. I'd stand behind them sad-faced to remind Bobchia of our separation. Defeated, Bobchia would *erase* her words in midsentence and then huff to the kitchen, drowning her anguish in shots of coffee. "If it weren't for you Sweetie, I'd box their ears good! I've never had to erase so much in my entire life! Mercy, I think I'm getting *bursitis!*"

As time passed we grew exhausted of trying to think of things for the boys to do. At least they quit saying they were 'bored' after Bobchia kept shoving dust rags in their hands, telling them to 'dust everything that is wood.'

To get them out of the Inn, sometimes she'd take us to get ice cream. The boys would sit calmly in the park's gazebo and listen to stories of Grampie David and Father, but when they were in the Inn, it was a different story. Bobchia said she thought she'd go mad listening to them fighting and complaining, screaming and tattling! One time when she was desperate, she hauled out her rolls of duct tape and told them to race them down the hallway. After a few minutes of thumping and hollering, a duct-taped Andrew crawled into the kitchen. After yelling at Logan, then erasing her words with a throbbing arm, Bobchia made up her mind to hold her tongue—to keep her erasing at a minimum.

The Saturday after that, Bobchia ordered them back outside as more of the tenants were threatening to leave.

Andrew crossed his arms. "Bobchia, we don't *stink!*"

"I know that, mercy! When I was your age I was always working and wished I could play outside. You kids *can* but *won't!* If you can't find something to do outside, I'll have to find some *work* for you to do in here!"

"We are out of here!" Logan said and they ran outside. Soon they were having a blast behind the red barn sticking nails in eggs and blowing the yokes into Rocky's food dish for his late-night snack. When they finished, they taped the ends of the eggs with red or orange duct tape and carefully set them in the creek, betting sticks of blackjack gum on whose egg would be the first to float to the covered bridge. They had just launched the last eight when the mail truck came down the lane. They ran into the Inn and sat on the stairs, placing bets on the first tenant to grab the letters and newspaper from the mail slot. The long shot was Homer. (Although he was generally the first to get to the door he'd forget why he was there and go sit in the mail truck.) Even-odds was Tall Cliff because he had the longest stride.

After cashing in their bets, they followed Tall Cliff to the kitchen for lunch, where he read the obituaries aloud to all, then we'd have to listen to the *fond memories* of whoever had died. After looking at teary faces across the table, the boys were unable to eat their American cheese sandwiches. Mother ordered us to take our plates upstairs. "From now on, we will eat our lunch there *every* Saturday if this 'morbid routine' continues!"

Bobchia told the mourners that on Saturdays the obituaries would be discussed when the boys were *hopefully* outside and Mother was *hopefully* at the library.

Every now and then, I'd receive a letter from Florida. Friends rehashing the Ty and Tiff romance, confessing that they had known all along but wanted to spare my feelings. The *deepest cut* was when I got a letter from Tiff with my old address as her return address. I cried as I looked at the envelope and scribbled RETURN TO SENDER on it, thereafter refusing any letters from Florida. I was in my new life now, and it was better than I had ever dreamed!

As I enjoyed the time of my life, Bobchia exhausted herself, trying to run the Inn while keeping peace between the tenants and the boys. Just when she thought they were acting respectful, they'd *stage fights* in front of the old ladies, using their cardboard shields of faith and swords of the spirit they got from Wednesday night church. The women would scream as the boys revealed their missing teeth (blackjack gum) and bloody mouths (ketchup)! By the time Bobchia ran to see what all the commotion was about, the boys had licked off the ketchup and were chewing gum, carefully jousting.

The old men were not exempt from their pranks either. Bobchia thought the boys needed a Father figure and had recruited Spike to babysit whenever a baseball or football game was on TV. Spike explained the games in great detail, and the boys seemed to truly find them interesting, cheering and jumping on the couches whenever points were scored. But what they were really doing was *shaking the change out of the men's pockets*. 'Search' was the game they were playing. For when the room had cleared, they searched the cushions—a game designed to fill their piggy banks!

The nights that Mother wasn't at the library were particularly stressful at the dinner table. Logan would usually start things off by sticking out his tongue with food on it, making Andrew laugh.

Things would escalate from there. Sometimes Andrew would come to the dinner table with his ball cap on and refuse to remove it.

Mother would plead, "Take your cap off, please."

"But it's my *favorite.*"

"Please take it off when you're at the table!"

"But it's my favorite!"

As their voices elevated, Bobchia would pray for patience as she watched tenants leave the table but the straw that broke the camel's back was the night Aunt Ardelle and Wanda left the table without finishing their meal!

"*Who is the adult here, Clair?*" Bobchia snapped. She grabbed the hat off Andrew's head, walked over to the potbelly stove and threw it in. She dumped a wastebasket of trash in with it, lit a match and threw it in and slammed the door.

Andrew banged his fist down on the table, sending a spoon full of noodles flying. "That's my *best* hat!"

"*Not anymore!*" Bobchia screamed back.

A noodle did a three-point landing on Antenna Man's *antenna.* He never flinched.

Mother's face burned. "Rhea, these are my boys not *yours!*"

"You had *no right to burn my hat!*" Andrew slammed his fist down again.

I'd never seen Bobchia so angry! She looked Andrew squarely in the face. "*No right?* For two nights we've heard nothing but you and your Mother *arguing over that stupid hat!* Do you see anyone else in here with a hat on? Don't you have *respect* for anybody? I am your grandmother! This is *my* home. I have tenants who *pay* to live here! You are welcome to eat at my table—but *without* a hat! Do I make myself clear?" Andrew started to whine. She continued, "If you insist on whining, young man, I will go up to your closet, get the *rest* of your hats and *throw them in the stove!*"

Mother stood up. "Rhea, please! Must you go over my *authority?*"

"Authority, what *authority?* There are *rules* in this Inn and in the world, and you had better start teaching those boys *right from wrong!* Not everybody is as *patient* as I am!"

Mother threw her napkin down. They stared at each other. Finally Mother broke away and ran upstairs sobbing. The boys giggled. Bobchia grabbed them by their ears. "*I've got a bone to pick with you two!*" She led them out of the room toward the parlor, calling over her shoulder, "Jennifer, see to your Mother!"

*"Yes ma'am!"* I ran after Mother, to our room. She was wiping her tears and looking up 'discipline' in her Bible's concordance. "Proverbs 22:6 says: **'Train up a child in the way he should go: and when he is old, he will not depart from it.'**"

"Bobchia told me that there are thirty one Proverbs, one for every day of the month and they'll make you smart because Solomon wrote…" She gave me 'the look.'

"Next *you'll* be wearing a cobbler's apron! You know as well as I that Paul disciplined the boys before he was ill. I know they are bad, but they *just* lost their Father."

"Mother, it has been almost *two years!*"

"I know I have to come to grips with that *every morning when I open my eyes.* I miss him so much." She hugged me and told me she could have never gotten through the last two years *without me.* I needed to hear those words! She wiped her tears, saying a little prayer under her breath, "God, please help me to be a good mother and help the boys behave. Amen."

We walked to the top of the stairs, arm in arm. All was quiet! We looked at each other and hurried down the stairs to the kitchen. The boys were sitting there eating like perfect gentlemen. Bobchia cleared her throat, and they said in unison, "I'm sorry, Mother."

Mother ran to the table and hugged them. "My little men!" That day to mother, was an *answer to prayer.* My brothers never told me what happened in the parlor, but from that day forward whenever they got out of hand, Bobchia would put her head down and look at them *through her eyebrows,* and they would immediately settle down.

The next day Bobchia intercepted a phone call for Mother from Miss Arlen, the school nurse. The boys had been up to their old tricks with the Black Jack gum, blacking out their front teeth and telling their horrified classmates that their teachers had 'punched them in the face and knocked their teeth out!' When Bobchia arrived at the school, the boys were getting a lecture from Mr. Fish. They were relieved when Miss Arlen had knocked on his door and announced that their mother was waiting to talk with him. "She'll believe us!" Andrew whispered to Logan confidently.

"She always d-u-z!" Their smiles turned into frowns as Mr. Fish held the door open for Bobchia, introducing himself to her as she came into his office.

"I am very pleased to meet you, Mr. Fish. I am their *proud* grandmother, Rhea Matkovich."

"They tried to *bribe* me, telling me they have money!" Mr. Fish said.

"Tell him you're sorry! Tell him right this very minute that you are sorry!" She walked toward the boys windshield wipering her fingers at them.

"I'm sorry right this very minute!" Andrew said.

"Sorry." Logan hung his head.

She held out her hands. They unwillingly filled them with pack after pack of Black Jack gum. "You *know* better than to chew gum in school! Mercy, there are signs posted all over the halls!"

"But Bobchia…"

"What?"

"*I can't read yet!*" Andrew said.

Bobchia threw the gum in the wastebasket, telling Mr. Fish that if he had any more trouble with the boys to let *her* know and the rabbit-ears would be removed from the television set! (A kid can live *without a lot of stuff,* blackjack gum included, but a kid can *never* live without good TV reception!) Bobchia went back to the Inn and confronted Spike, telling him to quit bribing the boys with gum to stay out of his leaf piles!

The rabbit-ear threat was an *educational turning point* in my brothers' lives as they started to improve in school.

Mother's loan finally got approved, when Bobchia put the Inn as collateral. (I kept my promise to not tell Bobchia, but Pat Whiteman, Bobchia's second cousin on her mother's side, is a loan officer at Penn Bank, and she let the cat out of the bag.) Bobchia acted *surprised* when Mother proudly told her after Bible study, that she would be starting nursing classes the next Monday. Mother also got hired to work at Pine Grove a few days a week. (Thanks to Bobchia's volunteer work there, she was a shoo-in.)

Bobchia confided. "I just pray your Mother isn't biting off more than she can chew!" She was thrilled to have more time with the boys and reassured Mother they wouldn't be any trouble while she was gone. She eagerly took on her role as full-time grandmother, without Mother looming over her. What she didn't realize was that Mother was more determined than ever to get us out of the 'three ringed circus,' as she called it. Living constantly under the threat of leaving again made my prayer life stronger and my knees a bit calloused. I couldn't bear to think of living anywhere beyond the walls of the Inn.

At Sunday dinner, Harold told Bobchia he had received a letter and that the reason the funeral home had burned down was because the hot wax machine he had plugged in to remove the hairs on Mrs. Archer's upper lip had faulty wiring. The insurance company had put a check in the mail to cover his loss. Bobchia got up from the table and went into the bathroom, coming out she handed him a pair of tweezers. "You won't have to plug *these* in. Use them on the next old gal you get with a *mustache.*"

The day Harold received the check he rushed to the Inn, pacing in the kitchen, waiting to talk to Bobchia. She and I had just put salve on Joan of Arc's paws, and when we walked into the kitchen, Harold started, "Rhea, I have some *great news!*"

"Oh, you got your neck brace off, good!" She slid the tin to me as I sat down.

"The brace is *not* the news!"

"Well, mercy, have at it!"

Harold glanced at me. "Oh…I have some homework," I mumbled and took a couple of cookies and went up two steps, waiting to hear the news.

"I got the check!" He held it up and walked over and kissed her. I leaned to see Bobchia, with my hand over my mouth. She smiled up at him. "Oh, Harold, I'm so *glad!*"

Harold beamed from ear to ear. "Sell the Inn and go to Vegas with me!"

"*What?*" Bobchia took a step back.

*"We can get married and retire out of the snow."*

I almost fell down the stairs straining to hear her answer. "I'm pleased as punch to think that you'd want me as *your wife,* but mercy, Harold, the Inn *is* my life! Now that Jen and the boys are here, a runaway horse couldn't pull me away! God gives everyone a purpose, and mine is right *here!* My Bobchia used to tell me, 'Bloom where you are planted; *do God's work where He put you!* Don't waste your life waiting around for some *important thing* to happen because that day may never come!' How could I ever leave this Inn? *My roots are deep here.* What if we get married and you move in here with me. How about that?"

Harold's faced drooped and he turned a little to the side. "I'm sorry. I don't think I could live in this *confusion."*

"I'm sorry, but *I can't live without it!"*

Harold pulled at the collar of his shirt. "Are you sure?"

"That's it, Fort Pitt. Besides, I could never live in that heat. It'd be like having a *permanent* hot flash. You know I like the snow."

"Well...I guess the only thing left for me to do is to deposit this check and open another funeral home."

"It won't be so bad. I'll help you when I can. I'm good with wallpaper!" She giggled. "I just went from a *wedding to wallpaper!* Sounds like a country western song to me."

He laughed and gave her a kiss, and she gave him a nice big piece of chocolate cheesecake.

That night after Bobchia rang the dinner bell, "Dinner in a *few!"* Mr. Pratt wheeled in an empty wheelchair. "Mercy, Homer, you forgot your wife!" Bobchia and I went in to get Mrs. Pratt. She complained that no one had come to get her for lunch. Bobchia apologized and said that she had gone to the store and had forgotten to leave a note on the coffee pot for Ardelle.

When Bobchia wheeled Mrs. Pratt to the table, Logan whispered to Andrew, "Let's get her to *talk."*

"She didn't last time. She probably won't this time either." They sat down across from her and watched her intently as they argued over who had the biggest drum stick.

Bobchia rolled her eyes. "Mercy, eat! They're off the *same bird!"*

Mrs. Pratt tried to back her wheelchair away from the table, but Bobchia got up and pushed her back to her plate, assuring her that the boys would be quiet as she looked at them though her brows. The boys were good throughout the meal until they got ice cream for dessert, soon to be a batch of gerish. Mrs. Pratt watched as they ate, sticking their *gerish* covered tongues out periodically and repeatedly saying, "*I wish…Mr. Fish…had some gerish.* I wish… Mr. Fish…had some gerish."

Mrs. Pratt snapped. She reached across the table, grabbed their bowls and threw them against the wall.

"Mercy! Mrs. Pratt!"

"Hey, look!" Andrew laughed. "*Ice cream gerish is starting to fall, starting to fall down the wall!*" Logan giggled and fell off his chair.

"*Boys!*" Mother yelled as she ran to the sink for the dishcloth.

Bobchia hurried Mrs. Pratt back to her room. Discovering a prescription for nerve medicine that had never been filled lying on an end table. That was when Bobchia made the decision to let Mrs. Pratt eat her meals in her room from then on—(or at least until the boys graduated from high school).

As we ate our pie, Bobchia offered the deer head parlor to Mother, saying that Cecil and Cliff would move her bed and desk downstairs. Mother declined and took her coffee to the porch. Venal and Izora got up and started doing the dishes. Bobchia poured a shot of coffee and turned toward me. "Your Mother probably doesn't want to be in that room because of Luella lying there in state. Honestly, Sweetie, if your Mother only knew how many people have *died* in this old Inn in the last hundred years, she'd probably go sleep in the *red barn!*"

I knew Bobchia would only laugh at Mother if I told her that the real reason she didn't want the room was…*the herd*.

I changed the subject. "Donna told me in school that a person only has to be *sixteen* to drive in Pennsylvania."

"What are you *driving* at?"

"Well, I'm not *driving* anything yet!"

"Very funny, I was wondering when we would have this conversation. What does your Mother say?"

"To wait until spring."

"That sounds like good advice to me. What's the hurry? We're so close to town you can practically walk to everything. Besides the roads are treacherous here in the winter."

"*Chee.*"

"Now, don't be mad. You can practice driving on that old tractor in the field when Spike's not on it. You can't hurt anything out there and that way you'll get a lot of practice before spring."

(I knew it was a losing battle to argue—*especially* because she and Mother, who never agreed on anything, *agreed on this*.) We walked to the porch and sat on the swing next to Mother who was visiting with Aunt Ardelle and Wanda in the rockers.

The boys were throwing stones in the creek. After a couple minutes they ran over to the tiny bridge and with their backs to us, urinated off of it. A car came down the lane, honking at them and parked. A man got out laughing at the boys, waving to Bobchia.

"Sweetie, this is one of the *funniest guys* you'll ever meet!"

"That's a matter of *opinion!*" Aunt Ardelle said grabbing Wanda's arm and pulling her inside.

A thin man around fifty walked up the steps carrying a suitcase. He bowed to Bobchia and kissed her hand. Minnie growled from the apron. Bobchia stood up. "Mr. McStall, I haven't seen you in a *coon's age!* Good to see you again. I would like you to meet my family."

Mother yelled, "Boys, come here for a second." They ignored her.

"Boys!" Bobchia yelled. Logan pushed Andrew. "Hey!"

Andrew punched him in the arm. "Ouch!"

They ran up the steps and stood beside Mother.

"He pushed me!" Andrew pointed at Logan.

"He punched me!" Logan pointed back.

I stood up.

"This is my daughter-in-law, Clair, and my grandchildren, Jennifer, Andrew and Logan. Clair, children, this is Mr. McStall."

"Hello." We said.

To the tune of '**Pop Goes the Weasel**' he put his hand out to shake Mother's only to quickly bring it back. He moved his feet from side to side and moved up and down in front of us he sang; "Hi! My name is Matthew McStall; I'll shake your hand to greet ya. I'm not very handsome or ve-ry tall, **but** I'm glad to meet ya!"

He jumped up startling Andrew. Andrew kicked him in the shin! He grabbed his leg. "Ouchhhhh!"

Logan laughed.

Mother scolded, "Andrew! Tell him you're sorry right this very minute! Well?"

"You're sorry right this very minute!" Andrew spit out.

Bobchia bit her lip and said; "Your room is ready, Matthew."

"Th-th-thanks." He got his suitcase and limped toward the door.

Bobchia looked through her brows at Andrew, windshield-wipering her finger at him. Then she said, "How about a nice big piece of peach pie to make up for the black-and-blue mark you're sure to have on your leg tomorrow Matthew?"

"O-o-o-k-k-kayyy." They headed for the kitchen. From that day on Mr. McStall was nicknamed Mr. T-t-t-tunes.

Mother held her head. "I never heard of a pie that fixed black-and-blue marks! *I've got to get a second job!*"

Logan broke her train of thought, yelling, "Andrew punched me!"

"Where did I p-p-punch you?" He laughed.

Logan looked at both of his arms and shrugged his shoulders. "I don't know, but the next time you do I'm marking it with duct t-t-tape."

"Boys! He will *hear you!*" Mother scolded. They quickly ran to the red barn.

A thought occurred to me. "Mother, have you noticed that Logan has *quit* spelling his words?"

"Come to think of it, you're right."

"I wonder why."

"It's this place. *It changes people.*"

# 6
# Play Ball!

Now that the boys were acting more like *normal* students, they were allowed recess privileges. This meant they could either play baseball against the big kids or play tag with the girls. They chose baseball. Lanny, the biggest kid, had the biggest players on his team. The smaller kids, better known as 'the shrimps,' were doomed!

Butch's girlfriend, Joy, worked in the school cafeteria and drove Lanny, Lucy and Ricky home every day and babysat them until Butch got off his shift at Cyclops. Every day I watched as Lanny tormented the shrimps. He'd jump out from behind the bushes along his property line and chase them until they reached the safety of Bobchia's property line. "*Hey shrimps!* How's come ya didn't catch any of those baseballs I hit in the weeds at recess?"

"Shut up, *ya big ox!* If you wouldn't get your *boogers* all over them, I might be able to hit them!"

"Don't call me names, shrimps!"

(I figured as long as the shrimps ran faster than the ox, I'd stay out of it.)

Bobchia looked concerned, watching from the kitchen window as the boys came through the door, totally defeated.

"I can't even do good at *recess.*" Andrew pouted as he washed his hands.

Logan shook his head. "*Me either.*"

"You do better than me! I *hate* recess."

They sat at the table slumping in their chairs.

"Mercy, not like recess? That was my best subject!"

"The big kids play ball better." Andrew lifted his head to answer.

"Well, they are older and have more experience than you. I'll get Harold or Spike to coach you. Harold played for the Pithole Oilers in high school and was in the *All-Stars*. He knows a little bit about the game. You'll be playing like the big leaguers before you know it!"

The boys perked up. "Honest, Bobchia?" Logan smiled.

"Yes, now have a cookie." They eagerly reached into the tin.

Bobchia winked at me and looked to the ceiling. "TYG the sun still shines!"

Unfortunately, when she asked Spike to teach the boys the art of baseball, he was in the process of doctoring his back. It had bothered him ever since his days at the Cyclops steel mill, and he'd reinjured it from stacking hay bales in the barn last summer.

Harold couldn't help either as he was busy trying to get a new funeral parlor in operation. He'd recently purchased Bobchia's friend Noni Standford's old house when she'd moved to Florida to be with her grandkids. The house was located on the other side of the burned funeral home, and Harold was busy supervising the Amish carpenters who were renovating the house for funerals. Harold was in a hurry to get it finished, as he explained to us at Sunday dinner. "With these hot autumn days, dead people are stacking up like *cordwood,* and I'm losing all my customers to the Planter Brothers Funeral Parlor in Pithole!"

Mother found Harold's talk about dead people at the dinner table appalling and made us take our plates upstairs. As soon as we left, Bobchia scorned, "Harold! You know she's *touchy!* Quit adding wood to the flame! Can't you think of anything else to talk about besides *dead people?*"

Harold shook his head. "Sorry, *dead people* are my life!"

"Couldn't you talk about the weather?"

"Well, I did say 'with these hot autumn days'…"

"Go on!"

"Oh yeah, I get your point."

Bobchia rolled her eyes and Harold promised he would never, ever talk about dead people again in front of Mother.

Bobchia was so desperate to have the boys fit in at school that she went to the extent of asking Homer (in one of his more lucid moments) to teach them baseball. He had played in college, before he'd been drafted into the war.

One evening after supper the boys waited in the backyard where Homer was supposed to meet them, but instead he walked right past them to watch the carpenters work on the funeral home. The boys ran in, complaining, "He don't want to play after all! He didn't even look at us one time!" Andrew said with his hands on his hips.

"Yeah, his eyes look *funny.*"

Bobchia sighed and ran her hankie over her face. She'd been trying to help Harold wallpaper his new funeral parlor, but it would just have to wait. The boys were her first love. She told me she didn't want to miss *one* more minute of their childhood (like she had mine), and if that meant playing ball with them, then she'd just have to play ball! She pushed the boys out the back door, saying, "Well, let's see what you kids are made of. Get your bat and glove and show me what you got!" She turned to me. "Sorry Jen, I'm going to have to put our walk on the backburner. They need a coach, and I've been elected!"

The boys eagerly ran to the station wagon and pulled out their bats and an old superman pillowcase, that held their baseballs, from under the backseat. Bobchia smiled as they dragged their equipment over the cobblestones toward her. "Play ball!" she cheered.

Bobchia started by having the boys play catch. She could not praise Andrew enough for catching and for throwing the ball right into Logan's glove. He didn't even have to move one inch to catch it!

"He can throw, he just can't *hit!*" Logan teased.

"I can too hit!"

"Cannot!"

"Can too!"

"Cannot!"

"Can too!"

"All right already!" Bobchia cut in. "Batter up! I can pitch pretty good. I used to play stick ball when I was a kid."

"*Stick ball?*"

"I'd even pitch to your dad when your grampie wasn't around."

Andrew reluctantly got a bat. Logan hunkered down behind him punching his mitt. Bobchia pitched ball after ball. They went whizzing right past Andrew and into Logan's glove. Logan laughed carrying them back to Bobchia.

"Quit laughing at your brother!" Bobchia reprimanded. "Remember, '*do unto others!*' Do you like it when people laugh at you?" Logan shook his head. "Well Andrew doesn't either!" Over and over Bobchia pitched to Andrew. Over and over he struck out. "Don't worry Andrew, you'll settle in. *Slow and steady wins the race.*

We'll work every night until you get the hang of it, and next summer, I'll sign you up for little league."

"I'll try to be good by *then.*" Andrew said with determination.

I felt a little envious watching them. I'd never imagined I'd have to share *my* Bobchia! I had missed her so much for the last twelve years that I thought we'd be inseparable when reunited. Yet Bobchia always acknowledged me in little ways, touching my arm when she walked past me or winking at me from across the table. Yes, I was **across** the table from her, now that she was the boy's coach! How she delighted in sitting between them, rubbing their backs while smiling down into their sweet faces as they ate. Did I say *sweet?* Well they were to her, at least for the time being.

One night after supper, while I was lying across the bed with Joan of Arc, writing in my journal, I looked out the window and a bulldozer was hauling out debris from the basement of the burned funeral home. Bobchia and Andrew watched from the sidewalk as they waited for Minnie to do her business. She then handed the pup to him and got a ladder from the shed propping it up against a giant oak. She climbed the ladder and reached into her apron pocket, pulling out a piece of twine with a whiffle ball dangling from its end and secured it to a limb. She climbed down and picked up the bat, trading it for Minnie. I admired her patience as she showed him how to stand and swing. She pulled her camera out capturing the moment as he halfheartedly swung the bat, lightly tapping the ball. I opened the window to hear her explain how to shift his weight for the 'maximum hitting power.' "If your grampie David were here, he'd show you, like he showed Paul how to hit it. Mercy, I only wish I could remember all the things he said to your father."

Again she showed him the proper stance and grip, but he didn't improve much.

Finally he sat down on the ground. "I'll never be able to hit it. You better *unsign* me up for baseball next summer!"

"Don't despise the days of small beginnings! You will get the hang of it. It just takes practice. Babe Ruth wasn't any good when he first started either."

Andrew lifted an eyebrow. "The candy bar?"

149

"No *ding dong*, Babe Ruth the famous Yankee ball player—your grampie's favorite!" Andrew nodded. "Now bend your arm. Patience is a virtue."

"What does that mean?" Andrew asked as he swung, limply tapping the ball.

"A virtue is a good quality in a person."

"Oh, one of *those.*"

"Come on now, let the weak say they are *strong!*"

Logan walked out onto the porch laughing as Andrew swung, missed and threw the bat to the ground.

Bobchia hollered at him, "Logan, *quit laughing* at your brother! He's got a long row to hoe and needs encouragement—even from *you*, young man!" It went in one ear and out the other. She turned her attention back to Andrew. "All you need is some practice. If you want to be good at something, practice, boy, *practice!*" Again, she showed Andrew how to stand and hold the bat. Logan motioned to Andrew to slug the ball upward. He did. The ball sailed up the tree and wrapped itself around a branch.

"That's the way! Good job!" While she climbed the ladder to untangle it with a stick, Logan raced over to Andrew and gave him a high five. She climbed down "Try it again!"

Andrew hit the ball again, and this time it went higher!

"I told you that you could do it! See? *Bobchia knows!*" As soon as she climbed down the ladder, he hit it again, tangling it worse. This was repeated several times as Bobchia rubbed the backs of her legs.

Andrew hopped up and down. "*I'm really getting good!* Oh Bobchia, it's way up there! I'm ready to hit it again!"

She climbed up and unhooked it and then climbed down, taking the ball off of the twine.

"Hey! You said that I need practice!"

"Just hit the twine, it's the right height. I need some coffee!"

The boys giggled as they watched her limp through the yard and slowly climb up the porch steps. *It's only a matter of time*, I thought, *until Bobchia catches on to Logan's pranks. Then the chicken feathers will hit the fan!*

Bobchia pitched to Andrew every night before the evening news. She even went to Hoppy's one morning and bought herself a ball glove so she could play catch with the boys after dinner. Slowly and steadily, Andrew improved. Andrew bragged to his friends about how Bobchia played ball with him every night after school but nobody knew what a 'Bobchia' was.

One night, Logan, always a showoff, wanted to impress Bobchia. "Pitch them to me *instead* this time, Bobchia!" Slam! Slam! Slam! One by one the whole pile of balls flew over the fence and into the pumpkin patch!

Bobchia smiled. "You both are getting so good that I bet I'll be watching you on TV someday! Speaking of the TV, I better 'fine tune' the set for the news, and you better get those baseballs and get into the kitchen. I've got a couple pieces of apple pie in there with your names on them! Tonight is apple pie a' la mode night, thanks to Cliff. He made ice cream today."

They slowly walked down the lane. "Why did you have to hit them so far anyway, dummy? You even hit my *special one* so you better find it!" Andrew demanded.

"Did you know Bobchia put our names on her pies?" Logan asked.

"Never did. *First trees, now pies.* She's funnier than most old ladies I ever knew in my life."

"Yeah. *Apple pie commode* don't sound very good to me. I don't think I want any!" Logan shook his head.

"Me, either!"

When they arrived at the pumpkin patch, Lanny and Ricky were running up their porch steps with their arms full of baseballs, laughing. Andrew kicked Logan. "Owe!"

"*See what you did!* How am I ever going to get my *special baseball back?*"

"I don't know! I'm telling mom you kicked me!"

Lanny pounded on the window of the porch, they looked up. He laughed at them while lining their baseballs on his windowsill. Logan stuck his tongue out at him as Andrew *growled* deep in his throat. Slowly they walked back to the Inn, defeated, dragging their bats to the kitchen porch.

"Somehow, I have to get my good ball back! It's all your fault, dummy!" Andrew said kicking him again.

"Owe!" Logan pushed him, saying, "As soon as I get in the kitchen, I'm putting duct tape on this leg *then* I won't forget the one you kicked, *then* I'm gonna show it to mom when she gets home, *then* you'll be sorry!"

"Shut up!"

The kitchen window suddenly went up. The boys looked over. In a high-pitched voice and to the tune of **Bali Hai**, Mr. T-t-t-tunes sang, behind the lace curtain with his hands and head coming through the lace curtain, beckoning them. "Apple pie is calling, with a scoop of ice cream, get your plate; quit stalling, It's not a dream, not a dream. Apple pie. APPLE PIE! **APPLE PIE!**" They threw dirt at the curtain.

Although fights over baseball caps at the dinner table never happened again, they were replaced by 'the clashes of the green vegetables.' Mother was slowly winning the respect of the entire household by the way she was handling the boys, but this was the *one battle* of the wills that she was never going to win! Desperate, she turned *into* 'Nurse Clair' spouting off definitions of diseases that lacked 'green vegetables' and when that failed she spouted; "you'll get *rickets,* if you don't eat your vegetables!"

"What a *ricket?*" Logan asked.

"Sounds like a bug! I don't want to get *bugs!*" Andrew said.

"Mercy, people are *eating* here!" Bobchia windshield wipered her finger towards them.

"Rickets makes your legs grow funny." Mother said.

"Can't I have some corn? I can *stand* a lot of corn!" Andrew said.

"Why can't we just eat meat and cookies?" Logan asked.

While plates of delicious food along with the side dishes of icky peas and green beans, was *bottlenecked* at the end of the table, to the tune of **Oklahoma**, Mr. T-t-t-tunes rode his chair like a horse, pretended to swing a rope, and sang; "Paaaaassss *me* the pot roast, potatoes and the black eyed peas… the horseradish, the cold cow's milk, the Rocky Mountain baked beans!" The boys clapped. He stood and bowed.

"Mercy!"

After dinner most of the tenants went to the great room to watch the news while we chatted. Mr. Pratt came in and sat down. "Homer, you just ate!" Bobchia exclaimed.

"Oh, I wondered why I wasn't hungry." He got up and left.

Harold laughed and poured himself another cup of coffee, pretending not to notice when the boys hid some of their vegetables under the chair pads.

Mother glanced up from her book and examined the boy's shirt sleeves.

"Were you two in a fight? You know I don't approve of fighting." The boys shook their heads vigorously. "Your shirt sleeves are tattered, and I don't have the money to buy you any more new clothes! If your Father…" She stopped and bit her lip. "I want an explanation of what happened when I come back from sewing these." She pulled off their polo shirts, leaving them in their tee shirts. "Now finish those peas or you *will* get rickets!"

Her voice grew faint as she climbed the stairs, complaining that she didn't have the right thread color and that she still had four more chapters to read. Bobchia watched her leave, shaking her head. "I never thought we'd get through last week when she was reading about 'epidemiologic infections,' remember?"

"That's when I was *itchy!*" Andrew scratched his neck.

"This week she must be studying *rickets of the world!*"

Andrew looked over at my plate. "How come Jen don't gotta eat *her* peas?"

Logan nodded. "*She* don't get yelled at because she's so *precious and beautiful all the time.*"

I shook my head at Logan. "Girls don't *get* rickets, so there!"

Bobchia laughed. "Yes, they do, but *girl* rickets are more precious and beautiful than *boy* rickets!" She snorted as she carried away our plates and dumped the veggies into the garbage.

Logan's eyes grew wide. "What will we tell Mother?"

"That's not what I'm concerned about. What I am concerned about is *what happened* at recess to get your shirts so tattered." The boys both looked so sad that *I* almost felt sorry for them! They stared stone-faced at each other, never to reveal the awful truth.

Bobchia put her hands on her hips, loving the challenge. (She used every bit of her grandmother strategy to unlock the deep, dark secret of their anxiety.) "Sweetie, in the pantry, behind the prune juice, you will find a cake carrier. I was going to donate that cake to the church bazaar tomorrow, but *this* serves a better purpose. Make sure you support the bottom of it!"

I walked into the pantry. On a wall, stuck with blue duct tape, was a row of blue ribbons that Bobchia had won for her cakes and pies over the years, and hanging under them was a row of cobbler aprons, one for each day of the week. I moved the prune juice and grabbed the carrier. (So help me, that cake weighed five pounds!) As I was leaving the pantry, a few marks on the wall beside the light switch caught my eye. There were lines at different heights with birthdates and names on them. I squinted and leaned closer to my four marks.

"Sweetie, can't you find it?" I brought the cake out and handed it to her. "This is your great grandmother Kay's idea of a *simple cake.*"

"When did she bake it?" Andrew asked.

"I thought she was *dead.*" Logan said.

"She is. I baked it using her recipe, *ding dong!*" She proudly set it in front of them and took off the lid.

"*Oh boy!*" Harold said.

Bobchia leaned toward the boys with her hands on her hips and a grin on her lips. The smell of the cake made us salivate. We stared at the chocolate, marshmallow, peanut butter, caramel, cherry cake with fudge icing. (This cake, if shared with the Russians, could bring peace between Russia and the United States!)

"It smells delicious!" I said.

Bobchia gave us each a big piece. The boys crammed cake into their mouths, and she quickly pulled their plates away from them. They reached for their plates. "Ah, do you want some more?" They shook their heads eagerly, licking their lips. "*Well?*" she said.

Logan swallowed hard. "Well…" Logan looked at Andrew and hung his head.

"Well, we play ball at recess." Andrew said.

"Mercy, *I know that!* What are you doing to *rip* your shirts?" She asked nervously, checking the hallway for Mother.

Andrew averted his eyes and continued. "The big boys say that if we want to play ball with them, we have to get the balls they hit into the *briar patch.* We try to jump and catch them before they go in, but Lanny hits them so *stinkin' hard,* then he laughs at us!"

"Lanny, huh?" She said shaking her head.

We try to find 'em, but if we don't, then it's a *stinkin' homerun!* I really try hard to find them, Bobchia." Logan said.

"Me too!" said Andrew as he pulled up his pantleg to show his scratched leg. Logan pulled his pant legs up too.

Harold shook his head as he cut another piece of cake. "That briar patch was there when *I* played on that field! You'd think they would have gotten rid of it years ago."

Bobchia's face dropped. "*Mercy!* There's some Mercurochrome in the medicine cabinet, Sweetie. Would you go get it?"

A piece of paper was duct-taped on the inside door of the cabinet, in Bobchia's writing. "**The spirit of a man will sustain him in sickness, but who can bear a broken spirit?**" Proverbs 18:14.

I returned to the kitchen and handed her the Mercurochrome. She applied it to their legs as they ate.

"That stuff hurts!" Logan complained.

"But it is *orange,* your favorite color. Come on now; put some frosting in your mouth. There, honey boy, that wasn't so bad." Then she turned to Andrew. "Get some cake in your mouth. I'll *blow* on your leg. There ya go, my other honey boy!"

Harold put his plate in the sink and licked his fork. "Let's go play some ball."

Andrew shrugged. "We don't got any baseballs. Lanny took them all."

"Well then let's go to the field. I'll show you how to get some *out* of the briars."

"Can we Bobchia? Can we?"

Bobchia smiled. "Sweetie, write your Mother a note and tell her we went for a walk." I grabbed a pen and paper as the boys shoved the rest of their cake into their mouths.

I made a face in disgust. "You eat like *pigs!*"

"You *are* a pig!" Andrew said as he stuck out his tongue with cake on it.

Bobchia looked through her brows. "You're wasting daylight. Hurry up!"

Andrew made a face at me behind Bobchia's back, and I made one back. She handed the boys sweatshirts to put on.

"Sweetie, rinse those cake dishes off and put the cake back before you-know-who sees it."

"Cool."

As the boys ran out the kitchen door, Pumpkin rushed past them scrambling up the big oak. They hurried back in. "Bobchia, Pumpkin got out and ran up that big tree!"

She put a hand to her forehead. "Oh no! I hope Ardelle and Wanda don't see her up there!"

"What if she can't get *down?*" Logan asked.

"Wonder if she *starves to death* up there!" Andrew cried.

Bobchia shook her head. "Mercy, did you ever see cat skeletons in trees?" They shook their heads. "Then there's your answer!" She got the cat treats off the fridge. "Here, tell Spike to shake the can and coax her down. Hopefully Ardelle won't see her." They ran to find Spike.

Bobchia dug in the closet and got out a couple of old flannel shirts and leather gloves. Harold met her on the porch, carrying a pail and hedge trimmers from the shed. "Rhea, we'll need a couple of flashlights."

She got them and came back out. When the boys returned, she handed them the flashlights and they immediately held them under their chins. (It wasn't dark yet.) As we walked past the Sterling's house, we saw Lanny in the window, standing behind the baseballs that lined the windowsill, laughing, pointing at the boys.

The boys averted Bobchia's attention. "Look at that sky, Bobchia!" Andrew yelled.

"It's my favorite color!" Logan cheered. Then they made faces at Lanny and ran ahead laughing onto the covered bridge and waited for us.

Andrew announced, "Logan and me *hate* Lanny!"

Bobchia put her hand on her heart. "Shame on you! We are to *love everyone that God does.*"

"Love Lanny?" Logan eyes grew big.

"Well at least *like* him. Try okay?"

Logan thought it over. "Okay, I will...but not too hard. I mean, I like other kids in the school okay—just *not* him."

"Oh? Who do you like?" Bobchia asked.

That got them started.

"Ah, Guy and Sarah." Logan said thinking.

"Ary and Josh." Andrew broke in.

"Molly, Carly and Emily."

"Gavin and Aiden and Doug."

"Joel, Max and Kelsey."

"Noah, Tanner, Taylor and Emmett."

"Don't forget Wyatt, Zack and Cole!"

Bobchia pursed her lips. "Hmm. Who are their grandparents?"

"They don't tell us stuff like that!" Logan laughed.

"Do any of these children have *last* names?"

"Maybe!" Andrew said.

"Do any of them go to Sunday School?" Bobchia asked.

"Some do," Logan said.

"*Ask* the ones who don't!" Bobchia said.

"Okay!" The boys ran ahead.

Five blocks later we reached the baseball diamond. Bobchia put Minnie down to play with the boys then she and Harold put on the flannel shirts and gloves and carefully waded into the briar patch. They stooped down with the flashlights and threw out as many baseballs as they could find.

"Hey some of these are my baseballs that Lanny stole!" Andrew cried. "See the red mark I put on my baseballs?" Logan nodded. "But I don't see the one that Father wrote on." Andrew said sadly.

"Hey do we get to keep these?" Logan asked.

"Just a few, I have plans for them." Harold said, popping his head out of the brush.

Bobchia came out. "There are all your baseballs, guys." They thanked her. "Harold, come on, what are you doing in there?" She put Minnie in her apron.

"I think I see a few more. You and Jen go on ahead. I want to give the boys some *pointers.*"

Bobchia waved her hand. "All right then. Come on, Jen, you can help me get the pies cut for Bible study tonight."

"Okay!" I smiled. "Dawnette is coming over early to ride Dollee. Then, can we ride her over the hill to Church for Teen Action?"

She nodded. "If your mom says it's okay."

When the boys returned they came running out to the barn chewing on blackberries as I was saddling up Dollee.

"*We have a secret, and we ain't telling you or Bobchia!*" Logan said.

"And you can't *make* us!" Andrew said.

"Who cares?" I said as I led the horse out of the barn. "Leave me alone. Dawnette will be here any minute."

"Don't ya want to *know* a secret?" Andrew asked with his hands on his hips.

Harold said "if Bobchia knew she'd be madder than a *wet hen!*" Logan laughed; "Whatever that means!"

"Okay, we'll tell *you*, but you have to promise not to tell Bobchia and don't cross your fingers either." Andrew whispered.

I promised. They said that after Bobchia and I left the field, Harold had cut and tramped little paths throughout the blackberry patch and had *strategically* placed baseballs along the paths so they could run in during a game and get them. He told them that he and his friend Slick had done the same thing when they were in the All-Stars and to keep it a *secret*. They wondered if it was *cheating*, but Harold said, 'Well, if Lanny *hits* a ball in here and you *find* a ball in here, who's to say it's not the ball he *hit* in here.'

The boys giggled as they ran through the field making plans for tomorrow's game.

The next day after they out ran Lanny down the lane, Bobchia was at the window cheering them on when they burst into the Inn. Andrew squealed holding up his ball glove. "Sign me up, sign me up for ball! I'm ready!"

That night at the supper table, the boys were so focused on talking about their 'big game' that they weren't even aware they were eating vegetables! Andrew was labeled 'The Blackberry Kid' because when Lanny hit a ball into the briar patch, he had hurried in, got *a* ball and then stood there chewing on blackberries while Logan franticly yelled at him to "*Throw the ball, stupid!*" He calmly waited, tossing the ball into his glove watching Lanny out of the corner of his eye clear first base, stomp on second base, and when he rounded third, confidently waving his ball cap like a big leaguer and was just a '*slide*' away from a home run, Andrew *sailed* the baseball into Logan's waiting glove at home plate and *wham!* Lanny was *out!*

"Man, it's the *mostest fun* of all, Bobchia!" Andrew beamed.

"I knew it! I just knew that you'd be a *chip off the old block!* One of these days Bobchia will be watching you two on TV!"

The boys had been dubbed '*the recess heroes*' making the dinner conversation the *mostest fun!*

"I do a *lot* better at recess now!"

"Me too!"

As they settled in, their grades improved. At least once a week that first year, only after the kitchen was in order, Bobchia and I would accompany the boys to the baseball diamond (instead of taking our normal walk up Red Barn Mountain). Bobchia always thought that it was *her* pointers that won them the day's game, then she'd offer up a tip or two for the next day's game.

Even though I was always by Bobchia's side, I realized the boys were slowly stealing her heart away. They looked so much like Father (each in their own weird way) and Bobchia was always laughing about something they had done. I suppose I was the most jealous when they laughed together, because laughing with her was my most cherished memory. I became very good at forcing smiles and trying not to envy the boys or to wish I was little again. I even convinced myself that it was good that they were learning from her. But I was the one who was really learning—learning to *share* my Bobchia.

# 7
# Critters In The Basement

Everyone was complaining about how hot the autumn was, except for me. I was used to it because my Florida clothes kept me cool. The mornings and evenings were especially chilly, but the afternoons were extremely warm. The school (like most in the north) didn't have air conditioning, but I was always nice and cool in my Florida clothes. Bobchia said, "One extreme always leads to another. With that batch of acorns on the ground behind the red barn, we're sure to have a doozey of a winter! You'll wish for this heat in a couple of months, just wait and see." She kept the Inn cool by closing the windows on the sunny side and opening them on the shady side, rotating as the day progressed.

One morning as we were getting ready to leave for school, someone knocked on the kitchen door. Bobchia eagerly opened it, thinking it might be an 'angel unaware', but instead it was Butch Sterling!

Bobchia looked up at the towering man. "Did Dollee Doll jump over the fence again?"

"Can she eat fifty-three pumpkins?"

Bobchia raised an eyebrow.

"Because our fifty-three pumpkins are *missing!* I want them back, and I aim to get them!"

"We *don't have* your pumpkins, Mr. Sterling! Where in this crowded place would we ever put fifty-three pumpkins?!"

"Why don't you ask those *brat* grandkids of yours?" Butch took a step toward her, putting his huge face in hers.

She motioned for us to get behind the door, and then she pulled out her only weapon. "*Sic him, Minnie!*" Bobchia held the tiny dog up to his face. Minnie growled and viciously snapped at his huge nose with her tiny teeth.

Surprisingly, he stepped back! "You *religious* old lady! I'm calling the police to get a search warrant!"

"Good! You can tell them to search your basement for that *homemade hooch*, you think nobody knows about! I'm sorry, Mr.

Sterling, but I would thank you to leave my premises *immediately!*"
She held Minnie up and out, walking toward him, and he clumsily
backed down the steps.

She glanced at us peeking around the door and then looked
back at Butch, lumbering down the lane. "Good girl, Miss Minnie
you sure showed him what for!" she said as she kissed her,
hurrying in and slamming the door. "See kids, just like David and
Goliath!"

Andrew shook his head. "But Minnie is a girl!"

She put Minnie back in her apron while spiting dog hairs out
of her mouth and looked to the ceiling. "Mercy, it's getting harder
and harder for me to 'love thy neighbor'!" She knelt down and put
her arms around the boys. "You kids don't know anything about
fifty-three pumpkins do you?"

Logan looked *nervously* at Andrew, then back at her. "Where in
this crowded place would we ever put fifty-three pumpkins?"

"*Exactly.*" Bobchia shook her head. "Let me grab the keys and
drive you to school today. I don't want you walking past Butch's
place for a while."

Andrew grabbed his stomach. "Bobchia, I'm sick. I don't think
I can go to school today."

She felt his head. "You don't feel hot."

"I don't feel good too."

Bobchia felt Logan's head. "You don't feel hot either."

I nudged her. "Well, I guess you can stay home today after that
awful scare. I suppose the kids on your baseball team don't really
need you two to get Lanny *out*. They can probably do it *without you
two!*"

The boys looked at each other, grunted until their faces got red
and grabbed their stomachs.

"Plug your nose, Bobchia!" I yelled and quickly stepped out
onto the porch.

After two loud burps, Bobchia scorned, "Mer-cy! How about
*excuse me?*"

"You're excused, Bobchia!" Andrew giggled. "I feel better
now!"

"Me too!"

The boys ran to the car. She came onto the porch laughing.

"Believe me, Bobchia, their farts are nothing to laugh at!"

"Sweetie, we don't say f-a-r-t in the Inn. Around here we have bouts of 'gastric hyperacidity.' They *smell* the same but it has a nicer ring to it."

As the days grew hotter, the daylight grew shorter, along with everyone's patience. The weekends were especially trying with the boys. Mother had picked up another course, so she spent her time studying upstairs in front of a fan with her feet in a pail of ice water. Not wanting to run the ovens, Bobchia made several kinds of cold dishes, while Spike and Cliff took turns manning the grill, anything to keep the Inn cool.

'American cheese, please' rang in Bobchia's ears. The boys, not wanting to get sweaty, stayed inside getting on everyone's nerves.

Bobchia fanned herself. "Mercy, you're going to be *bound up* for a month if you don't eat some fruit and get some exercise. Quit sitting around like bumps on a log! Smell the fresh air! You'll be cooped up all winter. Go play ball!"

Logan smiled. "I keep hitting the ball in the briars at school."

"That's a boy, Logan!"

"But not Andrew. He just watches the balls fly past his nose and strikes out!"

She turned toward Andrew. "I thought you were hitting the ball better!"

"I am! I'll show you, Logan! Bobchia, watch me out the window!"

The boys ran outside. Logan pitched five balls to Andrew, and he hit all five into the empty pumpkin patch. Lanny ran from the bushes gathering the baseballs adding them to the long line on the window sill.

"We're out of baseballs *again,* thanks to you, smarty pants! Now we can't play ball anymore!" Logan whined as they came back into the kitchen.

"Shut up!"

"Great job, Andrew!" Bobchia praised. "I'm very impressed. Now why don't you boys go for a bike ride or go play in the creek?"

Andrew shook his head. "It's *too hot* out there!"

While the tenants relaxed in the coolness of the great room, thanks to the shade of a gnarled oak growing along the north side of the Inn, Bobchia listened to the boys.

"I'm bored!"

"Me too!"

She fanned herself with the newspaper and rubbed the groove in her forehead, got an idea and went into the pantry reemerging with the birthday box then she blew up a balloon and handed it to Logan. Then she unrolled the paper towels and handed them the empty roll and told them, "Go play ball in the great room!"

That lasted until Mr. Hair complained that the boys kept stepping on his feet when they ran the 'pretend bases.'

"Don't you have respect for other people's feet?" Bobchia scolded.

Andrew was quick to offer a defense. "We did not step on that *weird guy's* feet, honest! We'll show you!" The boys pulled on Bobchia's arms, making her spill her lemonade on her apron. They guided her to a chair and repeated the homerun in slow motion, taking care not to step on *her* feet.

"Told ya, Bobchia!" Logan beamed.

"See? And we didn't step on *his* feet either!" Andrew crossed his arms.

Bobchia rubbed her forehead with one hand and fished an ice cube out of her glass with the other. She looked at the ceiling in thought as she dropped the cube into her apron pocket for Minnie. "I don't know what else you boys can do! You'll just have to go back outside and play."

"It's too hot, Bobchia. I'm already *slippery*, feel my head!" Andrew lifted his arm. "Smell me!"

"I can smell both of you from here, thank you! All I know is what my Bobchia told me whenever I complained of the heat: *'Get horizontal and pant!'*"

"What does that mean?"

"Lie down!"

"I ain't tired."

"I'm *not* tired, Andrew." Bobchia corrected.

"Me neither!"

"No, I mean…never mind. Ask Spike if he'll take you fishing."

Saturday was another scorcher. The boys complained for the millionth time about the heat. Again they whined it was too hot to put snakes in the claw-footed tub or to play in the creek. So when Cecil dug up worms for Jet, he dug up an extra can and took the boys fishing. They were only gone about an hour, and they returned with two big trout, swimming in a pail in the red barn. They ran through the Inn, excited to show them to Mother and Bobchia.

Logan giggled. "They ate the worms at *the same time!*"

"Yeah! I think they must be twin brothers." Andrew mused. "Hurry up! Come and see!"

By the time Bobchia had refilled her glass with lemonade and Mother had torn herself from the pages of her book, the fish had disappeared!

"The pail is turned over!" Andrew exclaimed in dismay.

"What happened to my fish?" Logan lifted the pail and frowned.

"Sorry, boys. It was probably Rocky; he just couldn't resist!"

Andrew was mad and grabbed Cecil's cans of worms and threw them off the little bridge. They hung over the railing watching them crawl on the bottom of the brook. Cecil stuck his head out of the barn. "Hey, those were *Jet's* worms! That's the last time I'll take you kids fishing!"

At lunch, the boys complained about Cecil and about having to eat pastrami, whining that they wanted their favorite—grilled American cheese sandwiches.

Bobchia shook her head. "Grilled cheese again? You're going to get constipated!"

"Come on Bobchia, please make me an American cheese sandwich."

"Me too! And not that other cheese when you tried to trick us, only *American* cheese this time, please."

Mr. T-t-t-tune, clapped his hands over his head and danced around the table, and in the worst Spanish accent, singing to the tune of **Only in America**, "I like grilled cheese that's *Amer-e-can,* macaroni and cheese that's *Amer-e-can,* ravioli with cheese that's *Amer-e-can,* pastrami with cheese that's *Amer-e-can!* Olay!" He slid across the floor on his knees, ending up eyeball to eyeball to

Minnie in Bobchia's apron. Minnie jumped at him and almost bit him as he scrambled to his feet. The boys applauded. He bowed.

"Mercy!"

After we ate, the boys started whining again.

Bobchia threw her hands up. "I control what goes on *in* the Inn, but I cannot control the weather!" She took a shot of coffee, shut her eyes and rubbed her forehead. "Hold the phone, Gert. I'll be right back!"

She came back down the stairs with a couple bottles of fingernail polish, laughing about the sight she'd seen out her bedroom window of Nikki burying the boys' fish beside the shed. She wiped her forehead with her hankie and got the flashlights out of a drawer. "Come on kids, follow me!"

The boys looked nervous, likely thinking they were 'in for it' again. They lagged behind as she walked toward the parlor. Then she made a sharp right, shifting Minnie in her apron. "Hold on, Miss Minnie!" She took the panting pup out of her apron and kissed her. "You're a little *hot* dog, aren't ya?" She giggled, spitting out Minnie's hair then stuck the pup back in her apron.

We followed her down the hall to the door beside the game room.

"Hey, look! A pool table!" Andrew exclaimed.

Logan leaned to look in the door. "Can we play?"

Bobchia ignored them. A sign above the basement door read, "KEEP OUT." Bobchia got onto her tiptoes to unlatch a slide lock and open the door. She told the boys to get ahead of her then looked back and winked at me.

The coolness of the basement felt wonderful at first, but the darkness was menacing as we slowly crept down the stone steps.

"Feels good down here, huh? Your, great, great grandfather, Edjew built this Inn in 1849 for his bride Mineya." She said stopping as she held the flashlight to a keystone with the date carved into the stone. "When everyone else was selling out to be in the Gold Rush, he bought this land cheap to farm it. He planted corn and wheat and raised cattle and pigs. This Inn used to be a stagecoach stop having a tavern and rooms to rent. In 1859, Colonel Drake struck oil just a couple of miles down the road."

Andrew whistled. "Wow, Bobchia, did you have that *memorized?* You sound just like TV!"

She giggled. "Drake's Well is what Titusville is famous for." She stopped and continued with the story. "Edjew's cousins—their

American names were Charles and Dewayne—gave up farming to drill with the Colonel."

"What was Edjew's American name?" I asked.

"Edward, anyway, a lot of their oil well blasting buddies would stay here. According to Edjew's journal, some of the men would walk into the dining room and actually eat their dinner with rubber bottles of nitroglycerin, sticking out of their shirt pockets. Can you imagine? When Mineya went to clean their rooms and saw the bottles lined up on the dressers, she made them put them in a bucket and hang them over the creek. It made her feel safe, but the truth is that even one of those little bottles could have blown off a side of a mountain. Mineya roped off the rockers on the creek side of the Inn until the men left town. Back in the day, lodgers got a real deal—a heaping plate of meat and potatoes and their horse groomed and fed for just a quarter. You can't beat that with a stick! Nowadays that would cost at least five fifty. We'll have to take a trip to Drake Well and check out the pictures in the museum, some of your relatives are in them."

"Groovy!"

We walked further down the dark staircase.

Logan got afraid. "I'm sorry I spit on Andrew!"

"I'm sorry he spit on me too!"

They tried to go back up the stairs, but Bobchia blocked his way. "Get back down there! I want to show you *the water!*"

Logan's eyes shone white in the darkness. "We can't swim in deep water very good!"

Bobchia held the flashlight under her chin. *"I know!"* Then she laughed an evil laugh.

"I'll be good!" Logan said.

"Me too!" said Andrew.

"Promise?"

"I promise!" They said in unison as we reached the bottom of the spooky stairs.

"I'll hold you to that."

Natural light shone in from the barred windows. "**1849 RED BARN INN**" was carved deep into the stone archway.

Minnie whined, so Bobchia put her down and she took off running.

"Minnie!" I yelled nervously.

"She's okay, Sweetie. She likes to run through the tunnels."

We passed a huge, round room containing several old barrels, milk cans, and church pews with metal junk on top of them. We heard a 'meow' and then a 'hiss.'

Bobchia crooned, "Tommy. Here, pretty kitty!" Tommy came running with Minnie on his heels. Bobchia scooped him up and kissed his back.

We took turns holding the big tabby as Bobchia went to a table and opened a can of cat food, dumping it onto a paper plate and set it on a bench. Tommy jumped from Logan's arms to eat. Bobchia scratched him behind the ears as Minnie tormented his tail, so back in to her apron she went. "Did you kill any critters, Tunnel Tommy, or did you just *scare* them away like I told you to?" Bobchia shook her head. "I'd feed you regardless, big guy."

Logan picked up a dead mouse by the tail. "I like dead stuff! Look at this cool dead mouse!" As he swung the mouse past Andrew's nose, he yelled a blood-curdling scream that echoed through the tunnels.

"Mercy, stop that Logan!" She said, looking through her brows at him.

"Sorry!" Logan held the mouse in front of Tommy, who batted at it a few times and then kept eating. He held the mouse close to his own face, studying every detail. "They're cute even when they're dead!"

After Tommy was done eating, Bobchia put him over her shoulder, hugging him.

"Meow." Minnie tried to bite his tail when it swung past her face.

We walked over to a slatted door on tiny wheels. Bobchia slid it to one side, revealing a small room that felt even cooler. "This is my root cellar, where I keep my potatoes and apples for winter. Cliff needs to get another couple hundred pounds of potatoes down here and we'll be set.

"Yea, winter!" The boys cheered.

"Can you remember snow, Sweetie?"

I thought. "Not really."

"You're all in for a treat. It is so beautiful here in the winter. If we get snowed in, we'll just eat and get a big quilt and *snuggle down.* Sometimes the schools close because of the snow."

That caught Andrew's attention. "Honest, Bobchia, honest?"

"Only because of *snow?* No kidding, Bobchia?" Logan looked up at her in excitement. "Oh, boy! Maybe it will snow so hard we won't have school all winter!"

Tommy heard a noise in one of the tunnels and fussed to get down, so we all petted him goodbye. He ran off, quickly disappearing as Andrew looked concerned.

Bobchia slid the door closed. "You'll see him again, honey boy. Don't worry; he'll be back."

Bobchia picked up the paper plate and food can and threw them in an old barrel. "Over here is the spring room." We walked into a long, narrow room with a water ditch.

"Bobchia, you got water in your basement!" I said in jest.

She giggled. "Edjew built the Inn over it. The stream that flows beside the Inn branches into the brook in front of the Inn and then flows into this stone ditch." The ditch was about three feet wide and a foot deep. It ran the entire length of the room and then out a pipe in the stone wall at the other end.

"What's on the other side?" I asked.

"The pipe under the kitchen window, where the water falls into the creek. You've seen it."

I nodded. "Oh, yeah."

"This used to be where your, great, great grandmother Mineya used to wash her clothes."

"What's Mineya's American name?" I asked.

"Mary Ann. You know, back in the day, a spring room was considered quite a modern convenience, kind of like our refrigerators. See those old metal jugs over there on the shelf? Mineya would put meat or milk in them and then put them in the water to keep them cold."

"Was her refrigerator broke?" Andrew asked.

"Mineya lived before refrigerators were invented." She squinted watching Logan twirl the mouse. "Let's say goodbye to the mouse."

"Goodbye mouse!"

"Goodbye mouse!"

Logan dropped the mouse into the water. The boys walked beside it as it floated, finally disappearing through the pipe in the wall.

"This is so cool!" Andrew exclaimed.

"Yeah, let's float some more dead stuff!" Logan looked around.

"Well, I don't think there is any more dead critters. Tommy puts all his *trophies* by the table where he eats so I will reward him. It's his way of thanking me for feeding him." Bobchia changed the subject. "Your Father and his friends played down here for hours when he was your age. He used to get nice cold drinks from there." She pointed and then walked over to a little cement well, where the underground spring came from the hillside. There, she pushed a cement slab covering the well to one side and pulled up a wire attached to a dented tin cup and took a long drink, smacking her lips. "Nothing like cold spring water on a hot day to cool a body down. Want some?"

"Yeah!"

"Yeah!"

The boys walked over and looked into the well.

Andrew shrieked. "There's a baby *alligator* down there!"

Bobchia laughed. "It's just a salamander. It keeps the water clean."

Logan pinched his nose in disgust. "Yuckie!"

"Try it, come on!"

The boys shook their heads.

Bobchia shrugged. "Here, have some, Jen."

"Thanks anyway."

"Where're the *toys* Father played with?" Logan asked.

"Toys? Well, they're right over here." She reached into the ditch and moved some rocks around.

"Nothing there."

I looked into the water. "What are you looking for?"

She flipped over another rock. "There, *see it?*"

"*A baby lobster!*" Andrew screeched.

"Actually it's a crayfish."

"Will they bite?" Logan asked as he put his hand in the water.

"Well, not exactly."

He pulled his hand out.

"You have to grab them by the back of their heads or they *will* pinch you." She leaned way over to catch one and Minnie fell in! We laughed and laughed as Bobchia hauled her out onto the cobblestone floor where she shook.

"She needed cooled off anyway!" She laughed as she stuck Minnie back into her apron, bracing it underneath with one hand as she flipped over more rocks with the other. "Take your shoes off and make a dam. Be careful, the stones are slippery."

Logan stuck a finger back into the water. "Will those things bite us?"

"They will *run* from you."

We quickly took off our shoes and waded in.

"It's wonderful." I said, splashing water on my arms.

"It's cold!" Logan said, moving his foot close to a crayfish to scare it over to Andrew but it swam backward instead, over Logan's other foot! He screamed, scaring Minnie so badly that Bobchia had to hurry and catch her before she hit the water again.

"Mercy, Logan! You'll wake the dead!"

His eyes got big.

"Erase, erase, kidding!"

Andrew picked up a stone and threw it at a crayfish.

Bobchia windshield wipered her finger at him. "Live and let live. If you kill them, you won't have anything to play with."

"Don't kill 'em!" Logan warned. "We'll have to go back upstairs!"

Bobchia handed Minnie to me, took off her shoes and waded in. "Paul used to race crayfish with his buddies. They'd be down here for hours on hot days like this. He would make a dam up here and down there."

Andrew put his hands on his hips. "Bobchia, you said a *bad word.*"

"I did?" Bobchia winked at me.

"*Twice!*"

"I'm sorry, Andrew."

Andrew cocked his head. "Yes, well next time *you'll have to talk with the Man Upstairs!*"

Bobchia giggled as she moved rocks to dam-up about ten feet of the ditch. "Paul would catch crayfish with his hands, but I think cans would be easier. Boys, go get me a couple of cat food cans out of the barrel." They eagerly got them and handed them to her. She put a can in the water, putting the lid in front of a crayfish. When it swam backward, she had it trapped.

"Yea! You got it!" Logan cheered. Andrew clapped.

The boys hunkered down and carefully watched as she poured the crayfish onto the cobblestones.

"This is the *mostest* fun!" Andrew laughed.

"It is!" Logan agreed.

The crayfish looked fierce holding up its claws high and open.

Andrew said excitedly. "It almost looks like the hermit crabs in Florida. We brought some to show you, Bobchia, but they must have crawled out of the car when it stunk so bad."

"Look at those claws!"

"I bet those claws could cut a fish's head off!"

Bobchia caught another and poured it next to the other one, then reached into her apron pocket and pulled out the bottles of finger nail polish. She dabbed red on the claws of one crayfish and orange on the other. Bobchia told the boys, "Now we need to wait a few minutes for them to dry. If you want to pile up some more rocks, go ahead. Jen and I will guard these critters for you."

Minnie whined so I put her down. She growled at the crayfish as they held their colored claws high in the air. She braced herself, straining to smell them and then backed up barking, sending echoes throughout the tunnels.

"Mercy, Minnie!"

"Are they dry yet?" Logan asked.

Bobchia scooped the red one into a can and handed it to Andrew. "Hold the lid over it." Then she scooped the orange one for Logan. "How do they swim, Logan?"

"Backwards." He said without hesitation.

She smiled and kissed the top of his head. "You'll never forget that, will you?"

"Nope." He said trying to wipe his head off.

She guided the boys to the front of the ditch. "Get set to drop them in. Ready? *Go!*" What a sight! The boys dropped the crayfish in then cheered and screamed at them and then at each other and then back at the crayfish! Bobchia took a picture.

Andrew's crayfish was the first to go over the other end of the dam. He hurried to scoop it back over to the other side. "I won! Yippie!"

"You cheated!" Logan countered.

"Did not!"

"Did too!"

"Did not!"

"Did too!"

"Did not! Ask Bobchia."

Bobchia shook her head. "You sound like Paul and his buddies, so I'm going to tell *you* the same thing I told *them*. I don't care who is right or wrong, but if you fight, that's the end of the races for both of you, *understand?*"

"We won't fight, will we Andrew?" Logan put his arm around Andrew.

Andrew shook his head. *"Never!"*

"You'll have a lot of fun down here. As long as you follow my rules, you are welcome to play here instead of upstairs in the heat."

Logan rolled his eyes. *"More rules?* Why is there always rules?"

She continued, unfazed. "Rule number one: you stay *only* in this room. As far as I know, the tunnels down here that were a part of the Underground Railroad are dead ends, but I don't want you wandering around and getting hurt."

"Trains ran down *here?"* Andrew asked.

"Not trains. Edjew made the tunnels to hide *slaves* after they made the long trip up north, following the Monongahela River. Funny, when God made that river flow backward from south to north, only *He* knew it was for such a purpose!"

"From south to north?" I questioned. "I never heard of a river going from south to north. *Are you teasing?"*

"It's as true as I'm standing here, Sweetie. If the slaves followed that river north as far as Pittsburgh, there they'd meet up with a network of free slaves and abolitionists called 'conductors.' They were God fearing people who accompanied the runaways further north through wooded country along the Allegheny River and streams to 'station houses.' I'm proud to inform you that this Inn was one of those 'station houses'!"

"A what?" Andrew asked.

"A *safe house* for runaways. It was the only one in this area."

"For real?" I asked.

*"For real!* They were few and far between. There were others in Franklin and Meadville. The 'station house' in Sugar Grove was the ancestral home of my dear departed Luella. If only these walls could talk, they'd tell you the stories of the brave runaways. Some arrived still wearing shackles! That barrel over there is full of them."

"Wow! You sound just like TV!" Andrew smiled.

"Well, I've heard David proudly talk of his grandparents to people over the years, inquiring about the history of the Inn. Did you kids notice the green light in the cupola the night you arrived?"

"Yeah, I thought you had Christmas lights up there," Logan said.

"I lit the green lantern to welcome you! David always lit it on holidays and on special occasions in remembrance of Edjew and Mineya. You kids coming here was my most special occasion but whenever Edjew lit the lantern it was to *signal* the runaways that it was safe to run from under the covered bridge and woods, down the lane and into the tunnels to hide, concealed beneath the cobblestones."

"Were they running from a *bully?*" Logan asked.

"The worst kind. As soon as Edjew saw Mineya drag brush in front of the tunnel entrances, he'd blow out the lantern and rush down to the tavern, it was beside the game room, to wait for the 'slave catchers' to come in."

"Who?" Logan asked.

"The *bullies!* They were relentless at rounding up slaves and taking them back to their owners for bounty money or they would just sell them. They'd chase them like animals on horseback following their barking dogs. They often tracked them here, but Edjew knew how to throw them off the track. 'What do you mean I'm hiding slaves?' he'd say, insulted. 'Why, I'd turn them in myself for the reward, if I knew *where they were!* It's a free drink you'll get from me for hunting the runaways!' Then he'd slip a pinch of sleeping powder into their drinks, giving Mineya the time she needed to move the slaves from the tunnels to the creek taking them to the next 'station house.'"

"He *lied?*" Andrew raised an eyebrow.

"Well he was trying to—"

"Do you really got a *bar* here?" Logan chimed in. "We ain't allowed to go to a bar!"

Bobchia sighed. "Is that all you got from my history lesson? No, there is not a bar here any longer! Mineya made him close it shortly after the *Emancipation Proclamation.*" The boys looked puzzled.

"That means after the government freed the slaves," I said.

"That's right, Sweetie."

"Wow! Mineya must have been as brave as Edjew!" I said decisively.

"She was small in stature but mighty feisty. And a member of the Ladies Fugitive Aid Society. They sewed clothes for the slaves and made quilts, hanging them over their porch railings but they weren't just for looks... Mind Ya." She snorted. "The quilts gave runaways *secret information.*"

"Wow! Quilts like the ones on my bed?" I questioned.

"No, these quilts were used as *codes* to the runaways. In the back of Mineya's Bible, which I have in my trunk upstairs, there are quilt patterns sketched in the back of it along with slave names."

"I can't wait to see it!" I said.

"Bibles passed in churches from one 'helper' to another was a way to communicate the names of the slaves that had passed through the Underground Railroad in an effort to reunite families at the various 'station houses.' The patterns on the quilts didn't mean a thing to the 'slave catchers', but for the runaways, they meant *freedom.*"

"I don't get it." Logan squinted.

"Well, most of the runaways couldn't read, so, for instance…" Bobchia stopped to think. "The North Star pattern with the flying geese was a 'code' that signaled them to follow the stars and the flight of the geese to find their way north. Another was The Bear Paw pattern. Those quilts were hung over the railings in the spring of the year, when bears emerged from their dens looking for food. That quilt told them if they followed the bears' footprints, they would eventually find food."

Andrew's eyes laughed. "And the bear!"

We laughed. "Mercy, I hope not! The Drunkard's Path pattern was a zigzag pattern, which meant go north in a crooked direction to throw the 'slave catchers' off your trail but the one they longed to see was The Log Cabin pattern with the *black square* in the middle, meaning they had arrived at a 'station house' where they would be safe. I can't think of any more patterns, but you get the idea. The clues were as plain as the nose on the 'slave catchers' face, but luckily, they never caught on!"

"Wow!"

"Wow!"

"Did Edjew and Mineya ever get caught?" I asked.

"No TYG! If they had been caught, we wouldn't be standing in this Inn today!

"They put the Inn and all they had at risk, believing firmly in Romans 12: 9-13:

> **'Let love be without hypocrisy. Abhor what is evil.
> Cling to what is good. Be kindly affectionate to one
> another in brotherly love, in honor giving preference
> to one another; not lagging in diligence, fervent in**

spirit, serving the Lord; rejoicing in hope, patient in tribulation, continuing steadfastly in prayer; distributing to the needs of the saints, given to hospitality.'"

The boys looked confused. "What does that mean?" Logan asked.

"Mercy, child. In short it means **The Golden Rule—Do unto others as you would have them do unto you!**"

"You sure know a lot of stuff!" Andrew said.

"Well, when I'm not reading the Bible, I can almost hear David's voice as I read the family's journals. You children should read them too. After all, how are you going to know where you are going when you don't know how you got where you are at?"

The boys looked more confused.

"We got here in the *station wagon!*" Andrew said proudly.

Logan looked around and asked, "Were they scared to keep people way down here?"

"I'm sure that Mineya and Edjew were on their knees more than once, especially after hearing of 'station houses' that mysteriously caught fire or whenever a 'helpers' livestock lay poisoned in the fields. Mercy, when I think of Mineya hiding slaves here and hauling food down those long stairs day after day, I wonder if I would have the courage to do it."

"Where did the slaves go from here?" I questioned.

"According to the journals, after they got a warm meal, coins and bread in their bandanas and after a quick prayer they'd head northwest to Erie with a map of landmarks drawn on a handkerchief or a newspaper." Bobchia stepped closer and acted out her story. "Can't you just see them pushing their way through the brush, peeking out at porch railings along the way, hoping to see a *Log Cabin quilt?* Otherwise, even without breaking to sleep, it would take days to walk fifty miles with children in tow, traveling through the woods in the rain and snow, avoiding the 'slave catchers.' When they finally reached Erie, they hid in the weeds along the lakeshore and waited for darkness, praying for a moonless night. At nightfall, in the distance, they heard the hounds of the 'slave catchers' closing in. The men ran to uncover the rowboats others had hid under the brush and driftwood along the peninsula. They dragged them to the water's edge and held them steady for the women and whimpering children to begin the long, cold trip across Lake Erie. They jumped in, rowing against the hard waves, looking skyward at the moon, peeking around the clouds revealing their location on the water to the 'slave catchers.' The mothers clutched their children praying aloud as the hounds got closer and closer jumping into the surf, swimming toward the crying children but with an *angel's hand,* disguised as a wave, the dogs tumbled back to shore. The enraged 'slave catchers' caught up to the hounds on their swift horses and fired their rifles into the air. Boom, boom, boom!"

We all jumped.

"You scared me!" Andrew whimpered.

"Me too!"

"Think of how scared the runaways must have been as they looked back at them on their horses pawing at the sand as the waves rocked their boats toward the shore. *'God help us!'* the men moaned as they strained with every stroke of the oar."

"Did they make it?" Logan watched Bobchia, motionless.

"They disappeared into the shroud of fog on the lake."

"What does that mean?" Andrew asked anxiously.

"They were safe in the small boats."

"*Hurray!*" They boys cheered.

Bobchia continued, "But they still had a long, twenty-mile trip to Canada ahead. They were exhausted and hungry, but they had been exhausted and hungry before, coming north from Georgia. I bet you can't guess what they did in the middle of that lake?"

Logan was ready. "*Fished!*"

I laughed.

"Mercy, Logan, they *sang to Jesus!* And as they sang…their faith grew and gave them strength as they followed the stars to Canada. It's always darkest before the dawn and as they stared into the fog singing praises to the Lord, they saw tiny green dots lining the shore of Long Point Ontario. They rowed closer and saw green lanterns swaying in the darkness. As they rowed closer still, they saw the lanterns swaying from hands of other free slaves, cheering!"

"I like that story!" Andrew said decidedly.

"It's not just a *story,* honey boy."

I was wondering on an earlier part of the story. "What if the 'slave catchers' didn't believe Edjew. What if they knew the runaways were down here in the basement?" I questioned.

"Then Edjew would shake a rope that he had hidden under the counter. It hung down from that hole in the corner over there. See it? The rope has long since turned to dust, but it used to have a big, old cowbell hanging from the end of it and when Mineya heard the cowbell ring, she'd rush the slaves out of the tunnels and head them toward Erie. It was *dangerous,* no two ways about it, but being from Croatia, they knew what persecution was, and that's what made them eager to help any slave traveling the Underground Railroad."

"What's a slave?"

"Yeah?"

Bobchia smiled at their innocence. "Let's see. A slave is a person that was made to work very hard but never got *paid.*"

"That's mean!"

"Yes, but enough history. I could go on all day, but I've got a million things to do. So let's see…Rule number one stay only in this room. Rule number two is that you have to have your homework done before you can play down here. Rule number three is that you have to feed Pumpkin *without* letting her out and rule number four is that you have to empty the kitchen garbage after supper every night."

"*Empty the garbage?*" Andrew made a face.

"Yes. Before you play, you have to do some *work*—just like the rest of us living here."

"*Kids don't work!*" Logan protested.

"If you lived back in the oil days, you two would be *Oil Dippers!*"

"You got the *dip* part right!" I laughed.

Bobchia ignored me and continued. "While fathers worked the oil fields and mothers were maids or worked in kitchens, kids that were strong enough to swing a bucket were tied to long ropes attached to tree trunks along Oil Creek. Their job was to skim the oil off the top of the water and pour it into barrels so be glad you have just *little* chores to do."

"But we're just *kids!*" Logan protested louder.

"Not only did kids do that, but—"

"Are we *your* slaves?" Andrew challenged.

I covered my mouth.

"No, you're not *my* slaves!"

"Will we get *paid?*" He asked.

With her hands on her hips, she explained "Let me put it this way. I will *let* you play down here *if* you play only in this room, *if*

179

you do your homework, *if* you feed Pumpkin and *if* you empty the garbage every day. Do I make myself *clear?* Deal?"

The boys looked at each other.

Logan started, "Bobchia, how about—"

"*It's my way or stay upstairs.* It's no skin off my nose. That's it Fort Pitt."

"Deal!" They yelled in unison. They gave her high fives and made it official.

Minnie growled. "Minnie even says it's a deal, so you'll abide by *all* my rules?"

They nodded. "Good. I'm taking one of these flashlights, and I'll be back in an hour. No fighting!"

We pretended to leave, hiding around the corner to make sure the boys didn't quarrel. They returned to their racing. Andrew's crayfish reached the wall first again. "I won!" He cheered.

"You did not! I won!" Logan whined.

Andrew reminded Logan not to fight. Bobchia smiled. "That redhead is sure a corker! I'm so glad Logan got cured."

"Cured?" I questioned.

"Of spelling!"

When the boys raced again Logan won and when they didn't fight, Bobchia motioned for me to follow her. "Let's go up this way. It's been years since I've gone up the back way."

"I think you should write a book, Bobchia." I said. "You have so many great stories!"

She chuckled. "I do love to tell stories, but I can't spell much better than Logan. When I was in school, I wrote my spelling words on my arm before tests. Besides, I'm just paraphrasing David's journals. He was the writer."

I ducked cobwebs as we walked slowly up the winding staircase, stopping for history lessons along the way.

"This passage leads to a little parlor inside the game room. It was used as a 'pass-out room.' Whenever Edjew would get men that were 'slaves to the drink' he'd put them in the parlor to sleep off a 'toot.' Mineya and the housekeepers would sneak in the parlor and drag the passed out men down these stairs to the round room, where the slaves held their church. They'd prop up the sleeping drunks in the middle of the church service, and when they heard the salvation message, they'd get *saved!* After all, *today* is the day of salvation!" We laughed. "In that round church room there hung a beloved painting called 'Now Freedom' that's now hanging over the mantel in the great room. I've seen you looking at it."

"The red barn looks so new in that picture."

"It was new back then. A freed slave named Andrew Franklin Lincoln painted that picture. Did you ever hear a more patriotic name than that?"

"The picture was painted by a slave?"

"*Freed* slave—there's a big difference! He worked here. When certain patrons found out that Edjew *paid* his help, they would pack up and leave the Inn without paying their bill! It makes me proud to live here and to have relatives who stood for what was right! Not a *mealy mouth* in the lot!"

"I have a question. What do cows and the red barn have to do with freedom?"

"Well, let me get back on the Underground Railroad track and I'll tell you." She stopped and held the flashlight under her chin. I giggled. "Hidden in that picture is a scripture, a code that *men died to protect* that reinforced the freedom that they longed for in their hearts, a code that only the U.R. knew. That's what Edjew wrote on the last page of his Bible."

"Well?"

Bobchia pulled on my arm. "I've never told this to another living soul." I leaned down. With her voice barely above a whisper, she looked deep into my eyes. "Under the cover of darkness, a 'transporter' of a slave wagon risked his all, even his very own children who would have to beg in the streets—if he was caught—transporting slave children to reunite them with their parents. With grain sacks tied with twine around the hooves of the covered wagon's team of horses, he followed tattered maps in the moonlight on his journey along bumpy paths and through shallow streams. Old men held the children, whispering stories to hush them inside the wagon, as crickets and bullfrogs disguised the muffled hoof beats leading them to a 'station house.' Whenever they'd approach a clearing, they'd stop to listen for dogs. Then the 'transporter' would jump from the wagon and sneak toward to the house. *Was it a trap?* Bravely in the darkness he quoted aloud the 'code', half the verse of Deuteronomy 23:15: 'Thou shall not deliver unto his master the servant'...then he'd nervously wait for the response that meant safety for the children or capture by the 'slave catchers.' A voice from the shadows would complete the 'code', saying, 'which is escaped from his master unto thee.'

There the children would be safe for the time being! They helped the children out of the wagon and into the home where they would hopefully be reunited with family members and get a hot meal. That is how they moved people from one 'station house' to another."

"Groovy," I stood up.

"Wait, I forgot one important thing." She pulled on my arm. I knelt down. "*Boo!*"

"Oh, Bobchia! Is all this really *true,* or are you kidding?"

"I know I embellish, but the stories are a fact. Your grampie donated most of his grandfather's documents and maps to the Smithsonian. He wanted to keep them for the family but felt obligated to share the stories with the world. We went there on our one and only vacation, searching for days in the huge Preservation of the African American Families of the Civil War books, finally finding the names that coincided with the names in Edjew's logbooks. I am proud to say that we did not find a single record of anyone having been caught and returned to the cotton farms from The Red Barn Inn! TYG! The green dome helped bring many a family safely down the lane and north to Canada. But I must say we discovered something that was rather amusing."

"Really… what?"

"It was hard to distinguish slaves when some had the *same names* and some had the names of their masters, but we knew we hit *pay dirt* when we saw with our own eyes the names of children that I suppose were either born here or were later named in honor of your great, great, grandparents—some were named Edjew and some Mineya *Matkovich!* Can you imagine that? Slaves with *Croatian names!* Now that's something you won't read about in your history books at school young lady! David sure got a kick out of it!"

"So then what happened?"

"After the U.R. days, the tavern closed and became a restaurant and eventually became a bakery. Mineya hired as many free people that she could, opening the Inn to anyone who needed a place to stay. No longer holding church in the round room, the congregation grew at the little brick church. They eventually built the big Christian Branch church on the other side of the covered bridge."

"Oh yeah."

"There's an oak pew in there with the name Matkovich on the back of it. Back then people paid for their pews. Anyway, from what I read, Edjew got saved and was baptized in the creek beside the church."

"Why don't you go to church there?"

"I go where David and I went. I don't know why his family quit going there. I asked him that question several times, but he always avoided it. Anyway, I don't know about you, but I'm getting claustrophobic, and my dogs are barking. Oh but look!" She pointed the flashlight to a boarded up door. "I always wanted to take those timbers down to see what was back there, but your grampie was a stickler for preserving the Inn as he remembered it when he was a boy."

"Why don't you take them down?"

"You know, that thought never occurred to me. Without David, well, it doesn't really matter what's back there. I haven't changed the Inn that much since he passed, except for giving the great room a deserved facelift. Your great grandmother was told that George Washington slept in the Harmon house that was on the property before the Inn was built. It burned for reasons unknown. Edjew heard stories and wrote a theory or two about the fire that you might find interesting, although nothing was ever proven. Some of the white stones of the foundation of the Harmon house are in the fireplace of the great room and in the fireplace in the blue bedroom at the top of the stairs."

"George Washington! Really?"

"You know it has to be true because I charge Mr. Pill an extra five dollars every month to sleep in that blue room!" I laughed.

"Watch your step, it gets narrow right here." She pushed on a wood panel, popping open a doorway into the parlor closet. "Don't trip over the roll-a-ways. Boy, I can feel the heat already!"

We hurried out a door onto the side porch, brushing off dust and cobwebs from our clothes and hair. "Ooo, Bobchia, do I have any spiders on me?" I asked.

"Only that fuzzy black one on your back!"

"Get it off! Get it off!" I shrieked.

She laughed and brushed my back. "Erase, erase. Do you think I would actually let anything *hurt you?*" I shook my head. From there we went to the kitchen to wash our hands and have a tall glass of lemonade.

"Can we leave the boys down there forever, pleeeeeease?" I begged.

"They *are* something to behold, but I think your Mother might miss them." She giggled then hit a tiny spider on her arm.

"Live and let live, Bobchia."

"Any bugs that venture inside my inn are fair game!"

"The Inn is so interesting. I had no idea! I want to learn all about it."

"Good, I was afraid you might get bored with all the details in my head."

"I *love* all the details."

"It's in your blood, Sweetie. You know, I've only told you the tip of the iceberg."

"I'd like to do a paper on the Inn for a school project."

"Now you sound like your Father. He wrote a thesis on the Inn when he was in college. There's stuff in there that your grandfather didn't even know about. Paul interviewed all the relatives and old timers in town. It's really fun to read. It's in my desk upstairs. His notes and journals are in his trunk in the attic. He was always jotting something down. You are *so* like him."

"Thanks. I'd love to read them! May I?" She nodded. "And if it would be okay, I'd like to look through his trunk. Only if it's okay."

Bobchia shook her head and with a quiver in her voice. "Yes, it's time to share those things."

# 8
# Our Secret

"Well, how do you like it here so far?" Bobchia asked as we sipped lemonade.

"I love it, Bobchia. This is where I belong!"

"*I know.*" She nodded.

"It's way *cooler* than Florida and—"

"It will get way *cooler* in a couple of months, for sure!"

We smiled, but I could tell she had something on her mind. "You've had it pretty easy since you came back. You liked caring for Joan of Arc?"

"Oh yeah, she's doing really well. Almost healed."

"Maybe you'll be a doctor, like your Father."

"Nah, too much school."

"So, what's on your agenda for today?" She slid the tin of cookies to me.

"Oh, I don't know. I want to go over to Beverly Jean's. Her Cocker Spaniel just had pups, and I can't wait to see them!"

"*Please* do not bring any home! Promise me you won't, and I want to see your uncrossed fingers young lady!" I promised. "Good."

"If it cools down, I'll probably ride Dollee in the woods later."

"What did you do last Saturday?"

"Let me think." I said, munching. "I went over to Dawnette's and met up with Beverly Jean and Kathy and we walked around town and ended up at Donna's. She got a job at Jane and Jim's Boutique. She gets a discount and showed us her new clothes. Why?"

"Well, for someone who didn't want any friends, you sure have turned into a *social butterfly!* I could use a little help today."

"I would be glad to help, although I do help with the boys, remember?"

"I know and I'm sure Clair appreciates it since she is always studying, but Venal and Izora could use some help in this heat, changing the beds, hanging out the sheets, taking them down, that sort of thing. It's too hard for us old gals in this heat."

"You don't use the dryer?"

"Mercy girl, on a *sunny day?* Bite your tongue! Don't you like the way your sheets *smell?*"

I shook my head thinking I must have broken the eleventh commandment: 'Thou shalt *not* dry clothes in a dryer on a *sunny day!*'

"Mrs. Dunham hung the towels out this morning, but it's too hot for her to take them down. The sheets are dry and need to be folded and put in the linen closet upstairs. Do you think you could do that for old Bobchia?"

"I'd do *anything* for you, Bobchia."

"Good! That will free me up for a game of five hundred bid with Ardelle, Wanda and Spike; that is, as long as the boys stay amused with the critters in the basement. It won't take you *that* long, Sweetie. I'll take the last load off the line, so you'll still have plenty of time to meet up with your friends later, okay?"

I nodded. She jumped off her chair, started down the hall and then stopped and turned. "Oh, if you change the sheets on Homer's bed and you happen to find tools under the mattress, just put them on the counter, and I'll have Harold take them back to the carpenters. That man is one big caution!"

"He's a *thief?*"

"Well, let's just say he's a little confused. Oh, and if you see any dirty dishes while you're in his room, don't hesitate to introduce them to the kitchen sink. There are sheets in the washer. Thanks for hanging them up!" She hurried down the hall rubbing her hands together. "Ardelle, deal the cards!"

I took the dry things off the line and hung the wet ones up and then went upstairs to help Venal and Izora finish making up the beds. Just as I went to knock on Mr. Pill's door, he swung it open, startling me!

"What do *you* want?" He asked, pulling his door back and sticking his head out.

"I, well I…I came to change your bed."

"I don't need any help from *you,*" he said as he kicked his dirty sheets through the narrow doorway and fell forward. I pushed him back and he snapped the clean sheets from my arms. I leaned forward to get a peek at the fireplace, but only saw a wastebasket overflowing with candy wrappers, then his wooden door as it slammed in my face!

"I was just trying to help you!" I said, insulted. I picked up his sheets and threw them into a clothesbasket. "*You old gastric hyperacidity!*"

I heard the sisters coming up the stairs. Izora hurried to the landing and impatiently looked down at Venal who was puffing her way up. "Hurry up! We're running behind! We've got to get the upstairs done before it gets any *hotter!*"

"Oh hush, Izora!"

"Don't you *hush* me! You're the one who is always saying she needs *exercise!* We should have done the upstairs first but no, you were too busy *flirting* with Ken! You better just pray he never gets his glasses *fixed!*"

"Shut up!"

"Now we'll probably faint up here, it's so *hot!*"

"Faint before I get there, will you?" Izora paced while I searched the linen closet for the perfect sheets for Bobchia's bed, "Here are some pretty green ones." I said tugging them from the bottom of the pile.

Venal finally reached the landing and bumped Izora with her hip, sending the delicate woman into the railing. "Sorry, Sis. My hip got away from me *again!*"

"You've said that *ever since we were in the womb!*"

I giggled while admiring the pile of embroidered pillowcases. "Groovy, daisies!" Venal finally reached the top step. She pulled back on the railing and propelled herself forward toward Bobchia's room. I rushed to Bobchia's door. She bumped me with her hip! "Hey! That wasn't very nice!"

"Sorry, I thought you were *Izora!*"

"*I'll do Bobchia's room.*"

"*What?*" She yelled, adjusting her squealing hearing aid.

Izora came over and yelled in her ear, "*She'll do Bobchia's room!*"

Venal covered her ears. "Will you quit *screaming?* I can hear, you know!"

"Sorry, Jennifer. My sister doesn't have any *manners*. But she sure does have *big hips!*" Izora then bumped Venal with *her* hip. It didn't faze Venal but Izora went bouncing down the hall!

Venal laughed. "Sis, it's all in the padding! *You need padding!*" She waddled after her, laughing.

I opened the door to Bobchia's room. Sunlight from the high windows flooded the dim hallway as I stepped into the most beautiful room in the world. Enchanted, I leaned on the door, closing it. Time had no claim on this room. It was preserved exactly the way Grampie David had painted it to surprise Bobchia on their wedding night. As a child, this room with green walls, a pink ceiling and a crystal chandelier hanging from a blue plaster oval above the bed, was 'a dream come true!'

I walked past the bed and looked out the French doors to the balcony. I closed my eyes remembering the evening tea parties Bobchia, Grampie and I had had with my doll, daisy, and his growling hound as it watched the deer walk the paths of Red Barn Mountain.

Smiling, I opened my eyes and noticed an overstuffed chair in the corner between the French doors and the night stand. Snug in the nook of one arm was a rust colored teddy bear wrapped in a baby's quilt.

"How sweet." I said picking it up. It had shiny black button eyes but a closer look revealed it to be as worn as the chair.

Centered above the chair hung a framed, cross-stitched poem titled; Daddy's Chair.

My knees sunk deep into its cushion as I climbed on, straining to read the poem.

## Daddy's Chair

Daddy's chair was big,
    A cumbersome thing to behold,
But I'd never part with it—no never
    Not for silver—not for gold.

It was an odd color
    And very threadbare,
I'd often sit in front of it
    As mother braided my hair.

I'd sink down in the seat
    With feet far from the floor,
That's when love surrounded me
    When my Daddy came through the door.

On his lap—he'd tug me up
In my face—he'd smile,
Then he'd hug and kiss me
And chat with me a while.

His big hand
Would pat my little knee,
And his laugh filled the room when asked:
"Daddy, will you marry me?"

Come Saturday mornings
I'd watch cartoons from there,
Under my cuddle blankie
With Cinnamon, my teddy bear.

Over the years—it faded more
The seats grew lumpy and worn,
I was so embarrassed
When friends noticed it was torn.

I begged him to buy a new one
Pleading; "It is beyond repair!"
"Oh honey girl, it was *my* Daddy's
Its kind is *awfully* rare!"

Daddy is gone now
But the big, old thing is still here,
As are the memories with it
Of my childhood so dear.

Silver or gold can't buy
That beautiful worn out chair,
For where else would I sit and think of *my* Daddy
... except *there?*

"This must have been great grandpie's chair and you must have been Bobchia's teddy bear!" I hugged it and sat on the bed.

I admired the massive mahogany headboard that Grampie had made, with the deep carvings of the Red Barn Inn emblem. Then my eye caught the bed steps he had made me as a child, half

190

hidden under a quilt. I rushed to them, remembering how I'd burst into this room crying during a thunder storm and how he'd inevitably throw the quilt back when he saw my pigtails fly up those steps! *'We've been waiting for you! Hurry, get in the safe place!'* I'd dive in between him and Bobchia, the quilt and their love surrounding me.

I fell back onto the bed, lacing my fingers behind my head. Such contentment I never knew from those days to these, since returning to my 'heaven on earth.' I lay there studying the sparkling chandelier, remembering whenever I was sick I'd beg to go to Bobchia's bed and what she did to cheer me. I sat up and there it was, across the room in front of the window, now sharing the marble table with an overgrown Christmas cactus, the fan, pointing to the chandelier. I turned it on, and the room exploded in dancing rainbows. *I was four again.* I jumped onto the bed and pushed the feather pillows under my head. "I bet this bedroom is more beautiful than any in the White House!" I lay there on a cloud until my eyes got heavy.

I thought I heard Bobchia say, "Jennifer! You're supposed to help change the beds, not sleep in them!"

I sat up and looked around the room. I should have known I was dreaming. Bobchia *never* calls me Jennifer! I reluctantly turned off the fan and stripped the bed. Then I put on the crisp, green sheets, careful to make hospital corners like Mother had taught me. I wondered, while shoving the pillows into the daisy pillowcases, if Bobchia could teach me to embroider anything so beautiful. While centering the large quilt to hang exactly in the middle of the green dust ruffle, I stepped on something squishy. "Ouu!" Thinking I had stepped on a Minnie surprise, I quickly lifted the ruffle, only to discover a duct-taped pair of bedroom slippers. Giggling, I fluffed the little lace pillows and arranged them on the pillow shams several times until I was satisfied.

After straightening the tiny blanket on Minnie's bed, I went into the bathroom to gather the towels and read the plaques framing the mirror.

**'Commit your works to the Lord, and your thoughts will be established.'**

**'If you search for good, you will find favor. If you search for evil, it will find you.'**

*Wow, Bobchia reads these every day so they must be important,* I thought. I read them again and then checked my hair for cobwebs in the mirror.

Then the most wonderful thing happened! I saw the reflection of my doll sitting on the bookshelf across the room. The last twelve years melted away as I rushed to her. *"Daisy! Daisy!"* I ripped the plastic, duct-taped bag. "Oh Daisy! I used to *cry* myself to sleep, I missed you so much." I hugged her over and over. "I never thought I'd see you again!" I touched her blond hair and gazed into her sky blue eyes. Then I lifted up her pink dress with white daisies on it, revealing that her underwear was on backward and she only had on one white shoe. Just the way I left her that last, horrid day. I hugged her again and again and wondered, *what else did my Bobchia save for me?*

I set Daisy on the bed and took some photo albums off the bookshelf sharing them with her. "This album must be all the cards I made for Bobchia." On the backs of them she had written, "From my Sweetie Pie" and the date she had received them. They all had daisies of every shape and size on the front, some with animals and red houses. (I was probably trying to draw the red barn.) "Look Daisy, I drew a picture of *you.*" I hugged her again.

The cards had scribbling inside and then the translation, "I love you awful" in Father's handwriting. I remembered Father dialing long distance so I could wish Bobchia happy birthday every year. She would tell me how much she loved her card and, *'It will stay on my refrigerator for a whole year, until I get another one next year!'* I could always hear the tears in her voice, and eventually the conversations would end with me crying, begging Father to take me to her. He never did. I feel cheated of all the wasted years and still struggle to forgive my parents for keeping us apart.

I wiped my eyes and opened the next album. Intrigued, I studied a black-and-white wedding picture of Bobchia and Grampie David smiling in front of an old car. He towered over her, even in her high, round-toed heels. Her long, curled, light hair was parted on the side, held back with a shiny barrette, and her pleated dress had white buttons down the front and a crocheted collar. She held a bouquet of daisies (minus the one in Grampie's lapel) with white gloved hands. She was beautiful, and he was handsome with a hat cocked on top of his thick black hair. On the next page was a picture of Bobchia holding a baby girl, my Aunt Jennifer, *my namesake,* who died from polio when she was only nine. Father had told us of her sufferings and of how the family had struggled to meet the doctor bills. He was only eight years old when she had died. After her funeral, he ran to her room and had hugged her picture, promising her he'd become a doctor.

The rest of the album was full of pictures of Father growing up—feeding chickens, hugging a calf, holding up a fish he had just caught with Grampie, kneeling beside dead deer, holding up their horns with Grampie and there was an older man, probably great grandfather, John Paul. There were more pictures with hunters and hunting dogs beside dead rabbits. Whenever I came across a picture of Bobchia, she was always holding up various orphaned animals to her cheek, with more peeking out of her cobbler apron. *Funny,* I thought, *she rescues animals, and he hunts them.* There were pages of pictures of Bobchia and grandfather with people at holidays, probably boarders over the years. I went on to find wedding pictures of Mother and Father, duplicates from their wedding album and only a few more of Grampie, he had passed away when I was little. I wondered about the mysterious blank pages, faded where pictures had been taken out.

I put the album down and looked curiously at a concave leaded-glass hutch across the room that matched the dish hutches in the dining room. This one held photos in antique frames with various things in front of them. A picture of Bobchia with Grampie in a wheelchair beside her made me sad; now she was the *taller* one. A purple heart lay in front of that photo. There was another picture of Grampie holding a rope to a workhorse and of Father, dressed in a cowboy outfit, shooting a cap gun in the air. The cap gun was sitting in front of the picture along with a toy horse. I looked intently at it.

"Hey, wait a minute! That horse looks like the one Andrew *found* in the cemetery! *Just like it!* How could that be unless…unless Bobchia was *at* the cemetery? She was in Florida and didn't come *to take me home?*" I stared at the toy horse, crying. *"Why didn't she come and get me? She must have known that I needed her.* She was all I ever wanted for twelve years, and she didn't even *come to see me!"* I slumped to the floor in tears. "Maybe this isn't like the one Andrew found…" I looked at the horse again through the glass. It was identical.

I got a tissue from the bathroom, and as I walked back to the hutch, a beam of light reflected off the chandelier and onto an emerald green, double-framed picture in the hutch. In half the frame was my Aunt Jennifer wearing a green dress with embroidered daisies, and in the other half was me in the same dress. Our hair was the same color and we had the same green eyes. In fact, we looked so much alike that if it weren't for her leg brace, it would be hard to tell us apart. Our bronze baby shoes were side by side on the shelf in front of the frame. A picture of me dressed like Miss Sunbeam was next to that one with a blue hair bow lying in front of it. A large picture of a tall man and Father proudly showing off his shiny Cub Scout medal was centered on a shelf with the polished medal lying in front of it. **Me and my scout master Larry Silvis** was written across the top. Then another picture of Bobchia and Grampie David as teens, laughing and wearing green top hats. She had a pin on her pretty sweater that read, **I'm proud to be Irish!** The pin was propped up on the picture. Other pictures of Father and Aunt Jennifer with carefully arranged pieces of their childhoods were sealed behind the thick glass—Bobchia's memorial to them.

I sadly gathered the albums to return them to their shelf, and while walking past a dresser, I noticed a heart necklace hanging over the corner of the mirror. I lifted the heart that said # 1 **Grandma**, wishing I could remember giving it to her. On the dresser, sitting on a starched daisy doily, was a picture of Bobchia holding me. The daisy dress cascaded over her arm, as I held a fistful of daisies in front of our faces, inhaling the petals up my nose. Her laughing face was the face I had longed to see for these past twelve years. I closed my eyes and tried to remember that day but could not. The thing I *could* remember was her love for me and the day that I had proudly picked her the biggest bouquet of daisies, was the day I wished I could *forget*.

Tears ran down my face and as I put the albums back on the shelf, I saw a little knob on the inside corner of a shelf. I tugged on it and discovered a hidden compartment. I reached in and pulled out a long, narrow, tin box with a jammed lid. I quickly took it to the bed and opened it, finding letters from Father to Bobchia with shaky writing, tied in a green ribbon and postmarked as recent as the month he died. I could only imagine that Father had asked Bobchia to watch over us if something should happen to him. I couldn't bear the thought of reading them, so I gently set them aside with the newspaper clippings of his obituary.

Wiping my tears, I continued looking through the tin box and discovered a medallion engraved **Debate Team**. I got excited remembering the day Father had told me about winning it. I was about five years old and had run into the living room crying over my stuffed toy puppy because it had lost one of its button eyes. He picked me up and sat me on his lap. I kissed the stuffed animal broken hearted.

I picked up the medallion, closed my eyes and heard his voice. *"Don't cry, honey girl. What's wrong?"*

"Fix Sissy."

"She looks good to me. I had a dog that looked just like Sissy when I was a boy. When I was in the eleventh grade my debate team traveled on a bus to Pleasantville to debate."

"What does that mean?"

"Debate means to discuss something, talk about something. Anyway, as the bus approached a bridge, I saw a puppy dart under it and begged the driver to pull over. He told me that he was not allowed to stop the bus between schools, so on the way back when I saw the bridge up ahead, I pretended to be sick, and he pulled the bus over. I searched under the bridge and found the puppy shivering. Luckily I had a piece of jerky that Mother had stuck in my pocket for the trip home, so he came right over to me. I hid him under my coat and got back on the bus, but I was sad when I looked at him because he was blind in one eye. That's why nobody had wanted him." I started to cry. "Oh honey girl, I didn't mean to make you cry! The puppy was *happy* I found him, he really was!"

*"He was?"* I said through my sobs.

"Yes, he licked my face all over!" I held Sissy to his face.

"I told that puppy, 'Don't worry little guy, you'll have a good home in the red barn with nice warm straw and good food to eat.' Then I snuggled him in my coat, and do you know what he did?"

"What?"

"He fell right to sleep in my arms."

"Look, Sissy fell asleep too! Daddy, did you keep him forever and didn't care even when he only had just one eye?"

"I did, and I named him Pirate!"

"Did he sleep in the red barn?"

"Nope, he slept in bed with me, just like Sissy sleeps with you! He was the best hunting dog I ever had! Well now, honey girl, Daddy has to go to work, so let's take Sissy to mommy to sew her eye back on."

"Daddy, I don't want it back on, and I'm going to call her *Pirate!* Do you think Sissy will like her new name?"

He'd kissed me. "Pirate is a great name, honey girl."

I opened my eyes. "I bet Pirate was one of the hunting dogs I saw in the photos with Father. *What else is in here?*" I pulled out folded drawings and Christmas decorations that Aunt Jennifer and Father had made. There were precious Valentine's Day cards with X's and O's all over them with hearts, signed with unsteady hands. I looked at trinkets, an angel pin, school pictures, a couple of Boy Scout medals, a few silver dollars, Indian head pennies, and a baby's gold ring. At the bottom were some important looking documents with fancy writing. I got them out and was looking curiously at them when Bobchia cleared her throat. I wasn't dreaming *this time.*

"Looking for something?" She closed the door.

Embarrassed, I sat up. "I…I…"

*"Those are the reason Paul left here."*

"What?" I asked timidly.

"Those papers are the reason we fought the day he took you away." She came over and sat on the bed next to me. "Paul never mentioned these to you?"

"No. I wasn't snooping, honest!"

"Oh?"

"I was so excited when I found *Daisy,* and I looked through that picture album over there, and when I went to put it back I found this tin box."

"Was it *lost* in my room?"

"Well, no."

"Then you were snooping."

"I really didn't mean to but…*I guess I was. I'm so sorry Bobchia.*" I couldn't remember ever doing anything to displease her. I hung my head and covered my eyes. She patted my hands.

"Bobchia, I know you were in Florida after Father died."

*"How could you know that?"*

"Andrew found a toy horse beside the headstone, and it's like the one over there on the shelf. Why didn't you come *after me?*" I hugged her, crying.

*"After you?* You didn't belong to me, Sweetie."

*"I do! I do belong to you!"* I screamed.

Bobchia took my face in her hands. "Listen to me! Look at me! Do you think your Mother would have let *me* take you? You wouldn't have been happy *here,* with her in Florida! Besides, I didn't come there to *take you away.* I just wanted to see my grandchildren, but once I got down there, I knew that if I ever saw you and the boys, I wouldn't be able to *leave*. When Paul was sick, he wrote telling me that he was going to make Clair promise to bring you here if anything should happen to him. After Paul died, I waited and waited to hear from your Mother. I sent letters but she never wrote back. After six months of writing, I thought I would go *mad!* I quit writing, still hoping your mother would write to me, but she never did. Was I ever going to *see you again?* Was I ever going to meet my grandsons? About a year after Paul's death, I went to the cemetery. It was terrible. I cried and prayed. Oh, how I wanted to see you! You have to know how *desperately* I wanted to see you and the boys—more than anything in the world! I thought, *I'll just go to the house.* Can you imagine what that would have been like?"

"Yes! *I would have loved it!*"

"And your Mother? She would have been outraged, and you wouldn't be here right now! Don't you see? She had to come *here* of her own free will and *bring my grandchildren to me*. That's what I *prayed,* and that's what God *allowed* to happen. It's not easy to let go and let God work, but you are living proof of answered prayer."

"*I don't ever want to leave here again.*"

"*I know.*"

"I don't want Mother to leave either."

"I know that too. I don't want you to *choose* between her and me. I never wanted that. She is your Mother. I just want to be *a part* of my grandchildren's lives, that's all. The most important thing is that you are all here *now,* and I thank *God* for that every day!"

"Do you thank God for Mother's being here too?"

"I…do."

"Bobchia, do you have your fingers crossed?"

"*I do.*"

"Bobchia!"

"Erase, erase. I'm kidding. Listen, I'm glad your Mother's here, because she's family and family *is* everything! You can have everything in the world, but if you don't have family, you don't have anything. Your treasure is where your heart is, and I can never have enough days on this green earth with you! *I love you so awful!*"

"*Me too!*" We hugged for a long time.

"Now as far as these bonds are concerned, you have a right to know what separated us twelve years ago."

(I could see I had hurt her in overstepping a boundary that I never knew existed.)

"Your grandfather and his father and grandfather before him never trusted banks, so they bought these bonds." She looked concerned and held both of my hands. "They are worth a lot of money if cashed in. Paul wanted to do just that, but your grandfather wouldn't let him. He thought it would be better for Paul to make his *own* future than to be handed one. They fought over them more than once. The first time was when he dated Clair. He sure fell hard for her, wanting to turn her head with a new car. Please don't mention this, but there was another young man interested in your Mother at the time and Paul was jealous. Your grampie told him that if it was God's will, he and Clair would be together, and if not, then it wasn't meant to be. Boy, he sure didn't want to hear that! He also told him that the bonds were handed down from his grandfather to his father and were seed money only to help those in need."

"What is *seed money?*"

"*Give and it will be given unto you.* That is a *promise* we have from God. Whenever a person has a need, I sow a seed and bless them. *God blessed me to be a blessing.* Remember to *never* spend your last dollar, Sweetie. *Give it away* and you've planted yourself a seed. God will see that you get it back plus more. *You reap what you sow!* I don't mean just money but love, kindness and mercy as well. *God blesses what He possesses!* Remember, you can *never* out give God." She looked at the bonds. "These were a constant aggravation. Paul wanted to give Clair everything, and he pleaded his cause more than once, only to be rebuffed by your grandfather. When Paul decided to go into medicine, we wanted to fund his education, but by then he would have no part of it. The big blowup was the day of your grampie's funeral. I couldn't handle one more thing that day, Sweetie, and when you were pulled from my arms, I felt as though *my heart had been ripped out of my chest! My life was over.*

"After you left, I locked myself in this room and prayed that God would take me to be with my David. When He didn't, I'm ashamed to say that I screamed at Him for taking everyone from me, then I threw my Bible in the corner. I was mad at the only Person who could help me, GOD! I cried all night. The next morning the sun filled this room like it always did, but my joy for living was *gone*. I remember thinking that all the wonderful days with my family, that I had taken for granted, *were gone forever!* Someone pounded on my door, wanting me to fix their breakfast. I got dressed and went downstairs, expecting to see you running down the hall, but you were *gone*. It was the strangest feeling to not have any family here. I didn't know what to do next. *What was my purpose?* What was I to do without my family? The only place I could think to go was the cemetery. I knew David wasn't *really* there, but I didn't know where else to go. I was alone for the first time in my entire life! *How could God let this happen to me?* I wondered. I always tried to do the right thing and treat people the way I wanted to be treated.

"I went to the cemetery and I stared at the graves, remembering our lives together, but no tears would come. I was separated from my family, *but God had not separated Himself from me!* Suddenly my life started playing over in my mind. I remembered the day when I had met David, our courting days, raising Jennifer, Paul and you, and by doing that, the *strangest* thing happened. I don't know how, but way down deep in my heart, I became *grateful to God* for letting me be a part of those lives. What an empty life I would have had if God had never let me meet David. *The more desperate I became, the more real He became,* He had given me a *blessed life!* I was overwhelmed, not with grief but with *gratefulness.* Right then and there in that cemetery, I praised the Lord, begged Him for mercy and asked Him for *forgiveness!*

"I had been there contemplating for hours when I faintly heard a woman weeping. I tried not to hear her or *care*. I had troubles of my own. I asked God to make her stop, but she kept weeping. I looked around but didn't see anyone. I got up and walked toward the sound. At the bottom of a knoll was a distraught woman, kneeling in front of four graves. I paused and prayed for her, but as I turned to leave, her sobs became uncontrollable. I couldn't bear it; *she was weeping for me!* I went to her side, and we wept together. Her daughter, her only child, son-in-law and grandchildren had been killed in a plane crash. All she had was *in the ground*. We talked until dark. I persuaded her to come back to the Inn with me. She stayed a few days, until she got the courage to go back to her *empty life* in New York City. She would never see her family again, but you and Paul were *alive* and that gave me *hope that I would see you again!* Weeping may endure for a night, but joy cometh in the morning! God knew that someone else's grief would make *me* appreciate my life. By sowing a *seed* in her life, God gave me the strength to want to *live mine!* She might have been an 'angel unawares', for all I know.

"That night after I got her settled in her room, I went back to my room and picked up my precious Bible off the floor. It was open to John 14, where Jesus said. **'Let not your heart be troubled, ye believe in God, believe also in me. In my Father's house are many mansions, if it were not so, I would have told you. I go to prepare a place for you. And if I go and prepare a place for you, I will come again and receive you to Myself; that where I am, there you may be also.'** That was all the comfort I needed! David and your Aunt Jennifer were together again, rejoicing in a mansion and *waiting for me!* I missed them, but it was just the *shadow* of death that separated us. They're waiting for me on the other side, in heaven! TYG! I will see them again, and then we'll be together for all eternity!

"This old Croatian woman was a lot stronger than I ever gave her credit for. That's when you really find out what you're made of—when you've lost everything and your back is against the wall! I had a spark of hope, a *mustard seed of faith* and as long as I had that, I knew that one day I *would* see you again! I learned a very important thing that day."

"What?"

"It's easy believing in God when everything is going your way, but saying what you believe and *living* what you believe are two very different things. Is there anything too hard for God? In one day, don't ask me how, He emptied my heart of grief and filled it to the brim with gratitude and *His perfect love!*"

"That's beautiful, Bobchia."

*"That's my King Jesus!"*

She looked at the tin box. "If you'd pull out that envelope, you'll see what is left of the daisies that you picked me. They're mostly powder now." She wiped a tear.

"Oh, Bobchia I love you awful!" I hugged her.

"I love you awful back!"

I opened the envelope. She sneezed.

"GBY."

She pulled her hankie from her sleeve and wiped her nose.

"GBY back! I'd like to think that you'll be as cautious with these bonds as your grandfather and I have been all these years. If you are, you'll be able to bless a lot of people and then pass them down to your heir, the one *who loves the Inn* as much as *we* do." I looked at her in surprise. "Well, mercy, you have to know that I have willed the Inn to *you*, don't you?"

"*You have?*"

"Well, who else would love this big, old, drafty place as much as I do?"

"*Me! I will! I do!*"

"*I know!* We'll just keep this under our hat for now, okay? It'll be our secret. I don't want your Mother going *completely* over the edge." Her eyes twinkled.

"*Our secret, Bobchia.*"

We hugged and then went through the rest of the tin box together, looking at her will and the deeds to the property beyond the covered bridge that she was leaving the boys. Then I pointed to the picture frames.

"I really liked your wedding picture."

"I was only *fifteen* and David eighteen when that was taken." I looked at her wide-eyed. "Yes, I was a young bride. Unfortunately, I also became a young widow. It's a hard picture for me to look at. He left for the army the next day, and nine months later Jennifer arrived. I don't recommend that path. Life was hard enough… then Jennifer got ill. When she was five, the doctor put a pin in her good leg to stop its growth so the leg with polio could catch up, but the doctor miscalculated and stunted the good leg. The dear girl had a terrible limp. Life was not easy, but we loved each other and were happy. Besides, I was also a young grandmother, and I certainly enjoyed that!"

We went through the rest of the picture albums. "Ah look, here's a picture of Tuffy, your grandfather's Chihuahua. He lived most of his life in my apron. Light as a feather, that one was. When he got old and lifted his leg to go sometimes he'd fall over!" She turned the page. "We could never butcher one of those pigs or cows. Paul had them all named, and they would follow him around like a pack of dogs. *Natural causes,* every one of them. It cost us a small fortune to keep them all those years ago."

"Just like now."

"*Just like now.*"

She turned another page. "Look at this picture of your grandfather in his cowboy hat. That was taken during his John Wayne phase. He'd make me go horseback riding with him at Wesley Woods, whether the dishes were done or not!" She pointed at another picture. "And mercy, look at him on the high school football team in that uniform, *the handsome thing!* He sure loved football. Even though he had to quit school in the eighth grade to work at Cyclops and the bakery, to help support the family, he begged the coach to let him play. He let him play all right—by making him *clean* the locker rooms. But he sure showed them! He turned out to be *one of the best players* that team ever had! In the yearbooks, he's just in the sports pictures in the back. I'll have to show you. I have some newspaper clippings of him in that other album over there when he played semi-pro-football for the Warren Red Jackets, until the Army called him. Look at this picture of the team. There's the gang—Matkovich, Zerbe, Deets, Rogg and Lytle—*unstoppable!*" She wiped her tears.

"I'm sorry that I got out the albums and reminded you of Grampie." I whispered.

"Oh, honey girl, everywhere I look in this Inn there's a memory of him. He was one of a kind and very comical." She smiled, remembering. "He kept a hat and coat on a nail beside the door. Whenever someone came up the steps, he'd grab them off the hook and open the door. If he *wanted* to visit he'd say, 'I just got home; come on in!' But if he *didn't* want to visit he'd say, 'Sorry, I was just leaving!' I sure miss the *old red head!*" She pulled a hankie from her sleeve and wiped her nose. "I always thought that we'd grow old together. You can make many plans but the Lord's purpose will prevail. He went way too soon. Well, TYG, I'll see him again *soon!*"

"Not too soon, okay Bobchia?"

She nodded then shared more memories of Father's childhood. We laughed and cried but it was what we both needed. Then I got up the courage to ask her to do something that had been bothering me.

"Bobchia? The pictures of me that are all over the Inn…"

"*Aren't they cute?*"

"It's…it's embarrassing."

"*Embarrassing?* How could those darling pictures be embarrassing? Why, they've been there ever since…"

"*I left.*" She nodded. "Well, I'm *back* now, Bobchia and I'm *never* going to leave again."

She shook her head. "*I know.*" She thought for a minute. "I'll sure miss seeing those pictures every day, as I walk by, but no need—I know them like I know the back of my own hand." We agreed that the pictures of me scattered throughout the Inn would be confined to the shelves and tables in her room.

She couldn't wait to show me through the old trunk at the foot of her bed for it held *her most prized possessions:* the old family Bibles, Father's Yankee baseball cap, Grampie's favorite hunting shirt, my pink baby blanket with the white fuzzy lambs on it, Aunt Jennifer's baptismal dress and the green daisy dress that we both wore. Bobchia proudly held up her wedding dress, now covering only the middle of her frame, then she hugged a stack of love letters tied in a faded green ribbon that Grampie had written her when he was in the war. All had yellowed with the passing of the years. She wiped her nose with her handkerchief before reaching into the bottom of the trunk and bringing out the pièce de résistance—Grampie's long artificial leg.

# 9
# Rule Number One

Later that night the boys raced through dinner without incident. Mother had eaten her supper upstairs in front of a medical procedure book and was on her way to the kitchen with her plate as the tenants stampeded past her to the great room to watch the local news. Mother sighed, sidestepping the crowd and put her plate in the sink. The boys ran to her.

Andrew hopped up and down. "Mother, want to know *our secret?*"

"We went to the basement!" Logan butted in.

"Shut up! *I* wanted to tell her!" Andrew shoved him.

"Can we go to the basement again? Can we?" Logan tugged on Mother's sleeve.

"The basement?" She looked at him through hazed eyes.

"Can we?" Andrew asked.

"Can we *pleassseeeee?*" Logan begged.

"Why? What's *down there?*"

"Dead rats and crabs with claws! It's so fun!" Andrew smiled.

"When were you down there?"

"Today. Bobchia took us."

Mother shook her head. "Did you say *rats?*"

Andrew looked nervous. "Can we go? Please? We'll be *careful.*"

Mother gave Bobchia a look.

"It's safe, Clair. I assure you that there aren't any rats, just a mouse or two. Paul used to play down there when he was a boy."

"Well...I don't want the boys getting hurt."

Logan shook his head. "We can't get hurt. The water isn't *that* deep."

"*Water?*" Mother raised her eyebrows. "*How deep is it?*"

"Just this deep." Andrew held his hand above the floor. "So can we? Pretty please with sugar?"

"Really, Mother, the boys are safe down there." I chimed in.

Mother dismissed my comment with the wave of a hand. "You want me to believe that *you* have your brothers' best interest at heart after what you said about them last night?"

"What did that pig say about us?" Logan demanded.

"I didn't say how much I *loved* you, that's for sure! Not after you threw those snakes on me!"

"Those were our *best snakes!*"

"Yeah, we'll probably never even see them *again* thanks to you!"

Bobchia cut in. "I assure you Clair, if it wasn't safe, I would never have taken them down there."

"*I would have,*" I said under my breath.

"Well, if they can't get hurt..." Mother trailed off. The boys jumped up and headed for the basement door.

In a low voice, Bobchia reminded them, "*Remember the rules.*"

Logan walked back. "I did my homework, honest."

Bobchia looked at Andrew. "I only had one page. We don't got much homework on the weekend." Bobchia crossed her arms.

Logan started inching away. "Andrew, I'll meet you down there!"

Bobchia called Logan back. "You *both* go or you *both* stay up here. Besides, there's something else that needs to be done before you go."

They ran to the sink and pulled the bottom cupboard door open, hitting Aunt Ardelle's leg as she poured a cup of coffee. "When I was a child, I was *not* permitted to *run* indoors!" She chastened.

"Boys, be careful!" Mother called.

"Sorry, lady!" They both said as they worked together to tug a full bag of garbage out of a small container.

Mother looked at them, "What's this?"

"We now have two *garbage men* in the family." Bobchia proudly announced.

Mother looked puzzled as they dragged the bag across the kitchen floor (dropping a few potato skins along the way) and out the back door. A few seconds later we heard a lid slam signaling, the job had been completed.

The boys hurried back in and stood in front of Bobchia.

"Now go get your homework," she said.

They raced to the desk in the great room and back.

"Ten and a half seconds," Spike hollered from the other room, after checking his stopwatch.

"Ha, ha, I beat ya!" Logan said to Andrew as he handed his homework to Bobchia. Andrew stuck his tongue out at him.

Bobchia handed the paper back. "Have your Mother check it. If it meets her approval and if you fed (she looked at Aunt Ardelle leaving the kitchen) *you know who*, then you can go."

"*We fed the cat!*" Logan yelled. Bobchia hushed him.

"Yeah, we did!"

They watched Mother intently as she looked through the jumble of papers. "I think your writing could be neater."

"Next time, I promise."

"Me too."

Mother smiled at them.

"Can we go now?" Andrew asked.

"Can we?"

Bobchia smiled. "Maybe your mother would like to see your new toys in the spring room. Show her where the key is."

Logan nodded his head vigorously. "They won't pinch you or nothing. Will you come with us, huh?"

Mother bit her lip. "I have *so* much reading to do."

"Please! It's just in the basement. It'll just take *a minute* to get there."

"*Pleeeeeeease,*" Andrew begged.

She looked into their faces. "Well, I guess I can spare a minute."

"Yahoo!" They cheered. The boys grabbed her hands and pulled her out of the kitchen.

Minnie growled. Bobchia fished into her iced tea and dropped an ice cube into her apron pocket. "Mercy, I can't tell if I'm having a *hot flash* or I'm just plain *hot!*"

(Heat wave or no heat wave, as long as Bobchia got up before the sun did, we'd have pie to eat!) She cut two big pieces of cherry pie, handed me one and sat down beside me.

"Yum, this is so good."

While Izora scrubbed the pan *in* the sink, Venal scrubbed the front of her blouse *over* the sink.

"Dear sister, why are you always trying to *feed your blouse?*" Izora smirked.

"Hush, Izora!"

The hall clock chimed six. Izora set the pan on the drain board then hollered in Venal's ear, "Venal, the news is on!" They scrambled for the doorway.

Venal's 'hip bump' sent the frail woman into the wall. "Sorry Sis, my hip got away from me *again!*"

"Quit throwing your weight around!"

Bobchia shook her head. "Mercy, those two are *worse* than the boys!"

After they left, Antenna Man stood in front of the kitchen window, gazing at the sunset. "It's so beautiful," he whispered over and over.

I cut another piece of pie. "You make the best pie, Bobchia. It is delicious!"

She smiled. "My Mother, Regeena—that's Croatian for Rhea—was the best cook and baker. Stop me if you heard the story before." I made no motion, so she continued. "She was one half Croatian, one fourth Polish and one fourth Italian. She met my Father, your great grandfather Mario Cannata, at Ellis Island when she came to America with her parents, Anna and Peter Vrabec, to escape the war and the persecution in Croatia.

"Mario only spoke Italian, and after using his last cent for passage to America, he had no money for food. Grandfather Peter spoke only a little Italian and had very little money, but he was rich with compassion and gave Mario some dried jerky. Upon learning that Father had no relatives or anywhere to stay in America, Grandpa Peter took him under his wing. They moved into Aunt Mary and Uncle Tony's little apartment above The Villa, their Italian restaurant, where Grady's is now.

"Mary was Grandfather Peter's sister and had previously worked with Tony's Aunt Marie in the silk mill in Croatia. She had desperately wanted to come to America, and when she had confided that to Marie, Marie told her that her brother, Tony, owned The Villa in America but *didn't* have a wife. Mary told Marie that she was a marvelous cook so Marie sent Tony a letter telling him of *beautiful cook,* Mary. Before long, without even knowing what she looked like, Tony sent for Mary, and married her as soon as she got off the boat. It was no Romeo and Juliet romance, but it was Mary's ticket to freedom, and freedom, as you know, is *priceless!* A lot of women were 'mail order brides' back then, well anyway, the next day Mary started to work in the kitchen. No matter how hard she tried, she couldn't *fake* making a good marinara sauce. Tony realized she *wasn't* a marvelous cook, but she *was* marvelous to look at! He taught her how to cook, and they grew to love one another. *Are you with me so far?"*

I nodded and got another slice of pie. She continued, "They worked hard, scrimping and saving every penny they could for passage for my grandparents and Regeena to come over to America. By the time they sent for them, Mary and Tony had had two children, Louisa and Anthony. They called Anthony 'Spike' because he had a cowlick like *Alfalfa.*"

"Who?"

"Alfalfa, you know, the guy with the hair that stuck up on the top of his head!"

I shook my head. "Sorry. Is Spike the same Spike that lives here?"

"One and the same. Anyway, Louisa and Spike were too young to help in the restaurant, so the very next day after Peter and Anna arrived in America, Tony fired his employees and put my grandparents, Regeena and Mario to work in the restaurant. They were 'old school,' working from sunup to sundown, six days a week, resting only on the Sabbath. Father learned English fast, while my grandparents scrimped and saved to pay Mary and Tony back for their passage with interest. Six months after their arrival to the new world, my grandparents and Mother were proud to be able to move into one of the row houses on Merrick Street of course taking Mario with them. Cyclops, a steel mill, is there now.

"Not long after they moved into their own house, Grandfather Peter caught Mario kissing Regeena in the pantry and because he had not *declared* for her hand, the family was *scandalized* and father threw him out! He went back to the only people he knew in America, Uncle Tony, and Aunt Mary. Even though they worked side-by-side every day in the restaurant, Regeena was told not to associate with Mario, and Grandfather Peter completely ignored him! Mario worked very hard to pay for his room and board, and he saved every penny for a ring to place on Regeena's finger. Finally he bought the ring, but it took him a month to get up the courage to ask Grandfather for her hand. When he did, Grandfather told him he was not allowed to be alone with Regeena until the following Saturday, for that was the day they would be *wed.* That day the restaurant was closed for an entire hour, long enough for a *proper* church ceremony. They returned to work as a married couple. *Romantic,* wasn't it?

"About a year later when Mother was pregnant with me, she had a horrible fall down the basement steps. By the time someone found her, I had come into the world! TYG I was healthy, but Mother had to have several operations—one of them being a hysterectomy. Sadly, there would be no sons to carry on the

Cannata name. While Mother recuperated, Anna was my *mainstay,* my Bobchia. Oh how I *loved* that woman! Even though our lives revolved around the restaurant, she made every day fun! When I was little and underfoot and told to leave the kitchen, Anna would wipe my tears and slide a chair over to the counter and let me pound the life out of the pizza dough while Mother sat at the sink doing dishes and Father bused tables. I can almost smell Anna's marinara sauce cooking on the wood-burning stove. I haven't tasted anything like it since!

"It was a hard life, but all gave thanks every day to God that they were in *wonderful, free America,* and they prayed for the relatives left behind in the old country. They hoped against hope that the money they sent reached their loved ones, but never hearing a word back, they feared the worst." She took a shot of coffee. "There, I've prayed all these years that I would live long enough to tell you these things and I have, TYG!"

I learned forward. "Please don't stop."

"I know more about David's family tree then my own, because my side *didn't* keep journals. The only thing I know is that my grandparents came over because *America is the greatest country in the world.* What my Mother told me, I'm telling you. In *God* we trust, not some dictator. We take living in America for granted, but believe me when I say that my parents and grandparents thanked God *every* day that they lived in America! I really think it was better they did not know why their letters were never answered. Sometimes, not knowing is a comfort in itself. We can't change the past, only the *future.* "

"I'm sorry, Bobchia."

"No need to be. I love my family tree and David's family and this Inn. It's a part of me and a part of *you.* For instance, this kitchen and dining room used to be the Polish bakery that David's parents, your great grandparents, John and Kay Matkovich, had. That is how I met your grandfather. They referred customers back and forth to each other's businesses.

"When I was a young girl, we went to block parties after church on Sunday, the *best* day of the week. The whole town, the Polish, Croatian, Italian, Irish and all ethnic groups, would come together and bring the most delicious food I have ever eaten. I wish I had some of *those* recipes! Anyway, the food that we did not sell at The Villa that week would be hauled to the tables in the park. That rascal David would tempt me by showing me a box of his Mother's pastries and saying that if I wanted one, I would have to catch him. Then he'd run to the creek with those long legs of his and hide behind the sweetheart tree, holding the box out, teasing me. Try as I might to grab it, I couldn't. Then he'd hold the box over my head, making me jump for it. Finally he'd offer me the box but made me promise to give him a kiss for every pastry I ate. Honestly, those pastries of Kay's would *melt in your mouth!* I would eat as many as I could hold, but he always said I ate a baker's dozen! That's thirteen, ya know! Mercy, *he was a good kisser!*"

"That sounds so romantic."

"I thought it was. Come to find out later, he would raid his Mother's bakery case on Saturday morning to get chocolate éclairs for me! Ah, those were the good old days," she said with a twinkle in her eye. "The people who were poor could have a good meal and forget their troubles and differences for at least one day. In the cool of the evening, it was delightful to listen to Grandfather's mandolin and to David's relatives playing their drums and trumpets. We'd polka and waltz until dusk.

"Those days were good, but they were also hard. If you were poor, as soon as you could read, write and do a little arithmetic, you had to *quit school* and find a job to help support your family. The older kids had to take care of the younger, whether you liked it or not. Back then nobody got a *free ride.* If you liked to eat, you *had* to work, and if someone got sick, you had to work twice as hard to fill in. We took pride in our work but TYG for Sundays!

"Church was not an *option* back then. I was made to memorize the Ten Commandments at four years old, which didn't hurt me one little bit! As a matter of fact, it helped me out of more than one situation. Pastor Jay always says, 'After memorizing scripture, work is the greatest deterrent of delinquency.' Of course, when I was growing up, the deterrent was *Father's belt!* I remember changing my mind about my course of action more than once as I watched him remove his belt and listened to him recite Proverbs 22:15, '**Foolishness is bound up in the heart of a child; the rod of correction will drive it far from him.**' It might have been painful, but *true* none the less, and it kept me on the straight and narrow." Bobchia paused and looked at the ceiling. "What was I talking about before I got carried off?"

"You were talking about meeting Grampie David. I don't know how you keep all these things straight in your mind."

"Well, most of the accounts were written down, and whenever the families visited, they'd have *storytelling* in the great room. Besides, all we had to talk about back then was family."

"Really?"

"It was *before* TV, Sweetie." I shook my head. (A day like that was hard to imagine.)

Bobchia thought. "Let's see, David's great, great, great....I don't really know how many greats, but anyway, *his* ancestors were boat builders in Poland. The story that was handed down to David was that in the spring of 1820, fifteen brothers and six sisters and their families sold their possessions and bought supplies and, with a boat they built with their bare hands, voyaged to the United States. The trip took longer than they'd estimated. Although some family members died on the voyage, they never lost their faith in God. They settled in Virginia late in the fall. America to them was not the friendly country they had heard it was. They were naïve outcasts who spoke little English. Because they were desperate for lodging before winter, they were cheated out of their gold in exchange for a team of horses and a small piece of land. With winter coming on fast, they cut logs and built a 'common house' and barn, where they all lived that first winter. In the spring they built log cabins within 'a stones' throw' of the barn. They trusted no one and relied only on each other and became farmers.

"One day as they were building a cabin, *a man of the cloth,* a Methodist minister by the name of Prentice Fritz, was leading his horse through their land because it had thrown a shoe. He was met with drawn guns. He quickly held up his Bible and quickly became their first friend in America. A while after that, the minister married Sedina Vancil, one of the sisters whose husband had perished on the voyage over, and helped her raise her seven children. That's how the whole family started going to the Methodist church but they barely understood what was being said until a young school teacher from Boston named Miss Pansy Mills *accidently* entered their lives."

Bobchia paused for another shot of coffee and then continued, "Pansy had just received a teaching position in the one room school house in nearby Tionesta, where the family bought seed and supplies at the mercantile. I saw a picture of her once. She was fine with thick auburn hair and deep-set, dark eyes. One day when she was walking home, your great, great, great grandfather Francisco was racing his buckboard against his brother's Edjew's buckboard, and he plowed through a puddle and splashed water on Pansy! He tried to make amends as he rode beside her, but he could hardly speak English. She ran into her house, and her father stormed out with a shotgun and threatened Francisco, kicking him off of his property, 'The next time you come here, you'll be *pushing up daisies!*' Francisco's honor was at stake, so he waited for Pansy every night after school with a big bouquet of daisies. Eventually she agreed to take a ride on the buckboard. Everything seemed to be going well until they came to the turn in the road that led to her father's shotgun. Anyway, in a nutshell, they eloped! Her family disowned her for marrying a foreigner, which broke her heart, but they had a love that surpassed family ties. She continued teaching, and they continued smooching on the buckboard ride home every night and when the farm work and the dishes were done, she taught him how to read and write by candlelight."

"Cool! Is that really the truth, Bobchia?"

"I *embellished* it a little with the daisies and the smooching, because I liked that part the best, but to my knowledge, it *is* the truth. They had one child, Edjew, named after his *racy* brother. Pansy doted on Edjew. He was smarter than a whippersnapper, reading while he plowed the fields, reading while he fed the hogs. He had a love for books and was the only one in the whole family to go to a university. Not far from the university was a restaurant, and in the restaurant was a Croatian girl named Mineya. She worked long hours while the owner made advances toward her. She braved it all in order to learn English and to learn to count money to help her family that had come over to America and opened a bakery, only to lose *dough* (Bobchia laughed) whenever the customers made their own change from the cash box. When Edjew realized Mineya's situation, he escorted her to her home and talked with her father. Her father didn't trust him at first, but when he offered to bring his textbooks to the bakery every night to teach Mineya English and to teach her family how to count money, he was a shoo-in!

"Edjew and Mineya soon fell in love and got married and moved to Titusville where he taught school. With the purchase of this land and the building of the Inn, they became well respected. After five long years of knitting baby clothes, John Paul was finally born. Mineya concentrated on raising little John and making the Inn a success. She loved baking Croatian pastries and cooking the Polish dishes that Edjew loved. She did her baking on Saturdays and Wednesdays, and through word of mouth, news of her baking talents spread. People traveled from near and far, coming down the lane on horses and buggies, to get the new kind of dessert. Mineya called them 'fried pastries'; you know them as *donuts* without the holes, of course! She sold them two for a penny, a high price to pay back in the day, but people were eager to pay for the delicious treats.

Mineya and Edjew had six more children, all girls. Their names are easy to remember because they were all named after flowers. The first was named after Edjew's Mother, Pansy, then there was Rose, Violet, Petunia, Lilly and—"

"*Daisy!*" I interjected.

"That's right! The bakery became well known, but with the children underfoot, Mineya found she couldn't handle all the work alone, so she hired free slaves. That's how they got involved with the Underground Railroad—using profits from the bakery to support slaves' passages to Canada. Edjew gave up teaching and opened a tavern in the back of the Inn as a *cover,* so he said, to watch for the 'slave catchers.' By that time, Edjew's parents were gone, and after the Emancipation Proclamation Mineya begged him to *close* the tavern and go to church with her and the children. Well, you know the rest of that story. *God does answer prayers!*

"Let's see, then little John married Kay and they had John Jr. who married Ardelle. John Jr. and Ardelle moved to Erie and had several children. Mercy, I can't keep up with the Erie family, but if you're so inclined, you can ask Ardelle about them.

"I hope I didn't *lie* to you about anything. It's hard to keep all this straight, but you can check the records upstairs. Kay and John then had David Paul late in life and then *we* married and had Paul David and Jennifer and so on." She poured another cup of coffee. "That is your father's heritage and yours. Be proud, not ashamed of your Croatian and Polish background! Mercy, I need a glass of water!"

"Father told me, well, *some of it,* and I'm *not* ashamed!"

"Good, I'm happy to hear that."

Mother came up from the basement. "Paul did tell me of the fun he had growing up here."

"But he was ashamed to be associated with this place and as an adult changed his name from Matkovich to *Matko!*" Bobchia countered.

"I didn't have anything to do with *that!*"

"Are you sure?"

Mother looked hurt at Bobchia. I slammed my fork down. "*Quit fighting!*"

Bobchia looked at me and then to Mother. She lifted her hand to erase but got a pain. "Erase, *ouch*. Sorry, Clair. I should not have said that. The children remind me *so much of Paul*. I never thought it would be this *hard*, but I see him in their faces and I miss Paul so much!"

Mother nodded slowly. "*I know. I miss him too.*" She looked at Bobchia as if waiting for her to make the first move, but when she didn't Mother said, "I don't want us to be a *burden*. As soon as I have the funds, we'll find a place."

I quickly looked at Bobchia. "Nonsense, you are family, and *this* is your place, such as it is, for as long as you want it to be."

"I appreciate it, Rhea. *I really do.*"

"I know it's not what *you're used to*, but it's good cooking, clean sheets and lots of company, and you must admit, *never a dull moment.*"

Mother smiled. "*It's all of that.*"

Mother heard Antenna Man counting at the window, and looked perplexed, walking over to him she looked over his shoulder. "What are you looking at?" I asked.

"Apples falling into the creek, and I think…potatoes? Eighty-four, eighty-five, eighty-six…" Antenna Man continued.

"*Oh no!*" Bobchia yelled, jumping up and gripping the bottom of her apron. Minnie looked like a baby kangaroo in a pouch as Bobchia sprinted toward the basement door. Mother looked puzzled. I shrugged and looked out the window.

Then Mother took off for the basement, but only got halfway down, meeting Bobchia escorting the boys up. She had each of them by an arm and was directing them onto the window seat.

"We did not break *any* rules! I keep telling ya!" Andrew defended, and Logan nodded.

She looked at them through her brows and windshield-wipered her finger in their faces. "Rule number one: *Only* play in the spring room. Remember?"

"We did! We played *only* in the spring room!" Logan insisted.

"What about my pie apples and potatoes? You had to have played in the root cellar, after I specifically told you *not to!*" She looked so fiercely through her brows that I thought she was going to break a blood vessel!

Logan pleaded, "We didn't *play* there, Bobchia. Honest!"

Andrew added, "We just *stood* in the apple room. We didn't play at all, just *stood* there and just *rolled* apples to the spring room, and then they *fell* into the water. It was the *mostest fun!* We done a million of 'em!" He said proudly. Andrew looked puzzled at Bobchia's stern face, not realizing the severity of his crime. "Did you know apples float really good in water, Bobchia?"

"*Float! Float!*" Bobchia got into their faces. "I hope you two don't have any *plans* for Saturday morning!"

"Just cartoons." Logan shrugged.

"Cartoons! Did you say *cartoons?!*" Bobchia's face reddened. Logan nodded hesitantly. "Well, I have news for you boys. There will be no cartoons for you on Saturday morning or maybe for *the rest of your life!* We're going to pick apples on Saturday, so be prepared to get up at seven. No, make that six-thirty! Or maybe I'll get you up at *six!*"

Mother slid her body between Bobchia and her cowering sons. Bobchia stood up, composed herself and walked over to Antenna Man, who was still counting, "One hundred and twenty-six, one hundred and twenty-six, one hundred and twenty-six..."

"Your needle is stuck!" She said, pulling the Q-tip from his ear *then stuck it back in.*

Early Saturday morning Bobchia came to my bedside and shook my arm. I pulled the covers over my head. She put Minnie under my blankets. "Okay! Okay, I'll get up!"

I handed Minnie to her, and she set her down in the closet to wake the boys. Minnie jumped on the mattresses, franticly licking the boy's faces. They got up without complaint, because they knew if they complained, they would never see their pet crayfish, *Scooter* or *Crabby*, again. They lollygagged a little while eating their breakfast, but Bobchia pointed them to the van and we were out the door and on our way by six-thirty. It was about a half hour drive to Wayne's farm, just long enough for a catnap that was interrupted by Bobchia opening the car doors. "Come on, the early bird catches the worm!"

Andrew rubbed his eyes. "Catch worms? I thought we were going to *pick apples!*"

Fog hung thick around us. We crawled out of the car. The boys blew at the fog, laughing as it parted ahead of them. We walked across the fallen leaves and dew-covered grass, as the boys pulled a wagon full of boxes behind us. The sun crept over the hillside, awakening the earth with golden light.

"Mercy, you sound like a *herd of elephants!* We might see some critters if you kids would be quiet." She walked ahead and motioned for us to stop as she peeked over a ridge and down into the apple orchard. She put a finger to her mouth then beckoned us to her side to see a doe standing on her hind legs, reaching for apples from the higher branches while twin fawns ate apples on the ground. She pointed to the end of the field where a large buck stood camouflaged among the brush, watching our every move. "He's a *ten pointer* for sure," she whispered. The buck snorted and jumped out of sight. The doe cocked her ears, sensed danger and took off in a dead run. We watched the three white tails disappear into the thicket behind the buck.

"Wow, did you see the size of that deer?" Andrew pointed to where the buck had been. "It was bigger than the deer at Deer Park!"

"As the deer pants for the water brooks, so pants my soul for You, O God," Bobchia said softly.

"I want them to come back!" Logan looked down at the apple trees.

"They are magnificent, but they won't be back as long as we're here." She said.

"Then can we come back later?" Andrew asked innocently.

"Not today. I'm behind my work as it is, thanks to you know who."

"*Who?*" Andrew asked.

"You and your brother, *ding dong!*"

"Can we sit on the porch in your room again and watch them walk on that hill?" Logan chimed in.

"I think that can be arranged at dusk." Bobchia smiled.

"Do these deer know your deer?" Andrew asked.

"No."

"How do you know?"

We walked down to where the fawns had been eating.

"Look at their footprints!"

Andrew pointed. "Look, they only got two toes! That sure is funny!"

"That's the way God made them so they can squeeze their feet between fallen trees and rocks."

"Bobchia how come you know so much stuff?" Logan asked.

"It's because she's *old!*" Andrew said.

She laughed and then lifted Andrew to pick the nicer apples.

It reminded me of when Bobchia and I used to clean her clothesline. She'd throw a rag over the line and then would lift me to grab both ends. Holding on to me, she'd run the length of the line. "Do it again Bobchia! Do it again!" I'd cheer.

She would laugh and say, "You are getting too big for me to lift you!"

"I not big, *I little!* Do it again!" She would do it, until she thought her arms would break.

"Smile!" 'Pop,' went the camera. Bobchia's voice brought me back into the present. She took pictures of us picking apples, running through the fields and playing tag and of me sitting high on a tree branch. These pictures would become her new fridge favorites.

The boys did a lot of chipmunk chasing as she picked and admired the lush fruit, while I was busy sampling it.

"Just look at God's design on this apple; it's beautiful."

"It's just *a crummy old apple!*" Logan said.

"Nothing about apples is crummy! An apple a day keeps the doctor *away.*"

"Is that in the *Bible?*" Andrew asked.

"No." She laughed. "If you eat an apple, it keeps you *regular.*"

"What does *regular* mean?" Logan asked.

"You won't get constipated and won't have to go to the doctor!"

"Oh, I get constipated, but I don't go to the doctor for that. *Just shots.*" Andrew explained.

"Mercy! You boys are the reason that we're here, so get busy and start picking before the yellow jackets wake up!"

"Bees?" I said. "I hate *bees!*" Just the thought of them made me pick fast and yell at the boys to do the same.

"I want to leave some apples for the deer so they won't *starve* this winter." Andrew sat down.

"Me too!" Logan looked back at the woods.

Bobchia narrowed her eyes. "Wayne makes sure they are provided for. Besides, look at this field, they'll have plenty. Now get to picking or no Andy Griffith tonight!"

"I like that show, besides he has the same name as me!"

Once the boys got in gear, the boxes filled quickly.

"That should keep us in applesauce and pies all winter," Bobchia said as she loaded the boxes into the car.

I held my stomach as I got into the car. "Oh, my tummy."

Logan laughed. "Bobchia, at least Jen won't be *conserlated!*"

When we got to the stop sign before going down the lane to the Inn, Bobchia tapped my leg and pointed to a cardboard sign reading 'Free Rabbits.' She quickly looked in the rearview mirror at the sleeping boys in the back seat and whispered, "I told Spike not to put that sign out on *Saturdays!*"

"You're giving them away...to be *eaten?*"

"Shhhh! For pets! For pets! Mercy, child! Don't worry, I ask them more questions than an *adoption agency!*"

"I did notice the locks on their pens."

"Meme is now *celibate,* as long as Spike has the key!"

After Bobchia had parked the car, she turned and smiled at the boys. "Wake up and smell the coffee! Boy, oh boy! I can hear a cup calling my name!" I watched her proudly watch the boys carry the smaller boxes of apples to the porch. The rockers halted as we witnessed 'the admiring of the apples.' Some were touched, some were sniffed and others were shined on a shirt before they were eaten. (To this day, before I eat an apple, I first appreciate its beauty.)

We were tired after our early morning outing but after a tin of chocolate chip cookies and a tall glass of milk, we had gotten our second wind and were ready to fly into our Saturday chores. I headed for the laundry room. Mother caught the boys before they went out the screen door. She lectured them, confessing, that while we were picking apples, she had confronted Spike about paying them nickels to rake leaves. (She was convinced their bones weren't developed for such a task as she was studying children's development that week.) They looked at each other and smiled.

Logan asked, "Can we go now?"

"Yes," she conceded. "But no more raking!"

The boys ran out the door and through Spike's leaf piles, laughing at *Mother's confusion,* for Spike did not pay her fragile, cherished little boys to *rake* the leaves; Spike paid the brats to *stay out* of the leaf piles! The boys ran to the red barn to find Spike and to strike a better deal.

Later, as I was taking towels off the clothesline, Spike yelled at them, "It's not my fault I can't pay you anymore, it's your mother's! Now stay out of those piles; this is the *second* time I've raked them today!" He came over to me. "Your brothers won't *listen!*"

"Sorry." I took another towel down. "They won't *listen* to me either, just Bobchia!"

"Yeah…well…I haven't talked to you lately. How do you like writing for *The Rocket Recorder?*"

"I love it!"

"That was some basketball game the other night, wasn't it? It was my sport when I was in school. I was a pretty good player until I had to quit school and get a job."

"I hope we can stay undefeated!" I said grabbing my stomach.

"What's the matter?"

"I ate too many apples this morning."

"There is bicarbonate of soda in the kitchen."

"I'll be all right."

The conversation drifted back to the boys and then to Bobchia. He told me that after Father's death, in anticipation of our arrival, Bobchia had had the great room redone and the red barn painted. "That was a while ago, but she never doubted your return, no, *not for a single minute!* Every afternoon she'd sit on the window seat, staring at the covered bridge, sipping on coffee, waiting for you. 'Today may be my Sweetie Pie's *coming home day*,' she'd say."

"Well, I'll never leave here *again,* I can tell you that!"

"That's good. I don't think Rhea could stand losing you *twice* in one lifetime. You kids coming here has sure been a blessing!"

"Thanks, Spike, but I'm the one who is *blessed!*"

He checked his watch. "I better get started on that ice cream I promised your grandmother I'd make for supper tonight." The boys shouted and Spike looked over. "I'm going to knock those kids into next week if they don't quit playing catch around my car!" He ran toward them with his rake in the air. *"Get away from my car!"*

At supper that night, I couldn't even look at the apple pie as it was being passed, even with Spike's homemade cinnamon ice cream on top.

Bobchia noticed. "Sweetie Pie, no pie?"

"I don't think I'll eat apple pie for the *rest* of my life!"

She smiled and fixed me a bicarbonate of soda. Luckily, she didn't believe me and saved me a big piece for breakfast dessert.

The next morning it gave me great pleasure to relish eating the delicious apple pie in front of my envious brothers, refusing to trade a *single* bite for their packs of Blackjack gum (they kept hidden from Bobchia in their socks).

# 10
# A Wild Sunday

Mother started to drive the boys to Sunday school early on Sunday mornings to avoid Mr. Hair *squeezing in* beside her in the van. Today she was leaving extra early so the boys could rehearse their songs with Lois and their Sunday school class before performing them in the church service. I heard Mother arguing with them in the hallway.

"Why do we have to go so early anyway?" Logan complained.

"Lois wants your class to practice your song before you sing in front of everyone."

"Where is Jen?" Andrew asked.

"She's primping. Go get in the station wagon!"

"No fair!"

"No fair!"

They got in and kicked the back of her seat as she turned the key in the ignition but the car would not start. Spike and Harold came out of the red barn. The boys got out of the car and slammed their doors. Mother kicked a tire.

"*What's the matter?*" Spike asked.

"Oh, who knows with this old thing! Lois wanted the boys there *early* to practice their song with their class. I guess I'll borrow Rhea's car, drop them off and come back."

"*I don't want dropped off!*" Andrew whined.

"Me either, you always *stay* with us!" Logan said.

"You're not babies."

"I can take you then come back and get the others," Spike volunteered.

"That would be wonderful, if it's no trouble."

"No trouble at all. Hop in the van." He pointed the way.

"Why can't we take your *red car* you're always waxing? I like it the *mostest* of all the cars here," Andrew said.

Spike looked up. "Not a cloud in the sky. Let's just do that."

The boys cheered and watched him proudly uncover his 1959 red-and-white Chevrolet Impala. It had a shiny white top with big white fins in the back and snow white leather seats. Spike buffed a fender with his shirt sleeve.

Mother looked worried as the boys piled in the back seat. "Rule number one, no *kicking* the backs of *these* seats, and rule number two, no clowning around! We'll be there in five minutes."

"I like this red car!" Andrew said.

"Me too! It's so red and shiny!" Logan agreed.

"*It smells like roses!*" Andrew sniffed.

Spike smiled proudly, watching them in the rearview mirror as they drove down the lane.

When they drove past the Sterling's porch, the boys stared at their baseballs lined up on the windowsill. Andrew *growled* deep in his throat.

"I hope you're not catching a cold, Andrew. Spike, would you mind rolling up your window, so he doesn't catch a chill?" Mother asked.

"Not at all."

"Andrew, is your throat sore?"

"No."

"Logan how do you feel…?"

Just then Spike spit tobacco juice onto his window, *ricocheting it back onto the boys!*

"Get this brown stuff *off* of me!"

"This stuff *stinks!*"

Spike defended himself, "*You* told me to roll up my window! I *never* have my window *up!* My window is always *down!*"

"This is disgusting! Just *disgusting!* Turn this car around *this minute!*" Mother yelled. Spike quickly made a U-turn and floored it back to the Inn.

The boys ran through the kitchen door screaming, almost knocking Mr. T-t-t-tunes over as he stood at the counter drinking coffee. *Bobchia screamed!* Harold covered his mouth. I laughed.

"Shut up, Jen!" Andrew spit at me, but I quickly moved out of the way and it hit the floor! "How do *you* like it?" He yelled.

"Andrew David!" Bobchia scolded. Mother hurried in with an apologetic Spike on her heels, wiping the tobacco juice off his face with his handkerchief.

Bobchia yelled. "Spike! You told me you *quit* chewing!"

He looked at his feet. "I did…*for a while.*"

Mother ordered the boys to the tub.

"I already had a bath this morning!" Andrew protested.

"Me too!"

"Well don't be mad at me! Be mad at *Spike!*"

"Thanks a lot, Spike!" Logan's eyes narrowed.

"Yeah, *thanks a lot!* I thought you were my friend but you're my *enemy!*" Andrew yelled.

"This is the most disgusting thing that has ever happened to us!" Mother said with her nose in the air pointing the boys to the stairs. "Hurry up and get in the tub. We're going to be *late!*"

"I'm sorry, Clair, *honest I am!*" Spike said.

Bobchia looked through her brows at Spike as he grabbed a rag from underneath the sink along with the rose-scented cleaner and hurried out the door. Bobchia watched him through the window squeezing the sides of the sink. Then it got *worse;* we heard the *washer* in our bathroom fill up with water! Bobchia stared at the ceiling. Her fingertips turned as white as the sink!

Harold saw the look on her face and quickly left the room, yelling up the stairway to Mother from the hallway. "I'll take you and the boys to church when you're ready."

Mother came to the top of the steps. "*You* don't chew *tobacco* do you?"

"Very funny! I'll wait for you in the Metropolitan."

Mr. T-t-t-tunes came stomping up the stairs to Mother, snapping his fingers and singing to the tune of *I'm Gonna Wash that Man Right Outa My Hair,* "You'd better wash that juice right out of their hair, you better wash that *nicotine* off of that pair, so people won't look and stare, when they go to church to-day!" He then slid down the banister, fell to the floor, brushed himself off and went out the door.

Bobchia paced back and forth in the kitchen, her face turning more and more red every second. Surely she would make an exception on *this* Sunday! (It wasn't even a *full load!*) I hurried and cleaned Andrew's spit off of the floor, trying to make amends for the *sin* Mother was committing. I poured Bobchia a shot of coffee, but she ignored it and me and continued pacing and staring at the ceiling. Spike had changed his shirt and was waiting impatiently in the hall for Ginger to find her spectacles, nervously looking toward the kitchen.

Bobchia huffed and grabbed her purse, and we got in the car with Wanda, Izora and Venal. She was deep in thought, weighing her words no doubt, as she drove us to church. I was a *nervous wreck* as we walked into the church and sat down. I looked at the cross, praying for Bobchia to *forgive* Mother. I leaned over and whispered, "Bobchia…Bobchia…" She patted my hand.

Spike arrived with the tenants, causing quite a scene as they filled the pews behind us. Bobchia gave Spike 'the look' as Lois and her daughters came in the sanctuary wearing bright pink shirtwaists, leading her Sunday school class into the sanctuary. Her class, *minus two*, stood beside her at the piano and faced the congregation as she accompanied them in singing; **Jesus Loves Me** and **Jesus Loves the Little Children of the World**. Afterward, the children joined their parents in the pews. Then as Lois played the introduction to **Onward Christian Soldiers**, Harold and Mother, embarrassed, squeezed past us and sat down.

"I'm really sorry, Clair, *really!*" Spike frowned.

Mother nodded at Spike who was sitting on the other side of me. Bobchia leaned forward looking past me to Mother. "Where are the boys?"

"In the men's room," Mother whispered.

While everyone sang, Bobchia and Mother were preoccupied looking at the back of the church for the boys.

Several times Spike said, "*Ouch!*" Bobchia turned, giving him 'the look.' I curiously watched Lois's shoulder flinch as she concentrated harder on her music.

"*Ouch!*" Spike said again. I turned and we both looked puzzled at a rubber band in his hand, and then I saw one *hit* his head. "Ouch!" Then one flew past his head and hit Lois on the arm! She *flinched* but never missed a note of music. She pounded feverishly on the piano keys, playing faster than the congregation was singing. I looked back to Spike and then looked up. The boys were in the balcony *flicking rubber bands at him!*

I tapped Mother on the arm, discreetly pointing to the balcony. With the grace of a bull elephant, she *plowed through our legs,* stepping on Bobchia's foot. "Mercy, Clair, *my corn!*"

Mother bolted up the aisle. Venal adjusted her squealing hearing aid loudly asking, "Is she going to the *bathroom?* I have weak kidneys. I'll go with her!" People started to snicker. Venal barely squeezed past us, swaying up the aisle.

Lois *desperately* tried to finish the hymn as her hair came undone and hung in her face. Just as she hit the last note of the song, Mother cornered the boys in the balcony. With everyone staring skyward, Andrew leaned over the railing begging, "*Pray for me!*"

Everybody laughed. The title of Pastor Jay's sermon quickly changed from **Heaven or Hell, It's Your Choice**, to **Honor your Father and Mother!**

When church was over I stood by the van. Beverly Jean and Dawnette ran over to me laughing.

"I'm so *embarrassed!*" I told them as I listened to Mother scolding the boys in the van.

"Don't be," Dawnette said. "My sister, Lou, tried to *make change* out of the collection plate once!"

We laughed. Then I heard Mother say, "I have never been so humiliated in my entire life."

"You said that *last time!*" Andrew said.

Then Bobchia said, "I am just *plain mortified!*"

"Well, I better get in the van," I told my friends. "Call me later!"

That day, Bobchia *beat* Harold back to the Inn, and as soon as the boys had one foot inside the door, they were made to apologize to Spike and to talk to the Man Upstairs!

Logan crossed his arms. "Why do we have to tell Spike we're sorry? *He spit on us!*"

"*He* never said *he* was sorry for spitting on me!" Andrew stuck his bottom lip out. "And we even had to learn two whole songs we *didn't* get to sing!"

"Don't *sass* me. Just do it!" Mother demanded. Bobchia stood behind Mother, looking through her brows.

The boys slumped out to the barn to talk to Spike then spent some time chatting with the Man Upstairs. They were up there quite a while, and when they came down, Mother told them that she thought it would be a noble gesture to rake Pastor Jay's yard next Saturday, since they had disrupted his church service.

"*You said our bones were too soft to rake!*" Logan protested.

The boys pouted and hung their heads during lunch, while the tenants whispered and stared at them. They were so upset they didn't even eat their American cheese slices. Bobchia told everyone, "Eat and leave the boys alone. After all, they weren't the *only* ones to break a commandment on Sunday!" Bobchia tried to erase her words.

Mother fired back, "If I had waited to wash those clothes until tomorrow, *they would have been ruined,* and they need clothes as it is!"

Bobchia slightly shook her head agreeing with her, and I breathed a sigh of relief that we weren't moving, at least not today, which would have broken the *fourth commandment* all over again!

After lunch, Bobchia and I took a walk down the lane and laughed about how good the boys' *aim* was! Well, I walked; she limped. When we got back, she went in to soak her corn, and I went to the red barn to saddle up Dollee, that is *until* I spied the tractor key on a hook.

That got me thinking. "Dollee, how hard can driving be? It can't be *too* hard. After all, I've spent my entire life watching Mother drive! We'll go up Red Barn Mountain later, okay?" I gave her a sugar cube out of Bobchia's threadbare barn coat, and shook my head. "Not only am I asking a horse questions, *I'm answering them!*"

Dollee followed me out of the barn and watched me climb onto the tractor. I stuck the key in. "Dollee, go on, get back!" I ground the gears again and again, and then all of a sudden, *it took off!* Up and down the field I went, trying to steer clear of Dollee, the bathtub and the chickens! I went around and around in circles until I thought I was going to *puke!* Then I busted through the fence, slicing through Grampie's rhododendron bush! "Oh no!" I looked over my shoulder and watched it fall to the ground. I made a big circle, maneuvering the tractor through the same hole in the fence that I had just made and ran over the bush *again!* I franticly ground the gears and the machine stopped! Dollee cautiously came toward me. I grabbed my stomach and her bridle and ran her to her stall.

I timidly peeked out a barn window, expecting to see Mother and Bobchia race out screaming, but they hadn't seen me! I ran to the prized rhododendron bush and pushed it up. *It looked fine.* I stepped back. *It fell down.* I looked to the Inn. My stomach churned as I ran to the barn, desperately looking for something, anything to tie it up with, when I saw Spike's tackle box on a shelf. I quickly got out the fishing line and pliers and ran back to the bush. Hugging it, I shoved the fishing line through the flattened bush over and over onto the sturdy branches of the bush beside it. I snipped the line and backed away. It stayed standing! I shyly looked to the Inn. Antenna man grinned at me from a side window. I waved but no response.

I held my stomach while dragging a long board to the fence, piling it onto the post. While dragging another, I heard Spike laugh, cough and spit tobacco juice. Blood drained from my face as I turned. "I was just...just..."

"I know you were *just* covering up for Dollee Doll! She's always *hated* this fence. Did you think you could fix it with *fishing line?*" He pointed to it in my pocket, laughed, choked and spit again. "Man, you'd think she was a *Clydesdale* by the looks of that board! I better get my hammer and nails."

My head was splitting and my stomach ached; I needed to lie down. I went into the kitchen and took a couple of aspirin. Then I headed to my room, but as I passed the archway to the great room, I heard, "Sweetie! Sweetie!" Bobchia and the boys were sitting on the love seat with Aunt Ardelle's and Wanda's bird, Lucky, on Bobchia's lap. Minnie strained from the apron pocket to smell Lucky's wing.

Bobchia frowned at me. "Sweetie, what's wrong? *You look as green as this bird!*"

"My head is splitting!"

"Take some aspirin."

"I did."

Logan said," I hope you *spit up* your cookies, Jen!"

"Shame on you, Logan!" Bobchia said.

"She laughed at us when Spike *spit on us!*"

I held my head. "Well, I couldn't help it. You both looked like a couple of *Dalmatians.*"

"Carolyn assured me *that* that will never happen again! She had a long talk with Spike when they came home from church, and he promised her that he would *never ever* chew tobacco again!" I started to laugh then grabbed my head. "Why don't you lie down for a bit before supper? Come on, get that afghan over there."

"It's *my* turn to hold the bird!" Logan nudged Andrew.

"You just held it!" Andrew pushed him back.

"Can I hold it again, Bobchia?" Logan asked.

"Gently, *very gently.* Every time I babysit the old thing, I pray it won't die. I think it's as old as I am!"

"Wow, and it's still alive!"

Bobchia rolled her eyes.

"Can I have this feather?" Logan held one up.

"*I* want it!" Andrew reached for it.

"You didn't *pull it* out of its duppa, did you?"

"No, *it dropped out of its hind-end all by its self*...honest. Ask Andrew if you don't believe me!"

Andrew with wide eyes shook his head.

Bobchia took a shot of coffee. "You two share it, okay? The poor old thing can't afford to lose any more feathers. I wanted to go to church tonight. Mr. McStall is bringing his children, Makenzie Grace, Darlene, Peter and Jeff, to sing tonight. They call themselves 'Sweet Life,' and they are really good singers. If Mrs. McStall shows up, maybe I can talk her into taking him back! Your mother thinks the boys should return to the scene of the crime to apologize to Lois and Pastor Jay, but here we sit with Lucky. I told Ardelle and Wanda I would watch Lucky while they went to Rose's and Jim's, it's Rose's birthday. Ardelle always cooks a batch of chop suey for her birthday. It's absolutely delicious—even better than Chinese Chins downtown! Anyway, your Mom has a test tomorrow, so she's not going to church tonight either, but when I asked her to keep an eye on the bird, come to find out, she *hates birds!* She is not much of an animal person is she?" She took a long breath.

"She got pecked on the head by a Banty rooster when she was a little girl. That's the reason." I explained from across the room.

"Oh well, anyway, here we sit with Lucky."

"*I'll watch him* for you," I said.

"Shut up, Jen!" Andrew said. "We'll have to go to church *twice* in *one* day again!"

I retorted, "You need to *go again* after the spectacle you made of yourselves in church!"

"*So do you!*" He yelled. (I couldn't deny it—not after what I'd done to Grampie's rhododendron!)

"Are you sure you wouldn't mind?" Bobchia asked me.

"I'll be here. What could be so *hard* about watching a bird in a cage?"

"Good." Bobchia carefully put Lucky back in his cage and covered it with a knitted brown blanket with orange smiley pumpkins Ardelle had made. "Sitting over here on the bookcase, Lucky's away from the draft. Come on boys, you can set the table for me."

"I want to watch TV!" Logan said.

"No TV tonight or for the rest of the week until you learn to *respect* your elders. That is what your Mom told me, so go wash your hands and get the table set for supper. They'll be coming out of the woodwork to eat before long, and it's going to be a *potluck* dinner tonight. I've got to unload the fridge before I cook anything else. Let's see, I can heat up the bean soup we had the other night, and—"

The boys made disgusting sounds with their hands in their armpits. I laughed and grabbed my head. Bobchia snorted and continued, "Plus there's salmon loaf, ham and some chicken."

"Will you grill me an American cheese sandwich?" Andrew asked.

"Me too."

"Wouldn't ya like a piece of chicken or some soup for a change?"

Logan scrunched up his nose. "Bean soup?" They made more noises.

"American grilled cheese, please," Andrew said.

"I guess I will if you promise to eat an apple before bed tonight." Bobchia relented.

"I want some chocolate milk too."

"Me too, with lots of chocolate!"

"That's something I keep forgetting to discuss with you boys. Just because Avenella's hand *shakes,* it doesn't mean that it's her *lot in life to stir your chocolate milk every day of the week! Understand?*"

"But she gets it off the bottom *real good!*" Logan defended.

"Understand?" She said sternly.

"I guess," Logan said.

"I'll make you grilled sandwiches if you don't mention American cheese to Mr. McStall! After what happen in church today, I am in no mood to be *serenaded.*"

"What's that mean?" Logan asked.

"Sung to."

"Okay, I promise, but I like it when he s-s-sings!" Logan giggled.

"Me too. He's f-f-funny!" Andrew fell off the loveseat laughing.

"Okay, settle down."

Minnie whined when Bobchia bent over and kissed my forehead. "Minnie wants to take a nap with me," I said,

Bobchia put her on the pillow, giggling as she licked my face. "If you need anything, just holler." She got the wastebasket and set it beside the couch, petting Minnie goodbye. "Just in case. Come on boys, let's wash our hands." The boys stuck their tongues out at me behind Bobchia's back.

"Lucky ain't even dirty!" Andrew held up his hands.

"Not even!"

"I'll just be down the hall, Sweetie," Bobchia said.

"Okay."

I had just closed my eyes when I heard someone enter the room.

"S-s-s-sorry! I th-th-th-thought I h-h-h-h-heard R-rhea's v-v-voice."

"She's in the kitchen, fixing potluck," I said without opening my eyes.

"Th-thanks!" He hurried down the hall. To the tune of **There is Nothing Like a Dame**, he sang, "There is nothing like potluck, nothing in the world. There's nothing that saves a buck, than a dinner of potluck! It could be something you like best, or something you detest, bites of chicken or a roast, scrambled eggs on burned toast, a slice of ham with pickled beets, a casserole of mystery meats, potato soup or pulled pork, use a spoon or a fork—"

"*Get out of my kitchen! NOW!*" Bobchia's voice boomed.

I held my pounding head, laughing then I heard him run down the hall. Mother came into the room but stopped short when she saw the birdcage. She took the long way around the couch and sat nervously beside me, watching the cage.

"Finally, your grandmother kicked Mr. McStall out of the kitchen!"

"I heard."

"Now maybe we'll be able to eat in *peace* around here! I've had *indigestion* ever since that man set foot in this place! Why doesn't your grandmother know any *normal* people?"

"She knows *us!*"

"Very funny! She'd be a great study for my *Psych* class!"

"Mother, can't you just *once* say something nice about Bobchia?"

She sighed. "Let's see…there has to be something, something…nice."

"Mother!"

"Well, she *is* generous to a fault."

233

I held my head.

"Logan said you had a headache. I think we *all* do after church today! Did you take any aspirin?"

"I did."

"Is there anything I can do?"

"I just want to rest for a while."

She rubbed my back. "Minnie is keeping me company." As soon as I said her name, the pup started licking my face again.

Bobchia came into the room. "Clair can rub your back until you *burp,* and Minnie can lick your face until you *puke!*"

"Bobchia! Stop! *It hurts to laugh.*"

Mother gave Bobchia 'the look.'

"Come on Miss Minnie, let's leave her rest. Get back into the pocket. Did you hear the song?"

"Yes."

"I regret the day I asked that man to *sing for his supper!* I think I need an aspirin!"

She went back into the kitchen. Mother rubbed my back until I fell asleep then went to study.

Later, Mother came back, once again evading the birdcage. "How's your head?" She asked.

"About the same."

"Can I get you anything? I know, I could bring my books to the kitchen later and—"

"Please don't do that. I just want to rest."

Bobchia came in. "How's your head?"

"Okay."

"Are you hungry, thirsty?"

"No, thanks."

Mother asked, "Are you sure you don't need anything, anything at all?"

"No, thanks. Go study. I'll be fine."

"If you're sure. Just holler if you need me."

"Mercy, you'll never *hear* the girl way up there!" Bobchia grabbed her school bell from the kitchen and rang it. "This will wake the dead!"

"Bobchia!" I held my head.

"Oh, sorry! I can't *erase* that." She set the bell on the puzzle on the coffee table. "Those puzzles of Ardelle's have me curious. Every one of them has a piece missing!"

"I just want to close my eyes. If I need you, Mother, I promise I will ring the bell, *I promise.*"

"Well if you're sure. I have five chapters to go over."

"I'll see you when I come up for bed."

She kissed me on the cheek and left the room.

Bobchia hesitated. "I hate to leave you, Sweetie."

"Don't be silly. I'll be in this exact same spot when you get back."

The boys came in. "Did ya puke yet?" Logan asked unceremoniously. Andrew pretended to puke in the wastebasket.

"Ouu, get out of here! Boys are so *gross!*"

They laughed and ran outside

Bobchia looked over the couch and out the window, watching them climb into the van. "They're waiting in the van for me. Mrs. Pratt is in her room. She wanted to go but didn't want to have a relapse in case the church was crowded, and Homer said he was going but then forgot about it, so he's flitting around here someplace. Minnie is done in, asleep upstairs. She doesn't do stairs, so if she whines at the top of the steps, you'll have to get her and take her out, but the boys just had her out about an hour ago and put her through her paces." She walked over to Lucky. "Oh mercy, I should have changed those papers. Now I don't have time!"

"I'll do it, don't worry."

"Well, if you're sure. Yesterday's paper is on the desk. Whatever you do, make sure that you don't let Pumpkin in here, and keep Lucky in his cage. Nothing can happen to him in there."

"Don't worry. Enjoy Mr. McS-s-stall's music."

She snorted walking past the couch, wiggling my big toe. "There's a chicken breast and stuffing in aluminum foil in the fridge with the *code word* on it if you get hungry. I love you awful."

"I love you awful back. Bobchia…?"

"Yes."

"Ah, nothing. Have a good time!" I couldn't bring myself to tell her about Grampie's prized bush. *I just couldn't!* I heard the front door close and the cars leave. I snuggled down into the afghan, falling asleep to the sound of Lucky scattering birdseed onto the hardwood floor.

I gasped and sat up from a dream in which I had *repeatedly* run the tractor into the rhododendron, *completely knocking down Grampie's hedgerow!* "TYG it was just a dream! And TYG my headache is gone!" My stomach growled. I went over to the cage and lifted the cover off the cowering bird. "Come on, Lucky. Let's get something to eat." I carefully set him on my shoulder. "You are too *sheltered.* You need to get out once in a while and *see the world!"* I walked over to the window and stood sideways so he could see out. "See that bush, Lucky? You can't even tell, huh?" I saw a cat prowling around the hedgerow, looking up at us. "Uh oh, Cutie Boy sees ya!" Lucky turned completely around on my shoulder, shaking. I laughed. "You are so smart! Sorry, I didn't mean to scare you. Don't worry, I won't let him in! *You're safe with me, little fella!"*

We went into the kitchen. "Aaaahhhhhh!" I screamed and jumped backward. Mr. Pill was standing at the sink, gulping down a plate of food. Lucky fluttered to the floor.

"I thought all you people were *in church!* Keep that *buzzard* away from me!" He said, kicking his foot toward the bird.

"*Stop that!* Lucky! Come back here!" I crawled under the tables. Lucky hopped through the chair rungs. "Oh please, Lucky, stop! Lucky!" I got him cornered under the butcher's block. "TYG you didn't go behind the stoves!" I got him securely in my hands and stood up. Mr. Pill was gone. The dirty dishes in the sink were the only indication that he had been downstairs.

"I should have listened to Bobchia and kept you in your cage!" I quickly put him in his cage and pulled the blanket over the back of it, setting the cage on the coffee table and leaned down. "There, you'll be *safe* in there. I'll be back in a *few."* I went to the kitchen and washed my hands and then got out the aluminum foil covered plate with the 'code word' *asparagus* on it, out from the fridge. (As long as nobody around here *liked* asparagus, I would always have a hidden treat from my Bobchia!) I put the chicken on a plate and looked for the mashed potatoes that were left from a few nights before but couldn't find any. The Pill had probably eaten them! I got out the cottage cheese and heaped ketchup on everything. A big dill pickle from the crock made the perfect garnish.

I hurried back into the great room and 'fine-tuned' the set, turning the cage toward the TV. I leaned forward to chat with the pitiful green bird. "Don't tell Bobchia I'm eating in here, okay? Sorry, *I hope I'm not eating a friend of yours.* TYG for this food. Amen." The theme music for **Bonanza** came on. "I hate westerns, but *I sure like Little Joe!"* The bird stared straight ahead, not even blinking. I watched intently as Little Joe rode into Virginia City on his beautiful pinto horse. "That horse looks a little bit like Dollee, don't ya think? Only I think Dollee is prettier!" Little Joe got off his horse and walked onto the porch of a big white house and knocked on the door. A pretty blonde girl greeted him holding a picnic basket. "He likes blondes. Good." I listened intently:

"You look pretty today, Wilhalmeana. Let me help you with that picnic basket," Joe said.

"I hope you like fried chicken and apple pie, Little Joe." Wilhalmeana smiled.

*"Is the sky blue?"* He said smiling as he helped her on to her buckboard.

Then he tied the reins of the pinto to the back. They rode along a quaint little stream until they came to a shady spot beside a waterfall. He helped her down and put a blanket under the shade tree.

Then a stupid commercial came on! I talked to the television, "I'll be back, Little Joe, don't worry. I have to get Lucky some cookies and milk. How about it, Lucky?" The bird stared at the Polaroid camera commercial. "Not very talkative this evening, are ya?"

As I walked to the hallway, I heard someone faintly knocking at the front door. I looked through the lace curtain. *What if an angel came and Bobchia missed it because she was in church? How could I keep it here until she came back?* (After all, they can walk through walls.) An older, stocky man stood on the first step with a suitcase, a sweeper and a smile. He didn't look a thing like Little Joe. (What I thought an angel should look like.) I didn't want to take a chance on *missing an angel,* so I opened the door. He removed his hat. I was four steps above him and couldn't help but notice that he had strategically combed his thin hair from his right ear across the top of his bald head to his left ear. (Would an angel have a receding hairline?)

"Hello, my name is Mr. Edwards," he said. "I was hoping you had a room to rent for the night."

He sounded just like a regular guy. (If this guy was an 'angel unawares', *I* was unaware of it!) "I don't know, I think so. My grandmother owns the Inn. She's in church right now." (If he *were* an angel, he would have probably known *that!*)

"May I come in and wait? It's starting to sprinkle."

"I guess."

He brought his things in and set them in the vestibule. Then he hurried to wipe off the sweeper with his handkerchief.

I looked at the sweeper. *"We're pretty clean here..."*

"I'm a sweeper *salesman!*"

"Oh."

We looked at each other. The commercial was over. I could hear Little Joe talking to the girl, and I was missing it! "Uh, I was just watching **Bonanza**. Would you like to watch it while you wait?"

"It's my favorite show! Can I leave these things here?"

"Sure."

*Good, I wouldn't miss Little Joe after all!* We walked into the great room. I sat as far away from him as possible. He tried to make small talk. I strained to hear Little Joe.

Another commercial came on. We smiled awkwardly at each other.

"So...do you *like* selling sweepers?"

"Yes!" He said with a huge smile. "Especially this one!"

*"This one?"*

He hurried to the hall and came back in with the Super Duper Sweeper, *"It's the granddaddy of all sweepers!* It has an extra-long hose with Super Duper suction, heavy casters, and it's made out of real steel from Cyclops, right here in *your* hometown! Just wait until you see the Super Duper attachments!" He ran and got his suitcase and while pulling out the attachments, he also pulled out a couple pair of boxer shorts! I giggled and turned to the TV while he put the attachment on, turned on the sweeper and stood on the desk chair to sweep the drapes. As he turned his head backward and smiled for my approval, his hair became *dislodged* from his left ear and hung over the top of his head in a semicircle. (For a split second and *only* a split second, I actually wished my brothers were here to see *Half-moon Man*.)

My head pounded from the noise. I looked at the TV. Little Joe was pushing the girl on a swing. *Where did that swing come from?* Little Joe stopped the swing. He was getting ready to *kiss* her. I motioned for the man to quit sweeping. He turned off the sweeper and proudly pointed to the curtain (which was clean to begin with). I forced a smile. He dragged the chair over to the other curtain and began sweeping it while smiling at me. I grabbed my head, aggravated. I franticly motioned for him to turn the sweeper off. He frowned as he got off of the chair, disappointed.

"Look mister, the only reason I would *ever* have to buy a sweeper is if it could *clean the bird crap of the bottom of that cage!*" I waved a hand toward Lucky's cage. He smiled, and before I could say 'Lucky,' he held the Super Duper attachment in the cage and the Super Duper Sweeper's suction, *sucked up Lucky!*

"*Aaaaahhhhh! Turn it off! Turn it off!*" I screamed. "*Oh nooooo! Bobchia is going to kill me!*"

"I'm so sorry!" He stood there stupidly holding the attachment.

"*Dump it out! Hurry uuuup!*" I heard a faint 'chirp.'

He dumped out the dusty, flapping bird. I picked up Lucky and blew the dust off of the bird and into the salesman's face. He sneezed.

"GBY!"

"What does that mean?"

That's when I knew for *sure* that *he* was definitely not an angel!

He pointed to the birdcage proudly announcing, "Look! Not a speck of bird crap left!"

"Look mister, I don't think we have an empty room. Let me think. Yeah, they're all *full up!* Why don't you try the Brady House downtown?" I hurried Half Moon Man and his Super Duper Sweeper with the Super Duper attachments out the door and into the pouring rain.

I scooped up Lucky and ran into the bathroom. "Please don't die! *Please* don't die, Lucky!" I put some water into the sink. He flapped in it. I ran back and picked up a green feather and put it in my pocket. Then I blew *the dusty crap* under the rug. I put papers in the cage, glancing at Little Joe. He was kissing the girl and I was missing it! I ran to the bathroom and grabbed the bird. "You sure *are lucky,* Lucky!" While running with him to his cage, I tried to *tuck in* his tail feather.

"**Chirp**!"

"*Ouuu, sorry!*" I set him on his perch and shut the cage door just as Bobchia walked in.

The boys ran to the TV. Bobchia walked over to me. "How are you feeling? Mercy, you look *flushed,* Sweetie. Do you have a fever?"

"No, honest!"

She felt my head.

"Chirp!"

"Lucky just chirped! Did you hear that? He *chirped!*"

"Chirp, chirp!"

"Not in the entire time that Ardelle and Wanda have lived here has that bird *ever chirped!*"

"Chirp!"

"Mercy, he's trying to *fly!*" Bobchia walked over to the cage. "Why is he all *wet?*"

"I, um, I let him take a *bath* while I put papers in his cage."

"Chirp!"

"Who would have ever thought that a *bath* is what the old bird needed?"

"Chirp!"

I nervously looked at the bird and then back to Bobchia and then back to the bird, waiting for him to *drop dead!*

"Chirp!"

"I can't wait until Ardelle and Wanda get back to hear him!" Bobchia smiled.

"Chirp! Chirp!"

"Oh look boys, another green feather." She picked the tail feather out of the cage.

"I want it!" Logan dove over Andrew.

"No, I do! You have the *other one!*" Andrew reached for it.

Logan looked back to the screen just in time to see Little Joe kiss the girl again. "Yuck and yucky! Why do cowboys have to kiss girls anyway, Bobchia?"

"Oh, I don't know...probably because their *horses* don't like it!"

"Chirp!"

# 11
# I Am Thankful

Veterans Day arrived on a stormy morning. Bobchia was upset at breakfast. She, Spike, and Cliff, were discussing how they were going to get the flags fastened to the fence, in the midst of the terrible thunderstorm.

"This will be the first year that the flags won't get up. I remember us putting them up in rain and in snow but never in an electrical storm like this!" Bobchia said as we dragged ourselves into the kitchen and sat somberly at the table.

"You all look bright eyed and bushy tailed this morning!" She said.

"Bobchia, I'm tired...and scared!" Andrew said.

"So is Minnie, honey boy. She hides under the sink when it thunders." We opened the cupboard door and peeked at the growling pup shivering in the pocket of Bobchia's crumpled apron.

"Aw, she growls so cute!" I said.

"I'm still tired, Bobchia. The thunder was too loud." Logan rubbed his eyes. "Do we have to go to school when it thunders?"

"Of course you do! I bet you don't know the good thing about storms."

"What could be good?" Andrew dropped his head to the table.

"I know, I know!" Logan waved his hand. "The flowers get pretty, and the trees get big!"

"Nope, the best thing is that it's raining *cats and dogs* out there, so to speak!"

"Really, Bobchia?" The boys ran to the windows. "Where?"

Bobchia snorted as she set plates full of hash browns, bacon, French toast and eggs on the table. "Erase, erase, I was teasing you!"

"Hardly anyone sees the flags anyway, Rhea." Cliff said.

"*I* see them," Bobchia said assertively. "If the rain won't let up, I suppose they'll call off the program at the football field."

"I'm sure. Maybe they'll move it to the Christian Center."

"I hope so Cliff. I look forward to hearing David's name mentioned at the ceremony."

Bobchia bowed her head as the boys took turns saying grace, thanking God for the food, the pets in the red barn and even the man who called the Inn by mistake last night.

"Who called last night?" Bobchia asked with her hands on her hips.

"I don't know." Andrew shook his head. "It was a *mistake,* but it was still okay to *pray for him,* right? I mean even if I don't know what he looks like, right?"

"That's right, honey boy."

Andrew threw a piece of bacon on my plate and split the rest between him and Logan.

"Thanks, that's *one more* than yesterday!" I said.

"Mother said we had to share, so *I shared!"*

Bobchia hugged my arm as she set a saucer of bacon beside me and out of the reach of the boys.

"How many slices did *Sweetie Pie* get?" Andrew mocked.

"Yeah!" Logan leaned to see my plate.

Bobchia windshield-wipered her finger at them as Mother came in.

"What's going on?" Mother asked.

Andrew immediately jumped in. "She got a whole plate of bacon, and I already gave her some!"

"The tiniest one on the whole plate!" I argued.

"Civilized people *do not fight over food.* I'm sure there is enough for everyone." Mother poured herself a cup of coffee and sat down while Bobchia stood behind her, windshield-wipering her finger at Andrew. "I've got a test today and I couldn't sleep a wink!" Mother said sipping her coffee.

After we brushed our teeth we came back into the kitchen. Spike offered to drive us to school in the van. Mother glared at him.

Bobchia watched the rain. "Sweetie, there's lots of *bumbershoots* in the hall closet. Try to stay dry." She said following us.

We went to the closet but didn't know what a bumbershoot was, so we got the umbrellas instead. Bobchia hugged us and handed the boys their lunch buckets.

"Are we allowed bananas *yet?"* Logan asked for the umpteenth time.

"Mrs. Dunham is making banana bread today." Bobchia smiled.

"You say that *all the time!*"

"Yes, well, be good." She patted Andrew's head. "And you be good too, and remember the Golden Rule!"

"I know it!" Andrew said proudly. "Treat people the *way they want* to be treated!"

"No, *dummy!*" Logan said, hitting Andrew in the arm.

"Ouch!"

"Treat people the way *you* want to be treated!"

"Good job!" Bobchia praised.

Andrew hit Logan.

"Hey!"

"Well you must have *wanted hit* because you hit my arm!"

"Okay, now you're even. No more hitting!" Bobchia kissed the tops of their heads. "I love you awful!"

"I love you awful back!" Andrew said.

"Me too!" Logan beamed.

They ran out the door, wiping her kisses off in the rain, screaming when it thundered.

I kissed Bobchia on the cheek. *"Me three!"* She smiled watching us hurry to the van.

By the time school was out, the sky was blue and the sun was hot. The boys had a sword fight with their umbrellas down the lane, until they got to Sterling's house. Then they ran as fast as they could, only stopping when they realized they weren't being chased.

Lanny, tossing a baseball back and forth with Ricky, called to them. "Hey, blackberry kid! I bet you wish you had these baseballs that me and my brother found on our property!"

Logan made a face at him.

Andrew *growled* deep in his throat and walked toward him. "I won't be little forever! When I get *old* I'm going to let you have it for taking our baseballs! You just wait and see, *ox!*"

"That day will never come, ya shrimp!"

Andrew hung his head as I caught up to them.

*"He stole your baseballs?"* I asked.

"Yeah, every single one of them, the big dummy!" Andrew kicked at the ground.

"They're probably BBs by now!" Logan said.

"*BBs?*" I asked.

"*Booger Balls!*" Andrew pointed to the baseballs lined up on Lanny's porch window. "Someday I'll get them back. I won't be little *forever;* I'll grow! *Somehow someday he'll be sorry!*"

Lanny hollered. "Hey shrimps! Who is *Paul David Matko* anyway who signed this ball?"

I looked surprised at Andrew. "Even your *special ball?*"

"Is he in the major league?" Lanny taunted.

"It's my *lucky* ball!" Andrew yelled.

I put a hand over Andrew's mouth. "*Shhhh!*"

Lanny had heard. "Oh, a shrimp's lucky ball! Your lucky ball is now *my* lucky ball!"

"Give it back to me, *jerk!*" Andrew shook a fist at him.

"You can have it back for *ten bucks!*"

"Ten bucks? *I ain't got ten bucks!*"

"Too bad so sad! Maybe I'll sell it to some other kid or just *pound it* with a sledge hammer!"

Andrew sobbed. "He's going to *smash* my daddy's name, Jen. Please, Jen, please, don't let him smash my *mostest special baseball!* Please! You're *old,* can't you think of somethin?"

"If I tell you and Logan what to do, will you *trust me?* Just this once?"

"Will we get hurt?" Logan asked.

"Not *now.*"

They looked at each other and nodded.

"Run down the lane and hide behind the tall bushes beside the red barn." I pointed.

Andrew looked unconvinced. "What for?"

"Just go do it! I'll let you know when it's safe to come out!"

"*Safe?*" Logan asked.

"Just do it, Logan. *Trust me!*"

"The last time I trusted you, you put grape jelly on my bologna sandwich!"

"Well, you *liked* it!" I countered.

"Oh...yeah!"

They ran down the lane and hid in the bushes. I walked to the ditch and watched Lanny throw the *special ball* hard to Ricky.

"Ouch! Dad told you to throw *easy*! You hurt my fingers. I'm going to tell when he comes home! Then *you'll be sorry!*"

Lanny stuck his tongue out at him. "Tattle tale, tattle tale, hanging on a bull's tail!"

Ricky ran up the steps and into the house and slammed the door shut. Lanny stood in the yard, throwing the ball in the air and catching it over and over. He saw me looking at him. "Hey girl, take a *picture*, it will last longer!"

"You can sure throw that ball *hard!*" I called to him.

"You want me to throw it *hard* at you?"

"You could, *but you'd miss!*"

"What do you mean? You're standing right there, how could I miss? Besides, *I never miss!*"

"That's not what my brothers said. They said you couldn't hit *the broad side of a barn!*"

"When did they say that?"

"Just now, before they left!"

"I'll show those shrimps the next time I see them!"

"I don't believe you could hit the broad side of a barn *either!*"

"Hey!"

"Well there's the red barn way down there. I bet you *can't hit it!*"

"I'll show you! I never miss!"

Walking over to his pail of baseballs, he tossed the *special one* to the ground. He wiped his nose with his hand and grabbed one out of the pail, got into his pitchers stance and threw it. One by one, he emptied the pail, hitting the red barn again and again.

"Told ya I *never* miss!"

"That was just plain luck! Too bad you don't have any *more* baseballs. I could count how many times you hit the red barn and then you could tell all your friends at school. But too bad. *You ran out of baseballs!* Oh well. See ya!" I started to walk away.

"Hey, girl. *Girl!*" He called after me.

I turned. "Yeah?"

"I have more baseballs, if you want to count them."

"Okay."

He ran up the steps into the house. I jumped over the ditch and into the yard to retrieve the *beloved baseball*, when the boys stepped out of the bushes! I hurried back down to the lane, motioning for them to take cover just as Lanny hurried down the steps with a box.

"Are you ready to count, girl?"

I nodded. He got into his pitchers stance, wiped his nose and threw fastballs, curveballs, knuckleballs and hardballs, hitting the red barn over and over. When the entire box was empty, he asked, "How many was that, girl?"

"Ah...oh, nineteen? That's a lot!"

"I told you I could *hit* that barn! How many do you think I threw before?"

"Around ten, I think. So all together that's twenty-nine! Too bad you don't have *one more to make it an even thirty!* Wow! I bet if you hit the red barn thirty times it would be some kind of record, *a world record for sure!* Nobody and I mean *nobody* has ever hit the red barn thirty times with a baseball!"

"*Really?*"

"You would be the *first,* and that barn is over a hundred years old!"

"Yeah, but..."

"Wow, a world record! *Think of it!*"

He hesitated. "I don't want to throw my lucky ball..."

"*Lucky?* Are you kidding?" I laughed. "What could possibly be so *lucky* about it? I think it's a *bad luck* ball myself. After all how lucky could it be since the shrimp *lost* all his baseballs to you?"

Lanny's face lit up. "You're pretty smart for a *girl!*"

"Thanks! Only *one* more and it's an even thirty! How about another curveball? You look just like that handsome big leaguer *Gib Lebmud* when you throw a curveball."

"Really?" Lanny smiled and then went blank. "Wait. *Who's he?*"

"Well...he plays for...the Ocean View Seagulls! You mean to tell me you never heard of the *hall of famer Gib Lebmud?!*"

"*Seagulls?*"

"Are you sure you never heard of him? I can't believe anyone that throws as good as you do never heard of *him!*"

"Well, now that you mention it, his name does sound a *little* familiar."

Lanny got in his stance and threw the ball, hitting the red barn again! "*Thirty!* How's that, girl?"

"Perfect! *Absolutely perfect!* I have never seen anyone in my entire life that is more like Gib Lebmud than *you!*"

"Really?"

"*Really!*"

"Thanks!"

"I guess my brothers were wrong. You *can* hit the broad side of a barn!"

"Don't forget to tell those shrimps that the next time you see them!" He said as I started walking away.

"You can tell them yourself! Hey, Andrew!"

Andrew came running from the bushes, holding his shirt out with baseballs piled up to his neck. In his waving hand was his *mostest special baseball in the whole world!* "*I got it Jen! Thanks! I got it!*"

Logan struggled walking to the lane with his shirt stretched to his knees heaped with baseballs, laughing and dropping a few as he yelled, "Thanks for all the baseballs, *ya big jerk!*"

"Yeah, thanks!" I said.

"Hey! *Hey!*" Lanny chased me to Bobchia's property line, shaking his fist. "I'll get you girl and you too, shrimps! I'll get you, *girl,* for this!" He yelled wiping his nose on his hand.

"I'm sooo scared! Hey, go home and write that famous ballplayer's name *backward,* and then look at yourself in the mirror with your tongue hanging out!" I yelled.

"I'll get you! I swear! I'll get *all of you!*"

We laughed as he threatened us from the invisible property line. I helped the boys gather the rest of the baseballs and then we walked along the flag-draped fence toward the Inn.

"Wow, look at all the flags on the fence!" Logan said.

"Is Bobchia going to have a *parade* on this lane?" Andrew questioned.

"With fire trucks and firemen throwing candy?" Logan asked excitedly.

I shook my head. "I don't think so."

"Man, she sure likes flags!" Andrew whistled. "Hey, we better hide these balls someplace and *fast!*"

"But where?" Logan asked.

"I know a great place!" I walked ahead of them to the porch and held up the lid of the storage bench. They glanced over their shoulders to Lanny's house while the baseballs fell from their shirts, all except the *special one.* "Believe me; they'll be *safe in there!*" I assured them.

Andrew looked at the pile of baseballs and smiled. "Wow! Now we can play *forever!*"

I closed the lid.

Andrew *kissed* his special baseball.

"*Gag a maggot!*" I said.

Andrew ignored me. "My special ball, I've missed you, but *that* was the *mostest fun* I ever had!"

"Don't play with that one anymore," I told him. "Keep it on your dresser so you don't get it mixed up with the rest."

"You're not my *boss!*"

"Did you see Lanny's mean face, Jen?" Logan asked. "He'll probably pound us real good after tricking him like that!"

Andrew nodded. "Will you walk close to us past his house every night after school?"

"Nah."

That night after supper, Bobchia asked us to go upstairs and put on something red or blue, as tenants, in patriotic attire, assembled in the great room. We passed inspection, coming down the steps, me in my blue-and-white striped blouse, and the boys in their bright red polo shirts. Bobchia said nothing as Mother walked past her with a smirk on her face wearing a *lime green blouse*.

Mother ducked as Bobchia's camera captured the proud moment. 'Pop!'

"My little patriots! Just call *me* Betsy Ross." She smiled, turning to give us a full view of her flag blouse, red skirt and flag shoes. "I wear this on Veteran's day, the Fourth of July and whenever I vote!"

She had a big homemade pin stuck to her blouse. I read it. *"Freedom only gets stronger when you exercise it!"*

Mother sighed.

Bobchia smiled. "I made that up then made everybody pins! Here, put yours on."

"Cool!" I pinned it on.

"Boys, come here."

Andrew stayed still. "It's almost as big as my *chest*. Besides, we exercise every day Bobchia!"

Logan nodded. "Yeah, we run down the lane so Lanny won't *pound* us!"

"That's not what this pin means. It *means* to vote!"

"Exercise means to *vote?*" Logan asked.

"Which reminds me, Clair, you'll have to get registered so *you* can exercise your freedom!" Bobchia handed her a pin. "Now let's get this show on the road!"

Mother sighed and pinned on her pin while Bobchia herded everyone out the door.

She looked skyward. "TYG! Look up *future voter*, not a raincloud in the sky! Look at those stars. God *named* every one of them! Did you know that?"

"Is there one with my name on it, clear up there?" Logan asked.

"Or mine?" Andrew tilted his head way back.

"Chances are! Hurry now. I like to get to the Veterans Day program early to get a good seat. Look, the flags are waving to us from the fence."

As we drove past the Sterling's house, the boys laughed, pointing to the empty windowsill. "Hey, Jen, *look!*"

"What are you kids laughing at?" Bobchia asked.

"Lanny," Logan said.

"You should be *praying* for him instead of *laughing* at him."

"For *him?!* I don't even like *him!*" Andrew said in disbelief.

"Me either! He's mean to us!" Logan echoed.

"That's *why* you should pray for him! God will bless you for doing that!"

When we reached the football field, the school marching band was playing ***America, the Beautiful***. Bobchia herded us to the front row. After we sang several patriotic songs, Pastor Jay led the program with a prayer, thanking God for our *Christian Nation,* the land of the *free* and the home of the *brave.* "God, I ask that you would bless the hundreds of thousands of brave men and woman serving in Vietnam. Please bring them home safe. *Blessed is the nation whose God is the Lord!* Through your name I pray, and all God's people said ***Amen***. I implore you to keep our armed forces in your prayers. Every day they put their *lives on the line* for the freedoms we take *for granted.*"

The school band then played the ***National Anthem,*** and then Mayor Wojtowicz read a poem entitled ***The Cost of Freedom***. Tears ran down Bobchia's cheeks as the mayor read the names of the heroic men and woman that had served our country from our community. At the closing, the band played ***God Bless America***.

When we got back to the Inn, Bobchia brought down a thin scrapbook. It was plain brown, not like the flowered ones that were in her room. On the cover was printed **June 6, 1944. D Day**. When she opened it, newspaper clippings fell to the floor. We helped her gather them and put them on the coffee table. She searched through the clippings and pulled out a letter. "Look here, the first love letter I wrote to your Grampie."

"Yuck!"

"Yuckie!"

"Mercy!"

Mother, recalling the album, said, "This is not for *little eyes*. Why don't you two go help Spike bed down the animals in the red barn?" The boys cheered and ran out the kitchen door, slamming the screen door.

"Bobchia are you really going to read us your love letters?" I asked hopefully.

"No, Sweetie. It's not the inside but the *outside* that gives insight." Bobchia looked at Grampie's shaky writing. Her bottom lip quivered. "He was no doubt nervous, but who in their right mind wouldn't be?" She bit her lip and read,

> **"In landing craft beside me is old 'grease monkey', Vince.**
> **Normandy-Operation Overlord. High tide—full moon**
> **116th infantry, 82nd air born division, USS Mayfield.**
> **Zerbe is headed for Omaha beach. Keep your head down**
> **friend. God's speed. I see the beach. Cutting engines.**
> **God give us victory!"**

Bobchia wiped a tear sliding the tattered letter back into the album. "He would have *died* if it hadn't been for Vince wrapping his wounded leg with his belt. Days went by before I even knew he was wounded and in the hospital. Months later, he came home. I just wanted him *back here with me*. It was our faith in God and our love for each other that got us through. Eventually things did get better. We enjoyed raising Paul, but when you, *his little Sweetie Pie,* moved in, you brightened his days more than you could *ever imagine!*"

She noticed my tears and patted my hand. "Now don't you be crying. Lookie here at your grandfather, the *handsome thing!*" She smiled at pictures of Grampie and his buddies in boot camp, playing football, playing baseball, in a jeep and on a ship. Then she turned a page and came to an eight-by-ten picture of him in his army uniform. *"The handsome, handsome thing!"* She held her breath as she undid the pasted corners of the picture and passed it to me.

The boys ran back in. Andrew said, "Spike told us to take a hike! Can we watch TV *instead?"*

Bobchia pointed at another picture. "Here's one of your grandfather with his artificial leg."

"He was born with a leg that wasn't *real?"* Andrew asked.

Bobchia started to tell of how Grampie lost his leg at Normandy, but Mother cleared her throat.

"How could anyone *lose* a leg, anyhow?" Andrew questioned. *"Doesn't it just stay up there somehow?"*

Bobchia closed the album. "When you children are older, you will appreciate the *sacrifice* your grandfather made for our freedoms. Just like Mayor Wojtowicz said, *'freedom is not free!'* This album will be waiting for you upstairs, when you want to know more about your grandfather."

The next day after school my brothers walked one on either side of me instead of running down the lane. If I ran, they ran. If I stopped short, leaving them unprotected, Lanny would jump out of the bushes and terrorize them until they got beside me again.

"Someday I'll get you shrimps *alone!"* He threatened.

"Bobchia says that you need to go to Sunday school and show *'spect* to people," Andrew replied.

"And Ricky too!" Logan added.

"Shut up, *shrimps!"*

On the Monday before Thanksgiving, we came home from school and walked into the kitchen filled with the aroma of cinnamon and apples. Bobchia wiped her forehead with her sleeve, welcoming us with hugs.

"Come in, come in, come in, said the spider...to the *fly!"* She giggled.

Four big boiling pots of apples were on the stoves, plus big porcelain bowls of applesauce were cooling on the counters. We watched Cliff carry a steaming pot of apples to the counter and pour it into a Foley Food Mill, a funny looking machine with a steel sieve, sharp blades and a wooden handle hanging on a wooden apparatus over a porcelain bowl. Cliff massaged his shoulder as he turned the handle.

"*I'll feed you* before I put you to work," Bobchia said.

"Work?" Logan looked worried.

"We have to *work?*" Andrew made a face.

"It says in the Bible, **'If you're able to work and don't work, you don't eat.'**"

"Oh brother, it says *that* in the Bible? I thought it just said stuff about *love* in there," Andrew said.

Logan pointed to himself. "*I'm just a kid!*"

"Does it ever say stuff about taking it *easy?*" Andrew asked. "And why do you always say stuff from the Bible anyway?"

"Because it's the truth, and the truth will set you *free!*" Bobchia winked.

"Don't ya got any other stuff memorized?" Andrew asked.

"Yeah, from *somewhere else?*" Logan hit his forehead.

Bobchia looked into the boys' troubled faces. "Well, Henry Wadsworth Longfellow once said, '**So let us be up and doing, with a heart for any fate, still achieving, still pursuing, learn to labor and to wait!'**"

"So what does *that* mean?" Andrew asked hopefully.

"Work first and *then* take it easy!"

"Oh brother!" Andrew rolled his eyes.

"I'm tired!" Logan slumped into a chair.

"Believe me when I tell you that there is nothing, *nothing* like doing something that others will enjoy! Everyone will sure enjoy this sauce tonight. And just think—all winter when we're eating it, you will remember how much *fun* you had making it. It will make you feel so good! Just you wait and see."

Andrew shook his head. "*Work, fun?* You can buy that stuff at the grocery store!"

"True, you can buy applesauce at the grocery store, but you can't buy *Bobchia's* applesauce at any grocery store!" She said.

"Because it's made with love?" Logan smiled.

"You hit the nail on the head!"

Logan looked at her puzzled. She kissed him on the cheek. He tried to wipe it off.

"Now, go wash your hands."

We hurried to the bathroom. The boys fought over the soap, the water temperature, and the towel, then ran out and jumped into the chairs. We licked our lips.

Bobchia got out three bowls, scooped warm applesauce in them and set them in front of us.

Logan looked at his. "You forgot the spoons!"

"You don't need a *spoon* to eat applesauce in Bobchia's kitchen!" She ripped off three big hunks of bread from a cooling rack and handed them to us. "Well, *dip it!* Go ahead!"

"Yummmmmm!" Andrew said.

"Yummmmmm!" Logan said.

"Delicious, Bobchia," I said.

"Nothing like it on this planet!" She beamed.

As we ate, we watched Ardelle, Wanda, Gladys, Cliff, Mrs. Dunham and Cecil rub their shoulders. Bobchia went from one steaming porcelain bowl of sauce to the next, mixing in just the right amounts of cinnamon, sugar, brown sugar and her secret ingredient. (I was sworn to secrecy,—a double shot of vanilla. *Shhhh…*)

Andrew pushed a little piece of bread around the bowl, shoved it in his mouth and asked, "Can I have some more?"

"Me too?"

"If you promise to eat all your supper tonight. I don't want to get on the bad side of your Mother *again*. I don't know why that woman got so *fired up* last night anyway, do you? A little snack before bed never hurt anybody around here before.

"I think it was the root beer floats and chips," Andrew said.

"I think it was the hot fudge sundae on top of that, is why we *puked on our mattress,"* Logan said. "That *really* made her mad!"

Bobchia nodded her head, filled our bowls again and handed us more bread, giggling.

Logan smacked his lips. "I think this bowl is even better!"

It didn't take long until the bowls were empty again. Andrew licked his bowl like a dog and begged like one for more, making us laugh.

"Your Mother will have my hide if I give you more!"

Andrew cocked his head. "Bobchia, why are you always cooking stuff?"

"Because I'm the *chief cook and bottle washer* around here."

"Really? The *chief?*"

Bobchia nodded. "Are you kids ready to crank out some sauce?"

The boys cheered, "Yeah!"

Cliff gladly relinquished his job to Logan, who spun the crank on the Foley Food Mill wildly.

"Mercy, Logan! I never knew you were so *strong.*" Bobchia felt his muscle, giggling.

"I can even go faster than that!" Andrew said as he walked over to Bobchia, holding up his arm for her to feel his muscle.

"You boys will have all this sauce made in *two shakes of a lamb's tail* for sure!"

Andrew looked puzzled but walked to Logan, eager to take his turn. "My turn!"

"I'm not done yet! Wait your *turn!*"

"You always have to go *first!*"

That night at supper, as a smaller porcelain bowl was being passed, the boys unwillingly had joined the elite club of *shoulder rubbers.* Bobchia sat between them with her arms around them, announcing with pride, "Wait until you taste this applesauce! It's the best I have ever eaten in my *life!*" They smiled up at her, flinching as she squeezed them tightly to herself. *Was it the best because it was made with love, or was it the best because her grandchildren worked at the mill? It was both.*

On Tuesday after school, we ran fast as we could past Lanny's house, not because we were afraid of him but because we were thinking of *warm applesauce and homemade bread!* We ran through the door to an empty kitchen and then scrambled for the cookie tin. I grabbed it and held it over my head. Andrew kicked me in the shin,

"Ouch! Brat!"

He quickly grabbed it from me when I bent over, tossing it to Logan.

I limped after them. "*Ouu, that hurt!* I'm sorry now that I got *that ball* back for you, brat! If I ever catch you...!" I limped around the tables until my leg hurt so bad I sat down to rub it.

"Had enough, *precious?*" Andrew mocked.

"Shut up!" I yelled.

They sat at the opposite table, divvying up the cookies.

"Five for you and five for me," Logan said.

"It wouldn't kill each of you to give me just *one!*"

"Why?" Logan asked.

I got up. Andrew grabbed his cookies and *quickly licked all of them.* Logan did the same.

"You can have one *now*, precious!" Andrew held one out.

"*Little maggots!* I'm going to look for Bobchia."

"Do whatever you want to do…*Sweetie Pie!*"

"Shut up!"

Of all places, I found Bobchia crying in the deer head parlor.

"*Bobchia, what's the matter?*"

She motioned for me to come in. (I knew the deer were alive—their bodies standing in the next room.) She motioned again. I *reluctantly* went in, their eyes followed me.

"Pull up that chair, Sweetie. Are you limping?" Bobchia asked.

"The brat kicked me!" I unwillingly sat down in *the death room*, under the deer heads next to the table with Rocky, the stuffed raccoon, poised to strike. I leaned toward Bobchia, refusing to look at it or up.

After taking a double shot of coffee, she told me the saga. "Your mother and I had a fight!"

"*A fight!* About what?"

"About you!"

"About *me?*"

"Yes. I wanted to buy you kids some winter clothes, and she hit the roof saying 'I was trying to *buy your love.*' I'm not, Jen. I just wanted to get you kids some *heavier* clothes. But *she* said that '*she'd* buy some as soon as *she* got some money, but that money doesn't grow on trees but that as soon as *she* got some, *she* would buy them!' I wasn't trying to buy your love!"

"*It's her,* not you."

"Really?"

"She feels as though she's freeloading."

"*Freeloading?*"

"Because she doesn't have any money. She wants to move out of here, you know."

*"Big surprise!"*

"Even when she can afford to move us out, I just can't ever leave you *again*, Bobchia. *I won't!* But I don't want Mother leaving either."

"I know." She patted my hand. "Now let's not borrow trouble. We'll cross that bridge when we get to it, okay?"

"I guess." Minnie stuck her head out of the apron, then her foot trying to reach me. I took her. She growled at the raccoon, straining to sniff it. "I think Mother feels that her dream was shattered when she didn't become a nurse because of Grandmother and Grandfather Brocious both dying in the same year."

"I remember that being a horrible time for her. They were such nice people. It's a shame that you never knew them."

"Then she quit nursing school when she became pregnant with me, and her and Father ran out of money then moved in with you and Grampie—"

"We *loved* every moment of it."

"I know. I did too, but I'm sure *she didn't!*"

"How did you get to be so smart?"

"Father told me a lot."

"Well, she's a proud woman, and now that I think of it, it's *very commendable* that she wants to clothe her own children."

"Boy, I could *sure* use some new clothes!"

"I know! Maybe she wouldn't object to my *buying your love* at Christmas! What do you think?" She patted my hand.

"You're funny!"

"All this crying has made me hungry. Let's get a snack."

"We're out of cookies. The boys hogged them all!"

"All of them?"

"I never even got a crumb."

"I was going to make some this afternoon when Clair threw a wrench into my plans. We'll make some tonight after dinner. In the meantime I saved you a piece of strawberry cheesecake in the fridge with the *code word* on it."

"Groovy."

"I need a Kleenex, Sweetie, my hankie is done. Look in the *Chester* of drawers, as the boys call them."

I handed her Minnie and looked. "Nothing in there."

"Look in the closet."

"Just the fan in here. Oh, wait, there's a box on the shelf, if I can just...reach it. It's *heavy!*" I handed it to her.

"Mercy, what on earth?" She opened it. Inside was several rhinestone pins, bracelets, two shoehorns, a rain bonnet, three hankies, barrettes, an envelope of bobby pins, a hair net, ink pens, a little flashlight, necklaces, men's handkerchiefs, nail files, a battery, dried out nail polish and a little picture frame with tiny seashells around it.

"Whose box is it?" I asked.

"Heaven knows!" She took one of the hankies and blew her nose one handed as she thumbed through the contents. "Oh, there's that ugly necklace that Gladys gave me one year for my birthday. I thought I gave it to Ardelle. Wait a minute. Wait...a... minute! This is *the bingo box!* We used to play bingo every Thursday night, and whoever wanted to play would donate something to the box. Then if you won, you could take your pick of these prizes. As you can see, nobody wanted this *junk.* We quit playing when I rented some of the first floor rooms to the Wesleyans one summer years ago. I have no way to get this stuff back to the owners, as if they would want it. Probably some of them are even dead by now. I guess I could give it to charity." She put the lid back on and set the box on the table beside the raccoon. "Guard the family jewels for me, Rocky old boy." She petted the raccoon. Minnie growled at the dead thing. "Shhh, don't be jealous. He used to be in my apron pocket before you were! He slept all day and raised *h-e-double hockey sticks* all night, like Rocky the II!" She scratched it under its chin. "I sure miss you, big guy." She petted it as if it were alive. Minnie barked at it. I immediately went to the hall; I couldn't bear to watch her pet *the dead thing!* "Mercy, Rocky, you're dusty. It has been a while since I've *swept* you. I'll get ya come Saturday, old boy." I looked nervously up the hall, hoping not to see Mother, because if she ever saw Bobchia petting and talking to a *dead raccoon,* she'd move us out before dinner—and tonight we were having *Swiss steak!*

In bed that night, I mulled over the fight that Mother and Bobchia had. It troubled me deeply that the two women that I loved most in the world couldn't get along. I couldn't sleep for thinking about it, so I went to talk to Bobchia. I got to the bottom of the stairs and heard Bobchia talking to Aunt Ardelle in the kitchen.

"Clair got *sour* with me for telling the boys to go out to play to get the *stink* blown off of them! She said, 'My children *do not* stink. Thank you very much!'" Bobchia explained.

"Sour over *that?*"

"Yes, and not only that. Harold wants to bring more *dead people here!*"

"*Oh, no!* You told me that was a *onetime deal,* remember?" Aunt Ardelle said emphatically.

"Don't worry, I told him he couldn't have any more *viewings* here for fear Clair would haul the kids out of here and I'd *never* see them again!"

"You can't chance it."

"And I won't! He's planning on having an open house next Monday evening at the new funeral home. Hopefully the Amish will have the leaky roof fixed by then. He's been paying them double time since he's been losing all his customers to the Planter brothers." Bobchia lowered her voice. "If I tell you something, do you promise *not to tell a soul?*"

"*I promise.*"

"You know Pork Chops, the meat market on the south side?"

"Yes."

"Well, Harold has a few customers *on ice* in the meat freezer over there!"

"*What?*"

I covered my mouth.

Bobchia continued, "I swear I will never buy any meat there again *as long as I live!*"

"*Well! I never heard the like in my life!*" Appalled, Aunt Ardelle went to the great room to watch Johnny Carson.

Bobchia was opening her Bible as I went into the kitchen. "Sweetie, I've been wanting you to get *acquainted* with your great grandmother Regeena's Bible. Look, here's a picture you painted me when you were little." She handed me her treasure, preserved in wax paper, hugging my shoulder. "It's my Bible marker. I can still see you at that table watercoloring it as I made pies."

"It's kind of faded."

"Only from my *eyeballs* being all over it for the last twelve years! I wouldn't take a crisp hundred-dollar bill for it! What's the matter? Can't sleep?" She asked concerned.

"I think it's all the *sweets* I've been eating."

She slid the tin to me and took a shot of coffee. "*Probably.* The thing that really relaxes me is reading the Bible. The Bible will keep you from *sin* just like *sin* will keep you from the Bible."

"It makes me nervous!"

"*Nervous?*"

"All those wars in there? I'd never sleep!"

"The Old Testament is the New Testament *concealed,* and the New Testament is the Old Testament *revealed!* Why not start in the book of John in the New Testament and keep reading? Every question you'll ever have, is answered in the Bible. Plus it will *relax you.* You'll learn *so* many wonderful things about our Lord and, believe it or not, about *yourself.* Draw close to *God,* and He will draw close to *you.* That reminds me, your father wrote to me years ago, telling me that you had said the *sinner's prayer.*"

"I did when I was eleven, at church camp."

"TYG! I'm so excited to know that we'll be together, *forever with Jesus!* Remember, asking Jesus into your heart is the *beginning* of the greatest friendship ever, not the *end.*" I looked puzzled and she continued. "Remember when you first met Dawnette, Beverly and Donna? That was just the *beginning,* right? Since that day, your friendship has *grown.* They've been here, you've been there, you've talked on the phone—you can't learn enough about them, right?"

"Right."

"Just meeting Jesus is wonderful, but to really *know* Him involves *spending time with Him,* reading about Him, and praying to Him. If you never do anything else I ask, promise me you'll *read the Bible.* Satan has no power to stop God's Word from making a difference in our lives, so he tries to keep us from reading God's Word instead. I've had friends I thought would never leave my side, but some did, which hurt me. That's when I realized that Jesus had never left me, and that's when *I made the commitment to read the Bible every day. What a friend I have in Jesus!*"

"I'll start reading my Bible again, I promise."

"Promise Him, not me, and write this date down in your Bible, and don't you dare let *anything* keep you from it everyday!"

"*I won't!*" I smiled.

"I know you won't!" She hugged me and poured me a big glass of milk.

She took a shot of coffee. "Now, my grandmother's intuition is telling me something is troubling you."

"Well…"

"Well?"

"Well, it's Mother, the way Mother and—"

"*I know* what you're saying! Some *vegetarian* she turned out to be! Did you see her put away those *two* big pieces of Swiss steak at dinner? I couldn't *believe* it either! Don't let it bother you, Sweetie. We *all* slip off the wagon once in a while. The trick is to get back on! There. Feel better?"

"*I do.*" I chuckled. "Thanks, Bobchia." After finishing the tin of cookies, after another glass of milk, and after *another* Bobchia hug, I went back upstairs and slept like a baby.

On Wednesday the boys and I were excited. We only had a half a day of school because it was Thanksgiving vacation! The temperature was falling fast, as we hurried down the steps of the school toward the warmth of the Inn. The boys ran ahead, waiting for me at the red light, then screamed through the covered bridge, trying to make an echo, and forewarning Lanny of their arrival.

"Let's hurry!" Andrew yelled. "I want to look for more nails from the roof! (Harold had promised them a penny for their banks, for every nail found in the yard from the shingles the Amish were pulling off.) They waited for me at the beginning of Lanny's property line. I jogged to them and saw Lanny hiding behind a bush.

"I don't see Lanny!" Andrew said to Logan.

"I think it's safe. Do you think it's safe, Jen?" Logan asked me.

"*Yeah.*"

"For sure, Jen?"

"*For sure.*"

"Let's make a break for it!" Andrew cried.

They ran down the lane screaming, when Lanny ambushed them from the corner of his yard. "Hey, shrimps! I want my baseballs back or *else!*" They raced past Bobchia's property line and stuck their tongues out.

"A bully is a *coward!*" Logan said.

"So there! Nah, nah, nah, nah, nah, nahhhh!" Andrew taunted.

"I'm gonna pound you shrimps one of these days! So you just better *watch out!*" Lanny started walking back to his house. He picked up a stone, tossed it and caught it. Then he saw me. "Hey girl, you tricked me! Now *I* don't have any baseballs to play with!"

"*Too bad, so sad!* Now you know how my brothers felt!"

He threw the stone, just missing my head. I chased him up into his yard.

"You are the *ugliest girl in the whole world!*" He yelled. "Well, aren't you gonna cry? Lucy does."

"No, I'm used to it. But do you know something I'm *not* used to?"

"What?"

"Someone else besides *me* pounding on my brothers, so *you* just better *watch out!*"

I jogged down the lane until I smelled food and then I ran as fast as I could over the little bridge and up onto the kitchen porch.

The door of the kitchen was propped open with a wooden chair, letting the wonderful aromas escape. I caught up to the boys barely inside the crowded kitchen, waiting as bent over Venal was getting the pumpkin pies out of the ovens. She stood and *slammed* the doors closed with her hip.

Bobchia yelled at her from the middle of the kitchen sitting on her step stool. "Venal, get a *grip* on your *hip! You are going to shatter the glass in my oven doors!"* Then Bobchia waved her dishtowel like a flag. "I'm over here, boys! *Over here!*" The boys squeezed past Venal, ran past the cooks, almost knocking Bobchia off her stool with their hugs. She giggled.

"Bobchia! We won't have to go back to school until *Monday!*" Andrew smiled.

She looked to the ceiling. "Mercy, please watch over *old people and tiny animals!*"

Andrew cocked his head. "Does that mean you're real happy?"

She faked a smile. "*Pleased as punch!*"

Logan said, "My teacher told me that my only homework was to eat turkey until *I explode!*"

"A thought she holds *near and dear to her heart,* no doubt!" Logan looked confused. "Your snack is on the coffee table. Also Ardelle finally finished that puzzle! Do me a favor when you're done eating and look around on the floor for a puzzle piece, will you?"

"Yeah," Logan said.

"Do we *have* to?" Andrew asked.

"Yes. Do it for me, okay?"

They nodded and took off running bumping into the crowded chefs.

"*Walk!* Mercy! You are like bulls in a china shop!" She hollered after them.

"Sweetie, on the counter you'll see some recipe cards and a green pen. You are witnessing the 'Red Barn Inn Thanksgiving Ritual.' *Learn from the best!*" She fanned herself with the towel and smiled as I went from cook to cook, trying to write down what they were doing, and make sense of it all. (There wasn't a cookbook or a measuring cup in sight!) After seeing several 'pinches of this' and 'palms full of that,' I gave up, realizing that I would never be able to duplicate the delicacies the women of the Inn were preparing. Aunt Ardelle made carrot cake and strawberry rhubarb pies. Wanda made a pumpkin cake and zucchini bread. Mrs. Dunham made ambrosia salad, baked beans and, of course, banana bread. Helen got the squash ready and made a big pumpkin roll and smuck-and-sutch (her version of cranberry salad). Izora and Venal made pumpkin and apple pies. Gladys made three kinds of homemade rolls while Ginger, just made *a big mess!* She was trying to make an old family recipe of beef and noodles.

Bobchia whispered to me, "That beef will be tougher than boot leather, and who ever heard of *beef and noodles* on Thanksgiving anyway?" Bobchia, on the other hand, made several Croatian and Polish dishes along with her traditional *Thanksgiving cuisine* of lasagna and pigs-in-the-blanket! Big bags of corn from Wayne's farm were defrosting in a bowl on the counter for corn pudding as Spike was shredding bread and soaking it in melted butter and onions to make his grandmother's famous onion and herb stuffing. Bobchia explained that at precisely nine o'clock tonight (not one minute before, not one minute after) she and Spike would stuff the huge turkeys and stick them in the ovens at two hundred and fifty degrees to reach perfection by one tomorrow afternoon. *Hallelujah!*

"I was sad today when I thought of Luella not being at my table tomorrow," Bobchia said. "Everyone enjoyed her sweet potato pie that she graced us with every year. I asked her several times for the recipe, but she always left out *the one ingredient* that made it different from everyone else's. I wish she would have *willed* the recipe to me. I cried today when I tried to make it. I think it is pretty close. Here, taste it." She shoved a big spoonful in my mouth. "What do you think?"

"Um, I'll take another, *please!*"

"That sweet potato pie, Sweetie Pie, was a coming attraction. You'll have to wait until tomorrow, along with everyone else!" She giggled.

My mouth watered as we carefully sealed the food. Bobchia directed some food into boxes on the floor to be delivered to the **Christian Center's Methodist Mothers'** Annual Thanksgiving Dinner tomorrow, while the rest was placed on trays and carried to the cold room, thus fulfilling the purpose of the mahogany shelves. (Not *an inch* of shelf space was wasted.) As Spike and I stacked the last bowl of *deliciousness* high atop a shelf, I thought this room might easily turn out to be my favorite room in the Inn!

Spike joked, "Rhea always makes enough to feed a small country!"

I walked back to the kitchen where the cooks were cleaning their part of the kitchen.

"Sweetie, did it all fit on the shelves?" Bobchia asked.

"*Just!*"

"You never know who will show up for Thanksgiving dinner around here!"

(I surmised she was hoping to eat dinner with a *band of angels unaware,* but one thing was for sure, angel or not, nobody would go away *hungry* from Bobchia's table!)

It was time to feed Joan of Arc and Pumpkin. Last night at the supper table Bobchia had told me I could move in with them now that Joan of Arc was doing so well. I mostly took my showers there anyway to get away from my *gross* brothers. Mother overheard us discussing the move and persuaded me to *let her* move downstairs instead, because Mr. Pill's trains made it impossible for her to concentrate on her midterms. It would only be for a month and then we could switch back.

Not the *cat lover,* Mother said, 'Moving the cats upstairs would not be a problem' Bobchia hated the idea of having cats just four doors down from *Lucky* and told me that I would have to keep them quiet so Ardelle and Wanda wouldn't find out.

"How on earth can I keep a cat *quiet?*" I asked.

Bobchia rubbed the groove in her forehead, listening to Mother talk about the move. I knew that without Mother upstairs, the boys and I would be a disastrous combination. (If I didn't *maim* one or both of them, it would be *a true miracle of God!*) Mother didn't have classes on Friday, so we planned the big move on the day after Thanksgiving.

As I fed the cats, I found the aroma from the cold room *impossible to resist!* How could I possibly *wait* until tomorrow to taste all that delicious food? (*I couldn't.*) I looked up and down the hall and then sneaked into the cold room. I ate a little piece of banana bread, cranberry bread and zucchini bread and a huge piece of pumpkin roll. (*If only I had a fork!*) Then I got brave taking a pig in a blanket away from *the rest of the litter!* Just the smell of the beef and noodles made me *gag!* By then, I was frozen and hurried back to Joan of Arc's room and snuggled under a quilt with the cats as they licked my fingers.

Mother knocked and opened the door. "Didn't you hear the dinner bell?"

I held my stomach. "No."

"How can you lie there and smell all that food next door?"

"It's not *easy!*"

"Boy, I wish I had your *will power!* Come on, supper is ready."

Pumpkin dashed out from under the quilt and ran past Mother.

"*Grab her!*" I yelled. She half-heartedly reached for her, not wanting to touch her. "Mother! If Aunt Ardelle sees her, she'll have to stay in the *barn!*"

"Pets belong *outside!* Now come on!"

I slowly trailed behind her to the kitchen. I couldn't possibly eat another bite of anything! Mother and Bobchia felt my head and threatened to call the doctor, knowing I must be sick if I didn't want to eat Cliff's homemade chicken noodle soup with its big, fat, noodles…*my favorite.* The smell of it made me nauseous. When the grilled ham and American cheese with mayo sandwiches were being passed, I put mine (where the boys would get blamed for it) under my chair pad. For dessert, a box of chocolates was passed around the table. It was a dessert fast. All the cooks were exhausted!

Bobchia was right; one extreme did lead to another. When the snow came on Thanksgiving Eve, it came fast and furious, leaving a full ten inches on the ground. Harold and Spike shoveled the sidewalks and the parking area only to find them filled once more when they went out to get wood. The boys ecstatically grabbed their jackets and ran outside like maniacs, careening up and down the yard throwing snow at each other. After a bicarbonate of soda, I was anxious to go outside to have a snowball fight with them until I saw the tenants lined up at the windows. They laughed and pointed at the boys as if they were monkeys in a zoo, watching them eating snow. (Like *always,* they were oblivious, and I was embarrassed.) When they made snow angels and soaked their flimsy jackets, Mother went out onto the porch pleading with them to come in and get into the tub before they caught pneumonia. They flat out ignored her until Bobchia stood at the window with her hands on her hips, looking through her brows.

"Logan, look! Bobchia's at the window!"

"I don't care! I don't *want* to go in!"

"We'd better go in, Logan. She will *hurt you!*"

Up the porch and into the Inn they stomped, with their shoes covered with snow, whining because they'd been forced to leave their wonderland. Mother pointed to the stairway.

"We never had to take this many baths when we lived in Florida, and it was hotter there!" Logan said.

"Yeah, and we *sweated* a lot more there!" They stomped up the stairs, dripping snow along the way.

When I went upstairs to get my purse, my socks got soaked. "Ouu, Brats!" When I came out of my room, I heard splashing and Pumpkin meowing from the bathroom. I quickly opened the door and saw Logan spitting water out of a shampoo bottle at Andrew, while he poured water on the kitten. I grabbed Pumpkin!

"Hey! That's *our cat,* not yours! Give it back and get out of here!" Logan yelled, with water falling from his mouth.

"Yeah! Get out of here! I'm telling Mom you're in here with our *private areas!*"

I wrapped Pumpkin in a towel and turned to go, but when I reached for the doorknob, water hit my back. The boys laughed, taking turns spitting water from the shampoo bottle at me.

"Stop it, *brats!*" I yelled at them, dodging the water.

"Sticks and stones will break my bones, but names will never hurt me!" Logan taunted as more water poured out of his mouth.

"You know that is *butt water* in your mouth, don't you?" I challenged.

"What do you mean *butt water?*"

"Well, little morons, your butts are *in* the water, and the water is *in* your mouths!" They gagged! I laughed! "Please don't forget that Pumpkin's butt was *in* the water and I hope you both *puke!*" I turned out the light and slammed the door. They screamed for Mother.

I hugged the kitten and sneaked her downstairs to Joan of Arc's room, passing Aunt Ardelle in the hallway.

"Whew! That was a close one!" I said closing the door. I dried Pumpkin off and held her in a blanket and watched the snow fall. The smell of the food next door gave me a headache, so I set the sleeping kitten on the bed and went to the kitchen for an aspirin.

Bobchia came in. "How do you feel?" She felt my head.

"Fine."

"I was just about to send a posse after you. We're in the great room, come on." She put her arm through mine. "You probably don't remember, but your Grampie had a tradition on Thanksgiving Eve, that everyone under this roof would reflect on their blessings of the past year." She kissed my cheek. "TYG! *This has been a banner year!*"

Spike and Cliff had arranged the furniture in a circle.

Bobchia smiled her approval. "Thanks, it looks so nice. Let's sit here on the couch Sweetie."

We watched Mother slowly come down the steps, with her nose in a book as the boys ran past her in their pajamas. The towels around their necks flapped wildly as they flew outside the circle, messing my hair.

"Stop it, brats!"

Mother stood in their path guiding them to chairs without lifting her eyes from the page.

Logan stuck his tongue out.

"That will teach ya to *turn off the light on us!*" Andrew hollered.

"Yes, Jennifer, *what were you thinking?* They could have slipped in the tub!" Mother reprimanded.

Bobchia giggled as the boys showed each other their muscles.

"Look Bobchia, those Supermen are so strong they can drink *butt water* and don't even *die!*" I smirked.

"Shut up, Jen!" They ran over. I defended myself from their fists.

Bobchia grabbed their shoulders. "Boys! Stop. Sweetie, hush. Come on boys and sit on the other side of me and *keep your hands to yourself!* We are going to have a tradition here."

Andrew's face brightened. "Is it good to eat?"

She chuckled. "Here, sit, and I'll tell you what a tradition is. A tradition is a custom and every year—"

"Like Christmas?" Logan interrupted.

"On Thanksgiving Eve we sit in a circle and tell of our *blessings* that we've had in the past year."

Mother sat in a straight backed chair next to Logan, thumbing through her book.

"Can I go first?" Logan asked.

"Why can't *I* go first?" Andrew asked Logan.

"You went first *last* year!"

"We didn't get here *last year!*"

"When did we get here anyway?"

Mrs. Pratt and Homer came in. Homer tattled to Bobchia that Mr. Pill was eating in the kitchen. "Quick, call the police! A man is *filling his face* in the refrigerator!"

"Homer, sit down." Bobchia pointed to a chair. "We're going to tell our blessings."

"Blessing? Where's the *food?*"

"You just ate. Look at the napkin around your neck."

"Oh, yeah." He got up, sat back down, got back up and left.

Bobchia rolled her eyes. "We'll wait a few minutes for Harold. Where is he?" Spike shrugged then adjusted the heating pad on his back.

Mr. Hair sneaked in at the last minute and sat on the other side of Mother. She tried to make Logan change places with her, but he screamed, humiliating her.

We heard Mr. T-t-t-tunes humming as he came down the hall. As soon as he saw Bobchia, he knelt in front of her with his hands clasped, singing to the tune of **Maria**. Rhe-a, the Innkeeper's name is Rhe-a. I'm *thankful* she can bake and cook a pounded steak for meeeee." The boys clapped. He bowed.

Bobchia smiled embarrassed. "Well, thank you, Mr. McStall." Yawns went around the circle. "*The Geritol is wearing off, Sweetie.* It's time to get this show on the road! Spike, would you please start?"

One by one, people told of their blessings. I impatiently waited to tell of my Bobchia, (my greatest blessing), but as I listened, that was the sentiment of almost everyone there. They were thankful

Bobchia had bought medicine for them or that she had paid their doctor bill. Someone had heard she helped a family who had come on bad times and paid their taxes. (The day she blessed Ken with a *new* pair of glasses was the day Venal got *dropped like a hot potato!*)

Bobchia's face turned red. "*Brag on God!* It's the Lord's doing, not mine. He's the one that brought us all together for a reason. We are all *His*, and as I look around this room, *I'm* the one who is blessed with all of *you!* TYG that me and my family are living under the *same roof!* I feel so blessed that my heart will *burst!*" She looked to the ceiling and squeezed my hand. "If right this very minute God would take me home, I'd *leave* a happy woman!" I looked at our hands joined together and then nervously looked at the ceiling.

Then it was Mother's turn, "Mother...Mother!" I whispered.

"*What?*" She looked up from her book, embarrassed. We waited for a revelation as she opened her mouth, but nothing came out. We all leaned forward to hear her whisper..."Children."

Harold kicked at the door. Bobchia hurried to open it. He held Nikki in his arms.

"Mercy!"

"Spike, here's your dog! *She's froze up!*" Harold hollered as he carried the dog into the center of the circle and carefully set her down. Minnie poked her head out of Bobchia's apron growling at the snow-covered *dog statue.* I couldn't believe my eyes! Nikki's right front leg was poised as if she was walking.

"Thanks for getting her!" Spike said.

Mother gasped, "*She's dead, frozen to death!*"

"Nah," Spike said, "She does this every year with the first freeze."

The boys were awestruck. They got on the floor with their chins in their hands and crawled as close to Nikki as Mother would allow them.

Logan stared at her. "She's not even *blinking!*"

"*Not even!*"

Mother told the boys to get back, but they didn't budge. "Don't you dare touch her, she might have *rabies!*"

"That heavy snow brought down some of your rhododendron." Harold told her.

"*Oh, no!*" Bobchia and I hurried to the window. "Not David's rhododendron! *Ahhh,* look at it on the ground."

"Just *one* piece, Bobchia. That's all!" I rubbed her back.

She took her hankie out and wiped her nose. "Ah, it's part of the pink one. What a shame. That's odd that it didn't happen when we got that heavy snow a couple of years back, remember Harold? When the county was declared a disaster area? I hope it doesn't *ruin* the hedge row!"

I looked at her misty eyes, wanting to tell her about the ride I'd taken that wild Sunday, but I just couldn't! "It won't Bobchia; it won't ruin the hedge row, *I just know it!*"

"I sure hope not, Sweetie. It reminds me so much of my David. Now then, don't *you* be so upset." She patted my hand comforting *me*. I shook my head in shame as we walked back to the circle.

Nikki stood in that same position for one minute and twenty-four seconds.

"That's a full twenty-one seconds longer than last year, but *remember she is seven dog years older!*" Spike bragged looking at his stopwatch. When Nikki heard Spike's voice, she walked across the room to him, shedding a clump of fur along the way. Andrew quickly picked it up and put it on her back. Then the old dog bumped into an end table and dropped to the floor. Everyone laughed. (Everyone except Spike, Cecil, Bobchia and me, because we knew *her story*.) She lay there with the boys petting her until Spike brought in her food. Then she stood up, ate and dropped into a heap.

"Andrew, this is better than *cartoons!*" Logan cheered.

Bobchia told Spike that Nikki was too old to be outside. "Get some straw from the red barn and put in a low box by the potbelly. If we keep her out of the cold, she'll last till spring!"

Spike shook his head. "But she wants to be in *Poochie's coop.*"

"I know, but it's for her own good and don't forget to fill the feeders while you're out there, please. The one is just hanging by a thread. If one of my gray squirrels decides to jump on it, it will fall to the ground."

"Fix it again? I hope *you* have some nails. The ones in the barn have *disappeared*"

"There's a few in the mason jar under the sink. Did I ever make you kids squirrel pancakes?"

"With *real squirrels?*" Andrew said wide eyed.

"No, no, no, *ding dong!* Out of pancake batter! Well, at least *I* think they look like squirrels!"

"Squirrels?" Spike laughed. "Is *that* what they were? I thought they were *dinosaurs!*" He chuckled as he put on his coat. "If only you'd let me *hunt* the stupid things, I wouldn't have to keep fixing the stupid feeders!" He slammed the door.

"Pay him no mind kids! Just look at that Nikki dog. Not much to look at now, but let me tell you that before she went deaf, she was the best guard dog in the county." The boys looked at the dog in disbelief. "One time, several years ago now, I was walking to my car to go to the bank to deposit my Inn money, when all of a sudden a man jumped out of a bush, grabbed my purse and took off running down the lane! I hollered, 'Nick, *go sic him, girl!*' She took off with a vengeance, circling him and growling as she waited for limping Poochie to arrive. When she did, Poochie viciously latched onto his ankle! The man hit her with the purse, dropping the money. I can still see the soles of his shoes as he raced down the lane to the covered bridge with Nick biting at his heels!"

"Wow!" Logan said.

"She would have caught him too, but she ran back to check on her friend, Pooch. She's as loyal as the day is long, that one is! That's why I reward her with straw every winter, plus milk bones to keep the teeth she has left, good and sharp, *just in case.*"

Spike came in at the end of Bobchia's story. He snuck up behind the boys who were lying on their stomachs petting Nikki, enthralled in Bobchia's story and stuck his cold hands under their Pajama tops onto their backs. Screaming, they scrambled to Mother. She gave Spike 'the look' over the top of her book.

"Cold hands, warm heart!" He chuckled, taking off his coat, then he sat in a chair and tugged the old dog to his lap. "Someone threw old Nick and Poochie out to die, but we fooled them, didn't we girl?" He hugged her. "*I'm thankful*, and I know Nikki is too for coming to the Inn all those years ago." He hugged her again. She gazed up with cloudy eyes, adoring him.

I looked around the circle realizing that Bobchia was a *collector of anything that needed a home.* Her heart *was* the center of this circle and of the Inn. (Another thing I realized that night…everyone had duct tape on their slippers.)

The boys were sleepy after their outing, holding their eyes open with their fingers as Mother told them their bedtime story of David and Goliath as she was tucking them in.

"Did Goliath's armor really weigh one hundred and fifty pounds, Mother?" Andrew asked.

She nodded. "It really did, and that's almost as much as you two weigh together."

"Wow!"

"Wow!"

"And you'll weigh more after dinner tomorrow!" Bobchia added.

"We will for real, Bobchia? Will we get hair on our chest after we eat turkey?" Andrew asked.

"You never know. I can't remember if the turkeys I got from the turkey farm are *chest hair turkeys* or not. We'll have to check tomorrow night at prayer time." She winked at me.

"I check every night after supper, but I just see a couple of freckles. See?" Andrew lifted his top.

"I see!" Bobchia nodded.

After prayers, they begged Bobchia to let Minnie sleep with them.

"We don't have school, remember? You promised, remember?" Logan pleaded.

"Please, pretty please? You said that sometime she could, and I think this is a *good sometime*, ain't it?" Andrew said holding his hands as if praying.

"I did promise to give you *another* chance, and being a woman of my word, and seeing it is *sometime...*" Bobchia took the pup from her apron, kissed her head and set her on the little blue rug between the mattresses—letting her make the decision, of which boy she wanted to sleep with.

"Here Minnie!"

"Minnie!"

She frantically ran from boy to boy as each tried to coax her to his mattress with a variety of animal noises. She licked their squealing faces until Mr. Pill pounded the wall.

"Old coot!" Bobchia said, pounding the wall.

Later that night when I got into bed, Minnie scratched at my covers. I was the one who got to *cuddle her to sleep.*

The next morning, instead of the wonderful aroma of bacon and cinnamon rolls, I awoke to a *horrible* odor. No matter how many pillows I put over my face, I couldn't go back to sleep. I stuck my head under the covers. Minnie licked my face. "You sure are a *bed hog!*" "What on earth *stinks* in here? Do you have to go potty?" She whined. I held my breath while struggling into my jeans and sweater, then I stepped into my slippers. I picked Minnie up and went into the bathroom. Mother was getting dressed.

"Happy Thanksgiving Mother!"

"Happy Thanksgiving. I thought Minnie was sleeping with the boys."

"She needs to go out."

I put the pup on the floor and hurriedly tied up my hair and threw some water on my face. "See ya in a *few.*"

I ran down the stairs with the pup in my arms to the back door and pulled her sweater on over her head. I tugged on Bobchia's barn boots then faced the cold, setting her on the sidewalk. The pine trees were beautiful, heavy laden with snow. I enjoyed the Christmas card setting until it was shattered by the image of two pair of *red, frozen, long johns,* stiffly swaying on the clothes line. I laughed as I made a snowball and threw it toward the creek bed. It blew back into my face. *That's enough snow for now!* I thought. I brushed myself off, waiting impatiently with freezing feet, as Minnie searched for just the right *sidewalk spot* to do her business, then I picked her up and we hurried into the kitchen. I cuddled her across the table from Mr. Hair, ready to do my favorite thing—eat! Bobchia was bent over the oven. "It's freezing out there!" I said to her.

"*Happy Turkey Day,* Sweetie Pie!"

"Happy Turkey Day to you!" I eagerly waited for my eggs, hash browns and bacon.

Bobchia pulled out three pans of cinnamon rolls. She dumped one pan full onto a plate and put it in front of me as she gave me a half hug with her arm. "Careful, they're hot." She took off Minnie's sweater and put her in the apron. "Eat light so you'll have room for turkey."

*Cinnamon rolls are eating light?* I thought. *I have to quit eating all this sweet stuff.* I looked down at my zipper that was stretched to bursting. "Thank you God for this delicious sweet roll, amen." I put a knife full of butter on top and took a big bite. "Yum!"

I thought I heard a man singing in the bathroom but dismissed it as the radio. Bobchia was folding laundry on the ironing board, which I thought *odd* because her scheduled laundry day was Saturday and she *never* varied from it. When he sang off key, I knew someone was in bathroom.

"Who's singing?" I asked.

"Caleb."

"Caleb?"

"Yes, Caleb!"

"What?" the singing man asked.

"It's just Jennifer asking me who was doing all the caterwauling," she hollered.

"If I'd known anyone was listening, I would have done my Elvis impersonation." He sang **Hound Dog** in a thick Elvis accent. When Mother came into the kitchen, Mr. Hair stood up to greet her, hitting a chair seat with his handkerchief. Just then, Caleb came out of the bathroom bare-chested. He was wearing blue jeans and cowboy boots and was drying his dark hair with a towel. He was *very* handsome with a short beard, and despite it being November, he had a great tan. I knew my eyes must have been popping out of my head, because Mother quickly commanded, "Jennifer, upstairs!"

"But I haven't finished my—"

"Upstairs, now!"

I grabbed my cinnamon roll and stole a fast peek.

"*Now!*"

I ran out of the kitchen and up two steps, straining to see him through the railing. I stuffed the roll into my mouth.

"Rhea, how *dare* you have a half-naked man in the kitchen. And on *Thanksgiving!*" Mother exclaimed.

"Well, now you know what *I'm thankful for!*" Bobchia quipped.

I choked. Caleb and Bobchia laughed. Mother was appalled. Through her laughter, Bobchia introduced them, "Clair, this is Caleb Martin. Caleb, this is my daughter-in-law, Clair."

"So *you're* Clair." He walked toward her, extending his hand. Mother looked away as she shook his hand. "Oh, sorry. I'll get a shirt on. I'll be right back."

"Your shirt is done!" Bobchia announced holding it up for him. He grabbed it and gave her a kiss on the cheek on his way back to the bathroom.

Mother glared at Bobchia. She smiled back. "What? *What?*"

Soon he came back in with his shirt tucked in, buttoning it. I took the rubber band out of my hair and combed it with my fingers. I hurried down the steps, then walked gracefully into the kitchen. I cleared my throat, getting his attention. I held out my hand. "Hi, I'm Jennifer."

"So you're the *one* I've heard so much about over the years." He shook my hand, smiling at Bobchia and then back to me.

"I *am* the one." I smiled.

"You're as pretty as your mom."

"Thank you." I blushed, blinking rapidly.

He laughed. Mother gave me a look that could kill a rhino!

He turned back toward Bobchia. "Thanks, Mom, for doing my shirt."

"*Mom?*" I asked.

"Well, Rhea is the *closest thing* I have to a mother. Mine left when I was only two—back when I was *really* cute!" (I was nodding my head, agreeing with every word the man said.) "But you can't *miss* what you've *never had.*" I took a bite of another cinnamon roll. "You'll lose your girlish figure if you eat too many of those," he teased.

"Oh, yeah? Well I saw a little flab around *your middle!*"

"Jennifer Rhea!" Mother said disgusted.

Caleb grabbed his stomach. "That's your grandmother's fault for feeding me so good and sending goodies with me when I'm on the road." He pointed to the side window. I eagerly looked out at the eighteen-wheeler that had a palomino horse painted on the side of it, leading a herd of horses with the name '**Trigger Trucking**' written across the image of a snow-covered mountain.

"Groovy!"

Bobchia came to the window. "It looks like Trigger could run right off the side of that truck, doesn't it?"

"Cool" I nodded. "I saw the barns you painted at the Turkey Farm and the article in *Look Magazine*. May I please have your autograph? *Pretty please?*" I asked blinking.

He laughed. "My fifteen minutes of fame."

A terrible commotion of screaming and laughing erupted on the stairs.

"Have mercy! People are *trying to sleep!*"

The boys ran into the kitchen.

"*I stepped in poop! I stepped in poop!*" Andrew screamed at the top of his lungs, running around the kitchen. Logan was laughing so hard he was crying and holding his stomach. We were all laughing except for Mother.

"Stop, *stop*, Andrew!" She yelled.

Caleb grabbed Andrew as he ran past him and held Andrew's foot out hurrying him into the bathroom.

"I have *poop* on my foot, man!" Andrew told him.

"So I see…"

Mother hurried in as Caleb stuck Andrew's foot into the sink, running water over it. Logan and I stood in the doorway laughing. Caleb put soap on it saying; "PU! That is just a shame!"

"What?" Andrew asked.

"If this won't wash off, we'll just have to *cut your foot off!*"

Andrew screamed.

"For crying out loud, Andrew, he's only *kidding!*" Mother said, trying to calm him down.

"*I am?*" Caleb smiled.

"*Yes, you are!*" Mother glared at him.

"Can Minnie sleep with me again tonight?" Andrew asked.

"Not after *this,*" Mother said.

He screamed again!

"What's a *Minnie?*" Caleb asked.

Mother quieted Andrew down, and he confessed that he had woken up first and seen Minnie's poop on *his side* of the rug so he turned the rug around so Logan would step in it, but Logan had seen it and turned the rug back around so Andrew would step in it!

"What's a *Minnie?*" Caleb persisted.

I looked back at Bobchia kissing Minnie and whispering to her, "I don't believe a word of those nasty things that Andrew is saying about you! My little sweetheart would never have a *bowel movement* on the boys' rug!"

"*What is a Minnie?*"

"*Rhea's dog!*" Mother said, annoyed.

"Oh, I should *have known,*" he said as he held Andrew up so Mother could dry his foot off, then he set him down.

"I appreciate you washing his foot."

"My pleasure, ma'am. After you." He held his hand out for her to go through the doorway.

Immediately Andrew kicked Logan.

"Ouch!" Logan punched Andrew.

"Ugh!" Andrew jumped on him.

Caleb broke up the fight. "Young man, if you want your mother to *even* consider letting Minnie sleep with you again, I'd suggest you and your brother start *cleaning* your room and those stairs, *pronto!*"

Mother crossed her arms. "I will *tell* my children what to do, thank you very much!"

"You have to strike while the iron is *hot!*"

"You've been listening to *Rhea* too much!"

"What's wrong with that?"

Mother gave him 'the look.' Bobchia giggled and handed the boys some rags she had sprayed with rose cleaner and a couple of bags. "Bring these back when you're done and put them in the garbage can. You both better talk to the Man Upstairs while you're up there!"

"Before I even *eat?*" Andrew pouted.

"Do *I* have to clean poop?" Logan asked. "I didn't even *spread* the stuff!"

"Well you turned the rug around so *I'd* step in it!" Andrew challenged.

"Well, you turned it *first!*"

Caleb looked through his brows. "*Just go do it!*"

They punched each other as they went up the steps.

"Hey!"

"Ouch!"

"Ouch!"

Caleb took Minnie from Bobchia's lap and held her up. "So you're what all the fuss is about! Are you sure this is a dog? She looks more like a *gerbil* to me! How can anything so *cute* do something that smells so *bad?*" Minnie licked his nose. "*I'm in love.*" Then she growled and tried to bite him. "Ouuu...*I knew a girl like you once!*"

Bobchia snorted. Caleb held the pup at arm's length, so she would take her.

"How do *you* know so much about raising children?" Mother asked, staring daggers at him.

"*A child feels secure in their accomplishments.*" Caleb said matter-of-factly.

"Oh, they *do?*"

"That's what Rhea told me."

"But how would *you* know? Do you even *have* a child?" Mother asked.

"Darcy's around here some place, probably in the barn with Dollee Doll. She loves that horse." That made my ears perk up.

Just then, Izora and Venal came in. *"There's my two girls!"* They squealed like schoolgirls. He went to hug Izora, but Venal bumped her out of the way with her hip, hugging him instead.

"You two didn't get *married* since I last saw you, did you?" Caleb asked.

*"Only in my dreams!"* Izora said embracing him.

Venal yelled, "What did he say? What did he *say*, Izora?" She asked, turning up the volume on her piercing hearing aid. Minnie howled.

"Mercy! Turn that thing *down* this minute!" Bobchia yelled in Venal's ear.

"Sorry!"

The boys brought down the paper bags and headed for the potbelly.

"Hold 'er there Newt!" Bobchia put out a hand.

Andrew looked at the bag. "But they're paper!"

"Are you trying to *spoil* the aroma of those turkeys?" Bobchia asked with her hands on her hips. Minnie strained to sniff the bags. Caleb laughed.

"Look, Bobchia, they look like *smashed tootsie rolls,* honest! Look if you don't believe me!" Andrew held open a bag.

*"Only they stink!"* Logan added, holding his nose.

"Mercy!" Bobchia rolled her eyes.

Caleb laughed louder and got a bag from under the sink. "Drop them in here, and I'll take them to the garbage can." He did it quickly and came back rubbing his arms. "Burrrr. Innkeeper, I need another cup of coffee."

"Right away!" Bobchia walked to the coffeepot.

The boys sat down stuffing cinnamon rolls into their mouths.

*"Did you even wash your hands?"* Bobchia asked.

They looked at each other, gagged and ran to the sink, and spit them out. Embarrassed, Mother escorted them into the bathroom. Caleb smiled when they walked pass him.

"You two *know better* than that!" Mother said, disgusted. When they came out, they ran grabbing cinnamon rolls before they even sat down, stuffing them into their mouths.

"Mercy, you didn't even *give thanks!*"

"Thanks, Bobchia!" Logan's voice was muffled.

"Yeah, thanks. These things are good!"

Caleb laughed looking at Mother, humiliated.

Bobchia warned, "Now don't get too stuffed. I have two twenty-five pounders in the ovens!"

Caleb peered into the ovens. "Ummm smells good. I can't wait!"

Mother didn't take her eyes off of Caleb, but neither did *anyone else.*

Darcy came into the kitchen carrying Pumpkin. Bobchia threw her arms around her, burying the petite girl's head into her bosom. Pumpkin 'hissed,' being pushed into a growling Minnie.

Bobchia took Darcy's coat and motioned for her to sit at the table. "That cat is a *Houdini,* always getting out!" Bobchia said laughing.

Darcy was pretty and looked to be around my age. Caleb introduced her, "This is Darcy." I said hello. She nodded.

"Hey, that's *my kitty,* not hers!" Andrew said to Bobchia.

"Sorry, Andrew," Bobchia said. "Remember, I told you that you could have Pumpkin *if* you fed and watered her. When was the last time you played with her?"

"I did feed her!"

"All I know is that several times I fed her and I know Jen has fed her and changed her litter."

*"I got busy."*

"How would you like it if I was too busy to feed you?"

"I wouldn't care!" He said stubbornly. Bobchia took his cinnamon roll from him. "Hey! I'm hungry!"

She gave it back to him. "Now you know how Pumpkin feels when you *don't feed her."*

"From my point of view, I'd call that a broken promise!" Mother said, hugging him.

"From the kitten's point of view, I'd call that *common sense!"* Bobchia said matter-of-factly. "When you get more responsible, you can have a pet. Do you understand?"

"I guess," he said sadly.

Darcy smiled at me as she played with the kitten on her lap. I realized she was deaf as she 'signed' words to Caleb. They had a conversation. Caleb told her who we were. Mother told the boys that Darcy could not hear. Logan asked Caleb what they were doing, and he said they were 'signing,' then told us what they were saying.

He looked at me. "Darcy knows you're Jennifer, because Rhea has shown her pictures and told her of you. She wants to know how long you're going to be here."

"*Forever!*" was my immediate response, prompting 'the look' from Mother.

Caleb signed my answer to Darcy. Caleb told us, "Darcy is taken with Pumpkin, because she can *feel* her purring."

Bobchia smiled. "Tell her if she sees Ardelle or Wanda, she's going to have to hide that cat in a hurry!"

The boys tried their hand at 'signing.' Bobchia got a kick out of it, but Mother put a stop to it.

Darcy 'signed' to Caleb again, but he didn't translate.

Andrew looked puzzled. "What's she saying now?"

"She's talking about you," Caleb said.

"About *me*? What did she just say?"

"She wondered why you eat with your mouth open."

Andrew stuck his tongue out at her with food on it. Bobchia got a kick out of that too, snorting as she set a pan of cinnamon rolls in front of Darcy. Mother threatened to send him to talk to the Man Upstairs again if he didn't straighten up. Darcy just shook her head.

Then Darcy signed again, as Caleb translated, "TYG for this food and for my wonderful Father and for Grandma Rhea, for kitty, for all my blessings and for this Thanksgiving. Through Christ, Amen."

Andrew looked at her. "Did God *hear* what she just said?"

Mother shook her head at him. "Of course He did!" Caleb smiled at Mother as she explained. "*He knows and hears everything,* you know that!"

Andrew kept staring at Pumpkin and Darcy. She handed the kitten to him then signed to Caleb. Andrew looked over at Bobchia who was stirring oatmeal, knowing she wouldn't let him keep her. Caleb said that Darcy didn't want to take Pumpkin if he would take care of her, that she would just love her and play with her while she was here. Andrew smiled and nodded to her.

The boys were ready for another snow experience, running to the window to check the thermometer.

"Wow! Where did the truck come from?" Andrew said.

"It's my rig," Caleb told them.

"Wow! I like those kinds of trucks!" Logan said.

"Look at that horse! Why is there RR on its rump?" Andrew asked.

Caleb explained, "That's the RR brand. It stands for *Roy Rogers, the king of the cowboys!* Do you know who he is?"

"Does he know Hoss?" Andrew asked.

Caleb chuckled. "Well, he might."

"Will you take us for a ride?" Logan asked.

"Sometime."

"Wow!" Andrew said.

"How about right *now?*" Logan grinned.

"I don't chew my cabbage twice—how about *sometime?*" Caleb grinned back.

Bobchia set bowls of oatmeal on the table. "Come and get it!"

The boys refused to eat.

Andrew pointed outside. "Bobchia, it's snowing! We have to hurry!"

"That snow won't melt until Easter, and you'll be *sick of it by then!*" She said.

"I'll *never* be sick of snow!" Logan said.

"*Never!*" Andrew confirmed. "I want to be a Mountie when I grow up!"

"Me too!"

Smiling at the boys' innocence, Bobchia said, "A Mountie, huh?"

"Yeah." Logan nodded.

"Well, let me tell you a *tall* story," she said. Caleb chuckled as he poured himself another cup of coffee. Bobchia launched in, "Let's see. Once there was a Mountie staying here." The boys' eyes grew big. "He was looking for a *real mean man* that he'd tracked from the north country." Their eyes grew wider. "His name was..." She looked at Andrew's hair. "Red, *Red the Mountie.* He was a big, handsome guy with red-blond hair, just like you have, and he wore a red uniform and rode on a big black horse that had a red saddle and bridle."

"*Wow!*" They said in unison.

"He stayed here a couple of days, and I asked him, I said 'Red, what makes you so big and strong?' He said, 'I take a vitamin every day." She handed them their vitamins, they choked them down. "I drink lots of *orange juice.*" They chugged all their juice. "And I eat all my *oatmeal* with honey on it."

"Honey?" They asked.

Bobchia put her hands on her hips. "Well, at least try it!"

They cleaned their bowls. Logan licked his lips. "Those Mounties know what's good to eat, don't they, Bobchia?"

"They sure do, *my little Mounties!*" She hugged them, trying to sneak kisses on their heads, but they quickly wiped their hair. "Now go upstairs and get your heaviest clothes on and I'll try to round up some heavier jackets and boots from some seaport." She took their jackets down from the line over the potbelly.

Caleb smiled at Mother, standing with her mouth open as she tried to figure out how Bobchia always seemed to get the boys to do *exactly* what she wanted them to do.

Mother helped Andrew pull on Logan's barn boots over three pairs of socks, for warmth, leaving Logan without boots. Mrs. Dunham lent him hers. They were short and black and had fake fur around the top. He called them 'sissy boots' until Bobchia told him that all the Mounties wore boots with fur on top, then they were perfect. Bobchia stuck some rags in the toes so they would fit. Tall Cliff gave the boys a couple of his wool sweaters that I'd accidentally thrown in the dryer, (on a rainy day), to wear under their flimsy jackets.

Bobchia and Caleb laughed. "Mercy, Sweetie, why on earth would you put *wool* sweaters in a dryer?"

"Well, I don't know," I said embarrassed. "We don't have wool sweaters *in Florida,* chee!"

The sweaters fit the boys' bodies, but the sleeves hung to their feet. They ran around the kitchen hitting each other with them until Bobchia cut the arms off and duct taped them.

Caleb looked at the boys' thin jackets. "Looks like you boys could use a couple of snowsuits!" Bobchia shook her head at him, as Mother gave him 'the look.' He quickly stuffed a cinnamon roll in his mouth muffling, "Sorry!"

Bobchia tied bright green and red babushkas around the boys' necks. After they struggled to manipulate several pairs of big gloves, she pulled heavy, gray socks over their hands securing them with rubber bands around their elbows.

Andrew held up his arms. "Socks ain't gloves!"

"They *fit* like a glove, don't they? That's it Fort Pitt!" Bobchia plunked a couple of grampie's orange hunting hats on their heads. What a sight!

"Ha! You don't look like no Mountie!" Andrew told Logan.

"So? You don't look like Sergeant Preston either!" Logan sassed back.

"Can we take Nikki out and pretend she's Yukon King?" Andrew asked.

"No! Where's my camera? Don't you *dare* leave this kitchen until I find my camera!" The boys stood with their arms around each other, smiling toothy grins.

"Pop," went the camera. Another fridge picture!

With spots before their eyes, they ran as fast as their bulky boots would let them to the mudroom and then out into the cold, slamming the screen door behind them.

Bobchia held Minnie up to the window, whispering the boys' every move, their heads moving from side to side following the boys racing around the yard. Caleb yelled at them to stay away from the truck more than once, reluctantly leaving the window when Spike recruited his help to put the heavy leaves in the dining room table. Bobchia giggled as the boys caught snowflakes on their tongues.

'Pop,' went the camera. The boys fell backward, making snow angels.

"Mercy!" Minnie whined. "It's okay, Miss Minnie. Look!" The boys pressed their noses to the window. "See, they're no worse for wear!" The boys waved at her then made snow angels while she cuddled Minnie.

'Pop,' went the camera. (I didn't realize it then, but this would be one of many fond memories of her. With everything she had yet to do, there she stood holding Minnie and doing the *mostest* important thing—enjoying her grandsons.)

"They are a handful!" Bobchia looked over her shoulder. "How Paul loved all of you."

"And you, Bobchia." I said back.

She got teary and put the pup in her pocket. She washed her hands and then pointed with her head for me to follow her to the dining room. There we found Caleb and Spike setting up card tables, talking of the afternoon's football game. Bobchia's eyes sparkled. "I wanted to surprise you, Sweetie. Grampie's cousins are coming down from Erie. They haven't seen you since you were a little girl. Do you remember Johnny?"

"No."

"It's their group picture that's on the side of the fridge. I'll show you when we go back to the kitchen." She opened a drawer to her china cupboard and proudly got out a pillowcase that held the most exquisite tablecloth I'd ever seen. "My Bobchia made it with love and gave it to me on my wedding day, and I'll give it to you on yours, but just in case I'm *in heaven* for that occasion, I wanted us to enjoy it together on this, your first holiday back." She smiled while unfolding it and whipping it into the air. The embroidered gold and brown tumbling leaves trimmed with flowing fringe brought the dark mahogany table to life.

"Oh, Bobchia!"

"*I know.*" She slowly smoothed the folds of the heirloom, enjoying the memories of decades past. "My Bobchia was the kindest lady I ever knew. The day she died, I sat on her feather bed, singing **Jesus Loves Me.** The angels came and carried her off to heaven with *me singing to her!* That's the way I want to go, Lord willing."

"Thank you, Bobchia."

"I haven't *given* it to you yet!"

"I didn't mean for the tablecloth."

Darcy and I got acquainted while drinking hot chocolate at the kitchen table. Bobchia gave her a tablet and a pen and told me that Darcy could read lips if I talked to her face to face. I didn't realize that I was talking so loudly to her until Bobchia said, "Sweetie, you're giving me a *headache!* She's deaf!"

I told Darcy I was sorry for *yelling.* She grinned. Bobchia laughed. She smiled and wrote, 'It's okay. I didn't hear you!' We laughed and chitchatted about Bobchia and school until we were asked to set the tables. Bobchia carefully handed us Grandmother Kay's dishes out of her hutch, telling how they were smuggled from Croatia on a boat in a *pine coffin.* I didn't ask any questions, hoping she wouldn't repeat the story around Mother. She gave us soft cloths to shine the silverware and the covered butter dishes. The green crystal dishes and glasses sparkled on the beautiful tablecloth, just as they had decades earlier.

Bobchia sent me to get a head count for the feast before getting out the everyday dishes for the card tables. I made the mistake of knocking on Mr. Pill's door first. After listening to his depressing speech of 'I have *nothing* to be thankful for, and I don't know why you do either! Half of your relatives are *dead*, aren't they? I don't even believe in God or holidays but at least I ain't no *hypocrite!*' I ran down the steps as fast as I could to tattle to Bobchia, hoping she would throw him out!

"Mercy! Where is the *mercy* in that?" She paused and smiled. "I should have warned you. It's nothing personal; he says the same thing every year, the old bat! I'll keep praying for him, and one of these days *he'll join us.*"

"I hope not! He's better off by himself!"

"How is he going to *learn* to love if we don't *show* him love? Love is patient and kind. Love is not jealous, boastful or proud or rude. It does not demand its own way. It is not irritable, and it keeps no record of being wronged."

"See, you said it yourself, love is not *irritable,* and he is *irritable!*"

"Your Thanksgiving Bible lesson is First Corinthians 13. Memorize it!"

"The *whole* chapter?"

"You know the words to all the Beatles records, *don't ya ya ya?* Although saying 'I want to hold your hand' *over* and *over* doesn't really count as *memorization* and yes, the *whole* chapter, then let it guide your life! Please don't ever think I got to be a *sweet* old lady on my own! It's only by the *grace* of God! Mr. Pill told me his family is all gone, and he blames God for everything bad in his life. We've all been there! *You've been there!* Now let's have a hug and please get me a head count!"

I walked up the stairs thinking, how did this happen? *He* is the one that is irritable yet, *I'm* the one that has to memorize a *whole chapter* of the Bible on *love!*

The Inn's head count was twenty-four. With Mary and Fritz, Helen's sister and brother-in-law and their kids and Bobchia's cousins and their kids, it brought the count up to nearly forty. As Darcy and I put orange and yellow tablecloths on the card tables, Bobchia handed me a picture of Grampie's cousins from Erie. "Here is our good-looking family! This is Johnny, Joyce, Fred,

Debbie, Sherri, Mike, Linda, Chucky, Frankie, Gail and Roger. The rest are husbands, wives and kids. Try to remember who they are. Mercy, I just thought of something. I hope they don't bring a batch of food here like they did last year."

The phone rang. Bobchia hurried to answer it, but Homer had quickly picked it up. When he saw her, he hung it up. Bobchia scolded him, "Go read the paper! It's yesterday's, but you won't remember it. Sweetie, sit by the phone. Hopefully whoever called will call back."

(Putting a teenager beside a phone is like putting Jackie Gleason in charge of the *candy store.*) I called Beverly Jean and then Dawnette, but as I started to dial Donna, Bobchia stuck her head out of the noisy kitchen. "Has anyone called?" She asked.

I hurried and hung up. The phone rang. It was a long distance call from Penny, Spike's daughter. They lived three hours away, as did Penny's twin sister Pam and her family. They didn't trust venturing out on the icy roads. Penny sent Spike and Carolyn their love and asked me to tell them she'd see them on Christmas.

I hung up, then Harold called and asked to speak with Bobchia. She talked for a few minutes and then hung up with a sad face. "His Metropolitan got stuck at the end of his driveway, and Wayne came over and pulled him out with his truck. Then he followed Wayne back in the hearse, *mercy,* to the farm so he could help him put chains on Jody's car and the other trucks. Jody talked him into staying for dinner, and the grandkids talked him into making snow forts afterward." She rubbed the groove in her forehead while walking down the hall. "He wants me to save him a piece of pumpkin pie."

The phone rang again, and I picked it up. It was Johnny wanting to talk to Aunt Ardelle. She hurried from the kitchen, wiping her hands on a towel. She conveyed the bad news to Bobchia. "They had a caravan of cars on their way to the Inn when Frankie's car slid sideways. He got turned around, but the roads are treacherous, so they went back to his place. They won't have turkey, but they're thawing out steaks and will eat the food they packed in the car to bring here. I told them we'd be up for New Year's Eve with bells on if the roads aren't bad!"

Bobchia's shoulders drooped. "Sweetie, if that phone rings again, don't you *dare* answer it! We hardly have anyone coming to dinner."

"For sure we have twenty-eight people!"

"What's twenty-eight people? I need at least thirty-five to put a *dent* in it! Come on, you and Darcy can clean some veggies and make some dip."

"Vegetables, with all that good stuff you made?"

"You're right! Your Mother would never touch them!"

The boys had been outside for a couple of hours when they got into a snowball fight over the fence with Lucy and Ricky. We watched from the windows in the great room. Mother and Bobchia cheered for the boys. (I secretly cheered for Lucy and Ricky.) Then Lanny came out and pulverized them! Mother begged the boys to come in and get in the tub but they refused and instead, got into a game of tag around the truck. Caleb, concerned, watched from the window.

I overheard Bobchia whisper to Caleb, "Watch this!" She took the towel off her shoulder and wiped the steam from the window. Then she knocked to get their attention and stuck her face to it, looking at them through her brows.

Caleb curiously looked at her and laughed. "Are you trying to *scare them to death* or what?" He went onto the porch laughing and yelled, "Get away from the truck, and get in the tub, *pronto!*" He held the door open. They ran in and gave Caleb high fives and then ran up the stairs. Mother and Bobchia looked at Caleb in amazement.

Mother brought the boys' wet clothes down and hung them over the potbelly.

"It's hot in here, but you'll need a bonfire to get those dry," Caleb said as he added wood to the flame, smiling at her.

"Thank you," she said.

"You are welcome, ma'am." He pretended to tip his hat. She smiled sweetly, noticing his dark eyes.

I went upstairs and got my hair dryer, curlers and clothes and took a shower downstairs in Joan of Arc's room. I looked in the mirror. I was disgusted at how tight my blouse and jeans were. (The cinnamon rolls and pies of the last weeks had finally caught up to me!) I set my hair, and while I was under the dryer, Darcy came in with her suitcase. I told her that it was *Bobchia's fault* that my clothes didn't fit. She got a paper and pencil and wrote that she always gains a few pounds whenever she stays here, but enjoys every moment of it!

When my hair was dry, I gathered my things and went upstairs to see if Mother had something that I could wear that was comfortable but wouldn't look *ancient*. As I looked through her dresser, I was surprised to see that she was fussing with her hair.

"What on earth are you looking for?" She asked.

"Something that is *loose!*"

"Me too! I think I have something." She pulled out a couple of sweaters.

"I've never seen those before! Aha, *new sweaters!*"

"No, no! Rhea lent them to me when I started night classes. You know how she carries on. 'You'll catch your death in those cotton blouses.' After today, I'll probably be wearing a *potato sack!*"

We knew we were about to eat the best dinner of our lives, so we promised each other we'd go on a diet tomorrow. Then Mother said, 'Don't forget the Leftovers!' That moved the first day of our diet to Saturday.

I held the sweaters up in the mirror. "This one isn't too bad, although yellow makes me look washed out, and the sunflowers are really ugly. I like the plain blue one better."

"*Age before beauty.* I'll take the blue one."

"Chee, okay. Who's going to see me anyway?" I took the curlers out of my hair and put it on.

I heard Ginger knock at Aunt Ardelle's door asking her to zip her dress. I had passed Aunt Ardelle on my way up the stairs, so I hurried to Ginger's aid. "Hi, Jennifer. Don't I look *pretty?*"

"*Ginger?* I hardly recognized you!" (Her cheeks were so rosy and her jewelry was so gaudy.) "Aunt Ardelle is already downstairs. Can I help?"

"If you don't mind, dear. What do you think about these finger waves? It took me all morning to get them in."

I smiled and looked at the big waves on the sides of her head, plastered down with hair glue. Tiny spit curls framed her face. "Groovy!"

"I'll get my braid out of your way."

"I've never seen your hair *down* before!" I stood on my tiptoes, struggling to zip the gangly woman's tight, red-satin, strapless, sequined evening dress that smelled of mothballs. The wires from her hearing aids hung down into the top of her dress, where they connected to square battery cases, making a pattern on each side at the top of her chest. "It must have *shrunk* in my closet!" She giggled.

"My clothes *shrunk* too!"

"It must be the washer. I had another dress that did the very same thing, but I chose this dress because I think a middle aged woman, such as myself, should look well-groomed coming *out of mourning*, especially on a *holiday.*"

"There you go, beautiful!"

She giggled and walked back into her room, reemerging with a black-fringed shawl that she flung around her neck, hitting me in the cheek. "Thanks honey! See ya in the *funny papers!*" She lifted her head and strutted down the steps.

I went laughing back to Mother.

"What is so funny?"

"Ginger is definitely *out of mourning!*"

"Why do you say that?"

"She's trying to look like she's twenty!"

Mother leaned forward into her mirror. "Aren't we all?" She threw her brush onto the dresser and pulled her hair behind her ears.

"I could ask *Mr. Hair* to come up and comb your hair for you."

"Jen, it's bad enough when the boys give *pet names* to people around here, but you're old enough to know better!"

"Chee, I was *only kidding!*" I fixed my hair as the boys came out of the bathroom laughing into the room.

"Come here for a minute," Mother said to them. "Did you brush your teeth?"

"Why do we got to do that when we're gonna eat and get them dirty again?" Logan asked.

"Because it is the civilized thing to do!"

"Why?"

"So your breath smells good when you're talking with some-one."

They turned and panted on each other.

"Atrocious!" Andrew gagged.

"Puke city!" Logan stepped backward.

They ran to brush their teeth and then ran back in. After smelling their breath, Mother gave them a crash course on table manners. Finally, the boys were ready to *meet their public.*

They walked a step in front of us going down the stairs. Mother tried to get Andrew's cowlick down with a little spit. He loudly protested.

"Hush, people will *hear* you!" She said.

Logan dodged her hand as she tried to do the same thing to his head, almost falling down the stairs. I laughed.

"I'm *thankful* that I only have *one* big dumb sister instead of *two* big dumb sisters!" Logan reached behind him trying to hit my knees with his fist. I looked sweetly at Mother.

"Jennifer, *don't you dare kick him, and I mean it!*"

Fans blew from each end of the kitchen, sending the aroma of the feast throughout the Inn. We walked through the archway of the hot, chaotic kitchen as Bobchia poured gravy into the china gravy boats. Aunt Ardelle, Helen, Izora, Venal and Gladys were busy lifting the potatoes, corn, green beans, squash, sweet potatoes and all the Croatian dishes (that I can't pronounce, let alone spell), while Wanda, Darcy and Spike were carrying salads, breads and pies from the cold room, lining them up on the counter. Caleb was busy carving the turkeys, piling the meat high on the platters.

Logan elbowed Andrew. "*We hit the mother lode!*"

Mr. T-t-t-tunes reclined on a window seat with one leg lazily swinging over the side. The fans blew his unbuttoned shirt along with his chest hair as he sang slow and deep to the tune of **Summertime:** "Thanksgiving time, prep-a-ra-tion ain't ea-sy. The cooks are jumpin', don't ya know, don't ya know, as I'm waiting to diiiiiine. Hot pumpkin pie and the stuffing is steam-y, so hush growling stomach, you'll eat on tiiiime!" The boys clapped. He stood and bowed.

Andrew looked at Mr. T-t-t-tunes chest. "Look Logan—he must eat a *lot* of turkey!"

"Quit singing and grab some of these bowls, and mercy, button that shirt or the Board of Health will *shut me down!*" Bobchia ordered.

He buttoned his shirt and helped carry the food into the dining room. Bobchia looked annoyed at Ginger.

Caleb spotted her. "Grandma?" She beamed as he struggled to get a turkey platter on the table, hurrying to hug her.

"*Buddy,* I had no idea you would be here in this snow storm! I've missed you!"

"I've missed you too! I didn't think I'd see you until Christmas, Grandma. Sorry about Step-Grandpa."

"He didn't linger, dear. His got up and go just got up and *went!* Buddy, I wore this dress for you!"

"You look absolutely beautiful, Grandma!"

Darcy ran over to her and gave her a hug.

"Darcy, I can't get over how much you look like your mother!" Ginger said. Darcy shook her head, Caleb smiled.

"Are you sure you're all right, Grandma?" He asked. "I mean, since the rescue of you and Grandpa Gilligan and everything that happened?"

Fit as a fiddle, Buddy boy, and ready for *love!*" He gave her another hug.

"Mercy!" Bobchia said under her breath.

Mr. Hair quickly came in and sat beside Mother until he noticed Ginger's long braid hanging over the back of her chair then he quickly moved to the seat beside her. Caleb almost sat on him! Everybody looked at Mother as if she would protest his move. She blushed.

Bobchia leaned across the table. "*You've lost your beau!*" Mother gave her 'the look.' Caleb sat across from Ginger and asked, "How's your arthritis, Grandma?"

"Old Art is just like every other man, *he won't leave me alone either!*" She giggled into her hand, while looking at Mr. Hair.

Bobchia noticed me wearing her sweater. "Hey, I like your sweater! Smile!"

'Pop,' went the camera. I took a deep breath as the spots circled my head. Bobchia turned her attention to the boys.

"My, don't you two look handsome today!" She moved the giant bottle of ketchup that was in front of their plates.

"Caleb said that turkey had *four* legs! Can we eat all of 'em?" Logan asked.

Bobchia laughed. 'Pop,' went her camera. The boys blinked several times at her.

"Mother *hockered* on my head earlier!" Andrew reported.

"Andrew!" Mother scorned.

"Well *you did!*

"She tried to *hocker me too,* but I wouldn't let her!" Logan showed us how he'd dodged out of the way. We all laughed at Mother's expense.

Darcy pleaded with Caleb to let her know why everyone was laughing. He 'signed' fast and furious, while Darcy shook her head with her hand over her mouth.

Bobchia waited for a quiet moment. "Okay, I am getting *older,* and the food is getting *colder!*"

Caleb took the hint, 'signing' to Darcy to stand with him and say grace, he translated. "Thank you Lord for the abundance of food at this table, and bless the hands that prepared it as we pray for the less fortunate. Thank you God for the Pilgrims who founded our great Christian Nation and for our daily blessings and for my family and my adopted grandmother." Caleb hesitated and then said, "And help those boys to listen to their mother! Through Christ, our Lord, Amen."

We all said amen, but Bobchia said it the loudest.

We ate and ate and then we had pie.

Finally we all sat there staring at all the leftover food. Well, everyone except for Mr. Hair, who stared at Ginger's braid.

"It took two whole days to make all this food, and fifteen minutes and forty eight seconds to eat it!" Spike said, looking at his stopwatch.

"It was just delicious!" Caleb said with everyone agreeing.

The boys were eager for another snow experience, but their clothes were still hanging wet over the potbelly. So instead they made do and followed Caleb into the great room, jumping on the couches and talking during the football game. Several times they made mad dashes through the crowd of women that were helping in the kitchen, to check the status of their clothes. Then they'd run back to jump on the couches and cheer some more coins into the cushions.

Disgusted, Caleb brought the boys to Mother. "I'm sure those clothes are dry by *now!*"

"Caleb, *touchdown!*" Spike yelled from the great room. Caleb ran out.

The boys tugged their clothes off the line.

"They're dry and hot!" Logan beamed.

Mother and Bobchia struggled to get the warm clothes back on the boys, lecturing them to quit pounding on the long, heavy icicles hanging from the corners of the Inn. They promised Bobchia they would quit *if* she promised to call them in when Charlie Brown came on.

"You'll be ready for bed by the time he is on," she said.

"Can't we stay out until then?" Andrew asked.

"*You'll* be an icicle by then!"

They hugged the boys, then out the door they ran.

"I should have had Cliff knock those things down, but I didn't think of it."

Mother and Bobchia stood watching at the corner windows until they saw the boys safely making a snowman, then they resumed their place in the assembly line of women that wound from the dining room into the kitchen, passing the plates, the bowls and the stories of Thanksgivings past.

I hollered from the kitchen. "Bobchia, we're running out of containers!"

She hurried in. "Mercy, why is it *still* so hot in here?" She checked the ovens. "I must be having a hot flash!" She opened the refrigerator and talked into it. "I need to have my head examined for fixing all this food for only *twenty-eight* people! Phew, feel better now!" She searched every cupboard for containers.

"I love leftovers, Bobchia!" I told her.

"It's a good thing, Sweetie! You'll probably be eating this stuff for a *week!*"

"Well at least *I'm* thankful!"

Bobchia looked to the ceiling and hugged me. "Oh Sweetie, erase. Me too!"

From a side window we watched the boys slide down a knoll and into the burned out basement of the funeral home on a piece of cardboard. Spike hurried outside to warn them they could get hurt, but as soon as he came back inside, they slid back in.

It took a while to scrub all those pots and pans and get the kitchen back in order. When it was done, the women gathered around the dining room table for a *conflab*. Bobchia sat down and asked me to take Minnie out because *her dogs* were barking. I braved the elements setting her on the sidewalk. "Hurry up, Miss Minnie. I'm freezing!" She stood there watching me shake. Finally I just picked her up and came back in and handed her back to Bobchia. She promptly put her in her apron to warm up.

"I wish I could fit in there!" I said. "By the way, she didn't go."

"Did you sing to her?"

"*Sing to her?*"

"Old Shep."

"You mean the song where the dog dies?"

"Well, I don't sing *that part!*"

I whispered, "Well, nobody had to *sing* to her this morning while she was leaving *tootsie rolls* on the boys' rug!"

"Mercy, Jen!" She peered in at Minnie, shook her head and then patted the chair next to her for me to sit.

My ears were still ringing from the *last conflab* we'd had two weeks ago Sunday. I could easily point out which woman had the grief of gallbladder, the suffering of sciatica, the hysteria of hysterectomy and the agony of da feet! (Bobchia) I limply sat down. Mother giggled, giving me a wink then rushed out of the room. We heard her scream on the stairway when she bumped into Lucky's cage, nearly knocking down Aunt Ardelle and Wanda as they were bringing Lucky downstairs. She raced up the stairs and slammed the bedroom door!

"My land! *What on earth is the matter with that woman?*" Aunt Ardelle asked as she picked up Lucky's knitted turkey blanket from the steps and shook it off. They hurried to the dining room. "My oh my! She certainly is a *different* kind of a person, isn't she? Nothing like you, Jennifer. Nothing like you at *all!*"

"Thank you!" I giggled.

Bobchia laughed.

Lucky chirped. "He *heard* you Jennifer! Do you want to hold the cage?"

"Thanks anyway," I replied. Lucky tweeted again.

"Every time he hears *your voice,* he talks!" Wanda said smiling.

The conflab had officially started with the placing of Lucky on the bookshelf. It was déjà vu. Anyone stopping to take a breath *automatically forfeited* her place in the conversation. I spied a Christmas S&H Green Stamp catalog and leafed through it, bored and half-listening to the women's various infirmities...verbatim. Finally, after two pots of coffee, a cookie sheet of peanut butter fudge and one and a half pumpkin rolls, the conflab was officially over. (I could feel my stomach creating stretch marks!)

I needed to walk off my dinner. I thought, *If only I could find someone to walk with me who was willing to leave the comfort of the Inn.* I shuffled down the hall, fed the cats while Darcy slept, and walked to the great room. It was pointless to ask Mother to go for a walk because it was too close to midterms. Glancing around the great room, I realized it was pointless to ask the lethargic crowd.

Bobchia limped down the stairs. "I just put a battery in one of those little flashlights from the bingo box and it worked, so I put it in the green lantern. *Voilà!* Now I won't have a candle to worry about up there. Remember, the green dome will lead you home! Boy, are my dogs ever barking now!"

"I guess that means you won't want to go for a walk with me."

"*A walk? Mercy!* Harold should be here any minute. Besides I have to get my *spiritual* food while I can still see straight. Caleb arrived before the sun, and I didn't have my devotions this morning." We walked to the kitchen where she cut Harold a big piece of pumpkin pie. "Want one?"

"Do I look *hungry?* My clothes don't fit, and I'm wearing *your* sweater!"

"It's never looked better." She giggled and thumbed through her Bible. "Maybe Darcy will go with you."

"She's napping with the cats."

"Well, can't you wait until tomorrow? It's not likely we'll have a *thaw* tonight. You should really wait until someone can go with you." She took a dish from the refrigerator and set it on the floor. "Nikki old girl, do I ever have a treat for you!" She petted Nikki as she ate. Minnie stuck her head out of the apron and whined. "If you ate that, Miss Minnie, you'd be *pushing up daisies!*"

My stomach hurt as I petted Nikki. "I think I'll go for a little walk by myself. I'll be fine."

"Well, if you must, stay on the sidewalks and under the streetlights. If anyone grabs you, yell *FIRE!*"

"Fire?"

"Yes, people always look when someone yells fire!"

"Chee, I'm just going for a little walk. Besides the green dome will lead me home!"

"That's right! Here's my coat and my babushka. My boots are by the door." She left and came back with two pairs of heavy gray socks.

"I am not putting those on my *hands!*"

"They are to keep your little pigs warm." I put them on. "There's also a hat in the pocket. Use it!"

"Chee." I took a carrot out of the fridge for Dollee and petted Nikki, with her head in Ginger's beef and noodle casserole. "Bobchia!"

"I know, I know, she's had enough *suffering* in her lifetime!" She laughed looking at the expression on my face. "Waste not, want not! That's the motto around here. Besides, somebody had to *eat it!* I just hope it don't push the old girl into an early grave!" She laughed until she saw the babushka lying on the bench. "Sweetie, come over here!" I sighed and slowly walked over. "Put your head down. I thought my days of doing this were *over*. There."

"Chee."

"Don't *chee* me! You're not in Florida anymore. Besides I read that a person loses eighty percent of their body heat out the top of their head. You'll catch your death if you don't keep your head covered! Now remember, yell *fire!* I love you awful!"

"I love you awful back."

A 'Be careful!' followed me out the door.

I took a few steps and looked back. She waved and then left the window. I took off the babushka and stuffed it into my pocket. It felt good to be out of the heat of the Inn; the cold air revived me. I walked with my head up catching snowflakes on my tongue until I bumped into the fence. Leaning over, I looked into the deep hole where Bobchia's prized bush once stood. "I'm sorry!" A gust of wind blew my hair and made me shiver. I put the hat on and ran to the barn. I could hear Caleb and Spike discussing the game as they made sure Dollee and the other animals that had wandered into Bobchia's life had food and bedding on this cold night.

Kittens scampered to greet me when I entered.

"That quarter back couldn't throw if his life depended on it!" Caleb said. He looked up from brushing Dollee. "Cool hat!"

I quickly pulled it off and looked at it. It was brown and gold and had a rocket on it with the words **Titusville Rockets 1938** embroidered across it. I stuck it into my pocket. "What brings you out on a cold night like this?" Spike asked.

"I thought I'd take a little walk. Anyone care to join me?"

"On a night like *this?*" Caleb shook his head.

"*Are you kidding?*" Spike asked.

"Darcy might, she likes the snow." Caleb said.

"She's napping."

"Turkey always makes her sleepy. Why aren't you napping?"

"I think it will be fun to take a walk." I said sheepishly.

"You could shovel while you walk. That would sure take the *fun* out of it!" Spike said, with a lip full of tobacco, laughing.

I ignored Spike and petted Dollee. I gave her the treat and a big hug. "I miss riding you around the barrels, Dollee Doll." Cutie Boy made his dramatic entrance, jumping from the rafter into Dollee's stall with his back up, hissing. "Don't worry! I won't hurt Dollee." I picked him up and petted him.

Caleb asked, "Does your grandmother know you're going for *a walk by yourself?* Did she tell you to yell 'fire?' She told Darcy the same thing, so she *signed* fire! *It was so funny!*" Spike spit into a can laughing. I laughed then waved goodbye.

Dusk was quickly turning into night. The moon peeked around snow clouds, illuminating the lane and the majestic pines bordering the Inn. I looked upward. "The green dome will guide me home! Groovy!" Geese honked overhead in perfect formation against the bright moon. "Cool!" Then all was quiet. I was appreciating the beauty of the snow when I heard my brothers fighting in the burned out basement.

"This was too a *station house!*" Logan said.

"Was not!"

"Was too!"

"Was not!"

I stood there for a moment wondering how different my life would be if they stayed in there forever. A charred oak with snowy branches hung directly over them. I snuck behind it and kicked it with all my might!

"Look! It's snowing wercer in here then out there!" Andrew pointed.

"Yeah!"

Covering my mouth I ran down the lane, past the empty windowsill and through the covered bridge, stopping on the other side to catch my breath. "I need to get in shape!" The fishing path beside the bridge was framed with low icy branches and would have been entirely concealed under the thick blanket of snow if not for several deer tracks leading down to the babbling stream. "TYG, it's beautiful!"

Everywhere I looked was breathtaking. The further I walked, the more I enjoyed the scenery, the solitude. The snow under the streetlights looked like great mounds of sparkling diamond dust. I paused at Murphy's store window where mannequins depicted the first Thanksgiving. Then I walked on, aimlessly. The snow clouds opened, making it harder to see. I put on Bobchia's hat and stuck my hands deeper into the barn coat pockets. A pickup truck went by with two men standing on the back scattering shovelfuls of cinders onto the road. Laughter came from children stacking a snowman inside the gazebo in the park. I walked across the street, curiously looking through the fence of the public pool, seeing snow where water should have been. The wind picked up. I shivered and gladly put the ugly babushka over the hat and turned for the heat of the Inn when I heard the faint sound of a radio and laughter. *Why would anyone be playing a radio in this blizzard?*

My curiosity got the best of me. I proceeded up the steep hill. All of a sudden a toboggan cleared the top of the hill and was aimed straight for me! I screamed and jumped back, but it rammed into my arm and knocked me backward into a telephone pole, lodging my foot between the pole and a rock! The toboggan slid sideways and came to rest at the bottom of the hill. Everyone laughed!

"Groovy ride!"

"The grooviest!"

"We knocked someone down!"

"We *did?*"

"Well, I thought I saw someone."

"We did! *That old lady up there!*" A guy ran up the hill, extending his hand. "Are you *alright,* ma'am?"

"My foot is caught, and it hurts," I told him.

He dug at the snow and moved the rock. "Can you walk?"

"I think I can." I put my weight on it, and he caught me as I teetered. "It really hurts!"

"I live over there," he said, scooping me up and carrying me to his porch. He set me on a covered wicker chair. "I'm sorry we ran into you, ma'am. I thought everyone in town knew about this street." He looked familiar in the faint light. He couldn't possibly be, but *he was!* The basketball player that *caught my eye* at the last game I'd covered for *The Rocket Recorder!* He was looking at *me!*

"I'm sorry, what did you say?"

"Didn't you know about the street?"

"*What about it?*"

"It's *Hotdog Hill!* Didn't you see it blocked at the bottom?"

"I guess I…didn't notice it."

A girl yelled, "Hey, Andy, we're going *again. Come on!*"

"Go without me," he hollered back.

She came running over wearing high-heeled leather boots, a long fur coat and matching hat and granny glasses. I recognized her as one of the snobs at school. He must be her boyfriend. "Andy, *let's go!*" She pulled on his arm. "Who is the *old lady?*"

When he turned to talk with her, I ripped off the babushka and hat, stuffed them into my coat pocket, and combed my hair with my fingers.

"She might *here* you!"

"I doubt it." She pouted.

"She hurt her foot. I can't just *leave her here!*"

"*Why not?*" She screamed and stomped back to her friends.

I tried to stand and caught myself on his shoulder just as a porch light came on and the door opened. Andy looked at me and blinked. "I'm really *not* an old lady!" I laughed.

"*I see that!*" He chuckled.

"What's going on out here?" A man questioned.

"Dad, we ran into her arm with the toboggan, and her foot got hurt!"

"Oh no!" He said. "Bring her in here and let's check the damage. I don't want a *lawsuit!*" Andy helped me through the door and onto a bench.

"*Why were you out on a night like this in the first place, young lady?*" He asked gruffly.

"I just wanted to take a walk in the snow, *that's all.*"

"On a night like *this?*"

"I was minding my own business when I got *hit by a toboggan!*" I said defending myself and rubbing my arm.

"Take your coat off and let's get a look-see." The man tugged at the old barn coat. When he saw the yellow flowered sweater he proudly said, "Andy, I bought your grandmother a sweater just like this for Christmas. What do you think?" He hesitated. (I could have died on the spot!)

"Well, I think *she* will like it," Andy said. "The flowers are kind of big, but yeah, I think she will."

"Pull up your sleeve young lady, and we'll take a look-see." I flinched as he moved my arm back and forth. "Well, I think you're going to have quite a bruise, but I don't think anything is broken there. Which foot is it?" (I was embarrassed in those old barn boots.)

"Dad's a doctor," Andy explained.

"If I could just use your telephone to call my Mother, she will come and get me," I said.

The girl stuck her head in the door. "Andy, *come on!*"

"Marcy, go *without me!*" Andy yelled.

"*I don't want to!* Please, pretty pleeease." Andy walked over and talked with her. She slammed the door.

"May I please use your telephone? I'll be out of here in no time." I begged.

The doctor pulled off my boot and the two heavy pairs of gray socks.

Andy looked with his eyebrows up. "*Cold feet?*"

His Father intently looked at my foot and gently moved it.

"OW! *Please* give me the telephone."

"It's already starting to swell. You probably just sprained it, but we should go to the hospital to make sure. I don't want to be *sued.*"

"Please, I just want to go home. My Mother is studying to be a *nurse!*"

"Well, that doesn't mean—"

"Bobchia will know what to do."

"Who?"

"My grandmother."

"Oh, well, if you are sure."

"*I am.*"

"Where do you live?"

"The Red Barn Inn."

"Oh. I know Rhea."

"You do?"

"Yes, she called me once years ago to help her deliver a breech calf. I believe…she talked of a son who was a doctor? She was sure *proud* of that boy!"

"That was my Father."

"Are you here for the holidays?"

"No, we moved here because Father died."

"Oh, I'm sorry to hear that. Andy, take her over there." Andy nodded. "Make sure you apologize, and if you need to see a specialist, young lady, I'll see to it. I don't want a *lawsuit.*"

"There isn't going to be a *lawsuit. I just want to go home,* I'll be fine." I put one sock on slowly and then tried to get my swollen foot into the boot, but it was impossible!

"Tell Rhea to put some ice on that, and stay off of it as much as possible. And *no stairs!* I know that place has a lot of stairs in it," the doctor said.

Andy smiled at me. "Put your hand on my shoulder. Go ahead." I did and instantly got a funny feeling in my stomach when he lifted me. Even though I was in excruciating pain, I wished he would carry me the whole way to the Inn!

"If you need anything, anything at all, young lady, call me. I'm in the book. Andy Williams is my name."

"Not the *singer!*" Andy said laughingly as he carried me through the doorway and to his truck. "If you could just open the truck door..." I reached over and opened it. I felt light-headed when he set me on the seat. "I can put the seat back further."

"It's fine."

He started to walk around the back of the truck when Marcy ran over. "Where are *you* going?"

"I'm taking her home."

"The *old lady?*" She asked.

"She's not so *old.*"

Marcy looked in my window. I waved with one hand while combing my hair with the other, and batted my eyelashes at her. She stomped back to Andy. "Where's the old lady? *Who is she?*"

He came back and opened my door. "I'm sorry. I didn't even ask your name."

"Jennifer." I smiled.

He walked back to Marcy. "Jennifer is her name."

"Well, isn't that just a *sweet* name?"

"Yeah, it is." He got in the truck, smiling. Marcy ran to his side of the truck, motioning for him to roll his window down, but he pretended not to see her and stepped on the gas. She screamed after the truck.

"Your girlfriend sounds *so* mad!" I said.

"She's *not* my girlfriend, but she sure *thinks* she is! Our mothers are in the same clubs and—"

"I know all about mothers in clubs!"

"My dad turned fifty and had his will drawn up. With a hundred attorneys in town, he had to pick *her* dad, and today of all days she brought the papers around. I think she *planned* it!"

"So your name is *Andy Williams* also?" I asked.

"Yeah, but I'm not the *singer* either!"

I giggled and stole a glance at his face when we passed under a streetlight. "I hate to ruin your evening."

"I ran into *you*, remember?"

"Oh, right." I shook my head.

"I caught your debate on arbitration after school the other day."

"*Really?*"

"Yeah, I thought I'd run into you in the hall and tell you how good I thought you did, but I never ran into you, well, not until *now* anyway!" We laughed. My heart skipped a beat.

"I have a copy if you ever want to read it."

"That's okay."

*(I have a copy. What a stupid thing to say!)*

"So you live in the Inn?" Andy asked.

"I *love* it there."

"I'm sorry about your father."

"Thank you."

There was an awkward silence as he turned down the lane to the Inn. He parked the truck. "Well, we're here." He smiled, turned the truck off and looked up at the dome. "I've always wondered about that green light."

"It was a lookout for the Underground Railroad. My great great, grandparents hid slaves in the basement, and that green light was a signal for them to run down the lane and hide in the tunnels under the cobblestones."

"*No kidding?*"

"Yeah, I'll show you sometime if you don't believe me!"

"Okay, but I believe you." He smiled at me.

I didn't know what to say, so I blurted, "And some of my relatives even worked with Colonel Drake!"

"Really? Wow! You must really be important!"

I could feel my face turn red when he chuckled and got out. I hoped he wouldn't notice the long johns on the clothesline in the moonlight.

He opened my door. I wished with all my might that I hadn't consumed all those chocolate chip cookies and pies over the last weeks! I sucked in my stomach trying to look thin. He cleared his throat and sang, "Put your *hand* on my shoulder."

"*You can sing!*" I smiled.

He laughed and tapped his shoulder for me to put my hand around his neck. I held my breath as I reached for him. "Hold on tight! Don't forget your boot." I could feel how strong he was when he bent over for me to get the boot. He closed the door with his hip.

I bit my lip and said, "I hope I'm not *too* heavy."

"You're like lifting weights."

*(Oh great. If his knees don't buckle, we might make it to the little bridge!)* I didn't dare look at him with our faces so close together, but I sure wanted to. Then I heard the brats behind us, laughing as they crawled out of the burned out basement.

"Hey, Jen, are your *legs broke?*" Logan asked.

"Did your *precious rickets* make your legs go *soft?*" Andrew crooned. "Or did you *lose* your legs some place?"

"Who are they?" Andy asked.

"I have no idea! Tell me, is Andy short for *Andrew?*"

"*Usually.*"

With little effort, he carried me up the porch steps. I pulled open the screen door and he turned the doorknob to the mud-room with his hand under my knees, then lightly tapped the door open with his foot. I reached behind us to close it.

"Hmm, smells good in here. Which way?" He asked.

"Straight down the hallway and to the right."

He carried me into the great room and set me on the loveseat next to Mr. Hair and Ginger, whose finger waves and braid had been replaced with long, flowing tresses.

"*Jennifer!*" Mother exclaimed.

"*Sweetie Pie! Mercy! What happened?* I told you not to *go by yourself!*"

I hit her with a toboggan," Andy explained.

Mother looked angrily at him, "You did *what?*"

"It's okay, Mother. It's just my ankle."

"It's pretty swelled up, ma'am," Andy said.

Mother demanded, "Who *are* you?"

I said, "Mother, this is Andy Williams, but he's not the *singer!*" I laughed; she didn't.

"I didn't see her until I *hit* her!" He said, defending himself.

"*Oh, really?*" Mother asked sarcastically.

He waited for a second and then said, "She needs some ice, ma'am."

"*I can see that!*" Mother hurried to the kitchen.

"I didn't hit her on *purpose!* My dad said she would be *fine,"*
Andy called after her. "Your mom looks *so mad."* He helped me off
with my coat. I smiled. (It's hard to look *beautiful* in an old red barn
coat, an ugly flowered sweater, and one barn boot while in
excruciating pain.)

"Here, lie down Sweetie," Bobchia said.

Irritated, Mr. Hair and Ginger moved to the couch where he
snuggled into her armpit. Caleb 'signed' the conversation to a
concerned Darcy as Bobchia looked through her brows at Andy.
"Your father wouldn't by any chance be a *doctor,* would he?"

"Yes, he is!" Andy nodded. "He said he knew you!"

"Well he doesn't know much about *cows,* I can tell you *that!*
And if he doesn't know about *cows,* how would he know anything
about my Sweetie's *foot?"*

(I wanted to die!) Mother rushed in with an ice bag and a
towel, as Bobchia removed my sock. "Looks like you got it stuck
in a *steel trap!"*

Andy looked at her, "Just between a telephone poll and a
rock." Then he looked down at it. "Man, look at the *size of it!"*

(I wanted to disappear!) Mother put the ice bag on it. Then
she, Bobchia, Spike, Caleb, Darcy and Harold, eating pumpkin pie
with whipped cream, stood in a circle around me, staring at my
foot as if it was going to *fall off!* I saw Andy's hand go up behind
Caleb's head in a wave as he quietly slipped away. I hadn't even
thanked him for his kindness! I could have, at the very least, asked
him if he wanted a Coke or pumpkin pie. Something. *Anything!* It
would be three long days until I would see him in school! I could
hardly wait, and I could hardly walk!

Thus by default, *I* would be the one to move into Joan of Arc's
room after all.

The next day at the breakfast table, Mother handed me some
aspirin and a fresh ice bag. "Thank you. After you're done drinking
your coffee, would you mind bringing some of my clothes down
so I can take a shower?"

"Okay, but it had better be a quick one. You're going to have
to stay off that foot and keep ice on it."

"But I will be able to go to school, right?"

"Right, luckily for you I just read about foot injuries last week, so I know what I'm talking about. I just can't believe the *nerve of that boy,* running into you!"

Bobchia added, "Then just taking off like that! I *told* you to wait until somebody could go with you. *Now look at yourself!*"

I sighed. "How many times do I have to tell both of you that it was an accident? An *accident!* I think I'd like to take my shower *now!*"

"Ah, come on, have another squirrel pancake. Look, a big bushy tail!" Bobchia tried to lighten the mood.

"I'll go get your clothes and then wash the others," Mother said.

"I never want to see that *ugly* yellow flowered sweater again!"

"The one you wore yesterday?" Bobchia asked. "What do you mean *ugly?* I'll have you know that that sweater cost me *five* books of S & H Green Stamps, young lady! Mercy, *I* thought it was beautiful!" She took a shot of coffee.

Bobchia noticed Caleb looking at Mother. "Um, Clair, as soon as Spike comes in from the barn, I'm sure *he'd* be glad to help you move Jen's things downstairs, even with his *backache!*"

"Darcy and I would be glad to help you move her things," Caleb offered.

"Oh, well, all right, if you don't mind. Thank you." He smiled at her. She blushed.

I got up. "Thanks, and please don't forget my favorite quilt." I hobbled down the hall carrying my ice bag to Joan of Arc's room where I propped my foot up on the bed. Pumpkin jumped up from underneath the bed to join me. I petted her and listened to Mother and Caleb laughing as they came down the hall. My thoughts turned to Father and her laughing together. When Mother opened the door, Pumpkin leaped out of my arms and ran down the hall. "Pumpkin!" I cried.

Darcy hurried in, tossed the clothes on the foot of the bed and ran after her. Caleb carried in boxes and set them on the floor. Mother arranged the closet. "There you go."

"Thanks, Caleb, for moving my stuff down," I said.

"No problem. I stayed in here once and had *nightmares.* Pink is not one of my favorite colors!"

"Well, Jen, I think that's everything that goes in the closet. Do you want me to help you unpack the boxes?" Mother asked.

"No thanks. I want to do it. Did you get my journals?"

"They're in that box on the dresser." Then added, "That ice bag won't do its job if you won't *keep* it on your ankle! I'll check on you later." She kissed me on the cheek and then joined Caleb in the hallway.

"Thanks, Mother."

"Thanks for helping me move her things, Caleb." I heard her say.

"Glad to, ma'am," he said in a thick southern accent. "How about you and me head for a cowboy coffee?"

"I should go study…"

"Today? *On Thanksgiving vacation?*"

"It may be vacation for you and the children, but I have to memorize the bones of the body."

I heard Mr. T-t-t-tunes come dancing down the hallway, singing, "The head bone is connected to the neck bone, the neck bone is connected to the back bone, the back bone is connected to the hip bone, the hip bone is connected to the leg bone, the…."

Darcy came in with Pumpkin securely in her arms, shut the door, sat at the desk and windshield-wipered her finger at the cat.

I got her attention by waving. "I hope you don't mind sharing this room. I don't mean to crowd you out."

She got a pencil and paper out of the desk and wrote, "I'm glad to have the company. I'll sleep wherever Grandma Rhea finds me a bed."

Darcy helped me put my clothes in the dresser drawers as Joan of Arc stretched out in hers. When Darcy took some of her things out of the dresser, I tapped her shoulder. "Please don't remove your things. I can use this other dresser." She nodded.

I almost tripped carrying a box when Pumpkin ran between my feet. Darcy was quick to grab her. "Thanks so much! This ankle is throwing me a little off balance."

I put my journals in the top drawer. Darcy set a box on the dresser with my most treasured items, and I unpacked it. Front and center, I placed the picture of Father along with the folded map, my Bible, the toy wooden horse, Daisy, and the little, white box from Pollards' Jewelry Store. Darcy smiled at the doll.

I explained, "She has been waiting for me upstairs in Bobchia's room for twelve whole years. Darcy, this is Daisy. Daisy, this is Darcy."

She shook the doll's hand and then wrote, "Grandma Rhea gave me a bride doll for my thirteenth birthday. She sits on my bed and—" The pencil led broke. Darcy looked in the drawers for another pencil but didn't find one. She turned back to me and said hesitantly, in a quiet voice. "Hi, Jennifer." I was shocked that she was speaking to me!

She explained, "I only talk with dad and Grandma Rhea but *sign* in public because my sister told me my voice sounds *awful!*" Her voice *was* a little different, but it certainly wasn't *awful!* It was great to have a real conversation with her. She looked at Father's picture. "You resemble him."

"Thank you. You resemble Caleb. And I'm jealous, you know!"

"Of *me?*"

"That you and Caleb are so *close*. My Father and I used to be really close. I miss him awful."

"Dad took a job near Pittsburgh, because my school is there and that way he could see me when he wasn't on the road."

I told her about Andy, which took me all of two minutes. She told me of a guy, Seth, who played in a Christian rock band. "I love music and concerts because I can feel the vibrations of the music and I blend in with the crowd." She pulled two framed pictures off of the shelf in the closet. "I was afraid Dad would see these," she explained. "This is Seth with his band. Isn't he handsome?"

"Yes, he looks like Fabian."

"I think so too." The other picture was of her and Seth on a park bench. "He has a little sister named Nita who is deaf and goes to my school. His band plays at the school benefits so the kids can go on outings. I'm afraid to tell Dad about him, because in case you haven't noticed, he is overly protective of me and still thinks of me as a child and not the woman that I am."

"I know the feeling! Oh, Bobchia just rang the lunch bell."

"I can bring you back something," she offered.

"Thanks, but I can walk." We walked slowly to the kitchen.

When we entered, Bobchia was teasing Caleb as he fixed a lunch tray then carried it up to Mother.

"Sweetie, something is *cooking* in the Inn and I don't mean the stew in that pot either!" She winked at me. "Boys, here are your sandwiches. Make sure you eat all your *fruit.*" They thanked her.

Caleb whistled coming down the stairs and into the kitchen. "What's this, sandwiches instead of *delicious stew?*"

"She makes us eat it!" Andrew said.

"Oh?"

Bobchia laughed. "I do make them eat the *fruit,* and tell Caleb why I make you eat your fruit."

"So we won't get *constilated,* that's why!" Andrew pushed his cup of fruit.

Caleb laughed. "Your grandmother's stew is the best!"

Logan made a face. "We *hate* stew!"

"I thought Mounties ate stew." Caleb made a confused face. "Didn't you, Rhea?"

"Red *always* did, absolutely!" She confirmed.

"What does it taste like?" Andrew asked.

"Oh, sorta like vegetable soup. Let's give you a taste." Bobchia got two spoons.

Andrew took a spoonful. "OW! Hot!" He gulped his milk. "It tastes good in my mouth with milk. Can I have some in a bowl with milk on top?"

"Me too?" Logan asked.

"That can be arranged."

Darcy made a face when I told her what was going to happen. Caleb winked at Bobchia as he poured a little milk over the hot stew and chuckled watching them eat it.

"Hey, Caleb, want to make a snowman with us?" Logan asked.

"Can do! I haven't made one since Darcy was little."

"Why?"

"I guess I was able to fight off the *urge!*"

"It will be the *mostest fun!*"

Behind the lace curtain of the corner window of her room, Mother watched Caleb build a snowman with the boys. *She laughed* when they turned on him, pelting him with snowballs as they chased him to the burned out basement, where he slipped and fell in! *She giggled* as he climbed out shaking his fist and caught the screaming boys, and gave them Indian sunburns. *She gasped* when he hugged and kissed them and fought tears when they *didn't* wipe his kisses off. (After that day, as much as she would try to concentrate on her studies, Mother's thoughts would inevitably drift to Caleb Martin.)

I enjoyed getting acquainted with Darcy, staying up late the next few nights, discussing our families. I described her in my journal as being like a butterfly emerging from a cocoon, a sweet, young lady with *deep emotions*. She confessed that even as a little girl, she'd never felt love from her mother. Caleb had tried his best to shelter her, but even as a child she knew that her deafness caused contention between her parents, making her feel responsible for their divorce. "It was like I had a hole in my heart that only the love of my mother could fill. But when I told Grandma Rhea about the hole in my heart, she told me about Jesus, and that *He* was the *only* one who could *fill it*. I repeated the sinner's prayer with her, and when I did, it *changed* my life! My heart still yearns for my mother's love, but now it doesn't consume my life." She confided in me how materialistic her mother and sister Mary were and how unbearable it was to be around them.

I told her of Father, my backstabbing friends in Florida and how I yearned for twelve years to be with my Bobchia. We read our Bibles together, and whenever we didn't understand something, Bobchia was in the kitchen eager to give us *food for thought*.

Sunday morning after a night full of conversation and after hitting the snooze button several times, we got up only after the aroma of bacon found its way around the corner, down the hallway and under the door. We hurried into our robes. Bobchia *cracked* her dishtowel on the table as we came through the archway scaring Homer out of the kitchen. "Come on sleepy heads. This is the day the Lord has made. We will rejoice and be glad in it! I was just about ready to pound on your door."

We eagerly sat down grinning as she heaped two big plates of food and set them in front of us. "How's your foot?"

"Not bad."

Mother came downstairs looking more lovely then she had in years. The boys, half awake, slid into the kitchen in their stocking feet, through the archway and bumped into Bobchia.

"Sorry!" Logan said without even looking at her.

"Sorry! I'll have stew milk, please." Andrew said yawning.

"I want dinosaur pancakes, please." Logan said.

Bobchia put her hands on her hips. "What do you think this is, a *restaurant?*" They nodded. "How about home fries, bacon, eggs and some *fruit?*"

"I guess, but I get five bacons this time, and he only gets four because of last time, Logan said.

"Mer-cy!"

Caleb came in all smiles. He poured himself a cup of coffee and slid into the chair next to Mother. We all stared when Ginger came through the archway, even taller in high heels, with her arm around Mr. Hair, looking up lovingly at her from her armpit. Except for her ponytail, they had exactly the same hair do— backcombed hair high and out. Ginger's tight blouse revealed pendulum bosoms hanging over the waistband of her flowered skirt. Caleb stood up, amazed. *"Grandma?"* He choked.

"Buddy, would you please do me a favor?" Ginger asked.

"Anything, Grandma. Name it." He walked over and put his arm around her.

"Please call me *Ginger* from now on!"

"You were always *too young looking* to be called grandma anyway!"

She giggled and hugged him. "Thanks, Buddy." He kissed her cheek.

Mr. Hair, annoyed, took his handkerchief and hit the seat of a chair several times, impatiently waiting for her to sit down. Caleb gave her another kiss, and when he tried to pull her chair out for her, Mr. Hair pushed his hand away along with the chair, causing Ginger to sit on the floor!

*"Grandma!"* Caleb yelled.

The boys laughed, falling off their chairs.

Caleb and Mr. Hair struggled to get her into the chair.

"Buddy, not grandma, *Ginger,* remember?"

"Whatever! *Are you okay?*"

"Yes. I don't think I broke anything, except maybe my pride."

Mr. Hair quickly ran to the other side of the table, stretched his body across the table, grabbed her hands and kissed them. "My darling, *darling* girl. Are you all right? My life would *never* be the same without you!"

Ginger looked sweetly at him. "You handsome thing, *I hope you never die!*"

"*Mercy!*" Bobchia quickly heaped two plates with food and set them on their hands. She looked over at the giggling boys and windshield wipered her finger.

She smiled and, 'Pop,' went the camera. Mr. Hair and Ginger put their heads together for a picture, but Bobchia ignored them, instead taking pictures of the boys and Caleb, as Darcy and I hid behind our napkins. Mother was annoyed about the pictures again, but this time it was because she was left *out* of them!

Mother and Caleb took the boys to Sunday school while Darcy and I got ready for church. Darcy told me she couldn't wait to see her Aunt Lois, Pastor Jay's wife. "My Mother and Lois are sisters, but Mother doesn't like church people much. I wish Aunt Lois would have been my mother instead; she is so kind."

Bobchia pounded on the door. "Mercy girls, quit primping! You've got five minutes tops! I'll be waiting in the car."

"Bobchia just pounded on the door! We better hurry!" I said. We rushed to the car.

"My two beautiful girls!" Bobchia beamed when we got into the car.

"How can you say that? I didn't even have time to put on my eye makeup!" I said.

"Youth has a beauty all its own, Sweetie." She looked at her watch. "Look at the time! Hold on, and don't you *dare* tell Harold!" We took off, arriving at church with time to spare. Bobchia hustled to sit with Caleb, Mother and the boys. Darcy and I sat with the youth group. While introducing Darcy to Bev, Donna, and Dawnette, Lois came into the sanctuary. Darcy rushed over and hugged her. Then Lois gave Darcy some sheet music, and she came back and sat next to me.

After two songs, Pastor Jay walked to the podium. A few Sundays back, Pastor Jay had started preaching a series on how the Lord knows each of us *personally* and on how we spend our *time* on earth. Last Sunday's sermon was titled, **Time Is *Not* on Your Side!** Pastor Jay continued this Sunday with the message, **How Much Time Do You Spend with the Lord?**

Deep into his sermon he held up a little alarm clock illustrating his point. "We all have the same twenty-four hours a day, seven days a week, three hundred and sixty-five days a year, and *each* of them is a precious *gift* from God! The Lord is *yearning* for you to spend time with Him. Do you *know* Him? He *knows* you! Why, He even knows the number of hairs on your head!" Just as he reached the crescendo of his message, the *alarm went off!* He threw the clock against the wall, smashing it to smithereens! The boys immediately fell to the floor, scrambling around under the pew! Caleb dragged them out by their ankles and sat them between him and Mother. Mother was so embarrassed! She and the boys sat with their heads down while the Pastor stared at them for the remainder of the service.

As Lois walked to the piano to play **Love Lifted Me,** she motioned for Darcy to join her. There Darcy 'signed' the words of the song to the congregation. The boys were captivated watching her, giggling when Bobchia wiped tears from her face.

When church was over, the boys disappeared so Pastor Jay couldn't shake their hands (or their scrawny little necks)! Mother and Bobchia bombarded the boys on the way home.

"And you're *absolutely positively sure* that you boys did not set that alarm clock so it would go off in the middle of the sermon?" Mother demanded.

"We are *ablute* and *positive* we did not, ain't we, Logan?"

Logan shook his head, sheepishly looking at Bobchia in the rearview mirror. Then he changed the subject. "Bobchia, why does God count our hair?"

"It means that He knows each of us *so well* that He even knows how many hairs are on our heads."

"Everyone's in the whole entire world?"

"That's what Scripture says."

Andrew thought for a second. "Does He minus the ones Logan *pulls* out of my head?"

"And the ones in our brushes?" Logan asked.

"Well, yes, to keep an accurate account, I suppose," Bobchia said.

"That would sure take a lot of time, *adding and minusing.*" Logan thought.

"Not for counting Tall Cliff's or Cecil's hairs! It would just take *a couple of seconds!*" Andrew added.

We laughed as we entered the door of the Inn to the aroma of a sauerkraut and pork dinner.

"Ick, what *stinks?*" Logan held his nose.

"*Stinks bad!*" Andrew agreed.

"That's Ardelle's sauerkraut and pork," Bobchia said.

"*I can't eat stinky stuff!*" Andrew explained to her.

Caleb laughed.

"Just wait until you taste it with a plate full of mashed potatoes and butter under it!" Bobchia said licking her lips.

"Can't I have a turkey sandwich with American cheese, Bobchia?" Andrew asked.

"Again?"

"Yeah! Please?"

"Please!" Logan cheered.

"Four days of turkey! Mercy, I was going to give it to Nikki tonight. You'll be *sprouting feathers!*"

At lunch, the boys *emphatically denied* having set the alarm clock, eating their turkey sandwiches one handed. (I looked under the table, their fingers were crossed!)

Before Caleb and Darcy left to go back to Pittsburgh, Darcy taught me how to sign the alphabet while sharing the cookie tin. Bobchia's curiosity peaked, watching Mother pour Caleb a cup of coffee, cut him a big piece of lemon meringue pie and then join him at the corner window table. Bobchia smiled as she gave Darcy and I a glass of milk.

"Sweetie, what was that noise?" Bobchia asked. "Did you hear that? Shhh, listen carefully. It's been years, but I think, I think it maybe, I think it is your mother *laughing!* Mercy! Look at her face. *She has nice teeth!*"

"Bobchia, quit!"

Caleb stood up, "I hate to leave, but I better get on the road. I have to stop at the courthouse in Franklin."

"Speeding ticket?" Bobchia quipped looking at Harold.

"No, my brother Deac is painting a mural in the courthouse of George Washington crossing French Creek where it meets with the Alleghany River. Darcy and I are chomping at the bit to see it. He's the *real* artist in the family!"

"Really?" Mother asked.

"Yes, I'll take you there the next time I'm home, if you would like."

Mother nodded. "All right."

"I should have left an hour ago," he said, looking out the window at the boys dragging an upside down wheelbarrow to the truck door. They struggled to get on it and then climbed into the cab.

"I better *hurry!*" Bobchia handed him a bag with enough leftovers to last him a week. He gave her a peck on the cheek, grabbed the bag and his coat and ran out the door.

"Pleasure meeting you, ma'am!" He hollered back to Mother.

"Bring back my containers!" Bobchia reminded him.

I walked Darcy to the truck. The boys blasted the horn. Everyone covered their ears, except Darcy. The boys wouldn't get out of the cab, so Caleb hauled them out, hugged them then brushed the snow off of his seat. He teased Bobchia, pretending to cry as he backed up the rig. Darcy 'signed' to Bobchia that she 'loved her', and Bobchia 'signed' the same thing back. Darcy signed, 'Goodbye, friend' to me, and I signed the same thing back—or at least that was my intention. She shook her head and waved until they disappeared in the covered bridge.

That night I tried on every pair of shoes that I owned, practicing to walk without limping. They all irritated my foot and made it swell even more. I tried wrapping it as tight as I could, but then my foot was too big for my shoes. I needed some ice for the ice bag, so I limped to the kitchen. Bobchia was sitting at the table reading her Bible.

"Oh, sorry. I didn't mean to interrupt," I said.

"Draw *near* to God, and He will draw *near* to you! I was just about finished with my four chapters anyway, *slow and steady.*" She poured me a glass of milk and slid the tin to me.

"I'm wondering why you never told me about Caleb and Darcy," I said.

"I never know when he's going to show up, and he never knows for sure where his work will take him. Last year he was here for about an hour and got a call to take a load of steel from Cyclops to North Carolina. He never made it back until spring. This year with all the snow, I didn't want to get my hopes up, and if it hadn't been for him getting behind one snowplow after another—" She hit her forehead with the palm of her hand and held her hands to the ceiling, smiling. "TYG! TYG! That's God answering my prayers *again!* It didn't even dawn on me when Caleb was telling me about what a coincidence it was having one snowplow and then another one in front of him, the whole way up from Pittsburgh, that it was a *Thanksgiving miracle!*"

Tall Cliff came in and said, "The bell is *hung.*"

"High enough so Ginger can't reach it?"

"She'd need a ladder!"

"Good. Thanks, Cliff."

"*Quiet dreams!*" He said, laughing as he left the room.

"What's that all about?"

"It started Thanksgiving day, ever since Ginger showed up in that low-cut dress showing off more chest hairs than Minnie!"

"Oh Bobchia, *you're awful!*"

"I know, but mercy! Dressing like *that* when she's old enough to be *my mother!*"

"How many times have you told *me* never to judge a book by its cover?"

"Erase, erase! Let me start over. Ever since Ginger showed up with that braid down her back, I've had to listen to Mr. '*If You Ever Need a Little Trim,*' knock on her door in the middle of the night. TYG she can't hear a *thing* without those hearing aids.' He wakes *me instead of her!* That's what *that* is all about! Haven't you noticed the dark circles under my eyes for the last three days?"

"I just thought it was because you were *old...er.*"

"Listen, there was no *hanky-panky* when your grampie ran the Inn, and there will be no *hanky-panky* while I'm running this Inn either!" Her face got red. "Well, you know what I *mean!* I'll throw him and his scissors out the door if he can't *contain* himself!"

I giggled.

She poured a shot of coffee and took it to the stairway turning her ear, then satisfied, downed her coffee then came back into the kitchen.

"How did you meet him?" I asked.

"The Brady House kicked him out for chasing the Rigby twins, Gail and Gracie. Their hair is so long they can actually sit on it! He was constantly chasing them, wanting to *trim their split ends.*"

"No, not *him,* Caleb!"

"Isn't he just the greatest fella?"

"I wish I could paint like he does!"

"If you think he is an artist, you should see some of the book covers his brother Deac has done and the beautiful murals he painted in Franklin. Beautiful! I saw it the other day when I went to Harold's hearing at the courthouse for speeding. Next time you can go with us and see it for yourself. It's remarkable!"

"*Next time?*"

"Sweetie, haven't you ever heard, 'You can't teach an old dog new tricks?' Well Harold *is* that old dog!" Her expression gradually changed from playful to serious. "Let's see. I don't mean this disrespectfully to Caleb because he's a lot different *now* than what he used to be *before* he knew Jesus, but then, weren't we *all?* Let me think. It was about ten, eleven years ago I'd say, when the dining room was still open to the public." She sighed. "When you left, the *only* thing I had was my faith in God. I kept praying over and over to see you again. Then one night Caleb and Darcy came in for dinner. You know me, I *had* to get to know that cute, shy, little girl. Caleb had just gotten a divorce and bought a rig. His wife had left him for a wealthy man and had taken the *'normal'* daughter, Mary, with her, leaving Darcy with Caleb as if she was so much *'damaged* goods.' Caleb was determined to see that Darcy had the best schooling that money could buy, so he got a second job and enrolled her in Pittsburgh's School for the Deaf and rented an apartment nearby.

"Every whipstitch they'd come to Titusville to visit with Mary. Afterward, Caleb would bring Darcy here for dinner. She loved coming here. I'd sit on the bales and watch her play with the kittens in the barn as Caleb paced back and forth, rehashing the day's encounter with his ex. I was like a mother to him. He just needed somebody to talk to, that's all.

"When they first came here, it was evident that he was still in love with Natalie, and seeing her with her *new* husband broke his heart. It made him so angry that sometimes he'd pound the table, as he told me about it. I couldn't have him doing *that* with patrons in the dining room, also it *upset* Darcy to see him angry and she'd run to my lap. I thought it better if they ate back here in the kitchen. I'd hold her and talk to Caleb about the Lord, but he had a *grudge against God* because of Darcy's deafness. Whenever they ate with me, I'd bow my head way down to say the blessing so Darcy couldn't read my lips. She'd beg Caleb to 'sign' to her what I was saying. He'd get mad at me but would finally 'sign' the blessing to her. I wanted the prayer to get into *his* heart. As I always say, 'A seed *sown* is hopefully a seed *grown.*' Yet the very mention of God would make Caleb so angry that he and Darcy would be scarce for weeks. I remember watching for them every weekend, and when I prayed for *you*, I prayed for *them* too.

"*Then a miracle happened!* One Saturday, I heard the rig's horn come from the covered bridge. Darcy was honking it and waving frantically! I ran to the truck. Her little arms hugged my neck. It felt wonderful. But…they weren't *your* arms. That night, while we watched Darcy play in the red barn, Caleb asked me a lot of questions about the Lord. He was so bitter over Natalie's having split up his family, *he cried.* I asked him, 'What are you *waiting* for? Why not give your heavy burden to the Lord? He has a plan for your life, and if you *confess* with your mouth that Jesus is Lord and *believe* in your heart that God raised Him from the dead, you will be *saved!*' That's exactly what he did! TYG! Right away I could see the difference in his face! The heavy burden he had been carrying was *lifted* off of his shoulders in that old red barn! You know, he even *stood* taller! I got him a Bible and told him to start reading in the book of John and to keep going, just like I told you. Now no matter how far away from Darcy he is, he is never *lonely!* He and the Lord have been truckers together for nigh onto ten years. And ever since Caleb accepted Christ into his heart, if he and Darcy were within yodeling distance, they'd be on my doorstep."

"*He took Father's place!*" The words tumbled out.

"No, child. Nobody could *ever* take Paul's place or your place either! You *know* better than that!" A tear rolled down her cheek. We hugged. "God does have a way with comforting me though, and He *always* answers my prayers! I remember how my heart broke when Paul and you left here. I prayed and cried until no more tears would come, and then one day Caleb and Darcy showed up! I sowed *a seed* in their life, and they *helped me* get through a bad time in mine. *God is so merciful to me!*"

"I'm sorry I said that, I just miss Father so much that my *heart aches!*"

"Mine too," Bobchia said somberly. "Now don't you cry or you'll have salty milk." Bobchia brushed away my tears. "Next to God, family *is* everything. Just ask some of the people who never have a single visitor or get a single letter. You have seen them rush to get the mail. It's heartbreaking. When a person is alone, I mean *really* alone, they lose their relevance, until…until…what?"

"*Until Jesus!*"

"Right! You are so smart! When my family was gone, I suppose that I could have resented the world and turned into a Mr.

Pill kind of a person, or I could trust in the Lord. I could be *bitter* or *better*. I don't know, maybe I just keep Mr. Pill here to remind me of what I would be like *without the Lord*. It depends on how a person looks at things. 'Two men looked through prison bars; one *saw dirt* and the other *saw stars!*' The glass is either half full or half empty."

I chugged my milk. "It's empty!" She smiled and poured me another.

"Bobchia?" She looked at me. "Do you think it's okay to pray for a boy to like you?"

"As long as his father isn't a *doctor!*"

"Chee, I mean really."

"Psalm 37:4 says, '**Delight yourself in the Lord and He will give you the desires of your heart.**' Why not pray that God would send you the boy *He* has picked out for you? God's purposes are for *us*—our purposes are not for Him. It may be someone you haven't even met yet."

"Or someone I *have.*"

"I suppose, but trust God. He knows what's *best* for you. He's preparing someone for you, like He did for your Father and like He did for me. *Trust Him.* Don't rush into anything, and make sure he's a *Christian* or there's trouble up ahead!" She hugged me goodnight.

As I left the kitchen, I made up my mind to pray to meet the boy that *God* had prepared for me. I wondered if it was okay to put a P. S. at the end of my prayer like I would in a letter. P. S. I hope I've *met* him already, and P. S. S. Can't it please be *Andy?*

On the way to my room, I passed Homer skipping down the hall, headed for the kitchen. I limped past the deer head parlor, turned and walked back and stood by the door. Slowly turning the doorknob, I pushed the creaking door open. The dim hall light shined a pathway to Rocky. His fierce silhouette was menacing in the window with the moonlight glowing on his fur. Never taking my eyes off of the raccoon, I searched the wall for a light switch, but there wasn't one. *Rocky is the light!* I froze. I could feel the deer's cold, shimmering eyes staring down on me, daring me to take another step! Above my hand was a wild boar's head, ready to gore me! I slammed the door! Beads of sweat formed on my forehead as I leaned against the door with my eyes shut, waiting to get brave enough to confront a *stuffed* raccoon. I opened my eyes. Homer stood in front of me, startling me.

"*Hot flash?*" He asked.

"No, I'm not having *a hot flash!*"

"The kitchen is dark, and I'm hungry!" He explained.

"Well, if you do me a favor, I'll get you a cookie."

"*Cookie!*" He said excitedly.

"Yes, if you go in this room and get me a box...Homer? *Homer!*" I shouted at him as he skipped to his room. I stood there gathering courage. "Okay, remember, Rocky is a *dead* raccoon!" I slowly turned the doorknob and pushed the door so hard it banged against the wall. Looking only at the floor, I hobbled as fast as I could, following the dim path of light to the legs of the table where the raccoon was poised to strike. My eyes slowly went up, up the legs of the table to his fangs glistening in the moonlight. I reached for the box beside him. I pulled my hand back, but then with all the strength I could muster, I yelled, "*Bingo!*" and grabbed the box! I turned to run out but the door was slowly closing. I hurried to reach for the doorknob, but my slipper bumped the door shut! "Ahhhhhhhhhhh!" I swung the door open and leaped into the hallway with the treasure box. Rocky slammed the door behind me.

The next morning my alarm went off at 5:30. Joan of Arc 'meowed' for waking her up so early. I leisurely took a shower in my very own bathroom and spent an hour in front of the mirror making a perfect flip while having a pretend conversation with Andy. My foot had swollen by the time I lathered my hair with spray and put on a pink blouse with a white skirt. (The season for white skirts had long since passed, but it was the longest skirt I had, to hide the ugly slipper.) I propped my hand mirror against the leg of my bed to see if I could hide the slipper under the long skirt, while standing on my good foot. After falling forward several times, I gave up and went to breakfast.

Bobchia set a plate in front of me with the cookie timer on it. It had a big black circle around the ten-minute mark. I looked at her as she windshield-wipered her finger at me. "You *know* the rule, *ten minutes or less* for showers, and if you *can't* take a shower in ten minutes young lady, we'll just have to *hose* you off in the driveway!" Ardelle and Wanda laughed.

"*Chee, Bobchia.*" I said embarrassed.

"Mr. Brown got up early this morning and was complaining of running out of hot water. He had to go to the hospital to get a *procedure* done."

"I'm sorry," I said red-faced, with my head down.

"Oh, I'm sorry too, Sweetie for being such a *grouch.* I didn't sleep very well last night. *Forgive me?*" I nodded. She hugged my shoulder and laughed. "When Mr. Brown first moved in, I had to remind him every two days to take a bath or I wouldn't feed him! Once he hid in his room for three whole days and was half-starved! Now he needs to lose thirty pounds, and smells like rose cleaner!" She filled a plate and set it in front of me. I said grace and pushed the food around on my plate. The boys slowly came down the stairs, shuffling their feet and stumbling into their chairs.

"Why do we have to go to school today anyway? You said the schools are closed when *it snows,* **'member?**" Andrew said.

"If the roads are *closed,* the schools are *closed. That* is the rule."

"Another stinken *rule!* You never told us *that* part. You just said we'd *eat and get under a blanket!*" Andrew said disappointed.

"Sorry, I didn't mean to misrepresent the school's policies!" She rubbed the groove in her forehead.

"We're tired!" Logan complained.

She filled two plates and set them in front of them. "Don't forget your blessing!"

They mumbled something and ate slowly, not even fighting over the bacon.

"Your vacation is over! *Hurry up!*"

They usually dove into their food, but today of all days, the very day that I wanted to get to school *early* to talk to Andy, the brats were, as Bobchia put it, '*Slower than molasses going uphill in January!*' The thought of seeing Andy had me so excited that I only had a tiny piece of toast. (Maybe I could lose some weight after all!)

Bobchia raised her eyebrows. "You feel okay, Sweetie?"

"Yes." Bobchia felt my head. I felt hers. *She looked awful!* "Are *you* okay, Bobchia?"

"I'm okay. I'm going to take a nap as soon as I get a break here. I'll have your Mother take you to school today, okay?"

"Okay."

She poured herself another cup of coffee, despite already having one in her other hand. She took a shot out of both.

"Bobchia, are you *sure* you're okay?" I asked.

"I didn't get much sleep."

"Sorry. I love you awful. See you tonight!"

"Love you awful back."

I looked out the window at the snow and then glanced at the thermometer—thirty-one degrees. I hurried and brushed my teeth and then went to the hall closet. Mother came up behind me. "Mother, *you look awful!*" I said.

"You would too if you heard a cowbell ringing in the middle of the night! How could anyone sleep with all that *racket?* Your grandmother *lost it last night,* screaming at Mr. Hair or *whatever* his name is, as he stood at Ginger's door holding long stem red roses! She *slammed* them against the wall up there!"

"Mr. Hair and Ginger?"

"No! *The roses!* You should see the mess! It looks like a *minefield* up there!"

"*No kidding?*"

"No kidding! Jen, I don't know if my *nerves* can stand living here *one more day!*"

"There, there, sit down. Everything will get back to normal soon, you'll see."

"*Normal?* What's *'normal'* around here? Have you *seen or heard anything normal* since we got here? People sing stupid songs or have Q-tips sticking out of their ears!"

"*Shh,* you'll be fine."

She rubbed the grove in her forehead. "What are sidewalks for, Jen?"

"What?"

"Tell me, what are *sidewalks* for?"

"For *walking?*"

"A person would normally think so, but not here, *nooo!* Here they are for *dog poop!*"

"*Owl mooses!*" I corrected.

"What?"

"Owl moose! The boys can't say *bowl movement,* remember?"

"That is *ridiculous!* You realize that is *ridiculous,* don't you?"

"I thought it was kinda *cute.*"

"*Whatever!* If the boys walk on the sidewalk, they step in owl mooses, and then Andrew tries to scrape the *owl* or the *moose* or the *poop* off of his shoe and gets dry heaves! Are you listening to what *I am saying?* I knew if I came back here I'd be ready for the *nuthouse!* OW! My head is *splitting!*"

"You need an aspirin! Mother, please go back to bed. I'll make sure the boys brush their teeth." Her eyes glazed over. "Mother? *Mother!*"

She shook her head. "Good idea. *I wish I knew what I just said.* I have to go to class later. Oh great! We're having a test on the digestive system, *and I feel like I'm going to puke!*"

"Go back to bed and *relax.*"

"*Only if I could!*" She went up stairs, came back down, and leaned over the railing. "Wear my coat; it's heavier than yours."

"You'll need it," I countered.

"Not until four."

"Okay, thanks."

"As soon as I get my check this Friday, I have to take the car back to the garage, but I should have enough left over to get you a heavy coat, okay?"

"Groovy!"

"*Or buy bus tickets!*" She rubbed her forehead, mumbling to herself as she went up the stairs. I heard something about a *funny farm.*

Bobchia met me in the hallway with a pair of Ginger's boots she'd borrowed. "They're the only ones in the *whole Inn* big enough to fit over your slipper!" They were clear rubber with a rubber band on one side that wrapped around the front and fastened over a button on the other side.

I scrunched up my nose. "Did these ugly things come over on the *ark?*"

"*Could have!*" She snorted. "When I was going to *buy* your love, I was going to *buy* you some boots too!"

"Please don't torture me, Bobchia!"

"The cowbell ring last night!"

"Mother told me."

"*It was not pretty!* You know Ginger can't hear a thing without those hearing aids, and she snores like *a storm trooper!* I don't know how she slept through the commotion, but she did! *Mr. Vidal Sassoon* had a pair of scissors in one hand and long-stemmed red roses in the other. That man is a legend *in his own mind!* The cowbell tolled at two-thirty!"

"He's in love, Bobchia!"

"*Love?* He'd probably love that *fox fur* of Gladys's if he ever got close to it! He's cleaning up the mess upstairs as we speak. I'm going over to the church later to talk to Pastor Jay about it. We'll likely either have a *wedding* here tonight or an *eviction!* Either one will *fit the bill."* She rubbed the groove in her forehead. "Where *is* your mother?"

"She went back to bed."

*"Back to bed?"*

"She's *uptight."*

*"Again?* Get your brothers in the car. I'll take you to school and nap later."

As soon as I set one ugly boot into the school, I hurried to take them off. I hid them under Mother's coat and stuffed them in my locker. I couldn't wait to see Andy! I scanned the hallways all day long. Finally, after fifth period I saw him in the hall talking intently to Marcy. I tried not to hobble as I walked toward him. Marcy scowled. The speech I had memorized earlier left my head as soon as I looked into his sky blue eyes.

"Thank you for being so kind to me the other night," I managed.

He smiled while I tried to hide the ugly slipper behind my good foot. He looked down. "Think nothing of it, *Skip."* He smiled and winked and started to say something but Marcy pulled him away, looking back and giving me a dirty look over her granny glasses.

"That's probably the last time I'll ever talk with him in my entire life!" I told myself as I limped over to my locker and kicked it with my sore foot. "Ouch, that was *stupid!"*

From that day forward, my heart would jump when I heard *'Hi, Skip!'* but whenever I'd turn to say something, Marcy would be there, glaring down her granny glasses at me and tugging on his arm. It was the way he said 'Skip' that made me melt.

Mother, wearing my coat, picked us up from school on her way back from the library. She confessed that she had spent most of the day there, studying and trying to regain her composure. At least she didn't look *as* rattled.

She said that after dropping us off at school, Bobchia had gone to see Pastor Jay. Then she'd had Cecil and Cliff move Mr. Hair's belongings down to the deer head parlor. Mother laughed as she talked like Bobchia, 'The next time you climb those stairs, your scissors and your clothes will be on the front lawn!' Mother laughed louder. "Rhea escorted him to the parlor saying that if she ever caught him near Ginger's room in the middle of the night again, she would add *his* head to *that* wall!"

I laughed while she drove down the lane until I saw the Pork Chops Meat Market delivery truck in the driveway of the funeral home. Mother looked concerned as she parked the car beside a blue VW with two dead deer draped across the front of it. One had four point antlers; the other had enormous horns.

"Wow! Look at *that!*" Logan smushed his face against the window.

"Wow! Dead deer where we can *really* see 'em!" Andrew exclaimed. The boys kicked their doors open and ran to the car.

"Hey! That car hit *two* deer!" Logan checked the front of the car for dents.

"Or they tried to *jump* over that little car and *missed,*" Andrew analyzed. "Man, just look at *those horns!*"

"I bet they could *kill a bear!*" Logan's eyes bulged.

"Hey, maybe the big one stuck the little one in the stomach and *ripped its guts out!*" Andrew jumped up and down.

"Yeah! Maybe they *ripped each other's guts out!*" They gave each other a high five then they looked curiously at the deer's empty stomachs and blood-stained fur.

Mother sighed. "Ah yes, *deer season.*" She reluctantly walked to the VW and grabbed the boy's arms. She struggled to pull them across the little bridge and onto the porch where we could hear laughter coming from inside.

"Can't we just *stare* at them a little bit longer?" Andrew begged. "Pleeeassssse."

"Honestly, wouldn't you prefer to see them *running* gracefully in the forest?" Mother asked.

"Nah, I'd rather see them *dead on a car with no guts!*" Logan yelled.

"*Me too!*"

We went inside. The boys ran ahead of us into the kitchen and right to the window, continuing to look at the dead deer.

"I can't see them very good now!" Logan complained.

Harold and two men in orange hunting suits sat at the table eating chili and apple pie. Bobchia filled their coffee cups saying. "Clair, Jen, boys, these are Harold's sons, Wayne and Dave."

They stood up. "Pleased to meet you," Wayne said.

"Nice to meet you," Dave said.

Mother forced a smile, and I said, "Hello."

"They got their deer and brought them in for us to see," Bobchia explained. "I think that ten-pointer might be the one we saw at the farm when we picked apples, *remember?*"

"Wow! We seen it *alive* and now we seen it *dead!*" Logan stared out the window.

"We seen some dead ones along the road, but I didn't think you could kill them—*on purpose* I mean!" Andrew said excitedly.

Spike hurried in to the kitchen dressed in an orange hunting suit. "Harold, did you bag that *big one?*"

"Nah, Wayne did," Harold said.

"It's a *beauty!* Where'd you shoot it?" Spike asked.

Harold blurted out, "He shot it on north ridge, just about a mile from the strip field where *Nate got that nice eight-pointer last year.*"

"On that steep slope where all the mountain laurel is?"

"Yeah," Harold continued, "It was snowing to beat the band, and I was freezing so I walked up to sit in the truck. I thought I saw something move behind some laurel about ten yards to my left. I couldn't see what it was, so I started walking toward it. I tripped over a log, and my gun went off. The buck stood up, and it was *huge!* It looked at me and then ran down the ridge. I dove for my gun!" Wayne was smiling with a mouth full of chili, shaking his head.

"Wayne was further down the hill and let him have it *right in the heart* about twenty-five yards from Dave," Harold finished.

"*Wow!*" The boys said in unison. Mother cringed.

Wayne continued, "Then Dave ran over to it yelling, 'It's a *big* one! It's a *big* one!'"

Dave shook his head and said, "I picked up its head to count its horns, but the darn thing started to *slide* on the snow. I held on to its horns but I slipped and fell over onto its back! I tried holding up the horns so they wouldn't break off when Wayne—"

"When I looked back and saw my brother sliding down the hill *on top of that deer,* I never laughed so *hard* in my life! I couldn't believe it! Luckily I was standing on a huge rock, and Dave was headed right for me! I jumped off the rock, and as the deer slid over the rock, I reached up and grabbed Dave's hunting suit and pulled him off. The deer kept sliding and got caught in the laurel. I was afraid Dave would *ride* that stupid deer down to the river and *go through the ice!*" He laughed. I wish I'd had a camera when he was *riding* that deer down that hill! That picture would be worth *a thousand bucks!*"

"Well, at least I got some good pictures of you standing *beside* the deer," Bobchia said. "As soon as I get them developed, I'll give them to Harold to give to you. How's that?"

"Thanks, Rhea, and as usual, I'll send you in some more deer steaks, how's that?"

She nodded. "They make delicious Swiss steak. I cooked the last of them a couple of weeks ago. People ate them like it was their last meal!"

Mother grabbed her stomach and sat down.

"Well we had better shove off," Wayne ventured. "Jody will be wondering where I am."

"You should stop at the newspaper office on your way," Bobchia said. "they'll put pictures of you with your deer in the paper."

"Good idea! Thanks for the chili and pie; it was delicious!"

"And please take one of those pumpkin pies over there on the counter to Jody and the kids. And there's a pie over there with your name on it too, Dave."

Dave smiled, looking at the pies lined up on the counter. "Wow, when you bake pumpkin pies, you don't mess around! Thanks again, Rhea."

"Yeah, thanks!" Wayne said.

"You're welcome! Stop in anytime!" The men left the kitchen.

The boys intently looked out the window as the men stood around the deer talking.

"I wish they could leave the deer here *forever!*" Andrew said.

"Where are they going to take them?" Logan asked.

"To the *Herald* to get their picture taken for the paper."

"To *Harold?*" Andrew asked.

She walked to the window and put her arms around their shoulders. "No honey boy, the newspaper office is called **The Titusville Herald**. It's spelled differently than my Harold, understand?"

Logan shook his head. "They sound the same."

"H-a-r-o-l-d is *my* Harold, but h-e-r-a-l-d means someone who *brings news*. Remember the angel of the Lord in your Christmas book we read last night? The angel who brought the *Christmas news?*" They looked up at her and shook their heads. Looking back and forth from face to face, she softly told them the story.

"Behold, I bring you good tidings of great joy, which shall be to all people. For unto you is born this day in the city of David a Savior, which is Christ the Lord."

"Wow! You *even* memorized stuff that Linus said in Charlie Brown's Christmas *too?*" Logan said, surprised.

"No, I memorize stuff from the *Bible!* So you know what *that means* don't you?"

"What?" Logan asked.

"Linus and Charlie Brown read their *Bibles!*"

"Wow, Charlie Brown must be really *smart* for a kid!" Andrew concluded.

"Yeah, he just *can't* play baseball very good!" Logan added.

Giggling, Bobchia sneaked a kiss on the tops of their heads. "Wash your hands. I made cookies this morning."

I washed mine at the kitchen sink as the boys pushed and shoved their way to the bathroom sink and then raced back and jumped onto chairs. Bobchia slid the tin, but I intercepted it, quickly taking out a couple of cookies before they touched them.

"Hey!" Andrew protested.

I slid the tin the rest of the way. They shoved cookies into their mouths. Andrew asked, "Bobchia, will you take a picture of me with the deer?"

"Me too?"

"Mercy, what for?"

"In case I want to show it to my kids," Andrew said.

"Your *kids?*" She laughed. "You ask your Mother."

Andrew turned to Mother. "Can I?"

"Me too?" Logan asked.

Mother lifted her head. "Well, if you *have to.*"

"*I have to!*" They said in unison. Then they grabbed more cookies and ran out the door with their jackets. Bobchia giggled and followed them with her camera. Mother got up and took an Alka-Seltzer.

"I would have sworn that was *beef steak!*" She said holding her stomach as she went up the stairs. "I'm going to lie down a few minutes before class."

I took the tin to the window munching and thinking that *only* Bobchia could make a Bible lesson out of dead deer, a newspaper office, an angel of the Lord and Charlie Brown and have it make *total sense!* I laughed watching her take pictures of the boys standing beside the deer, then holding the horns of the deer and the best one was with their tongues hanging out the sides of their mouths, like the deer. As soon as Bobchia got them developed, she taped them on the front of the fridge halfway down for the boys to enjoy and Mother to ignore.

After the kitchen had been put back in order, the tenants hurried to change into their Sunday best for their *outing* to **Parker's Palace of Peace II**, the open house for Harold's new funeral home.

"Sweetie, hurry up!" Bobchia yelled down the hall at me. "You know I want to get there *first!*"

"Coming!" I met Bobchia at the door.

Mother shouted down the steps as she herded the boys to the tub, "It's *disgusting*, just *disgusting*, to think that people would actually eat pumpkin pie with whipped cream while standing around a bunch of *dead* people!"

The red, white and blue neon signs announcing the open house hurt our eyes as we drove the five hundred feet to the funeral home. "That's one thing that attracted me to Harold," Bobchia said.

"What?"

"He's so *patriotic!*" Welcoming us at the front door of the palace was *Prince Harold* wearing a tuxedo. He beamed at us, bowed and kissed Bobchia's hand. She blushed like a *princess*. Then she put her arm through mine and guided me through the maze of repose rooms decorated in the shiny flowered wallpaper she had selected and hung. The floral arrangements were lavish and fragrant, and in the heat of the moment, a lot of money exchanged hands for many a *prepaid* funeral. The two-page advertisement that *Harold* had placed in The *Herald* had paid off, attracting people from both near and far. (Luckily most of them were *breathing*.)

# 12

# The Snowflake Festival

The next weekend Titusville kicked off the Christmas shopping season, as store windows were transformed from pilgrims and cornucopias to angels and mangers. The garage bill and Mother's textbooks took most of her paycheck, so instead of a coat, she bought me a heavy navy blue sweater to go under my jacket. She said the price of coats were *dear* and after Christmas everything would go on sale. I didn't mind. I liked the sweater; it was pretty and warm, and the color, navy, went well with my Florida clothes.

That Saturday afternoon, much to my delight, the Inn took on a festive spirit of its own. Harold, Wayne and Dave brought in a huge tree from Wayne's farm, cut to Bobchia's specifications to accommodate Grandmother Kay's delicate porcelain star.

"I hope this tree is *big* enough for you sweetie. Otherwise, we'll have to cut a hole in the ceiling!" She smiled.

"It's *perfect!*"

It took hours to arrange the furniture, move the piano and get the tree perfectly centered into the cove of windows.

When Mother came downstairs for a coffee break and saw the Christmas tree, she went to the mudroom closet and got out a bag containing *her* tree and dragged it into the great room.

I intercepted her. "Oh, Mother, we really don't need *that* tree. Look, we have a *real* one!"

"Nonsense," she said. "The boys *love* this tree and so do *I*. Help me get it out!"

I held the bag while Mother pulled out the dwarfed six-foot tin tree and its revolving, colored light stand and stood it beside the fireplace. Bobchia stared red-faced. "There, looks great, doesn't it?" Mother asked. "I'll get the decorations."

Bobchia was *erasing* the air as I walked toward her. She talked through her teeth. "A tin tree, a *tin* tree in the *Inn? Mercy!*" She looked to the ceiling and then at Mother bringing in shoeboxes of lime green, bright pink and turquoise glass balls carefully wrapped in fluffy, white garland along with thin boxes of tinsel.

"I'll send the boys in to help you decorate it," Mother said smiling at me. "It's time for them to come in anyway. Oh and please remind them that the ornaments are *glass*. I better reread the chapter on *cuts*, just in case." She left to get the boys.

"Did your Mother ever hear of a *Band-Aid?* Mercy, look at that *thing!* If I only knew having you here meant having a *tin* Christmas tree in the great room, I would have *reconsidered!*"

"Bobchia!"

She erased, laughing. "Sorry!"

"I've never liked the *ugly* thing!" I confessed.

"I suppose we'll just have to get used to it, *mercy!*"

The boys ran in and put the majority of the ornaments on the front of the tree, thus making the canister sweeper a part of our *decorating experience.*

Andrew turned. "See Jen, we're almost done!"

Bobchia rubbed her forehead as she watched the *expertise* of the 'Blackberry Kid' ball up box after box of tinsel and throw them onto the tree. Logan cheered. Bobchia quickly *hid* her tinsel behind the loveseat.

"We're done! I told ya it would only take *five* minutes!" Logan said proudly.

"But it don't look like last year." Andrew cocked his head.

"Four minutes and twenty-eight seconds to be exact!" Spike said laughing from the couch.

Logan crossed his arms "It's not *funny*, Spike!"

"Don't cha like *our* tree, Bobchia?" Andrew asked.

"Let me explain why an *evergreen tree* is used at Christmas," she said. "Come here, both of you. Now look out that window. Not a *tin* tree for miles! Tell me what kind of trees you see."

"I see a lot of branches," Andrew said.

"They look *dead!*" Logan said.

"That's right. Most of them look dead," Bobchia said.

"But the *pinecone trees ain't!*" Andrew exclaimed.

"*Exactly!*" Bobchia smiled. "That's why we use them at Christmastime to remind us that God's love is always *alive—evergreen*, get it?"

"Is that in the Bible?" Logan asked.

"No, but—"

"How do you know it is *true* then?" Andrew countered.

"Well, let's turn around and look at our trees. Which is prettier?" Bobchia asked.

"*The tin one!*" Logan cheered. The boys high-fived.

"Don't feel bad, Bobchia!" I said laughing.

She rubbed her forehead. "Let's break for supper."

After supper, the men carried long ladders inside and set them up beside the massive spruce. Tall Cliff and Cecil climbed up and patiently arranged the bubble lights as Bobchia supervised from the couch.

"Cecil, you missed a row! Your arms are too short! Go higher to match up with Cliff's row. Mercy, Spike, please grab Cliff's ladder; he's got a *longer* way to fall than Cecil, *heaven forbid!*" The men navigated the strings of lights so they met and then climbed down.

Spike turned off the overhead light, and when Cliff threw the switch to the tree lights, Logan had a *spelling relapse!* He ran around the tree pointing. "Wow! Look! There is r-e-d, g-r-e-e-n, y-e-l-l-o-w, b-l-u-e, p-u-r-p-l-e and w-h-i-t-e ones!"

Bobchia knelt beside him. *"Mercy, are you alright?"*

"Y-e-s," he said.

She made him lie down on the couch. "Is there anything I can get you, honey boy, anything at all? Just *name* it!"

He looked sadly at her. "Uh, American c-h-e-s-e please."

"Cheese it is!" She hurried to the kitchen.

Andrew ran to him. "Are you really *sick?*"

"N-o."

"Then how come you're getting cheese *again* when you just had some for supper?"

"I *spelled.*"

"Oh, I'm not very good at *that.*" Andrew dropped his head.

"Just spell cheese."

"I don't know how!"

"C-h-e-s-e. Make sure you look sad and talk real *slow.*"

Bobchia brought in a hunk of cheese with two big wedges of apple and handed it to Logan. With a full mouth, he shrugged at Andrew.

"Hey, Bobchia."

"What, Andrew?"

"C- -h- -s---e."

"I knew it was *contagious!*" She said.

Andrew smiled at Logan as Bobchia felt his head. Then she hurried to the kitchen. Andrew lay on the other end of the couch with hands behind his head, giggling. When Bobchia returned and handed him an identical plate, he did his best to look pitiful.

"T-anks."

Bobchia felt their heads again. "You both feel alright. Maybe I should have your Mother take you to the emergency room?"

"N-o, I mean *no!*" Logan said.

Andrew sat up. "No! We feel *better* now!"

"Make sure you eat all of that apple, okay? *Plungers* are on my Christmas list, in case you two are interested!"

The boys secretly gave each other high fives as Bobchia talked with Cecil and Tall Cliff. Then Bobchia carefully handed up boxes to Cecil on his ladder. He carefully handed the boxes on up to Tall Cliff who was on an even taller ladder. The boxes contained her priceless, sentimental Croatian, Polish and Italian hand-blown glass Christmas ornaments.

Sadly, for unnamed reasons (Logan and Andrew), the ornaments were to be admired from *afar* this year, adorning only the highest, safest branches in the towering *pinecone tree.* As tenants came into the great room carrying their family ornaments to be hung, they laughed at the tin tree. The boys raced over to turn it on. 'Click, click, click' went the unbalanced, revolving tree in the stand as it changed from pink to turquoise to lime green and back to pink. Everyone stared in *hideous* amazement. Some giggled. The boys looked hurt and went back to the couch and hid their apple slices under the cushions. Cecil and Cliff climbed down and carried out the ladders. Bobchia hurried and put **White Christmas** on the stereo and then clapped her hands. "Okay, everyone, the tree is ready for your decorations. Let's get this show on the road. Lawrence Welk and the hymn sing awaits!" The tree was soon a hodgepodge of decorations.

After the boys went to bed, Bobchia got out the *WD 40* oiling the 'click' in the motor. Then we redid the tree, hanging *her* boxes of long tinsel on it. "There's not much hope, Sweetie," Bobchia said. "Turn it on." The tree and the white garland changed color. "What an *eye sore!* Your Mother always liked the most *modern* things. I suppose your house in Florida was full of modern everything." I nodded. "Thought so. Well the tree is not good, but it is *better.*

Remember, *compromise* is the hardest thing to navigate through the waters of life!"

"Who said that, Noah?"

"Nope. You're *looking* at her!"

The next morning, Bobchia felt the boy's heads as soon as they came through the archway of the kitchen. They sat down without saying a word. Bobchia wondered, *Would they go through their whole lives spelling? Would they have children who would spell instead of talk? Would they even be able to have children?* Bobchia set platefuls of food in front of them. They bowed their heads. "Thank you for our food and for making our tree *look better* today," Andrew said.

"And for *straightening* out all the tinsel, Amen," Logan finished.

Bobchia breathed a sigh of relief, realizing she had worried for nothing. It had just been a twelve hour *spell.*

By now my nightly talks with Bobchia were a well-established *ritual* and had become my favorite part of the day. If being at the Inn was the *cake,* Bobchia was the *icing.* She amazed me. I don't know if she just didn't require a lot of sleep or if the caffeine kept her up, but whenever I'd come back down for a *second helping* of Bobchia, there she was, reading her Bible.

One night as I came into the kitchen she read, "'**He alone is my *rock* and my *salvation,* my *fortress* where I will not be shaken.'** TYG! There, that should help us both sleep! Did you read your Bible?"

"I did, but I'm still not sleepy."

"Good. Sit over here and keep me company." She reached under the sink and got out a bag.

"What *are* you doing?" I asked.

"I'm sure you've noticed the pretty decorations on everyone's door? Mr. Pill has taken it upon himself to be mule headed!"

"Oh, *him!*"

"Yes, he really is a *pill,* isn't he? He put a coat hanger on his door and keeps adding candy wrappers daily."

"The boys keep knocking them off! Anyway, I bent this hanger into a circle and thought I would make a wreath out of these wrappers."

"What for?"

"*For fun.* He has some sweet tooth that man does! I think it's the *only* one left in his head! I'll have to hide the candy bars again from the snoopy old thing. No wonder your mother's always tired; Mr. Pill's up half the night playing with those trains after eating all that sugar!"

I sat down with a thud.

"Want another piece of pie?"

"Nah, I'll just have some of these cookies. I'm trying to *cut down.* A cookie jar instead of the tin?"

"Ginger made those things for Mr. Trim. Don't eat them. They're harder than *Pharaoh's heart!*"

I laughed. "They *look* like yours."

"Don't you know by now that looks are *deceiving?* Mr. Trim chipped a tooth on them. Here's the good stuff." She got the tin off the counter and slid it to me. I took one out.

"There are only a few left."

"Is that a *hint?*"

"You make the *best,* that's for sure!"

"The boys were in them earlier. I'll make more tomorrow." I checked the cookies for slobber. "I better get rid of those other cookies while I'm thinking about it, before someone cracks their *dentures.*" Laughing, she dumped Ginger's cookies into the garbage can under the sink. They made a thunderous noise. "That probably woke Venal up! Ginger must get her recipes from the *KGB.*"

I choked. "That's *funny!*"

"Sorry, I'll get you some milk. How's your foot doing anyway?"

"Good."

"Are the kids at school making fun of your slipper?"

"Not really."

She handed me the coat hanger. "Try to think of a way to put these wrappers on here. I want to surprise him. He keeps trying to defeat me, but he *can't.* If you don't want someone to *get* your goat, don't tell them where it's *tied!*"

I laughed, making a mental note for my journal.

She went to her sewing cupboard and pulled out red ribbon and backing. Between cookies, I taped the backing onto the hanger and glued the wrappers to it. We pulled the ribbon back and forth through the wreath and then she tied a big bow and fluffed it.

"He tries my patience, that man," Bobchia said. "I lost a daughter, a husband *and* a son, but I am thankful and I refuse to give up my faith! You and the boys are my greatest blessings, did you know that?"

"Kinda thought."

She finished and held up the wreath. "There, what do you think?"

"I think that is the prettiest candy wrapper wreath I have ever seen in my entire life!"

"Good answer! I'll just put this on his door on my way to bed. But first I have to find a different hiding place for the candy bars."

"I bet I can find one!"

She laughed. "Goodnight, Sweetie Pie!"

"Goodnight, Bobchia." I kissed her cheek. Then I went up three steps straining through the railing and watched her feet give away the hiding place.

The nights Mother studied in her room, I studied at the desk in the great room to make sure the brats studied at the coffee table.

"This stupid puzzle makes my homework wiggly!" Andrew lifted up his paper.

"Put a tablet under it," I said without looking up.

Bobchia came in and chastised the boys for messing up Aunt Ardelle's puzzle.

Andrew pointed at me. "She's the one who told me to put a tablet *under it!* Yell at her!"

I looked up. "I meant under your homework, *not under* the puzzle, brat!"

"Pig!"

"That is enough!" Bobchia said. "Supper is ready. Why Ardelle insists on doing a puzzle down here when she has that big room up there is beyond me!" Bobchia volunteered me to help her work on the puzzle while the boys ate.

After dinner all gathered in the great room. Aunt Ardelle brought Lucky downstairs. This time, his cage was wrapped in a knitted blanket of angels and snowflakes. She fluffed it as she set him on the bookshelf, then lifted the front of the blanket so he could watch her and Wanda work the puzzle, waving to him now and then. "Boy Wanda, you've really gone to town on that puzzle!"

"I just sat down!" Wanda replied, astonished.

"Bobchia, can we string popcorn tonight?" I asked. Lucky chirped.

"Ardelle has a popper," Bobchia said.

"Why of course, Jennifer!" Ardelle said. "Did you hear Lucky? After what you've done for him, we'll string popcorn until the cows come home if you'd like!"

"Thank you." Lucky chirped again.

Ardelle went to her room for the popcorn maker.

Bobchia got out her sewing basket and asked me to thread the needles. Soon bowls full of popcorn were being passed around the room. The boys kept poking themselves with the needles so they quit, then they whined that they were bored so Bobchia fine-tuned the set to *I Love Lucy.*

It's funny how popcorn suddenly becomes *irresistible* when it *dangles* from a string. From his perch, Lucky witnessed the feeding frenzy right under everyone's noses and under the coffee table.

Conversations soon drifted to the Christmases spent during the Great Depression.

"We would get excited if we could afford the ingredients to make cookies," Bobchia said.

"And the *heat* to cook them!" Ardelle added.

"I remember my mother putting cardboard in my shoes so my feet wouldn't *freeze* on the way to school," Wanda reminisced. "In my lunch sack would be onion and mustard sandwiches and maybe a little square of sugar if I was lucky!" Ardelle said.

"We'd sing Christmas carols and read the Christmas story out of the Bible, trying to *forget* the Depression," Bobchia said.

The boys crawled out from under the coffee table looking sad.

(We hadn't had a happy Christmas since Father had gotten ill.)

"I need a cookie." I said, hurrying to the kitchen, wiping a tear.

Mr. Brown said, "I remember waking in the morning with frost on my blankets and crawling out of bed and onto a linoleum floor."

Bobchia hugged the boys and said, "No wonder they call it the *Depression!* I'm *depressed* just hearing about it!"

"I'm not *depressed* in the least!" Ginger announced, promenading down the staircase and into the great room in a flowing, strapless peach gown into Mr. Hair's waiting embrace.

"*Mercy!*" Bobchia rolled her eyes.

Logan stuck his tongue out. "Yuck!"

"Yucky!" Andrew covered his eyes.

"Jen," Logan said, "Lucy's back on! Bring me some American cheese please! Not the pepper cheese either, like *last* time, okay?"

"Me too!" Andrew called.

Bobchia smiled and windshield-wipered her finger at me as I came into the room, giggling, eating a candy bar. "You found the *candy bar stash!*" I smiled at her with chocolate teeth.

I gave the boys their plates of cheese and joined them in front of the TV and watched Lucy stomp grapes.

Ginger stood up in front of Mr. Hair. "See the way Lucy's skirt is, honey? The snow would be so high that I couldn't even see the road from my house, and I'd have to tuck my dress between my legs from the back and push it in my *belt* up front to make pants so my legs wouldn't freeze on the way to school. *Just...like...this!*" We all watched her do the dastardly deed. Bobchia stood up with her hands on her hips. Ginger quickly sat down. Mr. Hair stretched up to her for a kiss. Bobchia gave them 'the look', then went to the kitchen for a shot of coffee.

Mr. Brown looked at me. "Kids nowadays are *spoiled.* They have people to drive them to school, and they get everything they want for Christmas—*everything!*" People agreed.

I hurried to my room. "They don't know anything about *us!*" I kicked the bed. "The Christmas after we found out about Father's illness was the most depressing, and the one after he'd died was no picnic either!" I wiped my tears and smiled at the picture on my dresser of Father feeding Blacky, his little black squirrel. "God, I am *thankful* for all my blessings, *really* and *truly* I am. I'm back where I belong, and I refuse to let that old prune spoil one more minute of my life! The next time he says anything to me, I'll just say GBY. Thank you God, for every day spent with my Bobchia is as much fun as *Christmas!*"

The next night when the tenants started talking about the Depression, I got up to leave.

Bobchia quickly spoke up. "You're *boring* these poor children to death! How about if I clear the candles and fruit bowls from the dining room table and make way for the things you've made for the Snowflake Festival?"

"Good idea!" Mrs. Dunham said.

Everyone scattered to their rooms. Mother came downstairs for a cup of tea. "What's going on?"

"You'll see," Bobchia said.

Soon the big table was filled with exquisite embroidered pillowcases from Izora and tablecloths from Venal. Aunt Ardelle brought down a box full of knitted baby sweaters, gloves, hats and booties and rainbow-colored baby blankets that Wanda had knitted. Gladys had a box full of afghans and a snowman quilt she had made with Aunt Ardelle and Wanda. Harold brought in a box from the trunk of his car that was full of beaded ornaments that Jody had made. They were all beautiful! (I struck a deal with Harold for a pink pearled ornament for Mother and a green pearled one for Bobchia to be paid for later with my birthday money.) Tall Cliff had bags of dried jerky and fruit that he proudly put on the table. Halfway Decent Henry set two boxes on the floor full of jewelry boxes with whittled tops. (He gave me one on the Q-T with a horse head on it that looked like Dollee).

Mr. Hair collected key chains and said he'd be willing to sell some. Frank brought in box after box of Mary's slates that she had hand-painted. Some of the slates had red cardinals in snowy pines and others had various sizes of snowmen, with **Merry Christmas** or **God Bless Our Home** written across the top of them. Frank and Mary's daughter, Patty, had a variety of beautiful hand-crafted ornaments and beeswax candles that she had stored in the cold room along with boxes of yummy chocolate covered cherries that her daughters, Lisa, Shelia and Laura, had made. Unfortunately, the chocolates never made it to the festival! Frank walked around collecting money from the tenants, with the boys in tow checking the floor for *dropped* change.

Helen said she'd make creampuffs and apple dumplings to sell, closer to the festival date. Mrs. Dunham put a box of purple and pink African Violets (wrapped in silver and gold foil for a festive touch) beside the table promising to make loaves of banana bread. Dora proudly set shoeboxes full of watercolor Christmas cards on the table. Spike had stacked Cliff's little grocery wagon high with birdhouses that he carefully pulled into the dining room as Homer pushed Mrs. Pratt across the room in her wheelchair. She was clutching two framed oil paintings and placed them on the coffee table. One was an autumn picture of the covered bridge, and the other was of the Red Barn Inn in winter. Bobchia quickly confiscated the one of the Inn asking Tall Cliff to hang it over a couch. "It's beautiful, Homer, just beautiful!" She said. "No rent this month."

"We pay *rent?*" He asked.

Overall, it was quite an impressive array of soon-to-be-sold Christmas gifts. "Mercy, I forgot *my* pictures!" Bobchia hurried to the pantry and brought out a box covered with oilcloth that held several cross-stitched pictures of daisies and daffodils tacked in barn wood frames that Harold had made. She gently got them out and leaned them along the dining room wall, watching me admire them, taking note when I leaned down in front of the one with the handful of daisies tied in green ribbon.

"What is a festival?" Andrew asked.

"Well, it's a craft show at the Christian Center. It's a *fundraiser.* The town has one every year to raise money for the food bank and for Christmas gifts for the needy."

"*A food bank?*" Logan asked. "That's funny!"

"It's a place where people who need food can get some. The admission price to the festival is a can of food, and there are penny games plus craft tables to display Christmas gifts. We sell soup and desserts. Then there's a parade that starts on Main Street and ends at the center."

Andrew perked up. "A parade in the *snow?*"

"Are you *teasing?*" Logan asked.

"No."

"Wow!"

"Cool!"

"And after the craft show is over," Bobchia continued, "The high school kids come in and decorate for the Snowflake Dance."

"I didn't sign up to decorate because of my foot, but I'd like to go to the dance. Can I?" I asked.

"*To a dance?* With that foot?" Mother questioned.

"Well, all my friends will be there..."

"You mean *Andy,*" Mother said.

"Well, I don't know." I looked down.

Bobchia couldn't stand to see me disappointed. "I'll be there, Clair. Harold and I run the concession."

"Well, I guess you can go if your grandmother will keep an *eye* on you," Mother said.

"Mother, chee! *I'm sixteen!*"

"That's precisely why you *need* watching!"

Bobchia laughed. "Of course I'll keep an eye on her." She windshield-wiped her finger at me and laughed.

"Clair, the boys are eating the popcorn strings on the tree *again!*" Spike said disgusted, coming from the great room. Mother hurried in and chased the boys around the coffee table until she ran out of breath. Then she grabbed her tea and went back upstairs to study. The boys piled in front of the TV to watch Lassie save Timmy from the well…again.

"Bobchia, the festival sounds like so much fun!" I said.

"Oh, I almost forgot, they crown a Miss Snowflake at the dance. You could be a candidate for Miss Snowflake! I'm sure *you'd* get lots of votes!"

"Thanks, but no thanks." I shook my head. "What I am interested in doing is raising money for Christmas gifts, but I don't really know how to make anything. Do you have any ideas?"

Bobchia looked at the table of crafts for a moment. "Let's see, something *is* missing, but what?" She snapped her fingers. "I know! Luella's hard tack candy! We made it together every year. I wasn't going to make it this year because, well, I think I still have most of the flavors in the pantry. I'll check and make a list. As I recall, it was a good seller. I'll have Harold and Cliff get that big piece of marble out of the shed and put it on the corner table in the kitchen. There we can roll it out and cut it. We sold every bag we ever made! It will be fun!"

"Everything is *fun* with you, Bobchia."

Andrew whined, "I want to make stuff too!"

"Me, too! I want to have *fun!*" Logan said.

"Why, of course *you do!* What can you make?" Bobchia asked.

"*Nothing!*" Andrew hung his head.

"One time I made a macaroni necklace for Mother at summer camp, but it fell apart," Logan said.

"That's because you *hit* me with it on the way home." Andrew pointed to his shoulder.

"Oh yeah, I forgot."

"You could both make some; I'm sure they will sell like hot cakes," Bobchia smiled.

"Really?" Andrew asked.

"Really."

"Yahoo!"

"Homework *first,* crafts second, deal?" Bobchia said.

"Deal!"

"Deal!"

"Slow and steady—"

"Wins the race, Bobchia," Andrew said proudly.

"You're learning!" She smiled.

My next few nights were dedicated to making peppermint, cinnamon, anise, clove, wintergreen, and licorice hard candy. It was all so delicious that Bobchia had to keep reminding me to quit eating it or I wouldn't have any to *sell!* The kitchen was hotter than hot when Aunt Ardelle, Helen, Mrs. Dunham and even Ginger, (under Mr. Hair's watchful eye), baked pies, cookies and breads storing them in the freezer of the mud room. Bobchia had one hot flash after another. There were fans blowing from each corner of the kitchen, but they didn't seem to help. With my thin Florida blood, I enjoyed the heat as I rolled and cut the candy, while Miss Minnie's ears blew in the breeze from Bobchia's apron.

Bobchia patiently taught me the technique of candy making. I was proud of the colorful bags as I placed them into boxes.

"They're pretty, Sweetie." She held a bag up to the overhead light. "Look, they shine like Christmas lights!"

"Thank you so much for showing me how to make all these. Now I'll have money for Christmas gifts!"

"You did a great job!"

"I hope I'll be a *patient Bobchia* like you are, someday."

She patted my hand. "Sweetie Pie, you are a future Bobchia in the making."

The boys strung box after box of macaroni, using most of Bobchia's glitter. They talked of the toys they would buy when they each made a *million* dollars. Bobchia tried to slow them down, knowing *she'd* end up buying all their necklaces, bracelets and tie tacks.

"Boys, how much are you going to charge for one of your beautiful creations?" She asked curiously.

"One hundred dollars!" Andrew said proudly.

Logan laughed. "Are you kidding? We'll be lucky if we get *fifty bucks* for one of these things!"

"How much would you pay for one of those necklaces, Sweetie?" Bobchia asked me.

"Oh, *five cents*, I guess only if someone *twisted my arm.*"

"*Five cents* for all this *work?*" Andrew tried to kick me.

"Stop it, or I'll strangle you with one of those *ugly* things!" I said.

"You're just *jealous* because I thought of making them *before* you did!"

"*Hardly!*"

"Stop bickering!" Bobchia tried one on. "Well, boys," she said, looking at her reflection in the glass cupboard, "I think ten cents is a *fair price* for a macaroni necklace."

"*Just ten cents?*"

"*Ten cents?*" Andrew's face fell.

Logan looked disappointed then asked; "How many would we have to sell to get a hundred dollars?"

"How many dimes are in a dollar?" Bobchia asked him.

"Ten."

"And how many dollars are in a hundred dollars?"

"A hundred."

"That's right, so what is ten times a hundred?"

"Ten hundred?"

"What's another name for ten hundred?"

"I don't know. A thousand?"

"That's right!"

"Do you mean we would have to make a thousand necklaces to get a hundred dollars?" Logan frowned.

"Well, you'd have to *sell* a thousand necklaces to make a hundred dollars," Bobchia said.

Andrew looked at Logan. "Get that finger *out* of your nose and *string* that macaroni!"

The next day Harold brought ground pine from Wayne's farm and piled it in the cold room so Mother could make wreaths between her studies. Spike, still feeling the guilt about *the tobacco juicing*, went in after feeding the animals every morning and put some together for her. He even painted white tips on the pinecones that the boys had collected from the 'pinecone trees' in the yard, but he left the bow making to Mother. There were only two days until the festival, and it was getting down to the wire. Everyone was trying to finish their projects and help those who lagged behind.

The next night was Friday night, the big basketball game against the Pleasantville Falcons, our rival school. Beverly Jean had just got her license that week, and in study hall that day we *hatched* a plan on how to *convince* Mother to let me ride to the game with her. We wanted to get to the game early to sit in the seats behind our team, but because of the time it took for Mother to give Bev *the third degree* and the time it took for us to *persuade* Mother of Bev's safe driving record, we were running late. Mother watched as we hurried to the car. Bev inched the car down the lane, then gassed it over the covered bridge. Still, by the time we picked up Dawnette, Mary Ann, Betty Ann, Donna and Kathy, drove to the school, found a parking place, ran through the parking lot and saw the long lines stretching to the ticket counters, our hopes to get seats behind our team, were dashed.

"Oh no!" I exclaimed.

"Look at that line! We'll never get a seat behind the players now, and I promised Brian I'd sit right behind him!" Beverly Jean said defeated.

I looked at the 'Go Rockets!' signs plastered all over the walls. "Wait, I have an idea! *Stick to me like glue!* Excuse us! Pardon us! Sorry, *Rocket reporter* here!"

"Where's your *badge?*" A man asked.

"I don't remember *them* being reporters!" A girl said.

We struggled through the maze of people, finally making it to the front of the ticket line as I desperately searched the bottom of my purse for the badge. *"Ta-da!"* I proudly held it up to the groaning teens behind us and pinned it on, then nudged my friends toward the gym.

My foot throbbed after running and climbing the bleachers, but it was well worth the pain as we sat in the choice seats!

"You never mentioned *covering* the game tonight," Beverly Jean said.

"I'm not. See Rocket Recorder Ron over there writing in his notebook already? He is covering the game tonight. That boy is a 'living encyclopedia' of school history. He told me his hobby is collecting yearbooks. I bet he's writing about our *rivalry* with Pleasantville right this very minute!"

"I think he's kind of cute. He'll probably be a writer at **The Herald** like his father." Donna said.

"He didn't get the alumni pin for nothing! It's in his blood! Boy, his writing sure puts me to *shame*. But since my Recorder badge got us these seats, I better take notes on the game." I said pulling a little notepad out of my purse.

"What do you mean? I think you're a good reporter!" Dawnette said.

"I do too," Beverly Jean added.

"You just have a different style then Ron, that's all," Donna said.

"Thank you ladies, but…" I dug in my purse for a pen.

"Hey!" Beverly Jean said.

"What?" I looked up.

"Take note on *who* just arrived!"

Marcy and the other cheerleaders, dressed in their brown-and-gold outfits, came in with their noses in the air and sat on the front bleachers.

The gymnasium was packed shoulder to shoulder. The crowd erupted in cheers as the players ran out of the locker rooms dribbling basketballs. My eyes were glued on Andy as he ran up and down the court. He spotted me, smiled, shot, made a basket, quickly dribbled and made another! Marcy looked back at me over her granny glasses. He smiled at me again! I held my breath. When he ran to the other side of the gym, I turned to Beverly Jean. "Did you see that? *He smiled at me!*"

"I was too busy watching Brian."

Dawnette and Kathy didn't see him either because they were too busy debating on who was the cutest player—Mark or Randy. Betty Ann was busy watching Nicolas and Donna was busy watching *all* the other cute players. Mary Ann's eyes never left the shortest but fastest guy on the team, Casey, our star player. "He may not be tall, but he sure sends me!"

The game was about to start. The players stood beside the cheerleaders, facing the American flag as it lowered from the ceiling along with the state flag. Marcy squeezed in beside Andy pulling on his arm. He nudged her and put his hand over his heart as we sang the **National Anthem** and the school song. Andy turned. "Glad you could make the game, Skip. I'll make a basket for you!" I shook my head, speechless! He smiled and ran to his teammates.

I grabbed Beverly Jeans arm. "Did you hear that? Did you hear that? He's going to make a basket *for me!*"

"Groovy, I heard him, now quit squeezing my arm! Quit it! You'll give me *liver spots!*"

I watched the game intently, jotting down Andy's every move. When our team scored, we girls jumped! We screamed! We moved like hula girls as the basketball ran around the rim! "*We* can cheer just as good as *they* can!" Donna said excitedly. (We promised each other that we would try out for cheerleading next year!) It was a blast watching Andy score his five baskets!

Then, as time was running out, Joe blocked a player then Frank came from nowhere and stole the ball and threw it to Andy who dribbled wildly down the court, finding himself blocked from every side. Casey maneuvered through the tall players, but he too was blocked, so he got down and looked through the tallest player's knees at Andy. That's when the most unbelievable thing happened. Andy *rolled* the ball to Casey! Casey grabbed it and shot another sideways shot. Andy rebounded and rolled it *again* to Casey who made the last basket, giving Titusville the thrilling victory over Pleasantville—35 to 20! The crowd went wild!

Afterward, I waited with Beverly in the bleachers for Brian to come out of the locker room. The other girls left to stand outside, hoping to talk with the players they had crushes on. I looked at my notes. "I can't use any of these notes! I don't even know who *else* made baskets!"

"Brian made four!"

"And who else?"

"Frank, Joe and Casey."

"How many?"

"I don't know!"

"*See what I mean?*" In the next publication of the school newspaper, I admired the expertise writing of Rocket Recorder Ron's brilliant take on the game. He detailed every player's accomplishments and then encapsulated the entire game in one *brilliant* sentence: 'With a crowd of 500 sitting practically on the playing floor of the small gym, THS downed the plucky Pleasantville bunch with smoothly running passes.' (Writing is *definitely* in that boy's blood!)

Marcy stood in front of the locker room door waiting for Andy.

"Look at her standing *there!*" I scoffed. "Let's go!"

"I told Brian I'd *wait!*"

"Great!"

"Ride the wave, girl. She's a chaser; no guy likes a *chaser,* relax!"

"How can I relax?" I said defeated, looking at Marcy. "Drive me home!"

Bev changed the subject. "I'm so glad to have my license. At least I can get away from home for a while!"

"When's your mom going to have that baby?" I asked.

"*Every day* last week and *every day* this week so far! It is so, so, so *embarrassing!* My parents are so *old.* I didn't even know they still *kissed!*"

Andy had gone out the back door and came around to the bleachers through the side door. He walked over and sat beside me. I was thrilled! He looked over at Marcy shaking his head. Then he asked, "Skip, how'd ya like the game?"

"You played *great!*"

"Thanks. Pleasantville always gives us a good game." He smiled at my badge. "You can *quote me.*"

"*I will!*" I blurted.

He chuckled. "How's your foot?"

"Not too bad. How's your toboggan?" *(Why did I ask such a stupid question?)* He laughed. My heart fluttered.

Brian came out of the locker room, waved and walked across the gym to Beverly Jean. Marcy watched him and then spotted Andy.

Andy stood up. "I just can't *hide* from that girl, but I'll keep *trying.* Later, Skip."

"Later."

He jumped down the three rows of bleachers and jogged out the door. Marcy ran after him.

"*Did you see that?*" I said, grabbing and squeezing Bev's arm.

"I was sitting beside you! *Let go of my arm!*"

"Oh, Sorry!"

Bev and Brian dropped me off at the Inn. "Bev, *for sure* you're going to sit with me at Bobchia's booth tomorrow?"

"Yeah, I'll bring my scrapbook. I have pictures of the team. Andy is in them!"

"Groovy! I can't wait! Too bad Dawnette can't make it."

"She has to watch Lou Ellen again! They don't *dare* leave her home alone after *last time*. At least they still have their *pets!*"

"Thanks for the ride you two! Go slow; Mother is at the bedroom window. See ya at the center tomorrow!"

"See ya!"

After eating half of a tin of cookies, telling Bobchia about the game, filling up five pages in my journal, and saying my prayers, I had the *best* and the *worst* dream of my entire life. Andy and I were playing a one-on-one basketball game. He *praised* me for my over the shoulder shot, head bunt shot and hip shot. I even *kicked* it in for a five pointer, while Marcy, in her cute little referee outfit, constantly tried to get between us, blowing her stupid whistle. Slowly I realized her whistle was my alarm! I shut it off and got under the covers. The cats jumped on the bed, wanting to be fed. I pulled the covers down and looked into Joan of Arc's eyes. "All right, I'll get up!" When I sat up, I got excited. "Today is the Snowflake Festival! *I'll see Andy!*" I jumped out of bed, landing hard on my sore foot. "Ouch! Boy that hurt!" I fed the cats, put on my robe and limped to the kitchen.

Bobchia sat at the table reading her Bible. She held her hand up for me to be quiet then said aloud, "**'For now we see in a mirror dimly, but then face to face. Now I know in part, but then I shall know just as I also am known. And now abide faith, hope, love, these three; but the greatest of these is love.'** So true, so true! What could possibly be greater than *love?*" She hugged me. "What are you doing up at six on a Saturday?"

"You *read* in the morning too?" I asked as I sat down.

"Daytime, nighttime, sometimes both. I need more than *Geritol* and *caffeine* to run this place, ya know! God's Word makes me *strong*. Besides I like to read before the Inn gets loud."

She poured the last shot of coffee out of the pot and made another. "I knew a couple once that had fourteen children and never had a quiet minute until they all were in bed. They were always exhausted!" She took a sip. "He worked for Quaker State and was on the lease all day and could talk with the Lord any time he wanted while checking the wells, but she was housebound with the children! Think of it, fourteen children. Mercy! One day I decided to *bless* her with some pies. Even as I stood on their rickety porch, I could hear the commotion inside! I knocked and knocked. Finally one of her little ones opened the door and said, 'Come in, but Mama is praying.' I thought, *Praying? How could anyone possibly pray with all this noise?* I stepped into the kitchen and there Sally was, sitting in a chair with her apron up over her face, praying as her children played tag around her! It was the only way she could *make time for the Lord.* That made me ashamed of myself. No longer did I have the excuse that I was *too busy* to talk to God every day, so I started setting my alarm half an hour earlier, and now my quiet time with Him is the *treasure* of my day! I have a cup of coffee and a talk with God while the sun and the rolls are rising."

(That conversation was labeled in my journal as, **Lesson to Live by Number 27.**)

She put pans of cinnamon rolls in the oven and set the timer. "So what do I owe to this early morning visit?"

"I just thought it would be nice to *talk* with you."

"Oh good! What would you like to *talk* about?"

"Nothing in particular."

She waited and waited. After several smiles followed by shots of coffee, she jumped off her stool announcing, "The kitchen is *officially* open! Breakfast is now being served in The Red Barn Inn!" She buried her head in the fridge, stacking food onto the counter.

"Please just *one* egg and *one* piece of toast, *no* home fries," I said.

She stood up. "*No home fries?* Are you sick?

"No."

"You can have *all the bacon you want!* Your brothers won't be awake for hours."

"Just one, make that *two*, strips, please."

"*That's all?*"

"Yeah."

"Foot bothering you?"

"It was fine until I got out of bed." I went into the bathroom and got an aspirin.

"Here's some juice. I hope people don't dilly-dally this morning. I want to get there early to get the big tables. Ardelle said she'd man the stoves after I leave."

The timer went off. Bobchia set pans of cinnamon rolls on a wire rack, cut out two big ones and put them on a plate in front of me. "There ya go, for starters!"

I tried to ignore them, impatiently waiting for my egg and bacon hoping to somehow *miraculously* lose five pounds before the dance. I said grace and hurried through breakfast, staring at the rolls.

"Are you sure you don't have *anything* you want to talk about? *Any questions?*"

"I'm good, and so is this bacon." I said as I shoved it into my mouth. I stood up, looking at the rolls. Bobchia laughed when I cut one in half. "My jeans are *tight*. See you later."

She turned to the sink and watched in the reflection of the window as I grabbed the other *whole* cinnamon roll and left. "Thanks for the *talk*, Sweetie."

"You're welcome!"

I hurried back to my room, took a shower and set my hair. While under the dryer, I filled the pages of my journal with my anticipation of a chance meeting with Andy at the Christian Center. I imagined that on the mere chance of *seeing me*, he wouldn't be able to resist my *beauty*, and he'd run to me and *beg me* to go to the dance with him tonight. Anyway, it looked good on paper, and it was fun to think about! After a forty-five minute bake under the dryer, I took the rollers out and got back under for another five. Then I looked through my closet for just the right outfit. *The red blouse and the blue hip-huggers with the tiny roses should turn his head,* I thought. *That is if…I…can…just…get…them…zipped!* I laid across the bed and sucked in my stomach. The zipper *finally* went up. *"Whew!"*

I put my makeup on and combed my hair into a perfect flip. When no other shoes would fit, I stuck the ugly slipper on and went to the great room where the tenants were packing their crafts in to boxes.

"Hi, Mother," I said.

"Hi. I want you to stay *off* that foot today, young lady. Get your coat and boots on and warm up the wagon for me, will you?" She dangled the keys in front of me.

"Yeah, thanks!" I gladly grabbed them, thinking I'd drive it around the crowded parking area. (But remembered the *dead bush* and thought better of it.) I started the car. It startled me when it backfired. Thick black smoke encircled the car.

Mother got mad when she overheard Cliff and Spike, who were helping her pack the wagon, make bets on whether the station wagon would make it across the covered bridge, let alone to the festival!

Pretending to drive, I watched Harold and Bobchia pack the Metropolitan. Finally they carried the boxes of pies out, barely squeezing them in. Spike stuck his head out from the kitchen door and hollered, "Bev's on the phone!"

I hurried inside. "What do you mean you *can't* meet me there? Beverlyyy! I'll be *by myself all day!* Sorry, I know it's not your *fault.* No, honest, I'm not mad. I hope your mom is okay. Sorry you'll miss the dance tonight. I'm sure Brian won't dance with anyone, but if he does, *you'll* be the first to know! Call me later, and let me know if it's a boy or a girl. Okay. See ya!"

Sadly, I hobbled toward the car. Logan and Andrew ran ahead of me with blankets tied over their coat collars, slowly dodging the tootsie rolls on the sidewalk.

"*Hurry up!* My hair is getting snowed on!" I yelled at them.

"A *tornado* couldn't hurt it!" Logan yelled. They deliberately walked slower.

I got in the car and slammed the door. The boys got into the backseat yawning. Mother hurried and got in. "Brr!"

"Why do we have to go so *early* anyways?" Andrew yawned.

"Your grandmother has to do *everything* early! Surely you know that by now!" Mother turned to me. "Why did you shut the car off?"

"Because I went to the telephone."

"If this thing won't *start,* we'll have to take all this stuff back out!" She turned the key. It backfired, again, then the lights and wipers came on. With a thick cloud of smoke, the car started.

"I hope Rhea hurries up before this thing stalls!"

I told Mother of my bad news. "Bev's not going to the center because her Mother went to the hospital last night. She has to babysit her sister, Kathy. I wish you could stay with me at the booth. You could *read* there."

"I wouldn't be able to concentrate. It's just for a few hours. *You'll survive."* Mother rolled her window down. The smoke came in. We gagged. "Rhea," she called, "I think that coat rack will lie on top of the boxes in the back." Mother got out and helped Bobchia carry it over.

Harold came out complaining and yelling at Bobchia while carrying a heavy kettle of Cliff's chili to his car. "Hurry up, woman! I'm already *late* to sign up for the ice fishing contest! Frank left thirty minutes ago with Old Faithful!"

"Mary?" She asked.

"No, his *fishing pole!* Hurry up!"

"The lake is big and has plenty of big fish in it, and quit calling me *woman,* and don't you dare spill a drop of Cliff's chili. It's worth its weight in gold! It has a whole pound of bacon in it!"

It was a tight fit, but Harold got the kettle on the floor of the backseat of his car. Mother got back in the car and put it in gear. It backfired again. She turned it around, drove through the cloud of smoke and headed down the lane. All of a sudden, Harold honked and passed us, almost hitting the front fender of station wagon!

Mother laid on the horn. "What on earth is the matter with that *man?"*

"Step on the gas and beat him!" Logan leaned forward.

"Yeah, blow his *fenders* off!" Andrew cried.

I could see Bobchia hitting Harold's arm the whole way to the center. When we pulled up to the center, Bobchia pushed her door open with her foot. "Lead foot! Mercy! Are you trying to *kill* my grandchildren? *They just got here!* You deserve to get arrested *again,* and when you do, don't expect me to *bail* you out! You can just sit in jail and read books on *safe driving!"* He sighed and pulled the kettle out of the back of the car. "Try and get it to the kitchen *without* spilling it! I was going to charge a dollar a bowl, that is if there is anything *left* in the kettle to sell after that ride!"

Harold gripped the heavy kettle's handle with both hands as Bobchia opened the door to the center for him. The boys ran ahead of him, deliberately *stopping short* in front of him. He quickly grabbed the bottom of the swinging kettle. "Get out of my way or *wear it!"* They laughed walking slowly in front of him, until he was able to get around them, carrying the liquid gold to the kitchen.

Bobchia hurried in looking for the biggest tables, but they were already taken. She and Mother slid several smaller tables together while Harold brought in the boxes and the boys played tag around him. I casually looked for Andy.

"Sweetie, get those tablecloths and the glitter out of that box. Presentation is everything, you know, I read it in a **Betty Crocker Cookbook.**"

We spread the cloths, then sprinkled the glitter and arranged the bigger items in back. Bobchia arranged the baked goods in front. Mother displayed her wreaths on the coat rack beside the table. The boys pushed back the baked goods, along with my bags of candy carefully arranging their macaroni masterpieces. They *beautified* them even more with *extra* glitter, overflowing it onto their shirts. Bobchia grinned, as they *sparkled.* She reached into her purse and pulled out two, crisp one-dollar bills. "I think I'll take one of *you* and one of *you."* She pointed at each of the boys. "Here are my dollars"

"Thanks, Bobchia!"

"Thanks!"

She kissed the boys on their cheeks. They quickly wiped her kisses off and looked around to see if anyone had seen her kissing them. She windshield-wipered her finger. "Remember—"

"We know!" Andrew said.

"Chee!" Logan rolled his eyes.

Mother gave Bobchia 'the look', got into her purse and also handed each of them a dollar.

"Thanks, Mom!" Andrew said.

"Thanks!" Logan echoed. "Let's play that game over there!" When giving Mother a hug, they accidentally knocked Mr. Hair's box of key chains to the floor.

"I'll get them. Go have fun." Mother said. They ran to the penny toss games as Mother picked up the key chains. While arranging them on the table, she turned white reaching for a chair. "Rhea, look at *those!"*

*"Mercy, what's the matter, Clair?"*

*"Look!"* (Mr. Hair's key chains were *braided hair!)* Mother shivered and stood up. "I have to go study. *Bye!"* She hurried out the door.

Bobchia boxed up the key chains (they conveniently came up missing). We displayed Halfway Decent Henry's carved boxes and the rest of the items until our tables were full.

Across from us, on the biggest tables were store-bought items with *handcraft pricing.* A woman strategically placed silver ballot boxes with glittery snowflakes on them. In the middle of the biggest snowflake was a picture of Marcy in a long, red velvet dress holding two snow white poodles wearing tiny green fur jackets with little green bows on their ears. Underneath the picture was the phrase, '**Vote for Marcy Brown to wear the Snowflake crown!**'

Bobchia smiled at the woman, but she quickly turned her head. Bobchia looked to the ceiling, took a deep breath and said, "I better see what the ladies are doing in the kitchen and put back some pies for the dance tonight. I hope we have enough coffee. I'll be back."

Alison, a cute girl on my debate team, asked if she could put her ballot box on our table.

"Sure, I hope you win!" I told her.

"I think it's a losing battle," she said as she looked over at Marcy's picture. She handed me a shoebox with her name written across 'Size 8.'

"I'll vote for *you.*"

"You will? Thanks!"

When she left, I looked into Mother's wreath box and got out a roll of ribbon and some little pinecones that had fallen off of the wreaths. I wrapped red ribbon around the box, made a big bow, taped pinecones on the corners and wrote Alison's name in glue and sprinkled it with glitter. Then I set the box in front of the birdhouses with the note pad and pen I had in my purse. By then my ankle was throbbing, so I sat down and propped my foot up on a box. Looking at the ugly slipper, I unfolded one of Izora's flowery pillowcases, laid it over the slipper and studied the intricate embroidery.

"Hi, Skip! How are you going to dance tonight with a *pillowcase on your foot?*

I sat up red-faced, folded it and put it back on the table. "I...I..."

"Oh, I see you have your *precious jewels* for sale! Here's a beauty! Hold out your hand." He pushed a macaroni bracelet onto my wrist. "At least you won't go *hungry* while you're sitting here."

"*I will never eat this!*" I blurted out.

Marcy came over and pulled on Andy's arm. (It had occurred to me that his right arm had to be at *least* a foot longer than his left because she was always tugging on it.) Marcy noticed the ballot box. "*Alison? Oh please!*" She stuck her nose up and said, "I hate to break up this intelligent conversation, but we are wasting time. There are a lot of tables that have *more* beautiful things on them, such as *mine!*"

"Oh, I don't know, did you see these *beautiful jewels?*" Andy said as he picked up a macaroni necklace. Marcy grabbed it and threw it to the floor, breaking it into a million pieces!

Andrew ran over. "Hey girl, you owe me ten cents!"

"Ten cents for that piece of *junk?*" She laughed.

"*Junk?*" He kicked her in the shin.

"Ouch!" She looked at him with wild eyes.

"Andrew!" I tried to grab him, but he kicked her again.

"*You little snot!*" Marcy said.

"Hey, you can't talk to my brother like *that!* You called his necklace junk, what did you want him to do, *kiss you?*" I asked.

"Yuck! I would never kiss a *pig* in the face in my whole life!" Logan ran over laughing.

"Shut up, you *little snots!* I'll be lucky if I can walk tonight to get my crown!" Andy walked away, laughing. Marcy limped after him and yelled, "Well, are you going to pick *me* up, like you did *her?*" She pointed back to me.

"Not unless *I have to!*" He said.

She ran up to him, forgetting that she was hurt. He looked down at her leg. "It doesn't seem to be broken!" She pulled on his arm and hobbled beside him.

Andrew yelled, "What about my *ten cents?*"

"I'll give it to Skip tonight," Andy hollered back.

"Huh?"

"*You'll get it!*"

"I better, or I'll call the police! *Dumb pig face girl!*" Andrew looked upset that he'd been swindled until he noticed the bracelet on my arm. "You bought one of *my* bracelets!"

"Well, Andy put it on me."

"Then he owes me…"

"Twenty cents." Logan said.

"Hey I was *figuring* in my head!"

"We don't got *all* day! We got to go play that game again!"

"Do you really *like* that bracelet, Jen?" Andrew asked.

"*It's more beautiful than diamonds!*" I twirled it around my wrist.

"Honest? Than *real* diamonds?"

"Honest!"

They hugged me. (They had not done *that* since Father's funeral.) They started to walk away.

"Wow, more beautiful than *diamonds!*" Andrew exclaimed.

"Brother, are we ever going to *make money today!*" Logan high-fived Andrew, then they disappeared into the crowd. I stood twirling the bracelet and watching Andy weave around the room until I got a customer wanting to buy a birdhouse then I lost track of him.

Several times within that hour the boys ran over and asked me the same question: *"Have we made a hundred bucks yet?"*

"So far, *zero* dollars."

"What? Are you *sure?"* Logan asked.

They added more glitter on their macaroni and their shoes. Discouraged, not wanting to go home broke, they asked Bobchia to call Mother from the kitchen telephone, and begged Mother to deliver Joan of Arc for the pet show. (They had their eye on the five-dollar prize.) Spike brought the cat to the center in a towel. He handed her to me and then went to buy a bowl of chili. The boys ran over and demanded the cat.

"Gently, *gently,"* I told them. "She's scared."

Mother soon arrived to watch the contest. She asked the boys, "So you really think she'll win?"

"Mother, I *know* she'll win because she was so good to her babies," Andrew said.

"Uh oh, look at *her head!"* Logan pointed at her bald spots.

"We can cover it with one of *these!"* Andrew grabbed one of Aunt Ardelle's knitted, pink, angora, hooded baby sweaters and put it on her, while the cat meowed.

I laughed. "Wouldn't Aunt Ardelle be thrilled seeing one of her sweaters on a *cat!"*

Mother nodded and made the boys put an *IOU* in the cash box for the sweater. "What did you just spell?" Andrew asked her.

After the pet show, the boys hurried back to the booth with the cat. They were upset because Joan of Arc *did* win a prize, she won the two-dollar prize for the *ugliest* pet. To top it off, they still owed a dollar to Aunt Ardelle.

Logan tried to make the cat feel better as he held her. "You're not *as* ugly as the cat I seen dead on the road!"

Andrew petted her saying. "I know you're not the prettiest cat, but you are a *hero* cat, and that should *count for something!"* He started to tear up as he looked into her eyes. Mother pushed his hair across his forehead.

"It does *count*, honey boy. She is the most beautiful pet *inside* for she has the *unselfish heart of a mother.*" (Wow! Mother defending a *cat!*)

The boys struggled to hold onto Joan of Arc but she was determined to jump into my lap squirming to get to me.

"I'm going to buy you a toy for Christmas and some candy with my share of the 'roni money." Andrew told the cat.

"Me too, if we ever *sell* these *beautiful* necklaces."

"That would be sweet of you boys. You both share that two-dollar prize on something good to eat, okay? The chili has a lot of bacon in it." Mother smiled at them.

"Do we have to? Bobchia fed us a *couple of times so far.* Can't we use this on a fun game?" Andrew asked.

"Okay, but be good and listen to your grandmother. I've got to get back to my books. Give me a kiss."

They handed me the cat and looked to see if their friends were watching before giving Mother a peck on the cheek, then took off running. Mother smiled watching them disappear into the crowd. She reached into her coat and paid off the boys' debt. "How's your foot?"

"All right. I keep propping it up."

"I wish I would have thought to bring you some aspirin. Rhea probably has some in her purse. I'll check."

"Thanks."

"I have to give her the keys to the station wagon anyway. I guess I'll have to ride back with Spike."

"Make sure his window is *down!*" I chuckled.

"Very, funny! I'll be back."

I strained to see Andy, but the center had filled up fast.

Harold hurried over to me with a plaque, smelling of fish with frost on his eyebrows! "*I won!*"

"Good."

"I'll say! I caught a twenty-seven pound, forty-eight and a half inch Muskie! I beat out Frank and Kimbul! Can you believe it? My fish broke the record. *The record!* Thanks to *Old Faithful!*"

"Mary?"

"No, my *fishing pole!*"

I couldn't take my eyes off of his frozen eyebrows, going up and down. "Do you want to see the Muskie? It's in my trunk."

"Is it *dead?*"

"*Well of course it's dead!*"

"Thanks anyway, but the boys would probably like to see it," As I leaned backward from the Muskie smell, Joan of Arc leaned forward, out of her hood.

"Look at you in that fancy sweater." Harold said.

With her paw the cat reached out and pulled Harold's hand to her nose. She smelled it, licked it and then *bit it!* "*Ouch!* Is that anyway to treat your *rescuer?*" He asked. I laughed. "If you would have seen that cat carrying her kittens from underneath the porch it would have broken your heart! Poor thing." He tried to pet her again but she bit him again! "Ouch! It's *me,* Harold, remember? The guy that kept you and your family from *starving* to death! *Some grateful cat you are!*"

I hugged the cat as we laughed. Mother came back with two aspirin and a glass of water. "Take these." When she handed me the aspirin, she got a *whiff* of Harold and stepped backward. He told her about the Muskie, held the plaque out to her and asked her to take it with her to the Inn so it wouldn't get lost.

"Well, take it! Here, it won't *bite!*"

"It *smells* like it will!"

I choked.

"Oh never mind! I'll go show it to Rhea!" Harold took off for the kitchen.

Mother and I laughed as Joan of Arc struggled to follow him. "Now Joan of Arc, just because he *smells* like cat food, doesn't mean he *is!*" I told her, laughing.

Mother looked over the tables. "You've sold quite a bit, even some wreaths."

"Bobchia said that after the parade, it really gets busy."

Spike came over and laughed with us about *smelly* Harold. He said, "Rhea told him, 'If you plan on dancing with me tonight, you had better go home and soak in a tub of Old Spice for the next *six hours!*'"

Joan of Arc drew a crowd of kids who laughed and pointed at her bald spots. *If they only knew her story,* I thought, *they'd be petting her!* I shooed them away and put her hood back up. I had hoped to keep her for company, but the confusion had her on edge.

Spike took her. "Come on, girl. Let's see if we can tune in a football game while the boys are *here.*" Mother gave him 'the look.'

"Sorry, Clair. Are you ready? You drive, and I'll hold the cat. How's that?" He asked smiling.

"Spike, make sure Aunt Ardelle doesn't see her, okay?" I told him.

"Don't worry, they left early to go to Saturday card club at Jim and Rose's, and they left the old bird with the other *old birds,* Izora and Venal!" He laughed. "See you later!"

"Jen, keep your eye on the boys! Rhea's busy in the kitchen," Mother said.

"Okay. Wait you two! Come back! Don't forget to *vote!*" I motioned them back.

"For *who?*" I pointed to the box. "Who is she?" Mother asked.

"A cute girl on my debate team."

Spike looked over at Marcy's picture. "I think I'll vote for *that* cute girl over there!"

"Spike, *don't you dare!* Vote for Alison!"

"Okay, okay!" They did, and so did everyone else that I could *persuade.*

The parade that had started at the Christian Center an hour ago, with the school band playing **Silent Night,** was now returning and marching to **Jingle Bells.** Bobchia and I went to the window and looked at the floats that were lined up clear passed the gazebo. A gust of wind tore the strings off of the aluminum foil stars, scattering them through the street. Our church's float, with Pastor Jay as one of the kings and Lois with her choir of angels *(minus two),* scrambled into the center with their wings askew. It seemed like the whole town came into the Christian Center after the parade, dropping can goods off at the door, buying crafts, playing games, and eating desserts.

I saw Andy leaning on a wall beside the kitchen enjoying a piece of Bobchia's home made pie. He smiled at me then Marcy slid in front of him to watch him chew. That was the last I saw of him as people packed the center. By midafternoon I had sold all my bags of candy except for the half-eaten one in my purse, and our tables were almost empty. What we didn't sell we traded with other vendors. It was a great day for the food bank and for me! The boys were excited that most of their *fine jewelry* had remarkably sold at the *last minute.*

"A *miracle*, Bobchia!" Logan cheered.
"A *real true* miracle!" Andrew beamed.
A miracle, *indeed!*

Bobchia closed the kitchen around three so we had time to pack up before the teens came in to decorate. She and I gathered our purchases and put them on a table by the back door. "I ran out of desserts and had to sell some of the pies that I had put back for tonight, mercy, now I'll have to go home and get *Christmas pies* out of the freezer!" She tapped me on the shoulder and laughed. "I know what I'll do! I'll bring Ginger's pies tonight! *Warn your friends!*" She snorted. "I'll pull the car around; you get the boys. Grab their coats, will you?" She giggled as she pulled on her coat and headed for the door.

I limped through the center looking for the boys. I heard their laughter in the lobby, and peeked around the corner. There in front of the long, skinny door of the Coke machine stood Logan on a chair. He popped off the tops of the horizontal bottles of Coke, as Andrew beneath was catching the Coke in a paper cup, while he drank out of another!

In the deepest voice I could muster, I said, "*Stop, police!*" Without looking, Andrew ran out the door. Logan jumped off the chair, fell onto the wet floor and slid after him. I quickly hobbled to the back door and opened it. Bobchia was packing the station wagon. I watched Andrew run through the slippery parking lot, fall, get back up and run to the car. He hopped into the back seat and ducked onto the floor. Logan was not far behind him.

"Sweetie, I'll be back. I forgot the kettle," Bobchia said, passing me.

I got into the car and looked down at them cowering on the floor. I looked out the back window. "Man, I wonder what those *policemen* want? They're headed this way, and look really, really *mad!*"

"*Help us, Jen!*" Andrew whimpered.

"*Please!*" Logan said.

I threw their coats over their heads. They pulled them down tight. I rolled my window down. "Nope, no boys in this car, officers. You don't need to look in the backseat *either. No pop stealing boys are in here, no sir!* You're welcome. Goodbye." I turned around. "They're getting back into their police car. Oh no! They pulled up behind us. Uh-oh! I think they're going to *follow us the whole way to the Inn!* You'd better *stay down there.*"

"Okay!" Logan said nervously.

"You guys are way *too young* to work on *chain gangs!*" I told them.

Their voices were muffled through their jackets.

"Protect us, Jen! *Please!*"

"Don't let those *coppers* take us to the *big house!*"

"You two *owe me!* You got *that?*" I said.

"Okay, okay!" Andrew said.

I threw their blankets over their jackets. "Man, it's hot under here!" Logan complained.

Bobchia got in the car. "Where are the boys?"

"In the back on the floor."

"I counted the money you boys got for your macaroni necklaces. You made twenty-five dollars."

"Is that all, twenty-five dollars *apiece?*" Logan peeked out from under the blankets.

"No, twenty-five dollars *altogether!* That's a lot of money. That's twelve dollars and fifty cents for each of you, minus a tenth for the offering plate on Sunday."

"We have to give some away?" Logan asked.

"I ain't even *touched* it yet!" Andrew protested.

"*Or seen it!*" Logan added.

"A fool and his money are soon parted, so before it gets in your hot little hands we give to God the *first fruits* of our labor."

"Fruit?" Logan asked.

"God provides and we give some back to plant."

"*In the ground?*"

"In the offering plate! *Mercy!*"

"How much?"

"Ten percent. A dollar and a quarter from *each* of you."

Logan started, "But—"

"*God loves a cheerful giver!*" Bobchia said definitively.

"But—"

"Be cheerful! *That's it, Fort Pitt!*"

"Chee…"

"I'll tell you what Sweetie, there's not a doubt in my mind who will be *crowned* tonight! I saw Marcy's family stuffing the ballot boxes all day, just like they did for her cousin last year! Cheaters is all they are! Nothing but *cheaters!* They don't think anyone knows but who knows?"

"*GOD!*" We said in unison.

"That's right!"

I decided I'd rather stay home than have to see Andy watch Marcy get crowned, but I had promised all my girlfriends that I would be at the dance. Besides, Andy had said that he'd see me tonight. I could always have Bobchia drive me back to the Inn *before* the crowning. *That's exactly what I'll do!*

Bobchia parked the car. "Oh good, Ardelle's back. I bet she won every hand of cards!" She grabbed the moneybag and got out. "I'll have the guys come out and unload. I hope Ardelle has supper going!"

The boys popped their heads up.

"Those policemen parked behind us, so you better stay put until you count to *five hundred.* By then they'll think they followed the wrong car, and it will be *safe* for you to come out," I said pushing their heads back down under their coats.

"Good idea!" Logan said.

"I'm going in so they'll think the car is *empty.*"

"Thanks, Jen! One, two, three—" Andrew started.

"That's much *too fast!*" I told him.

"Oh, one... two... three..."

I got out of the car laughing and hurried inside. I relaxed on the window seat with the tin, munching and watching the car until the boys finally emerged. They crept across the yard with their blankets and coats over their heads, then bounded through the door and slammed it. They got down and crept over to look out the window.

"Whew!" Andrew wiped his arm across his forehead.

"They're gone!" Logan sat on the floor and heaved a sigh of relief.

"You're safe now, but they probably went back to the center to get *fingerprints!*" I told them.

"Oh no, like *Dragnet?*" Andrew's voice quivered. They hid under the table.

"Like Dragnet." I said.

Wanda and Mrs. Dunham came in and made salads as Aunt Ardelle stirred delicious pots of spaghetti sauce. Bobchia put cookie sheets of homemade bread sticks into the ovens and then poured boxes of (what else?) *angel* hair pasta into the boiling water. "Where are the boys?" Bobchia asked.

"We're under here!" They called.

"Mercy, get out of there and wash your hands! It's almost suppertime! After a few minutes, Bobchia took a fork, whipped out a noodle and flung it to the ceiling. "If it sticks, it's done! My Uncle Tony taught me that when I was a little girl." (That explained the squiggly marks on the ceiling!)

Bobchia could not resist the boys' pleas to *test* the noodles. She handed them forks. Everyone cleared the kitchen! The noodles flew on the light; they flew on the walls; they flew on Bobchia, Minnie and even into the hall! They flew *everywhere*—everywhere, that is, *but* the ceiling! "Mercy! Look at this mess! I would have thought all that *baseball playin'* would have paid off by now!" She snorted and confiscated their forks. They hurried to clean up the mess before Mother saw it then Bobchia cooked more angel hair. The dessert that night was—yep, *angel* food cake!

I ate in a hurry, needing every bit of the next two hours to look *naturally* beautiful for Andy. I took a couple of aspirin and hobbled to my room and fed the cats. Then I took a fast shower, washed my hair again, put on my robe, set my hair and got under the dryer. Mother came to my room carrying her plate. "Would you please keep an eye on the boys until you go to the center?" She asked. "I've got to study the parts of the brain." I looked down at her plate of spaghetti.

"*Ew*, yeah. I guess, *chee.*"

"They're eating in the great room. They begged Rhea to watch Shirley Temple. Thanks." I reluctantly got dressed and carried my dryer to the great room. They were eating on the towel-covered puzzle, intently watching Heidi. I put my hair dryer on a stool and plugged it in and sat on the floor in front of it. Then I stuck my head under the hood and turned it on.

"Hey! I can't *hear* Heidi! I'm telling *Mom!*" Logan turned the TV up so loud that *I* could hear it over the motor!

I yelled, "Who do you think told me to come in here and watch you two *roaches!*"

Andrew walked behind the dryer and *farted* into the air intake! I scrambled out choking! The boys were hysterical. "You little toad! You little toad!" I managed to hit Andrew in the arm as I jumped up.

"Help! Logan, get help! *Quick!*" Andrew took off. I chased him around the room and into the dining room.

Bobchia came in. "I don't care how *old* you are; if you break my Mother's lamps *I'll take a wooden spoon to your duppas!* If I could find one!" Around and around the table we went. "Jennifer, *stop!*" Back into the great room we ran. Bobchia hurried in and turned off the blaring TV.

Tenants raced to see what all the screaming was about. Andrew tripped. I grabbed his scrawny arms, pinning him to the floor. "You little *maggot,* you belong on a *chain gang!*"

"Say it, don't *spray it!*" He said spitefully.

"I'll get *even* with you if it takes *forever!*"

"You're spitting in my face, Pig!"

"Good, I hope you get *acne!*"

"What's that? Help! Help! I'm getting *acne!*"

Logan and Mother ran into the room. "Jennifer, get off of him!" Mother said. "*Get off!*" She *peeled* me off. I chased him again. "*Stop!*" I grabbed Andrew's arm and twirled him around.

Mother got between us.

"*My hair!*" I pointed.

Mother looked at the boys, disappointed. "You boys *promised* you would never *touch* your sister's hair again! *You promised!*"

"I didn't even have to *touch* it!" Andrew defended.

"Nope, he didn't *touch* it at all!" Logan defended.

"*Smell* my hair! Go ahead, *smell* it!" I told her.

She made a face. "*Ew,* what did you *spray* on it?"

"You mean what did *he* spray on it!" I pointed at Andrew.

"*What?*"

"He fa...*cut the cheese* on the dryer while I was under it!"

Mother asked, "He *f-a-r-t-e-d* on your *head?*"

"What did you just *spell?*" Andrew asked.

"Andrew, did you '*cut the cheese*' on Jennifer's hair?" Bobchia asked him.

"No! *I farted on it!*"

Everyone laughed! Bobchia looked to the ceiling.

Mother's eyes bugged out. "Andrew David! No TV all weekend, and *I mean it!*"

"*Is that it? No cartoons?*" I screamed.

"I can watch *cartoons,* can't I?" Logan asked. "I didn't *fart* on her head, *honest!*"

I sniffed my hair. "*Now I smell like him! Ouu, gag a maggot!*"

"Jennifer, quiet down!" Mother turned, looking at the crowd forming behind us.

Bobchia walked over and made a face when she got a *whiff* of my hair. Then she looked disgusted at Andrew. "Mercy, I told you to *eat fruit!* Clair, this child needs a *physic!*"

Andrew yelled, "I don't want a *physical!*"

Mother yelled, "You go right now and talk to the Man Upstairs and don't come down for an *hour!*"

I sobbed. Mother and Bobchia comforted me...at arm's length. "I've got to get the pies out of the oven and leave here in forty-five minutes, tops!" Bobchia said. "So, if you're going, Sweetie, I'd suggest you wash your head or *shave* it!" I cried louder. "Mercy! *Erase, erase!* I was only *kidding! Go wash your hair!*" We walked to the hallway.

I ripped the curlers out of my hair and threw them at Andrew, "I hope you're so *constipated* that you *blow up!*"

"Hey Jen, your head smells like a *terrr-let!* Nah, nah, nah, nah, nah, nah!"

"Shut up, *maggot!*"

I sobbed stomping to my room and slammed the door! I took another shower, scrubbing my head until it hurt then I towel dried my hair and combed it straight, trying to regain my composure. I thought of Andy as I put on the green blouse with my black and green paisley skirt that I had gotten for my birthday. I had only worn them *once* to school, and hoped Andy would not remember them.

Bobchia yelled at the door, "Ten minutes! Sweetie?" She knocked again.

"Come in." I said faintly as I put on mascara.

She looked me up and down. "I love that green outfit!"

"I *hate* my brothers!"

"Hate is a pretty strong word, young lady!"

"Well, what's to love about *them?*"

"Blood is thicker than water." She paused at the dresser, looking at Father's picture. "What a *handsome man* he was. And smart too! He took after your grampie for sure, and you take after both of them." She picked up the wooden horse and touched it to her cheek.

"Smell my hair, and tell me *the truth!*" I told her.

"Um, *strawberries.*"

"Good."

She walked to the mirror and fussed with her bangs using some hairspray. "I used to be as pretty as you when your grampie David and I went to the grange dances."

"I know. I saw the pictures," I said.

"Charm is deceitful and beauty is passing, but a woman who fears the Lord, she shall be praised. Your grampie had two left feet, but when he put his arm around, *my then,* tiny waist—I thought we were gliding on air!"

"Was it love at first sight?"

"Sure was! He was the *only* beau that brought me flowers. Of course he had to pass a *cemetery* on his way to my house..."

She got closer to the mirror and ran her hands down the sides of her face. "Now I look so old."

"No, you don't!"

"Well, now I know I'm old because it takes me longer to arrange the hair on my *face* than it does to fix the hair on my *head!*"

"That's funny, Bobchia!"

I looked closer at myself in the mirror. "I don't have any hair on my face."

"Not until you're *fifty,* Sweetie."

I towel dried my hair more. "That stink of Andrew's probably *rotted* the motor in my dryer!"

"Ardelle has a hairdryer up there, but you don't have time to use it; it's almost time to leave."

I threw my brush on the dresser. "I look *awful!* I can't go anywhere looking like *this!*"

She picked up my brush. "You look *beautiful!*" She brushed my hair straight down my back. "Just beautiful, *honest.* You really do! Has Bobchia ever *lied* to you?" I shook my head. "Trust me. These are some of the best years of your life, and you should enjoy them. You'll never look prettier or *younger,* I can guarantee you that! Tell me the Lord doesn't have a sense of humor! Having you in this room has really *backfired* on me, since I had planned for your mother to be clear *down* here and you to be clear *up* there! Oh well, the best-laid plans of mice and men! I like your hair like this. It reminds me of when you were little and how I'd brush your hair until you fell asleep, remember?"

"Sorry."

"It's okay. I guess I expect you to remember everything because I do. There." She put down the brush. "Your hair looks good just like that, trust me. I like it better like this than when it's curled and teased."

"Really?"

"*Really!*"

I rolled up my sleeve so I wouldn't break my macaroni bracelet.

"I'm proud of you for wearing that bracelet, especially after what Andrew did to you. A lot of girls wouldn't be caught dead *wearing pasta.*" Bobchia went into the bathroom and got the blue bottle of 'Evening in Paris' out of the medicine cabinet. She sprayed it on her neck and arms sending Minnie into a sneezing fit.

"Will you spray some on my hair, *just in case?*" I asked.

She sprayed a little on my hair and wrists. "Powerful stuff," she said raising her eyebrows up and down.

"Harold *loves* this stuff."

"Really?" Her face turned red. "*He's* the one that better pass the *smell test!* If not, he can just take Joan of Arc to the dance! He should be here any minute." She giggled and put the bottle back. I stuffed my swollen foot into a regular shoe and almost fell over. So I unwillingly put on the ugly slipper and a black shoe on my good foot. When we entered the kitchen, Harold was standing at the sink mixing Nikki's food.

Bobchia sniffed him. "You *pass* the sniff test, Harold."

"You smell pretty dog gone good yourself. And you *look* pretty good too!"

I smiled at Bobchia. She blushed and changed the subject. "Where is Nikki?"

"She wanted back into Poochie's coop, so I put her out there when we came back from the Christian Center. Don't look at me like *that!* She wanted out, and she has plenty of straw."

"Mercy! Hurry and feed her. I have to *get* back to the center!"

He grabbed the dish of food, went out the door and disappeared into the snowstorm.

While Bobchia packed the pies in a box, Aunt Ardelle came into the kitchen and handed me a Christmas package. "Merry *early* Christmas!"

"For *me?*"

"Go ahead and open it. I hope it *fits!*"

"Thank you!" I opened the box and pulled out a black felt slipper cover. "*It almost looks like a shoe!*"

"Good, that's what I had hoped for." I quickly put it on. "I measured *Ginger's* foot, so it should fit over the slipper." She smiled.

"*It fits!* Wow! Thank you so much. Now I won't feel so freaky, and it looks *groovy* with my shoe!" I gave her a big hug. "I can't believe you went to all this trouble for *me!*"

"I can't thank you enough for putting life *back* into old Lucky! He's been a totally different bird since you *bird-sat* him!" I couldn't look her in the eye. I stared at the slipper cover. "When Wanda runs the *sweeper*, he flies inside his cage! *He actually flies!* Sometimes we run the *sweeper* just so he'll get his exercise!"

I nodded. "Ah, thanks again!" I said.

"I put rubber backing on it so you won't slip while you're dancing. I remember what it was like to be young. I used to be quite the *flapper!*" She tried to do the Charleston, grabbed her back and sat down.

Harold kicked at the door and Bobchia opened it. He carried in Nikki and the food. "She froze up *again!*"

"Mercy, the poor old thing! I *told* you to keep her in the kitchen!" She hit him in the arm.

"Ouch!"

"Next time *listen* to me!" She petted the snow off of the dog's head.

"What about me? Pet my head!" Harold teased.

"We have to get the show on the road!"

"I'm covered with snow, does anybody care?"

"Well, you wouldn't be if you would have left her in here in the first place!" Bobchia scolded.

I followed them down the hall as they squabbled, taking Nikki to the great room. I was secretly hoping to get a chance to pinch Andrew.

As we entered, Spike was sitting with the heating pad on his back while stringing popcorn as the boys watched with their mouths watering. Mother was at the desk—memorizing the parts of the brain.

"*She froze up again, Spike!*" Harold announced, placing Nikki and her food on the rug in front of the fireplace.

"Hooray!" Logan yelled. The boys took their positions to watch the old girl thaw out.

"She'll catch her death out there!" Bobchia announced. "I want that dog in the kitchen until spring, *understand?* That's it, Fort Pitt! Let's head out!"

"Thanks for getting her, Harold. After shoveling I couldn't walk another step," Spike said.

I showed Mother my slipper cover. She made a comment about liking my hair but said that I had entirely *too* much makeup on and the perfume I was wearing was too strong!

"It's me Clair," Bobchia said.

"Oh. Keep an eye on her," Mother said. "She looks...*older* somehow."

"I *do?*" I smiled.

"Listen to your grandmother tonight!" Mother ordered.

"I will. *Chee!*"

The box of pies barely fit into the Metropolitan's trunk. We got into the car that smelled of Old Spice. Bobchia snuggled up to Harold and kissed him on the cheek, he quickly turned his head kissing her on the lips as he put the car in gear. Then he buried his nose in her hair and said, "You smell *real* good! You little French girl, you! *Vive la France,*" he said in a low voice as he stepped on the gas, peeled out and swerved down the lane.

Bobchia giggled. "Hot rod!" I covered my mouth in the backseat.

We drove past the park just as the mayor finished his speech, officially starting the Christmas shopping season, then he lit the tree in the gazebo with the snowman watching. Harold slowed down when the mayor threw the switch to light up all of Main Street with light strings zigzagging from lamppost to lamppost, causing the street to look like a glittery Christmas card.

"*Wow!* I love Christmas!" I said turning to look out the back window. I stared at the lights until we arrived at the center.

"Me too!" Bobchia said.

Harold pulled up to the curb to drop us off. "I'll get the pies, *Frenchie!*"

Bobchia giggled as we held on to each other walking up the slippery sidewalk. When we were safe inside, we hung up our coats, and I kicked off Ginger's ugly boots and put on the slipper cover.

"That was sure sweet of Aunt Ardelle!" I said, admiring it again.

"When they made her, Sweetie Pie, they broke the mold!"

We entered the gymnasium. Whereas earlier it had been filled with tables of crafts, now the tables were covered with red, green, gold and silver tablecloths. A turning mirrored ball, hanging from the ceiling, sent beams of light onto the shimmering snowflakes and the walls. Under the mirrored ball was a little silver porch swing decorated for *Miss Snowflake* with a big transparent bag filled with glitter and balloons tied above it. A Christmas tree with large snowflakes and colored lights filled the corner beside the band-stand.

"This is so pretty, Bobchia." I stood there, entranced.

"I think it gets prettier every year. I've got to try to get a knife through these *cement pies* and get the coffee made. We'll need *plenty* to wash these babies down! You have a good time, Sweetie. I promised your mom I'd keep an eye on you, so be good and stay away from that *doctor's kid!*"

"*Chee, I'm not a child.*"

"Just promise." I nodded. "I know you're crossing your fingers behind your back! Bobchia *knows* these things." She windshield-wipered her finger at me. "Just promise me you won't *ruin* our good family name. Come on now."

"I promise."

"Good girl!"

As soon as she left for the kitchen, I looked around for Andy. Dawnette, Donna and Mary Ann called to me. I tried to walk to their table without hobbling.

"I love your hair!" Dawnette said.

"Ooo, me too!" Mary Ann said.

"Really?" I asked.

"Honest!" Dawnette said.

"I think it makes you look sophisticated," Donna said.

"I hate it!" I confessed.

"Why? It really does make you look sophisticated!" Mary Ann agreed.

"Really? Groovy! Thanks!"

"You missed the show!" Dawnette said wide eyed. I looked at her questioningly. "Roxanne and Ryan had a *fight,* and she *threw* his class ring clear across the center!"

"*I can't believe it!*"

"Me either!" Donna said. "I thought he was the *love of her life!*"

Betty Ann and Nicolas came in and sat at our table.

"I like your hair!" Betty Ann said.

"Thanks."

Donna said, "I tried ironing mine once but it frizzed, and when I asked Karen how come hers didn't, she said she put a damp towel over it and *then* ironed it. How did you get yours so straight?"

"I just washed it and let it dry."

Donna shook her head. "Wow, groovy!"

The girls made me promise to dance with them, even *if* I limped.

The tables filled up fast. I positioned myself to watch the door for Andy. I knew he would be with Marcy, but I just wanted a *glimpse* of him.

Mary Ann said, "Karen called and said she was going to pick up the rest of the girls, and guess what?"

"What?" Betty Ann asked.

"Casey called me this afternoon and asked me to *meet* him here! I'm so excited! How do I look?"

"Beautiful," I said.

"I love your red dress!" Dawnette complimented.

"Thanks," Mary Ann smiled.

"Where did you get it?" Betty Ann asked.

"Jane and Jim's Boutique."

"I let her use my discount," Donna said. "You can use it too, Jen."

"*Ooo,* I love their clothes!" Betty Ann said.

Mary Ann stood up. "Casey is waving at me! Look Donna, Joe is talking to him."

"Later, I'm going with Mary Ann." Donna said, and they left.

"Jen, is there something going on that you want to tell us about?" Dawnette asked concerned.

"What do you mean?"

"Bev called me after she called you earlier."

"I didn't talk to her."

"I know, she said someone answered the phone and went to get you, but all she heard was *screaming and laughing,* and you never came to the phone! What was that all about?"

"*My little maggot brothers* is all! I wonder why she called? She told me this morning that she wouldn't be able to make it here tonight."

"She wanted you to save her and Brian a seat because she talked her grandmother into babysitting her sister for her."

"Oh, good!"

"Her mother finally had that boy that she always wanted."

"She had a *boy?* All I have to say is *poor Beverly Jean!*"

I watched the crowd coming through the door. Dawnette followed my gaze. "Who are you looking for?"

"Take a guess."

"Andy is at the Senior Class's booth with Mark and Randy." She pointed. "Oh, thanks." I turned my chair.

The Senior Class had a booth on the other side of the gym where they were selling pop and candy bars to earn money for their Senior Trip to Gettysburg in the spring. I searched at the bottom of my purse for a dime and made a beeline for the booth.

Everyone in line asked Andy the same question: "What kind of pop do you have?" He would go over and over the list with each person. I kept letting people in front of me, hoping I could be *alone* with him to have a conversation. Finally, Steve and Zack were done talking to Andy about last night's game. They got their pop and walked away. Andy had his back to me, opening boxes of candy bars.

"Pop please," I said.

"What kind?"

"Whatever you have the *most* of."

"A girl after my own heart—" He turned around. "*Skip!*" He popped open the top of a Coke bottle and handed it to me. I tried to give him a dime, but he wouldn't take it. He looked at the bracelet. "I see you're wearing the *family jewels* this evening." I smiled. I didn't know what to say. He smiled at my hair. "You look different tonight. *I like it.*"

I shook my head a little. "Thanks."

He leaned over the counter and admired at the slipper cover. "*Fan-cy!*"

I went to say something but Dawnette's sister, Lou, and some of her girlfriends crowded in front of me, all trying to walk in *borrowed* high heels. I looked down at their turned-in ankles and laughed to myself.

"What kind of pop do you got?" Lou asked.

"Bye, Andy," I said, leaning around them.

"Later."

*This is a good sign,* I thought, as I tried to walk without limping. "Later" meant *he'd* see me later, right? I sat back down at the table and watched him.

Soon Karen brought the rest of the girls in, Mandy, Laura, Ann, Jill and Keeley sat down.

"Oh, I love your hair!" Laura said.

"Me too!" Ann nodded.

"You look groovy!" Karen said.

"Thank you! Dawnette, I saw Lou in line to get pop. She was wearing these ugly high heels, and she almost fell over! You would have died laughing!"

"Were they black with little rhinestones on the front?" She asked.

"Yeah!"

"Those are *mine!* I looked for them all over the house before we left. That's why I had to wear these stupid brown ones with this black skirt! Wait until I get my hands around her scrawny neck! Did you see where she went?"

"No. Sorry for saying they were ugly."

"She must have sneaked them out in her purse. Do you see her anywhere?"

My eyes followed Marcy and her friends walking in, encircling the Senior Booth. Andy didn't acknowledge she was there. *Another good sign!* I thought.

The bandleader went to the microphone. "Good evening, one and all! Welcome to the Snowflake Christmas Ball! My name is Dick Tune, and when my wife Carol sings, she'll make you swoon! This is the grooviest band, number one in all the land! Get ready for some Doo Wop, everyone welcome the Tune-ups!" We applauded wildly!

The band started playing **The Twist**. Randy and Mark came over to get Dawnette and Kathy to dance. Zack came over and asked Laura to dance as Bill ran over and grabbed Ann's hand. "Come on, baby. Let's show them how!" Ann giggled.

The other girls coaxed me onto the dance floor. Frank, Steve and Zack along with others from the basketball team hurried over and twisted with us. Across the room, Marcy and her friends pulled Andy to the dance floor. I tried to think of something else, *anything else,* but *what else* was there to think of? I looked up at the boy I was dancing with, he smiled down at me. I looked over at Andy, who was watching us curiously. Knowing I had Andy's attention, I smiled up at the boy. My foot throbbed.

When the dance was over, my partner introduced himself as Kory and pulled up a chair. He was handsome and had a great smile. We chitchatted about school. He asked me if I'd like to go to the movies with him sometime.

"I might." I smiled.

"I'll get us a Coke," he said. "Anyone else want a Coke?" He asked the table.

The guys from our table went to the booth with Kory and visited with Andy. My girlfriends were excited to have the guys at our table and I pretended to be, but I *only* had eyes for Andy. The guys came back to ask us to dance as the band played **Only You** and **Chances Are**. Afterward we girls went to the ladies' room in a *herd,* lining up at the mirrors, sharing lipsticks and rouge. I wiped most of it off and ran my fingers through my hair.

"I've never seen your hair *move* before, Jen!" Betty Ann said.

"Me either!" Dawnette agreed.

"Andy said he liked it."

Betty Ann nodded. "Told ya that it looked good!"

"I'm going to quit curling mine too! I just hope it doesn't frizz!" Dawnette said.

Marcy's friends came in and sat on couches behind us.

"Hey, there's that girl that Marcy *hates!*" One of them said under her breath.

I turned and they quickly looked away changing the subject.

One of the girls, Barb said, "I hope Ira asks me to dance. I think he's *cute,* although Ed is a good dancer." Kari and Shari argued over Jeff as Cathy cried over some guy named Charlie! They got up and crowded around the other mirror, sharing make-up.

"We better get out there with Marcy, or she'll be *mad!*" Shari said.

"She's always mad about *something!*" Barb sighed.

I went around the corner to look at myself in the full-length mirror, and there was Lou, surrounded by her girlfriends, putting *baby powder* in her hair. I backed up and got Dawnette's attention, and pointed.

She walked around the corner. "Hey, Lou! Give me *my* shoes!" Dawnette pushed her into a chair and grabbed the shoes off her feet.

"*I'm telling Mom!*" Lou protested.

"I looked all over the house for *these!*" She kicked off her brown shoes toward Lou and put the black shoes on.

"What am I supposed to do, go barefoot? I don't want to wear *those!*" Lou made a face.

"Tough! Wear your boots!" Dawnette said. Lou threw powder at her black shoes. "You brat!" She grabbed the powder and dumped it on Lou's head! "That will teach you to steal *my* shoes, *Blondie!*"

We hurried out the door and to our table, laughing.

"What's with the *powder* anyway?" I asked.

"Last week she watched one of those 'Beach' movies on TV, and ever since she's wanted to be *blonde* like Connie Stevens, and now she's in love with Troy Donahue and *all blond boys!*"

"Look!" I pointed.

Lou came stomping out of the ladies' room, surrounded by a dust cloud. Everyone laughed. Dawnette yelled, "Hey Connie Stevens, you're turning *prematurely gray!*"

"Shut up, *jealous!*" Lou stuck her tongue out just as the band leader announced that the next dance was ladies' choice. Lou said, "I know *exactly* who I'm going to ask to dance." Then she stomped through the crowd as everyone laughed.

"My foot is killing me," I said. "I'm going to get a couple of aspirin from Bobchia." I went to the kitchen, but she wasn't there. Some of the ladies looked concerned when I looked through Bobchia's purse. "I'm Jen, her granddaughter," I explained.

"I've heard of you," one of them said.

"Where is Bobchia?" I asked.

"Who?"

"My grandma Rhea."

She pointed to the hallway with a big smile. I limped down the hall. When I didn't see her, I opened the door of the storage room. "Bobchia?" Minnie growled as I turned up the dim light. There she and Harold were necking, with Minnie and a coffee can between them.

Harold jumped back. "I was helping your grandmother *find the coffee!*"

"*Where? On her neck?*" I asked.

Bobchia held the coffee out so I could see it. "Now Jen, *I'm old enough to go for coffee!*"

"Mother wanted *you* to keep an eye on *me?* Cheee! *That's funny!*"

"Let's keep your *mother* out of this!" She said embarrassed.

I looked at their red faces. "Out of what? I didn't see a thing, not one *thing!*" I dimmed the light, closed the door and hurried back to my table, laughing.

Bobchia and Harold hurried to the kitchen. Harold announced, "*We found the coffee!*"

When I got back to the table, Kory asked me if I wanted to fast dance. "No thanks, I better sit this one out,"

"This is my favorite song," he said. "If you don't mind, I think I'll ask Mandy."

I nodded and he left. Dawnette looked curiously at me as I twirled the macaroni around my wrist. When a piece of it fell off, I put it in my purse.

"Bring a snack?" She asked.

"Andy gave it to me," I explained.

"Wow, *big spender!*" She laughed.

I looked at the booth. He wasn't there. He was probably on the dance floor with Marcy somewhere.

Periodically I would catch a glimpse of him at the booth, but Marcy was always standing guard. (Her bladder must be as big as Dollee's, I thought, because she *never* left his side, not even to go to the ladies' room!) She caught me looking at her once. I turned my chair.

Mother often told me that I was too self-absorbed, so I tried to talk with the girls about their problems, but we all had the same problem—*boys!* The girls and I danced a couple of fast dances with the guys, then I was ready to take my throbbing foot back to the Inn. I looked over to the kitchen, Bobchia and Harold waved at me, wanting me to know they were *behaving*. Kory and Mandy seem to hit it off right away. They laughed, danced every dance together and held hands at the table. Zack and Laura cuddled in the corner. Everyone seemed to be in pairs. Everyone but *me!* I was thinking of asking Bobchia to take me home when Beverly Jean and Brian came to the table with his brother, Tom, and his girlfriend, Mary Jane.

"I hear you have a baby brother!" I said to Beverly Jean.

"Yeah, Gary Ryan Phillips. He's a cutie!"

"They're all cute until they *talk!*"

"Speaking of which, I called the Inn and heard *screaming!*" Bev said laughing.

"Yes, well, I'll fill you in about the little *cuties in my life* sometime."

The band started to play a fast song. Beverly Jean jumped up. "Come on and get in the groove! I saw this on **Bandstand!** Come on, they're doing this dance in *Phil-a-delf-i-a!*" She motioned for us to get into a circle and then she got into the middle. To everyone's surprise, Roxanne ran over with Steve and got into the circle with us.

"*Deal the cards!*" Beverly yelled, pretending to deal us cards. We all did the same thing. "*Go fishing!*" She pretended to cast her line and reel it in. We all did the same thing. "*Baseball!*" She pretended to hit the ball and watch it leave the field. We all did the same thing. "*Water sprinkler!*" She put her one hand on her neck and stretched out her other arm, jerking it. We all did the same thing. "*Drive the car!*" She pretended to steer the wheel. We all did the same thing and had a *blast!* I hardly had to move my foot!

After the song, we went back to our table, laughing. We all talked at once. "That is soooo groovy!"

"What a blast!"

"You did a great job, Bev!"

Then Bev asked, "Hey, what's with Roxanne and Ryan?"

"That's what we'd all like to know!" Dawnette said.

The band played a couple of slow songs and then the bandleader announced that Miss Snowflake would be crowned after the **Jingle Bell Stroll.** I started to feel *queasy* and wanted to leave. Everyone from our table got up to stroll but me. I headed for the kitchen to ask Bobchia to take me home, but Beverly Jean and Dawnette grabbed me by the arms and turned me around.

"Come on, party pooper!" Bev said.

Reluctantly I got in line. Up and down the dance floor we went. When the song was over, I found myself standing beside the silver swing, the *last place* I wanted to be! The band did a drum roll. We turned to go back to the table, but Mayor Wojtowicz took the microphone and announced, "Everyone, gather around the Miss Snowflake swing." People crowded behind us. Dawnette laughed, pointing to the front of the Mayor's suit as he walked toward us and took his place behind the swing. His black suit had a round powder mark chest high. "Not even *blonde* people in *high places* are safe from my sister!" She laughed.

"Good evening everyone, and thank you for coming to the annual Snowflake Christmas Ball. Quit biting your nails, ladies, for soon I will reveal the name of Miss Snowflake 1967!" Everyone clapped. (I was *trapped* in seeing Marcy being crowned whether I wanted to or not!) "I'd like to thank all of the teens who decorated. You did another wonderful job this year!" Everyone clapped. "As the food bank chairman, I am proud to announce that the town's food pantry has once again been filled by the generosity of the citizens of Titusville." Everyone clapped. "On Christmas day the center will be open for a delicious dinner for those who are less fortunate, and gifts for them will be provided and placed under that Christmas tree. Please donate an unwrapped gift to the Methodist Church, where the Methodist Mothers will wrap and tag them. As usual, we are asking for volunteers to work in shifts on Christmas. Rhea Matkovich has the sign-up sheet in the kitchen. We appreciate your *sacrifice* to make this Christmas a special day for everyone. Your generosity is greatly appreciated." Everyone clapped.

The Mayor's wife walked over and whispered in his ear. That prompted him to brush the powder off of his suit with his handkerchief, then he proceeded, "After the dance, if you would all clean off *your* table, it would be greatly appreciated. The basketball team has generously volunteered to take down the tables and push broom the floor. The more hands that help, means less work for the regular volunteers—who are already stretched to their limit this time of year. Thank you." Everyone clapped. "Now," he held up a hand to hush everyone, "earlier today my beautiful wife, Kathy of thirty-nine years and I, counted the ballots for Miss Snowflake, and by an *overwhelming* majority," he looked to the band for another drum roll, "Miss Snowflake 1967 is...*Miss...Marcy Brown!*"

Marcy grabbed her face and *acted* surprised as Carol and the Tune-ups sang **Here Comes Miss Snowflake**. The spotlight followed Marcy through the crowd to the beautifully decorated swing. She yelled for Andy to help her onto it. Andy leaned against the booth and folded his arms. The Mayor put the microphone under his arm and awkwardly helped her up onto the swing, but when the swing moved backward, her foot kicked him in the stomach. "Ugh!" He clutched at his stomach and haphazardly tossed her crown onto her lap. She quickly put it on her head, as the swing hit the Mayor knocking him to the floor. Everyone gasped as he got to his knees and clung to the corner of the swing, that dragged him back and forth.

His wife hurried over and helped him up. He held onto the back of the swing, grimacing in pain, and pulled the ribbon tied to the bag of balloons hanging above the swing, without result. Marcy motioned for her friends to come over and congratulate her. When they did, her mother jumped on the swing next to her, almost knocking the Mayor to the floor again. The Mayor and his wife tried to get their balance as Marcy screamed at her friends to get out of the way so Rocket Recorder Ron's father, Mr. Sager, the owner of the Herald, could take a picture.

"Congratulations. Smile!" His camera flashed.

"When will my picture be in the paper?" Marcy asked excitedly.

"It will be in Monday's edition."

Marcy and her mother jumped off the swing, causing it to go up in the back, knocking the Mayor and his wife to the floor! Marcy's mother went over to her friends as Marcy ran to Andy screaming "*I'm Miss Snowflake! I'm Miss Snowflake!*"

Dawnette and I helped the Mayor and his wife to their feet. "If her father hadn't contributed to *my* campaign, I would never have voted for that spoiled brat!" Arm in arm, the mayor and his wife limped to their table.

We started to go back to our table when the band started playing, ***Put Your Head On My Shoulder***. I looked back at Andy and froze as he walked toward me!

"Put your *hand* on my shoulder, remember Skip?"

I nodded. "I remember."

"Well?" I shyly put my hand on his shoulder, and we danced slowly in front of the swing. Then he lifted me onto it and sat beside me. He smiled as we gently swayed, and then he pulled the ribbon. Balloons and glitter slowly fell over us and floated to the floor. I felt as if I was *dreaming!* It was as though we were on a cloud, drifting, but all too soon the song ended and Carol started singing ***Rockin' Around the Christmas Tree***.

Andy jumped off. "Hold on tight, Skip!" He twirled the swing tight then tighter, and then he let go! I squealed as it unwound. The slipper cover flew to the floor.

Everyone laughed. Andy stopped the swing and picked up the cover. I pushed my foot under the swing as he went down on one knee. "*Skipperella,* holdest out your foot that I mayest decorate it." I shyly held the ugly slipper out, and he put the glittered cover over it.

"It's so beautiful!" I said looking at it.

*"It sure is!"* He sat beside me. My heart pounded so hard I thought he would hear it! I didn't dare look at him or he would have known for sure that I had *fallen* for him. He put his hand on my chin and gently moved my face to his. I looked into his deep blue eyes. "Do you have any plans for tomorrow?" He asked.

"No!" I said quickly. Then added, "Church."

"Me too. I mean *after* church. My family is going to my Uncle Art's horse farm for a sleigh ride. Would you like to go?" He asked.

*"I'd love to!"*

"Do you think your mother will let you?"

"As long as you *leave* your toboggan at home!" He chuckled and looked past me to the booth where Marcy stared daggers. "How does around two sound?" He asked.

*"Wonderful."*

"I'll look forward to it!" He smiled. I held my breath as he helped me off the swing. "Tomorrow at two?" He confirmed.

"Tomorrow at two," I said all dreamy and then watched him walk back to the booth.

Beverly Jean rushed to me. "I saw the whole thing! It was so *romantic!* I thought he was going to *kiss* you for sure!"

Dawnette added, "That was so cool! Marcy got the *crown*, but you got the *guy!"*

"Wow! I can't believe it! I must be dreaming! Pinch me!" I swooned. Beverly pinched me. "Ouch! Chee."

"You said to pinch ya!" She giggled.

We walked through the sea of dancers as the band played **Goodnight, Sweetheart.** Roxanne and Ryan swayed slowly as she admired the class ring, once again, on her finger. Kory and Mandy were all smiles as he slowly twirled her, and Mary Ann snuggled into Casey's neck as we walked past them to our table. I could faintly hear Marcy's screaming above the band when Andy joined the others to help pack up the booth. She stomped out the side door and slammed it in her friends' faces as they tried to console her.

"He asked me to go on a sleigh ride tomorrow. I can't wait!"

"You'll have to call me and tell me all about it!" Beverly Jean said.

"Me too!" Dawnette added.

"I will! I will! I just hope mother will let me go. She just *has* to!" Suddenly the adrenalin wore off. "Ouuu, my foot is *killing me!"*

"We'll clean off the table."

"Thanks!"

"That's what friends are for! See you in church tomorrow!"

"Okay. See ya!" On the way to the kitchen I waved goodbye to Donna, who was all smiles talking with Joe. When I walked into the kitchen, I found *the lovers* slow dancing in a corner. Bobchia had her head on Harold's chest, with her body sideways so Minnie could breathe. Minnie gave me away, whining as soon as she saw me.

Harold quickly stepped back. "We were *just dancing!*"

I smiled at him.

"Did you have a good time tonight, Sweetie?"

"*The grooviest ever!*"

"Mercy, look at yourself!" I looked down and saw my skirt sparkling.

"I never had a *glitter problem* until you kids! Shake off before you get in the car."

After the center emptied, I turned the radio on in the kitchen. Andy along with his buddies, danced with the push brooms as the song **Dancing in the Street** blared. Bobchia curiously watched my eyes follow Andy around the room.

"Guard your heart above all else, for it determines the course of your life." She said to me.

"I really like Andy." I replied without looking away from him.

"I know, but there are plenty of fish in the sea." I didn't respond. "Don't put all your eggs in one basket." Again, I remained silent. "I didn't react to *my* mother *either,* when she said those words to me regarding your grandfather." She shook her head. "Hey, look at that dark-haired guy in the red shirt! He's pretty kippy and looks a little bit like Errol Flynn, don't you think?"

"Kory? He asked me to go to the movies," I said.

"Good, are you going?"

"No, he danced all night with Mandy."

"Oh, how about the cute wiry one running circles around the rest of them? Boy! Just look at him push that broom around!"

"Mary Ann has a crush on him."

"Too bad! He could have done my *hardwood floors* some good! What about—"

"I really like *Andy*, Bobchia."

She sighed. "I know. Well, let me ask you this. Is he a *church-goer?*"

"Chee, of course!"

"Good. *A Bible-preaching church?* It's trouble ahead if you're *unequally yoked,* you know!"

"I know. I didn't ask, but I will. I promise."

"That's my girl!"

She and Harold waited impatiently as the guys danced on. Bobchia turned off the radio and put her hands on her hips. Casey then threw a bottle cap on the floor, and the guys played hockey with the brooms until Bobchia and Harold stood at the door with their coats on. Harold motioned to them saying; "It's time to get this show on the road!" The guys got the hint and left. I waved at Andy's truck as it pulled out of the parking lot, not one minute before then, would I put on Ginger's ugly boots.

On the way home, Bobchia and Harold were apologetic about the storage room incident.

"If your mother knew about that, she would *never* let us go anywhere together again!" Bobchia said.

"*My lips are sealed!*" I promised. "Now, are we going straight home, or are we going to *Lover's Leap?*" I teased, twirling the macaroni bracelet on my wrist. Through the rear window I looked back at the center and the zigzagged lights, knowing that I would *never, ever* forget this wonderful night as long as I lived!

Harold pulled up to the Inn, and I got out.

"Sorry, Harold, about the glitter on the floor," I said.

He shook his head. "No harm done; it'll sweep. Goodnight."

"Goodnight!" Bobchia looked at me and then gave him a peck on the cheek then slid out of the car. He peeled out.

"The *old* teenager!" Bobchia laughed. We walked across the little bridge. Bobchia looked up and down the sidewalk with her hands on her hips. "Those little snoopers! A dead *giveaway!*"

"Huh?"

"They must think Bobchia is *stupid!*"

"I don't know what—"

"They *snooped!* They found their Christmas presents!"

"Huh?"

"Mercy, girl! Look at the tracks, *the tracks!* They found their skates and skis! I'll fix those *little snoops!*" She stomped up the steps and swung the door open so hard it jammed. Pumpkin made a break for it! "Grab her, Sweetie!" The kitten stepped on the porch, shaking her feet in the snow, cautiously smelling it. I limped up the steps trying to grab her, but she scooted between the rungs of the covered rockers.

"Pumpkin! Here, kitty, kitty!" I called. Then she jumped off the side of the porch. "Come back! *You'll catch your death!*" I looked over the side of the porch. There she was, buried in snow up to her head! She meowed at me. "I'll meow you! *Bad kitty!*" I slid down the side of the porch. "*Ouu, Pumpkin!*" The snow was deeper than Ginger's ugly boots. When I reached for Pumpkin, she sprang up then crawled through a tiny opening between the lattice and the stone foundation of the Inn. I panicked and dug at the heavy snow and tugged at the lattice but only managed to move it a few inches. I got on my knees. "I am freezing, you *stupid* cat! Pumpkin, come here *right now!*" With only the dim streetlight, I peered through the lattice. There was Pumpkin, sitting among *fifty-three other pumpkins!* "Oh no! *Oh no!* Why, those little *thieves!*" I laughed, then Pumpkin turned, jumping over several pumpkins going further into the darkness. "Kitty! Here kitty, kitty! When she turned to look at me again, I could barely see the reflection of her eyes. I dug faster at the snow. "*Pumpkin!* Here kitty, kitty!" I could hear the panic in my voice watching the tip of her tail move further and further away. I managed to get my arm past the lattice and quickly pulled a dried leaf from a pumpkin vine. I slowly moved it back and forth to entice her. I could scarcely see half of her face peering at me from behind a pumpkin. "Come and get it," I whispered. "*Come on!*" At first she didn't move, but then curiosity got the cat. Ever so slowly, she crept toward the leaf and shook her butt, then she pounced on it! I grabbed her and pulled her out through the tiny opening. She crawled up my coat. "TYG! So you thought you were the *only* Pumpkin at the Inn, huh? *Silly Kitty!*" Giggling, I petted the snow off of her. "My feet are freezing thanks to you!" I kissed her and brushed my coat, making my way to the sidewalk. Looking at the skate marks, I made a mental note to *torture my brothers* until they told me where the *Christmas stash* was. I hugged the kitten and went into the kitchen. Bobchia came out of the pantry carrying cans of prunes.

"Good, I see you found Pumpkin," Bobchia said.

"Oh, I found *pumpkins* alright!"

"Want a cookie and a glass of milk?"

"Can you stick a cookie in my mouth? I've got to get in bed to warm my feet!"

"Sure." She put one between my teeth. "There. Pleasant dreams, Sweetie Pie. Love you awful!" She kissed me on the cheek.

I mumbled, "Love you awful back!"

Joan of Arc met me at the bedroom door. "Too bad Pumpkin isn't *more like you*," I told her. I wrapped the shivering kitten in a blanket on the bed, hung up my coat, took off the ugly boots and tossed them onto the heat grate (hoping they would melt). I carried the wooden box that Halfway Decent Henry had given me and the gift-wrap into the bathroom, lined the tub with the wrap, got in and shook the glitter out of my hair. Joan of Arc jumped in and got *glittered!* "Oh, my!" I blew and petted it off as best I could and then put her on the bed beside the kitten, and went back into the bathroom only this time, I shut the door. I got back into the tub and shook the glitter off my clothes and put on my pajamas. I set the wooden box in the tub, folded the gift-wrap in half and lifted one end, pouring the glitter into the box. I gently added the macaroni bracelet and the broken macaroni pieces from my purse and then placed the box next to my other prized possessions on the dresser.

I was too excited to sleep, filling an entire journal with the night's events. I tossed and turned then finally got up. I looked into the box several times, never realizing that glitter could be so *reassuring.* I went back to bed, mentally trying to visualize an outfit for the sleigh ride, that would make me look beautiful and would keep me warm—but mostly that would make me *look beautiful.* Then I got depressed thinking of Marcy's wardrobe. I wished Mother would have let Bobchia *buy my love* when she'd wanted to so that I'd have something pretty to wear tomorrow. One thing I knew for sure: even if I got *frostbite,* I was *never* going to wear that heavy, ugly, yellow, flowered sweater of Bobchia's again! Eventually I fell asleep, with the moonlight shining on a glittery hero cat, on the pillow next to mine.

The next morning the tub was lined with glitter after my shower. I was glad Andy liked my hair straight because I was never, *ever* going to use *that* hairdryer again. (If the garbage men got *down wind* of it, they'd *refuse* to haul it away!) I got ready for church and then towel dried my hair in front of the fireplace in the great room. Mr. Hair kept peeking in at me, freaking me out until Ginger came down the steps and dragged him away by the scruff of his neck.

In church, I tried hard to concentrate on Pastor Jay's sermon, **Your Name Is Written on the Palm of God's Hand,** but I was too distracted trying to think of a way to tell Mother that I had *a date with Andy.*

At lunch my stomach was in a *knot.* I hardly touched the stuffed pork chop Aunt Ardelle had made.

Mother asked, "What's the matter, Jen? Does your foot hurt?"

"Kind of."

"Well no wonder! Whoever heard of going to a *dance with a twisted ankle?"* She shook her head.

I got up and took an aspirin. There was no way to *sugarcoat* the fact that Andy would arrive in an hour, so I just blurted out, *"I have a date with Andy at two o'clock."*

*"What?* Your grandmother was supposed to keep an *eye* on you last night! Weren't you, Rhea?"

I quickly added, *"I* wasn't *necking* with anybody last night, was I, Bobchia?"

Her face turned red. "She was a perfect lady."

"I just don't know about that boy; he seems *reckless* to me! Where is he taking you?"

"Sleigh riding at his uncle's horse farm."

Andrew whined, "I want to go! I love horses."

"I love horses too!" Logan said.

I gave them 'the look.' I wasn't about to say *a word* that would jeopardize my afternoon with Andy. "His parents are going to be with us. And his father is a *doctor!"* I smiled at Mother.

"Oh?" Mother brightened a little.

"*Some doctor!*" Bobchia said.

Mother looked worried. "What does that *mean?*"

I gave Bobchia 'the look.' She downed a shot of coffee. "Bobchia, maybe you should get more *coffee.*" I said looking though *my* brows.

"Thanks, but I'm coffeed out," she said.

"Maybe you should make a pot in case *Harold* shows up and *needs some coffee.*"

"*Harold?* Ah, you know Clair, um, I think, well, it would be *good* for Jennifer to go on a sleigh ride."

Mother looked confused. "Really? *Why?*"

Bobchia brushed her hair back. "Well, I don't know. In case she has to do a report on one at school, then she'll know all about it!"

Mother shook her head at her. "Where is his uncle's farm?"

"I'm sorry, I didn't ask, but I just have to go Mother, you have to say *yes*, you just have too or I'll *die!*"

"Well, I just think he's—"

"Please, Mother, *please!* We'll be with his parents, and I promise I won't get *hurt! I promise!*"

"Well...I guess it would be all right *if* his parents are going."

"Oh, thank you!"

Andrew said, "I want to go or *I'll just die!*" He fell off his chair. Logan fell on top of him. "Ouch!"

"I'll need his uncle's phone number, and he better not just *pull* into the driveway and *blow the horn.* You are *not* leaving this Inn until he comes to the door like a *gentleman.*"

"All right. Thank you, thank you, *thank you!* I have to hurry and change my clothes."

I searched my closet and came out in the heaviest blouse and black slacks I had. "Mother, does this look alright?"

"Yes."

"My clothes don't look anything like the *sleigh ride clothes* on Christmas cards."

Bobchia thought and said, "What about that yellow, flowered sweater. It's *heavy and warm.*" She said grinning.

"Thanks, but no thanks!"

Mother said, "What about that pretty green blouse?"

"I wore it *last night*, remember?"

"Oh, well, I guess I'll just have to give you an *early* Christmas gift."

"*You will?*" I smiled.

The boys' ears perked up.

Logan said, "I want my Christmas gift *early* too!"

Andrew cheered, "*Me too!*"

Mother went upstairs. Bobchia whispered, "I hope that doctor knows more about *horses* than he does *cows!*"

"Bobchia, *quit!*"

Mother came back down and handed me a box with the Jane and Jim's Boutique logo across the top.

"Oh, they have the *grooviest* clothes there!" I pulled at the box top.

"Sorry, I haven't had a chance to wrap it yet. I hope they fit."

The boys ran over.

Logan whispered, "It's probably some of *those* clothes."

Inside the box was a pink, mohair turtleneck sweater with stirrup pants to match.

Logan rolled his eyes. "*Told ya!*"

"Oh, they are just *beautiful!*" I held them up to me. "But I know they were *expensive.*"

"Try them on!" Mother smiled. "Go ahead."

I kissed her on the cheek. "*Thank you!*" I went to the bathroom to change, came back out and asked, "How do I look?"

"Pretty!" Mother said.

"Pretty in pink!" Bobchia said.

"Thank you!" I spun around.

Bobchia looked at Mother and then at me. "Clair said that *I* might as well give you your gift so you don't *catch your death* on the sleigh ride."

"*Really?*"

Bobchia went into the pantry and brought out a box covered in green foil paper with a big, beautiful, red bow on top. "Thank you, Bobchia!"

"You're welcome."

"Hurry up!" Logan said. "Don't *save* the paper, Jen!"

"Yeah, hurry!" Andrew said.

"Oh, wow! It's from Jane and Jim's Boutique *too!*" I lifted the lid.

'*Pop!*' Went the camera.

"Oh, a burgundy benchwarmer and high black boots!" I squealed.

Bobchia smiled. "I saw you looking at them when we walked past the window.

"More crummy stuff to wear! Didn't ya get her something *fun?*" Logan asked.

"These are so beautiful!" I kissed Bobchia on the cheek. "This is a great Christmas! I'm *so* blessed! Thank you both so much!" I hugged them. "I hope these boots fit." I took off the slipper, put on the cover and slipped them on. It was snug, but I didn't care; I was definitely *going for looks!* "Perfect!" I tried on the benchwarmer. "*Perfect!*" Everyone followed me into the vestibule where I admired myself in the full-length mirror.

'*Pop!*' Went the camera.

"*This is just the best Christmas a girl could have!*"

The doorbell rang. Logan answered the door with "*Merry Christmas!*" He caught Andy off guard.

"Ah, Merry Christmas!" Andy said.

Andrew walked over to him with his hand out. "*Where're my twenty cents?*"

"*Andrew!*" I chastised.

Embarrassed, Andy reached into his pocket, pulled out a quarter and handed it to him as I hustled to get between them. "Keep the change, little fella," Andy said fondly tapping Andrew's head.

"Thanks, but I ain't your *little fella!* Look, Logan!"

"Half of that is mine!"

Andy smiled at me. "Hi, Skip, good thing I got here early or you'd be *sweaty!*"

Bobchia spit her coffee into her cup into her cup, laughing, on her way to the kitchen.

"Her name is *Jennifer*, not *Skip*, young man." Mother reprimanded.

Andy nodded. "Yes, *ma'am!*"

Several curious tenants came to see who had rung the doorbell. Mr. Hair and Ginger came to the door holding hands. Their hair was in the same array of colors. Hers was teased so high that she was as tall as Tall Cliff! Aware that we were all looking at her hair, Ginger tilted her head sideways, patted it gently then winked at Andy. Andy tried not to laugh then he noticed Antenna Man peeking around the corner (*antenna* side out).

Homer came in. "When are we going to eat?"

*I was mortified* and wanted to get Andy out of the Inn before he got *scared off!* I dug into my purse on the bench and pulled out my little notepad and pen and handed it to him. "Would you please write your uncle's telephone number down for my Mother?"

"Sorry, I'll have to look it up in the telephone book," he said. I went to the telephone stand, lifted the lid, then quickly shut it. Embarrassed, I got the telephone book out and took it to him. I was even *more* embarrassed when I realized he was reading my comments about him during the last Basketball Game from my notepad. He smiled when I handed him the *1962* telephone book, held together with a rainbow of colored duct tape. He chuckled while looking up the number and jotted it down for Mother, who was looking out the window curiously.

"Who's in the car?" Mother asked.

"My parents," Andy said.

"What time might I look for Jennifer?"

"We won't be late. I have a report that's due tomorrow."

Mother hugged me. "Have a good time."

"We will, Mother! Thank you. Tell Bobchia I said goodbye."

"Goodbye, Mrs. Matko," Andy said. "It was nice seeing you again."

"Goodbye, *Andrew,*" she said.

"Hey! He's got the same name as *me* and my *grampie!* That's funny, ain't it?" Andrew said.

"Please call me *Andy*. Come on, Skip!" He caught himself, "Sorry, I mean *Jennifer.*" I giggled as he held the door open for me. When outside, he reached for my hand. We stretched our joined hands as we carefully stepped over the 'tootsie rolls' on the sidewalk.

Bobchia opened the door and called after me, "Sweetie Pie! Sweetie Pie, *come here!*"

Unwillingly I walked back to her. "*What?*"

"He *is* a gentleman," she said.

"You called me all the way back here to tell me *that?*"

"Mercy, no! Here, take this." She handed me a brown paper bag.

"*What is it?*"

"A couple of loaves of Ardelle's zucchini bread. Mercy! You can't go to someone's house with *both arms a-swingin'!*"

I walked back to Andy. "*Sweetie Pie?*" He asked.

"Yeah…She's called me that ever since I was a baby."

"It suits you," he winked.

"Thank you. Does your grandmother have a nickname for you?"

"Yeah…"

"Well? What is it?"

"Gram calls me…Angel Face."

"*Angel Face,* huh? That suits you."

That night when they brought me home, Andy walked me to the back door of the Inn so Mother, running from window to window, wouldn't be able to see *Angel Face* give *Sweetie Pie* a soft goodnight kiss.

At school, Marcy still tried to pull on Andy's arm, but he kept telling her to *back off.* She finally got the hint. Meanwhile, Mother wouldn't let me on the phone with Andy for more than fifteen minutes at a time. (Bobchia's *telephone rule* for all the tenants.) Andy would call and we'd talk for fifteen minutes. Then I would hang up and call him and talk for another fifteen, *whispering* on the upstairs phone. When Mother said 'Young love is painful' I did not realize *how* painful. Aspirin soon became *my friend* as I limped from the downstairs phone to the upstairs one, in an effort to *avoid* Mother.

I never had had so much in common with *anyone* as I did Andy! Mother tried to discourage me, saying, "Jen, it's just puppy love," but she could not discourage me (I knew in my heart of hearts that Andy was the boy that God had *prepared* for me.)

With Mother's time monopolized with studies and work, she and I had an *understanding.* I was allowed to see Andy as long as we were *always* in a public place. Bobchia didn't mind the idea of Andy so much after Pat Whiteman told her he was a Free Methodist, so Bobchia extended him an invitation to the Inn.

I hurried and called him and then waited impatiently at the door. "This is what I prayed for." I said.

He kissed my cheek.

When we walked into the great room, he said, "Wow, a *tin tree!*"

"It's Mother's." I said embarrassed.

"I kind of *dig* the motor. We had to build a motor in shop class." His eyebrows went up when he noticed the TV. And then he looked at the real tree. "Now that is what I call a *tree!* We used to get a real one but Mom went on a 'save the environment' kick with her club."

"It's beautiful, isn't it? It came from Bobchia's friend Harold's farm. They have hundreds of trees out there…on the farm." He smiled. (Why was I always saying something *stupid?*)

Bobchia came in and nonchalantly quizzed Andy. She asked *fill-in-the-blanks* questions on the patriarchs of Jewish history. He did pretty well, but she wanted to make sure he was the one for me, so she asked him about the difference between Methodists and *Free* Methodists.

"I don't know! *It's free!* We don't *charge* people to go there!" I laughed. She didn't. Then he quickly said, "Sorry, I don't know. It's the only church I've ever gone to." I took his hand and gave Bobchia 'the look.' Andy looked at me and shrugged.

Had he passed *The Bobchia Test?* Evidently not, because then she flat out asked him, "*Have you given your heart to the Lord?*"

"Yes. I did a couple of years ago at church."

That was the *only* right answer, thus allowing him to visit the Inn, me and her cookie tin.

After that night, Andy spent a lot of time in the great room with me, sharing the tin, helping me with algebra and watching Ginger and Mr. Hair *neck* on the loveseat. It amused us, but it made Bobchia *sick!* She said she felt like a *policewoman*—not because she had to keep an eye on *us*, but because she had to keep an eye on *them!*

For a change of pace, sometimes Andy and I would go to Grady's and listen to the jukebox or we'd sit in the gazebo and cuddle while watching the snow fall. That is where he gave me his class ring as big snowflakes fell all around us. It was like we were inside a snow globe. That night I took some pink angora yarn from Aunt Ardelle's yarn basket and wrapped it through and around the ring until it fit. I only wore it at school and in my room, careful to keep it out of Mother's watchful eye.

As Andy walked me to class one day, he noticed that I was wearing a shoe instead of the slipper. "Skip, you're not limping as much. Where is that fancy slipper cover?"

"In my hope chest."

"In your *hope* chest? Are you *hoping* to wear it again?"

"I *hope* not!"

Andy and I were falling hard and *fast* and we had to put the brakes on several times. Double dating and being involved in Teen Action helped us as Christian teens to maintain our integrity and purity.

As my late night cookie talks with Bobchia were mostly about Andy now, she sensed that our relationship was blooming.

"I wish Mother would like him. She'll *never* change!"

"You're right about that. She'll always have your best interest at heart!"

I rolled my eyes and munched cookies as she told me of the many happy days of her and Grampie's courtship.

"But you forgot to mention you were married at *fifteen!*"

"The United States was at *war!*"

"The United States is at war *right now!*"

"Mercy, how I regret telling you that I was a *child bride!* Listen, you'll be going to college in two years, and I know *his people* go to college." (She was right, he was destined to leave for college next year—something I kept putting out of my mind!)

"Mother and Father were married when *he* was in *college,* remember?"

Bobchia looked to the ceiling and then took a shot of coffee. "You are right, right as rain, so I think it is about *that time of your life* to pass on a *little tidbit of information* that my dear Mother passed on to me that she had gotten from her dear mother who spoke only Croatian." (*Oh boy, lesson to live by number 28!*)

Just as Mother walked through the archway, Bobchia said, "Sweetie Pie, Andy ain't gonna buy the *goat* if he can get *goat's milk* for *nothing!*"

I choked! Mother stomped over, grabbed my hand and practically dragged me down the hall, leaving Bobchia yelling, "What? *Clair?* Goat, *cow,* what's the *difference?* Okay, it was probably translated wrong, but the *gist* of the thing is the *same!*"

Mother pulled me into my room and slammed the door. At long last the Croatian wisdom of my great, great grandmother had *trickled down* through the generations to me, forcing Mother to give me the *purity talk* that she had long been avoiding.

# 13
## The Christmas Play

We kids were in luck! Mr. Fish had announced over the intercom that he was, 'forced to dismiss school early today, because the boilers had ceased to function.' This moved our Christmas vacation up, 'unless further notified,' an entire week, giving us a *longer Christmas vacation!*

Andy helped me and the boys into his truck, laughing as they climbed over me to get to the horn.

"A long Christmas vacation!" Andrew cheered.

"I like your white truck!" Logan said.

"Thanks."

"But I'd like it a lot better if it was *red*, rather than just plain old white." Andrew smiled.

"I'd like it a lot better if it were *orange!*" Logan confessed.

Andy looked at me. "And what about you?"

"White." I smiled.

"Huh-uh!" Logan protested. "*Red and green* is her favorite colors! Bobchia did the whole great room just for *her!*"

I shook my head and Andy smiled. "Well, I could paint the front of the truck red and the back green. How would that be, Skip?"

"*Skip?*" Andrew raised his eyebrows. Mother told you to call her *Jennifer*, remember? I'm telling!"

"Do you want to ride or *walk* home in the cold?"

Andrew sat back in his seat. "Okay, I won't *tell.*" He whispered to Logan to tell.

When we got to the Inn, the boys flew out of the truck, over the bridge, on to the porch, through the kitchen and up the stairs to their room. They swung the bedroom door open so hard it hit the wall, startling Mother at her desk. "What on earth is *wrong?* What are you doing *out* of school? Are you *sick?*"

"The boiler quit, and we get an extra week of *Christmas vacation!*" Andrew ran around the room.

"*Really?*"

Logan hopped up and down. "Honest! Ask Jen if you don't believe us!"

Mother dropped her head to her chin. "Oh, I believe you."

"Where is Bobchia?" Logan asked. "We want to tell her the *news* too!"

"I think she's in her room. She'll be...*thrilled*, I'm sure!"

The boys ran across the hall and pounded hard on her door.

"*Mercy, where's the fire?* Where's the—" She opened the door and peeked around it.

Logan took a step back. "Ouu, Bobchia, what is that *stuff* on your hair?"

"Where'd your *eyebrows* go?" Andrew asked. She opened her door wider.

"*It stinks!*" Andrew got the dry heaves.

"Mercy, back up and you won't *smell* it!"

"What is that creepy stuff on your *head?*" Logan asked.

"*It's hair color to make me look young and beautiful!* Why aren't you boys in school? Are you *both* sick?"

"The boiler quit, so we get a whole *extra* week off for Christmas vacation!"

Bobchia forced a smile as they told of their plans to make tents in her bedroom and stay up all night to watch TV *every single night!* She looked to the ceiling for help and then looked back to the boys. "Did you *warn*, I mean *tell*, your mother the good news?"

"Yeah!" Logan smiled. "She said you'd be *happy!*"

Bobchia rubbed the grove in her forehead and prayed under her breath. A timer went off.

"Are you making *cookies* in there?" Andrew asked.

"Mercy, no! I've got to rinse this stuff off! Where is Jen?"

"*Smooching* Andy downstairs," Logan said.

"There's a pan of brownies on the counter," Bobchia told them.

Andrew looked surprised. "Did you say the *B* word?"

"Have Jen cut them and pour you some milk. I've got to get in the shower! Have her find some cartoons on TV for you, okay?"

"Okay!"

"I've got to wash this stuff off *now!*" She shut the door.

Logan looked offended. "I wanted to ask her if Minnie could sleep with us *tonight.*"

Andrew was too excited to think about Minnie. "*Brownies and cartoons!*"

They high-fived. *"Yea, I love Christmas vacation!"*

*"Me too!"*

I cut the brownies, giving them and Andy each three. The boys shoved one after another into their mouths, demanding to watch cartoons. Andy laughed as I *fine-tuned* the set for the boys. Then his eyes followed Mr. Hair and Ginger as they strutted into the room and cuddled on the love seat.

"It's time for our soap opera, *The Young and the Senseless,*" Mr. Hair announced. "We watch it *every* day at this time." (In reality, all they wanted to do was, *gag,* neck!)

Logan put his hands on his hips. "Bobchia said we could watch cartoons because our school is closed, *so there!*" (I think the boys laughed more at *them necking* then they did the cartoons!)

An hour later the only thing that could have brightened Bobchia's day actually happened! Caleb called. I answered the phone and was asking about Darcy when Bobchia came down the steps, tying her apron as Minnie's head bobbed.

"It's Caleb!" I said holding the receiver up.

"Oh good!" She hurried the rest of the way down, eagerly taking the phone. "Why can't someone invent a telephone *without* a cord?"

Caleb had stopped at a truck stop for coffee and was on his way up from Virginia to pick up a load at Cyclops and take it to New York. He was about one hundred miles away and wanted her to stick a pie in the oven and put on a pot of coffee. It didn't take much of Bobchia's persuading to *convince* him to stay for dinner, and before she hung up, he had agreed to spend the weekend.

Bobchia came into the great room smiling at the boys watching cartoons. Mother was at the desk trying to read while keeping an eye on Andy and I who were keeping an eye on Ginger and Mr. Hair…necking.

Bobchia stomped over to the *lovers* with her hands on her hips. "Mercy, you act more like *teenagers* then *they* do!" She pointed at us. "If you two can't act like *responsible adults,* I will ask you kindly to *pack your belongings* and move to another establishment!"

Andy laughed and stood up. "Sorry…um…I'll pick you up around five to go to the Pizza Pan, okay?"

"Okay with you, Mother, if we go to the Pizza Pan with the gang?" I asked.

"Who?"

I sighed. "Beverly and Brian, Dawnette and Randy, Kathy and Mark, Donna and Joe, Mary Ann and Casey, and Betty Ann and Nickolas. And then we'd like to go to the movie."

"What's playing?"

I quickly looked at Andy. His face turned red as he shrugged his shoulders then said. "Umm, I think a Elvis movie."

Bobchia looked through the paper. "*Clambake,* starring Elvis."

"I guess you can go, but don't be late. Church tomorrow," Mother said.

"Why didn't you tell me that you liked *pizza?*" Bobchia asked. "I can make *better* pizza than the Pizza Pan."

Andy looked surprised. "You can make *better* pizza than the Pizza Pan?" He turned to me. "It's my favorite! She's *kidding,* right?"

"She's part Italian, and her pizza *is* the best!"

"My Uncle Tony's recipe *can't be beat!* How about a pizza party next week? Any day but Sunday, just let me know. Invite the gang over too," Bobchia smiled.

"Sounds great, Mrs. Matkovich. Thanks!"

Mother gave Bobchia 'the look' as I walked Andy to the door.

"*Good guess* about the movie," I said.

"Hey, do *you* make Uncle Tony's pizza too?"

"Ah...*is the sky blue?"* We kissed.

"See ya in a couple hours. Later, Skip!" Andy said as he headed down the sidewalk.

Little did I know that Bobchia's invitation would help me win Andy's heart or give him heartburn! (Depending, on *who made* the pizza.)

I walked back into the great room. "I can't wait to see Darcy," I said. (I wanted to tell her all about the Snowflake dance.)

"She's not coming with Caleb," Bobchia said.

"Why not?"

"She had to stay at school because of their Christmas benefit tomorrow night. She's on the entertainment committee."

"Ah, that's too bad." Somehow, I knew Seth's band would be the entertainment.

A commercial came on and the boys jumped up.

"Can I have another brownie?" Andrew asked.

"Me too?" Logan asked. They noticed Bobchia's hair. "Glad you *cleaned* your hair off."

"Does Bobchia look *young and beautiful* now?" She asked patting her hair smiling.

"Yeah...well actually...you look like an *old lady!*" Logan said.

They headed for the kitchen. I grabbed my mouth. Mother laughed. Bobchia gave her 'the look' and started to follow the boys to the kitchen when she got a whiff of something in the hallway.

"What smells?" She asked.

"Probably *the boys?*" I said.

"Mercy, Jen!" Bobchia looked up the stairway as Tall Cliff came down, mumbling to himself. Then she stomped upstairs with me close behind. "Mercy! Spray something up here, Ardelle! It smells like a *pig farm!*" She followed the smell to Ardelle's room where Aunt Ardelle was giving Venal and Izora their *Christmas permanent waves.* "Mercy, at least crack a window in here before we all suffocate!"

Wanda said in tears, "I can't crack a window because when I was cleaning Lucky's cage Cliff started the sweeper in the hallway, and Lucky flew out of his cage and into the bathroom! Please help Ardelle find him before *he suffocates!*"

We hurried to the bathroom, Ardelle was on her knees trying to grab Lucky from behind the toilet. He fluttered from the floor to the back of the tank cover and back to the floor. The timer for the perms went off. Ardelle yelled, "*Get your heads in the sink!*" Venal crowded out Izora with a push of her hip, sending the frail woman to sit on the toilet. Ardelle tried to get up, but got a kink in her back, and screamed, "Izora, to the tub, to the tub, *quick!*" Izora got on her knees at the tub and stuck her head under the faucet, turning the water on full blast, knocking some of her perm rods out. "*Turn the water down, for crying out loud!*"

Bobchia stood in the doorway of the bathroom, holding her nose. I laughed watching the spectacle. Bobchia went in. "Get out of the way, Ardelle!" Bobchia took the top off of the toilet tank and put it on the floor. Then she gently pulled the tank cover off. Lucky was holding onto it for dear life! "See, Wanda, *he's fine.*" Lucky fluttered and *fell into the toilet.* Ardelle and Wanda screamed. Bobchia said, "Sorry it's *your* toilet. You'll have to fish him out! Come on, Sweetie. We're going to the store. I know I need macaroni for sure."

Laughing, I followed her to the kitchen where she put the thawing roasts into the refrigerator and took out Gladys's blouses. She turned on the oven and searched the freezer, "Ah, here it is!

The only walnut streusel sour cream apple pie left! Wait until you taste it!" She shoved it into the oven. She reached into her apron, "Sorry Minnie!" and pulled out the timer and set it. "Just between you and me, Sweetie, *flushing* that bird would have *solved* a big problem around here!"

"Shame on you!"

"Erase, erase. Kidding, just kidding!" She laughed.

"Boy that perm stuff sure stinks!" I said.

"Every year at this time they get permanent waves, but they never smelled like *that* before! It's those new Helene Curtis Supreme permanents that Ardelle ordered for Izora and Venal. Their hair is the absolute worst—fine and *straight as a porker!* Ardelle does a really good job and only charges them five dollars! That's a pretty good deal, considering the Cut & Curl downtown charges seven dollars for the very same permanent. Get your coat. Caleb will be here soon." She grabbed her purse and put on her coat, and out the door we went to the grocery store.

(Although she would deny it, it was *evident* that Caleb had filled a void that Father had left.) Bobchia hummed through the store and the whole way home. When unpacking the groceries, she handed me the green stamps. "Mmm, smell that pie. In that drawer over there are some green stamp books, Sweetie. We have a dandy store downtown. You're welcome to use them for Christmas gifts, if you want."

"Thanks!" I eagerly got out the shoebox and counted out nine books, almost ten, and then finished pasting in the loose stamps that were in the bottom of the box.

The timer went off. Bobchia got her hot pads and carried the pie to the pantry. "*Mum's the word!* This is the last one of these I have, and it's just for *family*. The rest can have brownies and the spice cake I baked yesterday."

"Bobchia!"

"Well, I suppose you could give somebody *your* piece, if you want."

"*No way!*"

She hummed, glancing out the kitchen window now and then, while preparing the food. I set the table and was pouring applesauce into a bowl when we heard the rig's horn on the covered bridge. She ran to the window to watch the truck come down the lane. Caleb parked the truck and jumped down. Bobchia pushed the door open. Pumpkin greeted him on the snowy steps.

"What a welcoming committee!" He picked up the kitten. "Hi, Rhea! Hi, Jen!" He handed me the kitten and hugged Bobchia and kissed her cheek.

Venal and Izora yelled for Caleb at the top of the stairs hurrying down.

"Caleb!" Izora yelled reaching the bottom of the stairs.

"Caleb, come here!" Venal said out of breath, leaning over the railing.

He laughed, quickly going down the hallway where the two sisters proudly showed off their *'poodle hair.'*

"Girls, you look *twenty years younger!"*

"What did he say, Izora?"

*"You look twenty years younger!"*

They giggled. Venal twirled around, knocking the telephone off of the telephone stand with her hip. Caleb picked it up, laughing. Bobchia put her arm through his and guided him back to the kitchen. *"I* have a surprise for you," she said.

"What stunk back there?" Caleb asked.

"Perms. *Old ladies* get them this time of year." She said.

"I'm glad you're not *old!* You don't even have a *gray* hair!"

*"Never will either!"*

"Yum, smells a lot better in here. Could it be? I believe I smell *fried chicken!"*

"You do!" She laughed.

"You're the best! Thanks, *Mom!"*

*That remark shook me to the core.* I quickly took Pumpkin back to my room and looked at Father's picture on the dresser. "She said Caleb hasn't taken your place and nobody ever could—*ever!* She's never lied to me, so I know she's telling the *truth.* It's just hard to hear someone else call her mom. I miss you so much!"

I could hear them laughing from the hallway as I slowly walked back to the kitchen. Caleb was hunkered down, laughing at the fridge pictures. "You've been a busy girl! Who got the trophy buck, Harold?"

"No, Wayne, but you'd think Harold did! I've heard the story a million times, and the horns *keep growing!* I'll let him tell you all about it."

"I bet he was excited."

*"Excited* is not the word! The last I heard was that after measuring the horns, Cecil talked Wayne into joining the Boone and Crockett Club. Cecil still has ties with the Game Commission

and thought the deer would place high in the state record books, so we'll see. Harold can fill you in on the latest when he gets here. I've got more pictures in the camera and about four more rolls of the kids, but I haven't had time to get them developed."

"I just bet you do!"

Bobchia poured coffee for her and Caleb and they walked into the great room. Caleb shook the tops of the boys' heads. "I saw those *cool pictures of you and the deer* on the fridge."

"He was shot in the *heart,* and Wayne had to take the *guts out* before he even *dragged him out of the woods!*" Logan explained.

"Did you know deer have *real heavy guts?*" Andrew asked.

"*No,* that's a new one on me!" Caleb smiled with his eyebrows up and then looked over to Mother, who (I guess) was playing hard to get. "Hello, Clair."

"Oh, hello," she said looking up from her book, 'surprised.'

Caleb walked over and hugged Ginger and stuck his hand out to shake hands with Mr. Hair, who rudely turned his head away. Just then Mr. T-t-t-tunes came into the great room carrying a suitcase. He strutted, skipped and danced, and to the tune of **Singing in the Rain,** he sang, "I'm leeeaving the Inn, yes leeeaving the Inn. What a glorious feeling, she wants me back again! I'll get her some flowers and kiss her for hours. I'm leeeaving, yes leeeaving the Inn!" That time *everyone* gave him a standing ovation! He bowed.

Bobchia turned to me whispering, "Thank goodness he's leaving before he starts *butchering* the Christmas songs, like last year!" She walked him to the door and held it open for him to carry his suitcases out.

He turned to her. "T-t-t-thanks f-f-f-for e-e-e-every t-t-t-thing!"

"It was great seeing you, Matthew. Please tell Lana I said hello." He started singing a song to the tune of ***Auld Lang Syne,*** but she slowly inched the door shut before he finished.

After going to the Pizza Pan and to the movie, Andy and I followed Beverly and Brian to her house to take a peek at her darling baby brother. Then we went to Grady's for a quick soda. It was five minutes *past* my curfew when we drove down the lane. We saw Mother's shadow faintly through the lace curtain. Andy took his arm from around me, and I sat up straight as he parked the truck. He walked me to the door, but when he put his arms around me for a goodnight kiss, the porch light came on. He quickly stepped back and shook my hand! "Good night, *Miss Matko.* I enjoyed your company this evening, and I hope we can do this *again* sometime soon."

I was speechless. I watched him drive off and hurried in. Mother and Caleb were eating pie at the kitchen table. "Mother, you *embarrass* me!"

"Sorry, I don't mean to."

"Can't you think of what it was like *way back,* when you were a *teenager?*"

"Way back? *Yes*! That is *precisely* why I watch him!"

Caleb laughed as I stomped to my room.

"Mother is so ancient, ancient, *ancient!*" I went to bed, tossing and turning, missing my goodnight kiss and my goodnight snack! Finally in the wee hours of the morning, I got up and searched in the fridge and found an aluminum foil covered dish with the *code word* on it. As I unwrapped the big fried chicken leg, on the bottom of the aluminum foil—stuck with green duct tape—were the directions to the last piece of the coveted pie, hidden on the third shelf of the pantry behind the boxes of oatmeal in a soda cracker box. I eagerly pulled out the heart shaped dish with a note that read, "Sweet pie for my *Sweetie Pie!* I *love* my Bobchia!"

The sugar buzz lasted half the night, prompting me to hit the snooze button twice the next morning.

Bobchia put Minnie in my bed. "This is the day the Lord has made! We will rejoice and be glad in it!"

"All right already, okay, chee, Minnie, quit! I'll get up!"

After nodding through a sermon entitled, **Nothing Is Going to Change in Your Life, Until You Do,** I said my goodbyes to my friends and got into the station wagon with Bobchia.

Then Mother got in saying, "I thought the boys would be in the car by now."

"What's going on, Clair?" Bobchia asked.

"Lois wanted to see Caleb and the boys."

"What did they do *this time,* Mother?" I asked.

"Jennifer, you need to *change your attitude* toward your brothers! Lois assured me it was nothing to get alarmed about."

The boys came running out the side door, dragging garbage bags through the snow. "Oh yeah? I need to change my attitude." I said. "Look at them dragging the church's *garbage* to our car!" I slid down in the seat.

They shoved the bags into the car and got in. "Get this garbage out of here!" Mother said.

"Lois gave us our costumes," Andrew explained.

"*Costumes?*" Mother looked puzzled.

"For the Christmas play tonight," Logan said matter-of-factly.

Caleb got in. "They forgot them last week."

Mother's eyes grew wide. "*Tonight?*"

"We got stuff to say. The papers are in there someplace," Logan pointed.

"It's more than just singing carols like we did at school!" Andrew said.

"Mercy!" Bobchia shook her head.

"You'll go, won't you Mother? Caleb *promised* you would!" Andrew said.

Mother looked at Caleb. "You should *never* have told them that!"

"Well, I just thought that being that it's Sunday, you'd have time to—"

"I do not have time to do anything but *study!*"

"Please, Mother? Pleeease!" Logan begged.

"With sugar?" Andrew added.

"*See what you started!*" Mother said to Caleb. "I wish I could, honey, but I have to study for midterms."

"No fair!" They said in unison, kicking the back of Mother's seat until Caleb told them to "knock it off." Mother gave him 'the look,' then didn't look at him all through lunch, forsaking dessert to study.

I called Andy and he came over. Even though it was Sunday and the kitchen had just gotten back in order, Bobchia couldn't resist showing off her *culinary skills* by making Uncle Tony's pizza pies for Andy.

"Umm, Mrs. Matkovich, you were wrong. This pizza is *not better* than the Pizza Pan's pizza!"

Bobchia raised her eyebrows. "*What?!*"

"This pizza is much, *MUCH better* than the Pizza Pan's! *Yum!*"

"I knew you were smarter than your *dad!*" She blurted.

"*Pardon me?*"

"I mean, how many slices have you *had?* Here, have another!"

Andy smiled with his mouth full. *(TYG, he had won Bobchia's heart. Two hearts down and one to go!)*

The boys took their parts in the Christmas play *very* seriously, rehearsing their lines and getting on everyone's nerves. One by one tenants left the kitchen.

Andrew was to play a shepherd plus do the sound effects of the manger animals. He practiced 'baaing' without moving his lips, choking on his pizza. Harold listened as long as he could stand it, leaving to shovel the sidewalks.

When Mother came downstairs for coffee, she noticed that Andy and I were cuddling on the window seat and gave him 'the look.' Logan begged Mother to watch him play a wise man, but she had to "*study for the future,*" or at least that's how she put it. "After I become a nurse, I promise I will go to *all* your functions."

Caleb said, "You won't be a nurse for what, *two more years?*"

"A year and two months. I'm taking a *crash course,* if it's any of your concern."

"So listen to what you're saying! These boys need a mother *now;* they can't put their life on *hold* until you have a degree or have quote '*made it.*' They need a mother *today and every day!*"

"I'm the *oldest* one in my class, it's harder for me to retain all the medical jargon. Besides you have no idea what we have been through, and I don't see that it is any of *your* business anyway! They are *my* children, not yours! *I* am their parent!"

Bobchia gave Caleb 'the look', but he ignored it. "Then you had better start *acting like one* instead of being their *babysitter.* They need some *good old-fashioned discipline, and they also need to respect their elders!* They *can't* raise themselves!"

"I'm doing the best I can so I can get a job and buy them what they *want!*"

Andrew jumped in, "I don't *want* things, Mommy! I just *want* you to come with us tonight!"

"Me too! *Pleeeeeese,*" Logan begged. "Pretty please with *sugar?*"

Caleb couldn't stand to look at their sad faces and went into the hallway. Bobchia followed him and said, "Take it *easy* on Clair, will ya? I don't want them packing up and *leaving* again! Christmas is just around the corner, and I've waited *too* long to have them *here*. Promise me you won't say another word, Caleb! *Promise me.*"

"Okay. I'll *try* and keep my mouth shut."

She patted him on the shoulder. "I'm not saying you're *wrong;* it's just that I'm walking on *eggshells* here! I couldn't bear them leaving again, understand? I just…*I just couldn't bear it again.*"

"*Okay, okay!*"

Andy pulled me into the hallway. "I'm going to shove off."

"I'm sorry, Andy. My family is so embarrassing." I hung my head.

"You should hear *my* family sometimes. It is what it is. Your mom keeps looking at me as if I were going to *bite* you or something." He touched my cheek. I looked into his eyes. "Next time, *you* make me the pizza, okay?"

"Uh, *is the sky blue?*"

"I'll meet you later at the church."

"I'm sorry that she's in a *mood.* I'll miss you until then."

"Me too." He kissed me softly.

After waving to him until he crossed the covered bridge, I went to the kitchen, where Mother was pleading her case to Andrew. "I'm sorry, honey boy. I have to study for a quiz tomorrow. Besides, I don't have *anything* to wear. I have to get a good grade on this test because I *missed* the last one, when I took you to the doctor on Thursday for your cold, remember?"

"I remember. That cold was the *worst* one of my life!"

"Sorry." She brushed his hair across his forehead with her finger. "I just don't have a choice. Someday you'll understand."

Logan heard what Mother said and hurried upstairs and put a box on her bed.

Mother continued; "I'm sure you'll be *wonderful* in the play. Jennifer, Caleb, Bobchia and Harold will be there, so you won't even *miss me.*" She smiled.

"But—"

"No buts. You finish your cookie, and you can tell me all about it when you get home. I've got to study." She leaned over and kissed his cheek. He watched her leave the kitchen and wiped off a tear along with her kiss.

Upon entering her bedroom Mother saw the gold box wrapped with red duct tape lying on her pillow. Her fingers stuck together as she lifted the lid. "A red satin blouse! Oh, it's *beautiful!*" She held it up to herself in the mirror and then ran down the steps.

Caleb was helping Logan point like a wise man and project, "Look, look a star!"

Bobchia and I were helping Andrew with his animal sounds when Mother *threw* the blouse at Caleb. "I don't know who *you* think you are, but I *can't* accept this!"

Caleb looked surprised. "*What is your problem, lady?*"

"*You're my problem!*"

Bobchia tried to get between them, looking to the ceiling. Mother continued, "You waltz in here like you're *God's gift to women* with your hairy chest—"

"I didn't think you *noticed!*"

"Just because I didn't *swoon* like every other female in this place, you had to stoop to *bribery!*"

The boys tried to talk to her, but she ran upstairs with the boys after her and me after them. She went into her room and pushed the books off of the desk! Mr. Pill pounded the wall.

"*We're sorry!*" The boys said running to her and hugging her. Logan said, "We'll get you something *else*. Please don't be so *mad!*"

"I'm not mad at you, honey. It's, it's *that man!* He thinks he can use my kids to get to *me! Well, he can't!*"

"I'm sorry," Andrew said.

"*Quit saying that!*"

Caleb came to the doorway with Bobchia peeking around him. "*You are the most stubborn woman I have ever met!*"

Bobchia patted Caleb's back.

Mother looked at him through narrow eyes. "Why don't you just admit it? You *like* me!"

He laughed. "I did until you threw that *hissy fit* with your gums flapping so hard that *you ignored your own kids!*" Bobchia patted his back harder.

"I can't accept that blouse!"

He tossed the blouse on the bed. "If you would be quiet and *listen to your kids,* you might *learn something!*" He nodded to Andrew, folded his arms and leaned against the doorway. Mother gritted her teeth waiting for an explanation.

"You said you were *fat,* 'member?" Andrew said.

"And didn't have *anything* to wear," Logan continued. "*So we bought you that blouse.*"

"Yeah, Bobchia said you would *like it,* but instead you *hate it.*"

Mother shook her head. "*I don't hate it.*"

"You *threw* it at Caleb!" Logan pouted.

Andrew sat down on the bed. "You gave Jen her present *early,* so we gave you your blouse *early!*"

Mother looked lovingly at them. "You can return it and give Caleb back his money. You shouldn't have taken money from *him* in the first place!"

"We used our *roni money!*" Andrew said proudly.

Mother looked puzzled. "What is he saying, Logan?"

"The *macaroni money* we got from selling the necklaces at the Snowflake Festival."

"Oh," she said, biting her lip. She looked over at Bobchia peeking around Caleb.

"They are telling you the *truth,* Clair." Bobchia said nodding.

Mother hugged the boys. "*Please forgive me!*"

"Us forgive *you?* Chee, you're *funny,*" Logan beamed.

Caleb smiled at them in a huddle. "Come on boys, let your mother get ready. You've got fifteen minutes tops!" He said, looking at his watch. Caleb chuckled at Bobchia wiping her eyes. Then he patted her on the back helping her down the stairs.

Andrew whispered to Mother, "Are you *really* going?"

"Yes," she whispered back, wiping his tears away.

"*Yippy!*"

Logan looked at her seriously. "What about your test? You *better* get a good grade."

"I'll just have to burn the midnight oil."

"What does *that* mean?"

"I'll study when I get home because going to your play is *more important.*"

"Really?"

"Really!"

"*You're the best mom ever!*"

"I wish I was, honey, but I promise I'll *try* harder, okay?

"OKAY!" They said.

"Now you two go get into your costumes, and I will get into *the most beautiful red blouse in the whole world!*"

"*Wow!*"

"*Wow!*"

The boys ran out of the room and down the stairs, meeting Caleb and Bobchia at the foot of the steps with their costumes.

"We are going to be *late!*" Bobchia said, shoving them into the costumes.

"Don't worry, Rhea," Caleb said. "They won't start the play with only *two* wise men—*that's not biblical!*"

"I won't go if we leave without Mother," Andrew said. Then he baaed and mooed without moving his lips.

Mother talked to herself in the mirror. "*Why do I always think I'm right?*"

"Because you're old…er!" I quipped back.

She sighed, brushing her hair. I looked closely at her face in the mirror, looking for hair. "What are you looking at?" She asked.

"You could use some makeup."

"I don't have time."

"Bobchia wears it and says that even a *barn* needs painted once in a while!" I searched the dresser for her makeup bag and handed it to her.

"Well, I feel as *big as a barn*, that's for sure!" She said as she tried to get the new blouse buttoned. "Doesn't Rhea get on your *nerves* with all those ancient sayings of hers?" She put on some powder.

"No. Mother, do you like Caleb?"

"Well, he's *different.*"

"Don't you think he's nice?"

"I guess."

"Cute?"

"*Yes!*"

I made a beeline to my room, retrieved the bottle of the 'miracle fragrance' and hurried back up the stairs. Mother was picking up her books as I walked toward her taking the lid off of the bottle, when I slipped on a notebook! The bottle flipped in the air, splashing on her hair.

"Jen! Are you *okay?* Did you hurt your foot again?" She helped me up.

"A little."

"*PU! What on earth?*"

"Ouu, sorry!"

"My eyes are *watering!*" She said blinking.

"Well, at least your hair smells better than *mine* did!"

"That's a matter of *opinion!* What *is* that stuff?"

"It's called **Evening in Paris**. It's Bobchia's *favorite!*"

"Oh my!" She towel-dried her hair as best she could and brushed it. "I don't think this is *helping.*"

"We better hurry!"

She put on some rouge and lipstick, looking good for the time allotted.

We hurried down the stairs, but they were gone! Mother looked disappointed until we heard a blast from the truck horn. We grabbed our coats. Caleb met us halfway down the sidewalk. "Rhea and Harold left to save us seats. I hope you don't mind, the boys want to take the rig."

"I don't mind, but I don't think I can get up in it," Mother said. Caleb searched her face. "Why does everyone look at me like *that?*"

"You look pretty good for a *fat lady!*" He chuckled.

"Thanks, *cowboy!*"

He helped her up onto the seat. She slid in next to the boys, who were trying to turn the steering wheel and blasting the horn.

Andrew grabbed his nose. "PU! What *stinks?*"

"*Shhhhh!*" Mother hushed him.

Caleb then helped me up and jumped in the cab to stop the boys from blowing the horn again. He looked at Mother, rolled his window down, stuck his head out for a breath of air and said, "Boys, didn't you want to give your mother *something* else?"

"Oh, yeah, it goes with the blouse." Logan smiled. They tossed two little boxes on her lap.

"What pretty boxes." She opened them carefully, preserving the paper.

"*Hurry up!*" Andrew said.

Inside was the most beautiful, glittery red-and-green macaroni necklace and bracelet *in the whole world!* The boys took them and twirled them on their fingers, *glittering* the cab.

"*Gee whiz, guys!*" Caleb said. "*Give* them to your mom!"

They handed them to her, and she put them on. "You make me feel like a *princess!*" She hugged them.

(For the first time in their entire little lives, the boys were *speechless.*) When Caleb told Mother how beautiful she looked, Andrew and Logan smiled so hard I thought their faces were going to *crack!*

Mother was finally with us again—into the moment—later to be known as '*the macaroni moment.*' But the quiet was short-lived. Andrew started to *baa* in Logan's ear.

"Shut up!" Logan yelled

"You're just *jealous* that you don't have much stuff to *say!*"

"I'm a *wise* man. I don't need to say a lot of stuff; *I'm smart!*"

"Well, a shepherd has this pipe to *yank* the sheep by the neck, and a wise man just sits around and thinks of smart stuff to *think* about."

"It's a *staff*, not a pipe," Mother corrected him.

Andrew ignored her. "I'll yank *your* neck, Logan!" He tried to put the staff around Logan's neck, but Mother grabbed it, accidentally knocking a heavy cross, hanging from the rearview mirror, against the windshield. Caleb quickly stopped it.

"I'm sorry, Caleb." Mother said. "Now Andrew, I want you to settle down this *minute*. A shepherd does not *yank* his sheep. He *guides them* with his staff. If they fall over a ridge or get stuck in the creek, he *guides them* out with the staff. Now, do you know who *our* Shepherd is?" Andrew shook his head no.

"*Jesus,* because he helps us, *guides us* and protects us." Mother smiled.

"Did Bobchia make you *memorize* that?" Logan asked.

"I know a verse in the Bible!" Andrew said. "**Jesus loves me this I know. For the Bible tells me so. See!**"

"That's a *song! Jesus wept:* is a verse I memorized!" Logan bragged.

"Mother, do you have to study a lot to be a shepherd?" Andrew asked.

"I… I…no."

"Good, I think I'll quit school and save sheep by the *neck!*" Caleb leaned around the boys looking at Mother and laughed.

When Caleb pulled the truck up in front of the church's recreation center, the boys took turns blowing the horn, impressing their friends on the sidewalk. Mother asked them several times to *stop* but it wasn't until Caleb *threatened* to break their little fingers, *that* made them quit.

He smiled with remorse at Mother then jumped from the cab, brushing glitter off of his cowboy shirt. As soon as the boys jumped into his outstretched arms, he got *glittered* all over again! The boys rushed to their friends, as he brushed himself off again. Then he walked around the truck to help me jump to the ground.

"Thanks," I said.

He nodded. "You're welcome, ma'am."

Mother slid over to the edge of the seat. He held his arms out for her. She shyly reached for him and slid down beside him. He looked down at her. She smiled up at him coyly. *"You smell like Rhea!"* He said. "I better move the rig."

Mother's face turned redder than her blouse. *"Mercy! I smell like Rhea?"*

"And *sound* like her too!" I said, laughing.

Inside, Mother and I followed the glitter trail and caught up to the boys in the hallway beside the stage, where they rehearsed their parts once again for Mother. Lois came down the steps with Samantha, Amanda, and little Cora Rose who were dressed like angels.

"You sound like you know your parts boys, but the wise men *weren't glittery!"* Lois said.

"How do *you* know?" Andrew challenged.

"Hush!" Mother said, brushing them off.

Then I made the mistake of saying, *"Break a leg!"*

"Break your *pig face!"* Logan said.

"And your *pig back!"* Andrew said.

We were as embarrassed, as Lois was shocked!

Samantha and Amanda said in unison, "**Treat others as you want to be treated!**" Little Cora Rose said; "That is the *golden rule."*

Mother said, *"Apologize* to your sister! Go on! Tell her you're sorry right this minute!"

"You're sorry right this minute!" Andrew blurted.

"Me too!" Logan said.

When they hugged Mother's neck they stuck their tongues out at me then Lois ushered them behind the curtain to take their place with Mary, Joseph and the baby Jesus.

"We better get our seats," Mother said.

From the second row, Andy, Bobchia and Harold waved eagerly for us to join them. "Boy, you smell really *good!"* Harold said to Mother as she sat down. She rolled her eyes.

I sat between Bobchia and Andy, whispering a confession to her that I had spilled her perfume, and promised to replace it. She whispered back, "Don't worry, I still have the bottle that Harold got me for *Valentine's Day* and another bottle he got me for *Groundhog Day.* Oh, and the *one-pound bottle he got me for the Fourth of July.* He *loves* the stuff!" Her face turned as red as Mother's blouse.

Mother sat *round-shouldered,* trying to keep her gaping blouse together as Caleb came in. Then the lights dimmed.

"I had to go two blocks down to find a parking space *big enough,*" Caleb whispered apologetically.

Minnie peeked out of the apron whenever she heard the boys talking on stage, and growled whenever Bobchia took a picture. Mother got perturbed at Andy and I for laughing when Andrew's *baaing* drowned out Logan's lines and the angel's speech.

After the play we went downstairs to the social hall and enjoyed hot chocolate and platefuls of cookies. Lois's 'little angels' entertained us by playing Christmas carols on the piano together. Pastor Jay lavished praise on the children for their performances while Lois lavished her attention on Minnie. When her daughters spotted the pup, they ran over and fought over which one of them would hold her. After Minnie showed them her teeth, Bobchia quickly put her back into the apron. "Quit acting like a *dog,* Miss Minnie! Sorry girls, she is temperamental, this one is, but I promise that I'll put *your names* on the next stray pup that crosses my path. How's that?"

Samantha and Amanda shook their heads and said in unison, "Not *our names.* We'll name her *Queenie,* after Queen Esther."

"How appropriate." Bobchia smiled.

"How do you talk like that, and who is *Esther* anyways?" Andrew asked.

"Mordecai's orphaned cousin," the girls said.

"Bobchia?" Logan asked.

"What Logan?"

"It could be a *boy* puppy, right?"

"Well, of course."

"So there, it might be a *boy* puppy! What would you name it then?" Logan asked.

"*King,* after King Ahasuerus," the girls said.

"*Who?*"

"King Ahasuerus reigned from 485 to 464 B.C. He was king over one hundred and twenty-seven provinces from India to Ethiopia, and he made Esther his queen."

Bobchia smiled, raising her eyebrows. "*Wow!* You girls really *know* your Bible! Well, we had better head on down the pike. Goodnight."

"Goodnight, and have a *safe* trip home," they said smiling.

After Bobchia and Harold left for the Inn, Andy and I followed Caleb, Mother and the boys as they rode around town enjoying the Christmas lights.

We laughed when the boys blasted the rig's horn, causing a chain reaction of barking dogs.

When we got back to the Inn, hot chocolate and popcorn awaited us in the great room. The boys curiously walked over to Harold and watched him wipe off his face with his handkerchief.

Logan pointed. "Look, *blood!*" Harold turned his back. "What happened Harold?" He wouldn't answer.

Andrew took another look. "What happened to Harold, Bobchia? He's *bleeding!*" Andrew said.

"No, he's *not,* honey boy."

"*He is! He's bleeding!*" Andrew pointed.

"I seen dead stuff, I know *blood* when I see it! *He's bleeding!*" Logan confirmed.

"It's *lipstick,*" Mother said laughing, then she called the boys to the coffee table. "Please keep your cups on your napkins, and don't *spill* anything on Ardelle's puzzle."

Andrew looked back. "Lipstick *yuck!*"

Bobchia tried to avert their attention by giving them the cookie tin. "I am *proud* to have a wise man and a shepherd in my family!"

Mother's mind was definitely on Caleb—she actually allowed Bobchia to give the boys *more* sugar cookies after they had just finished off a *dozen* at church! She also deliberately sat as far away from Caleb as possible, sipping her hot chocolate while clutching the front of her blouse. I caught her staring at him as he and Andy wrestled with the boys on the floor. (Caleb was the *total opposite* of Father, rather rough-cut for Mother, but he was so kind and loving. How could she help herself? I no longer thought of him as 'replacing father' but a *God-send,* helping Mother, helping us all through a difficult time in our lives.)

"Baa, baa, moo, baa," Andrew said, jumping onto Caleb's back. Minnie whined in the apron.

Caleb reached around and pulled Andrew into a sitting position in front of him. "Okay, buddy, the play is over, and the manger animals are all *asleep.*"

Mother said, "That's right, and you should be too. It's almost ten o'clock."

Andrew looked at her. "So? We don't have school and don't have to get up early and take a bath or '*nothin!*'"

"Yeah, we're on vacation!" Logan said. "Can Minnie sleep with us? *If she poops, I promise I won't turn the rug! I'll just leave that poop right in front of my face and smell it all night, I promise!*" Caleb chuckled.

"Can't we stay up *just* until the clock strikes *one more time?*" Andrew begged.

Mother continued, "It's late, and the rest of us are tired. It's been a long day, so thank Caleb for taking you for a ride in his truck."

"Thank you, Caleb," Logan said.

"Thank you, Caleb. Sorry I blew that horn a lot!" Andrew said.

Caleb winked at them. "You are *so* welcome. *Thank you* for being so great in the play! I sure did enjoy it."

"All Logan did was *point,* but I had *real stuff* to say," Andrew said.

"I had *a* line, but who could hear me with that *big animal mouth of yours?*" Logan said.

"Well you—"

Caleb cut Andrew off. "You were *both* very, *very* good!"

Andrew looked at Mother. "Mother, did you *thank* Caleb?"

"No, but I will. Thank you, Caleb."

"You're welcome." He winked at her.

Mother turned her head to the boys. "Okay, bedtime."

"Can Minnie sleep with us, *pleeease?*" Andrew asked.

"Not tonight, okay?" Bobchia said.

The boys walked slowly past Andy and Caleb giving them high-fives. They started up the stairs, but Andrew ran back into the room and hugged Caleb. "Riding in your truck was the *mostest fun,* Caleb!"

Caleb smiled. "It *was* the mostest fun, buddy."

"*Will you play catch with me some day?*"

"*Sure will!* I'll hunt up my glove and throw it in the cab."

"Will you say *prayers* with me too?"

"It would be music to my ears, buddy. Run upstairs and get on your pajamas, and I'll be up in a minute."

Bobchia looked at me and Andy and pointed her head to the kitchen. I got the hint. "Thanks Caleb for the ride," I said.

"My pleasure, Jen."

"Later, Caleb," Andy said.

"Later, Andy."

Bobchia blew a kiss to Caleb. "See you in the morning."

We went into the kitchen.

Mother walked over to Caleb. "You made the night *special* for them. That was very kind of you."

"It was my pleasure, *ma'am*. Really, I get a kick out of them. Did you enjoy yourself?"

"It was so nice to do something besides study, and it was different. I have never ridden in a truck before."

"Maybe you'd like to go for another ride sometime."

"I should be studying as we speak. I have so much on my plate right now that I don't know if I'm coming or going. I haven't even had time to look up old friends. I've got to *ace* my midterms and then finally I'll be caught up to the rest of the class. Next semester I plan on doubling my classes. By then I'll hopefully see a light at the end of the tunnel. This place isn't the *best place* to raise children in."

"*Now hold it right there.* Before you start *slamming* Rhea, I want you to know that she is one of the greatest people I have ever known. I don't know what I would have done with Darcy if it hadn't been for her. She's like a *mom* to me!"

"I know, she has been a blessing to me too, and the children love her to death."

"And you?"

"Well, I'm older and a little *wiser* and understand her ways more than I used to. The children and I have had a rough time of it. Paul getting ill and us having to sell our possessions was, *I hope,* the worst thing we will ever have to go through. I want to get the children into a *stable environment;* that's why I'm working at Pine Grove when I can. I feel like a hamster in one of those wheels, and no matter how fast I go, I end up in the same place. I feel like if I stop, I won't want to get started again. It happened to me once before, and it's an *awful feeling.*"

"Do you always have to be in *control?*"

"When it comes to my children I do."

"I can respect that, but listen to what you're saying. You feel that you have to reach a certain point before the children can be happy and feel secure. Is that right?"

"Yes."

"Didn't you hear them tonight *begging* you to come with them? And didn't you notice how happy they were when *you did?* Did you *see* their faces and *feel* their hugs? The whole night's success depended upon *you* being there. Don't you understand? They needed their mother *tonight,* not when you get *your degree.* A degree is wonderful but not at the expense of your children. If you could just…slow down a little. Tonight is a memory they will have for the rest of their lives, and it's all because *you listened to what they needed."*

"So you're saying I should quit school and we should live here *forever?"*

"No, but they do need you to spend some *time* with them every day, even if it's just reading them a book or taking a walk with them."

"I feel *guilty* enough as it is, without *you* pointing out what *I should* be doing as a mother! And to top it all off, they're out of school a week *early,* and I'm trying to study for my midterms! *How am I supposed to do all that? I'll be a basket case!"*

"I could *help* with them."

"You…*could?"*

"Yes, I can keep them *busy* while they're out of school a few days this week and next week so you can study. Tomorrow I have to leave early to go to New York and then make a quick run to South Carolina. I could come back here for a few days before going back to Pittsburgh. I can be a *big help* if you want me to. Do *you* want me to?" He reached for her hand. "Now would be a good time to say *yes."*

She smiled. He looked into her eyes and kissed her. *"Yes,"* she said. He kissed her harder.

The boys yelled for Mother and Caleb to come upstairs for prayers. Mr. Pill pounded the floor.

The next morning Caleb and Mother were up early, laughing and eating breakfast together at the little corner table in the kitchen. I was surprised she was *sacrificing* her study time to be with him. Bobchia had a big smile on her face, trying not to stare, as they leisurely talked over coffee.

Caleb looked out the window and said, "It's snowing hard. I have to go. I *wish* I could stay, but I should have been on the road an hour ago." He put his coat on and kissed Bobchia goodbye. She handed him a sack full of goodies. Mother grabbed her coat to walk him to the rig. Bobchia and I stood behind the lace curtain amazed, watching them laugh and kiss in the falling snow. Mother even stood in the snowstorm, waving at him until he went over the covered bridge! We quickly sat down before she came back in.

"I *hate* snow! It's freezing out there!" She said as she stomped her feet.

"But you have your *love* to keep you warm, right Mother?" I asked.

"Very funny!" She smiled as she took her coat off and hung it on the line over the potbelly, poured herself a cup of coffee, then warmed her hands with it as she went up the stairs.

Caleb was true to his promise. He came back at the end of the week, making everyone happy, especially *me*. When he entertained the boys, I was free to hang out with Andy and the gang at Grady's and the Tic Toc Hop. When Mother thought I was doing too much socializing, Bobchia would whip up a pizza for us, that way Mother knew *for sure* what we were doing.

(There was, however, a persistent little question in the back of my mind: did Andy love *me or Bobchia's cooking?*) Anyway, TYG, Bobchia quit making *cow doctor* remarks to me about Andy's father, as Andy was becoming a 'regular guest' at the Inn. Andy lavished Bobchia with compliments on her easiest recipes as well as on her most elaborate Croatian dishes.

"Skip, do you know how to make this *delicious stuff?*" He'd ask.

"*Is the sky blue?*" I'd say, as Bobchia proudly set platefuls of rich food in front of him.

"Thanks, Mrs. Matkovich. I'm going to have to do *four* days of weight lifting instead of three to get in shape for the game on the fifth, after eating all your delicious food!"

"*Please call me Bobchia!*"

I gave her a surprised look. Mother gave her '*the* look.'

That night over the cookie tin Bobchia asked me again, "When are you going to *start* helping me cook the meals around here?"

"It *hurts* to stand on my foot."

"*Bologna!* That is no excuse! You know what I always say?"

"Wait, let me think. You can't fly until you *jump* out of the tree?"

"*Mercy!*" She snorted. "Although you have the right idea! You can *sit* and learn, ya know. After all Sweetie, *the sky is blue, but the kitchen is green,* and if you want to be a *good* cook, I expect to see you *in it*—and I mean *before* it's time to sit down and eat!"

"Chee."

"Don't *chee* me, young lady! There are a lot of your grandmother's Croatian dishes that are a little more *complicated* than pizza!"

"Your pizza is complicated enough!"

"We'll have fun, you'll see. After all, *the quickest way to the altar is through the kitchen!*"

"Is that in the *Bible?*"

"Mercy, child! No, that's what my Aunt Mary always said!"

"In that case, *reserve me a cobbler apron!*"

Bobchia snorted.

When Caleb arrived, the boys had the time of their lives! Caleb told them stories of the life he had on the farm in Texas where he was raised by his aunt and uncle. He'd take the boys to the window, point to Trigger on his truck, and tell them his favorite story of when he was just a boy and had gone to the state fair and saw Roy Rogers and Dale Evans in *person!* He told them of how beautiful Trigger, was with his long yellow mane and tail. Caleb pretended to be Trigger, dancing and pawing at the sawdust. He told of how Roy had ridden him around the ring, and how he had stood up on his back legs and pawed at the air! "Oh boy, how *I* wanted to be like Roy and have a horse just like *Trigger!*"

"Did you for *real paint* Trigger on your truck?" Andrew asked.

"*For real.*"

"Will you paint me a horse now?"

"I'll draw you one. How's that?" Caleb got his duffle bag out of the mudroom and pulled out his sketchpad. He showed them several of his drawings of rigs with horses on the sides of them.

"I like this horse with spots on its rump. It looks kinda like Dollee only the spots are just in one spot," Logan said.

"That's an appaloosa," Caleb told him.

"I like this black one. It's like Red, the Mountie's horse that stayed here. Remember?"

Caleb carefully ripped out the pages and handed them to the boys.

"Wow! Are these ours to *keep?*" Logan asked him.

"Yes."

"*Forever and ever?*" Andrew jumped up and down.

"Forever and ever."

"Wow, thanks Caleb!" Andrew held the drawing up.

"Thanks! Can we hang these in our closet?" Logan asked.

"Sure." Caleb dug around in a kitchen drawer and let them pick out a roll of duct tape.

They ran upstairs, and when they came back down, their first cup of *cowboy coffee* awaited them—along with the tin full of cookies.

After two nights of the boys crawling in bed with Bobchia and Minnie, keeping them both awake by tossing and turning all night; and then, asking her, at *three a.m.,* to make them bacon and cowboy coffee; Bobchia's *curiosity was peaked.*

She set the platefuls of bacon and eggs on the table while their caffeine levels and the moon was *high.*

"Come on quit throwing that ball in here and sit down! You put that spoonful of *sugar* back into that sugar bowl right now, young man! Andrew, I've never made cowboy coffee before. Tell me how Caleb makes it."

"Just plain old coffee with sugar," Andrew explained. (Just so you city slickers know the makings of cowboy coffee, it's only a *half* cup of coffee, with a *chuck wagon* full of sugar and a whole *lot* of cow! *Yee-haw!)*

That's fine for truck drivers who need to stay awake all night long traveling the interstate but not so good for young *whipper-snappers,* who should be snoring on their closet floor by nine thirty! Needless to say, Bobchia put the *kibosh* to Cowboy coffee!

The other *bur* that got under Bobchia's saddle was when Venal and Izora couldn't *find* the brooms to sweep the crumbs off the floor after breakfast. Venal crunched the crumbs to fine powder as they baked pies! Caleb (*the rustler*) had rustled the brooms to the red barn so the boys could paint them (their horses) like the pictures he had given them. They had eagerly traded their Superman capes for Caleb's red bandanas, and whenever they watched Roy Rogers' movies, they'd sit on their horses (the brooms). "What a hoot!"

'Pop!' Went the camera.

The next morning at breakfast, Bobchia rustled the boys' horses (brooms) back for clean-up duty. Andrew kicked at Izora and Venal as they swept the floor with *Trigger and Little Trigger*. After the floor was shinier than a *cowpokes spur*, Bobchia sent Tall Cliff to the hardware store to buy new horses (*erase*) brooms and then sent Caleb to play with the boys and their brooms (*erase*) horses to the basement while she made pies.

Roy Rogers verses the Mounties was only one in a long line of the boys' favorite stories that they acted out with Caleb as he told them of his childhood memories of his own broom (*erase*) horse. Caleb taught the boys how to jump their broom horses over the water ditch, and whenever they'd fall in, he'd sneak the *wet boys* past Bobchia in the kitchen and hurry them into dry clothes before she saw them, making the stories at the chuck wagon (dinner table) hilarious!

The Tuesday before Christmas, we were all relieved to hear that Mother had *aced* her midterms, but the following days were difficult for me as Mother and Caleb became *inseparable*. Andy and I watched through the lace curtain as Caleb, with a bag full of peanut butter cookies in one hand and an arm around Mother, walked to the rig. With a goodbye kiss and a horn blast on the covered bridge, Caleb left to pick up the load of steel at Cyclops. Then he was headed for Virginia and was going to stop on the way back to pick up Darcy on Christmas Day. I could tell by the way Mother was smiling when she came through the kitchen door that she was falling for him.

"Andy and I watched *you* from the window, Mother," I told her. "How do *you* like it?"

"Jennifer! *You embarrass me!*"

# 14
# Christmas

Christmas in 1967 was on a Monday, so on the Wednesday before, Bobchia made a list of what each of the ladies was going to contribute to the Christmas feast and of the ingredients that were needed. Deciding that the twenty pounds of sugar and flour in the pantry would not be enough, she sent Tall Cliff and Gladys to the Golden Dawn for more twenty-pound bags, plus spices and herbs. For that *reason* alone, I added stretchy stirrup pants and long mohair sweaters to my Christmas list. The laundry was the number one priority on Friday, leaving Saturday open for cleaning and baking so as not to disrupt the *Sabbath*. On Saturday, again, I attempted to write down the recipes of the blue-ribbon masterpieces that Bobchia and the ladies were pulling out of the ovens, but I was still confused, so with Bobchia's blessing, I opted to dust and sweep the great room.

I hurried out of the heat of the kitchen and into the fragrance of pine and bayberry that filled the great room. "Christmas smells so pretty!" I focused on the grandeur of the towering tree framed in the cove of red drapes, but the tree looked *peculiar.* From the star down to about four feet from the floor, popcorn garland gracefully hung from branch to branch, but from that point to the floor, big gaps of popcorn were *missing* only the limp string remained! "Oh *brother,* wait until Bobchia sees this mess!" I laughed getting the sweeper from the hall closet. Even though my foot throbbed no amount of pain would keep me from making this room shine for my *long-awaited Christmas in the Inn.* I bumped into the ugly tin tree several times, while I ran the sweeper, wishing I had a *super-duper sweeper* to *suck* the ugly thing up! "There, looks better already." I put **White Christmas** on the stereo and dusted the assorted tables and the roll top, looking forward to the birthday party tomorrow night. I looked at Bobchia's snow globe collection through the glass of her china cupboard. One by one I took them out and shook them and carefully arranged them on top of the piano.

I studied the oil painting **Now Freedom** as I dusted the mantel, trying to crack the *allusive code.*

"Sweetie, I've saved the *best for last,"* Bobchia said, as she came into the room placing a couple of big boxes with foreign writing on top of the puzzle. "These will be *yours* and the *boys'* someday. These are your grampie's and my favorite Christmas ornaments!"

"Thank you!"

"Oh, doesn't the piano look pretty? I forget how pretty the globes are when they're in the china cupboard. Well, tell me, did you figure out the code?"

"No matter how hard I study it, I can't get it."

"Give up?"

"No, well, maybe. I just don't see it. I've looked at it from every *possible* angle. I just don't see a Bible verse. It is written in *English*, right?"

"Of course, *ding dong!* Slide over that cane chair." She stood on it, gently holding the frame, lifting it from its nail hold. "Here, mercy, push that dust rag over the top of it when you get it to the couch." She watched me with her hands on her hips as I dusted.

I turned my head this way and that. "*I still don't see it.*"

"I told you to dust the *top* of it."

"I did."

"No, you dusted the *bottom.*"

"Huh?"

"When Edjew rang the cowbell and the slaves made their way through the tunnels and the 'slave catchers' searched the Inn, Mineya would turn the painting *right side up* and the code would *disappear,* keeping it from hate-filled eyes."

When she turned the picture upside down, she watched the unfolding of the code sweep across my face. As clear as day, from the treetops to the black-and-white cows standing beside the red barn, to the cows' reflections shining on the pond, was the verse that had saved many a precious life from slavery. "*I see it! I see it!* **Thou shalt not...deli-ver...unto his master the ser-vant...which...is es-caped...from his mas-ter unto...thee. *Yea!*"**

"Scripture is an amazing gift from God. For years a person can read the same verse over and over, but not until you really need it does the Lord *reveal* its' meaning, *changing our lives forever.*"

"Like proverbs and the parables!"

"You hit the proverbial nail on the head!" She climbed back on the chair. "Hand it here."

"Why don't you leave it upside down so people can read it?"

"It's not for *everyone's eyes,* just for family, *understand?*" I turned the picture slowly over, watching the words disappear, like snow settling in the bottom of a snow globe. "This place is full of mysteries, Bobchia."

"I think more *history* than mystery."

"I think *mystery*. For instance, our Christmas tree over there has something very *mysterious* about it..." I smiled as *she* solved the mystery.

"What do you—" She looked over and climbed down. "Mercy, *what*..." She walked over rubbing the grove in her forehead. "They think they got away with something, *don't they?* Don't you worry, Bobchia knows how to *fix* those little partners in crime! Old Bobchia has more than *one trick up her sleeve!*"

"See, you shouldn't have yelled at me last night for telling them they were *adopted!*"

She laughed looking at the tree. "Ardelle and Spike spent hours working on that popcorn string. Oh well, help me take this part off." We dumped the string in the wastebasket. "There, now come over here. I have been saving these for *you.*" She reached into a box and gently removed the tissue paper from each porcelain figure of the nativity. "These were your great grandmother's. Aren't they beautiful?"

"*They are!*" Carefully we set them on the mantel, adding gold candles and ground pine. "It's beautiful, Bobchia."

"They have been on that mantel *every* Christmas as long as I can remember."

"I will *always* put them there."

"*I know.* Now do you think your Mother would miss that tin tree if we *threw it out?*"

"Bobchia!"

"*Erase, erase.* Well, TYG. we're all different!" She hugged me.

Ginger came down the stairs, headed for the kitchen.

"Oh no! Not more *beef and noodles!*" Bobchia rushed down the hallway, yelling over her shoulder. "There's more stuff in the box to put out!"

I eagerly unwrapped the brightly painted wooden figures from Croatia, porcelain houses and trees from Poland, and a china horse and sleigh from Italy. While I strategically placed them on the tables and shelves throughout the room, I could almost hear Father's voice. *They're just for looking, honey girl, don't touch.* I walked around the room, coming to the conclusion that I'd make a better *Croatian, Polish, Italian interior decorator* than I ever would a *cook!*

If this was a Christmas dream, I *never* wanted to wake up! I inhaled deeply. The fragrance of the Christmas tree was slowly being over powered by the aroma of the Christmas feast. I followed my nose to the crowded kitchen. *It was déjà vu to the umpteenth degree* as I looked at all the pies, breads and rolls that were cooling on the counters. It was hard to believe that this banquet would *surpass* the one we had at Thanksgiving, but according to my Bobchia, *it would!* Aunt Ardelle put roasters of goulash into the oven for tonight's supper while Bobchia kneaded bread and curiously watched Mother…make fudge? (It was too good to be true, Mother and Bobchia cooking side-by-side—*a Christmas miracle!*)

My mouth watered as I walked over to my brothers who were frosting the gingerbread men at the corner table. Bobchia pulled up the stepstool beside them, fanning herself with a dishtowel. "I want to thank you boys for frosting the gingerbread men, but I don't think it's necessary to *lick your fingers* while you are doing it!"

"Frosting gets *on* them! I can't *help it!*" Logan said.

"Besides, it tastes good!" Andrew said.

"Look at that table, mercy, what a mess! Perhaps if you didn't put so much on at one time…"

Andrew scooped some frosting off the table with his finger and stuck it in her face. She licked it off, laughing. I couldn't stand watching them any longer.

"May I have a cookie? Is there one somewhere *without* your spit on it?"

"Jen, here take this one. I *hardly* touched it." Andrew said proudly, with bright red lips.

"Take one of mine, too. There's no *spit* on it either." Logan said, smiling with green teeth.

"Thanks, yum! *Delicious!* And this one too, *delicious!*" I licked my fingers.

"She gets to lick *her* fingers!" Logan protested.

"Did you like *mine* the best?" Andrew asked.

"They tasted the *same*—wonderful!"

"How could they taste the *same?* Mine was *green* and his was *red!*" Logan said.

Bobchia looked at the finished cookies. "I don't know if that frosting will ever set up in this heat! Sweetie, how's your foot today?"

"Pretty good. You want me to help carry the food to the cold room, right?"

"If you wouldn't mind. Cliff and Spike could use some help and I know you've had *experience.*" She winked at me. "Us old gals are running out of steam."

I gladly helped them carry all the scrumptious food, knowing that Monday would be a feast day to end *all* feast days! I watched Tall Cliff line the top shelf with the pies and secretly vowed to myself (*not* to God) that I would *not* go near the cold room without a *chaperone!* As I made the last trip down the long hall and back into the kitchen, my foot started to ache. Bobchia was laughing at the boys licking the last morsel of frosting out of the bowls, leaving more gingerbread men *unfrosted* than were frosted. Venal and Izora came in, quickly setting the tables. Then Bobchia rang the dinner bell. "Dinner in a *few!*"

I helped cut the big loves of steaming bread, piling them high into baskets for our goulash and honey bread supper. When everyone was seated, Bobchia asked the boys to say the grace. They refused, shyly looking at the tenants who were waiting.

"You say it, Bobchia," Andrew said.

"TYG for my family and the food that we are about to receive and this blessed, blessed Christmas season. May we *never forget the reason You were born,* and may we always praise the one and only Lord! Amen."

After dinner Venal and Izora started the dishes as tenants followed Bobchia into the great room to fine tune the TV set for the Bing Crosby Christmas special. I hurried and changed my clothes to go bowling with the gang, forcing my foot into a shoe. I wanted to get away from the aroma of the cold room so I waited for Andy with Bobchia and Mother in the great room. "I can't believe he's taking you *bowling* with that sore ankle of yours! Does he like to *torture* you?" Mother's eyes narrowed.

"Mother! Look how much better my foot is! I can wear a *regular shoe.*"

"I don't think he has any *common sense!*"

"It was *your* idea!" I protested.

"*My idea?*"

"You said we were spending entirely too much time in *dark* movie houses, remember?"

"*So?*"

"The only thing left in town is skating or bowling, unless you'll let us go to Pleasantville or Erie. We are *trying* to do what *you* want us to do!"

"Well…"

"Mother, *please* like him. He's so *wonderful* and his parents are nice. They go to church and even *pay taxes!*" I giggled.

"Very funny. Will you be home on time tonight?"

"No, *midnight.*"

"What?!"

I laughed. "The usual."

"Okay, be careful. The roads are slippery."

"He's a good driver, never goes past a hundred miles per hour, *honest!*"

She gave me 'the look' as I got up eagerly answering the doorbell. His blue sweater matched his blue eyes.

He smiled. "Hi, Skip. You look pretty."

"Thank you. I was just thinking the same about *you.*"

"Me? *Pretty?*" He laughed.

I blushed. "No, I mean *handsome.*"

"That's better."

"Goodnight, everyone," I yelled as I grabbed my coat and we went out the door. I could feel Mother's eyes on us as he helped me into his truck.

"Shall I kiss you in front of your Mother?" He asked.

"*Don't you dare!*"

We drove down the lane stopping in the covered bridge for a kiss.

The bowling alley parking lot was so full that we had to park along the road. He got his bowling bag from the back of the truck and opened my door. "I see you've done *this* before." I smiled looking at his bowling bag.

"You *haven't?*" He winked.

My foot ached as we crossed the long parking lot. We met up with our friends inside who were putting on their rented shoes. Andy watched me struggle trying to get my swollen foot into a size

7 shoe. Embarrassed I exchanged them for a size 8, ending up with a blister on my *good foot.*

Whenever we went on a group date, the guys would make some kind of *agreement.* Tonight's was, that whoever had the *lowest* combined scores with their date, would buy sodas at Grady's. I didn't think that my games of 48, 72 and 54 were too bad until Dawnette informed me in the ladies' room, that a perfect game was 300! How embarrassing! When we were walking back to the truck, Mark yelled laughing, "Andy's springing for the sodas tonight!"

"I'm sorry I made us *lose,*" I said, with both feet hurting, as he helped me into his truck.

"It's all right. We had fun. Besides, I just like being with you." He climbed in and kissed me and then drove us to Grady's. As soon as we got there, Andy hurried to the jukebox. ***Put Your Head on My Shoulder*** came on, I smiled kicking off my shoes, and we slow danced.

"Skip, are you limping *again?*"

"A little, but I'm okay."

As my curfew ticked closer and closer, Andy played our song *over and over,* receiving *boos* from the gang.

"I'm sorry I have to leave so early. My Mother is so strict."

"Quit being *sorry* all the time. *I want to be with you,* so it's okay, understand?"

"Okay."

He held me tighter, kissing me as we danced and then looked at his watch. "Honey, it's ten to eleven."

"*Already?*"

"I don't want your mother to get mad at me."

"Me either, but I don't want to leave."

The glow of the Inn reflected onto the snow-heavy pinecone trees surrounding it. "Isn't it pretty?" I said. "This is the most beautiful place to be at Christmas."

He looked over smiling. "Only when you are in it."

I snuggled closer until I saw a familiar shadow standing at the door. I quickly sat up. When he parked the truck, she left. "I had a wonderful time! You'll come tomorrow night to the birthday party, for sure?"

"For sure, Skip. What time? The guys want to go snow-mobiling in the afternoon."

"As soon as you can get here." We kissed and then he walked around the truck to open my door. I held my hand out, and he scooped me into his arms. He carried me to the porch, setting me down at exactly eleven o'clock.

"I can't wait until tomorrow." I said.

"Me either." He held out his hand for me to shake.

"Oh no, you don't! I *want* my goodnight kiss, Andy Williams!" We kissed. "Until tomorrow Skip."

"Tomorrow," I said all dreamy. I waved until the truck disappeared onto the covered bridge. Then I went inside.

The Inn smelled *different*. I walked through and found Bobchia in the great room stringing popcorn. "Sweetie, how was your date?"

"*Groovy!* He is so much fun! I bowled a 48, a 72 and a 54."

"Sounds like *Venal's measurements!*"

"Bobchia! That's so funny!"

Mother came in with a bowl of popcorn. "Want some?"

"As soon as I wash my hands." I came back and took a handful. "*Ouu! It's spoiled!*" They laughed, watching me spit it into a tissue. "Gag a maggot! *Mother!*"

"Good, maybe now the *boys* will leave it alone!" She handed me her Coke, laughing.

"We needed a *tester,*" Bobchia explained.

"*Thanks a lot!*" I said.

"Sorry, that wasn't very nice. Did you have a good time? How's your foot?" Mother asked.

"We had a blast, but I didn't do very well. I bowled a 48, 72 and a 54."

"How did Andrew do?"

"205, then 210 and then 190-something. I have the score paper in my purse. He's good at sports." I ignored her question about my foot and left to take an aspirin and to put a Band-Aid on the blister of my good foot. Then I poured a glass of milk and grabbed the tin.

Mother shook her head at me. "I see you're *limping again.*"

"Yeah, we should have necked in the *dark* movie house!"

Bobchia laughed. "*A **Wonderful Life*** is coming on! Have you ever seen it?" Mother and I shook our heads. "Boy, are you gals ever in for a treat! It's my favorite, next to *Ben-Hur.* It has an *angel* in it!"

"*Figures!*" I laughed. I cuddled with Minnie on the couch and emptied the tin as Mother and Bobchia strung popcorn.

The next day, I awoke to Bobchia patting my hand. "Sweetie, its Sunday! It's time to get up and get ready for church."

"Is it *Christmas?*"

"No, tomorrow. Come on."

I looked around, squinting. "I slept on the couch?"

"You were out like a light by the time Clarence jumped into the water, and we didn't have the heart to wake you."

"Who jumped into the water?"

"Clarence, the *angel* in the movie. Now come on, I got a stack of squirrel pancakes with your name on them." I rolled over.

"Hurry up now, before the boys eat your bacon. They're in there counting it out like marbles. This is the day the Lord has made; we will rejoice and be glad in it!"

I ate breakfast then took a shower. The blister on my *good* foot felt better. The wonderful aroma of the food next door tempted me, so I hurried and got dressed, put on my makeup and towel dried my hair in the great room in front of the fireplace and under Mr. Hair's watchful eye. I hurried past him to find Bobchia on the stool in the kitchen, sipping coffee and watching the boys play with Minnie while she waited for Ginger to find her spectacles. "Sweetie, fortunately for us it's Ardelle's turn to stay home with Lucky. She's going to make us chicken and biscuits for lunch!"

"Yum!"

"The death meal!" She giggled.

"What do you mean '*death meal*'?"

"That's what *Ginger* fixed for all *four* of her husbands before they *bit the dust!* Ginger confided in me the night I fixed the fried chicken for Caleb. She confessed she cooked chicken and biscuits for the millionaire, the professor, the captain *and* the bankrupt sailor before they 'bought the farm.'"

"What *farm?*"

"Mercy, before they *kicked the bucket!* Before they *passed* from this green earth!"

"And we're having *it* for dinner?"

"Yes, *Ardelle* could make a pie out of *wax* apples and it would be *delicious!*" As if on cue, Aunt Ardelle came down the stairs carrying Lucky's cage, wrapped in a bright green and red poinsettia knitted blanket. She set it on the bookcase in the dining room, where she'd have a view of Lucky from the kitchen and where he, (unfortunately) had a bird's-eye view of her *de-boning* the chickens.

In the van on our way to church, I whispered to Mother and the boys about the *death meal.* Bobchia smiled at me in the rearview mirror.

As the choir sang the Christmas cantata, **Born to Live in Our Hearts**, I was uneasy. The death meal *consumed* my thoughts. (This was the first time since my arrival, I was not looking forward to Sunday lunch.) When we rode home, I wondered how Bobchia could sing Christmas carols and be so cheerful... *knowing.*

The boys and I lagged behind on the little bridge as others (including Mother) rushed past us to change out of their 'Sunday best' and gather in the kitchen. Even though the aroma of the bubbling gravy was heavenly, I joined the boys in a dry American cheese sandwich.

While smiling at us, Mother and Bobchia heaped their plates enjoying every bite.

After the kitchen was back in order, everyone went to the great room to relax in its splendor and listen to Christmas carols on the radio. The boys and I followed, reluctantly waiting for the *death angel.*

Bobchia took a shot of coffee and said, "Ardelle, that chicken and biscuits melted in my mouth. It was delicious!" Everyone agreed.

"I'm glad you enjoyed it."

When Bobchia noticed us staring at her she stood up, grabbed her throat and fell onto the couch with her tongue hanging out! We ran to the couch getting on our knees in front of her.

"She's *dead!*" I screamed!

"Naw, *she's alive*, Jen, look!" Andrew said tickling her.

Laughing, Bobchia sat up and tickled the boys as I hurried to the kitchen and got a plateful of chicken and biscuits.

When the boys realized that nobody was going to die (at least *not* because of lunch) they ran to the kitchen, snatched their jackets off the line, jumped into their boots and raced out the door. I sat at the window seat stuffing myself, watching them make a yard full of snowmen. Bobchia hurried to the kitchen and grabbed her camera, taking pictures of them from the porch, then called for them to come in and get into dry clothes. She came back in handing Minnie to me. "Warm her up, Sweetie." I hugged the pup as we walked into the great room and stood in front of the fireplace.

"Did you ever see so many snowmen in one yard? It looks like a Christmas card out there! *Wooo,* is it ever cold!" She rubbed her arms.

Mr. Hair looked up at Ginger. "Not for me. I have my little *Gingersnap to keep me warm!*" He snapped his fingers, and she gave him a big hug and a kiss. "*Told ya!*"

Bobchia and Mother rolled their eyes at the same time. (*That* would have been a great picture!)

Steering clear of the cold room, I impatiently waited for Andy to arrive from the window seat. Harold came *barreling* down the lane in the hearse. The boys cheered as he slammed on his breaks sliding sideways, almost *taking out* the little bridge! Bobchia ran onto the porch as the boys ran to the hearse. "Mercy, what in the world is a matter with you? *The boys are out here!* Are you deliberately trying to kill my grandchildren?"

"They're in the *yard,* not in the *driveway!*" He said coming up the steps defending himself.

"A full-grown man acting like a teenager! You're a teenager! That's all you are, a *teenager!*" She hit him in the arm.

"*Ouch!* Now, honey bunch, you called me and told me to *hurry over!*"

"That was for lunch! You *missed* it, so don't you honey bunch me!"

"I thought you were in a hurry to see me! Well, I came as soon as I could. Here I am! *See me!*"

She came back in slamming the door in his face. He followed her in, laughing. "Now honey bunch, don't be *mad*. Come on, it's almost *Christmas!* Where's your Christmas spirit? Oh, I know why you're mad; it's because you haven't got me *under the mistletoe yet!*"

"It's in the *garbage!*"

"We can *pretend* it's hanging over your head! *Come and get some sugar!*"

The madder she got, the more we laughed. Harold blew kisses at her from across the room. The boys came in soaked, asking for a ride in the long car that was *longer* than the station wagon.

"*Absolutely not!*" Mother said, escorting them to the tub.

When the boys came back down, Harold was still teasing Bobchia. It was cute seeing him flirt with her as he carried the bowls of Tall Cliff's chili to the tables, as she was dishing them up. She resisted him through supper but kissed him on the cheek when he helped her clean the kitchen, the true mark of a *man in love*. They were all smiles when they walked arm-in-arm into the great room.

"Smells like *garlic* in here," Harold commented.

"Really, *mercy!*" She quickly went to the corner cupboard, got out several scented candles placing them throughout the room.

Spike turned on the tree lights and put a couple of card tables in front of the piano. Bobchia put bright red tablecloths over them adding a white lace one on top. Cliff and Cecil carefully carried in a huge double-decker cake. The boys walked slowly in front of them. "Get these kids *out* of the way!" Cliff chastised. Mother pulled the boys next to her.

"Mercy, Cliff, *bend* your knees or the cake will be *sidehill wampus!*" Bobchia called from behind him.

They centered the cake on the table.

"I can't wait!" Logan said.

"I want all the red flowers!" Andrew said.

"Bobchia, he can't have *all the red flowers*, can he?" Logan asked.

"Sweetie, light the gold candles on the mantel, and I'll turn on the stereo." Bobchia said.

"I want to light some candles too!" Andrew reached for the lighter.

"*Definitely not!*" Mother said.

"Look, it's the *Christmas Play* up there over the fireplace!" Logan cried.

Andrew looked at the nativity. "But that shepherd don't even look like *me!*"

"Let me see." Logan pushed him to the side. "Why are those wise men wearing purple? I wore *blue!*"

"Purple is a royal color, that's why," Mother explained. While she talked, they sneaked behind the tree coming out with *dry heaves.* Mother hurried them into the bathroom, laughing. Then she ushered them back with big glasses of ice water.

A wide-eyed, *windshield-wipering* Bobchia met them at the archway. "That will teach ya! You might have thought you were getting away with something, but Bobchia knows what goes on in the Inn—*remember that! I have eyes in the back of my head!*"

"Wow!" Andrew said.

"In the back!" Logan said.

*"Of her head!"*

They walked on their tip toes around her, then went behind the tree and shook packages. *"Get out of there!"* Mother said. They whined to watch TV. "Your grandmother has the stereo on."

*"So?"*

"So color. Do something *quiet* for a change." They unwillingly got their coloring books and crayons out from the window seat.

Wanda and Aunt Ardelle came down the stairs with Lucky, his cage covered in a kitted Christmas tree blanket with rhinestones in the star. Mother saw the cage then hurried to the hallway.

"What a beautiful cake," Wanda said.

Bobchia smiled. "Ardelle, tear down that puzzle, will you please? I've got a poinsettia daisy doily that has waited all year to sit on that coffee table!"

"We're almost done. It would be a shame to tear it down now."

Wanda set the cage on an ottoman and pulled the blanket back. "There, you can watch us finish the puzzle," she told Lucky.

"Can't you girls just *pretend* it's finished? I promise I won't call the police!" Bobchia teased. A movement in the tree caught Bobchia's eye. "Sweetie!" She turned her back to the coffee table, frantically pointing to the tree. In the middle, behind an orange ornament and popcorn garland, was a *camouflaged* Pumpkin, shaking her butt and getting ready to *pounce on Lucky!* I ran over and caught the cat in midair as Bobchia clapped and sang, "Oh! OH! *OH!* Jingle bells, jingle bells, jingle all the way! Everybody sing!"

The boys joined her. "Oh what fun it is to ride in a one horse open sleigh! Hey!"

Luckily, Aunt Ardelle didn't see the cat pinned to my chest as I hurried out of the room and down the hall. "You better not snag my sweater, you bad, bad kitty, or *I'll take you to the barn myself!*" Pumpkin meowed. "Sorry, *erase,* I didn't mean it." She meowed again. I hugged and kissed her. "How did you get out anyway? Dumb question! *Stupid latch!*" I hurried in. Joan of Arc was stretched out in her drawer, lifting her head to welcome us. "Joan of Arc, please keep Pumpkin in *here!*" She meowed.

I closed the door tightly and hurried back to the great room. Spike and Cecil came in carrying ice cream machines. "It's done!" I looked out the window for Andy then helped Bobchia get out her best china for the birthday cake.

"I love Christmas Eve just *awful,* Sweetie!"

"Me too, Bobchia!"

"Jen, can I see you when you're done there?" Spike asked grinning. I followed him outside then he switched-on the Christmas lights on the red barn and the fence. "Merry Christmas! For you Jen, your *first* Christmas back!"

"Wow! It's beautiful Spike, just beautiful! Thank you so much!" I hugged him.

"Merry Christmas Jen!"

Everyone looked out the windows. I stood looking at the lights until I was frozen then ran to the fireplace. The doorbell rang.

Mother was not thrilled when she answered the door and Andy stood there holding a couple of gallons of homemade cider. "Oh, it's you, Andrew."

"Merry Christmas, Mrs. Matko! Please call me *Andy.*"

She gave him a half smile. I hurried to the door, passing her. "Andy!"

"Skip! The lights look great!" He kissed me. "Look, my uncle Joey made this. It's still a little frozen, but I thought you and Bobchia would like it."

"Yum," I smiled. "I missed you today."

"I missed you *more.*" Mother called out to us, and he quickly kissed me again. Then we took the cider into the great room to Bobchia. "I thought you might like some cider." He said smiling.

"*How thoughtful.* Wait until you taste this birthday cake!"

"I *can't* wait."

I put my arm in Andy's and guided him around the room pointing out Bobchia's prized figurines, then we watched the boys put the candles on the cake. Spike lit them.

"I wish my mom could see all these antiques," Andy said. "She'd love it here as much as *I do!*" He looked into my eyes. I was speechless. Bobchia turned out the overhead light. He kissed my cheek.

With the bubble lights bubbling, the candles flickering and Andy sitting beside me, life in the Inn was *perfect!* Somehow everyone seemed closer, except for Mother watching Andy from the hallway.

"Your mother makes me *nervous,*" Andy admitted.

I looked over. "Me *too!*"

As Gladys played the piano, we sang happy birthday to Jesus. Just as the boys were blowing out the candles, Homer wheeled Mrs. Pratt into the room. She *screamed* when she saw the cake. Bobchia ran to her, desperately trying to calm her.

Ardelle, Wanda and Lucky went upstairs. "We'll have our cake in our room, thank you!" Ardelle said.

Mother helped Bobchia calm Mrs. Pratt, walking beside her and holding her hand as Bobchia wheeled her back to her room. Mother gave her a nerve pill and felt her pulse. "There, there, your pulse is down. *You'll be fine.*"

"Thank you."

"You're welcome. Now Mrs. Pratt, how about a big piece of cake and a spot of tea?"

"Sounds wonderful and you are a wonderful nurse!"

"Thank you very much."

"*I think you are too, Clair,*" Bobchia said.

"Why, thank you, Rhea."

When Mother and Bobchia came back into the room, the boys were fighting over which one of them would get the piece of cake with *Jesus'* name on it, so Mother cut it down the middle. "There. Now go sit down and *be quiet* for a change!"

Mother looked on as Andy filled the crystal cups with cider and I passed them out. When Ginger and Mr. Hair stood up to get a piece of cake, the boys slid onto the loveseat. When they came back they were mad so Ginger pulled two chairs together. Mr. Hair then leaned over the armrest, cuddling into her armpit as he ate his cake. Bobchia kept as close of an eye on them as Mother did on Andy and me.

When the boys were done eating, they sneaked behind Ginger's chair and made armpit noises. Embarrassed, Mother made them apologize, then they did the same thing to Andy and me. "Mother, get them out of there! *Mother!*" Mother never said a word! It amused Andy, but made me mad! "Get out from there! Go color, do something! *Go eat popcorn!*"

Andrew made a face. "It tastes awful!"

"Not *all* of it!" I told him. Then I whispered to Andy, "Bobchia put garlic on it to keep them away from it."

Andy laughed, then said. "My parents really like you a lot. Maybe you could come over to my house tomorrow afternoon!"

"They like me because I didn't *sue* them!" I looked over at Mother, who was staring. "Maybe, if you don't mind, it would be better if you came *here* tomorrow. Besides *I've waited so long to be here with Bobchia on Christmas.* I know you probably don't understand, but it would mean the *world* to me if—"

"Not a problem."

"You sure?"

"Sure."

Bobchia proudly brought over two big pieces of cake, each with big red flowers. "This cake will melt in your mouth, Andy. It was so pretty, I hated to cut it! It's a scratch cake—oh, not that I *scratched* while I made it!"

He laughed and took a big bite. "Mmm. Wow! This is sensational, Mrs. Matkovich!"

"*Bobchia,*" she corrected.

"Bobchia, this tastes like a *bakery cake!*"

"It's Jennifer's great grandmother's recipe for birthday cakes. They ran a bakery in this Inn for years."

"Really?"

"She never *told* you?"

"No. Skip, can you *bake* like this?"

Bobchia nudged me with her elbow. "I did *stir* it," I said.

"*Is the sky blue?* She'll make you one!" She blurted.

"*Great!*" Andy smiled as he ate. I sighed giving Bobchia 'the look.'

With a little persuading and "It's like riding a bike!" from Bobchia, Mother played the piano. The boys rushed to sit on the bench beside her. They were fascinated because they'd never heard her play before. She forced herself to take her eyes off of Andy long enough to read the sheet music to **Go Tell it on the Mountain, Silent Night** and **Hark the Herald Angels Sing**. Mr. Pill protested with the pounding of his cane on the floor, but he did not protest a big piece of Jesus' birthday cake when Cliff took him up a piece.

"See, Clair, you played wonderfully!" Bobchia said.

"Well there were those few times…"

"A great job, *really!*"

"Well thank you. What did you boys think?"

"You did the *bestest* job!" Andrew said without hesitation.

"A great job, but actually…not as good as *Lois!*" Logan said.

Mother quickly looked over at Andy and me.

"Boy, I wish I knew how to get on the *good side* of your mother!" Andy said.

"*Me too!*" We laughed.

Every time Mother looked at her watch, Andy would stand to leave and I'd *pull* on his arm to sit back down. He said that his arms were just starting to *heal* from Marcy and now I was tugging on them!

"Sorry! Hey, maybe you could go to church with us tonight." I said excitedly.

"I wish I could, but tonight is our Christmas with my brother Norm and his family. They come on Christmas Eve so that the kids can stay home on Christmas and play with their toys. Skip, don't look so disappointed."

"I'm not, how can I be? This is the *best* Christmas I've had in a long time!"

"Me too!"

"So you'll come over tomorrow?"

"Honey, wild horses couldn't keep me from being here! I don't know what time; my Uncle Tim and Aunt Sandy will be coming with the girls for dinner, but after that I'll be here! Sorry, I have a big family."

"Bobchia says that Jesus and family *are* everything!"

He looked over to Mother. "It's what your *mother* says, that is what I'm worried about. Well, I better shove off."

The boys ran from behind the Christmas tree, *gagging* and wiping their tongues off with their hands! Mother scolded them. "I can't believe you're eating that popcorn *again!*"

"Jen said to eat it!" Andrew coughed.

"*Jennifer!*"

"Liar, liar, pants on fire!" Andrew kicked at me.

"Pig face!"

Mother pulled the boys to the kitchen. "You laughed whenever *I* ate it, Mother!" I hollered.

Andy laughed as I walked him to the door. "It's a vicious circle, you know. They *will* get even with you. I *always* did with my brothers."

"I don't want to talk about them."

"What do you want to talk about?"

"Nothing."

"In that case…" He held me so tight I couldn't breathe and kissed me. "I'd better go. Sweet dreams, Skip."

"Sweet dreams." I watched him walk down the sidewalk backward, blowing kisses, then he fell and disappeared behind a snowdrift. I laughed so hard that Mother rushed to the window. I held my sides laughing when he stood up all covered in snow.

"That boy is *strange*, Jennifer!"

"That's why I lov—I mean *like him!*"

Andy brushed himself off and got into the truck. He waited until Mother left the window and then turned on the light and blew me a kiss. After he drove over the covered bridge I went into the great room for another cup of cider.

The boys were crawling around the tree, shaking gifts, whining to open them.

"Get out of there! Not until *tomorrow!* Can't you color?" Mother scolded.

"Color with all this neat stuff under the tree?" Logan asked.

"How do you know it's *neat stuff*? It might be bricks and two-by-fours for all you know." She said.

Andrew jumped in. "You are *so* wrong!"

Logan said, "Yeah, there's gifts under there all right! *Good ones too!* When I shook that long silver box over there, I know there was *skis* in it!"

"Yeah and I know for sure in that red box, there's some *skates!*" Andrew said.

"You sound awful *sure* of yourselves! You know what your Bobchia says, don't you?"

"Go water Dollee?" Andrew said.

Logan thought and said, "No, she says you can take a horse to the water, but you can't make him drink."

"Yeah!" Andrew nodded vigorously.

The saying I was referring to was, '**Don't count your chickens before they're hatched!**'"

"Why did the chicken cross the road?" Andrew asked Logan.

"*I give up!*"

"To get his gifts under the pinecone tree!" He quickly shook another box.

"No, gifts until *tomorrow*. Go upstairs and get into your pajamas, *without* the superman capes please. We're going to church in a while."

"*In pajamas?*" Logan asked.

"*We'll freeze!*" Andrew said.

"Well, you're going to wear your *coats!*"

"Oh."

They changed and ran back down while Bobchia fine-tuned the set. "Cartoons!" The boys cheered in unison as the Perry Como's Christmas special came on.

"Where's cartoons?" Andrew asked.

"On Christmas Eve we watch *Christmas shows* and listen to *Christmas music*, it is tradition." Bobchia explained.

"But—"

"That's *it*, Fort Pitt!"

After Perry Como the room mostly cleared, leaving just a few people who could stay awake *long enough* to go to the Christmas Eve service. At a quarter till eleven, Mother woke the sleeping boys from beside the tree and shoved them into their coats and boots then out the door into the cold air. Big snowflakes fell from the sky. The boys ran to catch them on their tongues.

"Boys, did you know that Christmas Eve snow tastes *better* than any other snow?" Bobchia asked.

"It does? Are you *teasing?*" Logan asked.

"*Gerish* is what mine taste like, Bobchia," Andrew said.

"Gerish? Really? Let me see." Bobchia tilted her head back and stuck her tongue out. "You're right, *Christmas Eve gerish*."

We piled into the van singing **Jingle Bells** as Harold drove us down the lane. Snowflakes filled the path of our headlights, leading us to the stone church we had come to love. We reverently went inside. Harold carried sleeping Andrew in and laid him on a pew.

The church was aglow with candles. Garland laced with white lights draped the sanctuary and the choir loft, and red poinsettias graced the wooden prayer benches. White poinsettias surrounded a little manger holding a single glowing candle in the center of the sanctuary. Logan fell asleep leaning on Mother's shoulder. The choir, wearing red robes, came down the center aisle and went up into the choir loft singing a thunderous *Joy to the World*. Then everyone sang *O Holy Night* and the *Hallelujah Chorus*. We all wondered how the boys slept through Lois's pounding renditions of the Christmas carols.

Pastor Jay opened his Bible to the book of Luke, reading of the birth of Christ. Then the ushers passed out unlit candles, and as the church bell tolled twelve, they turned off the lights and snuffed out the altar candles, leaving only the tiny manger candle lit. Pastor Jay took an unlit candle, lit it from the manger candle and held it up. "Merry Christmas! Jesus *is* the light of the world! Tell someone about Jesus!" Then he went to a lady in the front aisle seat and lit her candle. "Tell someone about Jesus!" She, in turn, lit the candle of the person sitting beside her, saying, "Tell someone about Jesus!"

*Christmas was finally here!* The whole church was filled with the light from a tiny manger, *as was my heart!*

After everyone's candle was lit, Pastor Jay held his candle up. *"God has given His greatest, most precious gift to us. He was born of a virgin and slept in a manger and then hung on a cross in our place.* If you do not know Jesus as your personal Savior, is there a better time than Christmas to invite Him into your heart? Repeat these words after me:

> 'Lord Jesus Christ, I have sinned against You and am not worthy of forgiveness, but You *love* me regardless of the sins I have committed against You. Please forgive me and come and live in my heart, and I will live my life for You. Thank You, Lord. Thank You for living in my heart,—*my* king, *my* redeemer and *my* friend.'

Now may the grace of our Lord Jesus Christ live in you now and forever more. Through Christ I pray, Amen. Merry Christmas, and God bless you!"

That Christmas Eve, standing between Mother and Bobchia, with their arms around my waist, I looked up at the wooden cross above the manger and *rededicated* my life to Christ.

Pastor Jay continued, "What is each and every one of you going to do?"

"*Tell someone about Jesus!*" We said in unison.

"Amen!"

We blew out our candles. Quietly the church emptied. People scurried to their cars. Spike scraped off the windshield as Harold and Tall Cliff carried the sleeping boys to the van. *TYG for this glorious night,* I thought on the way back to the Inn.

The men carried the boys upstairs for Mother laying them on their mattresses. We took off their coats and boots and pulled the covers over them. Bobchia took advantage of the situation, feeling their breath on her face as she softly kissed their sleeping faces and prayed over them. "May they *know your voice* like the sheep know the shepherd's voice. Lord, *lead them* like a shepherd and carry them in Your arms *forever.*" She kissed their little red-and-green stained fingertips and tucked them in. "They both so resemble Paul, but tonight I can see *you* in their faces too, Clair."

"Really?"

"Yes, yes I can. They are a *good mix.*" (Mother and Bobchia actually *smiled* at each other!)

I kissed Mother on the cheek. "Merry Christmas, Mother."

"Merry Christmas, Jen. Sleep good."

"You too."

Bobchia headed for the door, "Merry Christmas, Clair. See you in the morning."

"Merry Christmas, Rhea."

Bobchia hummed **Silent Night** as I limped down the stairs beside her. We stood in front of the nativity and warmed ourselves at the fireplace.

"There is nothing like going to church on Christmas Eve," Bobchia said.

"Or *waking up in the Inn on Christmas!* I can hardly wait!"

"Are you really that anxious for gifts?"

"*Gifts?* I don't *need* gifts. *I have everything I have ever wanted!*" We hugged.

She was speechless as she took out her hankie and wiped her nose. "The last Christmas you were here, your grampie and I gave you Daisy, remember? That doll was as tall as you were! I can still hear him laugh as he watched you drag that doll down the hall by one arm, banging her into the walls. I found her a couple of years after you left, in the storage bench on the porch. It was like finding a *diamond!* I kept her on the chair beside my bed for when you visited, but...well, you're here *now* and that's what is important! TYG! Now don't you be crying! I've got a million things to do before you wake up, so Merry Christmas, Sweetie! I love you awful, awful, *awful!"* She kissed my cheek.

"I love you awful back. Merry Christmas!"

I limped down the hall humming. I opened the door to my room and got a whiff of the cold room *deli.* The lace curtains were on the floor in a heap. "Trying to get out *again* I see!" I said to Pumpkin. She meowed. "Don't *meow* me!" I said, hanging them back up. "You're not fooling me, stretched out on that pillow, looking so *innocent."*

I bent down and petted Joan of Arc. "You need to teach Pumpkin some manners. *She's bad!"* I pulled the blinds and wrote in my Bible,

> **"December 24, 1967. I rededicated my life to Jesus Christ, standing between Mother and Bobchia at the Methodist Church. TYG! I will praise You forever and ever! My Lord and my Redeemer!"**

I pulled on my pajamas, washed my face and brushed my teeth, all the while trying *not* to think of all the food just on the other side of that *thin* pink wall. I brushed my teeth again and gargled with Listerine *twice.* (That should *kill* my sweet tooth!) I hurried into bed and pulled the covers over my head, but my sheets smelled like *food!* I said my prayers and visualized counting sheep, but they quickly turned into *meringue pies!* I lay there thinking about all the pies that Tall Cliff had lined on the top shelf. I figured I'd probably break my neck if I tried to climb up to get them. Then I had a revelation, a *wonderful revelation* that would *satisfy my sweet tooth* and keep me out of the cold room. *Eat chocolate chip cookies!*

I threw the blankets to the floor and hopped out of bed, grabbed my robe and hurried to the kitchen as fast as my bad foot would take me. I turned on the light, anxiously looking for the cookie tin, but it wasn't on the counter or in the pantry. Then I saw it sitting *empty* in the sink. *"Oh, no!"*

(The *old Pill* had struck while we were at church. The nerve of that old guy, eating all of *my* cookies and on my first Christmas back!) "I hope he gets *heartburn for Christmas! Erase, erase.* Mercy! I just got out of *church!*" I erased the air sheepishly and looked to the ceiling.

"I wonder where Bobchia put the gingerbread men. They were so good and *sweet!* She must have set them out somewhere so the frosting would set, but where?" I couldn't find them. Disappointed, I slowly walked back to my room, rinsed with Listerine *again* and hurried into bed. I stuck a pillow over my head. Even the embroidered flowers smelled like *food!* How could I possibly sleep? Then I got to thinking, talking into my pillowcase. "What would it hurt anyway? Just a *little piece* of zucchini bread or a *sliver* of pie. After all, it's *my duty* as a granddaughter to *help* my grandmother get *rid* of all that food so she doesn't get upset about having so many leftovers like she did on Thanksgiving. Half of the people probably won't show up for dinner, and then what? I'll be doing her a *real big favor!*" I quickly got into my robe and slipped into the hall, looking both ways, salivating when I opened the cold room door and quietly shutting it. I was like a kid in a candy store—I walked around turning my nose up at the scalloped corn and the cheese lima beans, the casseroles, the squash, the rolls and the *leathery* beef and noodles. *(Gag a gross maggot!)* I wanted the *sweetest* thing in the room—*the pies!* The *delicious* ones, the ones that Tall Cliff had put on the top shelves, not the ones Bobchia called *"coconut cream cardboard"* (Ginger's). I pulled a chair over and ever so gently took down a pie. "I wish I had a plate and a knife." I took the foil off of one. It was custard. *Ick.* I carefully put it back on the shelf and took another down. Funny, this one had a note on top of the aluminum foil that said, 'Asparagus pie.' *Who ever heard of asparagus pie?*

I lifted the foil to reveal a pie plate full of chocolate chip cookies, along with a note. **"Sweetie, Merry Christmas!** *Keep your fingers out of the food!"*

The next morning Joan of Arc jumped on my stomach. "Ugh!" I rubbed my eyes. "I'm not dreaming! I'm twelve years older, but I'm *here!* Merry Christmas, Joan of Arc!" I quickly got up and poured her and Pumpkin some food. (I hadn't felt this happy on Christmas in a *long time.*) I walked to Father's picture and bowed my head. "TYG for all the past Christmases that I shared with Father and all the Christmases in the future that will be spent with

446

Bobchia and Andy." I splashed water on my tears, got dressed and hurried down the hall. I caught a whiff of something that smelled even *more delicious* than the cold room. (How could that be *possible?*) I rounded the corner into the kitchen where eight large, golden-brown pastries were cooling. I ripped a big piece off of one. It melted in my mouth. *"Mmm!"* I ripped off another piece, ate it and then looked around for Bobchia. I couldn't resist taking another hunk. "Bobchia has to be here somewhere..." I walked to the window seats.

The sun was just coming up, splashing yellow onto the tops of the snow-covered pine trees. "TYG, I'm in the most beautiful place on earth!" A cardinal flew by the window. I looked at the bird feeders. I thought it *odd* that there weren't any birds at the feeder and then shivered when I looked at the thermometer reading—twenty-four degrees. Out of the corner of my eye, the sun reflected off of a *golf club* that Bobchia was swinging! (I did a double-take!) She was hitting Minnie's frozen *tootsie rolls* off the sidewalk and onto the frozen creek bed while Nikki stood motionless behind her in front of the steps, waiting to be picked up. I laughed, choking as I watched her pose, strike, walk two feet, pose and strike again! The birds looked like ornaments on the pines, patiently waiting for her to finish her *golf game*. *"Fore!"* She yelled, slamming the last one off the sidewalk and onto the ice, where it bounced and slid to the others. She turned, scooped Nikki in her arms and rushed onto the porch. I opened the door as she awkwardly came up the steps and through the door with the golf club flapping under her arm with Minnie's head sticking out of her robe pocket.

*"Merry Christmas, Bobchia!"* I said with my mouth full.

"How I have *waited* to hear those words! *Merry Christmas, Sweetie Pie!*" Bobchia looked at Nikki. "She froze up again and was only out there five minutes!" She blew a kiss my way, grunting while placing frozen Nikki on the plaid rug in front of the ovens to thaw out. We hugged. "Get me Monday's apron out of the pantry, will you Sweetie?" I promptly retrieved it. She took off her coat, revealing her green chenille robe with big, pink flowers, and put the apron on, transferring Minnie. "I bet ya didn't know old Bobchia could *play golf*, did ya? *I must have drove those suckers at least a hundred feet down that creek bed.* Of course they do *slide* a little. You can only hit them *if* it's *thirty-two degrees* or *lower,* and don't ask me

447

*how* I know that!" She snorted. I choked. "I see you found the kolache." I nodded and went for more.

"Help yourself. I have eight more in the ovens and eight more rising. Everyone just loves them around here. *How about you?*" I shook my head eagerly. "I'll try to get the recipe out of my head and onto a piece of paper for you. If Andy ever tastes kolache, you are a shoo-in to be the next Mrs. Andy Williams! *'Moon river whiter than snow...'*" She sang laughing. She covered her mouth quickly and went to look down the hallway. Then she came back and took a shot of coffee. "*Whew!* I'm glad your *Mother didn't hear me say that!* I better keep that recipe under lock and key—at least until you're out of *college!*"

"*You're funny!*"

She giggled as she washed her hands, asking over her shoulder, "Tell me, did you enjoy your *asparagus pie* last night?"

"Yes," I said, with a mouth full.

She laughed and hugged my shoulder. "I figured you'd be up to your *old tricks!* For *twelve* Christmases, I have prayed for *this* Christmas day! TYG!" I blinked back tears. "Now don't you be crying on Christmas!" She hugged me again. "Soon this kitchen will be packed with people. I'm glad you got up early."

"Me too." The timer went off. She walked over to Nikki. "And I'm glad *you* made it for another Christmas, old girl. Hold on." She grunted pulling the rug with the dog teetering on it, to one side, took out the kolache and stuck more in. Then, pulled the rug and the teetering dog back in front of the ovens. "There, you should be almost *done* yourself, Nikki, poor old thing." While petting Nikki's head, Minnie peeked out, sniffed at Nikki's nose and growled. Nikki blinked a few times, then walked stiffly to the potbelly and snuggled down in her low box. "*She's done to a turn!* What will we ever do for entertainment when old Nick kicks the bucket?" Bobchia washed her hands again and set the timer. "It will be fun when the boys get up." She saw the look in my eyes. "Sweetie! Don't you *dare* wake them up! *It's too early!*"

"*The brats!*"

"Sweetie! *Come back here!*"

I sneaked up the stairs, quietly limped past sleeping Mother, and went into the closet, kneeling down between the two mattresses. I studied their angelic faces. (How could toads be so *cute?*) I sucked on my index fingers and then stuck them in their ears yelling, "*Merry Christmas!*" They jumped up, fell over each other, and scrambled out of the closet *screaming*. Mother yelled for *quiet*. Mr. Pill pounded so hard on the wall that the boys' school pictures fell off! I was close behind, *laughing* as they flew down the stairs, fighting to get to the toys *first*.

"Yippee! It's Christmas!" Logan yelled.

"Yippee!" Andrew echoed.

Mother was in hot pursuit, trying to pull on her robe, *yelling*, "Boys, *be quiet! Boys!*"

Upon entering the great room, they dropped to their knees, sliding on the hardwood floor, and rammed into the Persian rug, causing the tree to shake. I grabbed the trunk of the tree, laughing as Bobchia came running in. "Mercy! You sound like a *herd of elephants!* You'll wake the *dead!*"

The boys yelled, *"The Man Upstairs! The Man Upstairs!"*

Mother hurried over to help me stabilize the shaking tree. Bobchia realized what the boys had said. "Isn't it wonderful that they are *thanking God for their gifts?"* Then she looked puzzled when Logan *flipped on* a switch and trains came on, *tooting and whistling*, with smoke pouring out of their smoke stacks. The open cars had little plastic animals in them, paired, two by two. On the lengthy tracks the train circled around the tree and under the coffee table, through the legs of the TV, with the giraffe's heads bumping the aluminum foil balls hanging from the duct tape, then the train came back around the tree again. Bobchia looked at Mother, she shrugged. Mother looked at Bobchia and she shook her head *no*. Just then, Mr. Pill teetered into the room, grinning with his one sparkly tooth! The boys ran and hugged him with such force that Mother and I *switched* from *balancing* the tree to *balancing Mr. Pill!*

Bobchia smiled to the ceiling, *"A child shall lead them..."*

Mother asked, "Boys, do you know who *he* is?"

"Yeah, he's *the man upstairs!"* Andrew said proudly.

Logan looked puzzled at her. "What do you *mean?* Chee, *you kept sending us upstairs to play with him all the time!"* We laughed as the boys held his arms, helping him to a chair. Then they slid back to the tree.

"We sure had a *great time,* didn't we boys?" Mr. Pill said.

*"We sure did!"* Logan said.

*"Boy, did we ever!"* Andrew said.

"They *taught* me about Noah's Ark, and I *taught* them about the trains," Mr. Pill said smiling.

Bobchia looked lovingly at him. "Mr. Pill, would you like a piece of kolache?"

He asked the boys, "Are you having some?"

"We don't have time! We have to open stuff!" Logan explained.

Mr. Pill yelled; "We don't have *time!* We have to open *stuff!*"

Bobchia looked at him, tight-lipped with her hands on her hips.

Logan read the nametags, throwing Andrew's presents at him.

"Ouch, *quit!*" Andrew said grabbing his.

They ripped the boxes open. "You opened one of mine!" Andrew protested.

"How do you know? You can't *even* read!"

Bobchia rushed to get her camera. 'Pop! Pop! Pop!' went the flash.

The clothes that Bobchia got them were exactly the same, just in different sizes. They threw them aside. She got them the same coloring books, paints and even the same angel ornaments. Then Logan pulled out the long, ski-sized box and ripped it open. "I can't wait for *these!*" He screamed looking at the two-by-four piece of wood with socks and underwear tucked around it. At the same time, Andrew opened his ice skates box, finding a brick with socks and underwear. They were *dumfounded!*

"Your mother and I worked hard to buy you new skates and skis, but when we went to wrap them, we saw they weren't *new* at all, but *used.* They were *scratched* and *dull.* We didn't think you would want them, so we took them *back* and bought you socks and underwear instead."

Logan screamed, "*Oh no!*"

Mother added, "We really felt *bad,* but we couldn't give you something that had been *used,* could we?"

Andrew started to tear up. "I used them. I'm sorry. I will *never snoop again!*"

"*Me either!*" Logan promised.

Mr. Pill got angry. "What is the meaning of *depriving* these children?" He stood up, pounded his cane on the floor, almost falling over but Mother quickly caught his arm helping him back into his chair. He tried to crack her on the knee with his cane but hit the coffee table instead.

She walked over to the sad boys and put her arms around them. "I think I see something beside the desk."

They ran over, grabbed the boxes and ripped off the paper, revealing skates and skis.

"Yea!" Logan cheered.

"Yippee!" Andrew hugged his skates.

'Pop! Pop!' went the flash.

The boys begged Mother to go outside. "At least wait until it warms up a little. Besides, there are *more* packages under the tree to open."

The timer went off. Bobchia handed me the camera. "Take pictures of the boys." She hurried into the kitchen. I got in their faces as they opened their Lincoln Logs.

"Yea! Mother will you help us build a cabin like *Honest Abe* lived in?" Logan asked.

'Pop!'

'Pop!'

"Hey! You're *blinding me!*"

"*I can't see!*" Andrew covered his eyes.

"Jen, put that camera *down!*" Mother chastised.

"You look great in that robe and that *hairdo,* Mother!" I teased, snapping a picture.

"You don't want to make me mad *today,* do you?"

"What was I *thinking?*" I put the camera on the puzzle.

Meanwhile, Spike had his mouth full of kolache and was pouring himself a cup of coffee when Bobchia entered the kitchen. "Merry Christmas, Rhea!"

"Merry Christmas. Pour me a shot, would you? I suppose *you* don't know how those trains got downstairs?" He winked at her. She took the kolache out of the oven and put more in. Then she took a swig of coffee and came back into the great room, handing me two bright red boxes with lavish green bows. "I hid your gifts in *another place* after the boys snooped."

"*See, pig face, I told ya I didn't know where your stuff was! You pulled my hair for nothing!*" Logan whined.

"*Mine too! I still feel bald right here!*"

"*Shame on you, Sweetie!*" Bobchia said.

"See! You told her about the *pumpkins* for nothing!" Logan said.

"Pumpkins? What did you say about *pumpkins?*" Bobchia asked.

"She might be in the *tree again,* Bobchia!" I pointed.

"*Oh no!*" She hurried to the tree. I pinched Logan's arm.

"Ouch!" He pulled away from me.

"Shut up! I *didn't* tell her...*yet.*"

"Have mercy! If Ardelle and Wanda see a cat loose in here, they'll have a *fit!* I don't see Pumpkin in here."

"Bobchia, I'm opening my presents *now!*" I said. She grabbed her camera.

'Pop! Pop!' Spots floated in front of my eyes as I looked into boxes of sweaters and skirts with stretch pants to match from Jane and Jim's boutique! "*Oh boy!* These are all beautiful! Thank you so much!" I kissed her on the cheek. She reached behind the tree and handed me a flat box. I eagerly opened it, revealing the needlepoint picture of daisies I had so admired.

"I saw you looking at it."

"I will treasure it *always.*" We hugged and then I pulled back a satin curtain, revealing a big bouquet of daisies in a coffee mug with Minnie's picture on it and a little box on the window sill.

Bobchia immediately held the daisies to her cheek and then got out her best porcelain vase arranging them, setting them on the mantel. "I don't remember ever receiving daisies on *Christmas* before. My, look how beautiful they look beside the nativity." She opened the box. "Aw, a green collar for Minnie, and what a beautiful ornament!" She hung the ornament, slid the collar over Minnie's tiny neck and took the mug into the kitchen, coming back sipping coffee. "Now that's what I call a *good cup of coffee!*"

Mother gave me boxes of skirts and sweaters from the boutique. "Groovy, but I know you can't afford these..."

"Quiet, if I couldn't, I wouldn't have bought them." We hugged then I got her package from under the tree and gave it to her. She carefully opened the box and held up the pink pearled ornament with a silver bangle bracelet around it. "How pretty, Jen. Thank you." She put the bracelet on. "It's *beautiful!*"

"I hoped you'd like it."

"I do. *I really do!*" We hugged and then she hung the ornament. The boys rushed over, jealously looking at the bracelet.

"It's pretty, but don't forget *we gave you a necklace and a bracelet already!*" Logan said.

"And we gave you your blouse early *too*, so even if you already *sweated* in it, it's still your Christmas present, *right?*" Andrew asked.

She chuckled and hugged them. They stuck their tongues out at me. "Yes, and I will treasure them *always!*" She reassured them.

The boys dug under the tree and together handed Bobchia a green box plastered with red and green duct tape. She giggled, slowly undoing the tape and folding the paper carefully while they eagerly waited. Finally she lifted the lid, squealing at a fuzzy pair of bright green bedroom slippers. *"Just what I needed! Beautiful green slippers!* Thank you!" She held them to her apron pocket windshield-wipering her finger upside down at Minnie. "See these? *No chewing* on these slippers, Miss Minnie, and *I mean it!*"

"We picked them out and wrapped them, but Mother said they were *the ugliest slippers she ever seen!*" Logan explained.

"I did *not!*" Mother protested.

"You *did!* You said, 'Those are the *ugliest green things* I ever saw in my life!'"

"Yeah, in your whole *entire life!*" Andrew clarified.

Bobchia laughed as she took off her duct taped slippers, threw them in the wastebasket and put the new ones on. "Well, I think they're *absolutely beautiful,* and my pigs are nice and *warm!* Thank you!" She hugged the boys and kissed the tops of their heads. They wiped the kisses off. Bobchia went to the closet and rummaged through it. "Now, I know for *sure* I put the boy's gifts in here. Where *else* could I have possibly put them?"

The boys ran upstairs and came back down with a shoebox full of macaroni necklaces, bracelets and tie tacks, handing them out like they were candy. Bobchia winced at the *sparkling* floor as they flung the necklaces around on their fingers. "You guys and *glitter, mercy!*"

I handed the boys boxes from under the tree. "Hey! I thought you *hated* us for *farting on your head!*" Andrew said. "I still have a black and blue mark on my arm where you grabbed me, see!" He pulled up his pajama sleeve.

"Well, it is Christmas, and I don't…well, I don't *exactly* hate you."

"You *don't?*" Andrew smiled. *"I don't hate you on Christmas either!"*

"I'm a little bit sorry for messing your hair." Logan said. "But I still might hate you if it's *clothes!*" Logan confessed.

"Yeah, it looks like a *clothes box,*" Andrew said.

They quickly shredded the paper, tied their new Superman towels around their necks and flew around the great room, *spreading cheer and glitter throughout.*

"Thanks, Jen," Andrew said as he glided past.

"Thanks. I don't *hate you* so much *now,* either." Logan said, then flew past Andrew.

I smiled. "You're welcome."

On his next trip around Logan threw a necklace at me. "Here's a macaroni necklace to match your bracelet!"

"And here's a couple of tie tacks (two pieces of macaroni with glitter). If you *glue* them to your ears, they'll look just like *matching earrings!*" Andrew explained. (I caught them on the fly.)

"Thank you."

"Welcome."

"Welcome."

Bobchia reached under the tree, handing Mother four boxes, three of them from the boutique.

"Can we open them?" Andrew asked.

"You boys *opened* your gifts, now let your mother *open* hers," Bobchia said.

"What do those stickers say, Mother?" Logan asked.

"You tell me."

He read over her shoulder. "**Don't open until Christmas!**"

"That's right! Oh my, Rhea, you shouldn't have, really."

"Why not, you are my *favorite* daughter-in-law, aren't you?" Bobchia smiled.

Mother was more than pleased, opening the boxes containing a red tam and scarf set with gloves that matched, a long, gray, tailored wool coat and high black boots. "They are *beautiful! Thank you.* They will be so *warm!*"

"You are welcome!"

Logan held up the next box. "This box says something different: '**Don't open until…until…**' what's that word Mother?"

"*Veterans Day!*" She laughed.

"What does that *mean?*"

"Well, remember the day the flags were on our fence (she actually said *our* fence!) and you wore red shirts to the football field?"

"And we prayed *outside* at night for the soldiers?"

"Yes! That day was Veterans Day!"

"So you got to wait until that time comes to open *that box?*" Andrew asked.

"That's what the sticker says!"

"Can you *wait that long?*" Logan asked.

"I guess I'll have to!"

"I don't think I could wait until then!" Logan said.

"*Me either!*" Andrew said. "Bobchia, can she open it now?"

"It is an awful long time to wait, isn't it?" Bobchia said.

"Does that mean yes?"

"Yes."

"Yea! Can we open it?" Andrew asked.

Mother nodded. "Go ahead."

They ripped into the paper and threw the lid off. "Clothes *again!*" Andrew tossed her the box. Inside was a flag blouse like Bobchia's, complete with a homemade pin that read, **Freedom only gets stronger when you exercise it!**

"How, (Mother swallowed hard) lovely. Thank you."

"You are welcome! I also took the liberty of getting you a voting registration form so you'll be able to *exercise* your freedom! It's underneath the blouse."

"I still don't get what that pin *says!*" Logan said.

Andrew shook his head. "*Me either!*"

Mother tried her coat on then put it on display under the tree, *hiding the blouse under it.*

I whispered, "Bobchia, you *bought her love!*"

"Mercy, *Jennifer!*"

I eagerly watched as Mother gave Bobchia the little oblong box she had been making payments on for weeks, from Waters Jewelry Store. Mother was right. It made her *speechless!* The charm bracelet had charms representing us kids, Father, Aunt Jennifer, Grampie David and Bobchia. She got teary-eyed looking carefully at all the little silver boy and girl head charms, with our birthdates on the back of them. "It's so...I never expected...*It's beautiful!* Thank you!"

Mother smiled. "You're welcome."

"But where's *your* charm, Clair?"

"Oh, I didn't think you'd want one of *me* on there."

"Why would you *ever* think a thing like that? You *are* a part of my family. Here, help me put it on. I'll wear it today but not again until you *add your charm* with the rest of the family, okay?"

"Okay." She handed Bobchia another box containing a picture of Father with us kids in an antique frame.

"Oh Clair, *I love it!* Thank you!"

"It was the last picture I took of Paul with the children."

*"This means more than words!"* She hugged Mother, put on her glasses and went to the nearest lamp.

As the tenants came into the great room, they looked suspiciously at Mr. Pill, clearly surprised that he was downstairs. Mr. Hair and Ginger arrived arm in arm, sporting the same big hairdo. She wore a slinky red dress with go-go boots, and he was wearing white pants and a black shirt with several gold chains around his neck. Mr. Hair extended his hand to Mr. Pill.

"Get away from me, you *dippy hippy!*" The boys laughed when Mr. Pill cracked Mr. Hair in the knee with his cane.

"Ouch!"

"Honey, are you *okay?*" Ginger asked. She carried him to the couch, covering him with kisses and an afghan.

Other people tried to talk to Mr. Pill, but he ignored everyone except the boys. When the boys *ate* kolache, Mr. Pill *ate* kolache. When the boys *drank* milk, Mr. Pill *drank* milk. When the boys *laughed,* he *laughed.* He had the best time watching them play with their toys. Then he told them to run upstairs and get the boxes out of his closet and bring them down. They came running down the stairs with big boxes wrapped in red foil paper and big green bows. He tapped his cane in front of his feet, they eagerly slid in front of him. *"Open them up!"*

They ripped into the paper.

"Oh boy, *snowsuits!*" Logan cheered.

"Yeah, *snowsuits and boots!*" Andrew pulled them out.

Mother walked over to Bobchia, standing with her hands on her hips and was leaning toward Mr. Pill. Mother whispered, "Aren't those the snowsuits *you* bought the boys, Rhea?"

*"You know it!* The snoopy *old thief* snooped in the closet!" She bit her lip, watching the boys give Mr. Pill the *hugs* that *belonged to her.* "Don't say anything, Clair. Look at his face" Mr. Pill beamed.

Bedroom slippers seemed to be the theme for the tenants' Christmas from Bobchia. Spike collected the old ones in a box, promptly taking them to the burn can to burn. While outside he thought he'd have himself a little pinch of *tobacco*. Meanwhile, Bobchia took Minnie out to do her business on the sidewalk. She saw Spike and called to him. He slowly walked over wondering if she had seen him. She laughed saying, "As cold as it is, I'll be hitting *those* off the sidewalk in an hour!" She pointed. Spike chuckled, swallowing his tobacco and choked. They walked inside together. She pulled on her slippers when they got into the mudroom. "Ya know, these slippers are *just about as green as your face!*" He ran for the bathroom. "Come back here when you're done!" She sat on the church pew, petting Minnie until he reluctantly came back into the mudroom. "Spike, I know you like *chewing*. I'm not sure if chewing will keep you *out* of heaven or not, but where would you *spit?*"

She shook her head and took a couple of deep breaths. "Well, I just so happened to be talking with Hoppy the other day, and he told me that you had been eyeing up a certain blue pole for ice fishing."

"*Just so happened?*"

She opened the closet door and handed it to him. "There ya go, but *mum's the word. I* feel like a *traitor!*"

"Thank you! It's a beauty! Well, won't *Blue Bird* here give *Old Faithful* a run for his money next year!"

"You already had a name picked out?"

"Of course!"

"Hey, no telling Harold, or I'll *never* hear the end of it!" She reached back into the closet and handed him a small box. "What's this?"

"Open it!"

"*Old Spice!*"

"For some reason, *they seem to go hand in hand!*"

They laughed as they came back into the great room. Spike hurried over to show the pole to Frank, challenging him to a fishing match on Lake Erie. Then Spike reached under the tree and gave Bobchia a box containing a green barn coat and matching hat. "This is my *green Christmas!* I've never seen a green barn coat before! They go great with these slippers! What do you think, boys? Sweetie, take my picture!"

'Pop,' went the camera.

"They are perfect. Thank you!"

"Bobchia, you ain't going to wear those slippers in the snow with that coat are you?" Logan asked.

"And ruin these *beautiful slippers?* No, honey boy!"

Mr. Pill banged his cane on the hardwood floor. Bobchia reached under the tree and handed him a cane with a muff on the end to cushion his floor and wall banging, which he didn't find amusing in the least! The boys gave him a dozen macaroni tie tacks, sticking them all over the front of his flannel shirt with scotch tape. He smiled proudly, showing off his shiny tooth.

'Pop,' went the camera!

Aunt Ardelle came down the steps carrying envelopes, as Wanda carried down Lucky's cage, draped in a red-and-green plaid Christmas blanket with an embroidered green parakeet on the front of it. Mother went into the hallway and sat at the telephone stand. Wanda wanted to set the cage beside the coffee table until she saw the glitter. "What is all over the floor?"

"Glitter!" Andrew yelled as he and Logan ran over. "Hold your hands out!"

They slipped macaroni bracelets on their wrists, sprinkling the lady's shoes with glitter.

"Oh…my. Thank you," Wanda said forcing a smile.

"Yes…thank you." Aunt Ardelle said shaking the glitter from her shoes as she handed the boys an envelope with a five-dollar bill in it. She whispered to Wanda, "Stomp your feet before you go upstairs!"

"A dollar!" Andrew waved it in the air.

"That is a *five dollar bill* young man!" Ardelle corrected.

"Can't ya give me pennies?" Andrew asked.

"That would be *five hundred pennies!*" Logan calculated.

"Wow! Five hundred pennies would *fill up* my bank!" Andrew told her.

"Mine too!"

Ardelle held a hand to her chest. "*Well, I never!*"

Mother hollered from the hallway, "Boys, that was very kind of Aunt Ardelle and Wanda. What do you say?"

"Thanks," Andrew said.

"Thanks, I like money." Logan said, lifting Lucky's blanket. "Hey, has Lucky *molded* yet? I don't see feathers, Andrew." Bobchia snorted.

Ardelle insisted that Bobchia take an envelope, from her and Wanda. "I don't...thank you. You *shouldn't* have, really." She gave them their box of slippers, and they thanked her.

I gave Wanda her present. "Seashells on a picture frame? Who would have thought that it would be so pretty. Thank you."

"You're welcome." Lucky fluttered in his cage and chirped.

Ardelle took the blanket off. "He heard *your* voice, Jennifer. Look at him!" She turned to Wanda. "Why don't we *will* Lucky to Jennifer? What do you think?"

"It would give us *peace of mind,* that's for sure."

"That settles it! I'm changing my will come the new year!"

I forced a smile, knowing it would be an automatic *death sentence* for the poor bird and said, "I don't think Mother would let me!"

"You'll be a grown woman with ten kids before us *old buffalos* kick the fence!" Ardelle laughed, handing me an envelope with ten dollars in it.

"Oh my, thank you," I said Lucky chirped again.

"You're welcome. Lucky wouldn't be the bird he is today if it weren't for *you!*"

I handed Aunt Ardelle her gift. "There's something in there for you *and* Lucky." Lucky chirped.

"You are the *dearest girl.* Nobody has ever given *him* a present before." She sniffed, wiped away a tear, took the paper off and opened the box. "How cute! A mirror with a *bell* on it." She held it up to the already frantic bird and shook it.

"Chirp, chirp, chirp, chirp!" Mother cringed.

Ardelle smiled. "He likes it! Thank you!" She put it on the side of his cage.

"You're welcome," I said. "And there is something else in the box."

Aunt Ardelle lifted the tissue paper, revealing a rhinestone broach. "Oh, look Wanda." She loudly whispered to Wanda, "This looks like one of the broaches that Mother used to give us every year for our birthdays!"

"*Those ugly things!* You always said her taste was all in her *mouth,* remember!" Ardelle elbowed Wanda. "Oh...pretty, very pretty."

"Thank you," Ardelle said.

"You're welcome."

After everyone had finished opening their gifts, Bobchia and I passed out the kolache. Aunt Ardelle gave Bobchia another gift—a compliment that meant more to her than the money in the envelope: "Delicious! This has to be what *manna* tasted like." Bobchia was again speechless.

The boys ate it until it was coming out of their ears and then ran to the window in the kitchen to look at the thermometer. Logan ran and slid to Mother in the hallway announcing, "It's thirty degrees out. *May I be excused* to get dressed and play outside?" She looked at him surprised.

"*Yes, you may.*" He ran upstairs then Andrew slid to Mother's feet.

"If I play outside, will you *excuse me?*"

"Yes, Andrew." He ran after Logan.

Soon they ran back down. "They were only upstairs eighteen and a half seconds! They broke their old record!" Spike laughed as he looked at his watch.

The boys slid in front of Mr. Pill. He *laughed* out loud! Every head turned, watching him laugh with the boys. Then Bobchia and I pushed and pulled them into their red suits and black boots.

"In the pockets you'll find gloves and scarves," Bobchia told them.

They pulled them out. "How did you *know* that, Bobchia?" Andrew asked.

"Oh, *lucky guess.*"

"Hey, *Man Upstairs*, do Mounties wear snowsuits like these?" Logan asked.

"Mounties? Well, yup."

"Can we play with the trains when we come back in?" Andrew asked.

"Trains? Well, yup."

Mother said from the hallway, "Thank you so much Mr. Pill for the beautiful snowsuits and boots."

"Snowsuits? Well, yup." He nodded.

"*Beautiful?*" Andrew scrunched up his nose. "Mounties don't look *beautiful!*"

"Yeah, Mounties are *tough*, aren't they *Man Upstairs?*"

"Tough? Well, yup!"

"See? Mounties are *not* beautiful, Mother!" Logan yelled.

"Sorry!" She pulled their hoods up as they walked to the door. "There you go, Mounties! Now keep those hoods up."

'Pop,' went the camera. The boys ran back into the great room and grabbed their skates and ski's then hugged Mother and Bobchia then ran out the door in their bulky suits. We went to the windows and watched Andrew skate on the sidewalk and Logan ski down the little knoll.

"Hey, they are *pretty good!*" Mother said, surprised.

"Remember, Clair, they've had *lots* of practice!"

"Oh, yeah. I forgot."

Ardelle said, "I *told* you, Wanda, that this puzzle would be the *same* as the others—*a piece is missing!* From now on I'm going to buy them at W. T. Grant's instead of Murphy's. Maybe theirs will at least have *all* the pieces!"

Wanda shook her head.

"Well, come on Wanda while the roads are good, we had better head out and pick up Rose and Jim. Then it's off to Erie."

Bobchia said, "Tell everyone in Erie I said Merry Christmas, and if the weatherman cooperates, we'll see them on New Year's Eve."

"Will do!"

"And tell Rose and Jim that the old Inn is still *full up*, but for *sure* I'm going to add on another wing in the spring, and next Christmas we'll all be under the same roof!"

"Wonderful!" Wanda said.

"Good!" Ardelle smiled.

Bobchia continued, "By then Sweetie will have earned her *chef's hat* and will be *rubbing elbows* with me in the kitchen!" Bobchia smiled, looking at me through her brows. Mother looked shocked. I was *in* shock!

"Now, are you *sure* that Lucky won't be any trouble?" Ardelle asked Bobchia. "I'd take him with us but he'd catch his death. I'll set him in the dining room, okay?"

"He'll be fine, Ardelle. Jennifer can keep an eye on him. And he'll be just fine in there. Not to worry!"

They stomped the glitter off of their slippers, then Bobchia ushered them into the dining room, reassuring them that the bird would be safe on the shelf. "Tell Jim and Rose Merry Christmas and to stop for supper the next time they're in town. When does he get the cast off of his arm?"

"In a couple of weeks." Wanda said putting Lucky on the shelf. "Oh no! He's not moving. I think he died!"

Ardelle shook the little bell wildly and he blinked. "He's alive! Cover him quick so he doesn't catch his death! There, now my baby will stay nice and warm. I've got to stop at the freezer on my way out and grab a couple of my pecan pies and then we're on our way. Merry Christmas!"

"Merry Christmas, and thank you again for the generous check."

Bobchia came back into the great room and chuckled watching them drive the old Thunderbird slowly down the lane. She turned from the window, "It only takes Harold forty-five minutes tops to get there. I hope they make it before midnight!"

Mr. Pill had fallen asleep in his chair. Bobchia covered him with an afghan. "Well, he's down for the count. Merry Christmas, you *old coot!*" Mother giggled. "Clair, *look!*" The missing puzzle piece dropped from Mr. Pill's fist to the floor. "*The scoundrel!* I bet he has a collection of puzzle pieces upstairs! The next time Cliff runs the sweeper up there, I'll have him take a look around."

It was nice hearing Mother and Bobchia laugh together. Bobchia completed the puzzle, then she tore it down. She went to the corner cupboard and stretched the daisy/poinsettia doily over the coffee table, adding a big box of ribbon candy on top. "There, that looks pretty. When is Caleb coming?" She asked Mother.

"He said early afternoon."

"Perfect, that will give me enough time to get the hams in the oven."

"I'd be glad to help, now that I don't have to study." Volunteered Mother.

"I'd appreciate that, Clair." They seemed to be getting along for Christmas, but I prayed for *forever.*

Bobchia got dressed and took her green barn coat and hat out from under the tree. I followed her down the hall. "Where are you going?"

"I've got to pick up Harold and take a few things over to the Christian Center. I'll be back at noon to start the potatoes and yams."

"Can I go?"

"I'd like to take you. We could always use extra hands, but it is depressing, rewarding but *depressing.* The people who go there, well, it is heart wrenching. You should recoup a little longer. Next year, if you're still here, you can help."

"*I will always be here,* Bobchia!"

"*I know.*"

We went into the cold room. Spike was packing food, clothing and toys into boxes from a secret compartment in the wall.

"Wow! *Another* secret room!" I peered in. "Look at all this stuff!"

Bobchia explained, "For a long time after you left here, I still bought you birthday and Christmas gifts, thinking you'd be back, but, well, I donated them knowing they'd put smiles on children's faces at Christmas time. It brought them joy, so I just kept doing it. Promise me something."

"Okay."

"Remember you can never *out give* God, *never!* It is so much fun blessing people!"

"I won't forget."

"How many secret rooms does this Inn have?"

"Hmm, five that I know of. I found a smaller one under the floorboards of a bathroom upstairs just a couple of years ago when we were putting in a new tub. It had a trunk with old newspapers, a jar of coins, a rag doll and rations from the Great Depression in it. There are probably more somewhere. If I don't find them, *you will.*"

"Where did you get all these toys?" I asked.

"Clearance sales throughout the year."

The boxes were piled high, some with names on the sides. I walked to a box marked *Sterling* picking up a bride doll out of it. "She's pretty."

"I got her for Lucy's bed. I thought it looked a little like her, but I'm at a loss as to what to give Ricky. And that Lanny boy, *mercy*, what could a person ever give *him?*"

"Let me look," I walked around looking on the shelves. "That ball glove for Ricky, and uh, do you have any baseballs for Lanny?"

"I think in that box over there, but I saw him playing catch with Ricky not so long ago." Spike said.

"I know for a *fact* that he doesn't have any."

"Oh, I'll check in that back box. Yeah, here's some."

Bobchia smiled. "Good, now I'll throw in a ham and a couple of pies from the freezer for Butch."

"Rhea, don't you think Butch might be getting a *little suspicious* after all these years, that *you're* the one leaving the box full of goodies on his porch?" Spike asked.

"You're probably right." Bobchia thought for a moment. "I'll give him a couple of *Ginger's* pies this year. That'll throw him off the track and probably in the *hospital!*" She laughed. "Hold down the fort for me, Sweetie!"

"I will."

"I've got to pick up Harold and get the hams in the ovens and the potatoes peeled at the center. I should be back around eleven, *if* my relief shows up. Get a head count. Spike, you might have to set up some card tables. With the roads being clear, we'll have an *Inn-full.* And don't forget to deliver the Sterling's box. The coast should be clear in a couple hours. They usually leave to go to Luke's around ten. Just so you know, Butch doesn't stand a chance with me *praying* for him and the kids. You mark my words, one of these Sundays he'll be sitting in a church pew, shocking everybody *but me. You mark my words!*" She looked to the ceiling as she went out the door, then up to the sky. "*TYG!*"

Spike carried the last two boxes to the car. As she drove off waving, he sneaked a pinch of snuff into his cheek before coming back in. "Your grandmother has a heart of gold. She'll go to the center and talk with the people today and plead their case at the employment office, come Wednesday. If I heard her say it once, I've heard her say it a million times: 'This country needs to give people a hand *up* not a hand *out!*' Don't be surprised if she brings someone back with her. A couple of years ago she brought back a young girl who'd just had a baby. Her parents had kicked her out. She stayed in your room for a couple of months, until she made the decision to give the baby up for adoption. Rhea helped her get a job and knows who adopted the little girl. It was nice having a baby in the Inn for a while. You know your grandmother—there's *always room in the Inn.*"

"I never knew about that."

"How could you? She'd like it if no one was the wiser, but with so many eyes..." He spit out the window. *"Sorry,* anyway, I've never seen her so happy!"

"Can I ask you a question?"

"Anything."

"You don't *like* my Mother much, do you?"

"Oh. Well, I really don't *know* her very well. I've been here almost ten years, and I've seen Rhea's reaction every time she would write or call your father. When he passed away, the rejection was hard on her, and I guess I might hold that against her, but I really don't *mean to.* Families *are* complicated. She was sure excited when your father wrote and told her that if anything should happen to him, he wanted her to take Clair and you kids in. She was excited but also suspicious that he wasn't doing well. When he died, it hit her like a ton of bricks! Her *only* hope was that Clair would follow your father's advice. She redecorated the great room in anticipation that *you'd be coming.* For two years I'd hear the same thing at breakfast as she gazed at the covered bridge: *'This might be my Sweetie's home coming day.'* She *never* lost hope but every day, she was *disappointed."* He spit out the window again. *"Sorry.* When she got the call from Clair saying that you were moving back for *sure,* I had never seen her so excited! All I heard was Jennifer this and Jennifer that, and she couldn't wait to see if the boys looked as much like Paul in person as they did in their pictures. It was great to see her happy, *really happy!"*

I wiped tears from my eyes, and held up my hand for him to stop talking. I couldn't *bear* to hear another word. "Thanks for filling me in."

"I didn't mean to *upset* you." I walked to the door. "I just thought you'd want to know." I shook my head and left.

I went to my room, crying in the shower for all the *lost years.* I put on my robe and wrapped my hair in a towel and hugged Father's picture as Joan of Arc purred against my legs. "TYG for all the cherished Christmases with Father. I miss and love him so much. Please give him a big Christmas hug for me. Amen."

I quickly went into the great room and took my red sweater and black ski pants from under the tree then rushed back to my room and got dressed. I brushed my hair straight and put on my makeup. As I was admiring my cross necklace, Pumpkin jumped onto the dresser and batted at it. "Curiosity killed the cat," I told her. She meowed. "Sorry, *erase, erase!*" I carefully put on the necklace and slipped on the macaroni bracelet. "Here, look, you didn't even notice my beautiful macaroni bracelet." I picked Pumpkin up and rubbed her ears. "I know it's not much to look at, but you should see the guy who gave it to me!" She meowed. "You're right! He is the *cat's meow!* That's funny!" I brushed my hair again and went into the great room and sat beside the fireplace, talking with Mother while she watched the boys play in the yard.

Bobchia came back at noon looking drained. I met her in the kitchen. "*I'm late!* The people who *signed up* didn't *show up,* Sweetie. But at least they're eating over there! I told them to lock the door on their way out. You should have seen the looks on those kids' faces when they opened their gifts! Oh well, I'll round up helpers from some seaport to help me clean the center tomorrow."

"I'll help you."

"I'll hold you to that." She took her coat off and checked out my outfit. "The minute I saw that red sweater, it had your name written all over it." She sat down. "I need to sit for a minute." She sighed. "The kids had a ball playing with Minnie. She's out like a light, look." She held her pocket open and I took a peek.

"Aw. I peeled the potatoes, the fire is on low, and I set the table for you."

"*That's my girl.*" She shut her eyes.

"Mrs. Dunham and Mother got the yams going, and the lasagna and pigs-in-a-blanket are on low with the hams in the ovens with the casseroles, and everything else is on the back burners until you make the gravy. Are you *sleeping?*"

"Bobchia's just *reading her eyelids,* Sweetie."

"Mother's in the side yard with the boys making a snowman." She scowled without opening her eyes. "Clair is in the *snow?*"

"They want to *surprise* Caleb."

"*Oh, really?*" Her eyebrows went up.

"I shined the good silver and set the tables with the poinsettia table cloths and napkins that were in the china cupboard. I hope that is what you wanted. Bobchia?" She snored. "*Bobchia?*"

With a blast of the rig's horn on the covered bridge, the old *blond* mare got her second wind! *"Come on, Sweetie Pie!"* She took off in a dead run with me hobbling close behind.

We pulled back the lace curtain from the kitchen window and watched the truck with a big wreath tied to its grill, come down the snow-covered lane. Darcy leaned out of her window waving to Mother and the boys, while Caleb waved his cowboy hat. "Merry Christmas!" He called.

"Merry Christmas, Caleb!"

Caleb parked the rig and helped Darcy down then he ran to the knoll and put the head on the snowman for the boys, giving them high fives. "I like your red snowsuits, and I see your Mother got a pretty gray coat for Christmas!" Caleb said.

Mother twirled as Logan ran to the creek bed to get stones for the snowman's eyes.

"Hey, did you bring your ball glove like you said you would?" Andrew asked.

"I did, little bud!"

"Yea!" He cheered.

"But how are we going to play in the snow? We'll lose the ball!" Caleb warned.

"We can play catch. I throw real good. I *never* miss," Andrew said.

"Never?"

"*Never!*"

Mother pulled a carrot out of her pocket and stuck it in the snowman's face.

"Looks great!" Caleb said.

Darcy signed "Merry Christmas" to Mother, and they hugged.

"What does a truck driver have to do to get a *Christmas hug?*" Caleb asked Mother smiling.

To their surprise, Andrew threw his arms around Caleb's legs. Caleb bent down hugging him tight. "Thanks, *little bud!*" Logan ran over and gave him a big Christmas hug almost knocking him down.

"Thanks Logan."

Mother held back her tears. Then the boys ran under the oak to get twigs for the snowman's arms.

Caleb stood up. "Merry Christmas, Clair." He held out his arms, and she eagerly went into his embrace.

"Merry Christmas, Caleb! I bet you could go for some coffee."

"Only the whole pot. I didn't want to stop when I had a beautiful woman waiting for me!" He put his arms around Mother and Darcy. As they started up the sidewalk, a snowball hit Caleb in the middle of his back. He turned.

"I told you I *never* miss!" Andrew smiled. "Let's have a snowball fight!" He said to Logan.

"Yeah! Let's get him!" They charged.

Caleb ran, dodging snowballs, to his truck. He climbed in and pulled out two sleds with big red bows and red runners. "Merry Christmas, boys!"

They were ecstatic. "Oh wow! Thanks!"

"You are welcome!"

"Thanks, Caleb!" Andrew stared with wide eyes. "Sorry I hit you in the back!"

"Sorry I knocked your hat off," Logan said. "Here it is!"

Caleb hit the hat on the side of his jeans. "I'll get even. Don't worry, little cowpokes!"

The boys, jumped onto the sleds and slid down the knoll, waving at the snowman as they slid by. Caleb climbed back into the cab and pulled out shopping bags. Mother walked toward him. "That was thoughtful of you. You didn't *have* to do that!"

"Those boys are the best, and *yes I did!* Don't you know that every boy *needs* a sled?"

"I don't know what to say."

"You don't have to *say* anything."

"This is the best Christmas the children have had in a long time."

"And *you?*"

"And me too."

"Good, and the day is just beginning! How about a walk in the snow later?"

Mother stopped, shivered and smiled. "I'd love to!"

He put his arm around her shoulder and then Darcy's, and with bags dangling, he kissed them on the cheek and walked up the sidewalk, dodging tootsie rolls.

Bobchia swung open the door. Pumpkin made a break for it! Darcy scrambled for her and grabbed her before she jumped off the porch.

Bobchia looked at Caleb. "Merry Christmas, *you handsome thing!* If I were just *thirty years younger!*"

He smiled. "Well, if I were thirty years younger, I'd be *nine!*"

She squealed when he lifted her up. "I'm a *back breaker!* Put me down!" We laughed.

Caleb smiled at me. "Merry Christmas, Jen."

"Merry Christmas, Caleb."

Bobchia looked impatiently at Darcy signing to her and pulled her into her bosom then Darcy pointed at my hair and nodded.

"Thank you." I said.

Then she pointed to Bobchia's green slippers, putting her hand over her mouth. Caleb looked down laughing.

"Quit laughing at my green slippers!" Bobchia said. Mother rolled her eyes. "The boys got me these, and *I love them!* They keep my pigs warm—not to mention they're better than the dust mop!" She skated around on the floor. "*Ta-da!*"

Laughing, we went into the great room and sat by the tree. Caleb and Darcy looked curiously at the glitter all over the floor. Darcy signed to Bobchia asking what had happened.

"The boys made macaroni necklaces and bracelets for everyone and then they twirled them around on their fingers, *that's* what happened! I don't believe in *sweeping* on Christmas so we'll have to put up with it, oh and try and act surprised when they give you your bracelet! Oh, speaking of bracelets, look at the one Clair got me!" Darcy looked at each of the charms. Bobchia touched Darcy's cheek to get her attention. "There is plenty of room on there for *yours and Caleb's charms.*

"Oh! I never thought…" Mother got Darcy's attention. "I'm sorry. I'll get yours and Caleb's on this week, okay? *I promise.*" Darcy smiled and shook her head.

"I'm only going to wear it on *Sundays* and special occasions," Bobchia said. "Otherwise someone might find a *head in their vegetable soup!*" We laughed. Bobchia hugged Darcy.

Mother went to the kitchen and came back with a tray of coffee and kolache, serving it to Caleb.

He turned to Bobchia. "I hoped you'd make *this!* I had my mouth set for it!"

"Dinner's just around the corner, ya know!" Bobchia cautioned.

He handed a piece to Darcy. She took a bite, patted her stomach and smiled at Bobchia. Mother handed Caleb a cup of coffee and checked her hair in the glass of the corner cupboard.

Caleb took a sip of coffee and then searched the bags, pulling out a tiny box, which he proudly handed to Darcy. She signed something to him.

"I know I already gave you a few things, but this is *something special for the sweetest daughter a dad could have.*" She eagerly opened the box and put her hand on her chest in disbelief. She turned the box to show us a sparkly pair of diamond chip earrings.

'Pop,' went Bobchia's camera.

Darcy hugged Caleb's neck, put them in her ears and ran to the vestibule to admire them in the full length mirror. Then she ran back and hugged him again, pulling her hair back to show them off.

'Pop,' went the camera. She signed to him.

"I love you back!" He smiled. "*You're the best thing that ever happened to me!*"

Darcy went to the corner cupboard, reached back on a shelf and brought out a little antique, blue box with a blue cloth ribbon tied around it. He untied it. "A Roy Rogers knife! Oh honey, *I've always wanted one of these!*" She nodded.

'Pop,' went the camera.

Caleb gave her a big hug and reached in the bag again. Reading the nametag, he handed me a little box.

"Thanks Caleb." I eagerly opened a darling pair of gold cross earrings. "Look Bobchia, they match *your* cross necklace!"

"Lovely!"

'Pop,' went her camera.

Caleb said, "Rhea, I didn't know you had a *cross necklace.*"

"I used to years ago, but Jennifer has it now."

"Thank you, Caleb. These are beautiful." I put the earrings in and pulled my hair back to show them to everyone. "I have a gift for you too, but I'll wait until Mother gives you hers."

Mother reached under the tree and handed a box to Darcy. "Thank you," Darcy signed.

"You're welcome."

Darcy lifted the lid, revealing a white mohair tam and scarf set, which she modeled for us.

'Pop,' went the camera.

Caleb told her how pretty they looked with her dark hair. When she hugged Mother, Pumpkin reached for the fringe on the scarf. Bobchia tapped Darcy on the shoulder. "Hold onto that cat for dear life! Lucky is in the dining room."

Caleb reached into the bag again and pulled out two boxes for Mother.

"Oh my, thank you." She took the gold paper off of a bottle of Channel Number 5. "I haven't had perfume in so long."

'Pop,' went the camera.

"Oh? I can still smell *Rhea* in my truck!"

Bobchia looked puzzled and turned around and smelled her armpits. Mother sprayed her neck and passed the bottle to all of us to share. Bobchia sprayed under her arms real good, sending Minnie into a sneezing fit.

Mother looked curiously at the other box, hesitating.

Caleb smiled. "I got this gift for you, but it's *mostly for me.*"

She looked puzzled at the ring box. Blushing, she opened it. "*A mood ring?*"

"Now all I have to do is check out the ring to see what kind of *mood* you're in. Well, go ahead, put it on."

'Pop,' went the camera.

"This will let me know if you're getting ready to have a *hissy fit* or not!" Her face turned red as we laughed. She put it on. We strained to watch it turn blue. "Blue, that's pretty good. No *thunderstorms* on the horizon…yet." He smiled.

He pulled out another box and read the nametag. "Is Ginger here?"

"No, she went with Mr. 'Would you like a little trim?'—soon to be number *five* and your new *grandpa.*" Bobchia teased.

Caleb waved his hand. "*Perish the thought!*"

"He took her to Grand Valley to meet his daughter, Harriet." We laughed.

"Do you think it's as serious as all that?" Caleb asked.

"Is the Pope *Catholic?*" Bobchia asked. "She wore her go-go boots!"

"*It is serious!* I was hoping I could talk her into making me some of her *chicken and biscuits* this trip!"

"Do *you want to be pushing up daisies?*" Bobchia asked.

Caleb laughed and put the box under the tree. He pulled out two little boxes from a bag. "Are Venal and Izora here?"

"Don't tell me you got them more *heavy earrings?*" Caleb laughed. "Those *lobes* of theirs can't handle any more *heavy* earrings!" He laughed louder. "Mercy! Why if those two women were ever in a wind storm, *they'd slap themselves silly!*" He laughed even harder.

"They're not *as* heavy as the ones I got them last year, I promise. Are they here?"

"They left yesterday to visit Nancy, in Virginia. They'll be back New Year's Day." He pretended the little boxes were breaking his back as he bent down to place them under the tree.

Caleb handed Bobchia the other bag. "This is *too much*, Caleb really."

"How do you know? It might just be *Q-tips!*"

"Good! I'm always running out, thanks to *you-know-who!*"

We looked over at Antenna Man who was content looking down at his new slippers. Bobchia pulled out a box from the bag and unwrapped it. "Boots? Mercy, I don't wear size eleven, but *Ginger does!*" She snorted as she lifted the lid. "Oh boy! Oh boy! *Oh boy!* A Polaroid camera and boxes of film! I really *needed* this!"

"*I know!*"

"Thank you so much!"

"Just think—you won't have to wait to get your pictures *developed* anymore!" He said proudly.

"I can't believe it! It's like the one I saw on *TV!* This will be *wonderful!* Would you load it for me?"

"Sure. There is more."

"Mercy!" She unwrapped an electric can opener. "How wonderful! It will sure save work for these tired old hands of mine. But I'll keep the old ones just in case we have a blackout!"

Caleb laughed, teasing, "I remember the last blackout we had. Everyone wanted *canned soup!*"

"Why Caleb Martin, *you fibber!* We have *never* had *canned anything* in this Inn!"

"*My point exactly!*"

"It's really way too much. Way, way *too much*, but thank you."

"That's not *all!*"

"*I think you've totally lost your mind!* What *else* could there be?" She reached to the bottom and got out a tiny gold box. "Caleb this is *way* too much!" She lifted the lid, revealing a dainty gold cross necklace. She wiped her tears. "*It's beautiful!* Did you by any chance *talk* to Jennifer."

I shook my head. "No Bobchia, *honest!*"

"Well now we'll match, Sweetie. Put it on me."

"Smile," Caleb said. We quickly hugged.

'Pop,' went the Polaroid camera. Caleb set the picture on the coffee table. We gathered around and watched the picture come into focus.

"The color is absolutely beautiful. We look so *real!*" Bobchia said. Caleb laughed. "Mercy, that line in my forehead has gotten deeper since—"

"There's something else at the bottom of the bag," Caleb said.

"You realize you're going to have to *hock* that rig of yours to pay for all this stuff! What else could I possibly have *need* of?"

"You'll see. Besides, it matches those wild slippers of yours!" She pulled tissue paper out of the bag and unfolded it. "Oh my! *Look at this!*" Smiling, she held up a red-and-green cobbler apron with a deep, flannel pocket, with **GERBIL** embroidered across the front of it. "*Miss Minnie, you hit the big time!*"

"I had it especially made for the *gerbil!*" Caleb laughed. "It has an *extra big pocket,* because I know her feet will never hit the floor and I don't want her poor little legs to be *deformed!*"

Bobchia snorted, hauled Minnie out of her apron and handed her to me. Then she took off her apron and proudly put on the new one, holding out the pocket for Minnie. We all took turns looking inside the pocket. The pup had snuggled down, nearly disappearing in the vastness. She growled when Caleb looked in.

"See, I knew the little gerbil would like it! Wait, hold the pocket open again and I'll get a picture. *Smile, gerbil.*"

'Pop,' went the flash.

Minnie jumped up trying to bite him. "*Man!* That's what I get for trying to *help a gerbil!*" Caleb set the picture beside the other one.

Bobchia laughed and took the camera from Caleb. "Go line up on the couch, everyone!"

'Pop!' She put the picture beside the other ones. She turned to the tree.

'Pop!' She threw the blanket off of frantic Lucky.

'Pop!' She came back in laughing. "I'll give this one to Ardelle! As Andrew would say, this is the *mostest fun!*"

Mother reached under the tree and handed Caleb a box. He caught her hand and looked at the ring.

'Pop!'

"Still blue, that's *good,*" He said as he took the paper off, revealing a Roy Rogers lunch box filled with the peanut butter fudge. "*Cool!* It's just like the one I had when I was a kid, except my old one had a dent on the side where I'd hit *Lester the Pester* over the head for stealing my sandwich!"

"Shame on you for hitting a kid on the head for stealing your sandwich!" Bobchia said.

"But it was *ham!*" Caleb protested.

"Oh! Well then…"

He took a bite of fudge. "Yum!"

'Pop!'

"Thanks, Clair."

"You are welcome."

Caleb couldn't quit oohing and awing over the lunch box. "Where did you find it?"

"Cara's Antiques, beside the park."

"I've looked all over the countryside for one of these things, and here it was right under my nose!" He winked at Mother and looked at the ring. "Green! She's *warming up,* folks!" I giggled. Mother blushed. I handed him his gift from me. He quickly ripped the paper. "A thermos to match!"

'Pop!'

He was delighted. I was amused that a grown man would make such a fuss over *kid stuff!* Bobchia pulled out a big box from under the tree and handed it to Darcy. She signed thank you, opened it, clapped her hands then held up a black bench warmer and boots.

'Pop!' She gave Bobchia a big hug.

Bobchia went to the desk, blinking back tears as she opened a drawer and handed Caleb a little, blue antique box with blue cloth bow. He opened it to reveal a cowboy string tie and slide with "RR" on it. "This is great!" He quickly put it around his neck and ran into the vestibule, laughing. He came back holding his head high, imitating Darcy. She hit him in the arm. "Ouch! This looks like a *Roy Rogers conspiracy* to me! This is really the best! Thanks everybody!"

"There's something else in the box, Caleb."

"Oh?"

Bobchia sang **Happy Trails** as he lifted up the cotton and pulled out a key on a **RR** key chain. "It's a **Roy Rogers** key chain and a key…to room five? But I stay here anyway."

"I know, but I don't want you to have to keep packing, unpacking and sleeping on a rollaway when all the rooms are full. I want you and Darcy *here* when you can be, and when she graduates in the spring, I want her here with me until you *settle down.*"

"I can't accept it."

"Don't say you *can't*. Just put it in your pocket."

Darcy was reading Bobchia's lips, begging Caleb in 'sign' to accept. Pumpkin tried to grab her fast fingers.

"But you're so *busy*, and the Inn is so *crowded,*" Caleb said.

"*There's always room in the Inn, especially for family!*" She said patting his arm.

He looked at Darcy, who held her hands together as if praying. "The only thing I can say is—*we accept!*" Darcy hugged him and ran to Bobchia. *We were all thrilled!* Caleb leaned over and looked at Mother's ring. "*Black*. That's...not...so...*good...* "

Bobchia looked at her watch. "Mercy, I had better get the gravy going, or I'll have to run the potatoes through a *sieve!*"

"Mmm, ham gravy," Caleb said.

We quickly went into the kitchen to help. Mother hollered out the side window to tell the boys that if they weren't in the tub in two minutes, they wouldn't see their sleds until *next* winter!

"Chee, what a *grouch!*" Caleb said smiling, glancing at the piece of *coal* on her finger. Mother gave him 'the look.' The boys bounded through the door.

"Why do we have to get in the tub?" Logan asked. "We ain't even dirty. *Snow is clean!*"

"And *white!*"

"We had snow suits on and nothin' on us even got dirty!"

Caleb stood behind Mother pointing to the stairs. They took off their suits and stomped up the stairs with Mother close behind. I looked at all the pictures that had been taken and quickly covered Lucky and moved him from the dining room to a knickknack shelf in the hallway where it was peaceful.

It was a snowy day, but the roads were clear, allowing a number of tenants to drive to their relatives. With the arrival of Frank and Mary's daughter, Patty and her family, bringing pies, and Spike and Carolyn's twin daughters, Penny and Pam and their families bringing more pies, the official count was thirty-eight people and eleven *yummy* pies!

"Mercy, you would *think* that they would *know by now* that I make enough to feed an army! What in the world are we going to do with all those pies?" Bobchia said.

"*Eat them!* The more pies, the merrier, Bobchia!" I gave her a big smile.

"Go ahead and smile! I know what you're smiling about! You won't have to *climb* the shelves tonight!" She hugged me laughing.

Caleb drained the juice from the hams into saucepans while Bobchia concocted the gravy. Tall Cliff, Darcy and I carried trays full of food from the cold room to the kitchen as Helen, Mrs. Dunham, Gladys and Mother lifted the food. Pans, hands and bowls were all over the kitchen as we took the food to the dining room for the *ultimate* Christmas feast. We heard *squealing tires* then Harold rushed in.

"*You're late!*" Bobchia scolded.

"Sorry, I dozed off in my chair."

To our amazement, the boys helped Mr. Pill down the stairs and into the dining room.

Harold and Caleb looked surprised and tried to shake his hand. He grunted at them.

"TYG!" Bobchia said. She was thrilled *until* he *took her seat* between the boys. I laughed and patted the chair next to me.

Harold asked Caleb to help him bring in a color TV set for us kids.

"*Oh, boy! A color TV!*" Andrew jumped up and down.

"I never could bring myself to replace the one that David bought," Bobchia said. "I guess I could use the old one it for a plant stand in my room."

"*Oh, boy!*" Logan cheered. (The days of fine-tuning would soon be a memory.)

Harold and Caleb carried the TV in and set it in the great room. The boys ran in and laid on the floor in front of it staring at the blank screen. "I'll hook it up after dinner!" Harold said, then boasted, "I'll have you know, boys, this is *no ordinary color TV set. This is an RCA Victor Color TV with a 19-inch tube and solid copper circuits!*"

"Wow! Real *copper* circuits!" Logan said.

Andrew nodded at Logan. "It looks *neat* even when it's *off!*"

Then Harold went back out to the hearse and came back in with a long box, handing it to Bobchia. "Can't this wait until *after* we eat?" He *begged* her to open it.

"Mercy, what did you do, *hock the hearse?*" He was like a little kid watching her unwrap the set of Paul Revere pans.

"There's the other kettle you were *wishing* for!" He winked at her. When she took the lid off, she found a huge bottle of *Evening in Paris* hidden inside. She quickly put the lid back on.

"Thank you, Harold. They are *lovely!*"

"Do you really like them?"

She smiled at me. "*Is the sky blue?*" We giggled, then she whispered, "Oh, Sweetie, this is all the *confirmation* you need!"

"What are you talking about?" I said.

"Well, with this set of pans, by next Christmas *you'll* be the best cook in the Inn!"

"Good!" I said surprising her.

"Good?"

I whispered. "You said, the quickest way to the alter is *through the kitchen!*"

"Are you taking notes on *everything* I say?"

"*I am!*"

"Mercy! Well *mum's* the word to your *mom* on that one!"

The tenants were getting impatient to start eating.

Harold tapped his cheek. "*Well, Rhea?*"

"Mercy, the dinner will be *ruined* if we don't eat it *now!*"

He kept tapping. "Then you better kiss me in a *hurry!*"

Mother and Caleb laughed as she gave him a peck on the cheek. Bobchia nodded to Darcy to pray and then held up her hand. "Hold it, Darcy! Clair, where are the boys?"

"Oh, the boys…" Mother went into the great room. "What on earth are you doing?"

"Were pretending to watch color TV!" Logan explained.

"Can't we stay a little longer? I think I see cartoons!"

"Yeah!" Andrew said.

Mother shook her head. "It's time to eat! Get to the table!"

"Sorry, Darcy!" Bobchia said. "Everyone's here now."

Caleb translated as Darcy 'signed' her prayer: "Thank you King Jesus for leaving heaven and being born and dying for us. Thank you for all our beautiful gifts and for this bountiful feast that we're about to enjoy. Thank you for bringing us all together this Christmas Day and for the love that we share. And thank you especially for *room number five!* Through Jesus Christ, our Lord, whom we praise, Amen.

It was like Thanksgiving all over again, only with ham instead of turkey, and just when we thought we couldn't eat another bite, Bobchia cut the pies! Luckily, no one missed Aunt Ardelle's pecan pie. (I *accidently* left it in the cold room for later!) The feast only took fourteen minutes and twenty-six seconds to eat, shattering last year's record according to Spike.

After dinner, Bobchia told Harold to turn his chair around and shut his eyes. Then she stood in front of him holding a needlepoint picture of his old homestead. "Open your eyes!" He was so excited that he jumped up and kissed her right on the lips in front of everyone!

"*Yuck!*"

"*Yucky!*"

"*Mercy, Harold!*"

"It's wonderful, just *wonderful!* It's when the big porch was on, when I was a kid! I'm hanging this in the *palace!* How did you ever...?"

"Wayne gave me a picture, and Homer drew it on the mat for me to needlepoint." Harold smiled at Homer and held it up. "Thanks Homer!"

"When are we going to eat?" Homer asked Harold.

"It brings back so many memories of when I was a kid," Harold said. "I can see mom and dad rocking on that porch. Thank you!"

"It was my pleasure," She said proudly.

In the assembly line to clear the tables, I couldn't help but notice Caleb flirting with Mother. Although she was like the Mountain of Gibraltar to start, the more he smiled that great smile of his, the more the mountain crumbled. By the time the leftovers were securely sealed and stacked in the refrigerators, the ring had gone through a *rainbow of colors,* staying on a rosy shade of pink, the color of Mother's face. She even flirted back a little. How could she help herself? He was a *cool guy.* But I had to wonder—why was his life such a *mystery,* and how could Darcy's mother just abandon her like that? Darcy was one of the sweetest girls I had ever known, a pure joy to be around. Nothing could have *prepared us,* for what was about to happen.

After the kitchen was back in order, Darcy brought Lucky into the great room and set his cage on the bookcase, not realizing that Mother *hated* birds. Mother quickly moved to a chair at the opposite end of the room. Darcy and I sat by the tree watching Pumpkin play with the tinsel, but we weren't the *only* ones watching her, for high on the bookcase, *incognito,* shivering on the floor of his cage and peeking through the slit of his knitted Christmas blanket, was Lucky, observing *every* little move the cat made.

After watching **Rin Tin Tin** (in *black and white* on the 19 inch RCA Victor *color* TV) and getting the wooden puzzles that Halfway Decent Henry had made them, together, the boys whined to go back outside.

"If your suits are dry, you can go out, but I want you to put all your toys under the tree so no one will trip over them," Mother ordered.

They shoved their puzzles under the tree, breaking an ornament.

Andrew picked it up. "Hey, Logan. Look, you broke your angel!"

"No, I broke *your* angel!"

"Oh."

They got their suits on, and out into the cold they went.

Andy called me around four. "Merry Christmas, Skip!"

My heart pounded in my ears. "Merry Christmas!"

"Mom is putting dinner on the table. Sorry I didn't call sooner, but we just got back from visiting Gram, and this is the first chance I've had to call you all day."

"That's okay."

"I'll be over in an hour or so."

"I can't wait!" I whispered.

"Me either! Is your mother going to *stare* at us?"

"Probably!"

"Good! I plan on giving you a *big sucker bite!* Do you think she'll *notice?*"

I laughed, just as Mother walked by. "I'll see you later then?"

"I'll be there!"

In that hour, I must have checked my hair and makeup a hundred times. Darcy told me that I looked beautiful and not to worry. I got the mistletoe out of the trash, rinsed off the coffee grounds and hung it up. (Bobchia had thrown it in the garbage after repeatedly catching Mr. Hair and Ginger kissing under it, but I didn't see any harm in hanging it back up since they were gone!)

Darcy and I sat on the window seat in the kitchen, a vantage point to the driveway, as she talked of Seth's New Year's Eve concert in Pittsburgh. She wanted me and Andy to go to it, so Caleb would let her go. I told her that knowing how Mother felt about Andy, it wouldn't happen. Besides, Bobchia had already made plans with Johnny for New Year's Eve. Five o'clock came and went. The telephone rang. I eagerly answered it. It was for Caleb.

I couldn't help but hear his side of the conversation, since the telephone stand was in the hallway. "We were planning on going to your mother's tomorrow like *usual*, why? Tonight? *Here?* Oh, I don't think...I don't know. *It's crowded as it is!* I know, I know, but I hate to spring that on Rhea. Well, I guess if it's the *only* time you have. Whatever. Yeah, goodbye." He was antsy after he hung up.

Harold came in and told Mother that the boys were *still* sliding into the burned out basement and that he wanted them to *stay out* of there! Mother got on her coat to go confront them.

When Bobchia came in to get coffee, Caleb cornered her, telling her of his dilemma. It was evident that she couldn't *resist* Caleb's pleas to help him out of whatever situation he was in.

I checked my makeup and gargled again. The boys threw a fit when they had to come inside. Mother directed them to the stairs to get into the tub—again! "If you can't listen, you can stay inside and get in the tub!" (You would have thought that someone had just *taken* Christmas from them the way they carried on.)

"Two whole baths in one day, *again!*" Andrew whined. "I never had to take two whole baths when we lived in Florida! I'm *not scrubbin' this time!*"

"Me either! Kids shouldn't have to take a bath on *Christmas*, should they?" Logan asked.

"*Never!*" Andrew said pointing at him.

They pushed themselves out of their suits leaving them in a pile by the back door. I relayed the conversation to Darcy.

The telephone rang again. I answered it, but it was Johnny and the Erie cousins, taking turns to wish Bobchia "Merry Christmas." They told her that the roads were getting bad and that Aunt Ardelle and Wanda had just left and were headed to Jim's and Rose's to spend the night.

Bobchia put her hand over the receiver and said, "Ardelle will be calling me later to give me *instructions* on how to take care of Lucky! I take care of a *whole Inn full of people,* and she's going to call me to tell *me* how to take care of a *little bird!*"

I checked my watch as I walked back to the window seat, eight minutes after six. I could barely see Andy jogging up the lane in the blizzard and rushed to the door. He hurried in red-faced, covered with snow. "Merry Christmas, Skip!" He kissed my cheek.

"Merry Christmas! *Ooo,* your face is freezing! Did your truck break down?"

"Nah, it was just blocked in our driveway. I don't mind, I needed the exercise anyway. I've put on a *few pounds* since I've been coming here."

"I know the feeling."

"But I did save room for a piece of Bobchia's *kolache* that you were telling me about." He took his coat off, shook it over the rug and hung it on a hook. Darcy smiled at him from the window seat.

"Andy, this is Darcy."

"I saw her on *toboggan night,* remember?"

"Oh yeah, how *could* I forget?"

"It's nice to see you again." He said to her.

Darcy smiled and nodded then went into the great room.

We passed Bobchia at the phone stand, and waved to her, then I steered Andy under the mistletoe and looked up. "Kisses before food?" He smiled. "That will be *our motto!*"

We kissed. "Okay now, where's the kolache?"

"Did you come here to see me or eat?" I questioned with my hands on my hips.

"Can't I do both?" We walked to the kitchen. "Man, who made all those gingerbread men?"

"The boys did. Would you like one or some kolache or this cake?"

"No contest, Bobchia's cake!"

"*Kidding,* you can have all three, but that will cost you at least three kisses!"

"No problem at *all!*" He kissed me. I cut him a big piece of cake. "This is delicious, but want to know something? *You* are the sweetest thing in this kitchen!"

"You asked me a question and then *answered* it!" We kissed. I licked the frosting off of my lips.

"This is *scratch*, right?" He laughed as he took another bite. "Mmm, must be. Delicious!"

"My kisses or the cake?" I giggled.

"Both! Did you have a great Christmas?"

"I did! How about you?"

"Now it's *perfect.*" We kissed again as Mother walked into the kitchen. "Hello, Mrs. Matko." I looked at Mother's ring, *black as the ace of spades!*

"Hello, you can take your cake in by the fireplace if you would like."

"In a minute, Mother," I told her.

"Okay then," she said as she stood there.

"*Okay then,*" I said back to her. She gave me 'the look' and left. "She makes me so mad!" I told Andy. "*She makes me feel like a child!*"

"It's because she *knows* how I feel about you, Skip." I hugged him. "*I...I love you, Skip.*"

My stomach did a flip. "I love you awful."

"*Awful?!*"

"It's the best kind of love."

"*Better be!*" He kissed me again and noticed my cross necklace. "I've never seen you wear a necklace before. Did you get it for Christmas?"

"No, Bobchia gave it to me. I hardly wear it because I'm so afraid I'll lose it."

"It's pretty, like you." He kissed me on the cheek. We went into the great room, and sat beside the fireplace and across the room from Mother, keeping her at bay.

The boys ran down the steps to Andy, trying to jump on his back, punching him. "Hey, how come you guys are in your *pajamas* already? Were you bad on Christmas? *Shame.*"

"Nah, we had two baths today and were running out of our *old underwear*, and our *new ones ain't been washed yet!*" Logan explained. Andy laughed. "Thanks for coming over to *play* with us."

"Well, actually, I came over to give your sister *this.*" Smiling sweetly, he reached under his sweater into his shirt pocket and pulled out a little gold box tied with a red ribbon and handed it to me.

"Thank you!" I opened it carefully.

"Is that *all* you got her?" Andrew asked.

"Just a *little* thing?" Logan asked. "Hurry up, Jen!"

"Rip the paper!"

Inside was a dainty heart locket. "*It's beautiful!* Thank you!"

"Open it, Skip."

On one side it said **Skip** and **Merry C. '67** the other side was blank.

"Let me see! Let me see!" Andrew pulled on my arm. "*What is it?*"

"A heart locket," I told him.

"Oh, I hoped it was a *frog,*" he said.

"Or a *compass,*" Logan added.

Andy whispered. "I don't want you to be afraid to *wear it every day,* that's why I bought it for you. We can go to Murphy's tomorrow and get our picture taken in the booth, and put it in the other side of the locket."

"It is so beautiful. *I just love it!* Please, put it on me." I lifted my hair so he could fasten it. Mother glared. When I kissed his cheek, I could see the reflection of the *black* ring in the mirror from across the room.

"Yucky!"

"Yuck!"

"*Go eat some popcorn!*" I ordered.

Caleb laughed and got on the floor, calling for the boys. "Horsey ride! Who wants a horsey ride?"

"Me!" Andrew said.

"I do!" Logan said.

"I said it first!" Andrew said.

"Well, I'm bigger than you, so there!" Logan pushed Andrew, then they jumped on Caleb.

"Gee, guys, take it easy! I'm not *Trigger,* you know!"

I held the locket as I got Andy's gift from under the tree. The boys ran back over. "Can't you boys *color* or something?" I said.

"Can I open it for you, Andy?" Andrew asked.

"Can I?" Logan asked.

"*Neither of you can!*" I said. "Go play with your Lincoln logs!" They stuck their tongues out and sat in front of Andy.

"The box looks like *clothes,*" Logan said.

I gave him 'the look.' "Go play!"

Andy eagerly opened the box and held up a bright red sweater. "This is *tough enough!*"

"I'm glad you like it. I hope it fits" I smiled.

"Told ya it was clothes!" Logan said.

"Look, Skip, *we'll match!*" Mother's eyes bulged as he took the brown sweater off and put the red sweater on.

"You look handsome." I put my arm in his and walked over to Mother to show her my locket.

"It's nice," was her forced response.

Bobchia hurried in. "Merry Christmas, Andy. I couldn't get Ardelle off the telephone. I never knew taking care of Lucky was so *complicated!*"

"Merry Christmas!"

"Bobchia, look at the locket Andy got me." I held it up.

"*How lovely!* Where did I put my new camera? It's great, Andy, wait until you see it! It develops pictures right in front of your eyes!"

"*Cool,* I've seen those advertised on TV."

"Here it is!" She grabbed it off a side table. "Get in front of the tree and put your heads together. *Smile!*" She quickly took the picture. "Now stand in front of the nativity. *Smile! Another good one.*" She handed them to me.

"Thanks Bobchia!"

"You're welcome. I have all kinds of leftovers in the fridge, Andy. I'll fix you a plate."

"Thanks, Mrs. Matkovich, but—"

"Bobchia."

"Thanks, *Bobchia,* I just got up from the table, but I did have a piece of your chocolate chip cherry cake. It was delicious!"

"If you get a *little hunger pain,* I want to be the *first* to know about it."

"You'll be the first, *I promise!*" He laughed.

We watched our images come into focus. My heart pounded so hard I thought he could hear it. "*Our first picture together!*" I whispered.

"I think we look *tough* together!" He said. I felt weak as he put his arm around me. Mother must have sensed the way I felt because she never took her eyes off of us. (Not even to blink!)

"*Me too!* Oh look, Andy, which one do you like the best?"

"*Both of them.*"

"Seriously, which one should I put in the locket?"

"The one you like, and the other will go in my wallet."

"I think this one will fit better. I'll get the scissors."

"I still think we should go to Murphy's tomorrow, or are you afraid to be in the booth with me *alone?*"

"Should I be?" I giggled.

I could tell Caleb wanted to confide in Mother as he watched her watch Andy and me. Mother suggested that Andy and I join the boys and Darcy as they ate a tub of Wanda's caramel corn. "No, thank you," I said. We sat awkwardly across the room from her until Andy got up and looked through the pile of games under the tree, pulling out Scrabble.

"I hate to tell you, but *I* hold the championship title at the *Williams' estate.*"

"Oh you do, do you? Well, I hate to tell *you* that my friends and I used to play, spelling *drawkcab!*"

"*In German?*" He asked.

"German?" I laughed. "No, *backward.* And besides that, I was the runner-up at the spelling bee in Ocean View out of over two hundred students, so as my Bobchia says, Mr. Williams, *'Don't count your chickens before they're hatched!'*"

"Wow! I never knew my girlfriend was so *t-r-a-m-s!*" He laughed. I got the card table from the closet. (I was impressed—he was a fast learner.)

The doorbell rang. Bobchia answered it and announced, "Caleb, it's for you!"

"I figured," he said disappointedly, 'signing' to Darcy. They passed Bobchia on the way to the door.

Bobchia came back in and said, "It's Natalie, *Caleb's ex,* and her little darling!"

Mother looked anxious and sat on the floor with the boys as they played with their Lincoln logs. "Caleb has *other* children?" Mother asked.

"He didn't tell you?" Bobchia said. "Believe you me she is the *total opposite* of Darcy!"

Bobchia mumbled something to Harold. He looked over at Mother.

Andy and I were so happy, enjoying every moment of our first beautiful Christmas together, and as he squeezed my hand and I looked into his deep, blue eyes...*it happened.* A *crash* came from the dining room, causing us all to jump up and rushed in! Horrified,

Caleb held the pieces of the hurricane lamp that had been Bobchia's *favorite.*

"*My mother's lamp!*" She said, with a quiver in her voice.

"*I am so sorry, Rhea!*" Caleb said, trying to fit the pieces of the base together.

"Why are *you* sorry? *You* didn't break it!" She put her hands on her hips and looked down into a tiny face.

Natalie walked over to her four-year-old daughter. "Angel, tell Rhea you're sorry." Instead, the little girl ran over to the matching lamp, taunting Bobchia. She pushed it a few inches on the table, then she pushed it a few inches more. *Bobchia froze.*

Andrew looked around the crowd of people. "*Wow!* Bobchia's *good* lamp! You are so in *trouble* now!" The girl's attention shifted. She walked toward him. Andrew looked at the plastic bag she was holding. "What's in the bag?" She held it up and showed him an upside-down goldfish in a spoonful of water. "*Your fish is dead!* Logan, come here and look at this cool, *dead fish!*" Logan ran over. The girl screamed!

Natalie hurried to her. "What's the matter darling?"

Andrew looked up at her. "Her fish is dead, *that's all!*"

She screamed again, holding the bag as high as she could for her mother to see.

Natalie said, "Remember darling, when you had Jonah on your bed and you *petted him to sleep?* And remember when I told you to put him back into his bowl?"

Angel shook her head, hugging the bag so hard that the remaining water gushed to the floor. Caleb took off his bandana and wiped it up. Natalie looked down at Andrew, gritted her teeth and said, "Well darling, *he hasn't woken up yet.*"

Andrew stared back at her, gritted his teeth and said, "And it will *never* wake up, *darling*, because it is dead. *Dead, dead, the deadest thing I have ever seen in my life!*" Angel screamed and punched him in the stomach! "Ugh!"

Mother pulled him back as he tried to kick her. "*Are you all right, Andrew?*"

"Let me *kick* her just one time!" Andrew pleaded. Mother held onto him as he widely kicked toward Angel, hiding behind her mother and sticking her tongue out at him. "Andrew, settle down! Are you sure you're okay?" Mother asked, looking daggers at Natalie.

"I'd be *great* if you'd let me kick her!"

Natalie got on her knees and hugged her daughter. "Angel, you have had *entirely* too much sugar!" Angel bit her arm. "Stop that or we're *leaving!*" She bit her again! "*Ouch!*"

Caleb quickly moved the other lamp into the great room and came back. Minnie whined in Bobchia's apron, causing Angel to run over and investigate. She stared at the apron, and when Minnie whined again, she tried to punch the pup in the pocket! But Bobchia caught her little hand and ever so gently squeezed it. "You need some *manners*, little girl!"

"*Oweieee!* You hurt my hand! *Oweieee!* You hurt my hand!"

"*Not as much as I'd like to hurt that little dupa of yours with a wooden spoon!*" (Unfortunately, her little dupa was *safe*. The wooden spoons were *under the porch* with the rotting pumpkins.)

Natalie looked at Bobchia. "Really, Rhea, that would be *child abuse!*"

"'**Spare the rod and spoil the child!**' She is a *perfect example*, that's for sure!"

Angel screamed, "Nobody likes *me!*"

Logan yelled, "No wonder!" Natalie gave him a dirty look.

Humiliated, Caleb suggested, "Let's move this visit to the *kitchen.*"

"Good idea!" I said. Lucky 'chirped' upon hearing my voice.

Caleb tried to herd everyone past the glass china cupboards.

"*Birdie! I want birdie!*" Angel cried.

I ran to the cage. "*Oh no! You can't have Lucky. Never!*" Straining, I moved the cage to the top shelf. Then I stood guard, folding my arms in front of me, blocking the little girl as she tried to go around me. "*Oh no you don't!*" Lucky chirped wildly.

She ran to her mother. "Birdie! I want birdie!" Angel hugged her mother, stomping the floor, demanding it. "*I want to stay in here! I want birdie*, Mommy!"

"*Okay darling,*" Natalie said.

Andy came over looking concerned as I stared down Angel. I quickly pulled Andy beside me, locking our arms to help guard Lucky.

Angel walked over, pointing and screaming.

"Mercy! *Quit screaming!*" Bobchia scolded.

"But I want *birdie!*" Angel sobbed.

"Too bad. Sometimes we can't always *have* what we *want!*" She screamed again. "Sorry, little girl, but this is *my* home, and these are *my* things." Angel screamed again. Bobchia quickly switched tactics, smiling sweetly. "Besides, all the gingerbread men are in the kitchen. *Wouldn't you like one, honey? They have oodles and oodles of frosting on them. Yum!*" Angel nodded vigorously.

"Rhea, Angel has already had way *too* much sugar today!" Natalie said.

"Oh, look at the poor little thing! Look at that darling little face, licking her lips in anticipation. Why, who am I to *deprive* Angel, the *dear little angel.*" She snorted.

"She can't have a *red gingerbread man!*" Andrew demanded.

"*Or a green one either!*" Logan said.

Mother felt sorry for the girl and handed her an apple from the crystal bowl on the table. "Here honey, maybe you should eat this instead."

"I want a cookie! *I want a cookie!*" she said, kicking at Mother making her jump backward, then she threw the apple at her. Mother ducked, and it sailed past Darcy's head.

Mr. Pill teetered through the room. "*That kid needs a collar and chain!*"

Bobchia said, "*Amen!*"

Caleb, red-faced, made another attempt to get her away from Bobchia's prized china cupboards, getting down on all fours. "Want a horsey ride?"

"*Horsey ride!*" She climbed onto Caleb's back, holding the bag with Jonah in front of his face. "Giddy-up, hi-ho, Silver. Come on, *giddy-up!*" She held onto the back of his shirt, kicking him in the ribs.

"*Ouch, easy, will ya?*" Everyone followed *Silver* to the kitchen.

Bobchia handed Angel a big gingerbread man. She quickly ate all the frosting off, then threw the cookie on the floor. "Mercy!"

Mother was in shock. The boys laughed! Caleb quickly got her off his back and cleaned up the mess, looking apologetically at Bobchia.

I had had enough of the little brat and whispered to Andy, "I'll beat you at Scrabble yet!"

"I bet you will!" He said, as he pulled me around to the mistletoe and kissed me. I could feel my heart racing. "I enjoyed our time together."

"Me too. Do you *have* to go?"

"Yeah, Mom wants us all together, you know how mothers are. You could come to *my* house. I'll walk back and get the truck."

"I'd love to, but I know Mother would have a hissy fit."

"What's a *hissy fit?*"

"Believe me you do *not* want to know!"

He kissed me again and thanked me for his sweater. "I *love* my locket," I told him. He put on his jacket, but when he opened the door, *the most unbelievable thing happened!* Marcy came bounding through the doorway in a plaid cape, her hands full of bags.

"*Andy!*" She squealed,

"How did you know *I'd* be here?"

"I...I...didn't!"

"*You didn't?*"

She looked at me. "What are *you doing here?*"

"*I live here!*"

She looked around. "In this *old dump?*"

"This is my grandmother's Inn! *Want to make something of it?*" Andy was surprised at my spunk and put his arm around me. She looked at us in our red sweaters. I looked at her. "What are *you* doing here?"

"I came here to see my *stupid* father. We usually meet at my grandmother's house, but she's in the hospital."

"Who is your *father?*" I asked.

"Caleb Martin."

"Caleb is *your* Father? You have got to be *kidding* me! Caleb, your *father!*"

She nodded. "I know what you mean. *You can pick your friends but not your family!*"

"Hey, Caleb's a *great* guy!"

"He was when he was married to Natalie *and* was the head of the **Titusville Bank and Trust Company** *and made lots of money.* Now he's just a *crummy* truck driver!"

"How can you talk about your father like *that?*"

"He's stupid and *my* father, and I'll talk about him anyway I want! Well, now that I think of it, I should be *nice* to him. At least until I get *all* my gifts."

"Caleb, *your father?*" (It would not sink into my head.)

"*Yes, moron. Are you deaf like my wimpy sister?*"

"Oh my gosh! I can't *believe* you talk about your family like this!"

"*It's easy. I just open my mouth and it comes out!*" She smiled.

"*You should be ashamed of yourself!*" I scolded.

"Honestly, Andy, don't you have a *better way* to spend your Christmas than in this old...old..." I doubled up my fist. "*Palace?*" She smiled looking over her granny glasses, blinking her eyes.

"This is the *best Christmas* I have ever had!" Andy said, squeezing my shoulder.

I felt a calmness come over me. "*Me too.*" I said.

"*Me three!*" Marcy said, lifting the bags so I would see them. "Look at all this *groovy stuff* Natalie got me! I had to leave part of it in my car. I *barely* had room to steer the wheel! I had the grooviest blast today. I can't wait to show Caleb and Darlene Christie. Where are they?"

"*Who?* Do you mean...Darcy?" I questioned.

"*Darcy?* Ha! She always has to *copy me.*"

"I thought Darcy's sister was named *Mary.*"

"*Mary Catherine* to be exact!"

"Oh, I get it now, *I think.* Marcy and Darcy, *sisters.*"

"You're a regular *Einstein.* Only I'm *not* deaf, and *I'm a lot prettier!*"

"Darcy is sweet and a good *friend!*"

"*Oh pleassse!*" Some of her packages fell to the floor. "If you were any kind of *gentleman,* you'd help me with these bags!" Marcy said to Andy.

He sighed. "Where do you want them?"

"Wherever Caleb is." Andy picked them up. "*Caleb, I'm here!*" Marcy yelled. With her free hand, she pulled on Andy's arm, looking back at me over her glasses. Andy pushed her off. She sneezed and sneezed. "Cats! They must have *cats!*" She sneezed again.

The boys came out of the kitchen laughing, but when they saw Marcy, they stopped in their tracks. She looked down at them scrunching up her nose. "*Ew, little snots live here too!*"

Logan looked at Marcy's bulky, plaid cape. "Andrew, look, *a real pig in a blanket!*" We burst out laughing! She kicked toward the boys while hugging Andy's arm. He dropped the bags.

Laughing, I went into the great room and sat at the card table where I had been so content before the *material girl* had arrived.

"But Andy! Caleb! I'm here!" Marcy yelled.

Andy sneaked up behind me, reached over my shoulder and spelled 'I EVOL UOY' with the Scrabble pieces. I looked up and kissed him as Marcy watched us from the hallway, sneezing. Caleb called to her. I quickly folded the Scrabble board and stood up.

"I had better go, Skip,"

"I wish you could *stay.*"

Caleb was excited to see Marcy and tried to hug her while she watched us walk to the door.

"I wish you could come with me. Thanks again for the tough sweater."

"Thank you again for the beautiful heart."

"You'll *always* have mine. Until tomorrow."

"Tomorrow," I said all dreamy.

We kissed again then he turned the door knob. "*I'm afraid to open it!*" He peeked through the lace curtain. I giggled. "Sweet dreams, Skip." I gave him a peck on the cheek and watched him jog down the lane, turning to wave before going into the covered bridge. I closed my eyes and leaned on the door, remembering his kiss. Marcy stared a hole through me! I walked past her to Mother who was looking sympathetically at Darcy.

(Then it dawned on me—I felt worse for Darcy being Marcy's *sister,* than I ever did for her being *deaf!*) Darcy was 'signing' to Natalie who had Angel on her lap. Angel kept moving Natalie's chin toward her so she wouldn't see Darcy sign. I couldn't understand a word. Mother shrugged at me as Caleb tried to calm everyone down. Angel ran over to Bobchia and even though Bobchia held Pumpkin as high as she could, Angel *still* managed to pull her tail, sending the cat out of her arms and onto the boy's log cabin.

"Hey! *You hurt my cat!*" Andrew put his hands on his hips. "Ain't ya got any *'spect for cats?*"

Marcy smiled at me as she showed her gifts to Caleb, an array of clothes that the queen herself would have been envious of.

"Well, Marcy, you sure had a wonderful Christmas!" Caleb said.

"Yeah, but it's not *over,* is it Caleb?"

He got a huge smile on his face and went into the kitchen, bringing back a box exactly like the one he had given Darcy along with a larger box for Angel. Angel quickly, pulled out a teddy bear and hugged it, then she ripped its eyes out and threw it on the floor. "You're welcome," Caleb said under his breath.

Then he handed the little box to Marcy. "I hope you like them." He kissed her on the cheek.

She rolled her eyes. "*Is this it?*" She sighed, boringly pulling off the ribbon and the paper. "*Earrings?*"

Bobchia, trying to spare Caleb's feelings, said, "I know, aren't they *beautiful?* Real *diamond* chips! Your father had them *especially made* for you and Darcy."

Darcy, reading Bobchia's lips, pulled her hair back to show Marcy her earrings. She 'signed', "Aren't they beautiful?"

"Well, *Angel* might like them," Marcy said. "We're getting her ears pierced on her birthday next month. Now if you want to see beautiful, look at my *necklace!*" We all looked at her neck, but when nobody responded, she flattened down her collar. Looking at our blank stares, she fished out a chain with a huge diamond dangling from it. We stared in disbelief.

"Is it *real?*" Caleb asked.

"Dear Caleb, you never could tell the *difference!* It's *just* a carat," Natalie said in a superior voice. Bobchia spit her coffee back into her cup choking. I patted her back. "I didn't want to get her anything *too* large. After all, she's still in high school." Darcy looked at Natalie, hurt. Natalie 'signed' to her, "I have gifts for you. You didn't think Natalie would forget her other princess, did you?" She handed Darcy a shopping bag. Darcy quickly looked inside and found a tiny box, eagerly opening it. There was an identical gold chain but *no* diamond. Darcy 'signed', "It's beautiful. Thank you." She opened the other boxes of sweaters and skirts.

Caleb was *furious*. He grabbed Natalie by the arm turning his back to Darcy. "*How dare you hurt Darcy like that!*"

"Really, Caleb, did you expect me to get *her* a diamond to wear to a *deaf school?* It probably would have gotten stolen, and where would *she* go to wear a diamond anyway?"

Caleb shook his head. "*I* got her diamond earrings!"

"Well, a thief would have to have a *magnifying glass* to see that they were real diamonds, Caleb."

He got in her face. "This takes me back to why we *split* in the first place!"

Mother quietly went to the kitchen, and I went to the TV where the boys and Angel were watching **The Grinch**. Bobchia put on the record **Silent Night**, turning it way up. Caleb's and Natalie's voices carried from the other room.

"You still don't get *it*, do you?" Caleb yelled. "The diamond is not the *issue* here! I will talk slowly so that *you* will understand." He smiled at Darcy and then turned away from her. "You shouldn't treat the girls *differently!* Darcy has feelings just like *you*, like *Marcy*, like *everybody!*" He walked over and looked at the chain. "It's beautiful, but it's not as *beautiful as you are.*" He said kissing her on the cheek.

Marcy watched them. "*Oh, please!*"

Angel screamed a *bloodcurdling scream.* Mother rushed from the kitchen to us, giving me 'the look.' I shrugged and said, "How is she going to know it *hurts* if nobody *hits* her back?"

"She hit me first, *honest.* And she broke my fireman too!" Andrew said, holding up the pieces.

"You *mustn't* hit Angel," Mother said.

"She *deserved* it!" Andrew screamed.

Angel screamed again, even louder. "He *hit* me! He *hit* me!"

Natalie rushed over, confronting Mother. "You should *teach* your boys some *manners!*" Bobchia headed straight for Natalie. Then she saw Pumpkin smelling Jonah on the floor, so she picked her up and set her on Marcy's lap. "Isn't she *sweet?*"

"*Achoo! Achoo!* Get that *fleabag* off of me!" Marcy protested. "My eyes are already swelling up!"

"Oh, sorry!" Bobchia took the kitten and handed it to Darcy, smiling.

Mother took a step closer to Natalie. "*Manners? That's the pot calling the kettle black!*"

"Yeah!" Logan said in her defense. "Wait. What does *that* mean?"

Bobchia came over and stood beside Mother, waiting for an opening. Natalie looked at both of them and sighed. "Well, I guess we should be going. Stewart will be wondering where his *little Angel* is."

"Don't forget about *replacing* my Mother's lamp," Bobchia said.

"Oh yes, *that.* I wonder where a person could find something like *that?*"

"You can check at Cara's Antiques beside the park," Bobchia told her.

"That *dumpy* old place?" Natalie said. "I wouldn't be caught *dead* in there!"

Bobchia shook her head and walked to the kitchen.

I unfolded the Scrabble board, took out the "I love you" pieces and picked up Andy's brown sweater that he'd left beside the chair. Marcy kept sneezing as Natalie and Caleb tried to talk, with interruptions from Angel. Mother gave the boys a lecture about hitting and how they should *walk away* and never throw the *first punch* and *never hit girls.*

"Even *Jen?*" Logan asked.

"Even Jen!" She said. "Jesus said we should turn the other cheek. In school, your father hit and taunted me. Boy, did I get *even* with him!"

"What did you do?" Logan asked.

"I kissed him right on the lips in the hall in front of his friends!"

"Yuck!" Logan made a face.

Andrew looked puzzled. "Was that before I was *received?*"

Mother smiled. "Yes. So if you don't want kissed on the lips in front of *your* friends, *do not* hit girls!" She looked at Logan. "You don't really think that my kisses are *yucky,* do you?"

"No, but when you were little they probably were!"

She shook her head. "Probably. Now you boys have had a busy day, so say goodnight."

"We don't have school! *It's Christmas!* Why do we have to go to bed *so early?*" Andrew said.

"Why can't we sleep with Minnie in the tent we made in Bobchia's room again?" Logan asked.

"Your grandmother is, no doubt, *exhausted,*" Mother said. "You can sleep in the tent tomorrow night, okay? Now tell everyone goodnight."

They hugged everyone except for Natalie, Marcy and Angel, who was hitting the apple around the floor with Mr. Pill's Christmas cane. Mother made the boys say that it was nice meeting all of them (*even though it wasn't*).

Andrew and Logan looked for Bobchia, but she was nowhere to be found.

"Send Bobchia upstairs," Andrew said. "I'm hungry, I want a gingerbread man."

"Me too!" Logan said.

Mother shook her head. "No more sweets, but you can have a piece of fruit." They whined. "It's fruit or nothing!"

"Can't we have a *banana instead?*" Andrew asked.

Mother smiled. "Sure."

They each grabbed one, sword fighting their way up the stairs.

Bobchia came in. She held her ear toward the stairway, hearing the boys laugh. "I had Minnie outside, and I didn't get my *hugs.*" She said to Mother.

Mother smiled and walked over to her, looking at her as if she had seen her for the first time. "You are really a *sweet person,* Rhea."

Bobchia surprised, looked shyly at her. "Thank you. Clair, I've wanted to say something to you, ...*apologize to you.*"

"*For what?*"

"Well, when you and Paul left and took Jennifer, I had a lot of time to mull things over."

"Oh, *well...*"

"*Please* let me finish. I have to get this of my chest. I, *I'm sorry I monopolized Jennifer.* There, I finally said it. It wasn't *intentional.* It just happened. She looked so much like *my Jennifer,* it was like she was *alive* again. I just couldn't help myself. I didn't realize what I had done until you were gone. Can you please *forgive me?*"

"*Of course I do.* I know I haven't been the wife you had *hoped* for Paul, but I sure loved him."

"Nonsense. You and Paul were *meant* to be together, I really believe that."

Mother looked surprised. Logan yelled down the stairs, "We're ready for prayers! Is Bobchia down there?"

"Yes," Mother hollered up.

"We *need* her up here too!"

"Okay, we're on our way up!" She turned back to Bobchia. "I'm sure that you wanted to wring my neck more than *once* over the past twenty years!"

"I can't deny that!" Bobchia said with a chuckle. I wiped my eyes, walking close behind them. Bobchia confessed, "Somehow I felt responsible for you and Paul getting together."

"*Responsible? How?*"

"It was nights just like this, all those years ago, when Paul would yell down that he was ready for prayers. David and I would trudge up and kneel at his bedside. He prayed for his Bobchia and Grampie and for all the animals in the red barn, naming them every night. Depending on how many we had is how *long* the prayer was." She chuckled. "Then David and I would take turns thanking God for our blessings. I would pray for Paul to be a *man after God's own heart,* and I'd pray for the little girl that *God* had picked out to be his wife. I prayed that she would be the way *God* wanted her to be, so I'm sure that you are."

Mother was touched listening to her as we walked through her room and into the closet. They boys jumped on the mattresses while eating their bananas.

"*Okay, guys!*" Mother said. They jumped off and got on their knees. I stood in the doorway with the Scrabble pieces in my hand, bowing my head and sniffing the cologne on Andy's sweater. Logan prayed and Andrew mumbled beside him. "Now I lay me down to sleep. I pray the Lord my soul to keep. God bless Andrew, Mother, Bobchia, Aunt Ardelle, Wanda, the Man Upstairs, Minnie, Pumpkin, Joan of Arc, Nikki, Dollee, all the animals in the barn, Caleb, Darcy, Spike, Harold and all the people who live here, and even Jen. Thanks for Christmas and all our stuff. Hug Father for us, and help that Angel girl to *act like one,* through Jesus' name, Amen. Your turn, Mother."

"Thank You for the gift of Christmas and for the little girls that will eventually be the *wives* of my sons and for the young man who will be the *husband* of my daughter and for Rhea. Through Jesus Christ, our Lord, Amen."

"I'm *never* getting married!" Logan said.

"Me *either!*" Andrew agreed. "Bobchia, it's your turn."

"TYG for Your birthday and my wonderful, *wonderful* family! Thank You for answering *all* my prayers and for giving me the desires of my heart and for this *joyful Christmas!* Thank You for blessing my family for a thousand generations. I will praise Your name *forever!* I love You *awful.* Through Christ Jesus, my Lord, Amen."

Bobchia and Mother tucked the boys in then hugged and kissed them goodnight. They franticly wiped their faces.

Mother windshield-wipered her finger at them. "Remember, Bobchia's kisses *never* wipe off! Good night."

Then Bobchia did the same. "Neither do *Mother's* kisses! See you in the morning."

Mother hugged me and Bobchia whispered, "I love you awful," as she walked past me. I followed them to the bedroom door and leaned on it, watching them walk down the stairs together was *a true Christmas miracle!*

"I will *never* forget this Christmas!" I said aloud. "*TYG soooo much!*" The boys ran and jumped on the twin beds, throwing their banana peels at me.

"*Hey, pig face, get out!*" Andrew said.

"*Shut the door!*" Logan yelled.

"Okay!" I turned out the light and slammed the door.

"*Hey!*" I heard a crash and hurried downstairs, hoping not to run into Marcy or the Angel *without* a halo.

I went to my room and hugged Andy's sweater, putting it on the dresser beside my treasures. I lay across the bed and arranged the Scrabble pieces to say 'I EVOL UOY' and then put my locket, my cross and my macaroni bracelet next to them. "Who *needs* diamonds? TYG. This is all the beautiful jewelry I'll ever *need!*" I closed my eyes, seeing Andy's face smiling back as I drifted off to sleep.

A slamming door woke me. I sat up straight and took a deep breath. "If Mother *marries* Caleb, Marcy would be my *stepsister!*" I thought of how I had been *steering* Mother toward Caleb and the way they had looked at each other. (*I definitely needed a cookie!*) As I approached the archway to the kitchen, I heard talking and peeked around the corner. Bobchia was handing Harold a big piece of cake. She leaned over and kissed him on the forehead. "What a *great* Christmas!" She said. "Aren't my grandkids—*grand?*"

"I hate confusion," Harold said.

"Confusion makes life, I don't know, *interesting!*" She took Pumpkin off the refrigerator and windshield-wipered her finger in the kitten's face. "Naughty kitty, stay out of the kitchen." Pumpkin licked her finger and then bit it. "*OW!* Bad kitty!"

Harold laughed with cake teeth and said, "Like mother, like daughter!"

Bobchia got a kitty treat out of the box and threw it down the hall. "Stay away from Lucky. *Scat!*"

I walked toward the great room. (When I didn't hear screaming or anything getting broken and *the Inn wasn't on fire;* I assumed that Marcy and Angel had left.) I peeked into the great room. Mother and Caleb were sitting across from each other at the card table. He was pleading his case. She stared at the fire. He reached for her hand, trying to get a glimpse of the ring, but she quickly put it under the table. (That ring must have been *blacker than black!*) He shook his head, broken-hearted.

I felt bad for him. He was such a great guy and the only one since Father that the boys and I had thought of in that way, but what if they did get married? Marcy would be my (gag a *million* maggots) *evil* stepsister! I grabbed my stomach. *But wait a minute!* If they did get married, Darcy would be my *wonderful, sweet stepsister,* and it would be worth putting up with Marcy, *right?*

I was in denial, not wanting to think about them or anything that would *spoil* the Christmas I had waited so long to have. The cookies in the tin were calling my name from the kitchen.

"Sweetie Pie! *Get in here!* I have great news!" Bobchia exclaimed as I walked through the archway.

Darcy shook her head *no,* and Harold started choking. Bobchia pounded his back.

"What is it?"

"Angel is going to stay *here* for an entire month!"

My eyes felt like they were going to pop out of my head. "Why would she stay *here?*"

"Natalie and Marcy are going to Europe for a month! What a *privilege* to mold that dear little child's mind!"

"I thought you said it was *great news?*" I said rubbing my forehead.

Harold started to choke again, squeezing out the words, "I think I'll visit my brother in Houston!"

"You *hate* Houston!" Bobchia chastised. "*You are not going anywhere!* Besides, it has to be a group effort to *love that child enough to teach her right from wrong!*"

"Why don't they get a *babysitter?*" I asked.

"Or put her in a *kennel?*" Harold said smiling with cake teeth. I laughed.

"But Sweetie, you *are* the babysitter!"

"*Oh no Bobchia, I couldn't do it. I just couldn't!*"

"They will *paaaay* you."

"Really? How much?"

"A hundred a week."

"*A hundred a week! Honest?*"

"Honest."

"*Groovy! Cool,* but I don't know if I have the *patience.*"

"It does sound like *mission impossible,* but that's why we all have to start praying *this very minute* so that by the time she gets here, we'll be *prayed up!* It will take *every drop of prayers we have,* so *study the book of Ephesians!* We'll have to keep our 'armor' on every single minute she is here! It won't be easy by any stretch, but we must remember that 'lessons taught with God's love are not soon forgotten!'"

"Is that *in* the Bible?"

"Probably. Well, no, well, *maybe* in Proverbs, or did I *make that one up?* Oh well, it is *true* just the same, isn't it? We'll have to run this past Clair. We better wait until her ring turns *pink* and *then we'll spring it on her!* After all, Angel didn't make such a *great impression on the boys.*"

"That's an *understatement!*"

"You'd have to keep your grades up..."

"I will, *I promise.*"

Bobchia smiled a sly grin. "I will have her until you get home from school *every single day.* Remind me to *hide* the other lamp, oh and I'll put *wooden spoons* on my list right now. *This will sure shake up the old Inn!* 'I can do all things through Christ who strengthens me!' That *for sure* is in the Bible! *Philippians 4:13!*"

"Well, Bobchia, it looks like you'll *finally* get what you have always wanted!"

"What's that, Sweetie?"

"An *Angel* in the Inn!"

# 15
# Bobchia's Birthday

# Epilogue

The phone rings, jolting me back to reality. I smile upon hearing my daughter, Lindsey's voice.

"Hi, Sweetie. No, you can't go to Rhiannon's after school, not today. It is Bobchia's birthday, remember? Yes, I have the daisies. We will be there in ten minutes. You and Logan meet us at the main door of the school, okay? Love you back!"

As I finish arranging the daisies in a plastic vase, Bobchia's song runs through my mind:

> **"You are the precious daisy in my garden, your heart is so full of love; like the sunshine that surrounds me, God has sent you from above."**

I look down and smile into the pocket of my cobbler apron at little Maddy, the newest addition to my family. She has finally fallen asleep after a scolding of chewing on my shoes and 'acting like a dog!' I carefully take off the apron and lay it in Maddy's low box in the pantry and quietly shut the door. I take the vase and set it on the window seat, arousing the curiosity of Skip, my lame cat. "Skip, those are for Bobchia, not *you*. Now quit batting the leaves!" I pick her up and rub her ears. "Remember, *scare* the mice away. I don't want any more dead ones surprising me in my slippers, okay? Besides, they are so cute!" I put my coat and boots on, but before I can grab the vase, the door swings open and my young sons, Andrew and David, rush in covered with snow bumping the vase knocking the daisies to the floor.

"Sorry." The boys say.

"*I'm freezing!*" Andrew shivers.

"Not as bad as *me!*" David rubs his arms.

"Shut the door boys!"

"My hands are froze! I need more gloves." Andrew rubs his hands together.

"Me too! These are soaked!" David holds his gloves up to show me.

"Mercy! You both went through two pairs, and that's all you have!"

"My hands are going to freeze *off!*" David says, blowing on his hands.

"*Do not move from this rug!*" I point.

Andrew grabs the cat. "Skip, warm my hands. Won't you, girl?" The cat worms its way out of his arms and limps after me into the pass out room, where piles of folded clothes wait to be carried upstairs. I grab a towel and two pairs of heavy socks and hurry back to the boys and dry the floor. "We have to go pick up Lindsey and Logan after practice," I tell them. "Thank you, David, for picking up the daisies."

"Did I put them in the vase good?" He asks.

"Real good, honey boy. Bobchia will like the way you arranged them. I'll get more water." I refill the vase. "There, now we better get this show on the road!" While holding the daisies and pushing Skip back with my foot, I manage to get the boys out the door.

"Here, put these on your hands." I hand them the socks as we go down the porch steps.

Andrew shakes his head. "My hands are cold, not my *feet!*"

"Yeah!" David agrees.

"Put them on your *hands!*" I order.

David pulls his on. "They feel like gloves, but they're *socks!*"

"They *fit* like gloves, don't they?" I ask.

"But—"

"That's it, Fort Pitt! Your uncles wore socks on their *hands* whenever their gloves were wet!"

"But you said they were *weird!*" Andrew protests.

"*And they still are!*" I turn and yell toward the red barn, "Andy, it's time to go!"

"Okay, give me a minute!" He answers.

"*Hurry*, we have to get to the school and Bobchia's before dark!" I push the boys into the car. "*Andy!*"

"Okay! Okay! We have *plenty* of time!" He hollers back, coming from the red barn. He hurries over the little bridge, and starts the car, scrapes the windshield and gets in. "What are you *smiling* about?"

"Just looking at *you*, that's all."

"Oh, really?" He leans over and gives me a kiss as he puts the car in gear. "Oh good, you got her daisies."

"When I was arranging them, I was thinking about Bobchia, which got me thinking about our first *kiss* and our first *Christmas in '67.*"

"Oh you were, were you?"

"I was thinking about writing a story about it." I pull the locket out from under the collar of my barn coat, smiling.

He leans over and kisses me out of the corner of his mouth without taking his eyes off the road. "It would be a *great* story!"

"It was a *wonderful time* in our lives, you know—the Mother, Caleb, *Marcy* story." I smirk at him.

"Don't even mention that *dip!*"

"That's not very nice."

"Well, she *was*, wasn't she?"

"*Yeah!*"

I point at the main door of the school. "I told Lindsey to tell Logan to be here."

"Maybe they're at the side door."

"I told her the main door. Be patient. Pull over here; they shouldn't be long."

The boys punch each other with socked hands in the backseat.

"Do you see them with those girls on the steps?" Andy asks. I shake my head.

A couple of minutes later the doors open, and teens pour out of the school. Lindsey and her boyfriend, Josh, slowly walk out and lean on the railing of the steps. Upon seeing Logan walk out, with Belle and Gabbi, Andy blows the horn. Logan quickly says goodbye, then runs past Lindsey and Josh carrying his gym bag and slides to the car. He opens the door, and throws the bag onto David's lap and jumps into the backseat between the boys.

"Ugh! *Hey ya big jerk!*" David says.

"David! That is no way to talk to your *brother!*" I scold.

"That thing *stinks!*" He yells.

Andy laughs, until he catches a whiff of it. "Logan, throw that bag in the trunk!" He orders.

When Logan gets back in, the boys jump on him and punch him with socked hands. "You guys are so *dumb!* You don't know your *hands* from your *feet!*" He pushes them to the floor.

"Ouch!"

"Jerks!"

Andy turns around and gives them 'the look' and they settle down.

"How was practice?"

"Coach Casey said I'll play *first string* next game!"

"Good thing! I was ready to buy ol' Case a pair of glasses!"

Lindsey couldn't bring herself to let go of Josh's hand. I roll the window down. "Lindsey, hurry up! We have to get to Bobchia's!" We watch them intently as they say their goodbyes.

"He's *too old* for her!" Andy says sternly.

"They are the same age *we were* when we met. Besides, she and I have had the *ytirup talk.*"

"Give me a sec, p-u-r-i-t-y! Well, *she's* not the one that *needs* it. Besides, *I don't like the way he looks at her!*"

"Mother never liked the way *you looked at me either,* remember?"

*"She still doesn't!"*

I laugh and slide closer to him as Lindsey gets in the car. "How was practice, honey girl?"

"Great! The play is sold out for *both* nights! **'The evil that men doeth lives after them; the good is oft' interred with their bones!'**" I nudge Andy.

On the way to Bobchia's, confusion escalates in the backseat. Andy looks through his brows more than once at the boys in the rearview mirror. "Logan, *quit* teasing your brothers! *Don't make me stop this car!*"

"Sorry, Dad."

Lindsey talks of Josh's plans for a toboggan party this Saturday on Hot Dog Hill saying, "I thought that since Grandma and Grandpa Williams *live on Hot Dog Hill* that maybe I could have a slumber party at their house. *Please!*"

"If it's okay with Grandma Jean, and the boys *stay outside,* it's okay with me," Andy says. "Who's going to be there?"

"Just the regular crowd," Lindsey says evasively.

"Who?" I ask.

"Josh of course."

"Of course. And?" I persist.

She sighs and looks at the ceiling "Kathy, Phil, Brandy, Sarah Grace, Ryan, Gary, Leah, Morgan, Mike, Patti, Sid, and Avery, plus some other kids from Pleasantville that Morgan knows."

"Just remember, *church on Sunday,* no matter how *sleepy* you are."

"Mother, I know, *chee.*"

I smile at her. "Hot Dog Hill is where I *met* your father."

"*I know for the millionth and oneth time!*"

Andy laughs. "Did she tell you that she had a *babushka* on her head?"

"For real? Mother! A *babushka?*" She giggles.

"Even looking like a bobchia, she still was *pretty!*" He says squeezing my knee.

As Lindsey talks on and on about Josh, I wonder how I must have sounded to Mother when I talked about Andy. Andy puts the wipers on. "Boy, the snow is *really coming down. I can hardly see!* I didn't think it was supposed to snow this hard until tonight."

Lindsey looks out her window. "Bobchia simply *loves* snow."

"That's because *she's not driving in it!*" Andy taps the breaks several times. "Put your belts on kids, it's pretty slick."

For a moment, the only sound is the fast, squeaky wipers as large snowflakes hit the windshield. The boys start wrestling again, oblivious to the dangers of the slippery highway.

When we reach Bobchia's, we see Harold's car entombed in heavy snow. His wipers scarcely move as the snow quickly fills the empty space that had just been cleared. We could barely see his orange hunting hat leaning against his window. Andy parks beside him, then blows the horn. We laugh startling him from his nap. He looks at us smiling then gets out of his car.

"Hi, Harold!" Andy calls.

"Hi Andy, Jen, kids." A familiar head sticks out of Harold's hunting coat pocket.

The boys scramble over to her.

"Minnie!"

"Minnie!"

"Careful now boys," Harold warns, "she's old and cranky, just like *me.*"

"*I knew you'd be here!*" I say, kissing his cheek.

Lindsey pushes the boys away and gently takes Minnie out of his pocket. We all receive Minnie kisses on our noses then Lindsey carefully wraps her up in her scarf. "Keep warm, Miss Minnie."

Andy shakes his head. "I can't believe that dog is *still alive!* She must hold the world record!"

Harold smiles. "She'll probably *outlive me!* She's always been carried around and has never had to *do* anything. Except now and then she does *doo-doo in my coat pocket.* But now and then I *doo-doo in my back pocket, so it all evens out.*" We laugh.

Logan gets the daisies out of the car and hands them to me.

Harold smiles. "Rhea sure loves her daisies…and you!"

"And *you!*" I say.

"And *me!*" Andy says.

"*Us too!*" The boys say.

Lindsey stands up straight, holds Minnie out, looks directly into her face and says, "*Bobchia loves everybody and everything that draws breath!*" (She's my dramatic child.)

"That pretty well *sums up* Bobchia!" Logan says as he opens the trunk, gets out the broom and brushes the heavy snow off of Aunt Jennifer's, Grampie David's and Bobchia's tombstones.

Andrew slowly reads the engraved words that Bobchia knew would witness to all who read them: "**Whosoever calls on the name of the Lord shall be saved!** Is Great Grandma really in the ground?"

"Is she cold?" David asks.

"She's in *heaven,* warm in Jesus' arms, honey boy," I explain. "Remember, we talked about *that.*"

"Will she please come back? *I love her awful!*" Andrew says.

"*She loved you awful.* No, honey, she's not coming back, but some day we will see her again." I hug him and look at Andy. He comes over and hugs both of us.

David asks, "Why did we come here? It's *sad.*" I'm unable to answer as tears roll down my cheeks.

Andy explains, "We came here because *we love Bobchia,* and this is her first birthday since she died. Your mother wanted to *honor* her."

"So she brought *daisies!*" David connects.

"*That's right!*"

"We might not do this every year, but I wanted to this year…just because." I kneel down to the headstone and pack snow around the plastic vase. A gust of wind scatters the daisies over the snow. Andrew and David run to gather them with socked hands and bring them to me.

"I'd like to come back next year and bring daisies. It makes me think of Bobchia and how much *fun* she was. Do you think she's *having fun in heaven?*" Andrew asks.

"Mercy, yes! She is with your Grampie Paul and Great Grampie David and Great Aunt Jennifer."

"*And the bestest, Jesus!*" David adds.

"That really is the bestest, *the bestest of all!*" I smile. "She'll be there waiting for us when we reach the end of our lives. *We will have quite the reunion!*"

"With chocolate chip cookies?" David asks.

"The best chocolate chip cookies *you ever ate!*"

"She's probably the cook up there!" David says matter-of-factly.

"If she has her way, she is. I do know one thing, she is in heaven, and we *have Jesus in our hearts, so we will see her again.*" I smile through my tears.

"And live with her forever and ever?" David asks.

"*We'll never be separated from her again, forever and ever and ever!*"

"What about my heart *now?*" Andrew asks. "*It hurts.*"

(Knowing the pain of being separated from her, I silently pray for him. *Help me, Lord to help him.*) "*I know how you feel.* How about when we get home we get out the photo albums and look at all the pictures of you and Bobchia together? Then you can pick out the one you like the best, and tomorrow we'll go to town and get special picture frames and put them on your nightstands. How does that sound?"

"I remember what she *looks* like." Andrew hangs his head. "It's her *hugs* that I miss!"

"*Me too!*" David agrees.

"*She sure was a great hugger,* but until we see her again, we'll just have to *hug* each other." I hug them, sobbing.

Harold wipes his face. "The first year is *always* the hardest with birthdays and Christmas because we have so many memories that she's in. Eventually we'll only remember the fun things, and you boys won't be so sad." He fondly rubs the tops of the boys' heads. "Come on, Miss Minnie." He takes her from Lindsey. She licks the tears from his cheeks. "I know, *you miss her too.*" Minnie whines when he puts her back into his pocket as if she knew what he had said. He fluffs the dishtowel around her until all we can see is two button eyes and a little black nose. "*Get toasty.*"

While we stand there looking at the daisies, we hear the distant sounds of cattle from the farm over the hill. It's dusk. The snow starts taking on a light shade of blue with the coming darkness.

Andrew blows his nose. "Can David and I make a snowman? Bobchia always liked *watching* us make them. Please?"

"Well, I guess." The boys race. "You better hurry; it's getting dark."

Logan rolls the snow fast, making the biggest ball for the body. Lindsey stands with her arms folded, glancing to see if anyone is watching. "This is so *juvenile!*" She complains.

Before long a snowman appears right in front of Bobchia's grave!

"I've never seen a snowman in a *graveyard* before," I exclaim.

"Me either. Bobchia would sure get a kick out of it!" Andy chuckles.

I smile. "Wouldn't she though!"

Logan brings some branches from under a big oak for the arms. David packs the daisies on the ends of the branches as if the snowman were bringing them to Bobchia.

"I wish I had my camera!"

"You sound like your Bobchia." Harold laughs.

"We need eyes, a nose and a mouth," David says. "Let's check in there!" The boys run to the caretaker's shed and squeeze through the door, that is ajar, blocked by deep snow.

"Mommy!" David yells. "*Come quick!*"

We rush over. Andy and Logan tug at the splintered door. Upon entering, we see a cat nursing kittens on a pile of dirty, cold rags as snow blows in from a broken window.

"*Oh, brother!*" Andy says. I walk over and pet the nursing cat. She's frightened but too weak to escape. I look at Andy. "I know, *I know,*" he says, defeated. "I'll get the carrier out of the trunk." He passes Harold on the way out. "No use in arguing about it. I lost this battle the day I said '*I do*'!"

Harold shakes his head, "*Just like you-know-who!*"

"*Exactly!*"

We gather up our newfound friends. Lindsey picks up mama kitty and wraps her in her scarf. "She's so *thin.*" Minnie's head pops out of Harold's hunting coat when she hears a weak "Meow."

"Honey, she can't hunt in this snow, and the kittens are draining her. She'll be fine as soon as I get some chicken into her." (I smile thinking of Joan of Arc.)

Logan returns with the carrier. "I want the *first pick.*"

"I get the *first pick.*" Lindsey says.

David gets mad. "Why does she get the *first pick?* I saw them *first!*"

Andrew gets in his face, "No, I saw them *first!*"

"Did *not!*"

"Did *too!*"

"Did *not!*"

"Did *too!*"

All I think about is my horrible brothers as I rub the groove in my forehead. "*David, get your dad in here!*"

Harold chuckles as Andy walks in and takes out the rags that David had shoved in next to the kittens. He replaces them with straw off the floor. David protests and Andy explains, "I know you meant well, but cloth *holds* in the cold and dampness, while straw will keep them *warm and dry, right Bobchia?*" He looks at me, smiling.

I nod. "*Right and mercy, don't forget it!*"

"I'll start the car," Andy says.

Under the windowsill of the shed are flowerpots, filled with dead flowers in sandy dirt edged in black stones.

Harold grabs a handful of stones. "Here's the face for your snowman, boys." They are too excited about the kittens to care. Harold walks out and gives the snowman a face and joins Andy beside Bobchia's grave. "How I *miss* that woman! You know there's not a day that goes by that I don't think of something funny she said. He looks down in his pocket into the face looking up at his. Well, Miss Minnie, are you ready to go home and sit by the fire?" Minnie pops her head out growling when Lindsey and the boys walk by with the cat and kittens, totally ignoring her.

"*Jealous?*" Andy says, rubbing Minnie's gray head. "The snowman looks good Harold."

I walk up to Andy and hug his back. "Harold, stop at the Inn on your way home. It has been awhile. I have a roast in the oven, *your favorite.*"

"And Minnie's." He says, smiling down at her.

I walk over to Bobchia's grave and touch her headstone, remembering the last thing she said to me as she squeezed my hand:

"**Sweetie Pie, don't you be crying. I've waited my whole life to be with Jesus! I'll be looking for you out of the kitchen window of my mansion.**"

"Lord, tell her I love her *awful* and hug her for me. TYG, Amen." *It's never been an easy thing for me to do, leaving my Bobchia.*

Sobbing, I walk away sadly, glancing back, then get in the car. Looking through the windshield we giggle at the snowman holding daisies like a beau coming to call. "Bobchia would have gotten a kick out of that snowman!" I say smiling back at the boys.

When we start to leave, a gust of wind blows the arms of the snowman over, palms up, as if he were *praising the Lord!*

"Did you see that? *Look at the snowman!*" I exclaim.

Andy backs the car up. "Wow! *Just like Bobchia in church!* How about that?" He said.

"*Just like my Bobchia in church!*"

A tear trickled down my cheek.

That night in the kitchen, when I finished reading a passage from Great Grandmother's Bible and mark my place with Bobchia's favorite marker, I think of her birthday last year when the Inn was full of her *love and laughter*. She was the *glue* that held this Inn together and I often wonder *which one of my children* will take the Inn over when I'm finally *with* my Bobchia again.

All those years ago, when Bobchia had told me of her will, I'd never dreamed of how *lonely* the Inn would be without her. I had some pretty big shoes to fill when she left me the Inn and the contents thereof. *I chuckle at the contents thereof;* Aunt Ardelle, Wanda, and Lucky (minus a few more feathers). They moved downstairs into the new wing of rooms next to Rose and Jim. Carolyn, Spike, Helen, Tall Cliff, Gladys, Mrs. Dunham, Cecil, Frank and Mary still make life here interesting. The rest had long ago gone to be with the Lord—except for Ginger and Mr. Hair who long ago ran off to Vegas.

People come, people go, but if they were here for Sunday dinner, then *they were in a church pew earlier!* Without hesitation, I send *all* sweeper salesmen to The Brady House, hoping I didn't miss out on an opportunity to entertain an '*angel unaware.*'

The antics of people traveling through, stopping for a night, a week, or a month, have kept us amused and have kept my journals *full!* On the four-legged side, I inherited all of Bobchia's cherished animals: Dollee, the cats, a couple of dogs, two goats, a sick veal calf, an abused pony, that Andy babies, a lame, white swayback horse that was headed for the—well, anyway, Bobchia headed him into the pasture. Oh, last but not least, that troublemaker, Rocky

III. I'm also the proud owner of a huge pile of wood and a shed full of roofing shingles, just in case a drifter happens by and *needs to work for a hot meal.*

Most of all, Bobchia left her *love* in all the hearts of the people she left behind. In every nook and cranny of this big, old Inn she left a *lifetime of memories to me.* Her ability to find meaning in the life of the most obscure person was a true *gift of God,* and how I *yearn* for those days again! She couldn't possibly have fathomed *my love for her,* for in all the nooks and crannies of the Inn, along the pathways I walk in a day's time, tucked here, tucked there, are an assortment of tables adorned with starched daisy doilies under pictures of her, *my Bobchia.*

Whenever I feel melancholy, I point the fan at the chandelier, get out my box of my journals, lie across the massive bed in a room that is more beautiful than any in the White House, and I am instantly transported back to 1967 with my Bobchia. *TYG!*

# Picking Bobchia Some Daisies

When I was a little girl
 Neigh to my Daddy's knee,
I'd pick daisies beside the red barn
 How *thrilled* my Bobchia would be!

She would unlock her china cupboard
 And get down her porcelain vase,
Arrange *each* single flower
 And sing softly into my face;

"*You* are the precious daisy in my garden
 Your heart is so full of love,
Like the sunshine that surrounds me;
 God has sent *you* from above."

Every summer the bouquets
 Were on her mantel—tall,
Until the daisies died
 And the petals—they did fall.

On my wedding day
 While pinning on Bobchia's dress
A corsage of little white daisies,
 She sang softly under her breath:

"*You* are the precious daisy in my garden
 Your heart is so full of love,
Like the sunshine that surrounds me;
 God has sent *you* from above."

Now *I am* a Bobchia
 And get down that porcelain vase,
For *fistfuls* of daisies
 And sing in my grandbaby's face.

*I still pick daisies for Bobchia*
    With regularity,
Placing them on her grave
    Singing as she sang to me:

"God needed another daisy
    In his precious garden of love,
*You* are the sunshine that surrounds me
    *As you watch me from above.*"

People are like grass; their beauty is like a flower in the field. The grass withers and the flower fades. *But the word of the Lord remains forever.* 1 Peter 1:24-25

# About the Author...

## Rhea Jean Fish

What makes for a good read? I've always heard that authors should write about familiar things, life experiences, etc. Even though this book is fictional, it contains within its covers a rollercoaster of emotions that I have had over my sixty-four years. I am a baby boomer (a literal child of the sixties). I've been married to David, a great Christian man, for the past 40 years. We are proud of our wonderful son, Andy, and his wife, Jennifer, and our grandsons; Andrew, Logan and Caleb, whose humorous antics are scattered throughout these pages.

I've also heard, but only halfheartedly believed, people on television when they say their book, movie or play was 'a labor of love.' Well, guess what? This one is a *revelation* of God's love to me. In writing it, I found out that I actually can *do* all things through Christ who strengthens me! I take joy in doing your will, my God, for your instructions are written on my heart.     Blessings to you!

# About the Artist...

## Deac Mong

Deac Mong (cover design & illustration) graduated with honors from the Art Institute of Ft. Lauderdale and has worked as an artist for the past 32 years. He has produced art for upscale hotels, businesses and private residences both nationally and internationally. Deac is a native of northwestern Pennsylvania where he lives with his wife of 34 years. They have 4 grown children and 7 grandchildren. He enjoyed working with Rhea because of her vision and spirit and prays that Christ's love would shine through every aspect of this project.

To see more of his work, please visit: **www.deacmong.com**